A
STRIVING
AFTER WIND

A Novel
By
Sharon Traner

For Mark

4

What does a man gain by which he toils under the sun? A generation goes and a generation comes, but the earth is forever. The sun rises and goes down and hastens to the place where it rises. All streams run to the sea, but the sea is never full.

And I have applied my mind to see and to search out by wisdom all that is done under heaven; it is an unhappy business that God has given to the sons of men to be busy with.

I have seen everything that is done under the sun . . .

And behold, all is vanity and a striving after wind.

Ecclesiates 1: 2-7, 13-14

CHAPTER 1

Annie hated the rain. All day, all night, it was raining.

She pressed her face against the window, watching the glistening rivulets trail down the glass in ceaseless, hypnotic succession. The window overlooked the street where an occasional car splashed by, disappearing into the abyss of an unusually dark, New York City night. Except for a few streetlights, which shed dusky umbrellas of light along the curbs, the only stationary thing that interrupted the darkness was Mrs. Blakemore's Christmas lights. They had been twinkling in the foggy gloom for hours. Annie tried not to look at them, irritated that their neighbor was traveling abroad and left an electric timer to remind them everyday, promptly at dusk, that the holidays had been miserable. She wished it was snowing. Maybe then everything wouldn't seem so bleak.

Her window perch was situated at the end of the long hallway that dissected the second floor of the large home she shared with her family. If she looked past the rain, she could see a distorted reflection of the corridor stretching out behind her. It was shrouded in somber shadows with faint, intermittent beams of light glowing through the open doorways.

Occasionally, the sound of voices intruded upon her solitude, but she did not respond. To speak required thought and interaction. She did not want to do either.

"I still don't understand how those damned doctors talked Pop into this," a voice cried. "Mother is too weak!" It was Mack, Annie's oldest brother. His voice was full of anger and frustration. Typical, she thought.

"That's why they took the baby early," a second voice retorted. "For God's sake, Mack! We've been over this a hundred times! It's like the doctors said--now they can treat the cancer!" That was Andrew, Annie's twin brother. He rarely expressed much emotion, but tonight his voice cracked on that word, *cancer*.

It was an awful word, a word that no one wanted to use these past few months. And although Andrew had not intended it, the sudden intrusion of that word permeated the restrained silence like a sudden gust of wind that blows out the one, remaining candle.

"Anyway," Annie heard him mutter, "there's no reason to get so mad. You're scaring the other kids. We'll know more when someone calls, right?"

It was a rhetorical question to which no one responded. Moments later Annie heard her twin escape down the hallway to his room. She could have given him a smile or nod to offer him absolution, but she didn't. There was only the rain.

She wondered why she wasn't crying. She wept oceans of tears since that day last summer when she first learned about the cancer. It was discovered when Mother visited her gynecologist to confirm her pregnancy. The overwhelming despair that had filled their lives since then was culminating tonight. Mother was undergoing surgery to terminate the pregnancy seven weeks early. It had not been an easy decision for their father, and Annie knew why. Mother was struggling to stay alive for the sake of the baby and once the birth was accomplished she might . . . .

Annie still could not say the word, even to herself. It was too awful, too final. She forced her mind to turn away from it. There was only the rain.

"Miss Annie?" a voice called. The sound was distorted as if coming from a deep hole. "Miss Annie," the voice called again, this time accompanied by a timid, hesitant pat. Annie recognized the touch before the voice. It was their nanny, Miss Grace, the elderly woman whose residence had been the bedroom off the nursery since before Annie and Andrew were born. "Do you want me to put the little boys in bed?"

"What time is it?" Annie murmured, still starring out the window.

"It's late, dear, after ten o' clock. Joey is asleep on Luke's lap. The others are just sitting quietly. I didn't know if I should disturb them."

"I'm sure they will want to stay up until we hear something. Let's wait a little longer." She turned away from the window for the first time. "I guess I should go to them."

They walked arm in arm down the hallway toward her

parents' sitting room, as mother called it, adjacent to the master bedroom. All eight of her brothers were there, even Andrew who must have rejoined them sometime after his heated exchange with Mack. Just as Grace said, Luke was sitting on the small sofa across from the fireplace with four year old Joey sleeping in his arms. The second youngest, Danny, was curled up close by. He gazed up with red, pained eyes and slid over to make room for her. She drew him near and hugged him, something she should have done hours ago.

It seemed natural that they were gathered here. The small room, furnished with Mother's antiquated things brought over from Ireland, was much more informal and intimate than the rest of the modern, sprawling house. The room normally teemed with energy and noisy confusion, but tonight, there was only suffocating silence.

Anxious to turn to her mind away from the agony mirrored in her brothers' faces, Annie seized upon well-worn and cherished objects that flooded her senses with happy memories. There was the wooden stool, which still stood in the corner near the fireplace. It had been brought up from the kitchen when Annie was three years old so she could stand upon it to brush her mother's long, beautiful hair. On the small, round table between her parents' favorite chairs was a stack of familiar children's books, partially covering the gashes from her brothers' ice skates and burn holes from her father's cigars. Annie inhaled deeply, hoping for a lingering scent of his Havana Specials. That smell was as much a part of this room as the pleasant sounds of the children's laughter and the somber voices of their parents holding court.

"I'm sure he didn't mean to do it, darlin'," mother would say, defending the latest transgressor. "He's sorry and promises to never do it again, right?" She would squeeze the culprit's hand with a reassuring smile.

"Well, you know how I feel, Kathleen," Daddy would retort. "You are much too easy on these children." That was as far as it ever went. The felon was excused, repentant and forgiven, and the incident forgotten. But those echoes of happiness had long since faded away and now this place was a waiting room.

"Man! Why doesn't someone call?" It was Thomas, Annie's fourteen year old brother. His face was twisted with agitation and bitterness. He jumped up from his chair and began pacing. "It's all because of the baby! If Mother had an abortion, they could have started the treatments months ago."

"Thomas!" Andrew hissed. "An abortion? Mother?"

Annie, as well as everyone in the room, knew what he was saying. Their mother's faith, her rigid Catholic beliefs, would never permit her to abort this baby even if it meant saving or prolonging her own life. Daddy had tried to talk to her about it, but he should have known she would never consider it, under any circumstances.

"Why don't you just shut up." Mack fired toward Thomas. "This is not the time to say anything like that."

Once again there was silence. Why were anger and guilt such a part of this, Annie wondered? It began when she came home from college last summer and suspected that Mother was pregnant again. The mere thought that her parents would consider having another child at this stage of their lives enraged her. Full of selfish indignation, she confronted her mother. "For God's sake, how could you?" she exploded one afternoon when they were alone in this very room. It was then that she noticed her mother's pained expression.

"Annie," Mother began, "I don't want you to be frightened, but Dr. Prichett found something else, too. He says there's a growth – here." Her hand touched her left breast.

The flood of fear and self-loathing that engulfed Annie at that moment became her constant companion. She stood by helplessly as the cancer spread to Mother's bones and lungs so that even breathing was difficult. Her hospitalizations became longer and more frequent.

And now tonight, her father or one of the nurses will call soon with news about the baby. The doctors said it should survive, but Annie was afraid for this baby, too. What if something was wrong with it? Mother's health had deteriorated as the pregnancy progressed. Annie knew enough about basic anatomy to know that anomalies in these situations were possible.

She stared across the room at little Joey. As usual, he was oblivious to the turmoil surrounding him. His cherub-like face gave no clues to his body's imperfections. He was born with twisted legs and a mind that developed slowly. No one dared use the word "retarded" around Mother. It was Daddy who seemed unable to cope, as though he felt guilty or ashamed. Mother never criticized him. It only served to make her devotion to the child stronger.

A wave of recurring panic swept over her. Would she be able to love and care for him as well as Mother? What about the rest of them? There were only questions with no answers and the rain.

* * * * * *

Like a shrill explosion invading the quiet, the phone rang.

Andrew, Annie, and the others crept close to it but no one touched it until Mack reached over and picked it up. "Hello," he murmured. "Yes, Dad?... Well, that's certainly good news...A girl. Yes, Annie will be pleased...She's right here...I'll tell her...Of course...Sure...Bye, now."

He hung up the receiver slowly and then cleared his throat before he turned to face the throng pressing against him. "Pop says the baby is doing well. It's a girl." His voice failed him then as he struggled to keep his composure. "She's almost four pounds, but that's pretty good, don't ya' think?" He managed a grin. "Mama must have come through it pretty well 'cause she's awake. She's asking to see you, Annie."

All eyes turned toward their sister. A brief instant of panic crossed her face, but then she visibly squared her shoulders and set about the tasks at hand. "Would you call William to bring the car around, John? And Luke, you'd better tell Miss Grace about the baby and help her put Joey to bed. Peter, Danny--you boys brush your teeth and go to bed, too." She was walking as she talked, leading them down the stairway into the foyer. It was easy to see how frightened they were. "Don't forget your prayers," she added as she reached into the closet for her coat and umbrella.

"But, Annie," her twin pleaded. "Shouldn't one of us go

with you? I could go."

"No, Andrew," she said, giving him a quick hug. "The other boys need you. And Daddy would have said if he wanted you to come. It's late. I'm sure you can see her tomorrow. I'll call you later if I can, but don't wait up, okay?"

She was trying to sound calm and matter-of-fact but they could see she was trembling as she buttoned her jacket. There were quick kisses all around and by that time, they saw the lights of the car waiting at the curb.

The boys stood huddled together and watched through the open door as she dashed to the car to be driven off into the rain.

* * * * * *

Mildred Francis O' Sullivan was a licensed nurse in New York, Canada, and back home in Ireland. She had the reputation of being a tireless worker and always reliable. And of course, she was also kind and gentle so that many of her patients asked for her by name at the private duty pool through which she worked. But here tonight, with this patient, she was simply, "Cousin Millie".

It was part of the bargain struck more than twenty years ago when she and her sister, Patricia, were young nursing students, struggling their way through school in Dublin. Somehow their cousin Kathleen heard of their troubles and started sending them money all the way from America. She had married a rich young man from New York City after the war. However, the O'Hara girls were proud and weren't about to take charity.

Cousin Kathleen sent a letter, insisting that they take the money as a loan. She told them how much money could be made nursing in the States. There were nurses, she said, who worked only a few months and made enough money to return home and live nicely the rest of the year. She herself was expecting her first child that summer. The idea of strangers tending to her and the baby was so worrisome that she wondered if perhaps one of them would be licensed and be able to come by then.

That's the way it had been ever since. Millie, Patty, and two others took turns coming from Ireland for three-month tours of private duty nursing. In return for the generosity shown those many years ago, one of them was always there for Kathleen when she gave birth or when one of the boys broke an arm or had the flu. Of course, Mr. Winston always insisted on paying generous wages, saying he'd rather pay them than a stranger.

Millie crept around the room, checking the flow of oxygen or the intravenous drip. She drew near when her patient stirred. "Don't ya' worry none now, Kathleen," she whispered, "Cousin Millie's right here." She had never minded caring for a dying patient. She had accepted the inevitability of death a long time ago. Although she had come to care deeply for many of her patients, she had never wept. Tonight was different. She whisked her handkerchief from her pocket more than once. Kathleen needed the touch of knowing, loving hands, and Millie would stay at her side until the end

.

* * * * * *

Annie crept down the corridor with slow, cautious steps. She was nervous about seeing her mother and didn't know how to keep it from showing. She rapped on the door and Millie ushered her in.

"She's been asking for you, darlin', but she just went back to sleep," Millie whispered. "Just sit with her for a few minutes. She'll wake up soon. I'll step out to that little lounge around the corner and check on your Da'. Now don't be frightened."

Annie stood motionless for a long time after Millie left. She could see in the dim light the pale body silhouetted beneath the ghostly, white sheets. Annie was shocked to see how thin and fragile her mother looked. Her colorless cheeks were sunken and her hair was matted and uncombed. There were all manner of tubes invading her body. Annie recognized most of them. There was the larger, bloody tube that appeared from beneath her sheets at Mother's mid-section, connected to the calibrated chambered apparatus bubbling at the bedside. Annie knew that was the chest tube, inserted to prevent Kathleen from drowning in her own fluids. There were also the familiar clear plastic tube bringing life-sustaining oxygen. Millie put cotton to cushion the tubing where it crossed Mother's cheeks, for even that minute amount of pressure could peel open her thin, nearly transparent skin. The repugnant odor of purulent drainage and diseased tissue permeated the room.

Annie was engulfed by a new wave of anger and self-pity. Why was she being forced to look at her mother like this? She envied her brothers back home in their beds. She would rather remember her mother as she was before. She moved with such elegance that most people thought she was royalty rather than Irish peasantry. When she dressed for formal occasions, Kathleen looked like a fairy princess going to the ball. Annie remembered sitting on the four-poster bed, chatting away while she dressed. And then, her father would come in and whisk her into his arms. He kissed her with such passion and adoration that it seemed to Annie they blended together in such a way that they ceased being separate entities. Theirs was a love that others envied.

Poor Daddy. How he suffered these past months. At first he refused to believe that Mother was so sick and then he began torturing himself because he was powerless to help her. What will happen to him now, Annie wondered. For the first time today, unchecked tears sprang to her eyes.

Just then Mother stirred. "Mama?" Annie whispered. "I'm here."

"Oh, Annie, I'm so glad to see you," Kathleen murmured.

"You mustn't talk now. You should rest so you can get stronger."

"Did you see the baby? I'm so glad it's a girl, but I'm worried about her. Love her especially hard," she pressed, a desperate urgency choking each word. "Help your father and brothers to understand it wasn't her fault."

"Yes, of course. I'll love her especially hard, I promise." She would have said anything just so her mother would lie back and rest.

"It won't be very easy for you, darlin'. You'll be thinking that it's all up to you to do the mothering. And maybe that will give you joy for awhile, but --"

"No, Mama, they need you. Sleep now so you can get better. Please!"

14

"Annie, listen, there's a whole wonderful world out there. You've got to go out and find yourself. Be happy, darlin'. Just be happy." Her voice became fainter as she struggled to breathe. "My Rosary. I can't seem to find it."

Annie's fingers crept under the pillow and found the well-worn beads. She sat numb and silent as Kathleen whispered the gentle words until she drifted off to sleep.

Chapter 2

Matthew Winston sat fidgeting on the green, vinyl sofa. "But I'm not tired, Millie," he insisted.

"Not tired, ya say," she retorted. "Ya' look like hell, if ya' don't mind me sayin' so. Annie is sittin' with Kathleen now so this is a good time for you to rest. Here, I've brought you a pillow and blanket. Now stretch out and nod off a bit." She didn't wait for an answer, but set to work placing the pillow under his head and spreading the blanket. Matthew allowed her to fuss, comforted by her care. He didn't want to be alone.

"Do you miss home, Millie--Ireland, I mean?" he asked.

"Why yes, of course I do. I hate like the dickens to be away from Brian and the girls, but the money is good and three months isn't so long, really."

"Kathleen and I went back there several times since we were married. The last time was five years ago. I can't imagine how she could stand living here with me in the city after growing up in such a beautiful place."

"Well, I know the answer to that and so do you. She loves you, and her life is here with you and the children."

"I know, Millie, but sometimes I wonder if she regretted it--marrying me, I mean."

"Why would ya' say such a thing? I never knew a happier woman in all my life."

"Yes, I suppose so, but I don't think she ever imagined when she took that job at the base that she'd end up marrying a guy like me."

"Oh, I suppose not. But you didn't expect it either, did

you?"

"Oh, God no. I was mad as hell when I was stationed there. I thought it was the most awful place I ever heard of." It was a well known family story. His parents were incensed when Matthew ran off and enlisted in '42. His father pulled some strings with the War Department and had him stationed at a small Naval base in Derry, Ireland.

"Kathleen was a clerk, wasn't she?" Millie asked, settling into a nearby chair.

"She was sitting behind the desk when I reported in to the O.D. I was spittin' mad, but she put me in my place, real quick. That's when I noticed her." He could recall the scene as though it was yesterday. Her face was flushed so that the pink in her cheeks gave her an attractive glow. Even though her hair was tied in a tight, severe bun, it did not camouflage her exquisite beauty. "I was smitten the moment she began talking. The other guys on the base said I didn't have a chance. Kathleen O'Hara did not fraternize with American boys. It took awhile, but I finally won her over."

"Oh, yes," Millie laughed. "I imagine you were quite charming."

"I thought so, but she was tough. I could tell she liked me, but she kept putting me off. Then she showed up one night at the Officer's Club. Every guy asked her to dance, but she only said yes to me." A smile of extreme satisfaction spread across his face as he remembered his joy when she took his hand and followed him onto the dance floor.

"It must have taken a great deal of courage for her to give into your advances, Matthew. Her grandparents were dead set against her having anything to do with you lads on the base, American or otherwise. Kathleen's own mother ran off with some brash radical from Northern Ireland and got himself killed. Poor girl was left to die alone with a newborn baby. It was quite the scandal!"

"Yes, Kathleen told me about it. That's why I kept begging her to take me home with her for a weekend. I wanted her family to meet me."

"I'm sure it took ever a bit of courage she had. I can still remember how intimidating my Uncle Patrick was. My goodness-- and you being a Protestant and all. It's a wonder Kathleen ever found the nerve!"

"Thank God she did. I loved it there. Remember how you'd come over the hill from the east and look down at their place? God, it was pretty." The scene was etched indelibly in his mind. The farm was surrounded by a horseshoe of purple and green Atrium Mountains. There were acres of heather blue grasslands and small vegetable gardens, divided by waist-high walls made from stones gathered by generations of O'Hara's. The whitewashed buildings with thatch roofs, wooden plank floors, and rough hewn doors and windows blended perfectly into the countryside in a peaceful harmony like nothing he had never known. "Kathleen warned me it would be a little primitive but I was a little surprised with the outhouse and fetching water from the well."

"Yes, well, I do remember that you made quite an impression on all the relation. You never acted like a cocky Yank, ya' know."

"No, Millie, I loved it there – the milkin' and bringin' in the turf. Those noisy chickens and the sheep. I think those were some of the best days of my life. Do you know that I never once slept in that house? I was given a heavy quilt and a pillow, and sent to the haymow. Of course, they never knew that –" He stopped, self-conscious of what he was about to say.

Millie only laughed and got up from her chair. "Yes, well, I think I should go look in on Kathleen. Now you get some rest!" She turned and left without waiting for a response.

Matthew lounged back, listening to her muffled footsteps disappear down the hallway, grateful for the quiet. Having been reminded of those days and nights back in Ireland, he yearned to submerge himself in those memories.

He vividly remembered the strong, sweet smell of his bed of straw and the tiny specks of moonlight that seeped in through the cracks in the timbers. He laid there, straining to hear the sound of Kathleen's footsteps. Then she'd be next to him and he would gather her into his arms for a night of love making.

Her grandparents seemed appreciative of Matthew's efforts

to please them, especially his willingness to attend Mass every Sunday. He would have done anything to make her happy and earn the blessings of her family. However, his parents learned of the situation and took steps to have him moved from the area. Since his father's company was one of the largest ship building outfits on the East coast, all it took was a phone call. In September of '43, Matthew received orders to report to the Naval Headquarters in London.

The last night in Ireland with Kathleen remained one of the most poignant memories of Mathew's life. It was a cool autumn evening, and Kathleen took him to her secret, rocky glen where she played as a little girl.

"This may look like any ordinary place with ordinary stones," Kathleen said, her soft voice resonating with child-like rapture, "but I know differently. These are the ruins of an enchanted castle. Over there was King Connor's great banquet hall where all the warriors of Ulster gathered to eat and drink. They would challenge each other in contests of skill and strength, and of course, the handsome, young Cuchulainn won them all!"

Although Kathleen had a barb's knowledge of Irish folklore and could recite dozens of legends about heroes and their ladies, her favorite was Cuchulainn and his beloved Elmer. They were star-crossed lovers long before anyone ever heard of Romeo and Juliet. "They met in a place called the Garden of Lugh," she explained. "They were a perfect match because he was the strongest, bravest man in all of Ireland, and she was the most beautiful woman he had ever seen. They fell in love instantly."

"What happened?" Mathew murmured, not wanting the magical aura to slip away.

"Well, one night – a night such as this – they stole away and proclaimed their love for one another. Cuchulainn looked down upon her chest and said, 'I see a sweet, soft place to lay my head.' But Elmer made outrageous demands on him, saying no man would rest upon that place until he had completed great feats of strength and courage. Cuchulainn boasted he would do everything she asked and more."

Matthew kissed her then and cupped his hand around her breast. "What great feats must I do before I can rest my head upon your soft, sweet place?" he asked as he began to unbutton her blouse.

"Just promise me this. You would sooner cleave every stone in this field than ever break my heart."

"Break your heart? My God, Kathleen, never!" He was startled by her response.

"You say that now, but you shouldn't make promises you can't keep." Tears streamed down her cheeks. "We come from two different worlds, Matthew. I can't leave my family, and what about yours? Do you do think they'll welcome me with open arms?"

"Then I'll stay here with you. As soon as the war is over, I'll come back. Look at my hands, Kathleen – calluses. I've never been happier than these past few months. I love the work. I love this land. You've been telling me I should be a farmer, so I will." He said those words with such fervor that she seemed to take heart and stopped crying.

They made love then with wild, reckless abandon as lovers often do during times of war. But their lovemaking did nothing to calm their fears. They clung to each other, trembling and afraid. Their secret sanctuary now seemed like a dark pit, and the moon and the stars, which had shown so brightly before, disappeared into an angry sky.

He left for London and was billeted aboard a destroyer, patrolling the North Atlantic. He made First Lieutenant by the time his ship became part of the huge armada anchored in the choppy waters off Normandy that cold, stormy day in June '44. Although he was miserable those months apart form Kathleen, he was proud to be serving his country. He immersed himself in his work and waited for the ordeal to end so he could return to Ireland.

However, a few months before the war was over, he was called home. His father had suffered a stroke, so Matthew was needed to assume responsibility in the family business, something he knew nothing about and cared for even less. As the only son, he was told it was his duty. In his letters he promised Kathleen it was only temporary, but his father never recovered and the pressures of post-war transition in the shipbuilding industry kept him in New York. His four sisters seized upon this opportunity to arrange a more suitable match. An endless procession of pretty young debutantes paraded past him incessantly. But he rebuked their efforts at every turn.

Finally, in the summer of '47, Kathleen sent word that her grandparents relented and gave their blessing. They couldn't stand to see her so unhappy. Matthew stole away to Ireland, and there in the Irish countryside, they were married. He brought her home to New York, and was then content to take his place as permanent head of the company.

That's the way it had been all these years. The only thing that changed was that their family kept getting bigger on a regular basis. There were ten children now, counting the new baby girl. He was a good father. His whole world revolved around that bulging brownstone. He was a dutiful son, going off to the office everyday for 26 years of boring meetings and anxious decision making. He was a good husband too, even a good Catholic. He loved the Church because she loved it. That probably wasn't the right reason, but he didn't care. He loved the way she looked when she draped her veil over her long, beautiful hair and knelt to light the candles, or the way she insisted on saying the Rosary each evening with her less than enthusiastic brood. It had been a good life, and he never regretted a minute of it.

Many times he tried to duplicate those happy days in Ireland. He had a greenhouse built at the back of the house where he dabbled in growing vegetables and flowers. He liked to feel the dirt between his fingers and watch the tiny seeds sprout and flourish. For summer vacations, he packed his family off to rural areas out West or upstate New York. Instead of sitting by the pool in resorts or country clubs, he'd go to taverns and drink beer with the locals. He'd ask them questions about hybrid seed and fertilizers or implements and livestock. Once he paid a farmer $1000 to let him plow his fields. How Kathleen would laugh at him, saying that God must have intended for him to be a farmer after all.

Matthew drifted off to sleep then, having found the peace that comes with remembering happier days gone by.

* * * * * *

"Matthew!" a voice called. "Wake up. Kathleen is awake and asking for you." He rushed to her room, not knowing if he should feel hope or dread. He could see she was weakening and having even more difficulty breathing.

"Oh, Darlin', how is the baby?" she cried. "I wish I could hold her. She's all right, isn't she? You're not keeping anything from me, are you?"

"No, no, she's fine, I swear." He took Kathleen's cold, frail hand and pressed it against his lips. "She looks like Annie. Her eyes and hair – beautiful like her mother."

"Yes, what a lucky pair we are." She sighed, but then gasped as a spasm of pain struck through her. Matthew looked at her, so sick and fragile, enveloped in a jungle of tubes and machines. He longed to carry her away to a place that was fresh and free.

"I'm worried about Annie," she murmured. "She's such a good girl, but it's not fair that she'll have to take all this on herself."

"But isn't that what we did? We always did what our families expected of us. It wasn't so bad, was it?" he whispered, stroking her cheek. "You know what I was thinking about? Those wonderful days on your grandfather's farm. Remember how happy we were? You teased me that I should be a farmer."

"Maybe you should have listened to me," she sighed. "What happened to all those dreams? Maybe now--" Her voice faded then.

Matthew was stunned. "What are you saying? Weren't you happy?"

"I would have been happy with you anywhere. I had everything I wanted and much more. But you – year after year, I watched you go off to that office, knowing you hated it."

"No, Kathleen, I was happy, too, as long as I was with you." He couldn't bear to watch her struggling to speak. Her breathing became so labored that her chest heaved with every syllable. "We don't have to talk about this right now. You should rest. We can talk more tomorrow, please."

"Matthew, listen. You had such wonderful dreams and now you have sons who are young men themselves. They have everything, but they don't know how to dream. You must show them…teach them…somehow." She grasped his hand harder then. "Oh, Matthew, I'm just so tired." She closed her eyes then and slept.

Matthew was left to sit alone, drowning in the echo of her last words. What was she saying? Why talk about old dreams now? He wanted her to awaken. She had to explain – to finish it, to help him understand.

"You wife needs her rest," some far away voice said, but he couldn't move. He watched her sleep, struggling for every breath. Her mouth was drawn and tight, her beautiful face, pale and sunken almost beyond recognition. Oh God, what an awful way to die. People were supposed to smile and then gently slip away. Not like this. He watched her until he couldn't any longer. He put his head in his hands and wept.

Sometime later, Annie crept in beside him. Together they kept a quiet vigil until the early morning hours when Kathleen slipped into a coma. Matthew insisted that his daughter return home and demanded to be left alone as he sat at Kathleen's bedside, allowing only medical staff inside the sacred confines of his wife's death chamber. When others begged permission to enter, he sent them away harshly. His grief was too private, his pain too profound, his spirit too broken to allow for any intrusion. He only spoke to her – pleading, urging, singing, cajoling, willing her to open her eyes one last time. But Kathleen never awakened to speak or even smile again. After two long, excruciating days, Matthew knew the end was near.

"Don't be afraid," he whispered, clutching her cold, lifeless hand. "I will rest my head upon your soft, sweet place again someday, I promise."

CHAPTER 3

Death, everyone said, is a part of living. It was all right to cry and let your grief flow. Grief. Mourning. What was it, Annie wondered, and how do you do it? She found no comfort in the words of the priest at the funeral Mass. He said they should feel joy that their mother's suffering was over and she was united with her God in a better place. And there was that cold, awful jolt when the coffin lid was slammed shut that final time. How can you just walk away? People said the conspicuous heaps of flowers were beautiful, but she thought they looked hideously discordant against the cold, steel gray, January sky.

Why would anyone urge you to cry and cast away that protective shield of numbness? The terrible fear and anguish rushed in and that was too unbearable. Perhaps knowing how to grieve came with age, but their father seemed to be having more difficulty than anyone. Maybe it should help having such a large family. Everyone said so. But Annie could not remember ever feeling so alone in her life.

The only comfort she found was to concentrate her attention on her younger brothers. Extra hugs and familiar stories seemed to be all they needed. Saying that they should get back to their usual routine as quickly as possible was easier than explaining her own urgency for normalcy. The funeral was on Thursday and the boys started back to school the next Monday.

Annie woke early that morning, anxious to make her brothers' first day as easy as possible. She knew they were confused and afraid, so she fussed over them and tried to convince them that everything was going to be all right. After they left, she wandered the house, looking for something else to focus upon. She came across Grace attempting to give Joey a bath.

"Grace," Annie cried. "What are you doing? You can't handle him by yourself."

The nanny was crawling on the floor next to the tub, trying to keep the thrashing boy from drowning, "But Miss Annie," she exclaimed, "he messed himself awful this morning --"

"Then why didn't you ask me for help? I don't want you

hurting yourself." Annie rolled up her sleeves and grabbed the struggling child. Soon he was bathed, diapered, and dressed. They laid him in his playpen and sat down in the nursery's two rocking chairs for a much needed rest.

"I wonder if he misses Mother," Annie murmured. "Do you think he even knows she's gone?"

"Of course, he does. Sometimes I find him laying in his bed, crying this most pathetic little moan. He misses her something awful, just like the rest of us." She looked away then, close to tears.

Unable to comfort another living soul, Annie changed the subject. "The boys seemed relieved to be going back to school today – except Thomas, of course, but I expected that. Why does he always have to be so contrary?"

"Yes, I heard him arguing this morning. To tell you the truth, I never understood that boy. He's been broodish since the day he was born. He's the only one of you children I was never able to get close to, even when he was a baby. He was never a happy child, and I don't see things improving."

"I suppose not – I mean, Mother was the only one who understood him. She always managed to overlook his rude behavior." They both knew that Kathleen insisted that the warmth and sensitivity Thomas was unable to express socially was abundant in his music. She arranged private lessons for him at an early age, and now he attended an exclusive school for the musically gifted. An accomplished pianist and guitarist, his first love was the drums. Annie was sure he practiced them incessantly just to irritate the rest of the family.

"I usually just ignore him," Annie sighed, "but I should probably try to talk to him – for Mother's sake." She made a mental note to make a special effort to ask her brother about his day when he returned home that afternoon. "Speaking of problems, I haven't seen Mack around, have you? I heard him and Andrew argue a couple of days ago and he stormed out."

She wasn't surprised her oldest brother was behaving like this. Matthew Macalister Winston, III, had thus far lived a charmed life with a cavalier attitude that served him well in his trendy social circles, but left him ill-equipped to handle anything serious.

"Yes, I heard the ruckus," Grace said, shaking her head in disbelief. "What is that boy thinking, staying away at a time like this."

"I don't know what's going to happen to him. He's twenty-two years old, and he has to start handling things like an adult – not just Mother's death, but everything. Pop said he will not take care of the Draft Board, and he meant it. Mack has to get back to college, or..."

The word Vietnam hadn't been mentioned much since last summer when Mother first became ill, but it was a very hot topic before then. This was 1970, and the war, or conflict as it was sometimes called, was dragging on much longer than anyone expected. How Mack managed to stay out of it this long was a mystery to them all and a source of irritation to his father. Although Matthew, Sr. revered serving in the military as a noble and patriotic duty, Mack dismissed it as a lesson in futility. He refused to acknowledge the grim truth that the longer this thing wore on, the more likely that he would get drafted, especially since his own father refused to intercede on his behalf.

"I wish Andrew would just leave him alone," Annie added. "I thought they would try to be civil to each other, at least for a while." She had been refereeing her brothers' scrimmages for as long as she could remember and was tired of it. "The only time Andrew came out of his room all weekend was to argue with Mack. I stopped by to see him last night and he acted like I was bothering him."

"He wants to catch up on his studies before he goes back to school."

"That's fine, but he could come out to see how the rest of us are doing."

"Well, dear, you know everyone copes with things in different ways. Andrew idolized your mother, and he can't face anyone right now."

Annie started to say it was absurd to think that Andrew loved Mother more than anyone else, but she said nothing. It was true. Andrew worshipped her. Wanting to please her, he declared his intention to enter the priesthood as a young boy and never wavered. He was at the top of his class at St. John's University, where he studied theology. Annie understood why the priesthood appealed to him. He would adapt to the rigorous discipline and he certainly was a kind and thoughtful person with deep convictions about God and the Church. But she also knew he had difficulty relating to people on a personal level. Annie never questioned it before, but she wondered about it now as he struggled with Mother's death. Surely being able to comfort and counsel should be a natural inclination for a future priest.

"My dear," Grace murmured, "you're taking too much of this on yourself. Your father needs to be handling these things. Perhaps in a few days, he will be able to look at things more clearly. He has to take care of the living."

The nanny's words were kind and well intentioned, but Annie did not hold out much hope in that regard either. Matthew wanted as little intrusion as possible. No one had seen him or spoken to him since Mother's funeral. He stayed in his and Mother's bedroom with the door locked. Even two of his sisters, Esther and Vivian, became frustrated that he would not admit them and stopped coming. Annie tried to keep as much decorum around the house as possible, but she resented her father barricading himself from his own family. She pitied him, but she needed his help.

"I think I'll go to the hospital and see the baby," Annie said, trying to sound more cheerful. "The nurses said I could come everyday if I want."

"That's a splendid idea. I'll keep Joey company, and I promise to get help if I need it."

Annie gave her a hug and turned to go, grateful to escape the dark pall that lingered throughout the house. As she walked down the stairs, she felt her mother's presence and knew how disappointed she must be in all of them.

* * * * * *

It became routine for Annie to visit the hospital daily. This sibling, at least, expected nothing except to be fed and held. Matthew named her Rebecca Elizabeth after their grandmothers,

26

but Annie called her Becky. It was amazing to see her growing so fast.

Try as she might, Annie could not get her father to accompany her. Perhaps Mother's worst fears were realized that he blamed the baby for her death. Annie knew him to be a loving father and hoped this crises would pass. Four weeks after her birth, Becky was ready to come home.

That morning Annie awakened early and went to her father's room with a tray of hot coffee and food. The door wasn't locked so she went on in. The room was void of light and color except the narrow shaft of light that invaded the darkness through the open door. She crept toward the large bed and began sifting through the rumpled linens. He wasn't there. Peering through the dim light, she spotted him, sitting by the cold, charred fireplace, asleep. There was broken glass and empty liquor bottles were strewn around him. The foul smell of whiskey and stale cigarette smoke hung in the air.

"Daddy," she called, shaking his shoulder.

He was slow to respond, mumbling incoherently until he leapt from his chair. "Annie, what is it?" he cried. "Is it your mother? What does she want?" He lunged across the room and then froze as he stared at the empty bed.

"Ann Marie, why did you come in here like this?" He sank onto the bed without looking at her. "What do you want?"

"I want you to come with me to the hospital to bring the baby home."

His hands fell limp onto his lap. "Honey, I can't –"

"No, don't say that. Please, come with me."

"Not today, Annie. Isn't that why I hired Millie? She can go with you."

"She's meeting us there. Besides, you have to sign papers. Come, please."

"I can't. Take one of the boys, or Grace. I just can't go back to that hospital."

"I know it's hard, but I can't do it by myself." She was close to tears but she didn't look away. She wanted him to see her desperation.

A glimmer of resignation softened his face. He took her

hand and squeezed it gently. "Hope you brought a lot of coffee."

Beaming, she poured a cup and sat very close to him as he took it with trembling hands. He said nothing as he drank the first cup, as though waiting for his eyes and head to clear a little. "I'm sorry, honey," he said as she poured another cup. "I really let you and your brothers down, didn't I?"

He gazed around the room as though seeing it for the first time. "My God, look at this place. Doesn't even seem like the same room, does it." He staggered toward the bay windows. He drew open the drapes and squinted as he tried to adjust to seeing sunlight for the first time in weeks. "Do you know your mother looked at dozens of houses before she found this one with the master bedroom facing south. I guess she wanted every ray of sunlight there was in a day." He smiled then, but Annie could see the depth of sadness in his eyes.

"I'd better shave and shower," he said, stroking his unkempt face. "Send Gilles in, would you, honey? Leave the tray." He took his daughter's hand and helped her to her feet. Taking her into his arms, he hugged her tightly. "You have such pretty hair," he murmured as he patted her long, red mane. "Really, thanks for coming and waking me. Tell those ruffian brothers of yours to behave 'cause the old man will be down at the breakfast table."

* * * * * *

As Matthew descended the stairs, it occurred to him that time had gone on without him. He surveyed his brood assembled at the table, really seeing them for the first time in months. Peter walked across the room and looked as though he had grown two inches. Thomas had different glasses and Luke's hair was much longer.

Then he noticed they were staring at him, too. He cleared his throat briskly, took his seat at the head of the table, and retreated behind his *Times*. There was an awkward silence for a few minutes, but they began to relax and resumed their conversation.

"So what if he does win," Johnny said, "it doesn't mean

anything."

"Sure it will," Andrew retorted. "He'll be the heavyweight champion of the world."

"Who will be?" Matthew asked casually from behind his paper.

"Joe Frazier. Tonight's the big fight, Pop," Johnny explained.

Of course, Matthew thought, his boys were discussing sports. With this many sons, most of the family discussions held at this table centered around athletics, especially when John was there. The fifteen year old was the family jock and resident sports authority. Matthew loved all of his children, but John's natural athletic ability was a particular delight. He was quick and agile and showed promise in several sports, but football was his favorite. Unfortunately, his mother declared the sport barbaric and had a European's preference for soccer. She never approved of boxing either, but it had long been a passion shared by John and his father.

"Frazier is going against Thomas Ellis over at the Gardens," John continued. "Frazier's a sure bet to win, then he'll be recognized as the heavyweight champion."

"And then that Cassius Clay character will be out, right?"

"Mohammad Ali, Pop, he changed his name to Mohammad Ali. Anyway, some of the guys at school say it's not fair."

"What's not fair? The guy refused to join up after he was drafted so the World Boxing Federation refused to recognize him as any kind of champion."

"People say sports are supposed to be separate from politics. What does him claiming to an conscientious objector have anything to do with boxing?"

"Well, for one thing," interjected Andrew, visibly bristling, "it makes a mockery of the whole process."

"Sure," Matthew said, "listen to your brother. When he decided to declare that to the Draft Board, it was something he took very seriously. Do you remember that Clay --er, Ali, fight I took you to last year, John? Remember how we talked about that look in his eye – like he wanted to kill the other guy? Conscientious objector, my ass. Any fool can see the only thing he cares about is saving his own butt. The Boxing Federation said no, and most of us red-blooded Americans and paying patrons of boxing, agree."

"Okay, that's it." Mack cried, throwing down his napkin. "I sat here and listened to your bullshit, but that's enough. We're having a nice conversation about boxing, and you turn it into a lesson about the Red, White, and Blue. Why would any man who can fight like that risk everything when he's the best boxer in the world. Maybe the best there ever was! He's no fool!"

"A fool? No, he certainly is not!" Matthew retorted, slamming his paper down on the table. "I bet before long he'll figure out a way to get it all back – the money, the championship, everything. But what makes him – or anyone else, for that matter – think they shouldn't do their share."

"Ah, Jeez, here it comes!" Mack howled as he leaped to his feet.

"No, now stop" implored Annie, rushing to stand by her father. "This arguing is ridiculous. Boys, get your things. It's time for school."

Matthew was struck by the horror in her eyes and was embarrassed by his actions. She was right. There has been too much tension in this house for far too long. He wanted to apologize, but Mack stormed out with Annie close on his heels. Matthew followed them, hoping to soothe an awkward situation.

Annie caught up with Mack on the stairs and turned him around roughly. "For God's sake, why did you do that?" she demanded. "The first day he comes down to be with the family and you pick a fight?"

"Pick a fight? Hell, he started it. Why is everything always my fault?"

"Oh, shut up. I don't care who started it. We just need some peace around here."

"Tell that to him," Mack sneered, gesturing toward Matthew who was standing at the bottom of the stairs. "There isn't going to be any peace in this house until the stupid war is over." Mack turned and leapt up the stairs.

Annie looked as though she was going to say something to excuse her brother's behavior, but Matthew motioned for her to stop. "Just go get ready, honey," he said. She fled up the stairs, too.

Matthew turned to return to the dining room and was startled to see Luke staring at them, a pained expression on his face. "Luke," Matthew called, sounding gruffer that he intended. "Why didn't you go to school?"

"Well," Luke murmured, as if shaking off a trance, "there's some kind of career assembly for seniors at school. I decided to skip it."

"Career, huh? Well, that sounds interesting. You'll need to make some decisions about your future soon." Matthew was dismayed to see that his attempt at making conversation did nothing to alter his son's solemn expression. "Did you ever send in that application to the Art Institute?"

Luke seemed surprised. That's my fault, Matthew chided himself. Luke was a sensitive, caring boy who always seemed ill at ease with himself. His artistic talents were of particular delight to his mother, but Matthew knew nothing about art and had difficulty knowing how to respond. The boy had always misconstrued this as disapproval. "I'd be happy to sit down with you and go over your application, Son."

"Sure, Pop, that would be great," Luke said, not sounding very convinced. "Anyway, I need to get to school. Good luck today. It'll be nice having a baby around here." He smiled then, waved goodbye, and was gone.

Would it really be good to have another motherless child under this roof, Matthew wondered. He began to feel panicked but he fought to push it back. This was a new day, a new beginning. Yes, it was true that he hadn't been there for his older children but he would try to do better with Becky.

* * * * * *

Matthew felt increasingly nervous the closer they got to the hospital. He knew Annie was watching him, probably praying that he wouldn't lose his nerve. He was not prepared for the tremendous changes in his daughter, who looked nothing like the small, sickly baby he had watched those anxious first hours of her life. Matthew was relieved to see that Annie was at ease with the situation and seemed to be in charge. Cousin Millie was there, too, going over the discharge instructions. Matthew was content to watch the proceedings from afar until Annie picked up the infant and placed her in his father's arms.

He stood awkwardly for a moment, as though he did not want to look at her. But then she began to fuss. Matthew drew her close and felt an unfamiliar sensation of moistness of his cheeks as he stared at the beautiful child – Kathleen's last gift to him. Maybe there was reason to hope after all.

* * * * * *

The rest of February was drab and quiet as the days passed slowly. Matthew was no longer aloof, but he didn't leave the house either. If Becky had a sniffle or a fussy spell, he'd sit in the nursery for hours, sometimes sleeping all night in Kathleen's rocker near the crib. He seemed to be over-compensating with the boys, too. He interrogated them when they arrived home from school. They knew he was trying to be concerned and interested, but he came off as interfering and domineering. The only one who escaped his stranglehold was Mack, who seldom came home at all.

Everything had changed and Annie was discouraged by her inept efforts to re-establish a sense of normalcy. There was never any pleasant conversation around the dinner table, only incessant arguing and acrimony. The meals themselves lacked their usual flavorful variety and festive fare because there was no one to guide Cook with menu selections. The servants seemed irritated and somewhat unhinged by the lack of direction. Annie always assumed the household ran itself, but she came to understand that it had been managed very skillfully by her mother. The bouquets of fresh flowers no longer magically appeared and the mail was left unopened. Annie knew the servants were hesitant to come to her with their questions because they viewed her as too inexperienced to make even minor decisions.

Sometimes Annie would sit in her room and stare into the mirror. She saw nothing that assured her of any inner strength or wisdom that would enable her to cope with these troubled times. Why couldn't she be more like her mother, she moaned silently. It seemed ridiculous to her that people used to comment how much alike they were. Her father always said, "My little princess – pretty as your mother."

She studied her reflection closely and saw little resemblance. Maybe their eyes were similar – large green ones. Annie had long hair, too, but it wasn't like Mother's. Hers was dark brown with soft, lovely waves. Annie's was red and irritatingly frizzy, a curse Mother said, she inherited from her grandmother, Elizabeth.

Sometimes she wondered what her friends were doing back at college. Her sorority sisters were busy with dates, classes, and all night gossip sessions. She hated going away to college at first, but now she missed it. *There's a great big world out there, Annie,* her mother said. *Go find yourself.* Where? How? What am I supposed to do? But no answers came back to her from the mirror.

Tension continued to linger in the air like a bad smell. Danny began waking up at night screaming with nightmares and the other boys' sullen faces told the grim truth that their problems were far from over.

Chapter 4

"Daddy, just hold still, and I'll help you with your tie." Annie followed her father as he darted around his bedroom. "You should let me fix the pocket of your dinner jacket. It has a big hole, so don't use it for anything important."

Mother would be aghast to see how her usually meticulously dressed husband looked tonight. There wasn't enough time to send his tux out to be cleaned and pressed, and his black wing tips hadn't been polished since the funeral. His mood and expression did nothing to enhance his appearance.

"I cannot believe those sisters of mine talked me into this," Matthew fumed. "The Foundation was Father's pet project, but so what? Why in the hell do I have to go?"

"Well, I suppose because you're the head of the family, as well as the company. These dinners are nice affairs," Annie insisted. "Look Daddy, I know you feel uneasy about this, but maybe it'll be nice to get out for a change." It had been several weeks since the funeral, and Annie wanted him to go. Perhaps that was a mistake, she thought, as she put the finishing touches on his tie. There was already an unmistakable odor of liquor on his breath. She had a feeling of impeding disaster.

Finally, he was ready to go. "You look fabulous, as usual," Annie lied as she helped him slip on his top coat. "And don't try any tricks, Daddy," she called after him. "William will give me a full report in the morning."

"Ha! Who signs your paycheck anyway," he muttered, pushing past the traitorous chauffer to open his own door.

* * * * * *

When Matthew arrived, the banquet hall was already glittering with lavishly dressed guests making sophisticated small talk. Matthew surrendered his topcoat and reached for a long-stemmed glass of Champagne and a cigarette. Damn, he hated these stuffy affairs. He and Kathleen used to watch who smiled the broadest or patted each other on the back the most. Then they scanned the business and society pages for those peoples' names in stories of cutthroat, corporate takeovers and newly announced divorces. Kathleen was always better at their game than he was. She had an uncanny knack for reading people. God, how he wished she was with him tonight.

His plan was to eat and make an excuse of an illness in the family to make an early exit. He stood back from the crowds, but unfortunately, he was soon engulfed by his four sisters. They chattered away as usual, until Esther, the oldest and most dominate, managed to take control and silence the other three.

"Well, Matthew," she chirped, "it's wonderful to see you tonight. But you know, Papa would absolutely—Matthew, must you smoke? You know it bothers me so!" she whined. And then, without breaking cadence, she continued. "Is that Harold Brinton's wife?"

"Not unless she's lost twenty-five pounds!" retorted Gertrude, the youngest. "I've heard he's been carrying on with his secretary, but I can't believe he'd show up here tonight with her, for goodness sake."

"Well, things have certainly changed in this town. There is no such thing as good manners any more," Esther said. "Look at her! It is obvious she has no class! I have no intention of saying one word to either of them all night."

"Look at Ruth Compton," hissed Vivian, Matthew's particularly sarcastic second sister. "I'd bet lunch at the Ritz that she had a face lift. She looks ten years younger than she did at the Christmas ball in December. There's probably bruising under all that makeup."

"Well at least she's with her husband," said Gertrude. "I heard she needed to do something. He was going to leave her, you know."

So it went, the tittle-tattle blabbing that had the whole room buzzing. Matthew began plotting a new scheme to escape before dinner. As he rehearsed excuses in his mind, he shook his head yes and no in accordance to his sisters' tones. Then he became aware that another female had joined them and was being introduced to him. The lady smiled demurely, batting her long, fake eyelashes.

"It's all been arranged," Esther announced.

"What has?" Matthew blurted.

"Well, Matthew, weren't you listening? Lucille will be seated next to you on the dais."

He stared at the woman incredulously. He was stunned because he thought Esther and the others had seemed bereaved by the illness and death of his wife. But, here they were, six weeks later, already playing matchmaker. The deep, scarlet in his cheeks and tight-lipped grimace were unmistakable evidence that he was incensed.

"Matthew, why are you so shocked?" Esther retorted. "You need a partner for dinner, and you've known Lucille for years. Don't you remember? Her husband was a partner at Wells, Juneau, Wells, & McKinley."

"Yes, Matthew," Vivian chimed in. "The poor dear just

lost her husband recently, too. Perhaps you can –"

"Ladies, I am sorry," Matthew interrupted, "but the only reason I came tonight was out of respect for my father and his foundation. But—Lucille, is it? You're going to have to find yourself another dinner partner. I really don't have much of an appetite these days, and I just lost what little I had."

"Matthew! Where are you going?" shrieked Esther as her brother walked away.

He could hear choruses of scolding from his matronly sisters and grunts of righteous indignation from the injured lady, but he paused only long enough to take two glasses of Champagne as he strode out the door. He burst out into the cold February night and hailed a cab, preferring to let William continue napping in the limo.

He crawled into the cab, flinging his tie and the two empty glasses into the slushy gutter. The night air was invigorating. Having left his sisters open-mouthed and embarrassed, he felt more unburdened than he had in a very long time. He wanted to stop off at home to grab some cash, but it was still early. Annie and several of her brothers would still be awake. He was in no mood for their well-intended meddling tonight. He gave the cabby the address of his office and instructed him to wait while he ran inside.

Rosetta, who had been the cleaning lady as long as Matthew could remember, was having a cigarette with Julius, the night watchman. When they saw the boss stride in, they jolted to attention like sentries caught napping.

He gave a playful, mock salute toward his father's portrait as he moved it aside to gain access to the stash of cash hidden behind the secret panel. Matthew's grandfather had it installed and called it "passion money". Considering the strict, straight-laced women his father and grandfather married, Matthew had a fair idea for what kind of "passion" it was intended. However, Matthew used it more than a few times to stake himself to a friendly poker game. He grabbed several handfuls without bothering to count it and returned old Dad to his customary place. On impulse, he thrust a couple of bills into the hands of the shocked Rosetta and Julius as he rushed back to the cab.

"Here's fifty bucks and I'll double it if you find me a good poker game, the higher the stakes the better," Matthew directed the cabby. He lounged back as the driver twisted his way through traffic until he came to a little corner tavern on the lower East side.

"Just say Mario sent you," the cabby said, waiting with an out-stretched hand for the promised reward. "Enjoy yourself and good luck," he called as he drove off.

Matthew walked in, rubbing his hands in lusty anticipation. He loved this kind of place. It reminded him of overseas during the war. The room was dimly lit with the unmistakable aroma of Italian cooking coming from the kitchen off the side of the barroom. Matthew suddenly had an overpowering appetite for a heaping plate of spaghetti, along with a bottle of house wine.

As he ate, Matthew watched the activity around the room with keen interest, taking care not to be obvious. He suspected he was being scrutinized, too, as was the custom in such places. There must be a game going on in the backroom, he thought. An expressionless sentinel stood outside the door as a waiter hustled in and out bringing carafes of wine. Sealed decks of cards was passed inside. Matthew finished his meal and pushed his plate aside.

"Are you sure I cannot get you something else, sir?" the waiter asked. Good, thought Matthew, This guy knows I have money and probably a good tipper. Matthew did not disappoint. He threw out a fifty-dollar bill, but placed his hand across it as the waiter reached to pick it up.

"Not so fast, young man" Matthew said, smiling. "I'd be glad to let you have this, but first you need to do something else for me. You see, I'd really like to sit in on that game going on back there."

The waiter seemed to be hesitating so Matthew decided he needed to be a little more persuasive. "My good friend, Mario, the cabby, told me this just might be where I could find a good. High stakes poker game." Matthew unbuttoned his coat so the waiter could see his bulging pockets of money.

The waiter approached the guard and they spoke in hushed tones for a few moments. The guard knocked quietly and stepped inside. Matthew smoked his after dinner cigarette unconcerned. Getting into these games was fairly simple if you had enough cash and you could convince them you weren't a cop. In a few minutes, the guard returned and gave Matthew the go-ahead nod.

* * * * * *

As Matthew sat down at the table, he didn't notice the young man standing in the shadows. He wasn't supposed to. The kid's job was to move around the room inconspicuously to attend to the needs of the players, and he did it very well. The regulars liked having him around. He was smart without being mouthy, confident without being cocky. He never drank or interfered in any way and could seemingly go for days without sleep. No one knew where he came from or where he lived, and no one cared. Hardly anyone knew his name. They just said, "Hey, you!" or "Injun' boy". He had high cheekbones, a square jaw, and a dark, expressionless face. He wore a rolled bandana around his forehead and his long, jet black hair. He was tall and lean with a presence of quiet strength.

Tonight, Sonny Jackson stood in his usual place away from the table, leaning on his mop. He had just cleaned up some broken glass, the end result of an "unfortunate accident" of one of Mr. Gonatelli's guests. The gentlemen had lost several successive hands and found himself relieved of all his cash. Perhaps that is why the boss allowed the stranger to enter the sacred confines of his private game.

"Gentlemen, your ante please," the dealer said. "The game is my old friend, draw with deuces wild".

It didn't take Matthew long to see that these were worthy adversaries. With an opening ante of $1000, this was the high stakes game he wanted. Although he managed to keep his poker face in place, inwardly he was having the time of his life. The necessary skill and concentration was a wonderful distraction. He had nothing to lose, except the money, which he lost rapidly. After the first hand, he found himself relieved of $3,700. The benefactor of Matthew's bad luck was the host, Mr. Gonatelli, a short, dark man with piercing eyes and a small, unsmiling mouth.

There was seldom much idle chit-chat around Mr. Gonatelli's table, but tonight only the barest necessities were spoken. There was a simple tap-tap if two cards were needed or a nod of the head as chips were piled on the table. The pots became enormous as ten to twenty thousand dollars were won or lost with each hand. Matthew began to think that this night would be cut short as his money dwindled fast. But then, toward morning, Lady Luck came over to his side of the table as he began winning more than he lost. One by one the other players dropped out, but no one left. At one point, Mr. Gonatelli dispatched an assistant to bring more cash from the safe. His jaw seemed to tighten with each successive hand as his cold, dark eyes stared across the table.

Finally, the edges of his mouth began to twitch a little. "I believe the dealer takes all." He laid down his cards and began scooping up his winnings. The cards on the table showed a straight flush, king high. It was the best hand he had been dealt in hours.

"Just a moment, please." There was only one possible way that Matthew could take this hand. Mr. Gonatelli stopped and glanced up at the stranger incredulously. His smirkish, half smile disappeared as the spectators pressed closer. Matthew laid down a royal flush – ten, jack, and queen of spades with two deuces wild.

Gonatelli rested his elbows on the table, pressed the fingertips together, and watched as Matthew retrieved his winnings. He nodded for a fresh deck of cards, shuffled them methodically, and presented them for the cut. He dealt their allotted cards and slowly picked up his hand. There was not a flick of an eyelash or slightest change in his expression to reveal what he saw when he fanned out those five cards. Matthew watched carefully as he, too, picked up his cards. This was probably the last hand, and he had a buzzard's taste to lick this arrogant bastard clean.

Replacement cards were dealt and then Matthew opened with the amount he knew Gonatelli had left -- $14,200. Gonatelli did likewise, leaving a vacant spot where excess of $100,000 had been a few hours ago. Matthew followed by adding several more thousand on the pile, inviting his opponent to either fold or call.

And then, it happened.

"Mr. Marconi." The words cut the silence like a thunderclap. "Would you please go back to my office and bring me the little red box?"

No one said a word as Gonatelli's assistant left the room and returned with a scarlet velvet box. The boss opened it and took out a folded, yellowed piece of paper. He laid it on the table for Matthew's scrutiny.

"This is a deed to 420 acres of prime land in the Mississippi valley. I, myself, won it in a game such as this a few years ago. I've never seen the place, but I must tell you, I consider this to be somewhat of a good luck piece. I do not wager it lightly. At $1,000 an acre, I'll bet it against everything you have."

Matthew fought mightily to keep his composure as he sat listening to Gonatelli speak. Hoping that no one noticed his hands were trembling, he picked up the document. The deed was for a parcel of land in Shannon Town Township, Dubuque County, State of Iowa. Still fighting hard to focus, he nodded his acceptance of the wager and pushed his pile of winnings to the middle of the table. His heart was pounding in his throat as he turned over his cards. He looked across the table. His answer came soon enough. Mr. Gonatelli's mouth became twisted and his cheeks flushed deep crimson. Everyone in the room knew he was beaten.

Matthew waited an appropriate time before gathering his winnings. "Mr. Gonatelli, I believe you have to sign this? Here on the back." Matthew presented the deed for the loser's signature.

Long, gut-retching moments passed before Gonatelli scrawled his name. And then, all eyes shifted toward the stranger. It suddenly occurred to Matthew that he was outnumbered in an enemy camp.

"It certainly is a pleasure to play with such gentlemen as yourselves," Matthew said, not wanting to sound cocky. He thrust the deed and the cash into the pockets of his dinner jacket and took side steps in the direction of the door. For a moment, it looked as though the guard was going to block his exit, but then he stepped aside. Matthew slid out, offering a friendly salute as he passed. In quick, wide strides he crossed the barroom and burst jubilantly into the brisk, early morning air.

He guessed it to be around 5 or 6 AM. It was Sunday so the streets were deserted and there was no cabs in sight. Not sure where he was, he turned from side to side trying to get his bearings. It was then that he saw several men step out of the shadows. Matthew recognized them to be Gonatelli's men. Quickly he spun around, but he was cut off there, too. He darted across the street and foolishly turned into a dark alley. They were on him in a flash. He kicked and struggled, but they held him down as they went through his pockets. Matthew knew what they were looking for, but was powerless to stop them.

Suddenly, a dark, blurry figure jumped into the fray. He flung one assailant against the wall and wheeled quickly to send another to his knees with a vicious blow to the gut. Matthew took on the third, grabbing the guy around the neck and bit his ear with all his strength. With his free hand, he picked up a brick and beamed him over the head

That left only the fourth and largest assailant and the stranger. They began circling each other slowly. Gonatelli's man had a long knife clutched in his hand. "Hey, Injun," he sneered, "the boss ain't gonna like this."

It was then that Matthew recognized the young man. He had brought in wine and cigarettes a couple of times. Matthew had no idea why the kid was helping him, but there was no time to ask questions. He flung his trusty brick at the huge man. It only grazed him but it gave Sonny Jackson enough time to kick the knife away. He spun quickly, smashing the guy's knee and then landed a vicious undercut to his jaw. The giant was stunned, at least momentarily.

"C'mon," Sonny cried, "we gotta get out of here. Let's go"

They ran out into the street, and by some act of divine intervention, there sat a cab. They both jumped in, ordering the driver to pull out…"and fast!"

"Young man," Matthew said breathlessly, "you're hurt."

There was a nasty cut across Sonny's upper arm, but he ignored it. "Did they get it?" he pressed, still gasping for air.

41

"Oh, my God, let's see! Where did I put it?" Matthew frantically searched his pockets, but then a slow smile spread across his face. "My daughter warned me not to put anything important in this pocket." Reaching deep inside the lining of the jacket, he found the much sought after document. He held it up jubilantly and kissed it. "She had no idea how wrong she was."

Chapter 5

Annie was sleeping in the window seat above the front door, but stirred when she heard something on the street below. There were loud voices and slamming car doors as her father got out a cab, supported by some stranger. She woke Mack and Andrew on the way down the hallway and then rushed downstairs. She met her father and his companion as they stumbled in the door. She was horrified to see their bruised and bleeding faces. "I knew it! I knew it!" she scolded as she drew near. "As soon as William came home without you, I knew you were going to do something like this. Just look at you!"

Annie turned to face the young stranger for the first time. His dark eyes were so intense she felt as though he could see right through her. She clutched her robe around her neck as she moved awkwardly toward him, turning her attention to the bloody wound. "It looks deep," she said, her cheeks beginning to flush. "You probably should see a doctor right away."

"It ain't deep, and I ain't gonna see no doctor." Annie withdrew her hand quickly, deciding she did not like this man and wished he would leave.

A steady stream of sleepy-eyed boys came down the stairs. They surrounded their father who sat down at the head of the dining room table.

"Sure glad you never fixed this pocket, Annie," he said. "They got everything else but not this." He took out the yellowed, tattered piece of paper and gingerly laid it out on the table. "Peter, go get a map of Iowa. No, not Ohio, Iowa. Look in the encyclopedia or something." He took the map, eagerly running his finger down the page. "There it is, right on the

Mississippi!" Matthew cried out suddenly. "See! There's our farm! Right there!"

Dazed, they looked at each other in total disbelief. "Farm! What farm?" they all said. "What are you talking about? We don't have a farm."

"Like hell we don't," Matthew rang out triumphantly. "You'd better hold onto your hats, because tomorrow we start packing! We're moving!"

This astonishing announcement met with another chorus of disbelief. They all looked to Mack to do their talking since he usually had the most luck arguing with their father. "Pop, we don't have any idea what the heck you're talking about!" he began.

"We're landowners now, son. By some stroke of extraordinary good luck, I am now in possession of 420 acres of the richest, blackest land on God's green earth." He kissed the paper like it was a holy relic.

Even Mack was speechless for a moment, but he recovered quickly. "You expect us to pick up and leave New York City to live in some God-forsaken hole in the ground? To farm? That is the most ridiculous thing I have ever heard." He waved his hand as though to dismiss the whole thing and turned to walk out.

Matthew's fist came down hard on the table. "Don't you walk out on me! No, I am not crazy. I'm not even drunk. I'm making more sense now than I have in a long, long time. Now you listen to me, all of you. You live under my roof and I support you very well, true?" He stood with his hands on his hips, surveying the little group fiercely. "All my dammed life I have done exactly what was expected of me. The only thing I ever managed to do on my own was to marry your mother. Well, I want this, do you understand?" He paused to take a deep breath and study each of their faces. "I wish your mother was here because she would have loved the idea. But she's not – all the wishing and praying in the world is never going to bring her back." He clinched the small piece of paper in his fist and waved it over his head empathetically. "But I am still alive and I am through sitting around, waiting to die, too. So now you just listen and listen good. This family is moving!"

He turned toward the liquor cabinet to pour a drink and remained with his back turned, indicating that they were dismissed.

Sonny watched the whole spectacle from a back corner of the room. Matthew motioned for him to sit down and offered him a cigarette.

"You probably think I'm crazy, too, don't you," Matthew said.

Sonny leaned over to light his cigarette from Matthew's gold lighter. "I think it don't matter what I think."

Matthew sat there, contemplating for a time, drawing deeply on his cigarette. "You can't go back to your job at the bar, right?"

"No, I reckon not."

"You're not originally from around here, are you"

"No. I was born on a reservation…..in Kansas."

Matthew mulled it over slowly. "Well, do you have any experience working on a farm or with animals?"

"Livestock? Yeah, I did a lot of odd jobs for farmers when I was a kid."

"I'd like to hire you. I need help to at least get started. I'd make it worth your while."

Sonny slowly surveyed his surroundings. "Let me get this straight. You want to take all this and all of them out to this farm in Iowa?" Matthew nodded. "Sure," Sonny said. "I'm in."

* * * * * *

Annie was still pacing around her room when she heard her father and the stranger come upstairs. Her worst fears were realized – this Sonny character had somehow involved himself in her father's crazy scheme. She went to the guest bedroom and knocked. She opened the door to find him standing awkwardly, holding his injured arm. She realized that would afford her a good excuse to open some dialogue. "Hello," she said. "I heard you come up. I thought perhaps you might need some help. I can bandage that for you." She moved closer to him, frustrated that she was blushing again.

44

"No, I'd like to take a shower and get some sleep," he said, turning away.

Annie knew she had been dismissed but ignored it. "Well, the bathroom's right here," she sang out cordially, as she flipped on the light. "I'll be back with the first aid kit by the time you're done."

She went to get her mother's much-used basket of bandages and ointments and then busied herself turning down the bed while she waited for him to finish. She expected him to come out with a towel wrapped around his waist, intimidating her with the well-defined muscles she suspected were hidden under his bizarre wardrobe.

But instead, he came out fully clothed with the sleeve of his wounded arm torn off at the shoulder. She opened the bandages clumsily, nearly spilling the whole basket. She could see the wound was clean and not very deep. She poured some of Kathleen's favorite cure-all ointment on it and wrapped it. He never flinched or even watched what she was doing, apparently regarding her actions as unwanted interference.

"I suppose we should thank you for helping my father. I'm sorry you got hurt," she said as she applied the tape sharply. "Why did you help him anyway? Did he offer you a reward?"

"No, he didn't. But he did offer me a job."

"So now the two of you are all set to go out there? Good God! That is the most ridiculous thing I have ever heard!"

"Maybe, but your old man sounded pretty sure of it to me."

Annie moved to the other side of the room and gazed out of the window. "Look, Mr. Jackson, I can lay my hands on a considerable amount of money. Why don't you take it and get out of here. My mother died a few weeks ago and my father is having a very hard time adjusting, but I expect soon he will realize he's making a horrible mistake. How about, say -- $10,000?" She turned to find him studying her again.

He didn't answer at first. He tied his headband in place, and then picked up his leather jacket and studied the damage to his sleeve. He moved in a slow, deliberate way that Annie found infuriating.

"Look," he said, "I think your father is going to do this

thing, with or without my help. And I already told him I'd go along with it for awhile."

"So what? I can get the money on Monday. Just take it and disappear. He won't where to find you, and then he'll give up this crazy idea of his."

Again, he did not answer as though he were choosing his words carefully. "Let's just go with this and see what happens. I'm a good worker and know a little about farming. I'll stay out of your way if you stay out of mine."

With that he turned away, looking as though he was going to disrobe. She had no choice but to leave, having accomplished nothing and feeling more unsettled than before.

* * * * * *

Annie only slept a couple of hours. Remembering it was Sunday, she decided she'd better get the family off to Mass. When she came down the hallway, she paused at the guest bedroom door. It was open and the bed made. There was no sign of Mr. Jackson anywhere. She hoped he had changed his mind after all and was gone for good. As she came downstairs, she was surprised to see her father already at the breakfast table, his faced glued to a book. Something about farming, Andrew mouthed silently. Mack was sitting at the other end of the table, looking very sullen. He was wearing the same clothes he had on the night before.

The doorbell rang and Giles admitted Sonny laden with an armload of magazines and newspapers. "I know a guy on Times Square who gets newspapers and junk from all over the world," he explained. "Here's a *Telegraph-Herald*, the paper in Dubuque. It's a couple of weeks old, though."

Matthew was obviously thrilled. "What a terrific idea!"

"Yeah, great!" Mack sneered. "At least our new hired can read."

Matthew ignored that last remark as he leafed through the piles of new reading material. Sonny turned to leave. Annie followed him to the front door where they were out of earshot of her father. "Where are you going?" she demanded. "You can't just leave!"

"I'll be back in the morning. I don't know, though. I bet I could make out pretty good here. You'd probably each give me $10,000." With that, he walked out the door.

Matthew looked up from his reading material and saw Sonny was gone "You'd better watch out what you say around him, Mack," Matthew warned. "He could take off your head without breaking a sweat."

"So I'm supposed to be scared of this guy?" Mack retorted. "I'll say whatever I damn please to the sonofabitch! Why do you trust him anyway? He's probably some two-bit hustler that'll take off as soon as he can get his hands on some of your money."

"Look, I don't care whether you like him or not, because I do. He saved my butt last night. He says he's from the Midwest and knows something about farming – I'm sure a hell of a lot more than any of us. He's smart and keeps his mouth shut, which is more than I can say about anyone else around here."

Matthew spent the rest of the day totally absorbed in all the material Sonny brought him. There was no use trying to reason with him. Mack slammed out the door that morning and was not heard from the rest of the day.

* * * * * *

Monday started with business as usual. "Peter, you need your winter coat and boots," Annie said, "and John, you left your history text on the dining room table." It was the usual before-school bedlam, but she noticed a few confused frowns. "Don't look so worried, boys. Everything is going to be fine and you have nothing to worry about. But boys, you probably shouldn't say anything to anyone, not yet." She was sure anyone who heard about their father's scheme would think he had gone berserk. Even the young ones seemed to understand and promised to not talk about their father's plans to anyone.

Matthew got up and dressed early. He took a pot of coffee into the library where he continued to pour over his stacks of reading material. Right on cue, Sonny appeared.

"Sonny!" Matthew called out happily. "Come on in. I cannot wait to get started." He patted the young man on the shoulder. "I've already read a lot of the material you brought over yesterday. Look here." He pointed to a small ad for the Shannon Town Pub and Grill, "Ah," he said, "I bet the beer tastes good there." He chatted on, pausing only long enough to yell upstairs. "Mack, get out of bed and come downstairs. We have to make plans!"

Mack came in and shuffled over the coffee pot, obviously suffering from a terrific hangover. There was a large purple hickey on his neck and a bruise on his lip.

"Annie," Mathew directed, sounding quite business-like. "Here's a pen and paper. You take notes. Sonny, Andrew, you too, Mack – let's sit down here and get started."

"Ah, ain't this cute," chided Mack sarcastically. "Matthew's round table."

"Okay, now," Matthew began, choosing to overlook his eldest son's attitude. "The first thing we ought to decide is when we will leave."

"Well, Daddy," Annie said. "Don't you think that we should at least wait till school is over. The boys have had enough upheaval in their lives." Matthew looked a little deflated, disappointed in his daughter's logic. He looked to Sonny for help.

"March is the beginning of the year on a farm," Sonny said, not looking at anyone. "You gotta have time to get ready for planting."

"Yeah, sure," Matthew agreed eagerly. "That makes sense. Hard telling what kind of shape we'll find things out there, right?" Again he was looking to Sonny for confirmation.

"Well then, how about this?" Andrew said, squirming a little in his seat. "How about you and Mr. Jackson go on out there and check things out. The rest of us can come when school is over in June. That's only a couple of months."

"Hey now! That is the best idea I've heard yet!" quipped Mack.

"No!" Matthew slammed his hand on the table. "We're a family and we'll stick together. We're going out there together.

I'm not giving you time to come up with more excuses. This is already the last week of February. We'll have to be packed and ready to leave by next Sunday – the first of March"

"That fast?" Annie gasped. But the look on her father's face told them the point was non-negotiable.

"Okay, then, what about transportation?" Matthew continued.

"Doesn't this place have an airport?" Mack asked. "Or how about a train? You can meet beautiful chicks on trains."

"But what about all the supplies and luggage?" Andrew asked. "There will be a tremendous amount of baggage with this kind of move."

"Jeez, Andrew!" wailed Mack. "You're sounding as nuts as he is! What do you think we're gonna do? Move this whole damn household – lock, stock, and waffle iron? You're all crazy!"

"No, we are not." Matthew gritted his teeth as though he was about to explode. "We are going to do this thing one way or another. So we just have to figure out the best way." He paused to compose himself. "And no, we're not going to take the whole household. That would be pretty stupid since we have no idea what we're going to find when we get out there. We'll just take clothes and a few household items. Everything else we can buy when we get there, or have a moving company bring out what we need. What I'm concerned about right now is deciding how we're going to get there."

"How about a bus?" Sonny suggested.

"A bus?" they all echoed simultaneously.

"What kind of bus, Sonny," Matthew pressed.

"A bus . . . like a school bus. You people are forgetting that where you're going, there's no kind of public transit or nothing."

"That's true," agreed Matthew. "What would we do when we get off this plane or train or whatever – hire cabs to take us twenty miles to the farm? So what you're saying is buy a bus, pack all the essentials, and go. Sounds like a good plan to me."

"Oh, God!" cried Mack in total disgust. Andrew and Annie were also exchanging looks of desperation.

"So, now we have to decide what to bring?" Matthew continued. This time they turned toward Sonny without bothering to answer themselves.

"Well, you'll need clothes mostly – jeans, good boots, warm coats, and sleeping bags, too."

"Sleeping bags!" Mack hooted. "What the hell for!"

"Because there's probably no electricity, heat, or furniture," explained Matthew. "Obviously, things like stereos and TV's would just be a waste of space. We can send for those things later. We'll have to pack very carefully." He began to pace. "Now, I've decided that we shouldn't tell anyone where we're going. If your Aunt Esther found out, she might try to stall us. And I don't need any more grief that I already have," he said, glaring at Mack. "We'll rent a garage for the bus and tell everyone we're going on vacation or something. We'll just say our plans are indefinite."

"What about school?" harped Andrew. "We should get the records from the teachers, and medical records, too--"

"Fine, fine. You and Annie take care of that. I've got to see about getting some cash and bank drafts. I'd better call Sid right away." Matthew left to call his banker.

Annie and her brothers exchanged worried glances when their father insisted on talking about money in front of this stranger. Sonny must have sensed their hostility, but didn't show a flicker of response. His cool, dispassionate demeanor made them even more nervous.

Just then, Angelica, the maid, came in. "Excuse me, Miss, but Grace said I should bring Master Joseph down to you for some breakfast. She seems to have her hands quite full with the baby."

"Of course, bring him right in." The timing was perfect, she thought. Let young Mr. Jackson take a good look at what he's getting into. No electricity, no heat. How ridiculous to think they could bring small children into an environment like that. She took the little boy onto her lap, struggling with him as always. He was never cooperative at mealtime. He'd thrash around and usually spit out his food. She hoped Sonny was watching, but he left the room, saying he had to make a call about a bus.

"Man, that guy is a real piece of work." Mack stood up and pulled on his jacket. "I do not understand why Pop trusts him so much. We have got to stop this thing before it's too late."

But he said nothing when Sonny and Matthew came back into the room. "Good news!" Matthew was beaming. "We already have a line on a bus. A guy in Jersey has it and says we can work on it in his garage. Great, aye? We're going over there to check it out." He flipped his car keys over to Sonny. "You drive. The less the servants know about this the better when people start asking questions." And they were gone.

"He's crazy! I mean, he's lost it – bad!" Mack cried.

"Yes, Mack," countered Annie, "we know what you think about this. You haven't exactly tried to hide your feelings. And you're probably right, for a change, but what can we do about it?"

Andrew began pacing at the opposite corner of the room. "Well, come on!" Mack demanded. "Let's hear the gospel, according to St. Andrew."

"Well, I agree," Andrew said. "The idea does strike me as ludicrous. But I think we're just going to have to accept it because I don't think we can change his mind."

"Jesus!" scowled Mack, sinking back into his char. "That was certainly earth-shaking. C'mon, we have to come up with some sort of plan here."

"Look, we're looking at this like Pop is insane. But maybe he isn't. I've heard of families deciding to turn their backs on good paying careers and affluent life-styles to move to the country or even the wilderness."

"Sure," sneered Mack, "like Canada?"

"No, really, Dubuque is not exactly the end of the earth. I've done some checking. It's a fair sized city. They even have three small colleges there. Maybe I'll start back to school at one of them next fall. Mack, you're the one who's supposed to be adventurous. How terrible can it be?"

"Pretty damn terrible!" exploded Mack. "You're as nuts as he is. So they have little colleges there. So what? What about nice bars and restaurants or good looking' chicks? Good God! You heard him. He's talking farming – like tote that barge and lift that bale. And Bozo there – our man Friday, he's talking blue jeans and work boots! Jeez! The old man can play out some weird fantasy if he wants, but you can count me out!" With that, he stomped out.

Andrew took a long deep breath. The silence was deafening. "What should we do, Annie? Do you think Aunt Esther could block this thing legally?"

"I don't know, Andrew. You heard what Daddy said. He said she especially can't find out. We can't do that to him, can we? He has that fire in his eyes again – he's excited. He really thinks once he gets us out there, we'll understand it and even like it. Maybe he's right." Her words sounded hollow without much conviction. "I agree with you, Andrew. We're gonna have to go along with it for now and hope he comes to his senses soon. We can't break his heart again. There's no way he can pull this off, but we have to let him try."

Chapter 6

They didn't hear from Matthew until he called early the next morning. He and Sonny worked all night, but he sounded upbeat and enthusiastic. "We started the modifications on the bus, but there's still several hours of work to do," he said. "We won't to be back until Wednesday evening sometime. I can't wait for you all to see this thing. This kid is really good with tools!" It was clear that Matthew was even more enamored with Sonny that before.

Annie wandered around the house, knowing there was probably countless things she should be doing, but she had no idea where to begin.

Wednesday night, Matthew and Sonny appeared. They both appeared bone tired, and their clothes were greasy and smelly, but their father was grinning from ear to ear.

"It's done!" he announced triumphantly. The bus is ready to go. Now, what did you get done while were gone?" he asked, noticing their blank faces. "You didn't do anything? This is Wednesday! We have to get going!"

"But Daddy, we had no idea where to start," Annie retorted.

Matthew brushed past them. "Giles! Bring me a drink – a

large one!"

Annie went looking for Sonny and found him in the library, reading one of the magazines he had brought Matthew. Pausing at the doorway to study him, she guessed him to be about Mack's age, early twenties, but he had a presence of self-assurance and wariness beyond his years. She had never known anyone like him before – his face was so intense, his features so dark and severe. As much as they mistrusted him, he probably mistrusted them more. He was looking at her then, so she turned away quickly, no match for those cold, penetrating eyes.

She sat the tray down and offered him some coffee. He nodded and took a cup, saying nothing. She felt the color rushing to her cheeks. Damn, she thought, biting her lip. Why do I let him intimidate me like this? She swallowed hard, determined to have a civil conversation with this man.

"Daddy's right, I guess," she started. "We didn't get anything accomplished. But honestly, none of us have any idea where to begin. You know, like specifically what we should bring and how much or --" Her voice trailed off. She had meant that to be a question but somehow he always made it impossible to speak directly. "You mentioned household goods before. Like what do you mean? Pots and pans? Linens?"

He sat sipping his coffee, still looking at the magazine. "I have some ideas, but it's going to take a lot to outfit a family with ten kids."

She bristled, realizing he placed her in that category. "Mr. Jackson, we can be organized. This family has packed for vacations many times. We just need a little direction to get started. You're supposed to be the expert here."

"Okay, sure, but I ain't no miracle worker."

"So, if it's going to be so hard, why are you going along with it? Is this some kind of sick joke to you?" He said nothing, which exasperated her even more. "Has anyone ever told you that you are a rude, conceited, over-bearing sonofabitch!" She fled, but she wished she had stayed long enough to see if that last statement registered any kind of reaction on that smug face.

* * * * * *

53

Every muscle in Matthew's body ached. He had never worked that hard in his life. He needed a shower and some sleep, but he stopped at the nursery door on the way to his own room. The sight of his baby daughter sleeping in her crib was a welcome sight. Matthew wondered what happy dreams were inside that tiny head. He reached down and gathered her into his arms.

The baby cried out upon being disturbed, and Grace came running into the room. She stopped short when she saw Mathew. He noted her look of disapproval, but didn't care. This was his child and he had the right to hold her if he wanted. As he sat down in the rocker, Grace turned to leave. "No, don't go," Matthew called after her. "If there's something you want to say, just say it."

She hesitated at the doorway, looking as though she wasn't sure she should stay. Finally, she sat down in the other chair, rocking in quick, jerky movements. It was easy to see that the gentle old woman was angry.

"Grace, we've known each other for a long time and I know you're upset. That's understandable, but --"

"What's understandable?" Grace blurted, purple showing in her sagging, gray cheeks. "That you're uprooting this family? Taking these children to God knows where."

Matthew did not answer at first, weighing his words carefully. "Grace, I know this sounds crazy – maybe it is, but I have to do it."

"For heaven's sake, why? Of course, you've been upset since Mrs. Winston's passing, God bless her soul, but is that any reason to make such a radical change? Surely, you don't think that we – the household staff, I mean – are going to go with you?"

"No, of course not --"

"Well, then what's to become of us? Are you serving notice? And who would hire us? Some of us have worked under this roof for over twenty years."

"Grace, I assure you that you can live here as long as you wish. I have no idea what's going to happen. We have to see how things are out there"

"But who's going to take care of the children – that baby

you have in your arms and little Joey. Who is going to look after them?"

"Annie? Me? We all will--"

"Oh, that's preposterous! Mr. Winston, you are a very smart man – or at least I always thought you were. How are you going to pull this off with no plan? You have no idea what you're doing."

"Grace, I don't expect you to understand – I'm not sure I understand myself, but this is something I have to do. I can't live in this house any more – not now, anyway. This was Kathleen's house. Everywhere I turn, every step I take, she's here."

"Of course, she is. She filled it with so much joy and love. I should think that would give you comfort."

"It's eating me up alive, Grace. I feel like I can't breathe. I have to do this, not just for me, but for all of us."

"You think this is going to be good for your children? How is that possible? You're taking them away from the only home they have ever known."

"Yes, I am doing this for all of us. I never told anyone, but Kathleen's last words to me were that our kids had everything, but they don't know how to dream. I didn't know what that meant then, but I think I do now. I look at the boys and I see a bunch of spoiled, pampered brats who have no idea what they want out of life. They've never had to work for a damned thing. Mack is a playboy, carousing all night. What is he doing with his life? Nothing."

"But Mr. Winston, Kathleen loved her children. She always--"

"Look, I'm not saying she didn't do a wonderful job. But now I'm on my own. They are my responsibility. I have to do what I think is best."

"I think you're making a mistake. This cannot be good for anyone."

"You may be right, Grace." He stood up and handed the sleeping baby back to her nanny. "But there's no way of knowing if we don't at least try." He left the room without waiting for a response. He had pleaded his case as best as he could. Maybe if he said it enough times, he might actually believe it himself.

* * * * * *

The next morning Annie sat at the kitchen table, talking with Cook. The question Annie had put before her was simple. "What would I need to cook for this family, like pots n' pans?" Annie's pencil stood poised, ready to make lists.

Matthew wondered in, nonchalantly pouring himself a cup of coffee, but then he noticed their faces. "What's going on here?" he asked.

"You're the one who says we have to get started packing, Daddy. I thought I'd get started on things for the kitchen," Annie explained.

Cook's round, horror-stricken face said things were not that simple at all. "Does she want to take things from this kitchen to that place-- that farm?" she asked, waving her stubby arms around her immaculate kitchen. This room had been her exclusive domain these past twenty-odd years.

"Now, now, Miss Daley, Annie doesn't mean that all," Matthew said. "We plan to keep this house just as it is. I'm sure Annie just needs to know what things she'll need to set up her own kitchen."

"Excuse me, sir, but do you mean Miss Annie is going to be doin' the cookin' for you all? Well, bless my soul, chil'. I didn't know you knew how to cook. Maybe we'd better go over some of my favorite recipes like--"

"No, no, that's all right," Annie said quickly, gathering up her things. It did sound absurd to think she could cook for this family. "I just remembered I have an appointment," she lied. "We can talk later."

She rushed out of the room and almost ran into Sonny who was standing in the doorway. Oh great, she thought. He's observed another little touching scene. She pushed past him, still determined to accomplish something. She went to the library, squatted down next to the coffee table, and spread out her papers again. There were thirteen neatly labeled sheets, one for each member of the family, one labeled "Essentials i.e. Household items" and one for "Non-essentials." They were each nicely titled but beyond that, they were empty.

"So, you like making lists, huh?" Sonny broke in, startling her.

"Yes, I do, for all the good it does me," she muttered angrily, trying not to cry. "I had such high hopes for today. I was going to get so much done!" She wished he would leave so she could throw a tantrum in private.

"I know, that's why I brought you this." He threw a huge book onto the table that said *Sears and Roebuck, Winter '70.* "Open it. It's got everything." He sounded sincere, but Annie still gritted her teeth. She could not stand his cocky intrusions. "You can go through and pick out stuff for everybody – clothes and boots, even coveralls." He turned the pages until he found pictures of men modeling heavy, one piece striped outfits, obviously work clothes of some kind. "Guess they don't sell these on Madison Avenue."

He was being pleasant enough and Annie tried to be appreciative, but suddenly it struck her funny. She envisioned her father standing knee-deep in mud, wearing one of these things – or Andrew or Mack. Oh, God, that was even funnier. She snickered and then broke into a full-blown fit of laughter.

Sonny obviously did not see the humor, which made Annie laugh even harder. He closed the catalog with a resounding thump and started to leave.

"Hey!" she called after him "I was just imagining my dad or Mack wearing one of these things, and it just struck me funny, that's all. I like this catalog idea. So, I make out the lists of what everyone needs. Then what?"

"Place the order and pay for it," he answered, somewhat condescending, she thought. "There's a Sears store on Staten Island. We can have the stuff delivered to the store in Iowa." He started to leave again.

"What? You mean we pay before we get anything?"

"You can trust Sears and Roebuck. They've been around at least as long as Bloomingdale's. I'll handle this," he said, picking up the sheets labeled, "Misc.- Essentials and Non". He went into the foyer and reached for his coat.

"But what about you, or do you already have your

'coverall'?"

He didn't bother to answer. Once again he left without saying anything.

* * * * * *

The rest of the day and evening, Annie wandered from room to room, checking sizes and making notes. She hated to admit it, but the catalog idea was great. It had everything in every size. Luckily, Mack was out all day. She dreaded explaining his new wardrobe to him. Better to let him be surprised.

Sonny appeared at their door again later that night. He swung the door open wide, calling, "Just put it all in here!" The Winston's watched as their foyer became transformed into at an Army Surplus store with stacks of trunks and boxes of every description. "Remember, be back here Sunday morning – 8:00 AM sharp," Sonny directed the two men as he dispensed a tip to each.

"Sonny, what's all this?" Matthew asked, looking very pleased. "If we take all this, there won't be any room left for passengers."

"There's thirteen trunks and large suitcases -- one for each of you. It should all fit in the rack we built on top of the bus. There's a tarp here somewhere to cover it all." He started moving through the piles. "I paid for all this with the money left over from the bus deal. Here's the rest." He dug into his pockets and took out some bills and change.

"No, Sonny," Matthew said, smiling. "Keep it for whatever comes up."

Sonny nodded and started to leave again, then turned to look directly at Annie. "You be ready at noon tomorrow." She felt as though she should salute, but he was gone as quickly as he had come.

They stood silently for a few minutes, surveying the mess. This was it – real, tangible evidence that this wasn't a dream. It was going to happen.

* * * * * *

Annie reminded the boys as they left for their last day of school not to tell anyone where they were going. "If anyone asks," she said as they were walking out the door, "just say we're leaving for a long vacation."

A few minutes later, Mack came thundering down the stairs, looking as though he was going to explode. Annie gestured toward the dining room. There was going to be another scene.

"What the hell did you do?" Mack screamed at his father.

"My, my," Matthew responded, still looking at the morning paper. "We're a little cranky this morning, aren't we."

"Yeah, you could say that. I get that way when I find myself twenty miles from home with no cash and credit cards don't work. How could you?"

"How could I what?"

"You know goddamn well what I'm talking about. And where in the hell is my car?"

"You lost your car?"

"Lost it? Hell no! I left it at the curb, and two hours later I come out to find it gone. My God, did you have it towed?"

"You're forgetting something, son. Legally, that is my car."

"The hell it is! You and Mother gave it to me for my 21st birthday."

"True, but if you bothered to check, you would have seen that it's titled and registered in my name. That nice policeman I talked to was very sympathetic when I reported it stolen."

"What? You can't do that."

"I already have. Your bank account and credit cards are frozen, too. Welcome to the real world, Mack."

"You're trying to railroad me into this farm thing, aren't you. Well, fuck that and fuck you. You can't make me go."

"Fine, but you'll need a job because I'm not giving you one cent."

"I can do that – get a job, I mean."

"How? You have no skills, no experience."

"I could work at your company, right?"

"No, because I wouldn't hire you, and neither would anyone else."

Matthew put down his paper and folded it thoughtfully. Looking hard at his oldest son, he put his hands together and rested his elbows on the table. "Mack, I am getting real tired of your whining."

"I'll go back to school."

"And do what? What are you going to major in – drinking and whoring?" Matthew got up and walked around the table. "I realize that in many ways I have failed in my responsibility in teaching you how to be a man. Have you looked in a mirror lately?"

"But, Pop, I'm only drinking because--"

"Look. I'll make you a deal. You stick it out until our first harvest – should be late October or early November. That goes for all of you," he said, waving his arm to encompass all three of his eldest children. "If you're still hell-bent to leave, then you can come back here with my blessing. You can go back to school or whatever, and I will continue to support you."

He squared his shoulders and took a deep, hard breath. "None of you have ever wanted for anything. You're adults now but you act like spoiled children. If you decide you really don't want to go with us, I guess that's your right. But if you're not there when we board that bus, I'll see to it that you're cut off without a dime, not even your grandfather's trust fund. It's time you learn about the real world, one way or another."

Matthew turned and walked upstairs. Mack said nothing, drank some coffee, and then left the house again.

Chapter 7

Sharply at noon, the doorbell rang and there was Sonny. Annie was ready. She grabbed her coat and purse and followed him out the door. "I took the liberty of calling a cab," she said. "If it's alright with you, I'd like to go down to Battery Park and ride the Staten Island Ferry." He said nothing as he crawled into the cab and continued the silent treatment the entire trip. His refusal to make polite conversation still bothered her, probably because she lived in a world of superfluous chatter.

Her world. Her life. She watched as the familiar sights floated past the cab window. This city was her home. For all of its faults, she loved living in New York City. She wondered when she'd ever see these places again.

They boarded the ferry. Sonny led the way, not looking back to see if she was keeping up. He made his way up the weathered stairs, pushed open the door to go outside, and headed toward the railing. Annie chose a spot on a bench nearby, but no one watching would ever suspect they were traveling together. The horn blasted and the old battered workhorse of the bay pulled away from its berth.

Annie gazed at the choppy water. A red tug scooted past. The Lady of the Harbor rose magnificently from her island. Annie's nostrils were filled with the pungent sea smells. The soft purr of the diesels was accompanied by the squawk of the sea gulls as they dipped and glided overhead.

Ever since she was a little girl, she loved to ride the ferry, especially with her father. Perhaps it was true he had never developed much affection for shipbuilding, but he loved ships and the sea. He would point out one freighter or another – ones his company built or others he wished they had built.

She felt tears welling up, more out of anger and confusion than sadness. This was the legacy her father had bestowed upon his children. And yet it was he who was taking it away. Why did everything have to change like this?

She hated being so angry with her mother for dying, but none of this would be happening if she were still alive. Her death that had pushed Matthew to the edge, made him start searching for something to belong to again. He believed this farm would help recapture some long ago dream, or perhaps it was just a desperate diversion from his pain. Annie wiped away her tears and looked out over the bay with renewed assurance. Maybe it did make sense after all.

How much does the success of this new enterprise rest on that man's shoulders, she wondered as she once again contemplated Sonny. Was he saying good-bye, too? Was New York his home or just a place he paused in his journeys? And why did her father trust him so completely? She knew why.

There was something about him. You could see it just the way he was standing there, his face into the wind, so damned self-assured.

She was certain that he intended to help them reach the farm, and then take the money and leave. Her father could hire a real foreman or hired hand or whatever you call such people. Perhaps they'd find a whole family – like on TV and movies. The husband does the farming, and the wife does the cooking and cleaning. Yes, that must be the way it's done. She felt relieved. Maybe things weren't as bleak as she first thought.

The ferry reached the Island and they disembarked. They took another cab to the Sears store. Once inside, he guided her to the catalog desk. Sonny was right. This was not Madison Avenue, Annie thought as she surveyed the plain surroundings. There were racks of flannel shirts and sweatshirts with hand written 25% discount signs.

"May I help you?" asked the crisp saleslady at the catalog counter as she glanced at them over the top of her horn-rimmed glasses.

Annie cleared her throat a little and said, "Yes, I'd like to place an order and have it shipped to Dubuque, Iowa, please."

"I see," the woman said, reaching for her order pad, putting the carbon in place with a great flourish. "You do realize that you'll have to pay for the entire order in advance."

"So I've been told." Annie cast a quick glance toward Sonny.

The clerk glared at Annie after she counted the four pages of neatly printed lists. "Young lady, is this some kind of joke? This is hundreds of dollars of merchandise?"

"Yes, I know. $954.66 See, it's all added up, including tax--"

"Look," Sonny broke in rudely, "do you want our business or not? If you're too busy to take care of this, I'm sure J.C. Penny's would be happy to handle this."

"Young man, I'd be happy to place this order except there are no weights listed here. We require those so that shipping charges can be assessed. It would take hours for me to find the weights for these items!"

Just then a pleasant looking young woman came up and tapped the clerk on the shoulder. "Miss Beamers, I'm going on my lunch break now, okay?"

Sonny blocked her path and waved a fifty dollar bill in her face. "Miss," he said, "how would you like to make fifty bucks on your lunch break today?"

"What?" she stammered, looking as though she wondered is she should call the police. "I'm meeting my boyfriend and --"

"Good! If he wants to help, I'll give him fifty bucks, too. We need weights for everything on this list."

"Oh, I see. Okay, sure. C'mon, we can go to the cafeteria." She took four of the huge catalogs from beneath the counter and led the way. Annie stood there, stunned, until Sonny grabbed her and pulled her a long.

One hour later, it was done. The manager of the store hovered nearby and offered any assistance they might need. When Annie reached into her purse and took out a stack of cash, a security guard was summoned because the cash drawer wouldn't hold that much money. "I'm afraid I'm a little short," Annie said, shamefaced. "I didn't know about the shipping charges."

"Ah, Jeez," moaned Sonny. "Here, I have it covered." The bill was settled and soon they were back out onto the street. Luckily, a cab was just letting off a rider. Sonny shoved Annie inside. He folded his arms across his chest and sat stone-faced.

Annie watched him out of the corner of her eye until she couldn't stand it any longer. "What are you mad about now?" she demanded.

He didn't answer at first, looking as though he wasn't sure he wanted another confrontation with her. "All right, then," he said, readjusting himself in his seat. "You walk into a store with nearly a thousand dollars worth of cash business and you apologize all the way through it. Christ! You should have had them kissing your feet!"

"Let me get this straight – you're mad at me? Why? Because I didn't get hostile right away? Some people might call that good manners!"

"You have to learn how to handle yourself in those situations! You're such a baby! What would you do if you were on your own?"

She sputtered and stammered but nothing came out. Never had she been so insulted! Sonny just leaned back in his seat and looked as though he was going to take a nap, which further infuriated her. So I have no guts, eh? No confidence? I have never had to make decisions before. I've always been taken care of and assumed I always would.

That is until now. Suddenly that familiar shiver of fright jolted through her and she fought back tears again. She wanted to cry obscenities at this egotistical jerk and pound upon his chest until he'd listen to her. I'll show him, she vowed, even if it kills me.

* * * * * *

Saturday morning everyone was up early. The boys were told to lay everything out on their beds and then Matthew, Annie, or Andrew could come around to check it. There were some tough decisions to be made. Peter couldn't decide whether to bring his rock collection or his baseball cards. Thomas was angry because neither of his guitars would fit in his trunk. At first Matthew stubbornly refused to make any exceptions, but was coaxed into allowing Thomas to bring one. Then he made a thunderous announcement that no one else had better ask for any other special compensation.

By supper, most of the trunks and luggage were packed and stacked in the foyer. There was a hush that fell over the house as even the younger boys seemed to understand the significance of this last night at home. Tomorrow they would begin what their father called their great adventure. Annie and Grace went through the baby things. Many of the blankets and sleepers held special remembrances so they found themselves recounting old stories as they packed, alternately laughing and crying.

Mack slipped down the hallway trying to get into his room undetected. He opened his door to find Andrew and Luke standing by his bed, which was piled with clothes and toiletries.

"Oh, God," he groaned. "What have we here? Daddy's little helpers?"

"C'mon, Mack, we're just packing your stuff," Luke

explained. "We're leaving right after Mass in the morning, and you don't have anything ready."

"Hey, who says I'm goin' to this funny farm anyway," Mack sneered.

"Shhh! Just pipe down," scowled Andrew. "In case you don't realize it, its late. So just shut up and decide what you want to bring along. We laid some stuff out already."

"You boys are just too good to me," Mack jeered. He picked up armfuls of clothes and flung them across the room.

"Okay, Mack, we get that you're drunk and in a vile mood, but we don't care." Andrew picked up some clothes off the floor. "You could try to be a little adult about this. Getting drunk every night doesn't help anything."

"Shut up," snarled Mack. "You make me sick, you hypocritical ass. You know this is the most fucked up idea you've ever heard, but you always go along with anything the old man says. At least I stand up to him!"

"Making my father happy makes me a hypocrite? He wants us to stick together. I can understand that. Why can't you?"

"Oh, hell, Andrew!" cried Mack. "You're going along with this lunacy for one reason, same as me – the money. He says he'll cut us off without a cent. That don't sound any better to you than it does to me. You couldn't survive 24 hours out there alone," he said, flinging his arms at the dark, cold world that lay beyond the walls of the brownstone.

"I said I'd go along with this plan long before he threatened to disown anyone. He said that solely for your benefit, and you know it. Now listen, I realize this is a terrible predicament for all of us. I just think we should try to get along and make the--"

"Ah, go to hell!" muttered Mack, flopping down upon his bed,

"Well, I can tell you why I'm going," Luke quipped. "Someone's got to go along to keep you two from killing each other." With that, they left the room. Mack would be passed out until the morning anyway.

.

* * * * * *

Later that night, as Annie was packing her own things, her mother was on her mind. Leaving the house made her feel like she was losing her mother all over again. As though he was reading her mind, Matthew wandered in looking a little wistful, too. "I can't help wondering what your mother would think about this," he said. "The past few nights, I wake up and I'd swear she's right there with me – I can feel her, smell her. I think she understands, I really do. She's probably the only one who does."

"No, Daddy. We understand, or at least some of us are trying to. Besides, if you feel this strongly about something you should go after it, no matter what. It's going to be a big adjustment, that's all. You just have to be patient with us, okay?" She smiled and gave him a quick kiss as he stood up. He looked tired and haggard.

"But anyway, we have a big day tomorrow, so I guess we'd better get some sleep, right?" He gave his daughter a big bear hug before he turned to leave. "I know I'm asking a lot, Annie. Please, just give it a chance. I know one thing, nothing is ever going to be quite the same again."

She tried to smile with as much reassurance as she could muster. She loved her father very much and wanted so badly for him to be happy. Maybe this was the answer. God alone knows, she thought. Better Him than any of us.

* * * * * *

Sunday morning dawned cold and gray. The family sat around the table, displaying a veritable smorgasbord of emotion from the little boys' excited chatter to Mack's glaring hostility. The usual chaotic confusion ensued but Matthew sat calmly reading his newspaper, just like every other Sunday morning for twenty-five years.

"It says here," he announced, " that the Supreme Court will hand down it's decision on whether draft dodgers have the five year statue of limitations. Those bastards!" he sputtered

"This is the land of the free and the home of the brave," sneered Mack.

The conversation might have escalated to a full scale confrontation, but Sonny and his friends reported promptly at 8:00 as instructed. All the baggage was loaded onto the truck. After Mass the family would be picked up by two airport limos. It looked very believable – the Winston's were going on a trip.

There were the last minute scrimmages, such as John trying to smuggle a basketball along and a couple of misplaced teddy bears, but finally, they were ready. They walked the two blocks to St. Gregory's, accompanied by many of the household staff. As usual, they made their tardy and noisy entrance. Everyone, even Matthew, fidgeted as the service dragged on.

Amid the cheers and well wishes from their teary-eyed servants and friends, the Winston's climbed into the two limos and were off. In a few minutes they passed through the Holland Tunnel and were soon delivered to their awaiting chariot. It looked like an ordinary large yellow school bus, except for the huge pile of baggage crowning the top. The interior had indeed been altered. Many of the standard seats had been removed and replaced by a table with four captains chairs and two small sofas. A refrigerator had been installed and the cribs for Joey and Becky were set up in the back.

Matthew wanted everyone settled and on the road by noon. Instead, there was mass confusion with the younger boys jumping and running about, and the older ones arguing over who should sit where.

"Hey, I'm hungry," called out one of the boys. "When we gonna eat?"

"It is noon," Annie said amid a chorus of hungry boys wanting lunch.

"I suppose we could eat now and then get on the road," Matthew conceded. "But let's make it quick. I want to get going as soon as possible."

* * * * * *

Their first meal on the road was a disaster. They weren't served half of what they ordered, probably because the poor waitress was so confused she was on the verge of tears. Everyone talked at once. Milk glasses were spilled. Thomas and John argued as though they were back home sitting in front of the TV. Little Joey nearly fell out of the dilapidated old high chair and wouldn't eat, shrieking loudly.

At that point, Sonny walked out. Through the diner window, Annie saw him trudging toward the bus. And by the way Matthew hustled everyone out of the place soon afterward, it was clear that he wasn't happy either. "Quiet down. Now!" he bellowed. Finally, the motor started and they were on their way.

Unfortunately, no one took their father seriously. Even before they reached the turnpike, the volume inside the bus had reached a dull roar. There was constant arguing, screaming babies, and a steady stream of requests for something to eat or drink. Someone even asked if they could pull into the first rest stop to use the bathroom.

There was so much wind resistance, especially with all the baggage on top, that Sonny was driving slower than expected. Less than 200 miles down the road, barely inside Pennsylvania, they pulled into a motel. Sonny said very little throughout the afternoon even though the noise was maddening and he was hit twice on the back of the head with a flying football. He sat quietly in the driver's seat while the others filed out.

Matthew stood back, looking dazed and annoyed. "Christ," he muttered. "I bet traveling by cover wagon wasn't this hard."

After more scenes of pandemonium in the motel lobby and restaurant, Matthew strode into the bar. Sonny was already there, starting at a half empty glass of beer. Matthew nodded in Sonny's direction and ordered his own. Neither man spoke.

Then Mack came in. "Well, this is going great, isn't it? The front desk called up twice because other guests are complaining. Andrew is trying to help Annie 'cause Joey and the baby are screaming bloody murder. Luke's got the rest of 'em. Lots of luck! I couldn't stand the little brats anymore." He turned to stare at his father, looking as though he was going to say, *I told you so.* But, seeing his father's expression, he thought better of it. He also sat down and ordered a beer, too, enjoying the relative peace and quiet of a noisy bar.

Matthew was on his third drink before any of them spoke.

"What we need is a plan," Sonny said. "Get some of this stuff organized ahead of time."

"Yeah," Matthew agreed, "like all the trouble we had in the restaurants today. I was thinking we should have teams. Divide the boys between Mack and Andrew. Luke can help Annie with the babies."

"How come he gets all the cushy jobs?" Mack muttered.

"Mack," Matthew continued, "you take Thomas and Danny. And Andrew can take John and Peter. Each team sits at separate tables – opposite corners, if necessary. Get it straight what everyone's ordering even before you walk in." He took several more swallows of his drink. "As I recall whenever we traveled with your mother, she always said we needed to allow time for the boys to work off energy. Like – eating lunch at a wayside and let them run around a little."

"And how about making sure we have motels with an indoor pool," added Mack "Let the little beasts work it off before dinner and maybe then they'll go to bed and shut up." Matthew and Sonny stared at him in utter amazement. "Don't look so shocked. I come up with decent ideas sometimes."

"Okay, then," Sonny said as he downed the last swallow of beer. "Sounds like we got a plan. I have to take care of a couple of things, so I'll see you in the morning."

Mack watched him go, scowling after him. "I suppose you told him where all the cash is, didn't you."

"Sure did – he helped me hide it." Matthew finished his drink and pushed way from the bar. "Just remember, Mack, this is my idea, not his. If you think we're having trouble now, just think what it would be like without him. I'm going to bed," he announced. "You coming?"

"In a while. I like the scenery," Mack said as he spun around on his stool, eyeing two shapely women as they walked by. "Don't worry, I can find my own way. I'm a big boy now."

"I know." Matthew threw money on the bar. "That's what I'm afraid of."

"Don't you think some of us should know where it is, too?"

Matthew turned to stare intently at his son. "Go to bed," was all he said.

Chapter 8

Matthew's team plan went into effect immediately. Breakfast went much better than the meals the day before. Once everyone was onboard, Matthew stood up and demanded everyone's attention. "Boys!" he called, "we have at least two or three days left of traveling, and I absolutely do not want any more days like yesterday. So just settle down, do some reading or something – anything as long as it's quiet. There will be no fighting, no throwing, no loud arguing, nothing!" He started to sit down but then faced them again. "Oh, yeah, I hope you all had plenty to drink at breakfast, gentlemen, because there will be no beverages served except at meal times. Any questions?"

"Yeah, Sarg, just one," muttered Mack out of his father's earshot. "When did I enlist? To tell ya' the truth, I don't remember doing it."

They pulled onto the Pennsylvania turnpike at 9:00 sharp. The next two and a half hours were relatively quiet. The boys actually talked and joked a little, except Thomas of course, who sat off by himself strumming his guitar. Andrew produced a deck of cards, asking if anyone would like to go a couple of hands. Matthew asked if he could sit in. "Your old man can handle himself around a deck of cards, you know."

"Yeah, we know," Andrew said, laughing. "That's what got us into this mess."

At 11:30, Sonny pulled into a rest area, over 150 miles further into Pennsylvania. The air was damp and cool, and there were still some patches of snow on the ground. Mack's team challenged Andrew's team to a game of football, so everyone went storming out for the game.

Annie was sleeping in the back of the bus until she sensed unusual movement. She was horrified to see Sonny bending over Joey. Having wrapped the boy in a coat and scarf, Sonny picked him up and walked toward the door.

"What are you doing?" She lunged toward them, ready to snatch the boy out of Sonny's arms. "It's too cold for him outside. Are you crazy?"

"I got him wrapped up." He brushed past her. "The kid's not made of glass, ya' know."

She watched as he hoisted the boy on his shoulder, heading the opposite direction from where the others were playing. He swung over the fence five feet from a "No Trespassing" sign and headed down to a nearby stream. What a peculiar sight, Annie thought. Sonny's expression was as grim as ever, but there he was, attending this fragile, helpless child. Across the park, Andrew, who had just taken a pass, pulled up and gestured in Sonny's direction. Everyone stopped to gasp. This stranger defied any logical explanation.

Whatever the reason for Sonny's uncharacteristic act of kindness, Annie resented it. She turned away from the window and began working over Becky who needed changing and feeding. This man did not have a sincere, caring bone in his body so why should he trouble himself with Joey? And now he'll probably get an ear infection or something. Just what I need, moaned Annie, a sick child.

A half hour later, when Matthew broke up the game so everyone could eat, Sonny brought Joey back to the bus. The boy had bright red cheeks and grinned from ear to ear. Sonny took off his wrappings without saying a word.

There were sandwiches, chips, and cookies for lunch. They ate hungrily and were soon on their way again. The boys settled down quietly, some even dropping off to sleep or just watching the picturesque countryside of western Pennsylvania slip by. They reached Ohio late that afternoon and pulled into their motel at 5:00 PM.

"Right on schedule," Matthew proclaimed triumphantly. Fifteen minutes later, he and his sons were jumping into the pool, squealing and cavorting to their heart's content.

When Sonny came carrying the last of the baggage into Annie's room, Joey was laying on the floor and seemed to reach his arms toward Sonny. Annie thought he was going to ignore the boy, but he did squat down to tousle Joey's curls. "What's the story with him anyway?" he asked.

"With Joey?" She took the boy onto her lap. "The doctors

would never admit it, but it was probably something that happened during delivery." She was trying to undress him, battling the tremendous spasticity. Even his feet were curled. It was difficult to separate his scissoring legs to change his diaper.

"How old is he – two, three? He still wears diapers, can't talk or nothing'?"

"Obviously he's – well, handicapped," she said curtly. What kind of stupid questions were these?

"You people have a lot of money, living in one of the biggest cities in the world – wasn't there somebody who could do something for him?"

"Like what? Sure they told my parents they should try this or that, go to this doctor or that therapist, but my mother hated it. He was always sick with colds and ear infections. He is a very frail child. That's why I'm so worried about living in a place that might not have electricity or heat or even running water. Now do you understand?" she demanded, fuming.

But he said nothing – just nodded disapprovingly and left. Once again, Annie felt cheated. There was so much more she wanted to say, but she was certain he didn't care enough to stick around to finish anything.

* * * * * *

Tuesday they drove across Ohio and Indiana, passing mile after mile of rich farmland, which normally would have been very boring to the Winston's. But this time, they gazed out their windows with much curiosity. Would their farm look like one of these – neatly maintained white fences and red barns with baby calves sleeping in the pastures? They could only hope.

They pushed on past night fall, stopping a few miles west of Chicago. All that lay between them and Mississippi was one hundred and sixty miles of Illinois. The word was passed quickly. Tomorrow they would be there.

After supper, Luke offered to take over the babies and get them settled for the night. Annie put on a nice outfit and even applied make-up. After all, she reminded herself, this is probably the last real civilization they would see for who knows how long.

She went downstairs to the bar, noting she turned a couple of heads as she walked by. She felt a little giddy and daring so she asked her father to order her a drink rather than her usual diet soda.

"Pop was just telling us his fantasies of how this place will look." Mack snickered. "He says it'll have a big rambling farmhouse over-looking the river, of course, and a minimum of two of those huge barns like we've been driving past all day. And, oh yeah, lots of animals, like cows and pigs and probably a few chickens. Right, Pop?"

"It's called livestock'," Sonny said, "and I can't wait till you're out there at 5:00 AM, knee-deep in mud and cow shit." He stood up then and finished the last of his beer.

Mack tried to appear undaunted, but he couldn't stop the color from draining from his face. He gave his father one of those rueful I-don't-believe-you-got-me-into-this looks. He then turned to give Sonny a piece of his mind. but he had already left. The others were laughing. "That sonofabitch!" Mack muttered, talking into his beer glass.

Annie fully intended to enjoy the evening. Her father was in very good spirits. They laughed and talked at the bar for a couple of hours. Later, when they were helping their father into bed, Mack pointed out that Sonny was not there. "Wonder what the hell that guy does off all by himself all the time?" Mack wondered, sounding accusatory. Andrew and Annie wondered, too, but they were too tired to debate it.

* * * * * *

March can be a very troublesome month – totally unpredictable, when any kind of weather is normal. The old saying is, "In like a lion, then out like a lamb" and vice versa, but most mid-westerners hesitate to put much credence in that old cliché, since experience has taught them that no rules apply when it comes to the month of March.

So far, the skies were mostly overcast and the winds were cold, but thankfully, there hadn't been any snow, ice, or rain, or mixture thereof – so far.

On their last day of traveling, everyone was rousted out of bed before dawn. Instead of hot pancakes and sausage, they were given stale donuts and juice, so that the grumbling began earlier that day. And then, just as they stepped outside to board the bus, they were blasted by waves of icy rain. They huddled in their seats listening to the torrents of sleet pelt the windows.

Sonny sat hunched over the steering wheel in a trance of total concentration as he negotiated mile after mile of slick pavement. They didn't stop for lunch. Sandwiches were passed around but no one seemed very hungry.

The sleet turned to rain as the sun climbed higher behind its curtain of steel-gray clouds. Trickles of chatter could be heard as their fear waned. They crossed the Mississippi into Iowa in early afternoon. There were still large chunks of ice floating in the dark, murky waters, making the river look very formidable.

"I'm looking for the turnoff to U.S. Highway 61." Sonny called to Matthew. "That'll take us north to Dubuque County." They turned off shortly and word was passed that they would be there in another hour and a half.

This new road was very choppy and uneven compared to the interstate. The bus bumped along, jolting and jostling its occupants mercilessly. Becky woke up screaming. Matthew bolted to the crib, picked up the infant, and began to pace. It was clear that he was too nervous to sit still any longer.

"I think it's breaking up a little, don't you think?" he said to no one in particular. "The rain is letting up, too." He tried to sound hopeful, probably trying to convince himself more than anyone else.

The reality of where they were and how far removed it was from anything they had ever known began weighing heavier. Even the names of things were alien to them, like the villages of Maquoketa, Otter Creek, or Zwingle, and a river called the Wapsipinicon.

"Hey, that's nothing," sneered Thomas, who was looking over a map. "This state has rivers called the Fox and the Turkey. There's even one called the Skunk!"

Shortly after they passed the sign that announced they were entering Dubuque County, they saw another sign that simply said,

HILL. "Maybe a decent hill is a big deal out here on the lone prairie," Thomas quipped.

But the snickering stopped as they swung over the top of that hill and dropped into a panorama of vastly changed scenery. The land bottomed out into beautiful wide valleys with peaked bluffs that rimmed the landscape as though to separate this little corner of the world from the rest of the planet. There were immaculate farmsteads etched into the hillsides and cattle grazing on the barren, rocky inclines where it was too steep to plant crops. Narrow gravel roads trailed off across the countryside, disappearing where the hilltops met the sky.

As they neared the city of Dubuque, the roadside became dotted with houses and gas stations. However, before they reached the city itself, Sonny turned south onto a narrow blacktop road by the sign which said, "Shannon Town: 18 miles".

Matthew let out a loud, unrestrained whoop. "We're almost there!"

The highway was part of a network called the Great River Road, which parallels the Mississippi's curves and meanderings. It takes travelers over high bluffs and across the valley floors. Even Mack and Thomas were quiet as they watching the intriguing landscape flow past the windows of the bus.

The first clue that they were nearing a town was a tall, white, spiraled church steeple rising above the treetops on a distant hillside. "Look, there it is!" someone cried. "That must be Shannon Town!"

The town looked to be incredibly small, only a few buildings nestled between the river's edge and high bluffs that towered behind it. The highway took them down the one main street that was lined with houses and businesses on one side and a riverside park on the other. As they drove along, they were through the town almost as quickly as they entered it. Sonny turned the bus around to head back. "We'll have to find someone who can tell us how to find the farm," Matthew said, still pacing.

Sonny pulled into a corner gas station. "Sure, this will do," Matthew agreed, standing poised at the door ready to leap out as soon as it opened. "Town like this, they'll be able to tell us right off."

Sonny followed Matthew inside. There were two men sitting by an old wood stove. "Good afternoon," Matthew began. "Would either of you happen to know where this place is located?" He showed them the deed.

They studied it for a few moments and exchanged surprised glances. "Well sure, mister. That would be the old Weatherly place," one of them said. "Everybody knows where that's at. Who's askin'?"

Matthew took the deed and turned it over. "That's me, Matthew Macalister Winston II," he said, pointing to his signature on the back. "I'm the new owner of the place. This is Sonny Jackson, my hired hand. We've been told that this is 420 acres of the richest, blackest dirt on God's earth." He finished with a grand flourish but neither man's expression changed. Matthew's smile faded, confronted by steady, scrutinizing stares.

He stepped aside so they could see the bus parked outside. "I've brought my family from New York City to come out here to live." The two men looked at the bus with all the children's faces pressed against the windows and then stared at Matthew and Sonny again.

A slow, twitching grin spread across the older man's face as he extended his hand. "Well, welcome to our little town," he said, shaking Matthew's hand. "I'm Jake Gibson, and I guess we'll be neighbors, if you're really serious about living out there."

"Oh, I'm very serious, Mr. Gibson."

"Ah, just call me Jake," said the old man, smiling. He leaned forward onto his cane. "I don't know what they told ya' when ya' bought that place--"

"I know it probably needs some work, but I'm very anxious to see it."

"Well now, how many youngsters you got? A whole bus full, aye?"

"I have ten children," Matthew said with strained politeness. "Now, if you could give us directions?" he pressed.

"Ten kids, huh." The old man rocked back and forth a couple of times, trying to stand up. "Well, listen, I guess the best way is for you just to follow me home." He opened the door, but then stopped to comment further. "But ya' know, we've had an early thaw so gravel roads are pretty soft. Mel hasn't had the maintainer out there yet. 'Course the school bus makes it out there without much problems. Bud's been driving that route for years."

He stopped again and began digging into his pocket. "That's all right, Jake," grinned the other man, apparently the proprietor, "You can take care of it the next time you're in. I think these fellas are kinda in a hurry."

Jake hobbled toward his old Ford truck. "Now, we'll be heading out south of town," he said, pointing with his cane. "I'll wait for ya' to get that thing turned around." Matthew nor Sonny answered. They just got in the bus.

"Now I know how John Wayne felt when he had to deal with Walter Brennan," Matthew joked.

Old Jake Gibson drove as slow as he talked and walked, and he didn't lie when he warned them about the roads. Once they turned off the highway onto what was supposed to he a gravel road, they swerved and slid their way for another three miles. Then Jake pulled into a driveway of a lovely farmstead and stopped. There was a collective hopeful gasp, everyone wondering if this was their place. But it wasn't. Jake got out of his truck. "Just keep going. It's right down the road there. See that stand of fir trees yonder? That's the place." He pointed with his cane. "You'd better not try the lane. It hasn't been worked in years. If there's anything you need, just come up here. Me and the misses are home most of the time."

Sonny revved the engine and pulled away. Everyone pressed their faces against the windows on the left side of the bus, straining to see the first glimpse of the place. The long row of large evergreens blocked their view, but as they drew nearer, they could see past them and there it was.

No one said a word as they stared at the dark and broken house, crowning the top of the bleak and colorless hill. Most of the windows and doors were broken. A few were boarded. Enormous trees surrounded the house, pointing their bare, sinister fingers as if to warn passing strangers to stay away. Across from the house, were several shabby, dilapidated barns and out buildings, each of them in worse shape than the next. The bus rolled to a stop at the entrance of a long driveway, its occupants sitting in frozen silence.

But then Matthew jumped to his feet and reached for the handle. "C'mon, what are you waiting for?" he cried as he threw open the door. "Let's go have a closer look."

No one moved at first. "Is he serious?" moaned Mack. "Man! This is worse, a hundred times worse, than I ever expected! Don't they have wrecking crews here?"

"Or matches?" sneered Thomas, standing up and reaching for his coat. "Or maybe these country boys just rub sticks together," he quipped as he passed Sonny, who was still sitting and starring.

Annie didn't move either, feeling nauseated and light-headed. Matthew tapped on her window and motioned for her to come. She opened the window stiffly. "Daddy, I think I'd better stay on the bus. The baby is asleep and Joey--"

"Nah, they'll be alright, Annie," he persisted. "I'll send one of the boys to check them every few minutes. Come on. Don't you want to see the inside of the house?"

She gulped frantically. No, she did not want to see the house at all. She was afraid she was going to throw up, but she reached for her coat and joined the others. Then, realizing there was probably no running water, she cringed at the sea of mud that laid between them and the house. "Be careful," she called. "Try not to get too dirty."

Undaunted, Matthew stepped forward, leading them slowly and tentatively at first. He seemed oblivious to their fears and horror. Then he began picking up the pace and they followed him, parading through the mud. He pressed harder, going faster and faster until they were all running, slipping and sliding up the hill.

And then they were there. They stood huddled together at the foot of the stairway leading to the wide, pillared veranda. No one spoke. The sound of their collective labored breathing was deafeningly loud. Matthew stepped forward and mounted the first step, but his foot fell through the rotten wood. He managed to pick his way up and approached the door. Ripping off the "KEEP OUT" sign, he tried to break away the other boards with his bare hands but they held fast. Sonny produced a hammer from beneath his jacket and together they managed to free the entrance. The door swung open, groaning appropriately.

They stepped inside into what appeared to be a large, high-ceiling foyer. There was an open stairway on the right side that swept gracefully around the far end of the room. Straight ahead, beneath the stairway, were four dilapidated French doors opening into the backyard. The Winston's stood gaping open-mouthed at their surroundings. They were surprised to see that this had probably been a lavish mansion in some earlier time.

Without speaking, they broke off into little groups and wandered in different directions. Annie took Peter and Danny by the hand and tapped Andrew on the shoulder to come along. She went to the right into what must have been a formal dining room. A long table stood intact down the middle of the room. Its dark oak finish was marred by deep gashes and weathering. The chairs were gone, and the stained glass panels were smashed in the buffets at the end of the large rectangular room.

She pushed through a swinging door, barely hanging by one hinge, and stepped into the largest kitchen she had ever seen. Of course, she hadn't been in many, but this one was huge. There was a pantry area to the left and to the right was a back stairway to the upper floor and a door which probably led to the basement. The remainder of the spacious, airy kitchen was bordered by long counters and cupboards. The large, rusted cook stove stood serenely in the rubble. Its pipes and parts were broken, and there were names, dates, and some vulgarisms scratched into its great belly. Still, even with the cobwebs and dust, there was a hint of warmth and hospitality in this room. They moved through the passageway-like indoor porch that took them outdoors.

Matthew and the other boys had gone left from the foyer into the living room. It apparently had once been quite elegant. The large fireplace was the focal point of the room with its marble mantle and ornate fixtures. Off this room was a smaller one, probably a library or study with bookshelves from floor to ceiling on three walls, now barren and broken.

Near the far end of the foyer they found another doorway into a small square room with much plainer furnishings. There was a large desk and pieces of a wooden roller chair. "This was probably the office for the estate," Matthew said. It had an exit leading outside, adjacent to where the doorways from the foyer and kitchen opened so that all the explorers rejoined each other there.

The porch winged off into long verandas that ran the length of the house. There were a few steps down to the stone walkway that dissected the backyard. The grounds, now covered with refuse and overgrown with weeds, sloped gently toward the edge of the timber. At the end of the walkway was a ramshackle structure that had once been a small gazebo sitting near the line of tall evergreen trees which served as a boundary between the yard and the woods. There, the terrain appeared to change, pitching downward sharply.

"This is the edge of the bluff," Matthew exclaimed. "The river and the valley must lay beyond. C'mon. There must be an opening here somewhere. " He followed the tree line to the right with the others close on his heels. The purposeful intensity illuminating his face drew them along.

They came to a large rocky shelf that jutted out over the ridge. The stony floor allowed little growth so it afforded an excellent alley-way to view the valley that stretched out before them. There were the acres of the rich, black farmland that Matthew had told them about. Beyond that was the river, dark and imposing even at this distance. Though the landscape seemed desolate and barren in foggy hues of gray, it was a spectacle that left even the most unbelieving gasping and spell-bound.

"My God, this is it!" Matthew proclaimed, his voice at first small and hallow but swelling rapidly until it was booming and exhilarating, He stretched his arms out as though to embrace it all.

No one said anything. It would have been useless anyway. They stood there, cemented by the resolve of one man. But then a cool breeze stirred the treetops, sending a shuddering chill through the little group as though reality was slapping them on the face.

"So now what?" someone said. None of them, not even Matthew, had the vaguest idea. As they had done already so many times these past few days, all eyes turned toward Sonny.

He was sitting astride one of the large tree trunks that served as a safe banister for this rocky balcony. He gazed over the valley with as much awe and reverence as Matthew. His jacket was open, but he seemed unaffected by the cold wind that swept over him. Then he became aware that they were all looking at him and his expression changed to business-like. He looked up at the threatening skies. "Well, we'd better get unloaded," he said. "It'll be dark soon, or worse, we'll get hit by a thunderstorm." Sighing deeply, he got up and led them back toward the house. It was time to get started.

Chapter 9

Their momentary feelings of optimism faded as they trooped back to the house. Walking with slow, muffled steps and heads hanging with an occasional panicked glance passing between them, they were led back to their house of horrors like the fabled sheep being led to the slaughter.

As they neared the back door, when most of them were wondering how their situation could possibly be any worse, a large savage-looking dog blocked their path.

Sonny stepped forward. "Get back!" he ordered, quiet but empathetic. "Move back slow – no sudden moves. Matthew, lean down and pick up that 2x4. Hand it to me, real easy like." Everyone did as they were told. "Nice doggie," Sonny kept saying. "Nice doggie." He reached into his jacket pocket and took out a half-eaten sandwich. He tore off a little piece and threw it toward the dog. "Nice doggie. No one's gonna hurt ya'. You hungry? Yeah, I bet you are. Good stuff, aye?"

The animal crouched to sniff at the crust thrown its way and then ate it. Sonny drew nearer until he was so close he could touch it, but he didn't. He threw the last bit of food. The dog looked at him quizzically for a moment, then gulped it down in one swallow and ran away.

"Where'd she go?" asked Peter with sincere concern.

"Ah, who the hell cares," Thomas said, picking up the board that Sonny had cast aside. "Mangy old mutt better stay away from here."

"She's a bitch with a litter here somewhere," Sonny said. "Just don't go poking under porches n' stuff. It's hard telling where she put her pups."

He led them through the back entrance through the foyer into the living room. He appeared undaunted, but the others were shaken. Annie felt sick again, standing in the middle of all the rubble. She was afraid she was going to cry. "You heard what Daddy said, don't go near that stairway," she cried. "And stay away from those dirty chairs and things. John, go check Joey and the baby. If they're awake, stay with them. No, wait!" she screamed, remembering the dog. "Mack or Andrew should go with you."

"Just hang on a minute," Sonny said. "This room is in the best shape. I think we should start out in here." He crawled into the fireplace and peered up the chimney.

"Sure," agreed Matthew. "The fireplace must work. Looks like some bum came through and used it recently. The windows are still intact or boarded up well. We all have sleeping bags so we can camp out right here in this room until the rest of the house is habitable." He made it sound so simple, but his children were not buying it, judging by the round of moans and groans.

"Habitable? When? How?" Annie exploded, glaring at her father. "How can we possibly make this run-down, drafty old house ever fit to live in? Since when do you know how to do plumbing and electrical work?"

"I don't, but we can hire people who do," Matthew said, that maddening eternal optimism radiating from his face. "We'll hire crews to do all the more technical stuff. We can get this place livable in a few weeks, right, Sonny?"

If Matthew wanted confirmation for his glowing predictions, Sonny did nothing to provide it. "Well, it'll take a lot of work and a lot of money."

"Yeah," jeered Mack, "and I'm just sure you'll help my father with the money part." Sonny turned away and didn't respond so Mack went on. "Besides, I'm sure there's a decent hotel within fifty miles of here where we can stay until this dump is renovated. Two or three weeks? Ha! No way!"

"Oh, yes, there's a way," Matthew retorted, "and you won't be sitting on your ass in any motel either. This is not New York, boys, where it's considered improper to get your hands dirty. We'd be the laughing stock of this whole town if we sit around while someone else does the work when we can do a lot of it ourselves. Now come on, let's get to work."

Matthew and Sonny began discussing how they should proceed. Work assignments were doled out. There didn't appear to be anything of any value left in the room so everything needed to be hauled outside and piled away from the house. Johnny and Peter were dispatched to gather firewood. Sonny took Mack and Andrew back to the bus to begin unloading. If Sonny heard Mack's incessant grumbling, he didn't pay any attention to it. He was having difficulty himself, trudging through the mud trying to carry the bulky luggage.

"Man, this is stupid," he announced, throwing down his load on the porch steps.

"For once we agree on something," sneered Mack.

"But wouldn't it be impossible to get the bus up here?" worried Andrew. "It'd never get through that muddy part."

"I bet our Boy Wonder here can think of something," Mack quipped.

Sonny said nothing as he scouted around until he found some planks and a wooden door. He picked up the door and motioned for the others to bring the rest. He positioned them across the sinkhole. Scraping the mud off his hands, he hoisted himself into the driver's seat and started the bus.

He didn't acknowledge Annie who was in the back of the bus, trying to bundle up the baby and Joey to get them out before the ride began.

"Don't worry," Sonny drawled. "Either we sink, or we won't. But if you want to walk through that mud hole again, be my guest."

Ann's feet were already cold and wet from the mud inside her shoes. "Okay, then, if you're sure it's safe. I mean, the worst that could happen is we'll have to walk part way if the bus gets bogged down, right?"

Sonny said nothing as he positioned the bus to point straight down the driveway. He gunned it and slammed down the muddy track. The bus swayed and groaned but the planks worked to maintain traction. Keeping a steady speed, he coaxed the bus up the hill. It was three-fourths of the way up before it ground to a halt. A brief but hearty cheer went up from the spectators. They all pitched in and had it unloaded within an hour.

A creaky, iron hand-pump by the well was functional so they were at least able to rinse off the worst of the mud and grime. Peter brought a cup and filled it to drink. "Oh, phew! This is awful!" He spat it out. "It's poison!"

Sonny splashed some water into his cupped hands and brought it to his mouth. "Ha!" he hooted. "You people been drinking city water so long you don't know the good stuff." He filled the cup and offered it to Danny.

The boy peered into the cup. "If it's such good water, why is it so red?"

"It's iron and minerals. It's good for you." No one was convinced. One by one they looked at the cup of clay-colored, filmy water and opted for milk.

There was a warm fire crackling by this time and cribs were set up near the fireplace. Sonny produced a large black cast iron pot from one of his supply trunks and prepared a pot of stew. Everyone say on their sleeping bags and ate quietly. Their bodies were weary, but the dark, shadowy room and strange assortment of noises kept them sitting upright until weariness overcame them. One by one, they succumbed into a deep sleep.

"Guess we didn't have to worry about excess energy tonight, did we?" Matthew mused as he moved among the heaps, tucking in the little ones. "I'm proud of my boys tonight," he said. "They had all worked hard with less complaining than I expected."

Annie moved around the room, too, picking up paper dishes and things. She trembled every time a hard gust of wind shook the house. It was as though the place was alive as it shuddered and groaned against the rainstorm. Rationalizing that the house had stood up to such storms before, she crawled into her bag and watched the light of the fire dance on the walls and ceiling, silhouetting the bowed figures of Matthew and Sonny huddled by the fireplace. She tried to concentrate on they were staying to drown out the whining wind and pounding rain.

Matthew talked about all the plans he had for this place. He was anxious to get machinery and livestock, and do some "real farming." Sonny listened for a while, but then said, "I don't think you have any idea how much work has to be done before one seed is planted."

Matthew reached over and tapped out his pipe. "Yes," he sighed, "I know what you're saying. I guess I just have to be patient. But now that I'm here – now that I've seen this place – why, it's even better than I hoped."

Annie smiled. Here they were, sleeping on a dirty plank floor in this run-down dump of a house on a dark and stormy night in the middle of nowhere, and her father is so excited he can't even sleep though he must be exhausted. Oh God, watch over us, she prayed. Keep us safe and warm, and most of all, keep my father from killing himself.

She tried to hear more of what they were saying, but the hum of their voices, the rain and wind, the creaking and groaning of the old house blended together to make a strange lullaby. Soon she slipped off into a deep sleep.

* * * * * *

Annie awakened gradually, recognizing the sounds and smells surrounding her. Coffee. Ah, that's what she wanted, even if it was brewed from that awful water the boys told her about. Sonny sat by the fire, perched on an upside down bucket, cooking what smelled like bacon. The rain and wind were gone now, and the old house was still. She thought the baby must have slept through the night, but then she saw empty bottles. Daddy or possibly Sonny must have taken care of her. She was thankful because she felt rested after a full night of sleep.

Sonny turned to see that Annie was stirring. She was pulling on her coat and boots hurriedly. "Hey!" he called, "you'd better take some Kleenex or something."

This guy really thinks he knows it all, she thought. The idea that he would take such liberties in personal manners irked her. As she stepped out onto the back porch, she couldn't help but pause to survey the view. It was a crisp, clear morning, and the sun was rising out of the valley. Even with the weeds and garbage strewn all around her, it was lovely. Wading through the mud and brush, she rushed to the dilapidated outhouse and wished she was one of the boys and could take care of business behind a nearby tree.

She lingered on the porch, listening to the morning sounds. After such a frightening night, she could hardly believe it was so tranquil. The river couldn't be seen because of the screening trees. She wondered if she could see it from upstairs. She climbed an outside stairway which led to the second floor balcony. Everything looks so different from up here, she thought. There was less contour and severity. Still, the wall of fur trees stood as a tall curtain until she maneuvered herself to the far right corner where she could see over the rocky place they had found last night. The river and valley came into full view.

The sun bathed everything in rich hues of gold, and even the large puddles of standing water from the spring melt were transformed into lovely, blue reflecting pools. And the river, though it was more than a mile away, shimmered in the morning light, looking less intimidating that it did last night.

She turned and saw there was a doorway that led into a bedroom. It was connected to another bedroom, which Annie guessed, judging by the few remaining snatches of pink and blue wallpaper, was a nursery. These were the perfect rooms for her and the baby. Plus, it had the best view in the place.

In the hallway, she found the back stairway to the kitchen, which would further substantiate her claim to this corner of the house. She explored on, finding there were four bedrooms on each side of the house. Actually, they'd have more room here than they did back home. Home. The word stuck in her mind like it was riveted there. Was this place home now? Most of the doors and windows were gone, and there were large gapping holes in the walls and floors. Never in a million years could this be home.

She turned her attention to the sounds of noisy confusion filtering up from the living room. Carefully, she descended the stairway, such as it was, and entered the living room just as Matthew was explaining how he had gone over to the Gibson's and was given generous portions of eggs, bacon, and bread.

"His wife is a really nice lady," he was saying. "Should see her pantry – just loaded with all kinds of food. Look at this bread. It's homemade!"

"Man," Luke whistled, grabbing his share like everyone else, "these farmer's wives sure know how to cook, don't they?"

"Yeah," laughed John, "and now Annie's a 'farmer's daughter' so she'll have to learn how to make all this good stuff – like baking bread and pies and stuff." They all snickered.

"Ha!" retorted Annie. "Baking bread for you guys would be a full time job – half a dozen loaves a day, at least." She squatted down on the floor and picnicked with the others. Never had eggs and bacon tasted better.

The baby was changed and fed, and breakfast was cleared away. It was time for a planning session.

"Obviously," Matthew began, "some of us need to go into town. We need a lot of supplies, and I need to set up an account at the bank and start talking to contractors – unless you want to live in this room indefinitely." Of course, the response to that statement was unanimous. "OK then, I guess Sonny, Annie, and I will go."

"Hey! That's not fair!" Thomas protested, loudly echoed by several others. "Why can't we all go, or at least some of us? C'mon, there's nothing to do out here!"

"Oh, yes, there is. Just look around. There's plenty to do!" insisted their father "You can start by hauling out garbage and junk from the rest of the house. Just put it on the pile we started last night. We'll burn it later."

"What?" Mack complained. "You're just gonna leave us out here in the middle of nowhere with no phone, no food, no nothing' -- except work? What are we? A chain gang?"

"Mack, shut up!" shouted his father. "What else is there to do? You said so yourself – no TV, no place to go. You boys get started. We'll be back by lunch, okay?"

No, it wasn't okay. The arguing continued. Sonny slipped away, picking up the pan of grease and scraps. He went outdoors and began looking for an opening underneath the porch. Peter and Danny were watching him, peeking through the broken windows in the office.

Sonny tried to coax the stray dog from her hiding place. Not seeing any sign of her, he put the skillet down on the ground away from the house and stood back and waited. It didn't take long. The appetizing smell was too much for her. She came out, crouching on her belly toward the food, keeping a watchful eye on the stranger lingering close by. When she began to eat, Sonny crept near her until he reached out and touched her.

"Okay, boys," called Sonny quietly. "Let her get to know you."

The boys were ecstatic. She tolerated their touching with indifference. "Just take it slow and quiet," Sonny said. As soon as the food was gone, she left.

"Do you think she's got a name, Sonny?" Peter asked. It was the first time the boy had actually spoken directly to him.

"Nah, probably not," Sonny replied. "But you can name the puppies when she brings 'em out if you want."

"Oh boy!" the little ones shouted with glee. Never in their fondest dreams did they ever expect to have a dog, much less one with puppies.

"Don't you boys go outside alone and don't go poking around looking for those pups, ya' here?" Sonny reminded them. "She'll turn mean real quick if she thinks someone's messin' around with her babies. You understand?"

"But how we're ever gonna see 'em?" Danny asked.

"She'll keep 'em hidden until she's good 'n ready to bring 'em out. That won't be until their eyes are open," Sonny explained. He picked up the skillet and started back toward the house, the two little boys close behind.

Then there was a loud slam of the door. "My God," Annie cried. "You fed it? You let them out here with that vicious dog?"

"She's not vic'us!" retorted Danny. "She let us touch her a little."

"And we get to name the puppies, too, when she brings `em out, right Sonny?" Peter said, excitement quivering in his voice.

"Boys, that is a very dangerous animal," Annie insisted, still glaring at Sonny.

"We know, we know – Sonny told us. Don't go out alone and don't poke around looking' for the puppies," Danny said. "We'll see the puppies when she brings `em out."

"And that won't be until their eyes are open," Peter added, sounding like an expert.

"Well, just so you're careful," Annie called as they scampered past her. She wanted to yell at Sonny but it was useless.

It was time to get started for town. They boarded the bus, Annie yelling out last minute instructions over the roar of the motor. "Wash all the pots and pans from this morning. Get more firewood, and don't let Joey close to the fire. Peter and Danny – stay by the big boys and don't go out alone."

And then they were gone, bulldozing their way down the driveway.

"Well," Andrew said leading the way back to the house, "we'd better get to work."

"Jeez!" Mack spat. "Maybe you're gonna swallow that bullshit, but I'm not!" He picked up a piece of wood and slammed it down on the ground. His brothers stared at the splintered wood and said nothing.

Once they turned onto the main road, Annie began to feel panicked again. She knew once they got into town she would be expected to make decisions about things of which she knew nothing.

She got a reprieve when Matthew insisted on stopping at the Gibson's to thank them for their kindness that morning. He tried to pay them before, but they refused. Plus, he wanted Annie to meet Mrs. Gibson. "You're going to really like her, Annie," he said.

"Just remember," Sonny sighed, "you told the boys we'd be back by noon. Sometimes these little visits can go on and on." It was obvious he would rather keep going into town.

Chapter 10

As they pulled onto the Gibson's yard, Annie couldn't help but notice the sharp contrast between this place and theirs. This was also a large, frame house on top of a hill, but it had neatly trimmed bushes and shrubs and bright, green shutters. She saw there was a wheelchair ramp leading up to one of the side doors. When she and her father started toward the house, Sonny lingered behind. "Gotta check something' under the hood," he mumbled. He appeared uneasy, his mouth set in that twisted, disapproving way.

Matthew knocked on the door, to which came an immediate, cheery response. "C'mon in, the door's open!" the voice rang out. They walked in tentatively, not accustomed to such open hospitality. "It's nice to see you again, Mr. Winston," their hostess said, smiling." "Jake should be coming right along. Have some coffee and cake."

"This is my daughter, Annie," Matthew said as he sat down at the table. "Ah, real coffee. We've had nothing but instant or restaurant stuff for days."

"Well, there's plenty more where that came from. If we run out, we'll just make another pot!" Ginny smiled as she cut generous pieces of a two-layer, chocolate cake.

Just then, Jake came in with Sonny in tow. "Well, hello there, neighbor!" he called grinning. "You'd better cut another piece of cake, Gin, 'cause we can't have this young fella go hungry in our own front yard. Pull up a chair there, missy," he said to Annie.

"We didn't come by to impose on you even more," Matthew said between bites of Mrs. Gibson's cake. "I just wanted to stop by to thank you for your kindness this morning. My boys just went crazy over that homemade bread."

"I'm glad," Ginny replied, "but was it enough? Jake tells me you have quite a family."

"Yes, I sure do! Ten in all. My oldest, Matthew, Jr. is twenty-two and the baby, my little girl, was born in January."

"Well, you'll have plenty of cheap help!" Jake said, laughing.

"Yes I do, if any of us can figure out what to do. None of us know anything about farming except Sonny here. I hired him to help us get started." Sonny looked up briefly in acknowledgment of the introduction and then went back to staring at his coffee.

Matthew continued. "You see, I ran my family's business in New York. I never cared much for it, but it was an obligation. My wife's people were farmers back in Ireland. I met her during the war when I was stationed over there. Anyway, when I got the chance to move out here, I grabbed it!"

"But how did you ever get your hands on the deed to the old Weatherly place?" Jake asked with unconcealed curiosity. "I mean, that piece of paper had been tossed around for more than forty years. Last we heard, some guy in Chicago owned it."

"I won it in a poker game. Honest to God! After I won everything else, this chap puts the deed on the table. He said it was his good luck piece, but it wasn't that night!"

"Well, for mercy sakes!" Ginny exclaimed.

"I'll be!" Jake whistled. "I can't imagine anyone thinking that place is good luck. I bet it's been owned by at least a dozen people since old man Weatherly's nephew died in '31."

"It hasn't been farmed since?"

"Oh, it's been worked by different folks through the years. Ronny Williamson and his boys rented it from that fella in Chicago up to two or three years ago, I guess. See, the owner let his boy take over the house for one summer and moved in with a bunch of his doped up, hippie friends. There was trouble over there one night, and the sheriff carted them all away. We had a real bad flood that next spring and we heard that the owner got into trouble with the IRS. Ronny said he didn't need the grief so he quit farmin' it. And it hasn't been touched since."

"Well, I own it now, and I aim to farm it, come hell or high water!"

Come hell or high water? Where did her father pick up that one, Annie wondered. She loved seeing him like this, so animated and excited. She leaned against the wall by the hot air vent of the furnace. The fan was blowing and she could feel the warm air swhirling around her legs. It felt so wonderful, but there was something she wanted even more that heat – a nice, clean bathroom.

"This cake looks delicious, but I was wondering if I could freshen up a bit first."

"Oh, for goodness sake! Where are my manners? I'm sure that old house don't have much in the way of facilities. The bathroom is down the hall on the right."

Annie took her time. She peeled off her jacket and washed her hands and face, embarrassed by the dark smear she left on the towel. Oh, God, she thought, I will never take a porcelain toilet for granted again as long as I live. When she came out, she was startled to see Mrs. Gibson sitting alone.

"They started talkin' farming and your dad wanted to see Jake's setup," Mrs. Gibson explained. "They said to tell you they'd stop in and get ya' when they're ready to leave."

Annie circled the table and studied the country kitchen with much interest. It was the most comfortable, inviting room she had ever seen. It was old-fashioned with square, paneled cabinets and faded green linoleum on the counter tops that matched the floor. Ginny sat at a wide open-hung sink, already rinsing the coffee pot and dishes. Annie guessed her to be in her late sixties, at least. She was a rather rotund lady with plump, rosy cheeks and a warm, gracious smile. Her gray hair was done up neatly in a braided bun and there was a knotted net across her forehead. She managed to fuss over her guests quite well while sitting in her chair, rolling back and forth between the table and the counter, her limp, lifeless legs dragging along.

"You have a lovely home, Mrs. Gibson," Annie said as she inhaled the wonderful aroma of the place. It was a blend of the sweet bakery smells, coffee grounds, bacon, and buttery toast and jelly. Annie slumped down in her chair and sighed. "It's so warm and comfortable. I can't believe that old wreck of a house of ours will ever be like this."

"Please, call me Ginny – us being neighbors and all." She rolled over to the table and folded her hands as though to signal her guest of her undivided attention.

"We're on our way into town to buy supplies, and I have no idea where to begin."

"Who did all the work back home in New York:"

"My mother – well, sort of. I never did much at all. Good grief – now I'll have to set up an entire household?"

It sounded preposterous when she said it aloud. And when Ginny started laughing, Annie couldn't help but laugh, too.

"Well, Annie, what are you shopping for? Groceries? Things for the kitchen? Gracious me, I can just imagine what that old house must look like. The cleaning alone would be such a job." The amazement that shone in her face told Annie that she understood the enormity of the task. "Your dad mentioned this morning that you were cooking over the fireplace, like a picnic or a barbecue. But for twelve people! For land sake, lucky you're so young. You sure got a mountain sized job ahead of you."

"Do you like it, Ginny? Living on a farm, I mean?"

"Well, I guess it just comes natural for me and Jake. He was born here, lived his whole life right here on this land. I grew up on a farm, too. I guess farming is the only life we know."

"Are those your sons?" Annie asked as she looked at the faded, silver-framed portraits of two little boys on the wall above the large cabinet across from her. The pictures were in colorless, gray tones and looked quite old. "Where are they now?"

Ginny said nothing for a few moments. Annie was struck by the sudden sadness that cast a long shadow across her face. "They're both dead," she said as she, too, studied the faded pictures of her two young sons. "The river took 'em – going on near 45 years now. Ben, the oldest, helped his dad set the catfish traps lots of times and he was such a good boy. Young Carl was more rambunctious and curious about things. He'd tag along with Ben ever' where he went. I guess Carl got into some trouble and probably fell in. Ben must have tried to save him. There bodies were found together a few miles down stream." She turned back to the sink and rinsed another cup and saucer.

"Sometimes, I can't help thinking' how different things would be if the boys were still alive. Like I said, this farm has been worked by Gibson men since it was first homesteaded in 1850's. Jake is working past his prime because he just don't

93

know what else to do." She patted her limp, useless legs. "Not only does Jake have to tend the farm, but he has to do a lot of housework."

"What happened – I mean, was there an accident, or --"

"No, just old rheumatis' I guess. Came on me the summer of '52. I was scared it was may be polio or something, but it wasn't. They don't hurt much, but they just don't move. I just thank my lucky stars that my arms and hands still work good. As long as Jake sets down everything I need before he goes outside in the morning, I can still manage to cook and bake. Jake thinks I'm a good cook, but that's just because he's used to it."

"Oh, no, this cake is marvelous. Do you think you could teach me how to bake things like this? I mean, you said yourself – I've got a lot to learn."

"I'd be glad to help in anyway I can," Ginny exclaimed. There was such sincerity in the voice that Annie knew she had found the perfect resource person. She had a million questions but just then her father called that they were ready to leave.

"It was so nice to sit and talk. Thank you so much for your help and your wonderful bathroom, and all that great food earlier this morning," she said as she put on her jacket.

"Well, like I said, what are neighbors for? You can come back and we'll talk some more. When you get to town, go to Bean's Hardware Store. Lori Bean works in there and she can help you a lot, I'm sure. Now take care," she called after her young visitor. "Come back to visit anytime – even it its just to use the bathroom."

Actually, Annie felt a lot better. Ginny's words "picnic or barbecue" stuck in her mind, as she thought that was a good place to start. She'd just have to remember what kinds of goodies Cook packed in those giant hampers when the family went to the park or shore. And there were things she needed for the baby, and cleaning supplies. Lists. The secret to managing all this was lists.

* * * * * *

Unfortunately, the ride to town took less than ten minutes, no time to write down anything. The bus rolled to a stop alongside the river front park.

"If we're gonna do any shopping," Matthew said, "I'd better stop by the bank first." He reached under one of the seats and pulled out a canvas bag full of cash and checks. Swinging the bag under his arm as he stepped off the bus, Matthew surveyed the little corner bank and smiled. "I think I'm just about to make somebody's day," he said.

He stepped inside and addressed the bespectacled, gray-haired lady behind the counter. "Hello, I'm Matthew Macalister Winston. My family just moved to a farm outside of town. I'd like to set up an account here. Do you suppose I could speak to your manager?"

The teller seemed a little miffed. "Mr. Winston, I'm sure that I can help you set up an account. If you deposit $200, you'll get a box of free checks, you know. Mr. Strong is also the mayor of our little town. He is a very busy man."

"I'm sure he is, but this is quite a substantial amount of money so I'd really like to meet the man and deal with him directly, at least the first time."

"A substantial amount? Just how much are we discussing here, Mr. Winston?"

"Well," Matthew answered evenly, "I have $40,000 in cash and several cashier's checks." He couldn't help but smile when spilled coffee ran across the counter and the lady's glasses nearly fell off when she jerked her head up.

Obviously determined to keep her composure, she casually wiped up the coffee and readjusted her glasses, saying, "Yes, well, I'm sure Mr. Strong would like to meet you and welcome you himself. I'll see if he can free some time."

As she spoke she was back peddling toward the door with the imposing sign which read, "Mr. Lewis J. Strong, Bank President" in bold letters. She excused herself and stepped inside. A few seconds later Matthew heard this rather loud "What?" blasting from Mr. Strong's office. The teller reappeared, announcing, "Mr. Strong will see you now."

The honorable Mayor Strong rose from his chair to shake Matthew's hand, smiling broadly. They exchanged pleasantries for a few minutes while Matthew unceremoniously unzipped his bag and began piling his money on the bank president's desk.

"I'm anxious to begin doing his business locally and thought the best way to handle it was with checks," Matthew said.

"Well, of course," Mr. Strong stammered, distracted by the impressive stack of $1000 bills. Matthew then took out the cashier's checks. "My goodness that is quite an impressive stack of money, sir. I daresay I am at a loss for words, something most folks would say was highly unusual." He picked up one of the checks and scrutinized it carefully. "In order to protect my investors," he said, sounding very professional and business-like, "I think I should call New York and verify these funds. No offense intended."

"None taken. Go ahead. Call. Ask to speak to Bill Kaplan, one of the Vice-presidents at First City. The phone number is 789-5515. That's 212 area code, you know."

Lewis Strong dialed the number. "Yes, hello...Yes, ma'am, this is Lewis Strong, President of the Shannon Town Bank and Trust. I am calling about a manner concerning Mr. Matthew Winston...Yes, Matt Winston...Oh, I see. . . Really. . . No, that's quite all right. I won't be leaving a message...You've been very helpful." He hung up the phone. "Now, Mr. Winston, what kind of an account would you like to set up with us today?"

Fifteen minutes later, Matthew emerged from the Shannon Town Bank and Trust, complete with his box of free checks. "C'mon, you two. Let's go spend some money."

They walked to the hardware store. The faded sign read, "Andy Bean & Sons, Hardware and Lumber Yard." There was a truck sitting at the curb with the same sign stenciled on the door but it also had a hand-written "For Sale" sign taped to the window. The place looked badly in need of repairs, considering the nature of their business.

Through the open gate they could see someone walking among the piles of boards, posts and plywood stacked in the decaying lumberyard. Matthew and Sonny headed out to the yard, which meant they expected Annie to go in and start shopping. By myself, she thought. What did she know about buying hardware, and the place looked so small.

The instant she stepped in she realized there was no need to worry about the amount or variety of merchandise in this place.

She had never seen anything like it. Every square inch of available space was covered. There were narrow aisles between shelves piled high with everything from tools to little ceramic knickknacks and music boxes. On the walls hung pots and pans, large basins and tubs, and clothes hampers. There were displays of everything from light fixtures and lamps to bikes and tricycles.

There was a young slender woman standing on a ladder sorting through some pots and pans on a high shelf in the corner. She was scolding someone, and Annie could hear a child crying. "Kevin!" she cried. "Why do you pick on your sister like that all the time? Now leave her alone!" Her voice was strained and she appeared upset.

Then she became aware of Annie standing nearby. She apologized as she descended the ladder and picked up the whimpering child. Annie saw that the woman's face looked tired and worn, and her eyes were red and swollen. "Can I help you with something?" she asked, forcing a smile.

"Yes," said Annie hesitantly. "Are you Lori Bean? You are? Well, my neighbor, Ginny Gibson, said you could help me."

"She did? Well, that was nice of her. I'll certainly try," Lori said, looking somewhat confused. "We carry a little of everything here. What are you looking' for?"

"That's what I need – a little bit of everything. I'm Ann Winston. My family is moving into the old Weatherly place. Yes, I know, it's not fit to live in, but my father is very determined. He's outside right now speaking with your husband. We need so many things. You see, there's 12 of us."

"Oh, my goodness," Lori murmured, letting the child slide off her hip. "So you've come in to buy supplies? Where would you like to start?"

"Well, I guess cleaning supplies."

"Like mops, brooms, er-- buckets and things? All that stuff is over here. How about soap and cleansers?" Not wishing to appear totally ignorant, Annie smiled and nodded agreeably to everything. Before long, there were piles of supplies on and around the counter.

At one point, Lori stopped and looked Annie straight in the eye. "I feel I must tell you something," she said. "There is a K-

Mart in Dubuque. Stuff is a lot cheaper there."

"No, no," Annie said as she studied a package of kitchen utensils. "I appreciate your honesty, but I see no reason to drive all that way when we can buy everything here."

Outside, Matthew and Sonny approached the man working in the yard. "Are you Charlie Bean?" Matthew called to him. "Mr. Lewis Strong sent me."

The man's face turned ashen. "Yes sir, I am. Can I help you with something?"

"Well yes, I believe you can. I'm Matthew Winston. And this is my hired hand, Sonny Jackson. I recently acquired the Weatherly farm. Guess you know the place, judging by your reaction. Anyway, I need to get the place habitable as soon as possible. And Mr. Strong mentioned you were quite capable of helping us with renovations."

Charlie relaxed. "Jeez, I thought you were bill collectors or the IRS. Anyway, I can sure do all that stuff for ya'. But it's only fair to tell ya' that there's bigger outfits in Dubuque that'd probably have everything in stock. I mean, I'll have to go there myself to get a lot of the supplies."

"Sure, I realize that, Charlie." Matthew sat down on a pile of 2x4's and lit a cigarette. "No, I'd rather deal with you than some outfit twenty miles away. I'll pay you to handle all that. Of course, it will require a lot of your time for the next few weeks, if you can manage the time away from the store."

Charlie looked away and grinned sheepishly like Matthew had just told a funny joke. "I don't think you have to worry about that, Mr. Winston. I'd be tickled t' death to sink my teeth into a real back-breaking job."

"Well, good," Matthew said, also smiling broadly. "Mr. Strong certainly gave you an excellent recommendation. But frankly, you're a little younger than I expected."

"Well, my granddad worked his whole life in this here store and my daddy after that. He died real sudden like a couple of years ago and left the place to Mama and us boys. She's too old to run the place and my brothers all went other places. So that leaves me to try to keep this place goin'." He wasn't smiling anymore.

"Okay, then, it's settled," Matthew said, reaching for his wallet. "Here's five hundred dollars so you know I'm serious." They started walking toward the store. "How soon can you start? If you're not doing anything this afternoon, you could come out and look the place over. You should see it," he said, shaking his head. "I wouldn't even know where to begin."

Sonny left Matthew and Charlie behind to talk about furnaces and ductwork and took his own list inside the store. He walked in to find Annie and Lori chatting away about everything from potato peelers to diaper rash. When Lori started to ask him if he needed help, Annie explained who he was.

"Ain't real friendly, is he," observed Lori.

"No, he's not," Annie said, nearly whispering, "But believe me, he's helping us a lot. Without him, we couldn't make it. Anyway, where were we? Oh, yes, about those canisters up there." She was pointing to a display of old-fashioned crock canisters, nearly hidden on a high shelf. "Ginny Gibson has some just like those in her kitchen and I'd like some, too."

"Okay, I'll fetch 'em down but they're heavy suckers. Tupperware makes some real nice ones – come in three different colors." She placed the ladder into position. "Tupperware?" she said again noticing her customer's blank expression. "You know, plastic storage containers. They're indestructible. Can't buy it in stores – gotta buy it at parties in people's houses. You know – Tupperware parties? Well," she murmured to herself. "I didn't think there was anyone in the civilized world that didn't know about Tupperware."

By the time Charlie and Matthew came in, Lori was standing behind her antiquated cash register, tallying the total. "That's $324.73, sir," Lori winced, appearing almost apologetic, but Matthew's expression remained unperturbed.

"There you are, Mrs. Bean. It was a real pleasure doing business with you. The first of many, I'm sure."

After everything was loaded, Charlie hoisted his boy onto his shoulders and Lori swung the little girl across her hip as they accompanied the Winston's back to the bus.

"Okay, Charlie, we'll expect you after lunch, right? Oh, I guess you won't be needing this." Matthew reached inside the truck and ripped off the "For Sale" sign. Everyone laughed.

The next stop was the grocery store. Annie intended to have some lists for here also, but the page was blank. There was no need to worry. Sonny went up and down the aisles, grabbing whole arm loads of everything.

Matthew was dispatched to the Grill and Pup to order twenty hamburgers, shakes, and a bag of fries. He chuckled at the now familiar reaction of the waitress and nearby spectators when he explained who he was, where he intended to live, and why he needed such a large quantity of food. After he ordered, he went into the adjoining bar.

The smiling, round-faced bartender introduced himself as the proprietor of the place, Billy O'Reilly. Since any stranger is apt to be noticed, Matthew was asked to recount his story one more time, but this time over a glass of foaming draft beer. Billy listened attentively, but instead of looking at Matthew with the usual shocked stare, he just stood there and shook his head sadly. "Well, what the hell took ya' so long? Should have come to your senses a long time ago," he said with mocked solemnity and then broke into uproarious laughter as his great red cheeks became even redder.

An half-hour later, Sonny pulled the bus to the curb in front of the store and instructed Annie to fetch him out. She found her father sitting at the bar talking with Billy as though they were life long friends. "C'mon, Dad," Annie said. "We'd better get back. Those boys have been alone for quite awhile.

Matthew slapped some money on the bar. "Billy, I intend to be one of your best customers."

"Good, cause I got a lot of regular customers, but they ain't all paying ones." He waved good-bye with his bar towel.

"These are good people in this town," Matthew said. "I'm going to enjoy spending my money here."

Sonny said nothing as he put the motor in gear and headed out of town, trying to maneuver the bus down the spongy roads. Annie wasn't listening to her father either. She found herself staring at her hands. They were soft and manicured. No wonder Lori Bean suggested several pairs of Playtex gloves. Ginny and Lori's were worn and callused. Is that what it takes for a woman to survive out here? Could I ever be like them, she wondered. Do I want to be? Yes, she thought, somewhat dubiously. She recognized the strengths and earthy wisdom in these women and yearned to have those qualities herself. She also realized that wishing for something is a lot different than actually having it.

Chapter 11

Andrew received no cooperation in getting anything accomplished after their father left. To make things worse, Mack led the opposition. Andrew yelled and argued until everyone rolled up their sleeping bags. But then, as soon as the room was cleared, Mack produced a basketball and the game was on. Andrew and Luke rescued the baby and Joey from courtside and escaped upstairs.

They climbed the front stairway cautiously and explored the layout of the rooms. Annie had already claimed the two rooms over the kitchen for her and the baby. Luke took out a small sketchpad from his pocket and drew the floor plan. Joey could have the small room across the hall from Annie, and the other two younger boys would have the fourth bedroom in that wing. Luke suggested that he share a room with Thomas, and Andrew and John could share a room. Then Mack would have his own room and their father would have what appeared to be the largest, master bedroom.

"Look at this bathroom," Luke called. "It's really a mess." He stepped aside so Andrew could see the rotted fixtures and holes in the floor. "The small bathrooms in Annie and Pop's rooms are just as bad. I don't know plumbing, but I know they need a definite total overhaul."

They followed the narrow stairs up to the third floor. There were some storage rooms and some small bedrooms with slanted ceilings and narrow windows. "These must have been for servants, right?" Luke whispered as though he didn't want to awaken any spirits of these long-ago occupants.

Andrew stared at the broken windows and crumbled

plaster. "If Pop saw this, do you think he'd still be as optimistic?"

"Yeah, probably," Luke said. "Nothing is gonna change his mind. But Andrew, look at this view! There's no people or buildings or cars – nothing' for as far as you see!" He grabbed his notepad again and started sketching.

Andrew chuckled at his brother's enthusiasm. "So it's quiet, but so what? We know nothing about farming, and we sure as heck don't know how to make this dump livable. Mack is right. This is crazy."

"Mack just doesn't like the idea of working. It's a new concept to him." Luke sketched as he spoke, a look of awe still upon his face.

"It's not the work that I'm dreading, Luke. I miss home, don't you? This is so far from everything – the libraries, my friends at school." He began pacing. "But Mack is ten times more upset than I am. The difference is I'm not going to be an asshole about it. I'll put in my time until November, like Pop said, and then we'll see who comes out on top."

They heard the bus so they made their way back downstairs.

"You didn't do anything around here?" Matthew shouted as he came in the front door. "My God, get out there and start unloading the bus. Put on your coats and boots. Use your heads, will you? You too, Mack!" The unloading was done quickly since no once could eat until it was finished.

As soon as Charlie Bean arrived, Sonny and Matthew took him down to the basement to inspect the monstrous coal furnace. It stood in the dirt and cobwebs like a giant octopus ruling its domain in the bottom of the sea. "Guess we should tear it out and install a new gas unit," Matthew said. They toured the entire house, measuring windows and doors, examining the roof and stairways. Charlie made a note to call the electric and phone companies as soon as he got back to town. Outside they determined the well was functional, but it would need a new electric pump and pipes. Charlie promised to round up some help and report for work early in the morning.

Meanwhile, everyone was given assignments, such as cleaning up debris strewn all over the house and yard. Matthew let them joke around as long as they continued working. "Better here than in school," the younger ones said.

Annie began to panic as the dinner hour approached, but Sonny came in mid-afternoon and unceremoniously browned some hamburger and poured in beans and tomatoes for chili. "Stir it every once and while," was all he said as he strode out of the room. Annie stood close by, stirred it as directed.

Everyone seemed to enjoy their supper, especially since Ginny had insisted on sending two fresh-baked pies for dessert. They made popcorn for snack later, and although there was some mention of having no television, the boys seemed content to sit around the fire and tell ghost stories. One by one, they curled up in their bags and fell asleep. There was no rainstorm bombarding the house, and even if there was, it probably wouldn't have kept anyone awake.

* * * * * *

There was joy in the Bean household for the first time in a long time.

Lori closed the store early that afternoon, took the kids home, and paced nervously around the kitchen, waiting for Charlie to come home. She heard the truck and a few moments later, he came tearing into the house.

"It's for real! It's all set!" he shouted, picking up his wife and twirling her around. "We're gonna make it! Where's the money? You didn't put it in the bank, did you?"

Lori took the money out of the Rice Krispies. Charlie wanted to touch it, smell it, and count it over and over again. They talked about going into Dubuque for dinner, maybe buying some new work clothes for Charlie. If he was going to work for a millionaire, he should at least look decent.

But in the end, they had ice cream at the Tastee Freeze and filled up the truck, which never had more than five dollars worth of gas at one time since they bought it. How sweet it was to have something to think about instead of bouncing checks and unhappy creditors. What a difference a day can make.

103

* * * * * *

True to his word, Charlie Bean drove into the yard at 7:30 AM sharp just as Matthew was reaching for his first cup of coffee. There was no bacon and eggs this morning. Boxes of stale donuts were passed around.

Matthew took his coffee and went outside. "Hi there," he called, putting on his coat and boots. "Bring along your own wrecking crew?" he asked, acknowledging the other two men getting out of the pickup with Charlie.

"Mornin', Matthew. Yeah, I figured we needed all the help we can get. This here is Skip Dunlevy and his little brother, Roger. We played football together."

Handshakes were exchanged. Matthew was amazed at the size of people here – wide, square shoulders, large arms and thighs. "They're truck drivers between jobs right now," explained Charlie. "They may look dumber than hell, but they're good workers."

"Well, we definitely do need help out here. I hope Charlie told you that this is not going to be a fun job," Matthew said laughing.

"He told us. We're used to it," Skip said as Charlie knocked off his cap. "Ya' see, I played guard and Roger here was center. We'd do all the work, made all the holes, and he'd got all the glory. We've been doin' the dirty work for this guy as long as we've known him."

"Good, because then we won't have to do it," Mack broke in, stepping out of the shadows with Andrew at his heels. The slim, delicate-looking city boys and the country giants faced each other. Andrew stepped forward and extended his hand. "Hi, I'm Andrew, one of Matthew's sons. Glad you came." He stepped back looking as though the men's grip had hurt his hand.

Mack leaned against one of the pillars and looked the other way when handshakes were offered. When the others had gone to unload the ancient but functional generator from the back of the pickup, Matthew turned to his oldest son angrily. "You rude, stupid idiot. We need these men, unless you want to do it all by

104

yourself." Matthew shrugged his shoulders, gave his son a parting scowl, and walked away.

"But, Father," Mack called after him, his voice dripping with sarcasm. "You didn't give me a work assignment."

Matthew sucked in a quick breath before answering. "Talk to Sonny," he said without turning around. "Maybe he has something simple you can do."

Sonny took his cue and stepped forward. "Yeah, do you think you could handle going into town? Here's a list of stuff we need, mostly from the lumberyard. Charlie's wife can help you." He thrust the list into Mack's hand and walked away, flipping him the keys.

Mack was rather pleased with this turn of events. He was getting away from here for a while. With any luck, he could hang around town until after lunch. Even a hick town was better than breaking his back around here.

* * * * * *

Annie's plan was to get the kitchen cleaned first, but she soon realized that was a joke. As soon as the generator was cranked to provide light, fifty year old dust came belching up from the basement. Sonny and Charlie were in and out. At least they understood the necessity of getting this room functional as soon as possible.

Mid-morning, Annie did a quick inventory and discovered Danny and Peter were missing. John was dispatched to find them. They were playing down by the barn. Just as she was calling them in to scold them and find them jobs, the electric and phone company trucks pulled up. At this point what had been somewhat chaotic became pure pandemonium. She was bombarded with questions that she had absolutely no idea how to answer, like, "Lady, where do you want the phone?...Where's the laundry gonna be?..."

It was obvious by their tones and expressions that these men were of the opinion that this house was a waste of time, effort, and money, but as long as Matthew was willing to pay, they were more than willing to oblige him. The electrician said he was only responsible for getting electricity from the high-lines along the road to the house. Matthew would have to find someone to come in and completely re-wire the interior. Hearing that, Matthew offered him triple wages that he made at the electric company to come back tomorrow and Sunday. And if he knew anyone who could help, bring him along for the same wage. A bargain was quickly struck.

By noon the driveway looked like a parking lot for who's in the area construction business. There was Fratney's Pump Service, the Skelgas LP Truck, and Lindner Brother's Sewer and Excavating, Inc. When they came with their thousands of questions, Annie sent them to Sonny or Charlie, who was certainly earning his commission.

At lunchtime, Lori Bean came out with a picnic basket of food for her husband and the Dunlevy boys. Everyone was glad to sit down to take a break and wash down the dirt with cold beer. Annie hastily put out some bread, lunch meat, and chips for her own crew and then approached Lori, asking her if she'd like a tour of the house.

"Oh yes, I was hoping you'd ask," she replied. Annie couldn't help but notice how much happier and more relaxed both Mr. and Mrs. Bean were today.

"Ya' know," Lori said, "when they get this old wood-burner out of here, there's going to be a huge space. You already have plenty of counters, so why don't ya' put two stoves here. You're gonna be doin' a powerful lot of cooking and baking. Which kind of stove are you gonna buy?" Lori laughed at her new friend's expression. It was obvious that the girl didn't even know there were two kinds, let alone how to use it. "Didn't you do any cooking back home?"

Annie sighed. "The closest I have ever come to any cooking was heating water for coffee or stirring Sonny's chili over the fire."

"Well, then," Lori concluded. "You'd better stick to flame cookin'. Get gas stoves." They both laughed.

Discovering the small room off the kitchen, Lori said, "Whoever designed this house was smart. They put in a good sized mud room." Seeing Annie's face drop, Lori said, "Well, honey, that's what ya' call it. The men and the kids will come in through here, kick off their boots, shed off their coveralls and things. Guess you could call it a washroom cause you'll probably have a sink back here for 'em to use before they come in to eat n' such. You wouldn't want 'em trackin' all that into your house, would ya'?" The answer seemed obvious, even to Annie.

"Ya' know," Lori continued, "I bet there's room for your washer and dryer in here. Sure would be better than making a zillion trips up and down the stairs to the basement. You're gonna need a freezer. Better get a 18.5 big chest freezer. You can put it in the basement. You're gonna need so much food, especially in the winter when you're snowed in out here and can't get to town for a couple of days." Anne was listening to all this in utter and profound disbelief. A mudroom? Snowed in for days? She followed Lori from room to room, trying to digest a fraction of what her new friend was saying.

"Don't put carpeting in the dining room, or at least I wouldn't. Kripes, how would you ever keep it clean? . . . The livin' room must have been beautiful but with all these kids, I'd think about puttin' in a family room in the basement or someplace, so they can spill and fight n' stuff down there . . . There's no bathroom on this whole floor. You're gonna need one someplace, don't ya' think? Like in the office, it's big enough. They could come in from outside and shower . . . "

"Wow," she whistled when they ended their little tour in the foyer. "Just think how elegant this place must have been. It's really going to be something when you get it fixed up again. I hope you don't think I made these suggestions to drum up business for my husband."

"No, of course not. Everything you said made perfect sense, even to me. Just look at it. What a mess! And Daddy wants it finished in a couple of weeks because he wants to begin working outside!" The situation seemed pretty desperate. "Lori, can you help me, I mean, even more than you have already? Go shopping with me to choose all the appliances and things. You already have a good idea what we need. Do you have to get back to the store?"

"No, no. Charlie's mom is taking care of the store and the kids this afternoon. She loves taking the place over. Sure, I'd be glad to help ya'. But..." she hesitated, biting her lip. "I hate spending' your daddy's money like this. Makes me nervous. Look! My hands are all a sweat just thinking' about it." They laughed then, giggling like mischievous schoolgirls. Annie reassured her that she shouldn't worry about the money. She was just so grateful for her help. They went out to find Matthew and Charlie to tell them their plans. Annie found someone to look after the babies, and then they were off.

"So, should we drive on into Dubuque or do you want to stop at Nick O'Brien's place," asked Lori. "He's the Skelgas man. His wife, Debbie, runs the store in town. They got real good stuff in there – you know, like Maytag and Whirlpool. Nick could deliver everything and set it all up for you. They're expensive as hell but...You know, worrying about money is just my nature" She bit her lip nervously.

"That sounds good to me!" Annie cried. "The easier, the better – that's my motto!"

Lori honked and waved when they passed the Gibson place. "They sure are nice people aren't they? What does the Good Book say? 'Blessed are the meek, for they shall inherit the earth?' I just hate seeing that woman sitting in that wheelchair. I used to clean for her when I was in high school. Paid me real good, too, they did. I figured I wasn't too good to scrub that woman's floors." Her words were sharp with a touch of bitterness. "Anyway, you're lucky to have such nice neighbors, cause not everyone around is as nice as them."

"C'mon, Lori. What do you mean?" Annie coaxed. "Everyone seems so friendly and easy going. Isn't that what small town people are like?"

"How come everybody thinks that about country folk? It's just like everywhere else – we got nice people and some not so nice people. It's just that there's no secrets in a town like this. I mean, it's a nice place n' all, and I can't imagine livin' no place else, but it ain't perfect either. But don't you worry none. You and your family is gonna do just fine here."

"Why, because we have a lot of money?"

"Yes, and you're Catholic, right? You got it made."

"I don't know, Lori. Aren't people going to think it's weird that we came out here when we know nothing about farming? I mean, I love my father, and it even seems strange to me. But he's not psychotic or anything, really."

"Nah. Don't worry about it. Rich folks can do anything they want. See, in a place like this, it's not what you are or what you do, it's who you are. You can be the biggest jackass in the whole damn county, but as long as you got yourself a good name, nothing else matters."

"You talk as though you know from first hand knowledge."

"Well, sure, I ought to. I lived here, or in other small towns like it, all my life. And down South, it's a whole lot worse. Me and my daddy moved to Shanny when I was fourteen. We moved around ever' couple years. But it don't matter much cause the rules are the same ever' where. Take Charlie's family for instance. His granddaddy started the business over seventy-five years ago, so John, that's Charlie's daddy, was well liked and well thought of around here. But the thing was, that man was about the poorest excuse for a businessman there ever was and everybody knew it. Him and Elsie, that's Charlie's mother, were big shots in the Chamber of Commerce, the Church, the Lion's Club, and all that. When he died, he was so much in debt you wouldn't have believed it. And now me and Charlie are left with the mess."

"But my daddy," Lori sucked in a long, deep breath. "Well, he never got nothing from nobody. Yeah, it's true, he drank too much, but he was a better man drunk than John Bean was sober. He was a truck driver. No matter what he did, folks just looked their noses down at him and me, too. People just couldn't believe Charlie married me. He says I'm nuts, but I swear that's the main reason people just don't stop by, unless it's seventy five cents of nails or a screwdriver or something." She sighed deeply then. "But that's all ancient history. I got a real good feelin' now. Your daddy probably saved us from goin' under. If we can put some money into the store and carry better merchandise, maybe people would come in by us. That's what Charlie says."

By that time, they arrived at the edge of town. It was very small. The sign at the city limits read, "Population: 568." Main street was about five blocks long. There were two grocery stores, a farm implement business, the bank, a large grain elevator and feed store, and two other churches besides the large, white steepled one on the hillside. The buildings were mostly neat and trim with an occasional shack dotting the small village.

As soon as they entered the store and introductions were made, it was clear that Debbie O'Brien already knew that money was no issue when dealing with the Winston's. She was quick to point out all the wonderful features of the most expensive models. "This Maytag is the top of the line," she said as she stroked the white appliance as though it was a fine sculpture. "It even has a delicate cycle for your dainties." She whispered the words as though she just said something scandalous. Lori rolled her eyes and moved on to the next machine. Soon a bill of sale was being written for two stoves, two refrigerators, ad 21.5 cubic foot freezer, two water heaters, and a washer and a dryer.

"Debbie," Lori said, "the Winston's will be paying cash, buying hundreds of dollars worth of merchandise. I think they would appreciate a 10% discount and of course, free delivery and hookup would be nice."

"But Lori, they're certainly getting a great price on these items. And of course, Nick would be happy to deliver everything and help in any way--"

"Oh, yes," Annie cut in quickly, becoming aware of the daggered stares passing between the two business women, "I'm sure all the prices are quite fair. My father will issue a check as soon as everything is delivered. Here is a five hundred dollar deposit-- I believe that's customary, isn't it? Lori, I think we should be getting back, don't you?" She wanted to get home. Weariness was beginning to set in.

"Cheapskate!" Lori muttered as she climbed back into the truck. "Wouldn't hurt her to give you a good deal. Do you have any idea how much mark up there is on stuff like that?" She stopped once to check in with her mother-in-law at the store, and then bought some beer at the Pub. Annie didn't argue when Lori insisted her new friend sit in the truck and relax.

Chapter 12

When they got back to the farm, they presented Matthew with the bill and the beer. Both went down easy. The men relaxed and reflected over the day's accomplishments. They had gotten a lot done. The old furnace was removed, the electric pump was nearly operational, and the trench was dug for the new septic tank. Brand new poles, strung with telephone and electrical wires, lined the driveway. So, at six o' clock as twilight set in, a caravan of weary men turned their trucks homeward, promising to return in the morning.

If these seasoned veterans were tired, the Winston's ached to the point of nausea as they spread out their bedrolls and fell asleep instantly. Annie tried to quiet the little ones, stinging with resentfulness. After all, her brothers weren't any more tired than she was. She struggled with Joey, finding him to be more hyper and uncooperative than usual. And then John, who always set out his clothes for the next day, made an appalling announcement. "I don't have any clean clothes for tomorrow." Annie knew the boxes of baby clothes were nearly empty, but she hadn't wanted to think about it. Now there was no avoiding the piles of disgusting, smelly, muddy, wet clothes, and it looked like it was up to her to do something about it. A rage began building from deep inside her – a totally frustrated, exasperated anger at the whole stupid mess. She began going from one corner of the room to another, finding more and more dirty clothes. She began throwing them, kicking them, feeling even more resentful as she moved among the motionless, sleeping bodies. What did they expect her to do – take the clothes down to the river and beat them on rocks?

Sonny tended the fire, expressionless as always. Out of the corner of her eye, she saw him watching her. He must have known what was happening and he probably had a solution, but she wasn't going to ask him. After several more minutes of her kicking and stomping, he finally said, "I'll get some crates from downstairs so we can haul it all into town."

"You mean there's someone in town who can do all this for us?" Perhaps her temper tantrum had been premature.

"No, we'll do it – at the Laundromat? You know, put in the clothes, put in the quarters? Maybe you don't know." He turned to go, sighing deeply.

They gathered all the dirty clothes they could find and threw them into the boxes. Annie was working with renewed vigor, fueled by fresh anger and resentment. Soon they were on their way into town, surrounded by great heaps of dirty jeans, shirts, and socks.

* * * * * *

Alice Simpson thrust the key into the lock just as the Winston bus stopped in the No Parking Zone in front of the Simpson Coin Operated Laundromat.

"Oh, ma'am," Sonny called, "we'd really appreciate it if you could hold off closing until we get our wash done." He and Annie climbed out of the bus. "Smile and talk nice," he muttered under his breath. Annie did as she was told.

"Oh yes, please," she said sweetly. "We're new in town and didn't realize you'd be closing so early--er, oh goodness, it is 9:00, isn't it? Could you make an exception just once?"

This formidable Mrs. Simpson stared at them. "What do you expect me to do? Sit here half the night?" she whined. "If you start now, you won't be done until after midnight. I run a very clean place here, ya' know. I can't have people thinking they can come in here all hours of the night and day. If I let you do it, then everyone else would expect it, too."

"Mrs. Simpson, we understand this would be an inconvenience for you," Sonny said smoothly, "so Mr. Winston would want to make it worth your while." He pressed several bills into her hand.

"Oh, well, I see," Mrs. Simpson gulped. "I guess, since this is an emergency. And goodness, I recollect that someone told me that you have several children in your family?"

"Yes, that's correct," Annie replied, smiling her most compelling grin. "There are 10 of us all together."

Apparently reassured, the elderly lady unlocked the doors and turned on the lights as Sonny began unloading boxes from the bus. Annie maneuvered Mrs. Simpson toward her car, promising to lock up when they were finished.

`"My, my, my," sneered Annie after Mrs. Simpson finally left, "you can be positively charming if you try, Mr. Jackson."

"No, not really, I just let your father's money do the talking. It's amazing how many doors it can unlock." There was no pun or humor intended. Clearly, he was as annoyed about this situation as she was. Soon everything was unloaded and Annie stood waiting for further instructions. "Start sorting," he hissed. "Like – jeans in one pile, whites in another, like that. You get it?"

"Hey, I'm not stupid. Yes, I get it!" She threw clothes in all directions.

"Yeah, sure. Why don't you go to the Pub next door and get some change." A county sheriff's squad car pulled up across the street. Sonny turned abruptly. "I gotta use the head," he said as he walked toward the bathroom. "There's a nosy cop out front. If he comes in here, just tell him to call down to the Simpson place."

The Sheriff drove off. Annie got several rolls of quarters and soon they filled every washer in the place and still had more piles of clothes on the floor. They emptied the vending machine of detergent, bleach, and softener. The jeans billowed great clouds of dirt and had to be washed twice. Annie's anger gave way to exhaustion. Her mind drifted back to the brownstone. How many times she had thrown clothes barely worn into the hamper and they would reappear in her closet, neatly laundered and pressed. She had taken so much for granted.

The time passed slowly, ticking to the rhythm of the churning machines, spinning and rinsing each in turn. She kept pacing because she knew if she sat down, she'd fall asleep. What a mundane job this was, exactly the kind of thing she'd expected to do on a regular basis. Her mind revolted at this revelation.

Once again she looked at her hands, small and pink. What

possible joy or reward could there be in laboring hour after hour, year after year, like this? She felt twinges of anger creeping in again.

As the washers finished, the clothes were carted over to the row of dryers. Annie moved around with unbridled resentment, crashing into things, flinging clothes here and there. She forgot that she had an audience. Then she turned and saw him staring at her.

"You really hate this, don't you?" Sonny said.

She was stunned by his perfect description of how she felt. "How am I supposed to feel? Honored? Grateful? I am so damned tired, I could drop. And don't you say I told you so, all right? Just leave me alone!"

They went back to work with no further words passing between them. At 1:20 AM they turned off the lights. She dropped off the key at the Pub as Sonny finished loading the boxes of clean, somewhat folded laundry back into the bus. He hoisted himself into the driver's seat and slammed the door shut. What an ass, she thought. He is daring me to give up.

As she slumped down in her seat, dazed and blurry-eyed, she had a vision of the little train that kept trying to climb the hill. Only the cars were cardboard boxes and the train's hissing sounded like the churning of a washing machine.

* * * * * *

Annie awakened Saturday morning to the familiar buzz of children laughing, bacon frying, babies crying, and men talking. Andrew was chief cook and baby watcher as it was he who was intently working over the fire. Matthew and Sonny were already up and out. She tried to move but found she was still very tired. No one was asking her for anything or telling her to get up, so she closed her eyes and pretended to still be asleep.

"They didn't get back till almost 1:30, so Pop said let her sleep," someone said.

Word was sent for Sonny and Matthew to come eat. They came in, talking vents and wiring. Both looked visibly tired and the day had just began. Mack was making a great show of his obvious disinterest. Thomas and the younger boys were giggling at his antics.

"So, Andrew and Luke can work in the basement with me and those other fellows. Mack can work with you and Charlie," Matthew said.

"Hey, I'm not going to crawl out there on that broken down roof," Mack cried. "It's full of holes and rotten spots. A man could get killed up there!"

"What's the matter, Mack," Thomas sneered. "You chicken?"

"No, but I'm not stupid either. You'd have to be crazy to go out there!"

"Well, someone has to do it," Matthew retorted, "and besides, you'll just be handing them supplies and tools. Think you can handle that? There's no use doing anything else upstairs until we get that damned roof fixed." He turned away, devoured his food, and went back to work.

"Hey!" Mack called after him, relentless as ever. "Don't you need anything else from town today? Does Annie need anything?"

"No!" Matthew barked without even breaking stride. "Charlie's wife is going with her again. I'm sure she is infinitely more helpful than you could ever be. So get to work."

The day was set. Annie crawled out of her nest and began readying for the day. She was glad Lori was coming with her again. Annie had enormous confidence in Lori's judgment, and it was wonderful having another woman near her own age just to talk with. Lori seemed friendly and warm-hearted, but at the same time somewhat reserved and on guard as though she was always afraid of saying the wrong thing.

Soon they were on their way toward Dubuque. "Lori, how old were you when Kevin was born?" Annie asked. "I mean, I was thinking that I'm old enough to have children of my own – I mean, lots of women have babies by the time they're twenty, right?" .

"Especially around here," Lori said. "There were two girls pregnant in my graduating class. Almost every year, there's at least one. Girls nowadays just walk up there in all their glory, in front of God n' everybody!"

"That happens everywhere, Lori," Annie said trying to sound worldly. She was aware, of course, that this happened to lots of girls, but she never knew any personally.

Lori went on. "I had a crush on Charlie since I started school here. But I didn't think he'd ever notice me. When we were juniors, he was flunking geometry so I helped him get ready for a big test. And then he asked me out. I couldn't believe it!" she said incredulously as though it had just happened. "The more we dated, the more heat he took from his mother and his friends."

"For heaven's sake, why?"

"He came from a good family and was the school jock. Everybody thought we were sleeping together, but we weren't. We didn't for a long time, not till the winter of our senior year. I guess we figured if we're gonna get blamed for it anyway, we might as well do it."

"His father died the summer after graduation. Charlie was all scared and he didn't know what to do. See, he was supposed to go to college and play football. But his father's business was an awful mess, and none of his brothers would come back to run it. They tried sellin' it, but no one wanted it."

"Then one night, he comes bustin' into my place and says, 'Come on, lets get married!' Just like that. He said we'd take over the business and raise our kids right here in Shanny. Sounded so simple, like the right thing to do."

"Wasn't his mother relieved that he stayed?"

"Hell, no. She told ever' body I ruined her son's life – I kept him from goin' to college. And still to this day, no matter what I do – I can work my fingers to the bone twenty hours a day – she just don't like me. Never will. But that's okay – I got Charlie and the kids. And if we can just get out of debt, I think things will be a lot better. Ever' fight we ever had was about money. They say money can't buy love, but having it sure makes loving easier."

Annie looked at her new friend a little wistfully. She had never known anyone like her before. This was a story of forbidden love, a young couple struggling together against great obstacles. It was like a story out of a magazine.

"Ya' know," Lori said, "I wouldn't probably do too much different if I could start over 'cause I was born to scrub floors and have babies. But you – are you sure you can handle all this?"

They both erupted into laughter. "See, I told you the whole thing sounds preposterous. You think we're crazy, too, right? Money or no money! But don't you see, you're better off than me. You know exactly who you are and what you want. I've always felt like something was missing in my life. I could have had anything I wanted, but what? I never had any idea."

"So I guess it is true," Lori said, laughing. "Money really can't buy everything." They pulled up to the stop sign at the junction with the main highway leading into Dubuque. "I bet you're excited to getting back to civilization, aren't you?" Lori asked.

"Truth is, I'm nervous. I am so glad you came with me."

"This is gonna be fun. I love helping you spend your daddy's money."

* * * * * *

When the traveler sweeps into the city of Dubuque from the south, he descends on a sharply curved highway carved out of a bluff. The skyline of the city is filled with a hodgepodge of smokestacks, church steeples, and glistening molasses and petroleum tanks by the harbor. The upper border of this picture is the imposing waters of the river with distant bluffs and villages on the Illinois/Wisconsin side. This place was meant to be hemmed in by natural borders, the Mississippi on one side and the bluffs on the other. There are seven of them, forming a definitive moon-shaped rim around the valley floor. But these steep hillsides had long since been conquered. Houses and businesses stair-step the terrain in perilous fashion. They're connected by a crazy, irregular system of narrow streets, many of which still showing cobblestones.

Dubuque boasts of being one of the oldest cities of the upper Midwest. Its urban existence was not born from a wartime fortress like many of her sister cities, but of a stubborn pioneering spirit of tenacity and capitalistic enterprise. The cracked limestone, ivy-walled buildings and wooden framed houses stand as silent testimony to the ability of a man to construct structures that endure longer than they who did the building.

Annie gasped when they rounded the last bend and dropped into the city. She could see the houses lining in the bluff high above them and the European style streets and old-world architecture. She was instantly enchanted.

Lori gave a quick travelogue tour as they drove through town. "There's the Fourth Street Elevator – the shortest, steepest railroad in the world. Down there is the ol' Shot Tower where they made lead bullets for the Civil War. Up there – see that big building up there on the hill. That's Mercy Hospital. I had both my babies there. Anyway, we're going downtown." She chuckled. "Downtown, Dubuque-style, that is. I'm sure it's a lot different from what you're used to. Let's go to Penney's first."

"The furniture is on the second floor," Lori directed as they walked in. "Let's do the big stuff. I can't wait to see that sales lady's mouth drop open when you tell her what you want," she giggled

The saleswoman in J.C. Penney's furniture department was the first in a long line of people who gasped when Annie announced what she wanted to buy. All she needed to say was "nine beds" or "ten pairs of boots", and there would be that increasingly familiar response. It wasn't only the large number of any one item, but also the speed and casual manner with which she shopped.

It was still early when they finished. Annie said she'd like to walk around the mall area a little longer. She was stalling. She explained her apprehension over Rocky Road at the 31 Flavors Ice Cream Emporium.

Annie told Lori the Staten Island story. "Sonny says I have to tell 'em to deliver it out to the farm. Will they do that?" she asked, biting her lip.

"Well, of course they will – free! No problem,"

"Okay then, let's go. Sonny makes everything feel like a test."

"So what? What ya' care what he thinks anyway?"

countered Lori. "He's works for you, don't he? C'mon, I'm sure they'll be very reasonable."

And they were. Of course, they would be happy to deliver such a large order, the clerk smiled. Would Tuesday be soon enough? Annie felt foolish worrying over something so silly. What must Lori think of her, she wondered.

Her friend just laughed at her. "You worry too much," Lori teased. "Maybe where you come from, everybody has a pile of money. But girl, around here, money talks. They want your business so they'll bend over backwards to keep you happy. When she said Tuesday, you should have said, 'No Monday or Sunday!' Sure, you should have made them get their tails out there on Sunday."

They went back downtown to the dock behind J.C. Penny's to load up a few items Annie wanted to take home with her today. Somehow, they managed to stuff in pots and pans, dishes and towels, and round dinette set for the kitchen. As they pulled away, Lori rolled down her window and started singing,

Next thing ya know ol' Jed's a millionaire.
The kinfolk said, Jed, move away from here.
Californiee is the place you oughta be.
So, they loaded up the truck and moved to Beverly --
Hills, that is...movie stars, swimming pools."

They were heading for the hills all right – Dubuque County hills – golden mounds, glistening in the spring sun. They made plans for their families to have supper together. "When you work this hard together, you oughta eat together, though I wouldn't exactly call what we did today work. We'll stop n' get some groceries and beer and make the men a nice supper," Lori said.

After selecting groceries, Annie automatically reached for her purse. "No, no," Lori said. "This is our treat. Besides I cut some coupons out of the Bugle yesterday. You know, coupons?" she said again, noticing her friend's blank expression. Lori showed her the small pieces of newspaper. "Beef steak – 99 cents a pound" or "Wonder Bread – 4 loaves for a dollar". But it was obvious that Annie knew nothing of the fine art of coupon clipping.

They picked up Lori's kids at the baby-sitter and headed out to the farm. They pulled onto the yard to a happy chorus of, "Hey, what ya' buy? Anything for me? What's for supper? We're starved!"

"Did you pick up any beer? I could sure use one right now – several, in fact," Matthew was bellowing from the other side of the house.

Annie did a quick head count and found that two of her brothers were missing. "Where were Peter and Danny?" she called

"Hey, don't look at me," Thomas said. "I was only in charge of Joey and the baby. No one told me to keep an eye on those two."

Before Annie could panic, the Gibson's Pontiac pulled onto the yard.

"I got a couple of escaped convicts here," Jake called. "I was wonderin' if there was any reward for catchin' two such dangerous varmints." He opened the door and out stepped the two little boys.

"Are you mad?" they said, searching their sister's face.

"Actually, if I'm angry with anyone, it's with your father and brothers." How could these two little boys be gone all afternoon, and no one notice?

Chapter 13

It was no one's fault, really. Considering the events of the day, it was almost understandable that two little boys might get lost in the shuffle, especially these two. Everyone agreed, even Mother, that these two were full of the devil. They had such imaginations, so what one didn't think of, the other one did. They were very close, especially these past few months. Annie tried to be attentive to them, but it was hard. They were always too noisy or dirty and needed scolding for things their brothers would never have dared to try.

They thought that moving to the country was a wonderful adventure, and on such a day, the woods were very inviting. Since no one was paying attention, they were on their own.

Ben had found them petting some lambs in the back pasture and invited them in for cookies. They sat at Ginny's big kitchen table and recounted their day's discoveries.

"But, boys," Ginny said, "you have to stay away from the river. Shouldn't we let someone know where you are?"

"Nah," Peter answered between bites. "Everyone is real busy. We were just getting in the way. But if Annie drives past, then we'd better get back 'cause she'll see we're gone."

"But she won't be back for a long time yet. She went shopping with Mrs. Bean," explained Danny. He took a long look at his hostess over the rim of his milk glass. He hadn't been around old people much except the aunts who clearly were of the opinion that children should be seen and not heard. He thought all old people must be like that, but he felt very much at ease here. "Maybe we could help you with something. We're stronger than we look."

Ben and Ginny exchanged glances. "Well," Jake said, "you fellas s'pose you could help an old man finish some chores? An ol' codger like me can use all the help he can get."

"The ewes – that's the mama sheep – aren't always good mothers," Jake explained as they leaned over the fence and watched the sheep graze. "For no reason at all she might not let her youngin's nurse. I swear, they are the confoundest, dumbest animals God ever put on this earth. But having a herd of sheep is easier for an old man than having to mow all the time."

He started his little Ford tractor and let the boys take turns steering it around the barnyard. He sent them into the hayloft to drop down a bale of hay. They strained and grunted, moving the obstinate bale to the edge and then pushed it over. Before coming down, they cast a wistful look at the stacks of bales, dusty rafters, and ropes hanging about. It didn't take an overactive imagination to see that this could be a wonderland. The old man understood.

"Is old Wilson up there?" he called, sitting down below, leaning on his cane. "That ornery, lazy ol' cat of mine. You boys ought to stay up there a spell and see if you can find him." Soon, he heard shrill laughter as they discovered the joy of jumping from haystack to haystack and swinging on a rope Tarzan-style, setting the pigeons into frenzied flight. The boys were so amazed. They didn't even know places like this existed.

So when Jake and Ginny delivered them home that afternoon, they knew they had just had the best afternoon of their young lives. And when Jake told them they should come back for a visit real soon, they wondered if tomorrow would be too soon.

* * * * * *

A lot of progress had been made around the house that day, but Annie was not particularly thrilled with the manner with which it had been accomplished. There was debris everywhere and the walls, even those which were previously intact, were dotted with holes where wiring and duct work had been installed. But she wasn't going to complain. There was electricity in part of the house including the kitchen so that the refrigerators now worked. There was a ribbon-cutting ceremony of sorts at the kitchen sink where everyone gathered to watch Annie turn on the water faucet for the first time. Trying not to appear unappreciative the Winston's were somewhat horrified to see that new pipes and pump did not magically produce clear water. They were still reluctant to drink it although everyone assured them that they would get used to it.

The LP gas was hooked up so that the new stoves were functional. The ladies had fun experimenting with all the new appliances. The menu that night was beefsteak, mashed potatoes with brown gravy, vegetables, salad, and a chocolate cake. Annie was amazed how quickly Lori put the whole thing together. Annie wasn't much help.

After supper, a very jubilant Matthew pushed away from Annie's brand new table and announced that he, along with Charlie and the "boys", was going into town to toast their accomplishments at the Pub. Soon after they left, the dishes were washed and Lori packed up her sleepy children to go home.

Annie made her rounds to make sure the boys were tucked into their sleeping bags and then went to check the baby. She needed to do something of which she felt confident, so she picked up the sleeping infant and cuddled her in her arms. Softly, she sang her mother's favorite lullaby.

> *Red and yellow and pink and green*
> *Purple and orange and blue*
> *You can sing a rainbow, sing a rainbow*
> *Sing a rainbow, too.*

Gradually, she became aware of faint sounds of Sonny's pounding and sawing in the kitchen. "God, doesn't he ever quit," she muttered. He had to be utterly exhausted.

She found him laboring on the cabinets. He murmured a hello, but there was no break in the tempo of his work. Annie poured herself a cup of coffee and sat down at the table. A week ago, even a few days ago, this would have made her uncomfortable, but now she knew this is what he preferred. Idle chitchat irritated him. She sipped her coffee and watched as he expertly fit the new counter tops into place. There were no wasted movements, only precision and concentration.

He finished one side and stood back to survey his work. He took out his cigarettes and shook one out, nodding when she poured him a cup of coffee. "It looks good," she said.

He said nothing, inhaling deeply on his cigarette. Finding the coffee too hot, he set it aside and crouched down by the old cabinets, easing his lanky torso inside. Turning onto his back, he tapped here and there until another section of the old counter was loose. He came crawling out, rubbing the dust out his eyes..

"My God, Sonny, how much longer are you going to work tonight?" she asked. It angered her that he was pushing himself like this, especially when no one else was.

"Look, this is ticklish work. Can't do it when there's a bunch of people hangin' around." Annie wondered if that remark was intended for her benefit. "Besides, I ain't that tired. I'm used to working late, remember?"

"Well, it's just as well you're getting some of this done because my father is already getting bored with the renovations. He wants to get started outside." She was going to say more but she could hear crying from the other room. "Sounds like Joey." Annie turned to attend her brother.

Moments later she reappeared, carrying the little boy who was still fussing. She thought for a moment that his expression changed when he saw Sonny, but that was absurd. She was going to give him some milk, but then she realized there was something else she had to do first. "I think I drank too much coffee. Here, watch him for a minute. I'll be right back." She thrust the little boy next to Sonny and fled.

She grabbed a flashlight on her way out but she didn't need it. The moon was bright and the night skies were clear. And she knew her way to the outhouse by now.

Coming back into the kitchen she was horrified to find Joey sitting on the counter unattended with tools nearby. "Joey!" she shrieked as grabbed the child. "Couldn't you stop working long enough to watch him? He could have hurt himself or--"

"Oh, for cryin' out loud. I wasn't gonna let him fall or nothin'."

"No? How were you going to stop it? Your back was turned."

"He was sitting there, watching me work. You treat him like baby."

"I told you. You have to watch him every second."

"That's stupid. He was fine." He went back to work.

But Annie persisted, refusing to be excused or ignored. "Stupid?" she cried. "Is that what you call having concern for my brother?" She wanted him to respond but got nothing. How dare he talk to her like that. This was the second time he had hinted that he disapproved of the handling of Joey. Annie picked up the whimpering child and stormed out of the room.

She sat down to rock the child but her jerky movements were even more unsettling. It took a long time to quiet him. Eventually, he fell asleep, his head heavy against her shoulder. She could feel wisps of his warm breath against her cheek. Yes, we do treat Joey like a baby, she thought, because in most ways he is one. It was true that his body had grown but he never spoke or crawled or did any of the other things a little boy was supposed to do. If Sonny knew how the family agonized over this child for

124

the last four years, he would never have said such mean, hateful things.

She stood to lay the boy in his bed and felt a familiar twinge in her lower back. He weighed at least 45 pounds and she often struggled to carry him. It occurred to her that in a few months she might not be able to lift him at all if he continued growing at the present rate. But he had seven strong, healthy brothers who could manage him easily.

She covered him with his quilt and bent over to kiss him. "Good night, my angel," she whispered. "There's nothing to worry about. I love you."

She crawled into her sleeping bag and listened to the chorus of different breathing patterns that surrounded her. She began to tremble as fear began to close in around her. Don't be such a coward, she thought. Why would you listen to anything that bastard has to say. Yes, their lives have taken a turn that no one would have predicted in a million years. But some things can't change. Old ideals and attitudes have to continue. They must.

* * * * * *

It was Sunday, but Charlie and the Dunlevy brothers pulled onto the yard at 7:30 just as they had the previous two days. Annie heard pick-up doors slam as she wandered into the kitchen, rubbing her eyes and yawning. Matthew and Sonny were dressed in their work clothes, having a cup of coffee. Matthew's eyes were red and there was the unmistakable aroma of stale beer on his breath.

"Daddy!" Annie exclaimed. "Mass is at 9:00. We have to get ready."

"Sorry, honey," Matthew said, gulping down his last swallow of coffee. "Charlie and the boys are already here. Besides, aren't you anxious to get some heat and plumbing in this old barn? I think God realizes the health and safety of my family is as important as going to church." He pulled on his cap and gave his daughter a quick kiss as he headed for the door. "Say a prayer for your old dad, okay?" He rambled out without waiting for a response. Sonny followed without comment.

Good, Annie thought, because I have no intention of talking to him. She was still smarting from last night's confrontation. She had to admit that she was pleased with the work he had completed. The counter tops were installed, the place was clean, swept, and ready to be used. She took a deep breath, squared her shoulders, and set to work. During the night she had remembered that today was Danny's seventh birthday. She was appalled that she and everyone else had forgotten it. Determined to make the day as special as she could, she was going to cook a big roast for Sunday dinner and attempt to bake her first cake. She should have gotten him presents when she was in town, but there was nothing she could do about that now.

Wishing she had written down Lori's detailed instructions, Annie searched through the boxes of kitchenware until she found the blue-speckled roaster. Buoyed by an unfamiliar sense of self-importance, she stepped to the sink to peel the potatoes and carrots. The task was not nearly as simple as advertised. The harmless looking device could viciously slice the skin off her fingers as easily as a potato.

After a few minutes, Annie found she needed to concentrate less so she was able to glance up from her work from time to time. She discovered a world that belonged to generations of farmwomen working at their kitchen sinks on such early spring mornings. From her window she could survey the yard. Birds flittered past and an occasional rabbit or squirrel scurried past. Everything was bathed in a heavy blanket of dew with the sprouts of new grass lending their deep, green color. Although the view was somewhat desolate and unkempt, Annie could imagine how it would look with painted fences, repaired buildings, and farm animals pacing about.

The deed was finally done, and the mound of meat and vegetables was pushed into the oven. The heated stove took the chill out of the morning air as one by one her siblings strolled into the kitchen, shocked that their Sunday dinner was already cooking.

There were brief scrimmages as the boys jockeyed for

position at the kitchen sink to wash and brush their teeth. No one could find anything. There was not much Christian love among the grim group as they marched toward the bus, ready to go to church.

* * * * * *

Since the whole town was buzzing with the news of the Winston's arrival and it was rumored that they were Catholic, the congregation of the small white church on the hillside was awaiting their arrival that morning with thinly veiled curiosity. Word was that they were a large family with a lot of money, so there was talk that the church might finally get new carpeting and the roof fixed. Wasn't it a shame the school closed some ten years past?

Precisely at 9:00, the organ finished the processional as Father James Fitzpatrick climbed the steps of the ornate, wooden alter. He turned to lead the congregation in prayer just as a loud commotion began building from the back of the sanctuary. Ten Winston's filed in, red-faced as they felt the stares directed their way. The kindly priest paused for a moment to allow adequate time as each one genuflected in turn and settled into their seats. The older Winston boys became aware of the scattered giggling as they got the once over by the young ladies and their mothers.

At the close of Mass, Fr. Fritz formerly welcomed the family into their congregation. "I see that Mr. Winston is not with you this morning," he noted in that priestly intonation meant to inflict guilt. "I hope to see him here next week." Ah yes, smiled the prayerful parishioners, we can't wait to meet this man who would move his family to a dump like the Weatherly place.

* * * * * *

Sunday afternoon was nothing like those lazy, peaceful days they had enjoyed back home in New York. No one was allowed to rest as saws buzzed, hammers banged, and drills whined from one end of the house to the other. Since the kitchen was now somewhat functional, Annie busied herself cleaning out the cupboards and putting away the things she had purchased the day before. She kept a watchful eye on her prize roast in the oven.

Just as dinner was almost ready, someone announced that a big truck pulled onto the yard. Annie checked the oven and went outside with the others just as Matthew and Sonny came up from the basement.

A large vehicle with an open cargo space and high walls came to a stop near the barn. It was a stock truck, loaded with various squawking and grunting animals. "What the hell?" Matthew exclaimed as he approached the driver. "You're Mr. McGruder, aren't you. I remember talking to you last night."

"Yep, that's me," the visitor announced, pushing aside the spectators as he walked toward the back of the truck.

"I know we talked about me buying some livestock, but we never made a deal, did we?" Matthew asked, obvious puzzlement clouding his face.

Mr. McGruder, who seemed to be a man of very few words, began opening the tailgate. "Where ya' want 'em?" was all he said.

"What?" Sonny roared with far more emotion that he had ever shown so far. "You can't even go to town for a couple of beers without getting us into a worse mess?" Angrily, he turned toward their visitor. "Mister, there's been a mistake here. We're not near set up for this yet."

"No sir," McGruder drawled. "Around here, a deal's a deal. I got a signed bill o' sale. Now, where'd ya want me to unload? I got t' hurry 'cause I gotta have this truck back by 6:00 and there's another load." He took some sort of small piece of paper out of his pocket as he spoke. He handed it to Matthew and then turned back to work.

"Oh, my God," Matthew sighed. It was a receipt all right, written on the back of a cheap, white napkin from the Pub. "Oh, my god!" he whistled again.

Sonny was standing with his hands on his hips, looking as though he didn't trust himself to speak. Everyone waited to see who was going to make the first move.

It was Matthew. "Oh, hell, my name's on the deed, so if I want to buy some goddamn livestock, I guess I can! Let's get these animals unloaded."

Mr. McGruder seemed quite intent on finishing his appointed rounds in the specified time. He swung open the gate and herded out five head of cattle, two of them with large utters.

"Milk cows!" Sonny roared. "You bought milk cows?"

"Yes, I did. Why in the hell should we buy three gallons of milk a day when we can just as easily milk ourselves?"

Mack, Andrew, and the others were beginning to get the picture, but there was no time to comment. The animals scattered as soon as they were unloaded. The plan was for the boys to corral the animals while Sonny and Matthew constructed some kind of fenced perimeter. The cattle were fairly easy to contain but the chickens and pigs were an entirely different matter.

A scene of pure pandemonium followed. Running after pigs through muddy ditches and prickly bushes, the Winston males uttered profanities Annie had never heard before. Even the normally suave Mack was chasing after the squealing, grunting, squawking barnyard animals along with everyone else. It was dark outside by the time the situation began to approach some semblance of control and the weary combatants drudged back toward the house.

Annie had dispatched Thomas to look after the little ones but hadn't thought about her Sunday dinner until she came back to the kitchen and was met with the awful stench of burnt food. "Oh, my beautiful roast!" she cried, heart broken. She looked at her scraped hands, now cold and caked with mud, and remembered how she had labored to prepare this feast for her family. She apologized to Danny for ruining his birthday. There was no cake, no presents, no anything, not even a chorus of "Happy Birthday."

Everyone was so dirty and tired that Annie thought Danny understood. But later, when everyone else sank into a state of near unconsciousness, he laid in his sleeping bag, staring at the ceiling.

"Hey, what's with you?" whispered Peter. "Aren't you tired? Or are ya' still mad about your birthday?" His brother didn't answer. "Ah, come on," Peter persisted. "birthdays aren't that big of a deal anyway. You know, I was thinking. You should have the pick of the litter – you know, the ol' dog's puppies. This being your birthday."

Danny aroused a little. "What if they make us get rid of 'em? They might, ya' know."

"Nah, they'd let us keep at least one, no matter what. I can't wait till that ol' dog brings 'em out so we can see them. She sure watches over her pups good, don't she?"

In the darkness, Peter heard quiet sniffles as his brother was trying to fight back the tears. "Peter, why do you suppose some of those sheep don't take care of their babies? Do you think it's cause she just don't want 'em or cause she thinks they're just dumb or somethin'?"

"Course not. It's got nothing to do with the lambs. Jake said it just happens sometimes. He don't know why. Besides, if she don't want 'em, they got ol' Jake to take care of them."

Danny was consoled by that last statement. He felt sleepy, but just before he closed his eyes he thought he would have to tell Ginny and Jake about his birthday first chance he had.

Chapter 14

The mood around the Winston household did not appreciably improve the next morning. There was more than the usual grumbling when Matthew rousted his unwilling sons out of their bedrolls

"Get 'em up!" Sonny blasted in Matthew's direction. "The fences are down and ever' last one of those damned animals are running all over the place. A couple of those cussed cows are all the way down to Gibson's."

"You heard him, gentlemen," Matthew echoed in his best John Wayne voice. "Let's get out there."

There was barely time to dress properly, much less eat. Two hours later, when they trudged wearily back into the kitchen, wet and caked with mud and other foul-smelling substances, it was not a happy group.

Sonny came in, carrying two large pails of what appeared to be milk, although it looked much thicker and more foamy than normal. "Here it is. What you're gonna do with it, I have no idea." He thrust the buckets onto the counter where Matthew stood drinking his coffee.

"I suppose we'll drink it," Matthew snapped, sounding equally agitated.

"Maybe you don't know this, but this stuff does not exactly come out of the cow as Grade A, pasteurized 2% milk." He left abruptly without waiting for a response.

No one spoke for a few minutes until Andrew cleared his throat and looked as though he was ready to make a rehearsed announcement. "It's Monday and only 8:30," he began. "This would be a perfect time to get the boys enrolled in school."

This proposal was received with a loud round of boo's and hisses, but Matthew waved them off. "Sure. All right. Get 'em dressed and out of here."

There were more groans and protests until the boys began to realize that maybe school was an appealing alternative to the mud and work. Mack graciously volunteered to drive them into town, reminding them that he was the only other driver besides Sonny and their father.

Annie was ill prepared for this latest turn of events and felt she should have been consulted before the decision was made. However, it probably was a good idea to get the boys out of here before things really exploded. Hopefully school would offer some semblance of normalcy. She managed to find the box of school records. Finding decent clothing proved to be much more difficult. An hour later, they were ready to go. They looked fairly presentable, she thought, although their clothes were wrinkled and shoes were stained with dried mud. She shuddered a little when she remembered the crisp, immaculate uniforms they had worn back in New York. It was becoming more apparent with each passing day that their new lives were becoming a never-ending succession of compromises and diminished expectations.

* * * * * *

The Shannon Town Community Schools were located across the parking lot from St. Patrick's Church. Set back in the woods on the hills overlooking the river, it had served as a serene and tranquil place for learning these past ten years since the merger of the public and parochial schools. Facing declining enrollment, the small congregation begrudgingly conceded that it was useless to keep St. Patrick's School open.

The two schools consolidated, using the new Catholic grade school building and construct a new high school with public bonds. The transition was accomplished fairly smoothly except for a few minor skirmishes such as deciding who should be the captain of the football team or the president of the school board. Of course, there was the constant threat of inter-faith dating which was the scourge of Catholics and Protestants alike.

Mack parked the bus, and they all sat quietly for a few minutes. The only noise was the gentle breezes rustling in the trees and the humming of a distant tractor.

"Jeez," Thomas sneered. "What is this – a convent?"

"No, I don't think so," whistled Mack as the girls' gym class came running past. They were giggling as they scampered self-consciously in the cool morning air. "Not unless nuns here are a lot different than the ones back East," he mused. "Not bad. I'll take the high school. You take the grade school." He checked his hair in the mirror as he grabbed his half of the folders.

Annie's job was easy enough. She herded her two charges into the grade school building on the right. They followed the signs to the principle's office. Soon they were being escorted to their respective classrooms. Principal Boris Meacham informed Annie of the students' high scores on national tests. "Our junior high sports' teams are closely overseen by the high school coaches," he said. Annie had no idea why that was important.

Mack paraded his three Winston's down the corridor. It was a standard, single level high school with classrooms down one side of the central hallway with the gym and cafeteria on the other. Arriving at the office, they were greeted warmly by Mrs. Chambers, the school secretary.

"No introductions necessary," she said. "I saw you at Mass yesterday." She called the principal, Mr. Rausch, to come meet their new students.

"Oh, we're so happy to meet you at last," he said, smiling

and shaking everyone's hands. "Oh, I see you brought school records. That's excellent. You should go see Coach Evans right away."

"Coach?" asked Mack, more amused than puzzled.

"Oh well, you see, Mr. Evans, our very fine guidance counselor, is also the varsity football and wrestling coach," Mr. Rausch explained. "Very, very fine coach."

"Of course," Mack said, his hand over his mouth trying not to laugh. They were ushered into Coach Evans' office, if it could be called that. The small windowless room was crammed with stacks of books and college catalogs, mixed in with baseball bats, football helmets, and various other sport paraphernalia. The illustrious Mr. Evans was lounging back with his feet on his desk. Since there was nowhere to sit, the Winston's stood awkwardly as he concluded a phone conversation with someone they assumed was a fellow coach.

"Oh, yeah?" he was yelling into the phone. "Who says, buddy! It's only March but already my team looks better on paper than your bunch ever will on the field . . . Well, there's always a first time . . . We'll just see come September 22 . . . I got the schedule right here in front of me . . . Hey, we'll be ready for ya'." After a few more friendly barbs, the coach finally hung up the phone.

He sprang to his feet. "You must be the Winston boys," he said as he scanned his three new students as though he was sizing up racehorses. "One of ya' wouldn't happen to be a good running back, would ya'? I could really use a good halfback."

"Well, sir," Mack said, still stifling his snicker. "I guess John here would be your best bet for that. He's the athletic one. Did real well in intra-murals last year." John said nothing, just stood staring at the floor self-consciously.

Mack continued. "Actually, they each have unique talents. Luke here is an excellent artist – I assume you do have an art program here?" His voice trailed off then because he wasn't sure Mr. Evans was listening. The guidance councilor was still gazing at John.

"Oh sure, sure, we have a really fine art program here," he said. "At least it'll get you by 'til graduation time in a couple months. And Thomas? What's he good at?" he asked, sitting his rather wide frame on the edge of his cluttered desk.

"Well, Thomas' interests lie mainly in music. He's taken private lessons for years, and he can play several instruments."

"Oh, well, that's fine. We have a mighty fine music department here. The marching band plays at all the halftimes and things."

"Oh, goody!" muttered Thomas under his breath, barely concealing his contempt.

"This is gonna be just fine for you boys," Mr. Evans exclaimed. "We may be a smaller school than you're used to, but we still offer a lot. And you know what they say--better to be a large frog in a small pond than vice versa, right?" Obviously, he must subscribe to that logic himself, thought Mack, or why else would he be teaching here?

Annie was waiting when Mack jumped into the driver's seat. "Those poor suckers!" he said as he turned the bus homeward.

* * * * * *

Annie and Mack entered the kitchen just as Sonny, Charlie, and the others came up from the basement. "Sorry, Matthew, but I gotta get back into town. I have to take care of a plugged toilet."

"We got some stuff to do, too," Roger Dunlevy said. "At least the furnace installation is almost done. Sonny can finish the wiring."

Sonny walked out to the truck with the men, talking about ground wires and circuit breakers. The remaining four sat in silence for several long, uncomfortable minutes.

"Well," Matthew grunted, stirring his coffee briskly. "I guess I really fucked up."

"Daddy!" Annie cried, horrified at her father's language. But the others were chuckling. Even Mack seemed to be enjoying this display of humility.

"Well, it's true. I do not believe there is a fence known to modern man that will keep those damned pigs penned up

134

anywhere!" But then his face softened and a wide grin spread across his face. "But did you see Peter catching that one slippery devil yesterday? He landed on his belly in the mud, but he'd be damned if he'd let go, even when he lost his glasses!" They howled with laughter.

"Now listen, all of you," Matthew continued, "I promise I will never do anything that stupid again. But why have this beautiful farm without some livestock?" His referral to "this beautiful farm" made them laugh even harder. "We'll have beef and pork for butchering, chickens for eggs and meat. That's what farming is all about. We'll be self-sufficient!" He looked more somber now, waiting for his irreverent children to settle down.

"But the truth is," he stammered, starking into his coffee cup, "I can't do this – not even start – without you guys. Mack, I know you never dreamed in million years I'd ask you to do anything like this. But I am asking now. Just give it some time. I need you to stay until the first harvest at the end of the summer. Andrew, I know that seems like an eternity. But I promise, you can go back to college in the fall." He sat quietly for a few moments trying to find the right words. "Don't you see, you have your whole lives ahead of you, so can't you spare me a few months?"

Sonny came in and went straight for the coffee pot. As was his habit, he preferred to hang back rather than sit at the table.

"I understand I need to be more open with you." Matthew said. "We're all adults so we should discuss things more. It's obvious that there needs to be more planning. So, what do you think? Should I call McGruder and tell him to take his livestock back?" He was addressing the whole group, but it was clearly a question Sonny needed to answer.

"Well," Sonny sighed, "the damn things are here now so we just as well keep 'em. McGruder wouldn't take anything back anyway." He blew across his coffee cup thoughtfully. "But we have to get some decent fencing."

"Yeah, there's no use trying to patch up the old stuff, " Matthew agreed. "I'll call in an order to Charlie right away. And maybe the Gibson's would know someone who has one of those separators for the milk. At least then we could drink the stuff."

It was amazing how hopeful he sounded. Skeptical glances passed between his children as they set about completing their assignments. Andrew went down the road to talk with Ben and Ginny, mumbling that he had no idea what he was asking them about. Matthew and Mack went into town to buy fencing, leaving Sonny to work on the furnace. Annie was happy to move about the quiet house, only interrupted by an occasional crying child.

The day went quickly. Annie was able to get a lot of cleaning done upstairs. Matthew surprised everyone by coming onto the yard with a new 4-wheel drive GMC pickup. "Took me about 5 minutes to buy it," he said, grinning. "It was the only one they had on the lot."

Their afternoon of concentrated productivity was loudly interrupted when the school bus delivered the five Winston students back home again. They each had their own stories to tell as the kitchen was swallowed up by noisy confusion. The one thing they all had in common was that they were starved and seemed genuinely glad to be back home. Annie smiled at their youthful exuberance. The lone exception was, of course, Thomas. He was brooding as usual. The teachers were awful, the students were hicks, and the music department was barely worth his time. But no one was paying much attention to his whining so he wandered off, still sulking.

The other boys were anxious to get outside and get more acquainted with the new animals. "Livestock," one of the boys corrected. "Farm animals are supposed to be called livestock." Peter and Danny thought each one should have a name. Annie was happy to see how excited they were because they were expected outdoors for another round of chores. They grabbed their sandwiches and cans of soda, ready to bust out the door.

"Hold it!" Annie commanded. "You have to change your clothes first!" This idea of "school clothes" and "work clothes" was still an alien concept.

The tired and hungry laborers came in after nightfall. Annie had managed to put a decent supper together with ice cream for later. There was homework to be done and a few other things to finish up before bedtime. Sonny had come in much later than the others. He took his plate and ate standing up by the counter. Then he was gone again.

Later, Sonny appeared again and sought out Danny and Peter. He mumbled something about following him outside. Annie started to object, but the they seemed so excited that she said nothing. They grabbed their coats and were outside for what seemed forever. She decided to investigate herself.

She stepped quietly onto the back porch, pulling her sweater around her shoulders. At the far end she could see flashes of light darting around and as she drew closer, she could hear the excited whispers of her little brothers.

"Oh, they're so cute," gushed one of the boys.

"They are still real little," Sonny cautioned. "Their mother won't like it if you handle them much. So I don't ever want to catch you guys down here alone, ya' hear?"

The boys promised, fondling one little furry ball after another. The mother crouched nearby, watching the proceedings carefully. Annie watched as the boys moved about, even reaching to pet the older dog. Annie's presence was so far undetected and she knew if she said anything, it would end in an argument with Sonny, so she slipped back into the house.

Later, when she was tucking the boys into their sleeping bags, she asked them where they had gone. They told her of the five puppies and how their eyes were open now. "Sonny says soon they'll be out playing on the yard," Peter said. "I can't wait!"

"You have to be careful around their mother," cautioned their big sister. "Are you sure its safe?"

"Oh sure. She's a dog, not a wolf or a fox or anything, you know," lectured Peter. "Sonny says the more she's around us, the more she'll trust us."

"Yeah," agreed Danny. "I think she's starting to a little. Sonny thinks so, too."

"Oh, he does," said Annie, tersely. It looked as though there were two more members in the Sonny Jackson Admiration Society, and that infuriated her.

* * * * * *

The next morning there was another scene of mass confusion. No one could find anything for school. The bus pulled up to the end of the long driveway and honked incessantly until all five boys were on board.

Just as that group of Winston's left, the "second shift" came in, already looking tired and cold from working outside since 6:00 A.M. Keeping the livestock corralled, fed, and watered with inadequate equipment was turning out to monopolize too much of their time. Even Matthew admitted it was much more difficult than he expected. The milk was a major disappointment to him. Even after Sonny got the Gibson's antiquated separator operational, everyone still complained the milk was too thick and creamy. Plus, Sonny was the only one who could milk the cows, which was an obvious waste of his valuable time.

For the second day in a row, they assembled at the kitchen table, trying to make plans for the day. Sonny took up his usual retreat in the corner. Thankfully, the Sears order was coming today so at least they would have some decent clothing. And the J.C. Penney's truck would be bringing the furniture today, also. Annie and Andrew would concentrate on the upstairs so everyone could sleep in beds tonight – if Sonny could get the furnace started.

By early afternoon, Annie proudly toured the second floor. It was cold and drafty, but the debris was cleared, cobwebs were gone, and the floors and walls were scrubbed. Her red hands were testimony to the hard work.

Of course, all the delivery trucks showed up at the same time. Sonny had to wade through the muck and mire of the low place in the driveway to drive the trucks through. Annie attempted to act as traffic cop, but chaos ensued and most everything got stacked in the front foyer. There were mattresses and box springs piled ten high with boxes of bed frames and bedside tables. Tools were dispensed and everyone except Sonny headed upstairs to assemble furniture. Once again, the time passed quickly.

They were working in one of the bedrooms when suddenly Andrew stood up erect, sensing something was different. Annie felt it, too. Then they realized it was the furnace, blowing bellows of wonderful warm air. And, to Annie's dismay, there were clouds of decades' old dust, too.

There were no sheets for the beds yet, no curtains on the windows or carpeting on the floor, but tonight they would sleep in beds in their own rooms. The boys took their sleeping bags and belongings upstairs. The house was dreadfully short of closets so piles of clothes and things were everywhere. At least, it wasn't all in one room.

Sonny didn't come in that night. One of the boys said they had seen him working in the shack across the driveway. About 9:00 he came in and picked up his few things and headed for the door. Matthew asked him where he was going.

"I got my own place ready," he said as he walked out the door.

Matthew began to protest, but then thought better of it. "It's true. We didn't think to assign him a room."

"So?" mused Annie. "I'm sure he prefers to be alone anyway."

Later, when the house was quiet, she looked across the yard from her bedroom window and saw a light coming from the broken-down shed Sonny claimed as his home. There was smoke rising from the chimney. Well, at least he won't freeze to death. She quickly reprimanded herself for worrying about him. He certainly could take care of himself. She crawled into her bed, feeling so tired she could hardly move. But she laid awake for a long time, unable to shut out the eerie ensemble of noises echoing all around her. After a week of sleeping on the floor with all those bodies so close, it felt strange to be in a bedroom alone. She began making mental lists of all the things she wanted to get done the next day. Gradually, weariness overtook her and she fell into a restless sleep with mops, brooms, and cobwebs floating in her dreams. There was no respite from the work, not even in sleep.

Chapter 15

The rest of that week was a tremendous transitional phase for the whole family. The drastic changes in the house certainly served notice that Matthew Winston was very serious about this venture. He was spending thousands of dollars without blinking an eye.

Annie soon discovered that when talking about the house, the operative word was "someday". The most obvious needs were attended to but only enough to get by. Modern electrical fixtures installed throughout the house, but there still weren't enough outlets anywhere. Some of the plumbing was updated, but Annie's bathroom and the one in the master bedroom were hardly touched. They were spending more time and effort in the bathroom being built in Matthew's office. Even he did not appreciate having to use the outhouse. It also had a shower, which theoretically meant most of the mud would not get past the back door. "Someday" the exterior of the house would be aluminum sided and the roof would be replaced. "Someday" the back porch would be restored and the beautiful fireplace in the dining room would be made functional. Right now, they'd take care of the necessities and get started with the farming. Everybody knew their father ached to begin.

There were other more subtle changes, too, like learning that "dinner", the main meal of the day, was at noon. "Supper" was the evening meal. There was accepting the fact that those long, leisurely showers they used to take in the morning just to wake up were a thing of the past. Showers had to be taken at night to wash off the day's sweat and mud and to sooth aching muscles. Their lives, which had once been so relaxed were now driven by the words "Hurry! Hurry!" Weather forecasts were no longer ignored. Rain was their enemy and warm days were relished. The sun dictated their days with relentless regularity.

A nice distraction occurred when the first of many freight trucks arrived, loaded with things from the brownstone. Dozens of prized possessions came, as dictated by the long lists phoned back East, sometimes daily. Since most of the staff had left for other jobs, the faithful servants who remained lovingly packed crates of books, sporting paraphernalia, and cherished keepsakes. Miss Grace told Annie she enjoyed doing it because it gave her something to do, but Annie wondered what the nursery looked liked without Mother's favorite chair and the mantle stripped of her clock. Annie was overjoyed to touch these things again and was comforted by their presence. She vowed never to request anything from Miss Daley's kitchen. How Cook would laugh if she knew how well the pigs and chickens ate because of Annie's disastrous adventures in cooking. It was a daily struggle, but she was determined to do better.

Annie found that her favorite time of the day was the second shift breakfast. As the boys left for school, Matthew, Mack, Andrew, and of course, Sonny, came into the kitchen for some hot coffee and a quiet breakfast. The talk across the table always centered around the plans for the day and work assignments. Annie could not remember her mother and father ever talking about his work. She really liked being a part of those round table sessions in her kitchen and appreciated having some idea where the men were going to be during the day.

Sonny never had much to say. But when he did speak, it was always a definitive statement. Mack could be depended upon to be sarcastic and argumentative. And Andrew, although he was a willing participant, paled at the mention of anything requiring the use of tools or heavy equipment.

Annie found excuses to visit Ginny nearly every day. She yearned for female companionship and she wanted to soak up as much of the lady's knowledge as possible. Most of what Ginny knew she called "just plain common sense". For instance, she taught Annie a foolproof way of making thick, country gravy. Just put milk and flour in an old mustard or peanut butter jar and shake it until all the lumps were gone. Pour that mixture into the skillet with the meat drippings and water. It was perfect every time.

Ginny also taught Annie some simple housekeeping rules. "You can't get a floor clean with a stick mop," she said, "especially the corners. You gotta get down on your hands and knees if you want to do it right."

"It's all such hard work," Annie said. "Don't you ever get tired of it?"

Ginny just smiled and didn't answer for a few moments. "Annie, I always figured God put us on this earth to work. Why else would a person bother to get out of bed in the morning? The Bible says, 'Vanity, vanity, all is vanity.' That means that a person who thinks he's bigger or more important than God will never be happy or satisfied. A person just has to do the best he can – the days and years take care of themselves."

Annie had a lot of difficulty accepting that explanation. "Weren't people put on this earth to try to make a difference?"

"Yes," Ginny said. "God put man here to think and plan and take care of things. But that's still plain old work."

Annie thought about that conversation many times. She struggled to try to understand, but she was sure Ginny's words should have some special meaning for her. Were these simple phrases the answer to so many of her questions? Someday they would sit and talk further with Ginny, but there was no time for that now. There was just too much work.

* * * * * *

The three high school students were learning to adapt to their new circumstance with varying degree of difficulty. One of the common problems they encountered was snap judgments and prejudice from their classmates. Their reputation as big city Easterners with money preceded them everywhere.

Luke was bidding his time until graduation. He enrolled in English IV, Civics, Latin, and Advanced Art. None of the classes really matched the curriculum of his school back East, but no one seemed to care. He had felt very uneasy going to art class that first day. The class, supposedly composed of the more advanced art students, was finishing their quarter projects which were oil paintings. As he looked at the easels around the room, he could see that there were varying degrees of progress. No one seemed to be taking it very seriously.

He was aware that he had some artistic ability. Normally,

he really enjoyed painting but he hadn't done anything since his mother died. He thought of her as he stood in front of his easel, feeling as empty as the canvas.

He decided the best thing to do was just do the work and keep to himself. There were already murmurings about "that New York hot dog". He finished the project the fourth day. He painted the view of the valley from the rocky place in the backyard. He thought it was decent but didn't want anyone to see it. He was afraid they'd think he was showing off.

Toward the end of the class period someone tapped him on the shoulder. He turned to find Margaret McDuffy, a rather short, plump girl with thick, dark glasses. Luke recognized her from Latin class and the bus route. She was biting her lip and wringing her hands.

"Don't mind them," she said as though she knew what he was thinking. "They all hate it when someone cares about art. This class is a joke." She gazed at his painting and gasped. "My painting has been done since yesterday but it's not nearly as good as yours."

He walked over to her easel. Her painting appeared to be a bird, probably a seagull, soaring through the clouds. Technically it was decent but he thought the lines were somewhat severe. He told her he liked it and she smiled in gratitude of his politeness. "It's Jonathon. You know – Jonathon Livingston Seagull. Have you read it? It's wonderful, isn't it? So spiritual, almost Biblical." Her face took on an enraptured glow that made Luke smile.

Then her face changed as though she just had a brilliant idea. "Say, I'm on this dumb art committee for the spring prom. Cheryl Swanson is supposed to be the chairperson but she hasn't done anything yet. She's the pretty one with all the guys hangin' around over there. We can use this art period to work on it, but believe me, no one wants to." She was looking at him quizzically now. "So I was thinking . . . maybe you could help me."

She lost him right after Jonathon Livingston Seagull. "What?" he stammered.

"Prom – you know, that ancient mating ritual, the biggest dance of the year. Didn't they have those where you came from?

Well, we're strictly low budget around here. We have ours in the gym. I'm sure that's nothing like what you're used to." Luke was trying to listen, but actually he was wondering how long she could talk without taking a breath.

"Everybody gets dressed up but mostly everyone just stands around because the music isn't very good and the food is awful. Anyway, this year's theme is 'Romance in Venice'. Pretty corny, huh? The planning committee wants a big mural on the back wall of the gym. What do you think of this?" She pushed her glasses back on her nose and then carefully unfolded a magazine picture of a Venetian courtyard. Luke wondered if she had any idea how ambitious an undertaking this would be. Once again, she read his mind perfectly. "You don't think I can do it, do ya'."

"Well, certainly not alone. What does the rest of your committee think?"

"Oh, they don't care. If I go ahead and start it, they'll sort of help out enough to get the credit," she said, a touch of bitterness in her voice. Apparently she had experienced this sort of thing before. Just then the bell rang. "Anyway, you think about it and let me know tomorrow."

The next day, she came hurrying up to him at the beginning of class. She had drawn the picture on a large piece of poster board and sectioned it off into smaller grids. Her plan was to make the mural in smaller pieces and then assemble it on the wall. It was a good plan and he said he'd help.

"Oh, good!" she cried. "It'll be beautiful, especially if you help."

He smiled at her enthusiasm for something which was by her own account, "dumb".

* * * * * *

John was likewise thrust quickly into the mainstream of school activities, under the watchful eye of the guidance counselor, Coach Evans, who just happened to be his physical education teacher. When John reported to the locker room that first day, Coach Evans was waiting with a smelly T-shirt and pair of shorts he had fished out of the lost and found box. "Move along, ladies," he said. "Get dressed. We're going out to the track today." There was a loud chorus of boo's which only served to deepen the scowl planted across Coach's face. "If you're lookin' for extra laps, keep it up!"

One of the boys dressing nearby came up to John. "Don't mind him," the boy said. "He's like that all the time 'cause he has to push some lazy butts around here. He's a good coach."

"Oh, yeah? You been on his teams?"

"Yep, I lettered in football and wrestling this year. I just moved here last summer so I made some enemies when Coach put me in at quarterback last fall. The other kid was a senior, so him and some of his buddies didn't like that – especially since we didn't win much. Wasn't my fault. Right now we're the laughing stock of the whole conference. By the way, my name is Kenny Beyers." He smiles and extended his hand.

"I'm John Winston," Johnny replied, somewhat hesitantly considering some of the responses he had gotten around school so far. "He said ... er, Coach Evans, I mean, said that he's looking for a running back. I never played on a real football team before except a little at school and with my family. I'm quick, or at least I think I am. Maybe he'd give me a chance to make the team."

"Hell," Kenny said, grinning. "He'll take anyone who knows how to hold a football. And listen, track is starting this week. If you make the team, you don't have to do this stupid phys. ed thing any more." They dressed and ran out to the track.

It was chilly and there was a lot of complaining. True to his word, Coach ordered extra laps. Randy and John pulled away from the rest, jogging along at a comfortable pace. Then came a whistle, calling everyone to assemble at the home stretch of the track. Mr. Evans wanted to clock everyone doing 100-yard dashes. "Winston, Beyers, up to the line."

They came up to the starting blocks and glanced at each other, the friendly conversation replaced by their innate competitive juices. The whistle blew and they were off. They both pressed hard, but finished dead even. They leaned over, their hands on their knees and gasping for air as the coach walked up, looking at his stop watch.

"Coach Stevenson starts track practice after school next week. I'll tell him to expect you. And I want you boys to get out there and bust your butts, you hear me? If nothin' else, it'll keep ya' in shape for next fall." He walked away, not waiting for any kind of response.

"Congratulations!" Kenny said, still breathless. "You made the team."

* * * * * *

When Thomas received his schedule, he said, "Are you serious?" He glared at the Mrs. Chambers, the school secretary, who had worked out his schedule. "Who said anything about me being in any band?"

"Well," she said, "Mr. Evans had mentioned to me that you are interested in music and can play several instruments. We assumed you would want to participate in music here at our school. Mr. Moore, the music teacher, would love to have you in his band, I'm sure. Why don't you try it? You can always quit later if it doesn't work out."

A band, Thomas thought. That's ridiculous. But he also knew that if he didn't at least try Annie would probably yell at him. He decided he would go for a couple days, find out how really terrible it was, and then he could go to Annie armed with some facts.

Tuesday morning he went to the music room where the other musicians were getting out their instruments. Girls mostly, he thought.

Mr. Moore came forward and introduced himself. "Mrs. Chambers said you play several instruments," he said, looking somewhat puzzled. "Did you bring anything with you?"

Thomas laughed, saying, "I'm sorry, Mr. Moore, but I don't think you'd have much use for the instruments I play. They're string mostly, classical violin and guitar."

Mr. Moore apparently caught the insinuation. "Yes, you're probably right. So why did you bother coming at all?"

Thomas started to say something like, I'm here because I have to, but the man's sharp glare cut him off. "I also play the drums," he said with thinly veiled sarcasm. He was directed to the back of the room where the rest of the drum corps was sitting up. Mr. Moore quickly introduced him to the other four drummers and went back to the podium.

The assembled group was called to order. As per usual, the rehearsal was started with several warm-up scales. Not even tuning the instruments, Thomas thought disdainfully, as he softly beat out a four-count as directed.

He was somewhat shocked when this small school director, who stood like a statue listening to every note, was able to call musicians out by name and tell them individually whether they were flat or sharp. The entire process was completed quickly so that they were able to open their folders and get down to work. One of the other drummers whispered to Thomas that they had three weeks to get ready for state contest.

He hated admitting it, but they weren't too bad. Of course, the music selections and arrangements were a lot different than the orchestra pieces he was used to because of the absence of the string sections. Here, the woodwinds played those parts – usually a little flat, he thought. At one point he must have been daydreaming because Mr. Moore suddenly began waving his baton frantically for the music to stop. "Drummers, would you please pay attention up here and let me sit the beat," he called out, obviously irritated.

They finished the first two pieces quickly. "OK, people, let's get to it," Mr. Moore sighed, throwing back his slender shoulders as though to brace himself. Thomas noticed a hint of nervous tension throughout the group. The dreaded music was set out before him on the stand. Thomas was astonished to see it was a classical piece, *The 1812 Overture*. He was invited to step up to the kettledrums. It was a fairly demanding part, even by his standards.

The band limped through the whole piece and then worked on several problem areas, especially the difficult racing parts for which the piece is famous. They were starting to make a little progress when the period was over and everyone rushed to put everything away. "I'll be here all day for anyone who wants to come down during free periods for extra help," Mr. Moore announced. Then he made his way to the drummers.

"Jimmy," he said, "you worked really hard to learn that snare solo. As far as I'm concerned, the part is still yours."

"Ah, nah," answered Jimmy. "I'll never be able to play it that well. I think Thomas should take it over." Thomas was shocked, first by the conductor's attitude and then by this boy, Jim. He seemed very shy and unassuming. It seemed obvious to Thomas that for the good of the band, he should play the part and wondered why it wasn't equally obvious to the director.

As the first week ground on, Thomas decided he understood his conductor less and less. The man certainly had a talent for music but never seemed particularly impressed with Thomas' abilities, or at least he never showed it. Thomas found this man, the band, and for that matter, the whole school, to be totally infuriating. Jimmy Mathers was no exception. Try as he might, Thomas was not able to brush him off. Jim followed him around like a puppy dog. No matter how rude or abrasive Thomas was to him, Jim never seemed to get the hint. Thomas found the entire situation exasperating.

* * * * * *

The second Sunday, Matthew decided to play hooky from Mass again. He had been standing on the edge, looking down at his valley long enough. It was a beautiful, crisp spring morning. He took off down the rutted road, feeling a little like Tom Sawyer sneaking away from Sunday school.

The road descended steeply along the rocky bluff wall, a narrow and shadowy trail through the trees and brush. It was obvious that it was undisturbed by man or machine for quite a long time as the road was barely passable, even by foot. Well, he thought, these squirrels and rabbits had better prepare themselves because soon there would be a steady stream of machines invading their sanctuary. His chest swelled and shoulders straightened at the thought of it. It was the backbreaking, hard work that he yearned for the most.

He picked his way through the ruts and weeds until he rounded the last curve and emerged from the timber into an expansive open field that stretched out for as far as he could see.

The land was as level and golden as the road had been steep and dark. Matthew blinked his eyes, trying to adjust to the sudden glare of sunlight. He walked out onto his land. And found it littered with debris left by four years of receding floodwaters. He squatted down and picked up a handful of dirt. More mud than anything else, he pressed it in his fist.

This was his – come flood, drought, war, or disaster, and no one could ever take it away from him. He walked, and then ran, to the middle of the field. He began to turn slowly and felt a rush of pride and fulfillment that he had never experienced before. "This is mine!" he announced at loud. "This is mine!" He stood motionless, suspended in time, sensing only the wind, the light and the earth beneath his feet.

Then he walked to the river, crossing through the border of brush and timber that separated it from his land. He stood at the water's edge, struck by its awesome power and size. He stared at its black, churning waters, swelled with the spring glut.

"You old river, we're going to be friends, aren't we?" Matthew murmured, feeling compelled to make his peace with it. "You just keep moving along and mind your own business and I'll do the same." This was his temple on this bright, beautiful Sunday morning. And his prayer was to his God – the God of this great river, these brilliant skies, and good earth. All things were as they should be. And for this, he was truly thankful.

Chapter 16

St. Patrick's Day was fast approaching. It had always been a day of enormous importance in the Winston household. Mother sang her favorite, traditional songs in her clear soprano voice as she floated around the house, decorating everything in emerald green. She never tired of telling the stories of Irish folklore. There was an especially wistful glint in her eye, reminding everyone how much she still missed her homeland after all these years.

So as the holiday neared, the family wondered what it would be like not having her with them. And for Annie, the extra stress compounded her feelings of frustration and weariness. Things just weren't going very well. Every day seemed more over-whelming and desperate than the day before. She had assumed once the house became somewhat habitable and modernized, it would become more organized. There was a loose routine of sorts, although every day brought its own surprises and disasters.

It was just that she never got anything finished – not the cleaning, not the laundry, not the kitchen, not anything. She felt especially inadequate when dealing with Becky. True, Annie was never schooled in the domestic arts of cooking, cleaning, and running an household, but she was supposed to know how to care for babies. So why was this one so fussy?

The baby woke up screaming during the night at least twice, sometimes more. There were times Annie cried, too, distraught and frustrated with the baby fussing in her arms. All those years Annie stood by her brothers' cribs, watching her mother and Miss Grace expertly take care of the babies, she never once remembered seeing anything like the rage she now felt.

And who was supposed to rescue her from all this, she wondered. Her father became more content in his new surroundings. He had Mack and Andrew outside working from dusk to dawn. Andrew, who seemed more aware of his sister's state of desperation than the others, did try to help her occasionally, but was always called outside. The other boys had chores and homework, and became increasingly more involved with school activities.

All of this meant that she was left standing alone in that drafty, dirty old house, and she hated it. She ached to be back home where the coffee was always fresh and she could lounge in bed in the morning as long as she wanted, surrounded by all her lovely things. The thing she missed the most was the sense of decorum that always wonderfully enveloped the old brownstone. How could she hope to ever cope with this? Sometimes she would cry out and even stomp her foot, but no one ever noticed.

So it was that on this particular St. Patrick's Day, Miss Ann Marie Winston was not at all festive. The day had been worse than most of the others. She had to beg Sonny to take her into town for groceries, so she could slave away in the kitchen to prepare the family's favorite holiday meal of corned beef and cabbage. After struggling to get everything on the supper table, she was hurt and annoyed when everyone hurried through the meal to go someplace else. Matthew and Mack were excited about attending the annual party at the Pub. Andrew was helping the church youth group put the finishing touches on the float for tomorrow's parade, so he and the other boys were dropped off at St. Patrick's.

Twenty minutes after she called everyone to the supper table, Annie sat alone, surrounded by stacks of greasy dishes and heaps of leftovers. A seething rage began building in her until she was ready to explode. She went upstairs to get Joey and the Becky ready for bed and sent Danny and Peter to their room. It was time to face the dirty kitchen.

She started to clean, but a cup slipped from her hand and shattered at her feet. She screamed at the suddenness of it, but then picked up another cup and threw it across the room. A plate sailed against the wall and then a bowl. She even threw a chair down hard onto the floor. Unfortunately, her tantrum did nothing to calm her nerves.

Afraid she was going to break every dish in the house, she turned away from the disgusting scene and bolted upstairs for a hot bath. Luckily, there was enough hot water to fill the tub. She poured in a half bottle of bubble bath and sank into the deliciously soothing water, wishing she had remembered to first pour herself a glass of wine.

* * * * * *

Sonny was asked to go along to the party in town, but as usual, he declined saying he had things to do. Whether it was shyness or a strict code of privacy, he always refused to socialize with members of the family. Plus, he had a new project, which kept him occupied every night. He was converting the bus into a strange looking flat bed truck. The closed forward cab had four rows of seats so that the whole family could still ride in it, but the back was removed. They desperately needed something to haul the loads of supplies from town. It was a huge undertaking, which he worked on alone after hours. This night, like many others, he trudged into the kitchen, looking for a cup of coffee.

* * * * * *

Annie felt wonderfully refreshed after her bath. She pampered herself by brushing her hair and even did her nails. She slipped on one of her father's long-tailed dress shirts, knowing he had little use for it any more. She needed to fill baby bottles for the nighttime feedings even though that meant going back downstairs. She decided she would ignore the mess and worry about it tomorrow.

The opened refrigerator illuminated the darkened room and it was then that Annie noticed the clean counters and swept floor. Startled, she gasped and turned quickly. Sonny sat at the table, drinking coffee. "Well," she said, "I hope you didn't get dish pan hands."

"You don't get dish pan hands with a dishwasher."

"Oh, boy," she cried, "you all think this stuff is so damned easy."

He didn't answer. Draining his cup, he got up to leave.

"You know," she called after him, "you are really something. You work hard all day, doing almost everything because we're all so damned useless. Then you come in here, find a gigantic mess, and you take care of that, too. Damn it, I was going to clean it!'

He stood at the door ready to leave, but then he turned and gave her a hard look. "Ya' wanna know what I thought when I walked in here?" he demanded, scowling. "I thought someone broke in or there was some kind of trouble."

"What?" she stammered.

"Jeez, there was broken glass and chairs knocked over. I went through the whole house to make sure everything was alright."

She had a mental picture of Sonny prowling from room to room, probably with a knife or some other weapon. She tried to remember if she had closed the bathroom door all the way, but pushed that thought out of her head as soon as it appeared. "Hey, I'm sorry, alright?" she said. "A cup fell by accident and the others, I threw. And I was going to break a lot more if I had to stay in this kitchen one more minute! So I went upstairs and soaked in a nice, hot bath. And I felt a lot better, too, until I came down here and saw you cleaned up the place!" She was sure that none of this was making any sense.

Sonny poured himself another cup of coffee and returned to his seat. "Did you ever stop to consider that you're going about this all wrong?"

Oh, man, Annie thought, here it comes! She braced herself for a lecture.

"Back in New York," he said, "how many servants did you have?"

"Well, with Cook and Miss Grace, five, I guess."

"With all these servants, were any of you expected to clean up your own rooms or help around the house?"

"Well, of course not," she said, somewhat shocked. "Angelica and the others took care of everything. My father wanted Mother to have a nice life. Besides, she was pregnant most of the time."

Sonny said nothing more, apparently believing he had made an important point. But she didn't understand. "Now, don't get all huffy again," he said. "Can't you see that you're trying to take the place of five servants all by yourself? And this place isn't nearly as nice as your place back East."

"Okay, so what are you saying? That I should give up? I can't handle it so I should run out and hire a maid and a cook? Oh, boy, wouldn't the people around here get a laugh out of that! We can work as hard as anyone else. That's what we're trying to prove – to you and everyone in this stupid town!"

"Jesus! Why do you have to prove anything? There's at least six other able-bodied people who eat and sleep in this house, plus Peter and Danny who romp around here like it's a summer camp."

"So? My father won't let anyone help me. There's much more important work outside," she cried, her voice dripping with sarcasm.

"I can take care of the old man. You just have to figure out some kind of system of running things without putting yourself into such a corner." He pushed away from the table and left without saying another word.

She sat there feeling as though she had just been struck by a thunderbolt. What an idiot she had been, placing all of this on herself. Why was she trying to do the impossible? She never asked any of them to do anything – to make their own beds, clean their rooms, or even put away their clean clothes. She needed a system, a workable plan of rotating duties.

She began to circle the table as the thoughts began swirling inside her head. She should be mistress and over-seer, not slave or servant. She decided to make lists of the new rules and regulations, which she would present to her father and siblings tomorrow.

Much later, when she was lying in bed, still too excited to sleep, she wondered why Sonny had said those things to her. Her father and brothers must have noticed how angry and depressed she had been these past few days, yet no one tried to help her in any way. But this man, this stranger, came to her rescue and made her see that she did in fact have options. Annie sighed wearily and settled into her bed. Ginny always said that tomorrow will take care of itself. Annie hoped that was true.

* * * * * *

All the Winston males knew there were drastic changes afoot the minute they came into the kitchen for breakfast. Their sister said a pleasant good morning to each one, but then asked, "Did you make your bed this morning? Did you bring down your dirty clothes?"

"What? How come?" were the sleepy-eyed, surprised responses. Was this some kind of a joke? However, her smiling but resolved expression soon led them to believe that this new attitude was something to be reckoned with.

It was Saturday morning. Matthew came hurrying in for breakfast and began rattling off work assignments for everyone. He was not happy when his daughter interrupted him and demanded a family meeting, but her tone of voice and terse expression compelled him to sit down without saying a word. Sonny took up his customary spot, leaning against the counter in the back corner, his arms folded across his chest and his face as expressionless as usual.

"I have decided to make a few changes around here," she began, sounding very authoritarian. "All of you seem to presume that I am responsible for everything that needs doing around this house. Well, that's ridiculous. I cannot do it all, nor should I have to. Therefore, I have come up with a plan." She took a deep breath. "To begin with, on Friday nights or Saturdays I expect each of you to clean your own bedrooms and change your sheets. I will still do the laundry but I will wash only the clothes I find in the hampers in the laundry room. That means, if you do not bring it down here, it won't get washed."

She paused for a few minutes to allow her first edict to be absorbed by the stunned group. "And there's more." She went on to outline a list of tasks that would be completed on a rotating basis, including bathrooms, dishes, and even babysitting. There was considerable groaning and grumbling as these latest laws were announced, but she made it very clear that it was non-negotiable.

"I still have a lot to do, especially taking care of Joey and Becky. I feel I have not been spending enough time with them and when I do, I'm so tired that I'm irritable. Look, I am not your maid, and I'm not going to kill myself trying to do everything."

In the chorus of moaning and arguing that followed, Matthew's voice could be heard the loudest. "These boys have responsibilities out--"

Annie cut him off before he had a chance to finish. "That's bull, Daddy! I need help, too. All I'm asking is that everyone does their share in this house just like outside."

"If you felt so strongly about this why didn't you come to me, and we could have worked something out?" Matthew persisted, looking offended.

She leaned across the table and stared at him, fighting hard to keep angry tears from falling. "I guess I was waiting for someone to notice how bad things were for me," she said, "but since no one did, I decided to take things into my own hands. It has been worked out – effective immediately!"

And so it was that the Annie Doctrine was adopted and implemented. She was aware of some rumblings of dictatorship, but she didn't care. It meant survival and more freedom for her. She was amazed how easily she adjusted to her role as "chief bitch and bottle washer."

Because Sonny helped her resolve her most major difficulty, Annie found that she had more tolerance for his rudeness. She was actually beginning to think that they had reached some kind of truce. But then, in a seemingly premeditated act of hatefulness, he managed to erase any thoughts she had of good will toward him.

* * * * * *

It began innocently enough. Becky had a bad cold, and then Joey kept her up all night, whimpering and crying with an apparent ear infection. The next morning, she got the name and number of the local physician from Lori Bean and called for an appointment. Luckily, she was told, Dr. Adams would be in "this office" that day.

In this office? Annie had no idea what that meant. She had serious misgivings about this country doctor, but she felt she should at least give him a chance. What choice did she have?

Her father was no help at all. When she told him she had made the appointments, he acted annoyed at the interruption. "Can't you reschedule for later? Mack just left for town, and I've got a contractor coming any time now."

"Well, then Sonny's going to have to take us," she insisted.

"No, I can't," Sonny retorted. "I have to be here to talk to the contractor, too. Just call back and say you'll be there as soon as your brother gets back." He and Matthew walked away as though the matter was settled.

"Pop, this can't wait," she cried. "You know how fast Joey gets sick." But he wasn't listening. So she turned to Sonny. "You have to take us now!" she called, grabbing his arm.

"No, I can't," he said, pulling away from her.

156

"Why not?" she insisted. "If you don't, it could become a lot worse. Joey will have to be hospitalized and think now inconvenient that would be."

"How could an hour or two make that much difference?" he muttered. "Mack will take you when he gets back." Again, he walked away.

"You know as well as I do that he might not be back for hours. Why are you being so difficult? Just take us into town!"

"No!"

Annie was incensed. She was talking about the health and well being of children. "Sonny," she pleaded, "Just take us in, and Mack can pick us up later. It'll take less than a lousy half hour."

He started to protest, but then seemed to change his mind. Soon, they were on their way to Dr. Adam's office. Annie was still seething with anger, but said nothing further.

When they got into town, Sonny pulled up to the curb in front of the office, staring straight ahead without turning off the engine.

"Can't you at least help me get them inside?" Annie implored.

"No," he replied without looking at her. "I'm gonna check on Mack to see what's taking so damn long."

Angrily, Annie carried one child inside, then the other. Sonny continued to sit behind the wheel, his cold, unrelenting expression frozen on his face. He gunned the engine and sped away the second she shut the truck door.

Chapter 17

Lori said Dr. Abe Adams was a "horse and buggy doctor," referring to his circuit of offices located in three other small villages besides Shannon Town. That fact that there was a "D.O." after his name instead of "M.D." was of no consequence to the people he had attended for the last 30 plus years. But Annie was apprehensive as she struggled to get her brother and sister into his office. She was grateful when Ellen, the receptionist/medical assistant/pharmacist, rushed out to help her and ushered them into the examining room.

"Miss Winston?" Dr. Adams asked as he followed them inside the small cubicle. "I understand we have some sick children here." He took Becky and began undressing her, cooing and smiling as he worked "C'mon, sweetheart, lets take your temperature." He loosened her diaper, gently slipped the thermometer into place.

Annie stared at him in utter amazement. She had never seen a doctor do that before. He began asking questions about their recent symptoms. "They had runny noses for a couple of days and Joey started running a fever last night. He's not eating or drinking."

Doc Adams took out the thermometer and held it at arm's length, trying to adjust his bifocals so he could read it. "102.6°" was the verdict. He took down the otoscope and carefully looked into the infant's ears. The problem was identified shortly. He glanced at the folders of medical records and then rolled over to where Annie was sitting with Joey. He tried to make friends with the little boy but finding that impossible, he had to go ahead with the examination while the others held him down. He confirmed Annie's suspicions that Joey also had an ear infection with a very inflamed throat.

He scribbled a prescription and handed it to Ellen who stepped out of the room and soon returned with two bottles of the cure-all pink medicine. Meanwhile, the doctor weighed and measured both of the children and made initial entries in the charts of his new patients. Annie explained how their mother had died of cancer shortly after Becky was born. They talked for a long time. Most of his questions were regarding Joey, such as what specialists and therapists had seen the boy.

"My mother always tried to protect him," Annie said. "He gets sick so easily, so she kept him home. Joey was very special to her."

By this time, Joey and Becky each had their initial doses of antibiotics and another patient, an elderly gentleman who was evidently hard of hearing, was shouting his displeasure of having to wait. "Well, I guess we should go," Annie said, but Doc Adams was no hurry to dismiss them.

"Ann," he said, "I am sure your mother loved Joey very much and wanted to take care of him the best way she knew how. I can tell by the way you speak of her that she was a wonderful mother, but Joey is growing. If he's this difficult to manage now, what about when he's ten or twenty? He won't fit in your lap much longer." He paused to allow her to comment or ask questions but she said nothing.

"Dubuque County has wonderful facilities to help young people like your brother. You should consider it, maybe for next fall. A van would transport him every day. You think about it over the summer and let me know."

* * * * * *

Annie was irritable throughout the evening. She had well-rehearsed snide remarks ready for Sonny. But he never came in for supper, so her father received the brunt of it.

Later, when she was too tired to be angry, she sought out Andrew and Luke. She was in need of solace and advice. Climbing the stairs to the third floor, she followed the faint glow of light down the dark, narrow hallway to the end room. Her beacon had been furnished by a propane lantern hanging from the ceiling.

Luke stood at his easel painting, and Andrew sat at a small table, reading. Both were absorbed in their work and did not hear her footsteps. She cleared her throat and when that didn't work, she knocked. They both smiled when they saw her. Neither one seemed annoyed at the interruption.

"What brings you up here, my dear?" teased Luke, with a heavy Transylvanian accent as he rubbed his hands with mocked fiendish delight.

Since Andrew's chair was the only one in the room, he offered it to her, bowing deeply. "Would madam care for some refreshments?" he asked, opening the window to reveal some juices and soda sitting on the outside ledge in the cool night air.

He tried to hide the large bottle of wine but she saw it. Instead of admonishing him, she said she'd take a glass, too.

"Makes it easier to relax," Andrew said, looking somewhat embarrassed.

"You don't have to explain anything to me. We're entitled. She told them the details of her meeting with Dr. Adams, trying to describe his demeanor as well as what he said. She also told them about the conversations she had with Sonny about Joey, too.

"C'mon, Annie, didn't it ever occur to you that Mother was too over-protective of Joey?" asked Andrew. "Her approach was pretty unrealistic, don't you think?"

Annie stared at him, unable to answer at first. "Are you agreeing with them?" she stuttered. "You think they're right, and Mother was wrong?"

"Annie, don't look so shocked," Luke said. "It's not a matter of right or wrong. None of us know how to help him. His behavior is so out of control, what's going to happen to him when he's older?"

"We all know how much Mother loved him, in spite of everything," Andrew added, "but I believe that eventually she would have sought some professional help for him. Her way just wasn't working."

Annie tried to repulse what they were saying as some kind of terrible sacrilege, but they kept talking to her in soothing, matter-of-fact tones until some of what they said began to penetrate. She knew they were trying to convince her because the decisions regarding the little boy were largely up to her now. Their father would consent to whatever she asked.

She had a lot to think about. Late that night, unwanted tears began streaming down her cheeks. Everything was too hard, and she was so tired of trying and failing. She tried to pray, pleading for guidance and strength, but a restless and fitful sleep was her only reprieve.

* * * * * *

April came and there was a real feeling of spring in the air. The days were still cool, but never that terrible, bone-chilling cold

160

like before. The temperatures at night seldom dipped below freezing.

Everything that was going to be done in the house in the foreseeable future was finished. Most of the completed work was functional, not cosmetic. Electricity, heating, and plumbing were restored, and all the windows and doors were repaired or replaced. At Lori's urging, Annie had managed to convince her father to complete a family room in one section of the cavernous basement with a TV and furniture for the boys. Another bathroom was installed down there, too. But elsewhere, little painting or decorating of any kind was attempted so the house remained drab and inhospitable.

Clearly, the decor of the house was the least of Matthew's priorities. There was only one thing on his mind – planting the first crop. There was so much preparation involved and he did not hesitate to buy whatever he thought would facilitate the venture. One day, three giant shinny green tractors rolled onto the yard, followed by two semi-truck flatbeds loaded with plows, disks, and planters. Teaching the intricacies of the mammoth machines was, of course, up to Sonny. Not only did he have to deal with Matthew's zeal and impatience, but also Mack's total disinterest and constant arguing. And then there was Andrew's total ineptitude with anything involving more than two moving parts. He nearly drove one of the big tractors through the kitchen wall, saved only by the large cement step by the doorway.

The contractors Matthew hired came with bulldozers and graders to work on the "bottom road". With passable access down to the fields, they were able to begin the preparatory work. They used the tractors and heavy chains to drag away the debris. The river level was monitored closely and the weather reports for the entire northern Midwest were of keen interest. The guys at the Pub said Matthew must be their good luck piece because it appeared there would be no late spring flood this year. But still, they said, he shouldn't worry about planting until at least mid-April because he might end up re-planting if high waters still came. Floods were a part of life here, the price they paid for the rich, high-yield bottomland.

Annie was taking interest in the earth herself. She wanted

a garden. The boys just laughed at her but she was very resolute. It started one afternoon she spent with the Gibson's, when Jake showed her his garden. It was time to put in the early peas, he explained. He pointed with his cane to where everything would be planted – rows of beans, carrots, radishes, lettuce, and Ginny's herbs and spices. Annie had seen their "fruit room" in the basement, which was lined with shelves loaded with canned goods. Ginny's homemade pickles were the best Annie had ever tasted.

The question of where she should plant her own garden was answered when she stumbled upon a place where she guessed there had been one before. From her kitchen window she could see some spindly pink blossoms on a few scrub fruit trees. One warm afternoon she decided to go exploring. The ruts on the field road were dry so she followed it toward the cherry blossoms. Past the house and barnyard, the road curved sharply and followed the crest of the ridge until it disappeared into the timber. Annie could imagine what the grounds must of looked like when the hillside between the road and bluff was mowed and trimmed with shrubbery and flower gardens.

She found the few remaining trees where once a fine orchard had been and also a large rectangular area of uneven ground. The perimeter of the garden was easily discernible as the ground was rutted and gorged where the topsoil had laid exposed for several years. It wasn't far from the house and the big stone barn was just across the road. All the traffic to the bottom would go past here so she would be able to keep track of everyone's comings and goings. The bluff dropped off sharply at the timberline so she even had full view of the fields below. It was perfect. However, she knew she couldn't do it alone. Now all she had to do was convince Sonny and her father.

As she expected, Sonny looked at her as though she was crazy. "Look, you have enough to do around here," he exclaimed. "It's a lot of work and I don't have the time."

"Who says you'll have to do it? You just have to help me get started," she pleaded. "All you have to do is run that big plow through it once or twice. Jake says that'll break it up pretty good. And maybe that thing with those big steel round plates? That would really help, and it would only take a couple minutes, right?"

"Yeah, right," he muttered.

"What about rototilling, the planting and weeding?" Matthew retorted. "You would have to work out there every day with the mosquitoes and hot sun. Are you sure about this?"

"Yes, I am. It's a lot of work but I want a garden. Just help me get started." She glared at Sonny as she spoke. She hated having to constantly ask him for help.

Sonny continued to vent his skepticism, but one morning he plowed her garden spot and disked it several times. Annie stood there beaming as she watched the unsightly weeds disappearing under the black blanket of soil.

He jumped off the tractor and came over to talk to her. "Do you see how bad it is?" he yelled over the roar of the engine. "I've disked it four times but the crust is harder than it is in the bottom."

So what, she thought. What did he expect her to say – forget it? Hell no! Her expression must have said it all because he stomped off without waiting for a reply.

Later that day, Charlie Bean delivered a rototiller, several hand tools, and bags of seeds. Nagging feelings of doubt began welling up inside the pit of her stomach when she saw the assembled paraphernalia, but she stubbornly pushed ahead. She wrote out a check and asked Charlie to unload everything by the garden. The wave of doubt was a little stronger this time, and for a minute she thought she was going to cry. But that would be pointless and a waste of time, she told herself.

One quick walk across the garden spot verified what Sonny had said that morning. The ground was still very hard. She turned to glare at her new machine. Charlie had given her some instructions. He even put gas in it and started it up. Looked simple enough. Over and over she pulled on the starter rope. The engine would almost start, then cough, spit a little, and then die. Annie became incensed that a brand new machine was so difficult to start.

It was John who came to her rescue. He sat nearby and read the manual. "It's the choke," he called to her. He described where the small lever was located and instructed her how to pull it out. She was amazed when the thing started running with one pull of the rope. Her hopefulness was short-lived, however, because she soon found that her problems were only beginning.

She had been told that the machine was self-propelled, meaning it pulled itself along, but the steering was quite another matter. She headed into the garden and started the blades churning. She was quite unprepared for the tremendous vibrating and pounding it caused as it tried to claw its way through the cragged ground. Try as she might she was unable to control the beast. She strained and struggled, trying to at least make it go straight. It was no use. Tears of frustration rolled down her cheeks, mixing with the dirt so that she could hardly see. She freed one hand to wipe away the mud on her cheeks but just that quickly the rototiller jolted and slid over onto its side, the blades spinning furiously. She strained to get the throbbing machine upright but it was too heavy and sent her reeling to the ground. She sat sobbing uncontrollably in the dirt and ruts until her face and front of her shirt was covered with a very unlady-like, black paste.

That's how Sonny found her. Coming up from the bottom, he must have seen both Annie and the machine on the ground so he stopped the tractor and raced over. "You ain't hurt, are you?" he asked as he turned off the rototiller. He extended his hand to help her up, but she jumped to her feet unaided.

"Do not say a word!" she screamed. "I don't want to hear any of your I-told-you-so's. I said I would do it myself and I will. But get rid of this damn machine! It's a stupid, worthless, noisy, horrible piece of junk! I'd rather do it the old-fashioned way!" She stomped over, picked up a hoe, and started hacking away. She realized she was making a fool of herself so she threw it down and ran to the house, every bit of her self-respect in shreds.

Sonny didn't come in for supper that night. After chores, he went back to the garden, started up the rototiller and began working it back and forth until the ground lay level like fine sand on a beach. Ann watched him, walking slowly behind the dreaded machine until sundown. She felt even more of a failure, but at least she'd have her garden.

* * * * * *

Spring meant Easter. Back home in New York, the stores teemed with beautiful clothes with matching wide-brimmed hats and purses. The stores and boutiques were filled with the wonderful aroma of huge bouquets of fresh flowers. Annie was intent on carrying on the tradition of decorating eggs and Easter baskets for the young ones. Mother always insisted on daily Lenten vespers but Annie didn't attempt it. Those prayer sessions had never been popular, and she felt she already faced enough unpleasantness and grumbling from her family.

Andrew, too, thought about initiating them, but he had enough problems getting everyone to be still long enough for a quick blessing at mealtime. Besides, family meals became less frequent with the older boys' extra-curricular activities at school and the men worked until after dark nearly every day. There was always an under-current of constant urgency in their home now. Andrew ached for the well-mannered orderliness they had known back in the brownstone. What he missed the most was the quiet.

He was already involved in the parish. The priest, Father Fritz as everyone called him, was a pleasant, middle-aged man who tended his flock like a wise and kindly shepherd and seemed to fully enjoy his life. He did admit that he once dreamed of leading a larger flock. "I guess every priest dreams of being a bishop," he joked.

Andrew did not understand. To him, dealing with the politics of a large church was the least appealing aspect of the priesthood. Being in a small parish like this seemed much more gratifying. Fr. Fritz had total control as he struggled to make the mortgage payments, get the organ tuned, and the grass cut.

Andrew was especially excited about the preparation for the Easter services. It was the community's fifth annual ecumenical sunrise service because after all, Easter belonged to all Christians. And if they combined services, then everyone could worship at the riverside park without forcing the other two congregations to go elsewhere.

* * * * * *

The world was beset with strife and tragedy that Easter in April, 1970. The Sunday newspapers tossed onto Shannon Town's lawns chronicled the facts that many places were not nearly as tranquil as their little corner of the world.

In the land of many of the ancestors, Ireland, Britain was sending in five hundred additional troops into Belfast after a week of disturbances. There were reports of many causalities . . .

In Viet Nam, there were also reports of causalities, American boys killed when the North Vietnamese launched a major offensive throughout South Viet Nam, ending a six-month lull in the fighting . .

In Massachusetts, the governor had just signed a bill challenging the legality of that conflict, stating that servicemen from their state may refuse to participate because of the absence of a Congressional declaration of war . . .

In the nation's capitol, 50,000 people were gathering to march to show support for that same war, preparing to clash with anti-war demonstrators . . .

But here, in Shannon Town, Iowa, the day dawned chilly and clear. And those who chose to leave their warm beds came together to pray for peace and understanding between all peoples everywhere. They knew that their show of non-sectarian, inter-denominational fellowship would have little impact on a troubled world, but they did it because it was a good thing to do.

Matthew told his children that attendance was not mandatory, although he himself was excited, the way he embraced everything new and different about this community. Mack graciously volunteered to stay home with the little ones. When Annie made the rounds that morning before dawn, Thomas resisted any attempts to be rousted out of his bed.

They drove through the still, dark countryside and met several cars and pickups turning up the road toward the little white church on the hillside. There was only a hint of daylight now in the east. The people filed in silently. The organ was still. Father Fritz, flanked by two sleepy-eyed alter boys, knelt at the alter. Then, at the appointed time, he picked up the heavy wooden cross that stood before him and lead the people out of the church. On the other end of town, Rev. Finney and his Lutheran flock left their church just as Pastor Grayson brought his small gathering of Congregationalists into the street. Slowly, quietly, they walked until the sects intertwined at the Riverside Park. The three men of God put down their crosses and took their places on the little bandstand, which was decorated with bouquets of flowers and purple banners, stirring in the breeze.

God himself provided the most stunning decoration of all. The sun chose that moment to rise above the treetops on the eastern shore and reached out to them with long fingers of gold and scarlet. The dark river was transformed by millions of brilliant diamonds dancing upon the water, as even the dew on the grass became lovely jade jewels.

An opening prayer called the people to worship and the first song was introduced. Joe McFlynn, the sometimes fumbling bus driver and part-time school janitor, stepped forward and waited for his cue. He began to sing in a rich baritone that drifted over the land and water.

Were you there when they crucified my Lord?
Were you there when they crucified my Lord?
Sometimes it causes me to tremble, tremble, tremble.
Were you there when they crucified my Lord? . . .

The story of the Passion was read. The homilies were simple, calling for the message of the Risen Lord of peace and understanding to be heard throughout the world. The three ministers prepared the Eucharist, each in their own way as dictated by the practices of their churches. Those who watched closely saw that there were many more similarities than differences. Joyful songs were sung and a Benediction recognized by all was said.

Many lingered, chatting quietly. Annie was surprised when one of the guitarists who had participated in the service, sought her out. "Is Thomas sick or something? We really needed him today," he said.

"Why, no," she replied. "You're Jim Mathers, aren't you. Thomas has mentioned you several times."

"Yeah, I bet," the boy said, blushing a little. "He really helped us a lot, ya' know. Taught us all the chords and helped us at practices. We kinda needed him – I guess he's our leader. We thought he was coming."

"Well, Jim, I thought you all did very well. The service was beautiful."

"It was real nice, it really was. I wish Thomas could have been here to see it. We tried to explain it to him." He sighed deeply. "He's really good, ya' know. I never knew anyone that could play a guitar like him, 'cept on TV or somethin'. He gets sorta short on patience sometimes, but I just hope he'll teach us more." The boy shrugged his shoulders and wandered off. Annie didn't understand what Thomas found so offensive about the boy.

Later that day, after the ham was eaten and the eggs were hunted, she had words with Thomas "We didn't you go this morning? You must have known the other musicians were depending on you."

"What musicians?" Thomas snarled

"Your friend, Jim Mathers and the other boys. You might be interested to know that I thought they did very well. But I don't think they have much confidence, which is further reason why you should have been there."

"There was no way I was going to be caught dead with those creeps," Thomas retorted. "And don't call Jim Mathers my friend. He's a sniveling idiot who doesn't know anything about music and certainly has no talent."

Annie was taken back by her brother's attitude. She started to argue but he sulked away. She found herself wondering for the hundredth time how someone so young could be so filled with hostility for no apparent reason. Mack was certainly opinionated and could be a jerk sometimes, but he was basically fun loving and could be downright charming. Thomas was never pleasant and acted as though he hated the world. Maybe he'd outgrow it, she hoped. She made a mental note to speak to her father about it, but she never had a chance that day and then another busy week started.

Chapter 18

The letters slide off the tongue rhythmically: M-I-S-S-I-S-S-I-P-P-I. The word conjures visions of freckle-faced Huck Finn's with fishing poles and corncob pipes, or shifty-eyed riverboat gamblers and pale-skinned ladies with pink parasols and hoop skirts. Gone are the days of the paddle wheelers and minstrel shows. Gone are the slaves whose prayerful spirituals once echoed across the waters as they sang to their God and to the river.

The Golden Age of the Mississippi was but a moment of its timeless existence. This "Father of Waters" was born not of clear blue lakes and streams, but of ice – massive plains of flowing glaciers that reached out like the hand of God to sculpt the land and divide the waters. Prehistoric people buried entire households in huge animal shaped mounds on its banks, perhaps worshiping the great mysteries of their time – the sun, fire, and the river.

Later, their less-primitive descendants lived and died on these same shores. The Sioux, Ojibwa, Sauk, and Fox stood beside the beautiful cascading waterfalls and ate of its plentiful bounty. They lived their lives to the rhythm of the river.

There is still a kind of cadence to life here. Many of the modern sights and sounds are mechanized and seemingly obtrusive, like the roar of the diesels straining to push a quarter million tons of coal or grain up stream, and the red and black buoy channel markers bobbing as guideposts on this great watery highway. But swimmers still swim and fishermen still fish in the muddy waters. Owls, hawks, and cranes still circle lazily overhead. On gorgeous spring days, the river mirrors what is good about the earth and the blue of the heavens is pale by comparison. Anyone who knows the river – really knows it – refers to it as "she", like a willful, beautiful woman who flirts, teases, and lies serene in the moonlight, and then suddenly rises up in a terrible fury, capable of consuming and destroying. Those people know you can love or hate her, bridge or dam her, pollute, ride, curse or revere her, but no one can ever possess her. Rather the river remains an implacable marker of time and space, a natural backdrop for human dramas, serving to remind those she touches how obscure and limited humanity is when compared to the boundless power of the river.

So it is that the sight of the first tow and barges making its way upriver is as much a part of the spring ritual as tulips, robins, and warm spring breezes. The Winston's had been told to watch for it. There was a pool at the Pub as to the exact day and time the first one would go past.

The cry went out one Sunday morning just as the family dressed for Mass. Peter and Danny, their good pants already dirtied, ran onto the porch and yelled through the open window. "It's coming! It's coming!" Matthew grabbed the binoculars and hurried down to the rocky place, with everyone close behind. They had seen pictures and heard stories of the mighty tows with upwards to fifteen barges cleated together. But what a sight it was to see. Even from this distance, it looked like a small island inching its way upstream.

"It's the *Sarah E. Thomas*," Matthew reported, looking through the field glasses. "She's got 9, no, 12 barges. Looks like she's running empty 'cause she's riding high." Reluctantly, he handed over the binoculars to be passed around. After a few minutes, he said, "C'mon, lets see if we can beat her into town." Everyone ran for the bus.

The Winston's were not the only ones who came to watch. There was a small gathering at the park. Billy had the ledger of this year's wagers.

"Here she comes! Here she comes!" the children squealed.

Billy looked over the ledger carefully and checked his watch. When the flagpole of the lead barge passed before him, he declared it official. "It is 9:32, Sunday morning, April, 19th. That means Charlie O'Leary is the winner – again! I swear that man must know somebody in St. Louie!"

It was a magnificent sight. It passed so closely that they could see the captain waving through an open window on the bridge. There was a great torrent of churning water left in its wake so that the waves beat upon the shore like the tide on an ocean beach. Then it was gone.

Spring was officially here. Annie and her brothers were aware of changing seasons before but they had never witnessed a spring so intimately as this. Daily, the landscapes changed as the spindly stark branches of the trees suddenly burst with green foliage. The lilacs bloomed and pastures were the playgrounds for newborn lambs, calves and squealing little pigs. All those whose chosen work it was to toil over the land were hard at work.

Driving his machine back and forth beneath his own patch of sky, Matthew marveled at the dozens of different shades of blue and the ever-changing clouds. The sun beat down relentlessly to warm the earth. The birds soared overhead. The constant roar of the tractor, which seemed so obtrusive at first, now seemed to settle into his mind, blending into every facet of his existence, even his sleep.

Matthew expected everyone to share his enthusiasm for this twelve hour a day job. Sonny doggedly labored beside him, working longer and harder than was expected. That angered Mack and even Andrew because they resented being expected to keep up this torrid pace. They had aching backs, blistered hands, and sunburn faces to show for their efforts.

The other boys could at least escape their father's demands while they were at school, which often created more problems as they became more involved in time consuming extra-circular activities. Old wounds were made deeper when it became evident that Matthew did not view each son's commitments with equal validity. Thomas was very frustrated when his father scoffed at the mention of the upcoming band contest, while John's track meets and practices were heralded events. Matthew and Mack even attended the first one. Annie sympathized with Thomas and tried to make him understand that it rained that whole day so they couldn't work in the fields. "Thomas, don't worry. I bet you'll be able to slip away for the day and everyone else could cover for you." But Thomas was not easily appeased.

John, on the other hand, was having the time of his life. At long last, he had some place to channel his competitive drive and athletic skills. He was amazed how much credence was given to members of the team at school, even in the community. The high school had been without a winning tradition for many years now, and everyone was hungry for victories.

The track team had been working under the watchful eye of Coach Nick Stevenson since mid-March. He had just been through a humiliating season as the head coach of the boys' basketball team and was determined not to allow his track team to likewise finish in the basement of the conference.

John Winston did what he was told without complaint. He pushed himself to the limit so he might finally discover exactly where that limit was. He and his new best friend, Kenny Beyers, challenged each other as their prowess on the track improved.

Rain fell all morning the day of the first track meet and threatened to cancel the four-school event. But by mid afternoon the storms passed and the team reported to the locker room as directed. As he dressed in his faded green and white uniform and laced his shoes, John had a queasy, nervous feeling in his gut.

"That'll go away as soon as the first gun goes off," Kenny said as they finished warm-ups together. That would be soon enough, as John was entered in four events: the 200-yard dash, low hurdles, and the 400 and 800 meter relays.

He crouched down in the starting blocks for his first race, trying to concentrate on everything the coach had taught him – coming out of the blocks, escalation, breathing techniques. But there was only the deafening pounding of his heart and the single-minded thought of running and winning.

And he did win, but only once. However, in the minds of the coaches, coming in second or third was a victory in itself. Kenny, John, and two other fleet-footed sophomores won the first relay. That was good enough for the team to finish second overall and no Shannon Town High School track team had done that in recent memory. The sophomores were the heart of the team, which meant the coaches had bona fide hope for the future. John and Kenny whooped it up in the locker room with the other boys. They had tasted victory and it was sweet. They came out of the locker room together and found their fathers chatting and congratulating each other on their sons' accomplishments. Luke lounged nearby, having completed his work on the mural and waiting for a ride home. Someone suggested they have supper together at the Pub.

* * * * * *

Kenny's dad, Harry Beyers, was a very likable man. He was, of course, aware of the background of the man sitting across the table. Harry was not intimidated by this eccentric millionaire who spent his family's money like water. As far as he was concerned, they had the same dirt under their fingernails.

"Your son tells me those garbage trucks I see around here are yours," Matthew said. "That's quite an operation you have there. Kenny says you designed and built most of the machinery in the re-cycling plant yourself."

Harry flashed a quick smile toward his son. Of all the things he strove for in his lifetime, the respect and admiration of his only son was one of the most important. "It wasn't that difficult" he explained modestly. "I traveled 'round a bit and visited some of the big operations out East. Most of it is just good ol' common sense. Why should I pay good money for machinery I can weld together myself?"

Matthew was in total awe. "You make it sound so easy, but you're talking to someone who finds it difficult to pound two boards together." They both laughed then. The boys cast relieved glances at one another. The conversation was rolling along nicely.

Then, just as they were finishing their meal, Walt Jamison sat down at their table. "Hey, Harry," he said. "Did you hear the news? They got those astronauts back."

"Who?"

"Those Apollo astronauts – they were supposed to go to the moon, but something happened. Man, I didn't think they had a snowball's chance in hell of getting' back alive!"

"Yeah?" Harry pushed away from the table. "Do you realize that little fiasco cost over a billion dollars of yours and mine money? I'm glad they got back, but they shouldn't have been up there in the first place."

"Yes, but, they say the Russians are gonna beat —"

"Beat us at what? Who can spend the most money the quickest? Well, I can tell ya', we're way ahead there. I just read the Russians already got a goddamn spaceship ready to go up this

173

summer that is unmanned and cost a third as much. Couldn't we have used that money somewhere else? Like in Vietnam -- end that fuckin' war."

Walt Jamison shut up then. Harry Beyers' views on Vietnam were well known around the Pub. It was useless to try to argue.

"But the government don't care much about our money or our boys," Harry continued. "I'll tell you what, if this thing keeps goin' much longer and they want my boy, I'll tell those sonofabitches to stick it up their asses."

There was murmuring both for and against his statement at neighboring tables. "Yeah," said another man at a nearby table, "I read that Nixon wants to do away with deferments for married men and maybe even doctors and such."

"Haven't you heard?" Harry said, sounding very sarcastic. "Nixon says he's gonna withdraw 150,000 troops by next spring. So don't worry – all our rich doctor and lawyer sons won't get drafted." A ripple of jeering spread across the room.

Matthew squirmed in his seat. He had heard these political discussions around the Pub before, but managed to avoid commenting. He learned that the people here had a good grasp of the complexities of politics and international affairs. Midwesterners turned on Walter Cronkite for the nightly news just like the high-rise dwellers back East.

It was also true that the people here had a different perspective. Most of them felt that they were sending their sons off to this war in far greater numbers than the college educated, upper class snobs on the coasts. And he knew that even though he and his family had been welcomed into the community, Matthew was still regarded as part of the privileged few. He felt their stares. Perhaps this would be a good time to speak up.

"You don't mean to tell me that you'd let those Communists beat us over there? I hate to see young men dying, too. I know I did in Europe during World War II."

Harry did not answer immediately. He ground his cigarette butt into the ashtray and said, "Your business back East, I heard it was shipbuilding. Did you have contracts with the Pentagon? And don't you have several sons? Why aren't any of them over there if you think it's such a good idea?"

"My wife was quite ill for a long time before she died recently. I thought it was important to keep the family together at that time." Matthew stood up then and threw some bills onto the table. He motioned for Johnny and Luke to follow him toward the door. "But now, since it does appear this thing won't be over any time soon, I do believe that one or more of my sons will be called. And they will go with my blessing."

* * * * * *

Two weeks and three track meets later, Thomas came downstairs early on Saturday morning and flung his black woolen band uniform across the sofa. He went to the window and scowled at the blue skies. Damn! It was going to be a nice day and his father would have everyone outside working all day. Thomas had stopped talking about the band contest, hoping the day would dawn dark and rainy. However, he had made up his mind he was going, whether his father liked it or not.

He sprawled on the sofa, eating a candy bar from his private stash hidden in his room. He stared up at his brother's track ribbons hung prominently above the mantle. God, he hated those things and the way his father strutted around, recounting what a magnificent jock his son was. And John was always so humble about it. It made Thomas sick to his stomach.

"Is that what you're having for breakfast?" Annie broke into his thoughts. "I see you have your uniform all ready to go."

"Yes, but I'm not going anywhere. It's a nice day. Pop won't let me go."

"Oh, stop it, Thomas. Why do you have to be so negative? I spoke to Daddy last night and he said you can go. What time does the bus leave?"

"7:30 – er, he did? How come? He doesn't care about my band contest."   "You're unbelievable, Thomas. I just told you some good news. Get out there and get your chores done early. Mack will bring you into town."

So it was that the Shannon Town High School band's star percussionist was delivered to the bus on time. As Thomas exited the car, Mack called, "Knock 'em dead, kid," almost as an after thought.

"Yeah, sure," muttered Thomas. He just wanted it to be over.

* * * * * *

There wasn't much fanfare when he came home late that night, either. Annie came out of the kitchen, asking how it went. "It sucked!" he cried as he slammed upstairs. The band got a II rating, but it should have been an I. They played better than they ever had before. Even the *1812 Overture* was decent. Yes, it was somewhat labored in some parts, but Mr. Moore was counting on the judges taking into account the difficulty of the piece.

Thomas tried to dismiss the whole thing as ridiculous. He was quite unprepared for the carnival-like atmosphere. He was used to the recital halls back home where competitions were approached with the utmost seriousness. But today, the crowded hallways were buzzing with spectators and participants directed by cardboard signs to libraries-turned-rehearsal halls and gymnasiums-turned-concert-halls. A gym? The thought of it still incensed him. Maybe those cavernous echo chambers were all right for basketball games, but not for judging the finer minutiae of classical music.

And Jim Mathers drove him crazy all day, following him around and talking non-stop. And then to make matters worse, Mrs. Mathers insisted on taking Thomas home. Jim's mom was a plain woman with a nervous, pinched face. The only time she smiled was when Jim told her that Mr. Moore told him he played his solo well.

"What did Dad say when he saw I was gone?" Jim asked but his mother only clinched the steering wheel tighter and said nothing. Thomas thought the whole family must be as uptight and dull as Jim. Thomas couldn't stand that bushy-haired kid anymore. Maybe he could rid of the little parasite now that the competition was over.

Monday morning, Mr. Moore read the comments from the three judges to his musicians. There were some favorable comments, but the reports sited particular measures of missed notes and specific passages that dragged. As he closed the session, he challenged his students to try harder and do better next year. "We'll be ready for 'em, that's for sure!"

"Oh, boy!" whistled Jimmy under his breath. "We thought he pushed us before! I have a feelin' we ain't seen nothin' yet."

Maybe you, sucker, Thomas thought, but not me. He did not plan to be around a year from now. When he turned to say something snide to his fellow drummer, he noticed a large bruise on Jim's forearm and cut on his lip. When he asked him about it, Jim shrugged his shoulders and said he fell. Thomas knew Jim was a klutz but was surprised he had hurt himself that badly. He would have pursued it but he didn't want to appear to care.

Chapter 19

Luke wasn't sure how it happened, but he and Margaret McDuffy were going to the prom together. He hadn't planned on going at all, but Margaret had mentioned it off-handed several times while they were working on the mural. Things got twisted around until it seemed he asked her. He didn't mind really and she'd be devastated if he tried to back out now. Besides, he genuinely enjoyed her company and they were certainly spending a lot of time together. The mural had turned out to be a tremendous job, taking many hours to complete, especially since the rest of the co-called artistic committee were less than dedicated. Luke managed to spend some time after school, and as it neared completion, he was surprised how professional it looked.

One morning about two weeks before the prom, Margaret waited for him outside the art room, looking red-faced and breathless. She blurted out her request as though she had rehearsed it many times. "My Aunt Betty wants you to come over for supper some night soon so she can meet you before prom. Don't worry, I already told her you'd probably say no." She paused then to take a breath, finally allowing him a chance to say something.

"Yes, I can come over and let her look me over," he said, grinning.

Margaret was shocked, obviously surprised he actually said yes. Arrangements were made for him to come next Friday night. "But remember," she kept saying, "you don't have to come if you don't want to."

* * * * * *

On the appointed night, he was more curious than nervous. The elderly Miss McDuffy had quite the reputation around the community for being difficult at times. Everyone gave her credit for at least attempting to raise her grandniece since infancy after her parents were killed in a car accident. The fact that the girl had always been a bit strange was believed to be the aunt's fault because of her refusal to accept modern changes in fashion and attitudes. My goodness, everyone whispered, she didn't even let the poor girl shave her legs.

Luke was aware of all this as he made his way to their place that night. The McDuffy farm bordered the Winston's place along the southern ridge. Luke knew of a path that led up the bluff to their backyard. Thomas teased him that he took the shortcut through the woods because he didn't want anyone to know he was seeing such an ugly girl. Luke ignored him. He knew the plump, round-faced girl was no Miss America, but he liked talking to her and was not at all put off by her aunt's request that he present himself for her inspection.

Margaret was in a state of sheer befuddlement when she answered the door, more red-faced than usual. She was perspiring so heavily that her glasses appeared to be steamed over. Luke grinned, trying to reassure her as she ushered him into the kitchen. Miss McDuffy instructed him to sit down across from her at the kitchen table so they could talk while Margaret finished supper.

Margaret bristled. "Aunt Betty, why don't you sit in the living room?"

"Oh no, this is fine," Luke said. "We can sit here."

"She's just nervous, ya' know," Miss McDuffy whispered. "She's afraid I'm gonna say somethin' foolish. Well, I'm an old

178

lady so I've got an excuse, don't ya' think?"

Luke liked his hostess immediately. It was easy to see where Margaret got her short, angular frame and bright, intense eyes.

They had baked fish for supper because Miss McDuffy believed in the old ways. "If we were supposed to give up meat on Fridays for all those years, I see no reason to stop doing it now," she said. After the meal, Luke helped Margaret clean up the dishes while the old lady asked him blunt questions about his family and background.

"Well," she said, "that old house finally got what it was built for – a family with a whole bunch of kids."

"Really," Luke asked. "What makes you say that?"

"Cause I can remember when that house was built like it was yesterday. I was just a little girl. I was interested in watching them put up such a grand place. Me and my brother, Freddy, would sneak over there – probably the same back trail you took coming here tonight, Luke. We'd go over there and just watch 'em for hours. Old Cap'n Weatherly brought in the best carpenters and materials upriver from St. Louie. I can still see him pacin' back n' forth with his hands clinched tight behind his back. He saw to every detail. To be sure, his house was going to look like those big plantation houses in the South. And it was beautiful all right, but it never brought him the happiness it was s'pose ta. Talk was, the place was doomed from the day he first laid eyes on it. Some even said he was in league with the devil himself so he'd never find any peace – not in that house anyway."

"The devil? In my house?" Luke gulped.

"Yes, you see, that place already had a history by that time. Different people owned the place since the time of early settlement in these parts, but no one ever made a go of it. There was always some kind of trouble so it was sold a lot. But in the spring of 1905 – I remember that was the year I started school – three families of Fox Indians arrived from a reservation out West somewhere. When they got here they said that the land, the place at the top of the hill where the house is now, had been some kind of special holy place for their tribe for generations, right up to the time their people got chased off. They were supposed to be direct descendants of the old chiefs or somethin'. I guess they worked and saved for years until they had enough money to buy the place."

"Indians bought our land? So what happened?" Luke settled into a chair across from his host.

The old lady paused a minute, gathering her thoughts, remembering things she hadn't thought about in years. She turned her mind back to a time when she was a small child, running and playing in the endless woods. "Those poor people were mistreated and blamed for everything that went wrong in the whole county," she continued. "They were snubbed and ridiculed so they mostly kept to themselves. They were called heathens and all sorts of awful things. Us kids were forbidden to go near the place, but me and Freddy, well, we didn't have any idea what any of that meant and we made friends with the Indian kids. Ah, they told such great stories and taught us wonderful things about the woods and the wild animals -- things my dad didn't even know." Once again her voice faded as remembered the Indian children's stories why the timber wolf cries so or why the leaves on the trees turn upside down when the rain is coming.

"Anyway, those three years they were here were bad times in these parts. Bad floods ever' spring, real hard winters. Some of the folks got it in their heads that the Indians were somehow to blame – that their strange chants and dances were evil. People started saying the Indians were aiming for all the farmers to fail so they'd be forced to sell. And then new Indian families would buy up more and more land, until pretty soon this town wouldn't be no place for decent Christian folks to live any more." Miss McDuffy struggled to find the words to explain to these young people, born in a different age of scientific technology, how people 60 years ago could be so desperate and frightened that they could blame their misfortunes on something so mysterious.

"So, when Cap'n Weatherly landed in town one day and announced he was here to buy that same land the Indians had, the people acted like he was their deliverer. He was really something, so handsome with all his fine ways and pockets full of money. He had his new bride along --a frail, pretty young thing from down South somewhere. He said he had been piloting on the river for twenty years and had often noticed that rocky hilltop shining in the sunlight when he came around that sharp bend in the river south of your place. And he knew the bottomland around here was the best there was. So when he decided to leave the river and settle down, he knew the perfect spot. He wanted many children so he planned to build a grand mansion."

"But the Indians wouldn't sell. Wouldn't even consider it, which of course, infuriated the Captain. So, him and his wife took up residence in town and spread his money around. He paid the merchants to stop doing any more business with the Indians. The rumors became more vicious than ever, probably started by Weatherly himself. They blamed ever' thing on those poor Indians, from the mayor's arthritis to babies born stillborn. Well, that next spring, one of the Indian children died and two of the families went back to the reservation. Maybe they were planning to get more money or supplies, I don't know.

"They left one family behind? By themselves?" Margaret asked. "Knowing this town, I bet there was trouble."

"Yep, there sure was. That spring, my father and some of the other farmers were missing cattle. They were sure the Indians were stealing 'em so they called a town meeting. I was afraid for them Indians and I laid awake, waiting for my dad. He came back late and his words were slurred. I knew he'd been drinking. The next day I heard that the Indian man had been beaten real bad, but he wouldn't admit to stealing no cattle. When I asked my papa about it, he looked me straight in the eye and said he had nothin' to do with it. And then he spanked me hard for being so disrespectful. Never could figure out why he did that – the spanking, I mean."

"The next night the church burnt to the ground and human remains were found. It was ol' Charlie Dorfmann, the town drunk. He probably wondered in there to get out of the rain since his woman wouldn't let him in their house 'til he was sober. The town went crazy. They said the Indian did it. Ol' Charlie probably did it hisself but nobody said nothin' about that. By the next night, people were out of control -- they came on our yard with torches and big talk. They yelled for my father to go with 'em but he said no. He'd had enough."

"So they went over there, hollerin' and screamin' for the Indian to come out. And when he didn't, they burned down his barn and were aiming to torch the cabin, too. They dragged him out and hanged him – right there on that big oak tree by the bluff. His poor wife and three little boys were standing there watching. Can you imagine such a thing?" She shuddered as though the whole horrifying spectacle had just happened yesterday.

"Oh, my God, Aunt Betty. They hung him? How come I never heard this story before?"

"Because most of the people around here were ashamed. It was cold-hearted murder, it was. His poor wife signed over the deed in return for some money and a guarantee of safe passage for her and her three children out of town and back to the reservation. Captain Weatherly got the land and started building his big house. His wife was sickly – couldn't tolerate this climate very good, I guess. She was never able to give the Captain any children. She lost three sons – some folks said they were like the three little boys who watched their papa hang that night. She died in childbirth with the third baby. After that, the Captain went rantin' and ravin' crazy. That big ol' house never hardly had no lights on anymore and the servants told stories of how the Captain saw demons and ghosts." She stopped then. There were more stories about the captain and his house but then she remembered that her young guest now lived there. "Course, I never did believe any of that. Anyway, one day the Captain just up and got on a riverboat docked in town and was never heard from again."

"And let me tell ya' something, Luke, I've lived here all my life. And I've seen people come and go. That place was sold time after time. 'Course, so have a lot of other farms around here. But one thing I know for sure 'cause I seen it with my own eyes – that next spring when all the trees leafed out, nothin' grew on that branch where they hung that poor Indian. It was deader than a doornail, but the rest of the tree was fine. The Captain ordered it cut off. But you can still see the scar on that tree."

* * * * * *

Luke repeated the tale to his family late that night. The younger ones were already in bed and Matthew had gone into town for a couple of drinks after supper. They sat spellbound as he told of the Indian families forced off the land and the building of this house by some seedy, mysterious riverboat captain. They tried to deny it but the story left them feeling uncomfortably cold. Even Sonny seemed restless and uneasy as he listened.

"C'mon, lets go see it," whispered Mack, grinning. He made it sound more like a challenge than an invitation.

"Mack!" Johnny cried. "It's dark out there!" They were all suddenly aware of the whining winds and creaking timbers.

"Nah, come on!" pushed Mack. "You guys aren't scared, are you?" He grabbed the flashlight and headed out. The others followed him, staying close together. They knew exactly which tree Miss McDuffy was talking about. When they stood beneath it, they gazed up at the massive thing with renewed amazement. Mack scanned the trunk with the light and there it was – a knarled scar where the fabled branch had been.

"Look!" Thomas said. "You can see an Indian's head, like on those old nickels."

"Oh, come on!" they all groaned. "You're seeing things."

A gust of wind seized the tree and its branches seemed to bend toward them. They rushed back to the safe haven of the kitchen and sat around the table for a long time. No one seemed to be in any hurry to go upstairs to bed.

"But you know what?" Andrew said. "Sometimes I do feel a sort of presence here, but it's never frightened me."

"Sure," added Luke. "I've read stories about this sort of thing. Ghosts don't have to be bad. Maybe our ghosts are of the friendly variety." Everyone laughed, though a bit anxiously.

"At least this explains some of the weird questions we've been getting around town," Mack said after a long period of silence. "You know, like, 'Heard any strange noises?' or 'Seen any ghosts lately?' I thought they were just trying to give us a hard time."

"Well," Andrew remarked quietly. "Regardless of what anyone says – ghosts or no ghosts, it'll take a lot to get our father out of this place."

"Yeah, ghosts," Mack called, talking toward the ceiling as though addressing unseen spirits. "You got quite a fight on your hands if you think you're gonna scare off our old man!" Everyone laughed again, this time a little more easily.

But everyone lingered around the table late that night and when they did finally go upstairs, they went in pairs.

* * * * * *

Much later, when the wind was full of night noises and the moon shone so brightly that any passing cloud cast an especially dark shadow across the house on the hill, a solitary, statuesque figure stood at the edge of the bluff. The half naked phantom defied the cold night air, his long dark hair whipping wildly in the wind, standing unafraid and unyielding, until the wind quieted and the clouds no longer interfered with the shroud of light glowing upon this place.

* * * * * *

It's amazing how, in the warm reassuring light of day, a tree is merely a tree, and the frightening sounds of the night are nearly forgotten. At breakfast, Luke told Matthew an abbreviated version of Miss McDuffy's story. It sounded much less mysterious over eggs and bacon. Matthew laughed, of course, saying he had picked up inferences of the storied legacy of their new home. He dismissed it all as harmless, small town folklore. But he did take his second cup of coffee outside and sat beneath the old oak tree. The others followed him, gazing up at it as it swayed harmlessly in the gentle breezes. They sat perched on the felled logs, sister trunks of their infamous tree.

"Wonder how old it is," Andrew asked. "It had to be a sizable tree sixty years ago so it has to be over a hundred years old."

"If this tree could talk." Matthew sipped his coffee. "Think of the stories it could tell."

"It felt like it was talking last night," Mack said, laughing.

So another tradition began. On warm mornings, with a couple of hours of work already done, Matthew would lead his troupe to the rocky place. They would sit and plan the day's work and survey the fruits of their labor of days gone by. Matthew never grew tired of gazing at the fields that stretched before him. Straddling the rough, splintery perch, he felt like a king on his throne, surveying his kingdom.

He was getting more and more impatient for the planting to begin. Sonny explained that even though much of the preliminary work was completed they still had to wait for the soil to warm, a purely natural phenomena that could not be altered or rushed by Matthew's money or his persistence.

Chapter 20

When prom night actually arrived, Luke had to admit he was a little excited. The gym, especially the mural, looked wonderful, and Margaret's sheer rapture was contagious. Annie insisted that he rent a tux with a white dinner jacket and order a pretty orchid corsage.

At the appointed hour, Annie came up to his room to see if he was ready. She fussed over him, fixing his tie and adjusting his cummerbund. She knew his brothers had been heckling him about his choice of dates, but she was proud of Luke for finding a lovely swan hidden inside an ugly duckling. Annie had spoken to Margaret at Mass and found her to be quite sweet.

She stood back and surveyed her brother. "You look very handsome," she smiled. "I wish Mama was her to see you. She always thought you needed to get out more and meet girls. And I think she'd approve of your choice."

"Oh, you do, huh." He grinned a little sheepishly. "Well, with Margaret I don't have to worry about finding something to talk about. She's good at that."

Annie gave him a sisterly kiss, reminding him to grab the corsage out of the refrigerator on his way out. His chauffeur, Mack, was waiting to take him to McDuffy's. Luke didn't have his license so Margaret was going to have to drive. That was a little embarrassing, but he'd survive.

He was a little early but he supposed she'd be pacing by

now. Miss McDuffy opened the door, smiling somewhat tersely, Luke thought, considering how friendly she was the other night when he came for supper.

"My niece is dressed but I think she wants to make a grand entrance or something," she said, shrugging her shoulders. "Now you know she is a damn good driver and she'll be doing all the driving tonight, right?" She took her shawl and sank down in her rocker. "Now you don't seem the type, but I'm tellin' ya' anyway. Don't try no funny business. This is her first date, ya' know."

"Aunt Betty!" Margaret shrieked from somewhere in the back of the house. She walked in then, trying to be elegant and graceful although those were by far the highest shoes she had ever worn. Her dress was lovely with a lacy jacket draped over her shoulders. Luke gasped appropriately which made her blush. He noticed right away she wasn't wearing her glasses, which probably explained why she nearly walked into the coffee table as she came across the room. Luke stiffled his smile as he knew how self-conscience she was about needing such thick lenses. He remembered the flower and he felt her trembling as he pinned it on. She had a boutonnière for him but she asked her grandmother to pin it on. Considering her limited vision, he was just as glad she had chosen that route.

They drove to the high school. Luke's earlier prophesy that they'd have no trouble talking proved false. She was too nervous. Perhaps the fact that she was driving on her first date bothered her more than it did Luke because she parked the car in the back corner of the lot. Unfortunately, that meant she had further to walk.

They, along with all the other young guests, were sent to the library where they mingled and drank some much-too-sweet punch. After much oohing and awing over dresses, hair-dos, and such, dinner was finally announced. The doors to the gym were swung open after weeks of secrecy. With the help of some well-placed lighting, cardboard Roman columns and plastic greenery, the place didn't look so much like a gym anymore. There was a false ceiling of blue and white streamers shimmering above them and even a bubbling fountain wishing well in the corner. All of this was designed to transport the fashionable ladies and gentlemen to an unforgettable night on the "Streets of Venice".

Luke and Margaret ate quietly. He noticed Margaret blushing from time to time when she saw her girlfriends, who were un-escorted, whispering and looking her direction. No matter how much he tried to put her at ease, he could see how nervous she was. The dishes were taken away and everyone turned their chairs toward the dais.

Raymond Harvey, the junior class president, was the emcee for the evening. He welcomed the faculty and senior class guests. Luke sat back and patted the carefully worded note tucked in his pocket. At the appropriate time he would have it delivered to the unsuspecting master of ceremonies. He put his arm around the back of Margaret's chair.

An important part of the prom program was the prophecy, prepared by a committee of juniors in which the future of each of the seniors was predicted. Most were comical but some bordered on cruel. Luke's name was mentioned in passing, something about him becoming a great artist who would be confused sometimes as to whether he should paint cornfields or skyscrapers.

Next was the senior class will, a tongue-in-cheek listing of gifts banqueted to lower classmen from the seniors. Again, some were funny, but many were less than kind. Luke sensed Margaret becoming increasingly tense as she waited for her name to be mentioned. She warned Luke that it might be a zinger. Then it came: "Annette Applegate wills the entire school library and her title as 'Class Brain' to Margaret McDuffy. Also, Annette would like to leave her the name of the optometrist who fitted her contacts." The two girls looked at each other across the room and shrugged their shoulders – it could have been much worse.

As the program appeared to be nearing completion, Luke excused himself and walked to the rear of the room where the underclassmen waitresses were hugging the wall, listening. He approached one he knew not to be at all shy and whispered something in her ear. He passed the note to her and returned to his seat to watch his bit of drama unfold.

Raymond waited for the applause to die down after the will

was read, preparing to make a few closing statements. Just as he was about to speak, the note was delivered. Luke felt no pity whatsoever as Raymond struggled to regain his composure as half the school looked on. Luke hated these egotistical types who always seemed to get their kicks by putting down others.

Raymond was destined for great things -- everyone said so. His father had some political pull in the area and was quite proud that his son was headed for West Point after high school. It was generally felt that the young man was well suited for such an honor. He excelled physically and scholastically. Well then, wondered Luke, why was this future general cheating in chemistry class – not once, but twice. The first time was a quiz and Luke thought he was probably mistaken. But the second time, he looked over to see Raymond staring at his answer sheet. Luke waited for him in the hallway after class.

He grabbed Raymond's arm as he went by. "I'm surprised at you, Raymond," he said, smiling deceptively calmly. "Why would you cheat on a chemistry test?"

"Cheat? Are you crazy?" the felon protested.

"I'm sure it would be easy to prove if the teacher compares papers. Too bad for you, I made a few really stupid mistakes."

"Hey man, I didn't have a chance to study," Raymond pleaded. "We got home real late from the track meet last night. Just ask your brother."

Luke considered his options carefully. Since he was the new kid in town it probably wouldn't be real smart to get one of the school's stars in trouble. "Alright, I'm not going to fink on you, not now at least," he said. "But just remember, you owe me big. And don't ever cheat off me again!" Later that night, when he and Margaret were working late on the artwork for the prom, he realized he had the perfect opportunity to collect on Raymond's IOU.

Raymond thrust the note into his pocket and began reading the long list of committee's and individuals responsible for the success of the evening. Luke knew the suddenly sweating host was going to have to be careful because his date, Cheryl Swanson, who had been the chairperson of the art committee, was sitting nearby. Raymond hesitated for a moment and drank a sip of water. Then he said, "And we are certainly impressed with all the art work on display here tonight. I am told that much of the credit goes to Margaret McDuffy who designed the murals and wall decorations that you see here tonight."

Many people looked at each other like they thought Raymond must have made a mistake. Others, who knew he was telling the truth, applauded enthusiastically. Margaret smiled, but Raymond's date was not amused.

"You had something to do with this, didn't you," exclaimed Margaret, her face beaming. "What was in that note?"

"Wouldn't you just love to know!" Luke laughed.

The program was over, and the tables and chairs were cleared away. A little four-piece band was now ready to take over the show. Luke and Margaret found a corner table where they could sit and observe the festivities. A full half hour after Raymond's announcement, Margaret's smile had not faded. She seemed to have recovered some of that old spark.

The band opened with a loud, albeit barely recognizable, version of Neil Diamond's "Sweet Caroline," followed by a slower "Crystal Blue Persuasion."

"Would you like to dance, Margaret?" Luke asked. He hoped she could manage a slow dance with those shoes. He led her onto the dance floor, feeling her tremble as she touched her hand to his shoulder. Luke sang along as he gently propelled her around the dance floor.

> *Crystal blue persuasion*
> *It's a new vibration*
> *Crystal blue persuasion*
> *Crystal blue persuasion*

> *Maybe tomorrow when He looks down*
> *Every green field and every town*
> *All of his children, every nation*
> *There'll be peace and good brotherhood*

Luke thought the music might start Margaret talking about pollution or world peace, two of her favorite topics, but she was concentrating so hard on dancing that she couldn't speak. The dance floor filled with the slower song so the band launched into another ballad, Peter, Paul, and Mary's "Leaving on a Jet Plane." Luke and Margaret limped their way through it, but were happy to return to their table when the band exploded into a raucous rendition of "Mama Told Me Not To Come." Luke watched the adult chaperons to see if anyone objected to the lyrics. Mr. Rausch and his staff were so busy standing guard over the punch bowl and making sure that no couple was dancing too close, that they weren't listening.

Want some whiskey in your water?
Sugar in your tea?
What's all the crazy questions you're asking me?
This is the craziest party I've ever seen
Don't turn on the light cause I don't wanna see.

Everyone seemed to be having fun, so the band tried "Eli's Coming" and "Proud Mary." When the band finally took a break after the first set, a Simon & Garfunkel album played softly over the loud speaker, leading off with a much more subdued, "Bridge Over Troubled Water."

"That band is awful," Luke said. "I can't believe those kids are actually enjoying it. If my brother was here he'd probably march up there, take that fat drummer's sticks right out of his hands, and have him arrested for impersonating a 'percussionist'."

"I'd definitely agree with Thomas. But they were cheap which was one of the main criteria for hiring them. And I don't think it's the music that has everyone all giddy. It's whatever is in those little flasks they're passing around. And there's probably a woodsey later on tonight, too."

"A 'woodsey'? What's that? A local colloquialism, no doubt."

"Oh yes, very local. I don't think you'd find it in Webster's. But let me see. Hmmmm." She thought for a minute, trying to assimilate a proper definition. "It is when a person or persons, usually minors, procure large quantities of liquid refreshment, usually cheap beer. And said persons meet at some

190

pre-arranged site, usually in some secluded, wooded area, and consume said beverages and engages-- er, well-- in whatever extracurricular activities which might ensue." She finished a little red-faced, but Luke was laughing.

"Beer, huh? You ever tasted it?"

"Beer? Oh, no. Aunt Betty would have a fit. Her father drank and she'd kill me if she ever found out I came near the stuff."

"Well, it is pretty foul. My dad lets us taste a little sometimes. He claims it's an acquired taste, whatever that means." They sat and watched a little longer until suddenly Luke stood up, took her hand to lead her out. "C'mon, I know where there's more beer than these punks could ever dream of, and it's not cheap, either. My dad won't miss a can or two. Miss McDuffy, how would you like to taste your first can of beer? What your Aunt Betty don't know, won't hurt her, right?"

Margaret knew she should protest, but she didn't want to. Luke escorted her to her car and motioned for her to slide over. She handed him the car keys without a second thought. "It can't be too much different than driving a tractor, can it? I'll be careful, honest!" She didn't care. He could have said let's hop a jet to Tahiti and she would have said yes. She felt him sitting close to her, flashing that wonderful grin of his. She hoped there was at least someone who noticed them speeding away, sitting side-by side like all the other couples.

They drove out of town talking easily about beer and beer drinkers they have known. When they arrived at Luke's place, he turned into the driveway slowly and turned out the lights as he drove up the hill. He whispered for her to wait while he ducked inside his dad's office and took out a six-pack from the little refrigerator. When he came out, he took her hand again and lead her to the gazebo. Leaning on his arm, she hopped along, taking off those awful shoes. The cool stone felt refreshing to her tormented feet. Luke bowed and dusted off a place for her to sit, and then popped open a can for her and one for himself.

"We should make a toast," he said in mocked solemnity, lifting his can. "To new experiences! To 'Springtime in Venice'!" They clicked cans, saying, "Here! Here!" and then

Luke leaned back against a post and watched her take her first swallow. He laughed when she gagged and nearly spit it out.

"Oh, that's awful," she cried. But she took another sip, determined to drink the vile stuff.

They both looked up and noticed the moon, which was nearly full and shining so brightly that they could see the outlines of the buildings and the timber shrouded in a hazy glow. It seemed to Margaret that the whole world was enchanted. It was a warm evening, but her nervousness and the cold beer made her shiver a little. He took off his coat and wrapped it around her shoulders. "I didn't know this little gazebo was here," she said. "I've lived next to this place all my life and always imagined that the inside must be beautiful."

"Nah, it's pretty old and creaky, but it's home sweet home. Everything needs work – everything. My poor sister has lists of things that need fixing, but Pop and Sonny just keep putting her off. All they're concerned with right now is getting the planting done." He reached up and shook loose a board that was hanging above him. "This should be white with thick green vines growing all over it, don't you think? Well, maybe someday."

"So, you're staying? I mean, the talk around town is that you're a bunch of discontented, rich people who came out here on a whim. Everyone's wondering if you'll stay."

"Ha!" laughed Luke. "Anyone who says that has never met my father. He's serious about staying, all right. And he's stubborn enough to pull it off. Oh sure, this place is a dump right now, but he's decided it's what he wants whether we like it or not!"

"But you do like it here, don't you, Luke? I mean, I've never heard you say anything like you hated it or that you wanted to go back East – right?"

"No, no, I like it here. But I'm in the minority, I think. Not that it really matters what we think. My dad's not listening to anyone."

"Didn't you know? My aunt and your father belong to this exclusive club – the I-know-what's best-for-you-club. At least you're lucky cause you're graduating in four weeks. What are you going to do then? You're not going away to school or anything

192

are you?" Shy, wistful hope was ringing in her voice, although she was trying to sound casual.

He didn't answer at first. The sudden clouded look on his face frightened her. "I'm not sure I have much choice," he said. "I'll be eighteen in two weeks." The reality of that didn't need explaining.

Margaret's heart seemed to skip a beat at that instant. Vietnam had always seemed unreal to her. But here it was, crashing down into this night of nights. "Oh Luke, not you! You couldn't do it, could you? Go to war?"

"Somebody has to do it, right? Isn't it like a duty? That's what my old man says. Where would we be if his generation didn't fight World War II?"

"It's not the same, and you know it. We have no business over there."

"I don't know what I believe. Here's my dad constantly preaching all this patriotism stuff, but Mack says its all a bunch of bull. He'll never go. And Andrew – he can't go. He's going to be a priest. So that leaves me, I guess."

"So all of this is because of your dad? What do you want, Luke?"

"I have no idea. Guess that comes from being born into a family with money. I don't have any driving ambitions. Or at least I didn't think so until we came out here. I really like the idea of farming, living out here in the country."

His mood changed suddenly then and he leaped to his feet. "Hey, you want to see a really cool spot I found back in the timber? This is supposed to be a woodsey, isn't it? C'mon," he insisted, pulling her to her feet. "What about your dress?"

"I have some jeans and a sweater in the trunk." She got her things out of the trunk and soon her dress was laying in heap on the backseat.

He started up the car and drove down the bottom road until he spotted his secret trail. He lead her down the pathway until they came to a creek. He flashed the light on the plank bridge he had built. Bowing deeply, he announced, "The draw bridge is down, my lady." She curtsied and danced across. He took her hand and helped her up a short, steep incline until they stood in a large clearing.

"See, it's a huge rock surface," he said, pounding his foot to punctuate his words. "Guess some glacier dumped it here. I found it one day when I was looking for those damn cows. I don't know if you can see it but there's a wide break in the trees so you can see all the way to the river." He took the blanket he brought from the car and spread it out so they could sit. He opened two more beers. "I think this would be a great spot for a cabin -- a nice A-frame cabin with lots of windows and fireplaces." He knelt on his knees and stretched his arms out dramatically. "This could be my private kingdom. Wouldn't need to go anywhere or do anything else – just live out my days right here and live happily ever after."

"King Lucas, aye? Just live here in your castle and slay any dragons that try to cross your moat. Well, let me tell you, sir, the local aristocracy does not look kindly upon strangers laying claim to parcels of our kingdom. First, you must be deemed suitable. Come hither and be knighted." She picked up a nearby stick. With a great dramatic flourish, Luke knelt before her. "Sir Lucas, because you have proven yourself to be a Doer of Good Deeds, rescuer of maidens in distress, and chivalrous and kind, I pronounce you King Lucas, King of the Realm of the, er-- Rocky Castle." She touched his shoulders softly as she spoke. The deed having been completed, they both collapsed onto the blanket, laughing. "Oh God, I've never acted so silly in my whole life. You got another beer?"

"Sure do. Didn't take us long to acquire the taste, did it?" He rolled over onto his back and stretched out, looking up at the night sky. Margaret was looking up, too, thinking that if she had wished upon a million stars, she could never have wished for anything more wonderful than tonight.

"What about you?" he asked after a long pause. "Now that my future has been settled and I've been solidly installed as Lord and Master of my kingdom here, what are your plans?"

"Me? I do think about it a lot. I want to go to college, obviously. I'd love to go to someplace like Berkeley or Radcliffe – just go as far away from here as possible. But I won't, of course. I have to stay close to my Aunt Betty. I'm all she has.

She raised me, you know, so I have to take care of her now."

"You hypocrite! You give me hell because I feel I have to do something for my dad. But you're doing the same thing. It's a bunch of bull anyway, you know. If you were free – to do anything or go anywhere you wanted, where would you go? You'd be scared shitless – we all would."

"I would not! I'd go to some exotic place, let my hair grow and walk around bare-footed. Live free and careless, even, be open to new experiences."

"How come you can't do all that here?"

"It's not possible. Nothing spectacular could ever happen to me here cause I could never get out of the rut I'm in. None of the kids here like me cause I'm too smart. But school is easy for me and it's the only thing that keeps me from being totally bored. I can't change my hair or anything cause I've looked like this for so long everyone would just laugh at me if I tried to change now." She sighed deeply. He seemed interested, so she continued.

"And besides, you can't believe how strict my aunt is about everything. I mean, I love her dearly but she just doesn't understand. I'm always gonna be remembered as the girl with the thick glasses, dumb clothes, and sensible shoes." Her exasperation was almost comical, and she knew it. She started giggling again, the beer making her feel a little giddy and dizzy.

"God! I must be a real creep to even be seen with you!" Luke teased. "But you know what I think? I think you're probably suffering from the grass-is-greener syndrome. It's not an uncommon phenomenon, you know. It's like your life is on hold. You just can't wait to get out in the big world and prove something – to yourself, mostly."

"How come you aren't anxious to get out on your own and try out your wings? You're so sensible and practical all the time. I thought artists were supposed to be romantics."

He laughed softly. "So, that proves it once and for all – I'll never be a great artist. I'm the down to earth sort. I paint only what's real." He shrugged his shoulders, still smiling. "Well, anyway," he said, "it's getting late. We probably should go, Maggie – you don't mind if I call you that, do you?"

"No, I don't mind," she purred. "That was my dad's pet

name for me when I was a baby. Just don't say it around school. I think 'Margaret' probably fits my image better." She gathered up her things as she talked. But when she looked up, he was suddenly very close and she realized he wanted to kiss her. She could scarcely breath when he reached out and drew her nearer. And then their lips touched. It was not a long kiss, but a kiss just the same. She felt a wild flutter in her stomach like she had just gone over the top of a Ferris wheel.

She didn't know how she was supposed to react or what to say, but he handled it masterfully. He took her hand and helped her to her feet. They both laughed as they found they were a little drunk. He put his arm around her quivering shoulders and they stood for a moment, gazing out over the misty countryside. It was bathed in silky moonlight, looking like a still-life painting of some mystical place. But then they returned to the real world.

* * * * * *

Maggie was so happy and excited that she hardly slept that night. She played the wonderful events over and over again in her mind, trying to memorize every word and gesture. It was the night her first love gave her a first kiss and taken her to a private, magical place. And for days and weeks, whenever she thought of their night together in their stony kingdom, there was one special song that kept playing in her mind:

> *In truth there's simply not*
> *A more congenial spot*
> *For happily ever-aftering*
> *Than here in Camelot."*

Chapter 21

Matthew's drinking buddies at the Pub reminded him it was only early May and there was no reason to panic. However, he was getting more short tempered and frustrated as the ground preparation and actual planting was taking twice as long as he expected. The gross inadequacies of his crew was hindering their progress. He and Mack argued daily, and Andrew, although somewhat more congenial, was not coping with the situation very well either. He longed for privacy as much as his flamboyant brother craved the all night parties. They were both waiting for summer to pass so they could return home.

Their dependence on Sonny didn't seem to lessen as the weeks went by. It was no wonder he had insisted on his own separate living quarters. "Sonny's shed", as it was called, was the only place of solitude he had. He did have one companion. The burly, unsociable dog chose Sonny to befriend. "Mutt" as Sonny called her, followed him everywhere, whether it was in the yard or round after round behind the tractor in the fields. It was rumored that Mutt and her five puppies had taken up residence in Sonny's shed during one cold, rainy night. No one knew for sure since they were never invited inside.

Annie began noticing that Sonny had another unlikely devotee. Every since that day in the way-side park when Sonny had bundled up Joey and taken him for that walk, the little boy's face would light up every time Sonny walked into the room. At first glance, it appeared that the affection was non-reciprocated, but Annie caught glimpses of Sonny bending over the boy, quietly talking to him. On rare occasions he even picked Joey up and cradled him clumsily in his lap. It remained a mystery to her why he paid any attention to this child. She suspected it was probably because Joey never bothered him with constant problems.

Annie certainly did not share her father or anyone else's high opinion of Sonny Jackson. He never ceased to annoy her. One particular source of irritation was his indifference toward her garden. She had so many questions and tried to talk with him at dinner one Saturday afternoon, but he snapped at her rudely. True, they were having a bad day. One of the tractors was broken and the gas truck hadn't showed up to fill up their diesel barrel, so they were running low. Plus, the dark clouds in the west were threatening stormy weather.

Annie was still determined to put in her garden, with or without Sonny's help. It seemed to her that her garden should be a high priority, too. Danny and Peter were her only available draftees in this enterprise. The three of them worked all afternoon, attacking the incessant weeds, which seemed to thrive much better than her vegetables. They began making some progress when word was dispatched from the house that Joey had messed himself and Thomas refused to change him. Annie had no choice but to throw down her hoe and stomp off toward the house. "Don't stop working," she called. "I'll be back in a minute."

Since the boys were less than enthusiastic about doing battle with the bumper crop of weeds, they chose a more entertaining sport. From her upstairs window Annie could see them sword fighting with the sharp hoes, jabbing and lunging at each other. She was just going to yell at them to stop when she heard Peter scream, and both boys came running toward the house. She could see blood dripping from his hand even at this distance. As she reached for a towel to wrap the wound, she dispatched the frightened Danny to fetch Sonny.

Just a few minutes later, the tractor came roaring up the hill full throttle. Sonny tore into the kitchen just as Annie was applying a dressing. Sonny stood motionless in the doorway, staring "You sent Danny to get me for this? A little band-aid cut?" he demanded, his face turning a darker shade of purple.

"It was bleeding very badly! How was I supposed to know it wasn't deep?" she sputtered, trying to vindicate herself.

Again, he stood for a long moment, just glaring at them. "What the hell do you think I am – your goddamn nursemaid?" He was yelling now. "Do I have to wipe everybody's butts around here? And you two. What in the hell were you doing out there? These are tools!" He shook a hoe in their faces. "You've been warned about this kind of shit before. Here, take these and get to work!" He thrust the hoe back into the boy's hand and stormed out, slamming the door behind him.

Left in the wake of the sudden triad, the boys looked as

though they were going to cry, but trudged back to work. Annie sat a while longer, shocked at first, but then angry. No one had ever talked to her or any member of the family like that before. How dare he use that tone and language with them. How was she supposed to know the boy wasn't going to bleed to death? She intended to speak to her father about this, but she doubted he'd do anything. They all knew that their father was convinced that without Sonny, they didn't have a chance of making it. However, it was also true that without this family, Sonny would still be pushing a broom instead of driving $75,000 tractors.

Her anger began to ebb as she worked in the warm, afternoon sun. The tiny beans, peas, and cucumber seeds were carefully placed in the furrow she made along the string stretched between two stakes as Sonny had taught her. She patted the dirt over the seeds as though she was tucking a child into bed. Her hands were raw and caked with mud, but she didn't mind. She surveyed the day's work and felt a deep sense of accomplishment.

She went happily back to her kitchen and began making a nice supper for her family, humming and smiling as she worked. About 6:00, she noticed John and Thomas doing the chores, apparently alone, telegraphing to Annie that the men were working late in the fields. She fed the little boys and put the baby to bed. Of course by now, the salad was wilted and the meatloaf and vegetables were drying out in the warming oven. The rush of excitement and satisfaction was now giving way to the aches and pains invading her body. Dark was descending over the land and the house was quiet. She sat on the back porch, becoming angrier the longer she waited.

Two hours later, the incessant humming of the machines became nearer as they made their way up the hill. She could hear her father and the others yelling at each other over the roar of the engines. Then there was silence and they came lumbering into the kitchen. They hadn't even noticed her sitting there and she ignored her father's calls until he got so loud she was afraid he'd wake up the children. "I'm out here!" she called. "What do you want?"

"You got a bunch of starving, hard-working men here. How about some supper?" He was obviously in a great mood.

They must have finished planting, at long last.

She didn't budge. "There's cold meatloaf for sandwiches. Feel free to help yourselves."

"Damn it, girl!" Matthew blasted. "We're tired and cold and hungry. Now, come on in here and cook us something hot. Boys, go shower and she'll--"

"No, 'she' won't!" Annie blurted angrily, trouncing into the room. "A nice, hot supper was ready three hours ago, but you missed it! This cook clocked out a long time ago!"

"Now listen here, young lady," started Matthew, as much surprised as he was angry. "We decided just to keep going since we were so close to being done. It's all planted. I am so happy and so proud of your brothers. They worked their asses off."

"Well, so did I! Got half of my garden planted and I would have done more except I thought I had to come in start supper. Maybe next time you'll take five lousy minutes to tell me what's going on around here." She slammed back outside again.

It took a few moments for Matthew to recover enough to speak. "Well, boys," he said, "let's go have supper in town."

Annie sat cross-legged, wrapped in a blanket in the porch swing, listening to them move around the house until they were gone. She sulked a little longer but decided it was stupid to sit out there, freezing to death. She went back inside the dimly lit kitchen and poured herself some hot coffee.

Later, Sonny came in. She could hear him in the mudroom, throwing aside his jacket and washing up at the sink. He went to the refrigerator, stared at its contents but didn't take anything out. Pouring himself a cup of coffee, he noticed her as he turned to sit down.

"Everyone else went into town for supper," she said, sounding defensive already. "Why didn't you go along?"

He stirred his coffee slowly and said, "I had to finish up out there. The boys were having trouble with that damn pump again." He lit a cigarette and slumped in his chair.

Annie looked away, choosing to ignore his obvious state of exhaustion. "If you want something to eat, there's some meatloaf in the oven."

"Nah, I'm not hungry." He took his coffee and cigarette

and got up from his chair slowly. "How's the boy's hand?" he asked as he neared the door.

She was surprised he mentioned it. Could this be an indirect apology? Probably not. "Oh, it's fine, just fine." She followed him to the door. "Ya' know, Sonny, I am trying to be more self-reliant, and I think I'm doing pretty damn good!" In response, he brushed past her and reached for the handle. "Aren't you going to say anything?" she pressed.

"I think I said enough this afternoon," he said as he opened the door. He clearly was in no mood for any meaningful dialog.

She blocked his retreat. "Yeah, you did have a lot to say this afternoon," she cried. "And I was pretty damned mad, too. But you'll be glad to hear that you taught me an important lesson. Don't worry, Mr. Jackson, I won't be bothering you with trivial matters any more." She was glaring at him, but his expression never changed. He disappeared into the night, leaving her angry and alone once again. If she was going to show him as well as every other egocentric male around here, she needed a plan and she knew where to begin.

* * * * * *

As she went about her Sunday morning routine, Annie was still a little icy. Skipping down the stone steps of the church after Mass, she made a surprising announcement. "Daddy, you and the boys are on your own today 'cause Lori Bean and I have plans for the day. I have no idea when I'll be back."

With that the two young ladies were off, giggling as they walked toward Lori's car. Looking equally perplexed, Charlie approached them asking for a ride home for him and his two kids. He had no idea what was going on either.

Annie came home later that evening, still grinning. She kissed her abandoned father on the cheek and asked about his day. But before he could answer, she floated dreamily upstairs.

"If I didn't know better," mused Mack, "I'd guess she was having an affair." He hesitated for a moment and then said, "Nah, it couldn't be."

Her behavior was chalked up to a female whim and not

discussed further. But when she left with Lori Bean for several hours twice more that week, she really had them wondering. When she announced she was leaving again Friday afternoon, Matthew demanded to know where she was going, but Annie just smiled and told him not to worry. "You'll understand soon enough," she sang out happily. She trotted out the door when Lori pulled onto the yard.

The boys and Matthew called after her. "Hey! What about groceries? We're out of everything! What about the baby?" It was useless. She left.

Then about 8:30 that night, the household was aroused by a loud honking. There was an unfamiliar car coming up the driveway. "Hey!" whooped Mack. "It's Annie! My God, my little sister is driving a car!"

"Hello, gentlemen," she called, stepping crisply out of the car, enjoying their gapping stares. "Help me unload these groceries, will you?"

"Where did ya' get the car. When ya' learn to drive?" they all chorused.

"Lori Bean!" deduced Matthew. "She's been teaching you how to drive and took you to get your license, didn't she. But where did you get the car?"

"Isn't it great?" she gushed, beaming. "It's a nine passenger wagon, V-8, automatic transmission, completely rust-proofed. And they gave me a great deal cause I paid cash."

"Cash? What cash?" demanded Matthew, envisioning her writing out a check for the total amount of the car.

"My own money from the trust fund in New York," she explained. "Well, it was my money to spend any way I chose, right?" Then she looked pointedly at Sonny and said, "Now me and the kids won't need anyone to cart us around any more." Sonny didn't acknowledge that comment was directed toward him. He simply picked up an armload of groceries. She realized she wasn't going to get any satisfaction this round either.

It was amazing to Annie how owning something of major value could change your outlook on life. All her life she had been totally provided for, pampered and spoiled. She didn't have to scrimp and save in order to buy it, but she felt like the car was her trophy for accomplishing and contributing. The blisters on her hands and her position in the family structure made her feel as though she was earning some measure of respect. With this car, she felt very independent and self-reliant. It was also a sign that she was one of the adults in this new coalition and a force to be reckoned with.

* * * * * *

It was a Friday night and Matthew wanted to take a quick run down to the bottom before supper. He cajoled Sonny, Mack, and Andrew into riding along. He still hoped his oldest sons would share his sense of accomplishment when they saw the young seedlings sprouting in the fields.

They were gone longer than they intended. They hurried into the kitchen hoping that they would not receive another tongue lashing for being late. But there was no supper cooking and Thomas was there, fussing with the baby. "Hey, where's Annie?" Andrew asked.

Matthew was standing at the sink. "Yeah, her car's gone. Is she gonna leave all the time now?" he asked, sounding annoyed.

"She had to take Danny and Peter into town," muttered Thomas. "God, babies are so hard to feed! Anyway, you won't believe what happened. You know how you told those boys not to play in the weeds and old buildings behind the barn? Well, guess what, they did anyway. The stupid Danny got into a big ol' beehive out there. Should have seen it – Peter came screaming across the yard for Annie. And there came Danny, totally surrounded by this whole swarm of bees. Yuk!" he winced, "it was awful!"

It took an instant for what he was saying to sink in. Matthew recovered first. "Danny's hurt?" he bellowed. "My God! What did she do?"

"Should have seen her!" Thomas exclaimed. "She grabbed a blanket off the washer and ran out there. She wrapped it around him and smothered most of 'em. She and Peter got some stings, but not near as bad as Danny. She loaded them both in the car and told me to watch the kids. She even had me call Dr. Adams' office to tell him what happened and that they were on their way. I haven't heard anything since they left."

The men stood there, staring at each other in total disbelief trying to process what they had just heard.

"I gotta get to town," Matthew said, heading out the door.

"I'll go along," insisted Andrew. And they were gone.

"I knew all that junk out there was gonna be trouble," Sonny said. "I told them damn kids to stay away from there." He stood up then and headed for the door with a look of purpose on his face.

"Where are you doing?" demanded Mack.

"I'm gonna level that son of a bitchin' mess out there!" Mack followed him and together they put the scoop on the front of one the big tractors to bulldoze the whole everything into a giant pile several hundred feet away from the barn. Then they set it on fire. There were several small buildings and two large decaying corncribs. The weeds were so high and tangled it was a wonder the little boys penetrated it.

The flames were still leaping into the dark sky several hours later when Matthew and Annie's cars drove onto the yard. Annie was met by an anxious reception committee.

"Oh, my God!" moaned Mack, looking at his sister's face. It was red and puffy, her eyes nearly swollen shut. Even her arms and hands had welts from bee stings.

"Don't look so shocked. It's not as bad as it looks. Help Daddy with Peter. He got stung, too. Poor Danny. He has to stay overnight in the hospital. Andrew is with him." John helped her walk toward the house. "There's a bag full of medicines in Daddy's truck. I just wanna go to bed." Then she stopped, noticing the fire behind the barn. "What's that?"

"Sonny bulldozed that whole mess and torched it. He's still out there, watching the fire." Annie couldn't help but smile. Leave it to Sonny to take care of the problem.

She didn't remember how she got upstairs, undressed, and into bed. The next thing she knew she awakened to a dimly lighted room. Her clock radio said 1:52. She became aware of a hazy figure sitting in the corner. It was her father, sleeping in the chair. She felt stiff but otherwise not too bad. She threw back the blankets to get up.

Matthew stirred. "You shouldn't be getting up, honey."

"Oh Daddy, I just need to walk a little. I don't feel too bad, honest. Did you call the hospital? How's Danny?"

"He's fine. Fever's down and he's sleeping. He should come home in the morning." Looking very tired and haggard, he sank down on the edge of the bed, running his hands through his hair. "You should have stayed overnight at the hospital, too. But you kept saying, 'I want to go home.' "

"Yeah, I did. Why? Does that surprise you?"

"Well, I thought a nice clean hospital might appeal to you after a couple months in this place." He looked around at the unpainted, un-carpeted room as he spoke. "Maybe I was wrong to bring you all here. I was thinking of myself so much I lost sight of what's really important."

"You'd better not let Mack hear you talk like that," she teased. "You just had a bad scare, that's all. We're fine. Look at what we've accomplished. You should be very proud." She kissed her father on the cheek and said. "Go to bed, Daddy. You're tired. I'm gonna stay up for awhile. Don't worry, okay?"

She walked him down the hallway to his room and kissed him again as she sent him off to bed. She looked in on Peter, who was sleeping soundly. She touched his cheeks and was relieved that they were cool and less swollen.

She went downstairs to the kitchen and found Sonny drinking coffee. There was no open hostility between them since their last run-in, but she hadn't forgiven him for his insufferable arrogance. "Hi. Mind if I join you?"

She reached for a glass, but it slipped from her hand and shattered at her feet. He poured another glass and said, "You'd better sit down." He cleaned up the mess, poured himself another cup of coffee, and sat down again.

"Thank you," she said, feeling a little uneasy as she felt his dark eyes inspecting her. "I'm alright, ya know. You don't have to nursemaid me, really." She emphasized those last words, in obvious reference to that other conversation they'd had days before.

He took a swallow of coffee before he answered. "Well, it worked, didn't it? Getting your license and that car was the best idea you ever had."

"Oh, you're taking credit for that? That was your doing?"

"No, but if I said something to rile you up, then I'm real glad."

Annie started to get angry again, but decided she didn't have the energy. Besides, he wasn't sounding sarcastic or condescending.

"So, what were you trying to do today, driving in that condition?"

"I was careful. I surprised myself, even – I mean, I just reacted. There wasn't time to get help. I didn't even realize I was stung until everyone started fussing over me."

"Well, you did damn good," he said with just a hint of admiration in his voice. "But next time, send someone to find one of us. You went from one extreme to the other. Just settle in the middle somewhere, alright?"

His words and mannerisms caught Annie totally by surprise. She didn't even know how to respond, especially when a small, half-grin stole across his face. She pushed away from the table and moved tentatively toward the stairs. He didn't make a move to assist her. She wasn't surprised. They had reached a new understanding – he'd help her if she fell flat but only long enough to put her back on her feet again and send her on her way.

Chapter 22

Annie's bold bid for independence had not gone unnoticed by anyone, especially Luke and Andrew. Both of them decided they wanted driving licenses as well. Luke talked about it excitedly to Maggie the next morning before school.

"You have to take a test -- a driving test, I mean, in a car, ya' know," she reminded him. "It's not very hard but you should practice a little first." Her mind was churning furiously, trying to think of a way this could lead to spending some time together. It had been three weeks since prom night, and she was disappointed he hadn't asked her out again. "Why don't we take my car into town and you can drive it around?" she asked bluntly, not able to think of a more clever way to approach it.

"Wouldn't that be illegal? I mean, what if we had an accident or something. I don't have a learner's permit and you aren't over 25, right?"

"So what. We won't have an accident," she said trying to sound reckless. "You never do anything unless you can do it well. Don't you want to get your license soon?" That would be so wonderful, she thought. They could drive around town and she'd sit close to him and be like a regular dating couple – if he'd ever get around to asking her out, that is.

Luke phoned her later to ask if she'd like to go out that night. She knew he meant out driving, but she preferred to think of as going out, like on a date. Her aunt made it very clear she did not approve of them going on a school night but didn't forbid it, either.

When Margaret picked him up, he was all slicked up from his after-chores shower and jumped in the car eagerly. She drove to the other side of Shannon Town and turned the driving over to him. She quizzed him from the driver's manual as they drove. They laughed at some of his incredibly stupid answers. The radio dial was set on her aunt's favorite FM station.

"I can change the station if you'd like," Margaret said.

"That's okay. Don' tell anyone, but I'd take Neil Diamond over Three Dog Night anytime." That's something else we have in common, she thought.

He drove through the city streets of Dubuque with no trouble just as she predicted. And when they were driving past the mall on the West end, they noticed that a new movie, *Easy Rider*, was showing. "I heard it was really different – lots of music," she hinted.

Luke grinned, knowing full well what she wanted. He pulled into the parking lot and ushered her into the theater. She fairly quivered with excitement. She had never gone to a show with a boy before. She loved movies, especially the old ones on late night TV. Her aunt remarked more than once that for such a sensible girl, Margaret certainly was emotional when it came to Alan Ladd or Gary Cooper riding off into the sunset, or Judy Garland and Bing Crosby crooning some heart-wrenching love song. However, she was also no coward when it came to trying new things.

"Well, what did you think of it?" Luke asked her as they crawled back into the car. But she was so stunned by the movie's violent and sudden ending, she could hardly speak.

"It wasn't as though those two guys were solid citizens or anything. But to just shoot them like that?" she exclaimed, choking back the sobs. "I just wasn't prepared, that's all."

"I had heard about the ending," Luke chided himself. "I should have insisted we see *True Grit*." He could see she was deeply affected so he slid his arm along the back of the seat and drew her near. They headed toward home.

"Do you think they're right? About being free, I mean -- to be that uninhibited and not tied down?" she asked.

"Heck no. Would you really want to be gorked out of your mind on drugs and travelin' around the country like that? They were so dirty and threatening, people wouldn't even let them eat in their restaurants. C'mon, Maggie, that's not exactly your style, is it?"

"Maybe not like that, but I don't want to end up like my Aunt Betty – tied to one place for seventy years. She's hardly been across the state line."

"You talk about freedom. She is one of the freest persons I know. She does and says exactly what she pleases. It's about feeling good when you get up in the morning, feeling good about who you are. And having choices – that's what this country is all about."

"Well, I guess you really didn't care for the movie, huh?" she said in a small, hollow voice. But then she started giggling and he started laughing, too. She turned on the radio and flipped to another channel. They were talking and not really listening until a newscaster broke in with a news alert. The sense of urgency and drama in his voice caught their attention.

"Tragedy on a college campus today. Officials from Kent University in Kent, Ohio, report that there were four deaths and nine young people wounded on their campus today as the result the Ohio National Guard firing into a crowd of demonstrators. The Guard had been called there over the weekend after the student protesters had disrupted the town, burned the ROTC building, and prevented firemen from controlling the fire. Large scale demonstrations have been building on that campus as well as on many others across the nation in response to the president's nationally televised announcement last Thursday that he was sending troops into Cambodia to destroy Communist bases of operation there. In response to today's tragedy, administrations of colleges and universities across the country are bracing for what they fear will be widespread rioting. Student organizers at the University of Iowa say there will be a vigil tonight-- "

Maggie turned off the radio and clutched her stomach as though she was physically sick. Luke drove on, staring straight ahead, also shaken by the news.

"They were just kids!" Maggie cried. "They're probably just a little older than us. How could they shoot them down like that?"

"Maybe there's more to it. I can't believe they would shoot into a crowd without some provocation. I just can't believe that!"

"You can't? Most college students I know don't carry guns. Aren't we supposed to be free? Isn't that what you said? Can't students demonstrate without getting killed? Can't people ride down the highway without getting shot in cold blood? I just don't understand any of this!" She sank into her seat, angry and confused. They didn't talk any more. He drove on home and pulled into his driveway. He turned off the engine and sat in silence a while longer.

"I don't understand it either," he said. "Everything just seems to be changing so fast. Things that are supposed to be important, aren't any more. No one knows who or what to believe. I'm going to be graduating in two weeks, and this is supposed to be one of the best times of my life, but it isn't. How can it be when I don't know what's real?" His fists were clinched and his mouth, tight and drawn. "Do you understand what I'm saying?"

She opened her arms to him and held him tightly. They clung together like survivors in a lifeboat. But then he tore away abruptly and bolted out the door. But after a few steps, he turned and stuck his head through the open window and kissed her hard. And then he was gone.

It was just a moment, really – gone so quickly. She wanted to cry after him to come back, to hold her and need her a little longer. But that was too much to hope for.

* * * * * *

The memory of that night was still very vivid in Margaret's mind when she and several hundred others including most of the Winston clan, squeezed into the gymnasium for the high school commencement. Luke marched in with the rest of the Class of '70, looking somber and ill-at-ease, as seventeen or eighteen year old young men often do at these occasions. Across the wall, above the stage, was a large banner with the chosen slogan printed in three-foot letters. "We have gone far, but we have further to go," it said. Maggie studied the words intently, wondering what it meant.

It was a hot May evening and it was very hard to focus on the tedious lecturing of the guest speaker. He told them this was indeed one of the best times of their lives, so they should enjoy it. The gentlemen lamented his own mis-directed youth in one of those if-I-knew-then-what-I-know-now speeches, pleading with the 64 graduates to work hard to secure a brighter future.

Incredibly, he made no mention of what was happening in the world beyond tiny Shannon Town, Iowa. It was as though the turmoil and conflict that spread across the country since the Kent University incident should have no impact on their lives. The speaker congratulated the many graduates who were planning to enter colleges next fall without commenting on the over 500 colleges and universities that were forced to close early that spring because of student strikes and rampant chaos.

If the arguments and conflict were consuming campuses

and political arenas, it also raged across many dinner tables, super market counters, and country fences. Luke was right when he said everything was changing. Perhaps it seemed magnified to him and his peers because they were being thrust into the middle of it, ill-equipped to make decisions and form opinions that would affect the rest of their lives. What they had learned in history classes in those very classrooms no longer applied. It had been easier for earlier generations of American boys in other times, in other wars. Even just four or five years earlier, scores of young men had marched willingly onto Asian-bound transports with the noble ideal of stopping the Communists, once and for all. But the illusion of that notion had evaporated long ago. Now Americans were forced to struggle with the question, do you agree or disagree? Is it right or wrong? The debate raged while mothers, wives, and sisters of young men wept.

* * * * * *

Annie was glad school was almost over. The daily ritual of getting every one up and out to do their morning work, then fed, clothes changed, and ready for the bus, was becoming progressively more difficult. There was so much work to be done that everyone was treating academics like an inconvenience. She was tired of fighting it.

What was especially tiresome was the constant arguing. Most of it was caused by internal family matters such as Danny getting into Peter's things or the endless verbal sparing between Thomas and John. But there were also the external conflicts that intruded into their home every time Matthew turned on the news or picked up the newspaper. Debating the state of national affairs and policies was an ongoing battle between him and his oldest son. Annie was sick of it. She hated the word Vietnam, and she hated the hallow, pained expression that sometimes flickered across Luke's face at the mention of it. He said very little but she knew the pressure on him was mounting. She prayed that the whole thing would end before he would be forced to make any decisions.

He, at least, was spared, the last ten days of school. There is no vaccine for spring fever and the boys had a severe case of it. Finally, all that remained was the traditional awards assembly that last day of school.

John was sorry to see it end -- the track season, not the class work. When talking to Kenny that morning, his friend laughed and reminded him that school would soon start again after three short months. Football practice would begin mid-August. "You're excited about that?" he laughed. "Just wait till we have two-a-days, with a zillion calisthenics with thirty pounds of pads in 90 degree heat."

"Well, if I want to make the team, I'd better stay in shape this summer," fretted Johnny.

"Ah, c'mon Winston, you're gonna make the team and you know it. And after I'm done with you, you'll know the plays backwards and forewords. Let's go to the stupid assembly and get our track letters. And man," he said, smacking his lips in lusty anticipation, "this is only the beginning."

* * * * * *

Perhaps it was an illusion but it seemed as though the strife and hostility seemed to melt away in the warm June sun. Life seemed to settle into some semblance of routine. Boredom breeds contention, but there was no danger of that. Matthew came to the table every morning, armed with work assignments like a drill sergeant. Now that the planting was done, most of the work involved trying to clean up the place. They had to get the barn ready for the bales of hay that would soon be stacked in the haymow.

Annie kept busy with the housework and her garden. They were already eating lettuce and radishes, and the peas and onions were almost ready. The flowers were a particular joy to her. Soon she'd be putting bouquets of pansies and marigolds on the table.

It seemed to her that the baby was blossoming, too. Becky was six months old now and thriving beautifully. Annie bought books and magazines to help guide her. The raising and nurturing of this baby was her highest priority. Becky had been given to her by her mother like a sacred trust, and she did not want to fail.

She was thinking about that one evening while upstairs bathing her. It was still 80 degrees at 6:00 at night and the baby was irritable. Annie knew a nice bath would settle her down even though that meant supper would be late. They would just have to wait.

She came downstairs just as her father came in. He was in a great mood tonight, she thought. He had just been down to the bottom and was telling everyone that most of the corn was a half foot tall already. Sonny and Matthew were discussing how soon they'd have to start cultivating the weeds which were as tall as the corn.

"Is the mail here?" he asked as he sat down at the table with a cup of coffee. Annie handed it to him. There was the familiar manila envelope, which meant their lawyer in New York had forwarded mail from back East. "Mmmmm, what have we here? An official looking letter for Mr. Matthew Macalister Winston III. If I am not mistaken, this is from your friendly neighborhood draft board." The room was suddenly silent as everyone turned to look at Mack.

"Hey, that guy's a good lawyer. Tell him to take care of it!" He was trying to sound cocky but couldn't stop the color from draining from his cheeks.

"And how is he supposed to do that?" his father countered. "You can't be exempt for school any more. So what are you going to do?"

Mack appeared to become further irritated by his father's calm demeanor. "Hey, this is serious!" he cried. "I am not going to get drafted! No way! You're acting as though this is a joke!" he screamed at his father.

"A joke? Young men fighting for this country? What makes you think that you're too damn good to do that? Who in the hell do you think you are?"

"I think I'm a guy who's smart enough to realize that it would be damn stupid to go over there and crawl around in some jungle for no good reason! I could get fuckin' killed over there, for what? Nothin'!" He was pacing around the table, flinging his arms empathetically. "Hell," he said finally, "there's always

Canada!"

"Huh!" grunted his father. "You'd find it awful damn cold and lonely up there. No friends, no family, no money." He punctuated that last word so that the inference would be unmistakable. He threw the letter at his son. "You have until the first of July to reply or they'll issue an arrest warrant. Maybe you can catch some terminal disease before then." He lit a cigarette as he stood up to go back outside. "We have a while before supper so let's get something done." With that he went outside, the screen door slamming behind him.

Mack stood there, frozen with anger. His father's attitude incensed him. "Hell no!" he shouted after Matthew. "I'm not doing a damned thing! Why should I bust my butt around here!" He was screaming now, but his father did not turn around to acknowledge him, which was more infuriating. Mack picked up an empty beer can and flung it at the door.

Sonny turned to leave. "Hey!" Mack exploded. "Where in the hell are you going?" Sonny said nothing. He opened the door and walked out.

"Hey! I'm talkin' to you," Mack yelled. He ran after Sonny and grabbed his arm. "There's one thing no one's ever asked you, Mr. High-and-Mighty. What about you? How come you've never been drafted?"

"You don't know shit about me," Sonny replied, meeting Mack's stare evenly.

"That's right, we don't. You come along and take over everything – our father, our home, our whole lives, and we don't know a fuckin' thing about you, except you're a stinkin', arrogant, son-of-a-bitch. And I've hated you since the first time I laid eyes on you!"

Sonny showed little emotion and turned to walk away. Again Mack stopped him. "Guess we know one thing about you, you're a fuckin' coward!" He grabbed Sonny's shirt.

Just that quickly, Sonny slapped Mack's hands away and flung him onto the ground. He seemed to weigh his words carefully before he spoke. "Listen punk, it's none of your damned business. I came here to do a job and I'm doin' it. So just stay out of my way!" Again, he turned to walk away.

But it wasn't over. Mack lowered his head and charged Sonny like an enraged bull. They both went down, wrestling and rolling around in the dirt. Mack was badly outmatched as he tried to slug Sonny across the face, but was unable to land any solid hits. Sonny finally brought him under control and yanked him to his feet.

"Listen, you worthless, piss ass jerk," he said, spitting the words. "Just stay the fuck out of my way and never touch me again!" He flung Mack back into the dirt and walked away.

Matthew watched the whole episode from the barn door. He couldn't hear what was said, but he could guess. Good, he thought, the kid needed that.

* * * * * *

Later, just after sundown, Matthew and some of the boys were sitting around the back porch, enjoying the cool evening. Danny and Peter were playing with the puppies, with Mutt sitting nearby.

"I sure wish that dog was more of a watchdog," Annie called from the kitchen window. "The raccoons are getting the chickens, Dad."

"The dog's not the answer," Matthew said. "You have to shoot the little rascals. And they carry rabies, too, so I don't like them around the yard." He sat quietly for a long time, watching the smoke from his cigarette curl up into the dark sky. "By the way, somebody has to go into town early and pick up a order from the lumber yard. It's been ready for three days."

"I'll go," Mack said, stepping out of the shadows. "Anything's better than hanging around here." He turned and walked into the house. Ordinarily, Matthew would have called him on his sarcasm, but not tonight. Mack had enough wounds and hurt-pride for one day.

Chapter 23

Mack woke up early. The shadows were deep with the sun just beginning to peer over the horizon. He paused at the refrigerator to drink milk from the pitcher. Now that he was used to it, he liked the fresh stuff.

He grabbed some cookies and sauntered out onto the back porch. He had a lot on his mind. His whole body was still smarting from the beating he took from his archenemy yesterday. How the hell was he supposed to beat a common street brawler? He must have been crazy to even try. And this draft thing. It seemed inevitable now. He tried every trick in the book these past two years and managed to stay out of it this long, but not any more. Oh well, he thought, getting drafted couldn't be much worse that being stuck here in the middle of nowhere with a bunch of stinking pigs. Still, the lush, glistening valley did present a certain tranquility. It was pretty, sure, but it also represented a tremendous amount of hard work, which was against his nature. Yes, maybe the Army would be a better alternative.

He was afraid that Sonny or his dad might surface any minute, so he decided he'd head into town. He'd have a leisurely breakfast in town while he waited for the lumberyard to open. He jumped in the truck and headed out. As usual, he drove too fast, especially for gravel roads. He punched the truck around the three, tight curves before the highway, swerving and sliding. As he came out of third curve, suddenly out of nowhere, a rider on top of a beautiful black horse bolted onto the road. Mack stomped on the brakes to keep from hitting them and laid on the horn to voice his displeasure.

The horse was already spooked and reared up at the sound of horn. The rider tried to stay with his mount until he suddenly found himself sprawled on his backside in the middle of the road. It was then that his cap flew off and a mop of beautiful, long black hair fell down over the young rider's shoulders. She stood up and dusted herself off, glaring at Mack the whole time. "Hey, I'm sorry!" he called, leaning out of the window. "But you ought to watch where you're going."

She did not reply. She took the reins of her horse and hoisted herself up into the saddle in one sweeping motion. Giving Mack one last parting sneer, the rider and her horse flew across the road and sailed over the pasture gate. Mack, mesmerized by the wonderful spectacle, got out of the truck just to watch them glide up the hillside. Horse and rider were as one as they sped along. The girl rode expertly, leaning forward and swaying with the rhythm of the horse, her hair like a wild mane flowing behind her. And when they reached the ridge, they slowed and turned so that she might gaze down at her perpetrator from a safe and lofty retreat. They formed a beautiful silhouette against the golden hue of the sunrise brightening behind them. Time seemed to stand still. Mack could scarcely breathe as he stood staring at them. But then they were gone, disappearing over the hill. He was left wondering if she was real or just an exquisite vision.

He hoped she would reappear. He pulled the truck to the side of the road and waited for almost an hour but she never did. He even thought about walking to the crest of the hill to search for her, but he decided it was probably useless. He vowed to somehow find out who she was and where she lived.

He drove on into town and parked in front of the hardware store. He sat there for several minutes until Charlie came out. "Hey, Mack, we got that order ready for your dad." Mack must have looked a little strange because Charlie added, "Hey, are you sick or somethin'?"

The posts and rolls of fencing were loaded, and Mack headed for home. He turned off the highway onto the gravel road slowly and drove down the mystical stretch, hoping to catch a glimpse of her. She seemed to have evaporated with the dew on the grass and the dark, cool morning shadows. He realized then that he had been gone a long time and he hurried home.

Luke greeted him as he pulled onto the yard. "You'd better get a move on it, Mack. Dad's already in a foul mood this morning I don't think he expected you to be gone this long." He took a double take at his brother's face. "Are you sick or somethin'?" he asked. "You look weird."

"No, I am not sick. Never felt better in my life!" He stumbled out of the truck like a drowning man in water. "I think

I'm in love."

"Oh Jeez. I should have recognized it."

"Lordie, you should have seen her. This gorgeous goddess comes flyin' across the road right in front of me. I almost hit her. She fell off, right in the middle of the road."

"Fell off what? You almost hit her?"

"She fell off her horse! She had the tightest blue jeans and the cutest ass you ever saw!"

By this time, Andrew and John joined them and Mack explained again his encounter with the beautiful woman on the horse.

"Oh God," moaned Andrew, grinning. "Here we go again – another mystery lady. You really go in for this kind of thing, don't ya'? Like the pretty brunette in the sport's car last summer. And that cute little salesgirl at the bookstore? What'll you bet, this one's married, too."

"Yeah, look at the poor sucker," Luke said with a laugh. "Same old symptoms – dreamy eyes, flushed face, rapid pulse -- Jeez, I think he has it real bad this time."

"This one's different," sighed the tormented Mack. "You should have seen her. I gotta find out who she is."

"Well, you're not gonna live long enough to find out anything if you don't get out there and get to work," said Andrew. "Here comes Pop."

Making hay on a hot, June morning was fast becoming their least favorite job of a long list of despicable jobs. This was their third day and their father complained about their slow progress. He rolled past them and slowed down only long enough for them to jump on board. And they were off.

The field they were working in wasn't even their own. It was an adjacent acreage belonging to Jake Gibson. One day last spring, the two gentlemen farmers were having a neighborly, over-the-fence discussion when old Jake complained that he was having trouble finding someone to put up his hay. Of course, Matthew immediately volunteered to take care of it. He was going to have to buy the hay for his livestock anyway.

Jake had gone out the beginning of the week and cut the field of ripe alfalfa. He went back over the field with his racking machine that gathered up the fallen shafts into long neat rows. The air was pierced by the poignant sickeningly sweet smell of fresh mown hay. Then Matthew drove the tractor pulling Jake's ancient but functional bailer that sucked up the grass and spit out neat, compact bales of hay. The boys took turns driving the tractor pulling the hay wagon while the others walked behind it, slinging the heavy bales up on the wide, flatbed wagon. The bales were stacked like piles of huge bricks, until the wagon was over-flowing. Those bales were unloaded, one by one, onto a conveyor belt, which delivered them up to be stacked again in the haymow.

The boys thought there surely had to be an easier way of doing this. Why didn't he just buy hay and have it delivered, they grumbled. None of the boys had been more vocal than Mack. But not today. He ran around the field like some crazy, juiced up fool, working rings around his brothers. Annie noticed it when she brought a jug of cold lemonade out the field mid-morning. "What's with him?" she stammered. "After what happened yesterday, I expected him to be even more cocky than ever.

"Oh, him?" grunted Andrew. "It's just a momentary lapse of sanity. He thinks he's in love. Don't worry. It'll blow over and he'll be his same old bitchy self soon enough."

The day progressed much more smoothly with Mack's infectious good mood. A water fight at noon cooled everyone down and lifted everyone's spirits. By 3:00, the last bale was stacked and the machines stilled. Matthew was pleased. He passed out cans of cold beer, even to John and Thomas. "You boys worked like men so you deserve a man's reward. Just don't tell your sister."

* * * * * *

Sunday morning Mack woke up at dawn again. He intended to go back to the place in the road where he saw the girl yesterday and wait there until he saw her again, even if it took all day. As he headed toward the pickup, he saw Sonny nearby, carrying the toolbox across the yard toward one of the tractors. Mack was in such a good mood that he called to him. "Hey, Sonny, what's broke now?"

Sonny appeared startled to see Mack up so early. "The engine seems to be missin'," he said. "I want to finish the cultivating this afternoon."

"Missing, huh? Looks like it's there to me."

Sonny jerked his head around sharply to glare at the intruder of the early morning quiet, but Mack was grinning, not sneering. Sonny returned to his work. "Aren't you gonna miss your Mystery Lady if you don't get goin'?"

Mack was startled. He had no idea Sonny had paid any attention to the conversation yesterday. "Yep, you're right. I'd better get going." He didn't want to be late. He drove too fast again, but when he turned the third curve he slowed to a crawl. His heart was pounding in his throat. He knew the whole thing was ridiculous but he didn't care.

Then he saw her. She and the black horse were standing on top of the hill. Was it possible she was waiting for him? He got out of the truck and began leaping into the air, waving his hat. "Hey," he called. "Come down here."

She sat motionless, though her horse pawed restlessly in the dirt and threw his head about. Then suddenly, she drew up her reins and they started running across the crest of the hill. They flowed along, the magnificent stead and it's beautiful, graceful rider. Mack jumped back into the truck and drove down the road, staying parallel with them as long as possible. But then they disappeared again.

"Oh damn!" he yelled as he jumped out of the truck and slammed his cap onto the ground. "Oh damn," he said again, this time more softly. Why had she teased him like that? Was she a beautiful witch sent to torture him? Maybe she wasn't real at all.

There was nothing to do but go back home. Sonny and the tractor were gone. Matthew and the others were beginning to move about, starting the chores. Mack joined them, but his light-hearted mood of yesterday was gone.

Sundays were more relaxed now that there were no major jobs. Annie made a big dinner for the family to eat together around the old dinning room table. Only Sonny labored throughout the long, hot afternoon. He came up from the bottom at sundown and came into the kitchen. Annie had set a plate aside for him and offered to warm it up, but he took it outside to sit on the porch to eat it cold. Mack sat in the porch swing, as though in a trance. "Don't mind him, Sonny," Andrew said as he left to go to inside. "He's been like that all day.

"The Mystery Lady, huh," Sonny said, settling down on the step with his sandwich and a cold beer. A hush had fallen over the place. There were only the gentle night noises and the creaking of Mack's swing.

"She was there this morning," Mack said. "She is so beautiful, but she's playing games. She waited for me, sat there for a few minutes, and then rode away. A she-devil, that's what she is, a devil. I cannot believe my luck."

Sonny ate his sandwich and then said, "Why don't you just go into town and ask around. Someone will know who she is."

"Yeah, I know," moaned the despondent young man, "but I know what'll happen. Either they'll say she doesn't exist, or she's married. That's what usually happens. I've had rotten luck with women lately. I'm beginning to think that all the good ones are taken – especially around here."

Sonny chuckled softly. Neither of them noticed but it was the first civilized conversation they had ever had with each other.

But just then, a frightened scream broke through the silence and they could hear loud crashing noises coming from the direction of the barn. As they both raced across the yard, they heard growling, snarling animal noises. It was the dog, fighting with a fox. Peter was standing nearby, crying and trembling. The battle was soon over, and the dog lay bleeding and badly wounded. "What the hell happened?" Sonny yelled. "Peter, what are you doing down here?"

"It wasn't coons," the boy cried. "I knew it wasn't and I was afraid Pop was going to kill 'em. So I sneaked down here, just to watch. When the fox came up, it saw me. I thought he was going to come after me! But then Mutt came out of nowhere and they started fighting. Is she dead?"

"No," Sonny said, working gently over the animal. "She's not dead, but pretty damn close. Peter, did the fox act crazy, like it might have rabies?"

Mack didn't wait for the boy to answer as he took off

running toward the house. "I'll get the shotgun out of the office and see if I can find it. You'd better take the dog to the vet right away." His father's shotgun stood in the back corner of the closet in the office. Mack picked it up and started to leave when he realized it probably wasn't loaded.

He had only handled a gun once before in his life. Matthew had taken several of his sons to a shooting range when they were spending the summer in upstate New York. Target shooting was not his idea of a fun afternoon, so he made sure he did poorly so his father never asked him again. He barely remembered how to load it or even how to hold it. Clumsily, he filled the chamber with cartridges and snapped on the safety. He grabbed the flashlight, and started down the bottom road in the general direction the fox had gone.

He crept along in the stillness of the night, surprised that he had such predatory instincts. He darted here and there, panning the area with the light. He saw Peter's friends, the raccoons, and various other fury creatures, but there was no sign of a fox. The adrenaline rush began to wane quickly as fatigue took its place. What in the hell was he doing out here in the middle of the night with a gun, looking for a fox who was probably miles from here by now. He began to worry about getting lost and rabid animals lurking in the bushes. This is really stupid, he told himself. He was ready to turn around and go home.

Then he saw it. The animal's eyes were like bright, glowing gems reflected in the light. Mack knew instantly it was the fox. He froze for a moment, not sure what he should do next. The fox fled and Mack chased it, running blindly through the brush. The animal seemed to be taunting him, as it darted ahead and then stopped to peer back at him. At one point, Mack hastily put the gun to his shoulder and tried to fire, but the safety was on. Hurriedly, he fumbled to disengage it. By that time the fox scurried into the bushes again. As he tried to run after it, his feet became tangled in something that felt like a log or maybe some wire. He tried to free himself but he began to fall.

Then, at the same instant, there was a strange, burning sensation in his lower right leg. There was no sound, no flash of light, as sank into the darkness. The wire. He was tangled in some wire. He reached down to free himself.

What's this, he wondered. Something wet and sticky. Mud? No, it's blood. The wire. The wire must have cut my leg. No, the gun -- the gun went off. My leg. Oh God, my leg. I shot my leg. You'd better see how bad it, he told himself. He tried to roll over but both legs were still ensnared in the barbwire. Struggling to clear his head and to think, he rolled this way and then another until he was able to half sit up. He reached for the flashlight and pointed the light toward his legs. Jeez, he gasped. His right lower leg and foot looked like hamburger and were bleeding badly.

Why in the hell didn't he pay more attention during those damn first aid classes in school, he chided himself. A tourniquet, that's what you're supposed to do, a tourniquet. Wait a minute. That's only if the bleeding is severe and the limb is likely to be lost. Yeah, it's really bleeding. You'd better do something. Your belt, use your belt. God, I must be getting weak. Maneuvering to get that belt off was tough. Tighter. Make it tighter.

He knew the situation was serious and he also realized his best hope was Sonny. Just my luck, he thought, the person who can't stand my guts is going to have to save me. He felt confident that Sonny would return from town soon and would check if he was back. Sonny's dogged persistence would lead him intuitively down that road. He won't stop until he finds me, Mack thought. It better be pretty damn soon. His leg was starting to throb. "C'mon, Sonny," he called out loud. "Come and find me!"

He knew it would be easier for Sonny to find him if he could somehow get back to the road. He tried to get up, but his feet were still caught in the wire and he was too weak to free himself. He slumped back onto the ground and began to tremble.

He stared up at the stars. They was so clear he felt as though he could reach out and touch them. "C'mon, Sonny," he whispered, "I don't want to die like this." He said the words over and over again until he was swallowed up by the cold, the pain, and the darkness, and he lost consciousness.

Chapter 24

Sonny wrapped the dog in a blanket he took off his own bed and lifted her carefully into the back of the truck. Peter pleaded to come along. The sleepy veterinarian treated them kindly and was very gentle with the dog. One leg was especially mangled, and there were several deep gashes. Mutt would have to stay at the clinic for a few days. She would be quarantined and watched for any symptoms of rabies. Sonny assured the trembling Peter that the dog was in good hands, and there was nothing more they could do for her.

When they got home, he walked upstairs with the boy, sending him off to bed. Then he checked Mack's bedroom and saw that he still was not back. The shotgun was not returned to its place, either. Sonny went outside and paced on the porch, trying to decide what to do. There was an uneasy feeling building in his gut. He had been a fool to let that hot headed, green horn go out into the woods alone. Mack was probably lost by now. Sonny grabbed another flash light and headed down the same road Mack had gone down three hours earlier.

He walked up and down the main road several times, calling Mack's name and becoming increasingly frustrated and worried. He knew several paths through the timber that Mack might have taken. He tramped through the woods for hours. There was one more area he hadn't covered -- the trial along the ridge by the property line.

He was startled by a noise in the bushes behind him. It was only a rabbit scurrying away, but there was something shinny reflecting in the flashlight beam about twenty feet off the trail. He moved closer to investigate.

Pushing through the brush he nearly stumbled over Mack's body. He quickly knelt to check for a pulse. The kid was still alive but barely. Sonny twisted the tourniquet even tighter and moved him so that his head was downhill. He took off his own shirt to wrap around Mack's cold, limp body. And then he bolted up the hill toward the house.

He tore up the stairs, pounding on Matthew's door first and

then the others. "Wake up! Wake up!" he called. "Annie, call for an ambulance and call the doctor. Tell 'em Mack's shot himself in the leg. It's real bad." He was already leaping back down the stairs. "Andrew, get the other boys and meet me outside. We'll get him up the hill by the time the ambulance gets out here."

"Up the hill?" Andrew called. "Where is he? What happened?" But Sonny didn't stop long enough to explain anything. Everyone sensed the urgency in his voice and did what they were told. Only Matthew and Luke stood frozen in the hallway.

Annie saw their faces and realized what they were thinking, but refused to even consider such a notion. "No, Daddy," she cried. "Don't even think that. It must have been an accident. Wait till we have more details."

Andrew, John, and Thomas jumped on the back of the wagon as Sonny spun past. It was the same wagon that Mack and his brothers cavorted around just a couple of days ago. Sonny screeched to a stop halfway down the hill and led them through the woods to where Mack was lying. It was nearly dawn now and light enough that they could see their brother's ashen face and the bloody mud pooled around him. "My God," whispered Andrew. "Is he still alive?"

"Yeah. He's still breathing, ain't he?" Sonny cut the wire from around Mack's feet. "Come on, we gotta carry him to the wagon. Don't just stand there. Move!"

They used a blanket as a giant sling and carrying him toward the road, struggling over the uneven terrain. They laid him on the wagon as Sonny revved up the engine and tore up the hill. They got to the yard the same time the ambulance arrived. It wasn't really an ambulance. It was a hearse driven by Mr. Jenkins, the local funeral director who doubled as an ambulance driver in emergency situations. Mack was laid on the stretcher and loaded into the back of the hideous-looking thing, amidst the throng of horrified onlookers.

No one immediately climbed in to ride along. Matthew, Andrew, Annie, and the rest stood as though paralyzed. "Sonny, you'd better ride along," Annie said. She was visibly trembling and frightened. "We'll get dressed and follow in a minute."

Sonny climbed into the back to sit along side the stretcher as the ambulance pulled away.

"Pop, listen to me," Andrew pleaded. "He's going to need surgery. We have to go to the hospital right away." Matthew still said nothing, looking dazed and bewildered, but he allowed himself to be led back into the house. He dressed and ten minutes later they were on their way toward Dubuque.

* * * * * *

It was a clear and crisp morning. Miss Penelope Lamp woke up early and walked outside in the fresh morning air, dreading closing up the cottage and driving into Dubuque to go back to school. It infuriated her that they had classes all summer. They only do that, she thought, because they need the student nurses to staff the hospital.

She brushed her long, black hair as she hurried along, and then wrapped it around the top of her head to make a bun that would fit under her nurse's cap. The nuns hated her long hair, but as long as she kept it up, there was nothing they could say. She went to the barn to say good-bye to her best friend, Mr. Phipps, her large, jet-black gelding. She gave him a lump of sugar and whispered a few words in his ear as she turned to leave. Mr. Conrad, the neighbor who was the caretaker of the place, was just driving up as she was getting into her Jeep to leave. "Take good care of my boys," she called. "I'll probably be back next weekend. Maybe my dad, too -- he's been wanting to do some fishing."

She drove down the long winding lane, stopping to look carefully both directions at the entrance onto the main road. It was a blind entry and cars came around the bend very fast. She paused an extra long time, smiling, remembering the tall, dark and handsome stranger whom she had encountered here the last two mornings. She blushed as recalled the unabashed way he had stared at her. She wondered when they might meet again and how she would handle it this time. It was intriguing to consider the possibilities.

As she pulled into the hospital parking lot, she noticed that her father's car was parked in it's reserved spot. She drove to the student nurses' dorm which was adjacent to the hospital. She ran upstairs to her room with only fifteen minutes to report to duty.

Her roommate, Jenny Alston, was already dressed and ready to go. "God, Penny, cuttin' it a little short, aren't we?" she nagged. "As usual, your luck is incredible. I heard an ambulance about a half hour ago. I bet it's an exciting case – maybe a real bad car accident or something!" Penny shot her a look of disgust. "Well," Jenny whined, "you start your follow-through today, right? C'mon, I'll walk you over to ER. I'm on 3-West. Miss Prentice is still there. I thought they'd discharge her over the weekend, but no such luck."

They walked across the parking lot toward the Emergency Room area. Jenny didn't have time to satisfy her curiosity as she hurried off to another part of the hospital. She guessed right, though, Penny thought as she walked in. It must be a big case. Nurses and technicians were scrambling here and there with a sense of urgency in the air. Mrs. Friar, her instructor, grabbed her, talking in that irritating high pitched tone she used when she was excited.

"Miss Lamp, this is a very good case for your follow through – a gun shot wound, self-inflicted, they say. They're getting him prepped for surgery right now -- a BK amp. That's a below the knee amputation, you know. Your father has been called in so why don't you ask him if you can watch the surgery? You will be assigned to this patient in recovery and post-op." She seemed almost pleased with the situation. "It should be an excellent learning experience for you, Miss Lamp," she squeaked. "I have to go check on the other girls."

Penny nodded in agreement. Thank God this woman was an instructor, she thought. At least she can't hurt anyone.

She went into the treatment room where her father was working over the patient. "Dad," she called, "Friar wants me to take this patient as my follow-through. Is that, er--" She stopped mid-sentence as she looked down at the young man's face. She gasped as she thought she recognized him.

"Penny, maybe that's not such a good idea," her father said.

"Do you know him? Maybe you've seen him around Shanny. He's the oldest son of that family that moved here this spring. Honey, are you listening?"

"Yes, Dad, I'll be alright, really. I think I may have seen him before but I don't really know him or anything," she stammered, trying to regain her composure or her father might not let her stay. "He's alright, isn't he?"

"Well, he laid in the mud for several hours until someone finally found him. He's extremely shocky – hemoglobin is down to 5. He's on his third unit of blood, so we'll take him to the OR soon. I have to talk to the family and then scrub. I guess I'll see you there, if you're sure you're alright with this."

She nodded as convincingly as possible. "How about vitals?" she asked, trying to sound business-like. She hoped no one had noticed that she was purposely not looking at the bloody, mangled leg the other nurse was scrubbing. Please, she begged inwardly, don't ask me to do that.

* * * * * *

Matthew, Annie, and the others were sitting grim and stone-faced in the waiting room when Dr. Lamp came in and introduced himself. "Mr. Winston," he began, "I'm sorry but there is no way we can save your son's lower leg. We need to perform the amputation quickly so we can stop the bleeding. He's already lost a dangerous amount of blood. But, once we complete the procedure and replace the blood he's lost, he should recover nicely." This announcement was not met with the looks of relief and gratitude doctors usually receive with this kind of news. There were only icy and angry stares.

Annie tried to cover for her father. "Oh, thank you, Doctor. That is good news," she said. "Has he regained consciousness yet?"

"No, unfortunately not. He's in shock so I don't expect him to wake up until after the surgery." He excused himself to go the surgery area.

Matthew signed the necessary papers just as whisked Mack away. They got a glimpse of him as they rolled him past. He looked ghastly. There was nothing to do now but wait.

Sonny hadn't spoken to anyone yet. He sat apart from the rest and ignored the heated discussion emulating from the Winston's corner of the room.

"Sonny," Annie called, "come here and tell Pop what happened to Mack out there tonight. He has completely the wrong idea."

"I already told you what happened," Andrew snapped. "Mutt got chewed up by a fox. Sonny took the dog to the vet, while Mack took off with a gun to kill the fox. They were afraid it had rabies. Mack got tangled in an old barbed wire fence and shot himself. For God's sake, I saw Sonny cut the wire from around Mack's feet. It was a dumb accident!"

"Yes, an accident!" Annie cried. "Mack would never do anything like that on purpose – not in the middle of the woods where he could easily bleed to death before anyone found him! For God's sake, Sonny, talk to him. Maybe he'll listen to you!"

Sonny finally seemed to understand Matthew's attitude. "They're right," he said. "It was an accident. It was my fault. I should never have let him go out there like that!" But Matthew's expression never changed.

"C'mon, Pop," Andrew coaxed, deciding to try a new approach, "let's go get some coffee. There's nothing we can do here anyway. You need some time to think this through more clearly." He maneuvered his father toward the door as he spoke.

"This isn't right," Annie murmured after they left. "We're acting like crazy people. Poor Mack. How's he going to handle this?"

She had directed her comments toward the only other occupant of the room, but Sonny did not appear to be listening. He was pacing, appearing frantic at times. "God, hospitals give me the creeps," he muttered. "I can't breathe. I swore I would never set foot in one again."

Annie shook off her numb bewilderment to try to focus on him. She had never seen him like this before. "When were you in a hospital?"

It was obvious that he was very uncomfortable. "My grandfather died in one of these places."

She was surprised at his openness. "I know what that's like. My mother just died a few months ago." She wanted to thank him for saving her brother's life, but he turned for the door.

"I gotta get out of here." He dug in his chest pocket for a cigarette.

Before he could exit, Dr. Adams strolled in. Annie was so glad to see him. Though she had few dealings with him, her instincts told her he could be trusted. "Oh, Dr. Adams, thank you for making all the arrangements this morning. Mack is in surgery now. There was no way to save his leg." The words were so difficult to say.

"Yes, I know. I stopped by surgery on my way here," he said, patting Annie's hand. "His vital signs are improving. He's going to be fine."

Sonny bolted for the door. "I'm goin' for that walk now."

"That was our hired hand, Sonny Jackson," Annie explained. The thought flickered past her mind that his behavior was odd, even for him. Maybe he hates doctors as much as he hates hospitals.

Matthew and Andrew came back then. Dr. Adams offered to stay and answer any of their questions, but Matthew continued his stony silence.

* * * * * *

Penny was surprised how little time it takes to cut off a man's leg. She knew would never forget the awful sound of the saw, drilling through the bone. The mangled and lifeless foot was separated and carefully wrapped to be taken away. What they do with those pieces of people's bodies, she wondered. The bleeders were tied off as the spit of the cauterizing tool was heard frequently. A flap of healthy skin was brought down over the wound and stitched into place. The word "fortunate" was used often. Penny wondered if Mack would think so.

He was taken to recovery room. She stayed nearby, searching his handsome face for signs of consciousness. She did all the usual nursing procedures – monitoring his vital signs every fifteen minutes, checking the dressings and the IV's. The blood was slowly dripping life back into his cold, pale body. Gradually, some color and warmth returned with periodic movement and restlessness. The morning wore on. She stood close, watching and waiting.

She rehearsed over and over what she would say when he woke up, but when his eyes finally did flutter open, she panicked. "You're in the hospital," she stammered. "There's been an accident. You've just had an operation."

She could see he was struggling to concentrate, trying to remember. "They cut off my leg, didn't they." He turned away and closed his eyes.

He was in the recovery until noon. His status stabilized and he was ready to be transferred to his room. Penny stopped at the family waiting room.

"Hello," she said. "You're the Winston family, aren't you? I'm a student nurse, Penelope Lamp. Yes, Dr. Dennis Lamp is my father. I've been assigned to take care of Matthew today and the rest of his hospitalization. We're taking him up to his room now."

Annie stepped forward and was immediately warmed by the girl's smile and sincerity. "I'm Ann, Mack's sister. Is he awake? Is he alright?"

"Oh, yes, he's becoming more alert. He's already had some pain medication. He seems to be doing well, considering--"

"That's what I mean. Does he understand what's happened?"

Penny hesitated before she answered. "Yes, I think so. He seemed surprisingly calm."

Matthew walked away then, his anger illuminating from his face and posture. Penny could see the worried glances that followed Matthew across the room. "Of course, he's still very groggy and weak," she said. "He's going to room 316 on the west wing. Wait here about fifteen minutes and then come on up." She excused herself and left.

The little group sat silently until the assigned time had lapsed. "It's time. Let's go, Pop," Annie coaxed.

Matthew signed heavily. "No, why don't you go on. I can't

231

see him just now. Tell him I'll stop by in a day or two. I want to get back home."

"Daddy, no," Annie cried. "Why are you being like this? Mack needs--"

"No, Annie," Andrew interjected. "He's right. It would be better if he waited – better for both of them."

"Yeah, I'll take him home," Sonny said. "We can get things settled at home and I'll drive in and get you tonight, okay?" Annie watched them walk away. Actually, Annie thought, it was a relief to see her father go.

Chapter 25

Luke was in charge of things at home. He behaved uncharacteristically sullen with angry outbursts. The chores were done late, the kitchen was a mess, and everyone was irritable. Finally, he threw the dishtowel across the room, walking toward the door. "John, Thomas, I'm going out for awhile. You guys take care of things while I'm gone," he ordered, ignoring their contemptuous glares. "No, I don't know how long I'll be!" He hurried across the back porch into the office. He dialed Maggie's number with a trembling hand. "Meet me at the place," he said when she answered. "Yes, now! Think of some excuse and come right away." He slammed down the receiver.

He bolted out the door and down the bottom road toward his secret place. He ran all the way, his heart pounding in his chest. Gasping for breath, he pushed himself until he broke out into the clearing. She arrived soon, flushed and breathless.

He bent over, his hands on his knees. "Did you hear what happened?"

"No, I didn't. We were canning all morning and haven't talked to anyone. What happened?"

"It's Mack. Sonny found him laying in the woods early this morning with his leg all shot up. Should have seen my father. He was so angry. Mack just got his draft notice, and he shot off his own leg!" He turned to look at her for the first time. "It was probably a dumb accident. All I know is he'll never go now. He can't."

Margaret could barely breathe. "You think you should enlist, don't you," she whispered. "No, Luke, you can't."

"God, Maggie!" He walked away.

"What did you expect me to say? 'Fine, go ahead! Have a nice time at the war!' You do not believe in this thing any more than I do. Luke, listen to me. You can't do this!" she begged, trying not to cry.

"Why not? I told you before, someone has to do it, so why not me?"

"You're doing this because of your father. You think you have something to prove."

"What's wrong with wanting your father to be proud of you? You should have seen him – at the restaurant, talking to Ken Beyer's dad and all those other men. He said one of his sons will go with his blessing."

"What are you talking about?"

"The night we had supper in town after John's track meet. Mr. Beyers was trying to insinuate that my father company was making money off the war, but yet none of us enlisted. The whole town heard it. My father is proud he served during the war. He went off to the war even when his parents forbid it."

"Luke, that was different. This is just a political maneuver – it's a farce! It's a war we can never win!"

"Who says? You must be reading different newspapers than I am. That offensive in Cambodia is going very well."

"Oh, sure, and did you see the casualty numbers?" She was talking loudly, almost screaming, but he was unyielding. "I don't care about any of that, anyway," she said more softly, trembling. "I don't know why I'm standing here shouting a bunch of political rhetoric. It's all garbage. The only thing I care about is -- is you, Luke. Don't do this, please."

He took her into his arms then and held her close as she let her tears fall unchecked. "Maggie, it's not like I have any choice," he whispered. "I'm eighteen. I'm gonna get drafted sooner or later. I just want to get it over with."

They sat down upon the cool stone of their rocky place. Luke gazed at the valley and river. "I need your help, Maggie," he said. "Could you drive me into the recruiter's office? Look, if you don't, I'll get there some other way."

She inhaled deeply before she answered, not knowing for sure how she should handle this. She didn't want to push him away. "Sure, okay, we can go next week." She hoped Mack would be home from the hospital by then, and Luke would calm down.

"No, I want to go right now. I see no reason to wait. I'm not going back home until I get this thing settled." He stood up with a resolute look fixed upon his face.

"Okay, then let's go." Fifteen minutes later, they were off.

* * * * * *

Three and a half hours later it was done. The Recruiters' office carried out the procedure in a precise, well-practiced manner. The Sergeant even got him in for his physical at the doctor's office, which was conveniently located in the same building. There were some written exams and other preliminaries to take care of, but all went smoothly.

"Well, if everything checks out, and I'm sure it will," the accommodating Sergeant said, smiling, "you could be sworn in soon."

"How soon?" Luke pressed.

"Well, how soon do you want? We do have eleven guys leaving this Thursday, but -- "

"Why can't I go then?"

"Well, son, it will take some time to process these papers. Is there any particular reason why you're in such a doggoned hurry? You're not in any trouble, are you?"

"No, it's nothing like that. The sooner I start, the sooner I'm done. I'm sure you can get my papers all in order by Thursday. That's three days."

"OK, I can do that, I guess. Why don't I call you tomorrow and-- "

"No, I'll call you Wednesday afternoon to make sure everything is set. My family is having some problems right now – one of my brothers is in the hospital. It would just be better if you didn't call my house, that's all."

234

The sergeant slapped Luke's file on the corporal's desk. "This kid's in a hurry, so process this as soon as possible," he commanded.

"What's the rush," asked the corporal, yawning. "Some kind of trouble with this one?"

"Nah, he's squeaky clean. I have no idea why he wants to go so quick. But I ain't gettin' paid to be no damn psychologist. He wants to leave on Thursday. Make it happen."

* * * * * *

Maggie had been sitting numb and sullen in the corridor, catching glimpses of Luke being shuffled from one appointment to the next. He came out and sat down beside her. They sat silently for several minutes, until finally Luke said, "I guess we can go now."

She handed him the keys and climbed into the passenger side, sitting very close to her door. She wanted to say something, but she was afraid of the answers to her questions. They rode along silently, each afraid to say anything.

About halfway home, she said, "There's one of those scenic overlooks up there. It's one of my favorite places."

He saw it and pulled in. She got out of the car and hoisted herself onto the rock wall, staring out over the wide, green vista spread out before them.

"Well? Aren't you gonna say anything?" He picked up a stone and threw it over the wall. "You could yell or something."

"You dope, I'm not saying anything cause I'm afraid I'll--" She didn't finish but they both knew she meant she was afraid she was going to cry. She got up quickly and moved to the other end of the stonewall. She took a deep breath and said, "I think you are making a terrible mistake, but your motives are honorable. I don't want you leaving and thinking I'm mad or anything." She waited to continue until she could trust herself to speak without trembling. "And I guess I'm scared."

She could feel him coming nearer until he stood behind her. She whirled around and buried her face in his chest. He held her as she cried. "Hey, I'm scared, too. Don't worry, Miss Margaret

Ann McDuffy, I don't want to be no hero, no dead one especially." He took off her glasses and cupped her face in his hands, waiting till she brought up her eyes to meet his. "Hey, maybe they'll make me a cook or a truck driver or something." They both smiled a little and he kissed her softly. "C'mon," he said, "we gotta get back."

They drove to the entrance of the driveway. He stopped the car. "Will you drive me back Thursday morning?" he asked, staring straight ahead.

"Sure, I can, but why not your dad or one of your brothers?" He didn't answer. "You're not going to tell them, are you."

He opened the door and got out. "I can't, Maggie. Everything at home is so screwed up. It's better if I just go. I'll leave a note or something." It was useless to argue so she started to drive away. "Maggie," he called after her. "Thanks." There was nothing else to say.

* * * * * *

Andrew and Annie did not leave Mack's bedside as the long afternoon wore on. Each time he stirred, they drew near, wanting to comfort him. He said very little, sometimes asking for a drink or what time it was, and then drifted back asleep. They found themselves casting quick glances at the place where the mound beneath the blankets abruptly stopped.

Penny performed her nursing duties with her usual proficiency. More and more Andrew found himself watching her. He was fascinated by this attractive young woman as she flowed around the room. Andrew had never paid much attention to girls, except on an intellectual or academic level, but he was definitely attracted to this one. Her warmth and genuine caring made her all the more beautiful. He offered to help whenever he could just so he could be close to her. He helped her reposition Mack and even held him on his side so she could give him the pain shots. He watched as her fingers gently touched her patient. Of all the things he had begrudged his brother, this was the most agonizing -- he would gladly lay down and take Mack's place for just the promise of her touch.

Dr. Lamp came in and tried to speak to Mack but he turned away. So the doctor talked with Annie and Andrew, reiterating that their brother had come through the surgery well. He would need therapy, of course, but for now the main thing was for the incision to heal and for him to rebuild his strength. Then the doctor turned to his daughter. "They tell me you've hardly left your patient's beside all day. Don't you think you should at least eat something? I'm sure there's someone who could cover for you for a little while."

"Oh, Daddy," she cried, embarrassed.

"Actually," Andrew blurted, "I was thinking about going to the cafeteria myself. Why don't you join me so I won't have to eat alone." Annie gasped at her shy, reserved twin's uncharacteristic forwardness.

"Well, I suppose I could step away for a few minutes." She checked the IV drip and the needle site. "His next vital checks aren't for another half hour. And he seems pretty comfortable."

"See," Andrew pressed. "This is a good time then. Annie, why don't you call home and see if Sonny can come get you. One of us should stay the night and I'm sure you're needed at home more than I am." With that, he followed his dinner partner out the door.

Penny accepted Andrew's suggestion because she realized this would afford her a great opportunity to get more information. Officially, she had good reason to ask questions because she had to complete the social and family history interview, which would be part of her report. But truthfully, she wanted to know more about Mack on a personal level. She led Andrew down to the coffee shop and ordered impatiently.

"Tell me about your family, Andrew. I gather its a large one from what I've heard around town-- er, Shannon Town, that is. I spend weekends down there because my family has a cottage in the area. You're the family that moved into the Weatherly place, right?"

"Oh, so our reputation precedes us, aye? Yes, there are ten of us kids. Mack's the oldest. Then comes Annie and me-- we're twins, and then six more brothers, plus the baby, Becky. My mother died soon after her birth in January."

"Oh, I'm sorry, Andrew. How awful for all of you."

"Yes, well, thank you. But anyway, through a rather bazaar turn of events, we found ourselves moving out here to become farmers."

"Oh, wow. That's incredible. What did Mack think about all this?"

"Mack?" Andrew laughed. "He hates it. My father told us that if we stay until the first harvest this fall, then we can go back East if we want."

"You mean, you'd all move back to New York?"

"No, I doubt my father will ever leave, but I'll go back to college. I'm not sure what Mack's plans were. He just got his draft notice a few days ago, and now this happened."

"You don't think he did it on purpose, do you?"

"No, he was trying to shoot a fox that has been eating our chickens and chewed up our dog. It was a stupid accident, but try telling that to my dad."

He chatted on about how he had declared conscience objector and his studies at Georgetown University, but she wasn't listening. She was thinking about Mack and his father's cold, strange behavior in the waiting room. Now she understood.

* * * * * *

Sonny parked the car in the circle drive in front of the hospital and waited for Annie to come out. "I haven't eaten anything all day," she said wearily. "We could eat here at the coffee shop and then go up and see Mack one last time before we go home."

"Naw, you've been here all day," he said. "I know a place we can eat and its a lot better than here." He started the car up. End of discussion.

"Guess it doesn't really matter anyway," she sighed as they drove along. "I don't think he cares whether anyone is there or not."

"He cares," Sonny said.

He pulled into the McDonalds parking lot and instructed her to wait in the car while he ran in to get some food. She didn't know if she could stomach greasy fries and hamburgers, but she was too tired to argue. When he returned, he threw the food on the seat between them and drove to the outskirts of town. He turned off the highway onto a little side street that curved first through a residential area and then across a wide valley floor. The road abruptly turned to gravel and lead up a long, steep hill. It ended in a small wooded park.

Sonny stopped the car. "We can eat here before we head home."

Annie was shocked. He was being pleasant – almost thoughtful. "Where are we?" she asked when recovered her powers of speech.

"C'mon, I'll show you." He grabbed the food and lead her down a winding path which lead to a round, tower-like structure built at the edge of the bluff. "This," he said, slapping the rough-hewn stone blocks, "is the Dubuque Monument." He led her around to the other side where there was an opening covered by bars. There was a plaque explaining that Julian Dubuque and an Indian, Chief Peosta, were buried there. Sonny motioned for her to sit down and handed her some food. "You see, they say this guy founded their town," he explained. "But really, there was no city here at all until after he died. The Fox Indians didn't let any other white men on this side of the river, just him."

Annie was intrigued by the story. "So who was this Chief Peosta?"

"I guess when he wanted to be buried next to his buddy. I think his daughter was married to ol' Julian. Unfortunately, the people of this state have decided that's not right, so they want to dig up the bones and separate them. The chief is going to be buried somewhere else."

"Well, that's pretty stupid," she said, nibbling on her sandwich. "Obviously, this is where they wanted to be buried so they should just be left alone." Sonny said nothing. "Guess this is pretty interesting to you since you're – you know, an Indian, too," she said. "How'd you find this place? Have you been here before?"

"Sure, sometimes I come into town before the stores open so I stop for some coffee and a newspaper, and come sit up here.

There's no place back home that's quiet – not like this."

He vaulted over the barrier fence near the sign that warned of danger beyond that point. He stood on the stone out-cropping, gazing at the panoramic view that stretched out before them. There were deep gullies on both sides. The Mississippi laid serenely below, framed by the surrounding woods. Off in the far distance was the city named after the man buried here.

Annie settled back against the cool stone and relaxed. It was very peaceful, so far removed from the trouble in the real world. "I can see why they chose this place," she mussed. "It's so beautiful and isolated."

"Yeah, well it was a big deal to be buried up here," Sonny continued. "See, down there is Catfish Creek. This was a sacred place for the tribe."

"How do you know all that?"

"I read stuff," he said, "and some of it I can guess. The chief wouldn't be buried just any old place." He spoke easily, not that cocky, sharp tone she was accustomed to. There were a million questions she'd like to ask him, like where did he come from and did he have family somewhere? But the time wasn't right, and she didn't want to spoil the moment. It had never occurred to her before that there might be a past or history, even a legacy, attached to this stranger – and she still did consider him a stranger.

But was he, she wondered. The way he moved, his moods, the inflections and tones of his voice -- these things were as familiar to her as those of her father or her brothers. She knew the way he stirred his coffee and tapped the spoon before he laid it down, and how he always turned the kitchen chairs around and straddled them backwards. His enormous strength, his stubborn resolve, and the way his quiet, steadying presence enveloped a room whenever he entered it – these were things she had come to rely upon. Suddenly she couldn't remember why she was supposed to hate him so much.

She stared at him, but it didn't matter because he wasn't paying any attention to her. He sat down with one leg dangling over the edge of the high ridge, with the other leg bent and his elbow resting upon his knee thoughtfully. He was not an intrusion upon this place, but rather seemed to complete it. He was handsome, in that raw, rugged sort of way that had always seemed severe and daunting to her before. And as she watched him, something stirred inside of her that made her heart soar and her palms sweat. She felt frightened and wildly excited all at the same time. Was it Sonny, she gasped? Was it possible she had feelings for him?

Her mind began racing. All this time she had thought of him as being so uncaring. The man has no heart, no soul. She had muttered those words a thousand times. Was she wrong? Or was he a man like any other with passions and vulnerabilities, desires and dreams. If he did, he certainly had them locked away. Perhaps that mysterious part of him was what intrigued her the most.

She realized then that he was talking to her. "Look, its a tow. Got a full 15 load." He was pointing down at the river where a tow was slowly flowing downstream. "Bet if we hurry, we'll get down home before her." He stood up then. "C'mon, we'd better be getting back anyway."

He was right, of course, but she didn't want to leave. She didn't understand what had happened to her during the past few minutes, but it was a seductively delicious feeling that she hoped wouldn't go away when they left this mystical place.

CHAPTER 26

Mack had a very restless night. He slept for short periods, asking for hypo's frequently. Andrew stayed at his side, trying to help in any way he could. Mostly he acted as a buffer between Mack and the nurses. They explained over and over the phenomena they called phantom pain. Even though the leg was amputated and the nerves severed, the brain doesn't program it that way so the pain he was still experiencing in his lower leg and foot was very real.

When Penny got to the floor that morning, the report from the night shift was not encouraging. "He had morphine every three hours and it's barely holding him," the nurse said. "Maybe he could have something stronger. And be sure to ask Dr. Lamp for a repeat on his sleeper, will you? He had a miserable night."

She crept into his room. The breakfast tray was untouched. He was lying back with his hands clasped behind his head, still looking very weak and pale. His cheeks were sunken and his lips were drawn tightly across his mouth. Andrew was dozing in a chair in the corner, but he bristled awake as soon as he sensed her presence.

"Good morning. I'm glad you're back," Andrew said, perhaps smiling a little too broadly considering the circumstances. "We didn't have a very good night, did we."

"No, 'we' didn't," Mack replied sarcastically.

"Andrew, you look exhausted," Penny cooed, having absolutely no idea what affect she was having on the young man. "Why don't you go home for a while. You can rest and come back this evening for a visit if you want."

"No, no, I would be glad to stay and help. I mean, you nurses are really busy-- "

"Well actually, Mack is my only patient. And I would probably be asking you to step out of the room for much of the morning anyway. Is there someone you can call?"

Andrew's heart sank then. He had hoped to stay all day, but for purely selfish reasons. He wanted to spend more time with the beautiful Miss Lamp. But realistically, his presence wasn't having much affect on his brother. If anything, he seemed to be more of an irritant than a help. "Well, I guess if you put it that way, I could call someone to come pick me up. Is that alright with you, Mack?" he asked. "I'm sure everyone back home is waiting to hear how you're doing anyway."

Penny watched Andrew leave and smiled a friendly "Good-bye" his direction. Then she turned her full attention to her patient. "Hi. Good morning," she began. Oh God, too sugary-sweet, she chided herself. Start over again. "Remember me from yesterday? I'm Penny, a student nurse." Again, nothing. "Hey," she called, maneuvering herself in front of him to get his attention. "Most people like having the students because you get more attention."

He still refused to look at her. "Can you give shots? Isn't it about time for one?"

"Maybe. I'll have to check your chart. I'll be back in a minute." Once outside the room she collapsed against the wall. He hadn't recognized her, barely looked at her. She didn't know whether to feel relieved or disappointed. That's good, she scolded herself. He has enough to cope with already

The morning went very badly. No matter what approach she used, the only response she could illicit was his refusal of everything – a bath, bed change, food. Later her father came in and she assisted him with the dressing change. They knew it is not unusual for new amputees to not look at their stumps, so they said nothing when Mack leaned back and stared at the ceiling. He gave curt "yes" and "no" answers to Dr. Lamp's questions. The only thing he said at length was to complain that the pain shots weren't strong enough.

"That's an angry young man in there," Dr. Lamp whistled when they stepped into the hall "Good luck, honey."

"Don't worry, Daddy." She smiled, trying to appear confident. "I always did love a challenge."

That afternoon, Andrew and Annie came for a visit. They brought in some personal things. Annie had packed some slippers and took them out. She wondered if he noticed. His answers to their questions were just as caustic as everyone else's. They had no idea what they should do or say.

* * * * * *

Tuesday morning the report from the night nurse was the same as the day before. The patient was restless and easily agitated. He requested hypo's every three hours, continuing to complain of a lot of phantom pain. Penny found him openly hostile. After trying to convince him to bathe and shave to no avail, she announced that his doctor ordered him to "dangle" twice.

"What the hell is that?" he snapped.

"You have to sit with your feet-- er, your foot to – well, dangle, at the side of the bed." she gulped frantically. "It's important that you start moving because – well, you could get pneumonia. And then you'll really be sick!"

"Well, we wouldn't want that, now would we." He threw back the sheets. "C'mon, let's get this over with so you'll stop bothering me!" He pretended not to be affected by the white-bandaged stump and tried to move to the edge of the bed. He cried out when he accidentally put pressure on his wound. He was moving so quickly that he wasn't giving her a chance to help or explain the easiest way to do it.

He sat perched on the side of the bed for only a few seconds when he began to sway with dizziness. "Oh God, I'm going to throw up," he wailed. "Let me down right now. This is a bunch of bull!" he cried. "I want a hypo right now! I don't care if it's time or not!"

This time Penny decided to hold her ground. "Let me tell you something about morphine. Dizziness and nausea are side effects. You might feel better if you could just try to cut back a little-- "

"I don't give a shit!" he screamed. "Don't you stand there lecturing me about nothin'! Just get the hell out of my room and send in another nurse!"

She stepped back, defeated. She had to go to class anyway so she reported off on another nurse and finished up her charting. This was not going well at all.

Later, she called home to tell her mother she had decided to come home for dinner that night. She needed to confer with her patient's surgeon.

Her father's car was already in the drive when she arrived. It was a large, impressive house on Grandview Avenue, one of the old, prestigious residential areas of the city. But both Penny and her father preferred their country cottage to urban life.

Penny gave her mother a quick peck on the cheek when she walked through the kitchen, trying to whisk past and avoid the standard bombardment of criticism regarding her clothes, her hair, her lack of make up, everything.

Penny and her mother did not see eye to eye on much, but it was the opposite with her father. She measured every man she met against him, and none of then came even close. She knew he had wanted her to follow him into medicine, but she decided on nurse's training. She didn't have the desire or the patience for all those years of study.

She found her father in his study, his newspaper open to the sports' page. "Hi honey," he said. "To what do we owe this unexpected pleasure? You need money or have a lot of laundry?"

"No, Daddy, I just wanted to talk to you about my patient. You know, the emergency amp. It's been three days and he's still uncooperative. He's not moving or eating – I don't think he's even had a bath! He's just vegetating."

"Penny, first of all, three days is not very long. The only other amputees you've dealt with have been elderly diabetics. This is a young man who has been severely traumatized. How do you think you'd react if it was you?"

"Oh, I'd be mad as hell, but I'd want to fight it, not wallow in it!" She was pacing, punctuating each word with a wave of her hand.

"Honey, why are you getting so worked up over this case? Perhaps you're losing your professional objectivity. I told you in the ER that you-- "

"Oh, Daddy," she moaned. "Now you sound just like those bitchy instructors. They're always preaching at us not to get too involved with out patients. I just thought you might have some ideas or some new approach. I just want him to get off his butt and start living again. Is that so wrong?"

"No, it's not. Just remember, empathy, not sympathy. You'll be more effective if you do not get so emotionally involved. You just have to be intuitive and sensitive enough to know when to push and when to hold back." He rose from his chair to give her a quick squeeze. "C'mon, that's the third time your mother has called us for dinner. Let's go have a nice meal and try not to talk shop. You know how excluded she feels."

They sat down to eat and had a pleasant evening. Dr. Lamp walked his daughter out later that evening and gave her a parting hug as well as some advise. "You have good instincts, Penny, so go with them. And remember, your own fears and feelings will not do this young man any good." Penny gave her father a kiss as she jumped into her Jeep. Too late, Daddy, she sighed inwardly. I can't turn off my emotions now.

* * * * * *

Luke could not sleep. Luckily, Thomas was a sound sleeper or he would have been bothered by Luke's incessant tossing and turning. Lying there, listening to the night noises, he could admit he was scared. He had never been one to seek out new adventures or experiences. Rather he preferred to stay close to home and family and be a candid observer of others' exploits.

Maggie's words kept echoing in his mind. "You're doing this because of your father. You think you have to prove something to him," she said. Yes, he wanted his father to be proud, but prove something? Prove what – that he wasn't a coward? Is that what he was doing? He turned over and punched his pillow and tried to sleep so he wouldn't have to think any more.

Somewhere off in the distance, he could hear the faint clattering of a train traveling along the track on the other side of the river. The eerie echo of the whistle at the crossing pierced the night air and sent a cold chill down Luke's back. The words of a familiar folk song began playing in his head.

> *If you hear the train I'm on*
> *Then you will know that I am gone.*
> *You can hear the whistle blow*
> *a hundred miles.*
>
> *A hundred miles, a hundred miles*
> *A hundred miles, a hundred miles*
> *You can hear the whistle blow*
> *a hundred miles.*

Involuntarily, his mind jumped to another verse which ended:

> *This a way, this a way.*
> *This a way, this a way.*
> *Lord, I can't go home this a way.*

He wrapped the pillow around his head, trying to drown out the sounds of the train, the song, and his own thoughts. But as the morning drew near, he was as intent as ever to follow through with his plan.

He got up about 5:00. He knew that Sonny might get up soon and he didn't want to chance a confrontation with him. He left his bed unmade so no one would suspect anything for a while. His dad would growl about him not being there for chores, but no one would get concerned until mid-morning. He hiked down the dark driveway to put his carefully worded note in the mailbox. They would find it at noon when they came to get the mail, and by that time he'd be on his way.

It was still 45 minutes before he was supposed to meet Maggie, so he headed down the hill road to the path for his secret place. Even in the darkness, he could find it easily. He picked up the pace until he was running, the thick brush and weeds slapping him along the narrow passageway. Then he was there. He wanted to memorize every inch of it – every smell of it, the feel of it, the sound of it – like a picture he could recall in an instant. The sun was just beginning to pink up the sky over the river. The woods were alive with the sounds of hundred different creatures.

"Luke," a voice called, startling him. He jumped, but he knew immediately it was Maggie. "I'm sorry. I probably shouldn't be here but I couldn't sleep. You couldn't either, huh? I'm sorry," she said again. "I'll go wait in the car,"

"No, don't be silly." He shuffled his feet and said, "I'm glad you know where this place is, ya' know? You can keep an eye on it – I mean, I know this ol' rock has been here for at least a million years, but don't let anyone change it, okay? Like cut down any trees or anything, alright?"

"You're not sure about this, are you?" she blurted. He didn't answer so she knew it was useless to proceed. "Well, anyway, I promise – about this place, I mean. I swear, no one will touch even a twig. You'll build your cabin right here someday. It'll be beautiful."

"Yeah, I know," he said. "C'mon, it's getting late. We'd better go."

The sun was up now. There were golden streaks gleaming

through the trees and the distant river was transformed into a glistening pool of orange and scarlet gems. Luke's heart was pounding in his throat until he could barely breath. And then he turned away and left.

They drove into town and talked about meaningless things. Neither of them said anything about stopping for breakfast. There was no room in their stomachs for food. Finally, the last four or five miles, they said nothing.

"You know what I'm really sorry about?" he said as they were rounding the last curve at the edge of Dubuque. "I won't be here for autumn – all the color and the corn picking – and winter with everything all covered with snow. I don't think there's any turning leaves or snow in the jungle." He laughed, but it wasn't a very good joke.

They were early. It was too hard to sit in the car so they walked to the park across the street and sat down on the steps of the bandstand. There was an empty beer case nearby. Luke ripped open the cardboard box and started sketching. Maggie marveled as he casually stroked a wonderful drawing of his place in the woods. He penciled in the cabin, complete with a swing on the porch and flowers in the window boxes.

By this time other inductees were arriving with their families. It was time to go. He finished up the picture and handed it to her. "Here, take this," he said. "I'm really glad you helped me with all this. I would have done it somehow alone, but you made it a lot – you know, nicer." He moved closer to her awkwardly. She threw her arms around him tightly.

"Luke!" she whispered. "You don't have to do this. It's not too late to change your mind."

He stepped back and pushed her away. His shoulders heaved and the pained expression on his face was unmistakable. "Damn it, Maggie, don't do this! Just trust me -- I have to go – for a lot of reasons." His face softened then and he wrapped his arm around her trembling shoulders, ushering her toward the waiting bus. "You gonna write me every once in awhile?"

"Sure, if you want me to. I'd like that. But how will I know where to send it?" She tried not to cry as her words choked on swallowed tears.

"I guess you'll have to wait until I write you first."

The recruiter began to bark out instructions. As he read off the names, the young men should board the bus. He explained to the families that the bus would be stopping at a few more places on route to Chicago where they would be sworn in and then taken by an Army transport plane to Ft. Leonard Wood.

There were eleven other names on the Sergeant's list. Some were brash and cocky, while a few were visibly nervous. One by one the names were called. "I'm used to being at the end of roll calls," Luke whispered. Winston, Luke Gregory, was the last name on the list. By that time, tears were streaming down Maggie's face. She held his hand tightly. Even after the last kiss good-bye, she didn't want to let go. But he wiggled his fingers free and stepped inside the bus.

The sickening hiss of the Greyhound door jolted her as a nearby stranger gently moved her back out of the way of the giant wheels. Some of the boys were sitting with their faces pressed against the windows, waving and throwing kisses to loved ones. Maggie walked along the bus, searching for a glimpse of Luke until the bus began moving too fast and disappeared from view as it pulled onto Bluff St. The throng of well-wishers were left in its wake, looking pained and frightened.

"Damn him! Damn him!" Maggie muttered at loud as she stomped over to the car. "Damn Nixon! Damn the Army! Damn the whole damn world! The one good thing that has ever happened to me and he goes off to some damn war!" She realized immediately how childish that sounded and quickly said a prayer seeking forgiveness for her selfishness. "Please, God," she whispered. "Keep him safe. Keep them all safe."

Chapter 27

The day started normally. Matthew was in his usual foul mood, which was even worse since Mack's accident. Chores were late that morning. Someone mentioned that Luke was nowhere around.

"I'm not surprised," Andrew mused, reaching for some

sausages. "Don't you think he's been acting strangely? He's been brooding all week."

The all nodded in agreement. Mack's accident was upsetting for the whole family, but Luke seemed to be especially affected.

"He's been pretty damn irresponsible if you ask me," Matthew muttered. "He's probably off daydreaming in the woods somewhere."

Annie thought in passing that it was unlike Luke to shirk his duties, no matter what was bothering him. She made a note to spend some time with him when he reappeared, but she had a busy day planned. After breakfast, she put Thomas in charge of the house and hurried out to her garden to do battle with the hordes of weeds. She had to resort to crawling down the rows in hand-to-hand combat. Her biggest fear was that she wouldn't be able to tell the difference between the vegetable plants and the weeds and pull out the wrong thing.

The scorching hot morning wore on. At lunchtime she went back to the house, wishing she could stay but she had plenty of housework to keep her busy inside all afternoon. She noticed the mailman's familiar blue pick-up stopped at their box. Peter was already running down the lane to fetch it.

He came running back with more than his usual enthusiasm. "Look!" he called. "There's a funny letter here with no stamps or anything. See?"

Annie saw immediately it was Luke's handwriting. She stared at it with a terrible sinking feeling in her stomach. It couldn't be anything good.

> *Dear Dad, Annie, and everyone,*
> *I have enlisted in the Army and will be on my way to Ft. Leonard Wood by the time you read this. Don't worry. I'll write or call as soon as they let me.*
> *Love,*
> *Luke*

"Oh, my God," she cried. She read it over twice just to make sure. "Peter, go get Pop. Quick! And Mack and Andrew!

Tell them all to come!"

She ran into the house and flung open the Dubuque phone book, trying to find a listing for the government or the Army or someone who could help stop this thing, but her fingers weren't cooperating. She called information and asked for the number for the recruiter. She had to say it twice because her voice was so choked that the operator couldn't understand her. Finally, she got through. A crisp, military sounding voice answered the phone.

"I'm calling about my brother, Luke Winston," she stammered. "We just found out that he's enlisting. This is a terrible mistake. Is there anything we can do? He just turned eighteen last month!"

Matthew, Sonny, Andrew, and the others came stomping into the house. "What was so urgent we had to come right away? Only had a half hour-- "

"Shhhh!" she hissed frantically, straining to hear the voice at the other end. "Now listen," she cried into the phone. "I am going to find that number in Chicago eventually, so why don't you save me a lot of time and trouble and give it to me . . . Well, he hasn't signed anything yet, has he? . . . So, it's not too late to talk to him, right? . . . Yes sir, I have it . . . Thank you very much."

She hung up the phone and looked so devastated and panicked that everyone knew that something was very wrong. She turned accusingly toward her father. "It's Luke – he's enlisted in the Army. He's on his way to Chicago. Once he gets there, he'll be sworn in and then flown to Ft. Leonard Wood. My God, are you satisfied now?"

"He enlisted?" Matthew stuttered. "What do you mean, am I satisfied?"

"You know damned well what I mean," she cried. "For months, you've been talking about duty and honor and having one of your sons in the middle of it! For what?" She was screaming now. "That sweet, sensitive kid – my God! You have to stop him! Here's the number. He hasn't gotten there yet, so you can forbid those people from doing anything until we get there."

Matthew stared at his daughter for a few moments, but the turned away. "No," he said finally. "I'm not going to do anything. He's eighteen. He knows what he's doing. I'm not going to embarrass the boy by running after him and dragging him home."

"Embarrass!" she cried, tears streaming down her cheeks. "You're not going to call? Well then, I will." She picked up the phone, but her father's hand stopped her.

"No, you're not," he said. "He probably would have gotten drafted anyway. They're still calling up hundreds of boys every month. You think just because he's your brother they should make an exception? Well, it doesn't work that way." He strode out of the room then, slamming the door behind him. "I'll be back for dinner in a half hour," he called. "C'mon boys, this place won't farm itself."

No one moved. Annie looked at each of them, silently pleading with them to do something. Andrew was the first to speak. "Maybe I could talk to Pop, convince him to at least call and try to talk to Luke."

"He'll never do it," Thomas muttered angrily. "He don't care."

"No, that's not true!" John retorted. "He just thinks this is something Luke has to do. I heard Pop talk about it one night at the Pub. He said if one of his sons enlists or gets drafted, it would be with his blessing."

"But why? I do not understand why this is such a big deal to him!" Thomas threw his gloves across the room.

"Hey, he joined up even when his parents forbid him!"

"Just stop it!" Annie cried. "I can't stand any more fighting. Just go outside and do as he says." They did as she asked, except Sonny.

She looked up at him, still sobbing and trembling, afraid of what he might say. Please, don't scold me, she pleaded silently. These past few days, since those magical few minutes in the park, she had begun to see him in a whole new way. Sometimes, when he came near her or inadvertently touched her, she felt as though her heart would burst. She had come to realize that it was true, she did have feelings for him. And two of the things she adored the most were his strength and earnest presence. He made her feel like he could fix anything. Could he fix this, she wondered.

For the first time during the entire time they had known each other, Sonny retreated from her gaze. Maybe he sensed what her tears were begging him to do, but they both knew he was powerless. There was genuine concern and anguish showing in his face. Maybe that was enough, just knowing he cared. She turned away and went back to her cooking, releasing him from any unspoken requests. He left with no words passing between them.

* * * * * *

They ate in stony silence. Annie put the food on the table and went outside. After a few minutes, Andrew came out and sat next to her on the swing. "I think we should go to the hospital and tell Mack," he said. "I don't think we should put it off. He'd just be more upset."

"Okay, but – I mean, I thought Dad might-- You're right, it would be better coming from us," she stammered. "It'll just take me a minute to change."

When she came out a few minutes later, she found Andrew sitting beneath the sympathetic old oak tree by the rocky place, looking pensive. Just then Sonny and their father came out of the house and headed across the yard toward the tractors. On the surface, Matthew seemed undaunted and no different than any other workday. "I wonder how he really feels," Annie said. "I hope he's proud."

"He was just being realistic – sooner or later one of us would get drafted. But I think he's pretty shook up. I mean, it's so sudden."

"I wish Luke would have talked to one of us. I knew there was something bothering him. I was just thinking I should make a point to sit down and talk to him. But there just wasn't time." Annie started crying again.

"I can't believe he did it," Andrew cried. "Maybe I should – I mean--"

"Oh stop it, Andrew. What are you saying? You thought long and hard before you filed for conscience objector. You made the right decision."

"Oh really? I'm not so sure. It was so damned convenient to hide away in some library. Good ol' St. Andrew – always does the good and righteous thing. I'd never have the guts to do what Luke did."

Annie could hardly believe what he was saying. "My God, don't do this! I can't handle this right now. I need you to be who you've always been. Don't we have enough craziness around here already? C'mon, we have to go. We can talk about this later, I promise."

* * * * * *

Penny found her patient the same as the two previous mornings. The night nurse reported that he had another restless night. He refused everything and was very rude except when he needed a shot.

This is getting ridiculous, she thought, as she collected her linens and things on the way into his room. She decided that today she would try a firmer approach. She ignored his surly scowl and removed the untouched tray without comment. She went right to work, setting up his bath on the bedside table and pushing it directly in front of him.

"Hey!" he exploded. "What the hell is this?"

"You need a bath," she replied crisply, pushing the controls to raise the head of the bed. "It's been three days." Of course, he didn't budge. She expected that. "Now look, in a half hour you're due for your next shot. Cooperate and I'll make sure you'll get it promptly."

"You can't blackmail me like this!" he retorted. "I don't have to do a damn thing."

"Matthew, you've been vegetating in this bed for long enough. If you don't start moving around you're going to get a lot sicker than you need to be. Now c'mon, start a little soap and water action here, and I'll get your shot."

She left the room without waiting for a reply. She paced in the hallway, trying to stall as long as possible. When she returned to the room, there were bubbles floating in the wash basin and the towel was damp. She asked him to roll over so she could wash his back Hmmmm, she thought, nice buns, and shoulders, too.

When that was done, she handed him the washcloth, asking him to "finish up". He took it and reached under the sheets. Was that a faint blush on her cheeks, he wondered. She was cute with a decent figure. But that did not discount the fact that she was a bitch. Probably the only reason she got by being so mouthy was because of her father. "Okay, that's done. Now where's my shot?" She didn't answer, pretending to be preoccupied with cleaning up the bath things. "Well?' he demanded.

"I have it drawn up, but first I thought you could get up for awhile. That would give me a chance to change your bed." His face changed drastically and she could tell he was very angry, but she was prepared to stand her ground. She flung back the covers and moved the wheelchair into position.

"This was not part of the deal!" he cried. "Why can't I have the shot and get up later?"

"Mack," she started, "I've tried to explain to you that it's the medication that is making you dizzy and nauseated. Just try it for a few minutes."

She took his arm to support him while he pivoted into the chair. Moving very quickly, she stripped the bed. She wasn't going to push her luck and have him up too long. Out of the corner of her eye, she saw him take quick glances at the stump. It was time, she thought.

She was nearly finished when another student nurse came running in. "Mrs. Benson fell," she wailed. "I need some lifting help."

Mack appeared fairly comfortable so Penny ran out with her friend. "I'll be right back," she called as left.

But she wasn't. He became increasingly more impatient and angry, so he wheeled himself over by the bed and tried hoisting himself back into bed. He managed to get himself to a standing position but the wheelchair started rolling. He tried to fling himself onto the bed but missed and fell hard onto the floor.

In that same instant, Penny came in and found him. There was bright red blood showing on his dressing. "Oh my God!" she exclaimed, running to him. "You forgot the brakes, didn't you." She pulled the emergency call light.

"Get away from me!" he howled. "Don't touch me. This is your fault!" She stood back while the others helped him get back into bed. "For God's sake, get me a shot – now!"

Penny turned and fled. "Miss Lamp," a voice called after her. Good grief, it was her instructor, Miss Friar. Penny had no choice but to stop and wait for her to catch up.

"Of course, you know the procedure. You must make out an incident report and call the doctor." She was squeaking again. "The patient appears to be quite agitated. Perhaps we need to discuss your approach." She was smiling that sickening syrupy smile that Penny detested.

"Well, yes, of course. But right now I have to call the doctor. The incision is bleeding so someone needs to look at it right away."

She paged her father and told him what happened. She was waiting with the dressings supplies outside Mack's room when he arrived. She was bracing herself for re-entry into the battle zone, but her father took the supplies. "I can manage this myself," he said.

She sat in the charting room, waiting nervously. She had written up the report, outlining the details of the situation. After a few long minutes, Dr. Lamp came out and sat down beside her. "There was a tiny opening on the incision line," he said. "I put a butterfly across it and it should be fine. I gave him my standard lecture about getting up more with less medication. But he seems to think that I'm covering for my daughter." He snapped the chart shut. "Penny, I know your motives are well intentioned, but I'm wondering if another older, more experienced nurse shouldn't take over."

"He told you he doesn't want me around him anymore, didn't he. But, Dad," she protested stubbornly, "everyone's just babying him. Anyway, I have class all afternoon and Friar wants me to see her later. I'll see what happens."

She had lecture all afternoon and when she got back to the dorm, there was a note from Miss Friar that she report for a conference before 3:30. She took a long, leisurely shower instead. It was so wonderful to get out of that starched, turtle-shell uniform and free her hair from beneath that cap. She put on jeans and a T-shirt and sat in front of a fan to dry her long hair. It flowed on the sensuous streams of air like when she was riding – the freedom, the carelessness. She closed her eyes and she could see him standing there, laughing and leaping into the air--

"Penny," a voice broke in, "Miss Friar called. She's waiting for you."

"Oh, damn. Tell her you don't know where I am."

"No, I told her you were here and she wants you over there – now!"

"God, why can't she just wait until tomorrow!" Penny took her white, clinical smock and started down the hallway.

"What's the matter?" one of the girls asked sarcastically. "Ain't Friar gonna roll over and play dead this time?"

Penny kept walking without commenting. She had no idea why so many of the students resented her so much, but she really didn't care. If this school didn't have rules against it, she'd live at home.

Miss Friar had the incident report and Mack's chart in front of her when Penny entered her office. She frowned disapprovingly at the student nurse's attire.

"Sorry, Miss Friar," Penny said quickly, anticipating the criticism. "I thought it was more important to hurry over so I didn't change. Angie said you wanted to see me right away."

"Hmmm, yes. I am very distressed over the situation with your follow-through patient. I spoke with the young man earlier and he seems pretty angry. Frankly, I'm surprised. You're normally very kind and considerate. But he tells me that you have been rude and insensitive. What do you think?"

"Well," Penny began, "I realize that this is a very difficult time for him, but I think he is jeopardizing his health by his failure to co-operate with his post-operative care. This is his third day post-op and he's hardly been out of bed. He's still taking Morphine like its candy. At least I got him to take a bath and get out of bed. I don't want to back down – unless you take me off the assignment. Are you?"

"Did you discuss it with your father?"

Penny knew that was coming. "Yes, I did, and he agrees with me that something has to be done. He didn't say anything to

257

make me think I should change my approach." Well, it wasn't really a lie because he hadn't said anything about that. "I'd really like to come back in the morning and try to work it out with Matthew. I'll be a little more gentle, but still persistent."

"Okay then, but remember he's a young man who's suffered a tragic loss. Perhaps it's just too soon for him to try to cope with this in a constructive matter." Miss Friar smiled smugly, apparently feeling very wise, indeed.

Penny thanked her and then offered to return the chart. She was anxious to check today's lab results and read her father's notation from this morning. She walked down the hallway slowly, her head buried in the chart.

It was then that he saw her. Whether it was the tight blue jeans, the long, black hair, or the way she walked – but he knew it was her. He was sitting in his wheelchair in the doorway of his room when she went by. His heart seemed to stop beating for a moment, unable to believe what he was seeing. He propelled the chair further into the hallway so he could watch her. She was leaning gracefully against the desk, absent-mindedly tapping one foot behind the other. She put the chart away and turned back.

He tried to move the chair back into his room, but it caught on the doorframe. She took a couple of steps but then saw him. Their eyes met for a moment as they gazed at each other awkwardly. She recovered first and hurried toward him as he frantically tried to propel the chair back inside his room, but she blocked his retreat.

"So! The cold-hearted bitch is really the mystery lady." He spit the words angrily. "Why in the hell didn't you tell me?"

"When? Tap you on the shoulder in Recovery Room and say, 'Hi, I'm Penny Lamp, the girl on the horse that you nearly hit the other day. Oh yeah, too bad about your leg.' And anyway, how was I supposed to know if you even remembered."

Mack wheeled his chair back inside his room and went straight to the window so he could stare out rather than look at her. He hated this. He had such wonderful fantasies about her and what this moment would be like. But this was all wrong.

"You must be tired, and the nurses are pretty busy with supper. So why don't you let me help you back into bed." There was no response. "How about supper?" she tried. "I can see you weren't exactly thrilled with the corned beef. I could go down to the snack shop and get us a couple of hamburgers." Again, he didn't react or answer. She moved around him and sat on the edge of the windowsill, directly in front of him. "Damn it!" she cried. "Look at me. You have a right to be angry. And maybe I pushed you too hard, but I couldn't stand seeing you like this. I wanted you like you were before, only up close this time."

"But I'm not like I was before, am I."

"Yes, you are, or at least you can be. It'll take some time, but you're gonna get through this. C'mon, I'll help you get back into bed"

He didn't answer but moved the chair to the bedside, snapping the brakes into the lock position. She started to put her hand on his arms to assist him, but he jerked away from her and pivoted into bed smoothly, unassisted. She fused over him, straightening the sheets and rearranging his bedside table.

"I didn't forget," he said. "Sometimes, when I was all juiced up on the shots, I'd wonder if it was true or just part of a dream. I just can't believe it's you, that's all."

"Why, because you think I'm a monster? I didn't like being like that, honest, but your case called for drastic measures. You probably won't believe this, but most of my patients love me – they think I'm great!" She was trying to be pleasant and upbeat, but it was useless. He wouldn't even look at her. "Anyway, what about those hamburgers?"

"Nah, I'm not hungry, but thanks for asking." He stared at the ceiling.

"You haven't eaten in days. How about some soup -- "

"No! I don't want anything to eat!" he cried. "I don't want you or anyone else hovering over me. Get the hell out of here and leave me alone!"

"Excuse me," a third voice broke in. A second shift nurse came into the room. "Oh, hi, Penny," she said, noticing Mack had a visitor. "Mr. Winston, you haven't had a shot since this morning. I could get something if you'd like."

"No, I'm fine. You people should make up your minds. First you say I'm taking too much, and now you're offering it."

He turned toward the wall, dismissing them both.

Penny watched him closely. He was tight-lipped as usual, but instead of being cocky and self-indulgent he seemed subdued. And he was refusing shots? The staff nurse left, and Penny knew that if she was smart, she'd leave, too, but she could not walk away. "C'mon, Mack, I'm not such a bad person, really."

"Don't take this personally. There's just a lot of stuff going on right now. Annie and Andrew came this afternoon to tell me that one of my brothers left home this morning and enlisted. Luke – he just turned eighteen-- " His voice broke then for a moment. "He's a nice kid who has as much business running off to the Army as-- "

"As you? Is that what they told you?"

"No, they didn't have to. Luke took the old man seriously with all that patriotism-stuff. And after my accident, I bet Pop was mad as hell. Luke probably thought he was taking some of the heat off me! Dumb kid!"

Penny could see the guilt twisted across his face. She didn't understand the dynamics involved, but she sensed that Mack's accident had touched off emotional undercurrents, especially between him and his father. She had no idea how to respond to all this. "So now what?" she asked finally. "I mean-- "

"I know what you mean. Am I going to get off my ass and start trying to handle this thing? Yes, I'm going to start therapy in the morning. And I'm going to try to lay off the hypos so maybe my head can clear up a little. I want to get out of here and go home." He looked up at her then. "Penny, are you, er – I mean, will you still be my nurse in the morning?"

"Well, sure, if it's alright with you." They smiled shyly at each other. "Well, you have a big day ahead of you so you'd better get some rest. I'll see you in the morning." She wanted to reach out and touch him, but it didn't seem right, so she turned and left.

Chapter 28

Penny reported to the floor a half hour early. "He had a terrible night," the night nurse said. "He refused all medication until I convinced him to take a sleeper at 2:30. Last time I made rounds, he was finally asleep."

Penny crept into his room. He was still asleep but not deeply. She could tell by the rumpled sheets that he had a fitful, restless night.

If the night had been bad, the day was even worse. First there was a bath and the dressing change. The crusty, bloody dressings had to be pulled away from the tender suture line. Then it was time for therapy. His stubborn knee muscles were massaged and stretched, and some one-legged standing to begin his new balancing act. Penny went with him and watched warily as he pushed himself, continuing to refuse any pain medication. Occasionally, glimpses of his humor surfaced, but mostly he remained quiet and subdued. He asked the therapist about a prosthesis. They introduced him to another patient who had one, who was able to maneuver flawlessly. Mack was reminded that his stump needed to be conditioned first.

Penny and Mack spoke very little except about matters directly concerning his care. "Is anyone coming by to see you today?" she asked when they arrived back at his room. She hoped it would lead to some dialog.

"Nah, I called them to tell them I'd be in therapy all day."

She surmised that he did not want to face anyone yet. Emotionally, he was in worse shape than ever. He seemed intent on suffering alone.

Friday was much the same, except he seemed more cheerful, but also more focused. At the end of his afternoon therapy session, the therapist noted that there had been considerable progress. She showed him some exercises he could do on his own over the weekend. After another week or two of hard work, she was sure there would be drastic changes, especially with his stiff knee.

Mack rolled down the hospital corridor toward his room. He was becoming very proficient with his new mode of transportation. Penny followed him, her hands clasped behind her back. He vaulted into his bed, showing off a little, she thought.

"Hey, why the long face?" he chided her.

"Well," she said, "I just came in to say good-bye. My shift is over and we don't work on the weekends. I don't think I'll be assigned to you next week. You're doing so well."

The color drained from his face, but he managed a forced smile. "I don't think I'll be here much longer anyway. You'll still be around, won't you? I mean, taking care of other patients, right?"

"Sure. I can stop in and see how you're doing, okay?" She turned to leave.

"Penny," he called. "You goin' out – riding, I mean?"

"No," she said without turning around. "I have a lot of homework." That was the first reference of their earlier encounters in two days. But he said nothing further, so she left.

She went to the dorm, showered and changed. She tried to take a nap, even went for a walk, trying to get him out of her mind. She found herself trying to think of excuses to see him again. Before long, she found herself heading back toward his room. She decided she'd just peek in. If he was sleeping or anything, she wouldn't bother him. By now it was suppertime so she was counting on his supper being unappetizing so she could get those hamburgers she had talked about a couple days ago.

* * * * * *

Penny was surprised to find that Mack had visitors. Andrew and Annie were there, looking pale and frantic. She also recognized their father from their brief, strained encounter the day of Mack's surgery.

"Your place is at home now," he was saying. "You don't have any tubes or anything, and you look pretty strong. I'm going to call your doctor and make arrangements to get you out of here."

"Excuse me, can I help you?" Penny asked, stepping into the room. "Mr. Winston? Hi, I'm Penny Lamp, the student nurse who's been taking care of your son all week. I couldn't help but overhear – you want to take him home? I don't think you understand-- "

"Oh, I understand," Matthew retorted. "My son needs to be home with his family. He seems to have recovered very nicely. You can get around on your crutches until you get your new leg, right, son? I'm going to have the nurse page the doctor," he announced as he left the room. Annie took one look at Penny's panic-stricken face and ran after her father. "Maybe I can talk some sense into him," she murmured.

"Miss Lamp," Andrew said. When she didn't respond, he tired again. "Miss Lamp, my father means well, but--"

"Mack!" Penny exclaimed. "You have to tell him no. You need more time, more therapy -- "

"No, I think he's right. I just as well go home. I'm not doin' nothin' laying around here except feeling sorry for myself. I just as well go home," he said again. Who was he trying to convince, me or himself, Penny wondered. "Since you're here why don't you teach Annie how to do the dressing changes."

"You could show me, Miss Lamp," Andrew said. "I've never done that sort of thing, but I'm sure you could teach me."

"Yes, someone had better learn because you know it's going to start bleeding again. And what are you going to do if you get an infection in there? And what about the therapy?"

Just then Matthew came stomping into the room with Annie at his heels. "Damn doctors!" he muttered. "They always think they know everything. Absolutely no way are you going to stay in here another night, much less two weeks. Christ, no wonder doctors have so much money!"

Penny couldn't stand it any longer. "That 'damn doctor' happens to be a terrific surgeon and also my father!" she retorted. "How are you qualified to know what's best for your son medically. He still has stitches, for one thing, and there's still some bleeding. And what about therapy? And if you're thinking about taking him out of here A.M.A. -- Against Medical Advice – then you should know that then my father does not legally have further responsibility for his care."

"Young lady, is that supposed to be a threat?" Matthew asked, staring at her incredulously. "And why are you so angry?

263

Your dad's coming so we can work something out, okay?"

Right on cue, Dr. Lamp strolled in. Obviously, he was less than enthused about the situation, but he didn't appear angry either. But then Penny had never seen him really mad. She wished he would be this time.

"Mr. Winston," he smiled, extending his hand. "As I said on the phone, I have some real reservations about discharging your son now." He walked over to the bed as he talked and folded back the covers. Matthew appeared shocked at the sight of his son's severed leg. "You see," the doctor was saying, "it's not healed yet. The stitches should stay in for three or four more days. And more importantly, he needs therapy – see how he keeps the knee bent all the time. That could be very serious if he doesn't get those muscles loosened up."

"I understand, but couldn't all of that be done as an outpatient?" Matthew asked, refusing to be deterred. "I'll make sure he comes to your office next week to have the stitches removed and we'll set up some therapy, too. I want him home, and I will do whatever is necessary to get him there."

"Very well then," Dr. Lamp said, much to the disbelief of his daughter. "I'll write out the prescriptions. You can get them filled right here at the hospital. And you'll need some dressings supplies, too." The two men walked out of the room, still chatting.

Penny stared at the three remaining Winston's in total astonishment. She was outraged, and it showed on her face. She didn't know if she was angrier with Matthew or her own father.

Andrew finally broke the silence. Clearing his throat, he said, "Miss Lamp, perhaps you should show us how to change the dressings now."

"We could ask one of the other nurses," Annie said, seeing how angry Penny was. "I'm sorry about this. You probably think our father is some kind of raving lunatic, but he has his reasons. And I suppose he's right – it would be better for Mack to be at home right now."

"Better for whom? Mack, or all of you?"

"Oh, get off your damn high horse, lady," Mack cried angrily. "How do you get off talking to my sister like that? I'm going home and that's all there is to it."

Shocked by his tone, Penny was jolted into calming down and tempering her behavior. She knew her father was using logic in co-operating with Mr. Winston's demands because then at least he'd be able to do the follow-up care plus gain the trust of the family. "I'm sorry," she murmured, trying to sound sincere. "I'd be happy to show you."

Annie paled at the sight of the bloodied, ragged stump, but Andrew appeared to get physically sick. The color drained from his face and sweat rolled down his temples. Annie managed to watch intently as the procedure was explained, but poor Andrew began to wobble as though he was ready to pass out. He made an excuse and made a hasty retreat. Annie sighed a deep breath of relief when at last the ordeal was over, and then she, too, left.

Penny handed Mack his clothes. She tried to assist him as he labored to get dressed, but he shrugged her off. Penny stepped back from the bed, smarting from his anger "Mack, I said I was sorry."

"I thought nurses were supposed to be kind and even a little tactful. God, do you have a lot to learn!" He struggled with his blue jeans, trying to pull them over his hips. He was nearly done when he inadvertently pushed down on his stump. He sucked in his breath for a few seconds, waiting for the pain to pass. "And I don't appreciate people standing here talking about me like I was a piece of meat at the butcher shop!" he added. "Get the damn chair so I can get the hell out of here!"

She dutifully brought the chair to the bedside. Mack stood up and started to pivot before he had caught his balance. He began to fall, but Penny grabbed him and they both toppled over onto the bed. Their faces nearly touched, and for a moment neither of them tried to move away.

"We'd better try this again," Penny said hoarsely. This time it went smoothly. He didn't look at her again. He grabbed his paper bag of belongings and propelled the chair into the hallway. Annie, Andrew, and Dr. Lamp were talking nearby.

"Okay, Mack," Annie called out. "Daddy went to the pharmacy and will bring the car around. So I guess we can go on down. Thank you so much, both of you, for all your help. We'll take good care of him, I promise." She was smiling a little too bravely, Penny thought.

"Here, why don't I go down with you," she offered.

"No, that's fine," Mack objected quickly, still not looking at her. "We can manage. Dr. Lamp, thanks again. I'll see you early next week." He started down the hallway.

"Yes, thank you," Andrew echoed, lingering behind the others. "Perhaps we will see each other again, but under less trying times," he said. But she wasn't listening.

As they left, Penny felt an awful sinking ache in her stomach. She wasn't ready for him to leave, not like this. Her father wrapped his arm around her slender shoulders and gave her a hug. "They'll be alright, honey," he said kindly. "Don't take it so personally. It's not the first time a patient thought he could do better at home than in here. And you know what? They usually do. Are you going to the cottage this weekend?"

"No, I can't. I'm going to write up this case study and get it over with. I'll just stay in the dorm this weekend. Don't tell Mother though. She won't give me a minute's peace." Her father left to finish his rounds, leaving her standing alone to stare down the empty corridor. She was glad he had accepted that excuse and not pressed her for more explanation. How could she explain why she couldn't go back there? Around every corner, at every crossroads, she'd be looking for him – the tall, dark, handsome stranger with the laugh that still echoed through her dreams. She didn't know how or when, but she would see him again.

* * * * * *

They rode along in silence for a long time. Matthew clinched the steering wheel and looked very uncomfortable. "I made a mistake," he began. "Sonny took me to the place where you fell. I didn't want to see it, but he insisted. It's a miracle he found you that night. I don't know how I could have thought you did such a thing on purpose, and I'm sorry. That's why I wanted to bring you home tonight. I couldn't say it there." He glanced at his son, looking truly remorseful. Mack did not answer him immediately. Please, Annie prayed, say something pleasant. Don't fight.

266

"I know, Dad. I'm really glad to get out of there," he said. No one said anything further until the pulled onto the yard. Mack was engulfed by a jubilant welcoming committee. Everyone was trying not to stare at his stump, but it was difficult not to. Peter and Danny seemed to be the most affected by the sight of the rolled up pants leg. "Hey, guys," Mack said. "I'll have an artificial limb in a few weeks that will make me good as new. You'll see."

As everyone made their way into the house, he hung back waiting for Sonny. "Hey man, how are you managing around here without me?"

"It's tough, but we're makin' it," Sonny answered, smiling.

Then most amazing thing happened. Mack leaned heavily on his crutches and offered his hand to Sonny. "Thanks for saving my life, man. I could have died-- "

"It was no big deal," Sonny interrupted. "I'm glad you're back. It was too quiet around here without your whining and bitching." They laughed then as they headed toward the house. "Hey, I was thinking," Sonny said, "since you're gonna have trouble with the stairs in the house, maybe you'd like to bunk in my shed for awhile."

"Sure, that's a good idea," Mack agreed, surprised at the offer. "Frankly, I could use some peace and quiet. Since you're not exactly a chatter box, I think it'll work out fine."

Annie was especially happy with these new arrangements since she'd now have an excuse to visit the secret confines of Sonny's shed. She made her first trek down there that night when she brought Mack some of his things. She was disappointed Sonny wasn't there. Mack was sitting in the darkness, smoking a cigarette. "Here's your toothbrush and stuff," she said, wondering where she should put them. The room was sparsely furnished with no dressers or closets. Sonny had hastily framed a crude bunk bed together and put an old chair nearby. "Mack, how am I going to know if you need anything down here? Maybe this wasn't-- "

"C'mon, Sis, I'm gonna be fine down here, really. I'm not helpless, you know." He drew deeply on his cigarette. "You know, I was just sitting here thinking that I never paid any attention to the sounds and smells out here – except the ones I complain about, that is. Maybe it's because I hated being stuck in the hospital, but it honestly feels good to be back here. Wouldn't Luke laugh if he could hear me now." He flicked the ashes from his cigarette onto the floor. "Annie, I'm sorry to do this to you," he said, trying to change the topic of conversation as well as the mood. "I mean, this is all you needed – another job to do. Maybe in a couple days I'll be able to do the dressing changes and stuff myself."

"Don't worry about it. It's late so you'd better turn in. Good night." She kissed him softly on the forehead and left just as Sonny came in. They murmured good nights to each other as they passed.

"Just yell if you need anything," Sonny said as he hoisted himself onto the top bunk.

"Yeah, sure," Mack said. He was looking at Mutt and her five puppies sleeping in the corner. He laughed to himself, noticing that she looked great. Your leg got chewed up, he thought, but look who's missing one. He tried to settle down but the throbbing pain was tremendous. He reached out and found the bottle of pain pills and swallowed two pills. He laid in the darkness until finally he drifted off to sleep.

* * * * * *

It was very late. Even Annie had gone to bed. Danny waited until everything was quiet to crawl into Peter's bed. He was surprised Peter didn't chase him away. Mature ten year old boys hate sleeping with their little brothers – well, that's what Peter said. Except tonight. When Danny braved a quick glance his direction, he saw that Peter was still awake, too.

"I was cold," Danny offered lamely. That was his usual excuse.

"It's June and it's hot," Peter pointed out. But he still didn't insist that Danny leave his bed. They lay silently for awhile, both staring at the ceiling and watching the shadow of the curtain swaying with the breeze through the open window.

"What you thinkin' about," the older one whispered hoarsely.

"Mack's leg"

"Annie said it had to be cut off or he'd bleed to death."

"But what they'd do with it?"

"Do with what?"

"Mack's leg. Where'd they put his leg."

"I don't know. Never thought about it. Only you would be dumb enough to ask a question like that." It was an interesting question, but it was kind of creepy talking about it while lying in the darkness, listening to the night noises around them.

"I bet Mama would know if she were here."

"Yeah, probably," his brother agreed, "but don't go asking Annie about it. I hear her, late at night, crying sometimes. So don't go asking her any dumb questions, alright?"

"I know, Peter. You don't have to tell me that," Danny retorted, angry that his brother would think that he would knowingly make their sister cry. "I won't ask her, but I wish someone would tell us where Luke went. I miss him."

"They told you. He went to Boot Camp."

"Boot camp! Who ever heard of a camp like that?"

"It's not like summer camp or nothin', dummy. It's a Army camp, where you learn how to be a soldier."

"Why would Luke want to go there?"

"I dunno. He just wanted to, I guess."

"Why? How come he'd leave us like this?"

"He didn't leave us. It's not forever. He'll be back."

"This kid at school, Greg Hodges, showed me a picture of his cousin. Greg said he got killed in the war." The boy's eyes were big and round, and full of fear and questions. "Luke's going to camp, not war, right?"

"You ask too many questions. Just go to sleep," Peter scolded, trying to sound gruff. But as he turned over, his arm fell across his little brother's chest and he didn't move it. "You worry too much," he whispered.

They both yawned and nestled down close together. Annie found them lying together when she checked on them during the night. She studied their sweet, angelic faces and was awed by their contentment. Children are so lucky, she thought. No heartache and no fears.

Chapter 29

Perhaps Matthew was right when he insisted that Mack come home from the hospital. It seemed like a signal that everything was going to be all right, and the family could go on with the business at hand. On the surface everyone was coping with Mack's handicap by ignoring it, as though it was perfectly natural for him around the house while everyone else was working. He reacted by maintaining a facade of good spirits.

But he was having a rough time. Learning to get around on crutches was very difficult because his balance was off. It frustrated him because he always thought of himself as being reasonably athletic and agile. The incisional area wasn't healing very well. He didn't want to subject himself to Dr. Lamp's frowns and lecturing so he skipped the office appointment. Sonny took out the sutures with his pocketknife.

The constant pain, especially the so-called phantom pain, was especially troublesome. He dreaded the nights. He'd lay there in the darkness and swear his big toe was itching or his heel was aching. He'd toss and turn, taking pain pills and sedatives, which were working less and less effectively.

One night, when he was fumbling in the darkness for more pain pills, he noticed Sonny's legs dangling over the side of the upper bunk. He jumped down and turned on the lamp. He got a glass of water from the bathroom and then sat down next to Mack on the bed.

"You're takin' more and more of those things," he said.

Mack started to deny it, but he knew it was the truth. "Can't help it. The sucker hurts like hell. And the part that hurts the most isn't even there any more. It screws up your mind!"

"I believe ya' but this can't go on forever. What are you gonna do when these pills run out?" Sonny wondered at loud. He turned off the light and jumped back into bed.

"I'm sorry if I'm keeping you awake at night. At least when you ran my ass all over this place, I was dead tired at night. I feel so damned useless!" He waited for some kind of reply, but Sonny said nothing.

The next morning, Mack sat in the kitchen having his fifth cup of coffee when Sonny came in. "C'mon, Mack" he said. "Come out here and help us out." Both Annie and Mack stared at him open-mouthed for a moment but then Mack grabbed his crutches and followed Sonny outside.

The little tractor was sitting in the driveway. Sonny showed him how he had fashioned a hand-controlled lever on the throttle. He and the other boys were working behind the barn, cleaning up the junk. Mack could drive the tractor, pulling the wagon. When they came in at noon, Mack was grinning and shirtless, trying to deepen his already dark skin tone. "It'll drive the girls crazy," he laughed. He sat down and ate two helpings of everything. Once again, Annie would have liked to express her thanks to Sonny, but approaching him on a personal level was as impossible as ever.

She busied herself around the kitchen, sneaking an occasional glance at Sonny's direction. The fact that she was developing a huge crush on this man was having little impact on their daily lives. It was useless to think that he might reciprocate any affection. They seldom spoke. Annie was trying very hard to be self-sufficient and bother him as little as possible. She wondered if he even noticed.

Annie was not the only one who was suffering. Andrew seemed to be operating in a fog and no one knew why. He seemed distracted and unusually quiet, even for him. Annie wondered if it was because he missed his accustomed academic environment so she encouraged him to investigate college campuses in the area. When he announced that he was enrolling at Loras College in Dubuque for the fall semester, he got no resistance from his father. Matthew was overjoyed that Andrew was content to stay nearby instead of insisting in returning back East. After that was settled, it was hoped his spirits would improve, but he remained subdued.

No one would ever have imagined that Andrew's

preoccupation was a certain young lady. He couldn't get Penny Lamp out of his mind. It was driving him crazy. It was a sensation totally alien to him and he wasn't coping very well. He had fantasies of taking long walks with her, holding her hand, even kissing her. His heart was nearly bursting, but he had no idea what he should do about it. Perhaps this fall after classes started, he'd casually call her up. Or maybe he'd see her somewhere, like in a store or along the street. But the wait for September seemed like an eternity.

* * * * * *

That sentiment was shared by someone else waiting to start college. Margaret McDuffy surprised everyone by announcing she had decided to skip her senior year of high school and enrolled at the University of Iowa in Iowa City. Her aunt was absolutely aghast, but Maggie was determined. She argued that she had enough credits to graduate so her last year at SHS was nothing more than a formality and a waste of her time.

Margaret made up her mind to do it the first time she had dared to go to Luke's special place in the woods alone. She began crying the instant she sat down on the rocky surface. This is dumb, she reproached herself. It was true that she missed him terribly, but she thought it was stupid to sit around feeling so miserable all the time. Perhaps she was jealous that he was out in the world on his own. It was then that it occurred to her that it was time to make some decisions about her own future.

She raced home and tore open the large envelope of information from the University. The next morning she drove to the Registrar's office and enrolled. She was proud of herself. Now she'd have something really big to tell Luke when he wrote or called. She was counting the days.

Annie and the rest of the family were watching the mail, also. Surely, he would contact them as soon as possible, they hoped. They found that they began watching the nightly news with renewed interest. Even though Nixon had promised to bring home 500,000 troops this year, this was no sign that the war would be ending any time soon. Many people believed he was playing pre-election politics. Most of the news coming out of Southeast Asia centered around Cambodia. Administration sources said the offensive was a brilliant success. But others said that since it was well publicized that since the U.S. was committed to withdrawing by the end of June, the Communists were just waiting for them to leave so they could rebuild their bases. It was a foolish waste of time and American lives.

The Winston's were wary of the word games the politicians were playing in Washington. Luke wasn't in Vietnam, but Annie was convinced that he would volunteer to go if given the chance. It was one of those gnawing fears that no one said at loud.

They viewed the upcoming 4th of July celebration with mixed emotions. This holiday, which was supposed to commemorate patriotism, seemed a little too personal this time. But it was hard not to get caught up in all the town's plans. There would be a carnival in the Riverfront Park, a parade, a corn roast, tractor pulls, and a fireworks display that was hailed as being the biggest and best in the county.

Lori Bean had invited them to eat with her family that evening. As the day was fast approaching, Annie knew she should be making plans and preparing food. Instead, she was trying to think of excuses so she wouldn't have to go into town at all that day. But the boys were excited and Lori, who was her closest friend, was counting on her.

On the surface, things were improving for the Beans. The store had a remodeled front and better merchandise that had customers coming back for more. Charlie was strutting around like he had the world in his hip pocket. He was now an officer in the Jr. Jaycees and active in the Lion's Club. His mother acted as though Charlie was a financial genus. But at home, Charlie and Lori were fighting more than ever. She did all the bookkeeping for the business and knew they were getting over-extended. She was especially peeved that Charlie was so quick to give credit. "He's just as cocky as his father," complained Lori. It seemed as though the happiness, which had eluded her all her life, was as distant and hopeless as ever.

Bean's Hardware and Lumber Yard was one of the co-sponsors of the big tractor pull to be held the afternoon of the 4th, so Charlie would be busy all day. Annie knew that was why Lori was so persistent that the two families should spend the day together. She didn't want to disappoint her friend, but she was still dreading the whole affair.

The day before the big celebration, Annie and some of her younger brothers drove into town for groceries. They were amazed how the town was decked out with flags and streamers everywhere. The carnival had pulled into town during the night, so the boys begged to go watch the roady's assemble the Ferris wheel. She did her shopping quietly, trying to ignore the excitement around her. These people really take this holiday seriously, she thought disgustedly. She planned to find her brothers and go home as soon as possible.

"Hey! Wait up!" a voice called. It was Lori, rushing to catch up with her. "What time you'al be comin' into town tomorrow?" she asked.

"Oh, I don't know Lori," Annie sighed. "Daddy and the boys want to come in early. Tractor pulls and corn roasts – that's all new stuff to us and they don't want to miss a minute of it. But, it's so hot and the baby-- "

"Oh, no, you're not gonna weasel out of this," Lori insisted. "What's wrong, hon. Ain't you heard from your brother yet? How long has it been?"

"He left over two weeks ago. It seems like an eternity. Mrs. Nelson told me that she heard from her grandson the first week. Damn him! He should know we're sitting on pins and needles waiting to hear from him. And tomorrow's a holiday so there won't be any mail."

"Well, don't pay no ever mind to ol' lady Nelson – don't you know that her grandson is close to perfect? And besides, that woman has more money than she'll ever spend and that boy knows who butters his bread. Listen, Luke is probably trying to be very conscientious about all the rules and such. He'll write as soon as he can, I'm sure he will. You just get your butt into town early tomorrow and we'll have a great time. Worryin' about things don't fix nothin'. Good advice, hey? I should listen to it myself!" They both laughed.

Annie had to admit she did feel more enthused. They had

to stop by Ginny's on the way home for a potato salad recipe. As usual, compiling a list of specific portions and directions was difficult. Ginny made these things for so many years that she cooked them by sight, consistency, and taste rather than measurements. The boys ran off to find Jake, leaving Annie and Ginny to talk about mayonnaise and mustard. Before long, the morning was gone. Annie kept looking out Ginny's front window.

"Watching for the mailman?" Ginny asked. "That's him now, isn't it?"

The familiar blue pick up stopped at Ginny's box. Annie jumped into her car and followed him to her box. She tried not to get her hopes up, but then she saw the handwriting she was praying for.

June 27,1970

Dear Annie, Dad, and the rest,

Well, I made it through the first ten days. No sweat. It's really not very hard once you get used to it. I was sort of worried about all the physical stuff. But it hasn't been bad at all, except for the poor "city kids". Luckily, I haven't been singled out or yelled at much at all, which is fine with me.

Annie, the food here is terrible. I really miss some of those great TV dinners you used to cook for us. I really miss you all. Don't worry about me. I'm fine.

Love,
Luke

It was the kind of letter she expected, vague and casual. She read it over and over until she had it memorized. Maybe she was overly concerned. He was going to be all right. It was going to be a great 4th of July, after all.

* * * * * *

The mailman was a very popular man that day. After he stopped at the Winston's, he traveled on south to the McDuffy place.

June 27, 1970

Dear Maggie,

 Sorry if this is hard to read. It's dark in here, but there's enough light coming in through the window to write. I'm doing fine here. Luckily, I don't get upset very easily because they go out of their way to try to make you mad. It's like they're trying to wear you down so you lose your individuality, so you can conform to their way of walking, talking, eating, sleeping, thinking – everything! It's been rough on some of the guys, but I'm doing fine – honest!

 It's really hot down here. The grounds here are real open. There's some woods way off in the distance, but they just as well be on the moon.

 Guess I should go to sleep. We get up at 5 am here.

Take care,
Luke

It was a short letter, but he had sacrificed his sleep time to sit in the darkness and write. He didn't say he missed her or anything real affectionate, but still it was very personal and she was thrilled. The return address was written very clearly on the front of the envelope, so she was sure he wanted her to write. She ran to her room and started composing her reply letter.

Chapter 30

 The weather was perfect for the 4th of July. Warm and the skies were a brilliant blue. Spirits were high and community pride was soaring. The sights and sounds of the small town celebration were woven in a rich blend of children's laughter and local politicians arguing with barbecue sauce dripping down their chins.

 The Winston clan had a wonderful time. The only causality of the afternoon was Danny who had vomited, necessitating the halt of his record sitting nine consecutive rides on the Octopus. The four ears of sweet corn, huge slice of watermelon, and cotton candy he had consumed shortly before he climbed aboard probably contributed to his misfortune.

Food remained one of the focal points of the day. Even Annie's potato salad was heralded as sensational, though Annie herself doubted that it tasted as good as Ginny's. The day flew by. When the fireworks display started, both Becky and Joey were already asleep. Not even the crackling and popping of the Rocket's red glare disturbed them. Matthew was in the beer tent, toasting everything from the flag to Roger Dunlevy's new truck. A lot of talk around the bar centered around the huge harvest that was expected in the fall. Everyone's corn was better than knee high on the 4th of July, the river was behaving, and that new fungus that was showing up further south was staying away so far.

Annie began to gather up her up her brood to go home. Thomas was with a group of boys, apparently friends of his. Annie recognized Jim Mathers, and Thomas mumbled quick introductions of the other two. There was a band setting up for the big street dance and Thomas wanted to stay. Annie was so thrilled that he was at last making some friends that she happily agreed. He could catch a ride home later with their father as John was doing.

Thomas was relieved to see the station wagon pull away. Now he was going to have some real fun. First things first. They ducked into the bushes and poured vodka from Thomas' small flask into cans of 7-Up. They could saunter around the park and drink, and no one would be the wiser. Jimmy was, as usual, hesitant.

"Jim, you nerd!" Thomas blasted him. "How's anyone gonna find out? We're just drinking soda, er -- I mean, pop, as you people say. Vodka doesn't even smell on your breath. C'mon, loosen up! Who knows, you drink enough of these and you might have enough nerve to ask Linda MacLeish to dance with you." They all laughed.

The four-man combo on stage cranked out loud, opening bars of something that Thomas' guessed was supposed to be Neil Diamond's *Cracklin' Rosie*. "Oh, God," he howled. "Doesn't anyone around here know how to play music? They'd be better off with the radio."

They hung around the perimeter of the dance floor, sipping their spirits from their pop cans. To Thomas's utter amazement, these people were dancing on Main Street. His repulsion for these local musicians was intensified when they inserted some Marty Robbins and Hank Williams into their program to accommodate the cross section of ages and tastes.

During a break between sets, Thomas hoisted himself onto one of the tables and gulped down the last of his drink. "You know what, I bet if someone put a band together they could make some decent money around here. There'd be bookings for weddings and parties, not to mention the dances at school. I mean, these guys stink and they're suppose to be the best around, right?"

"Yeah?" Kevin mumbled, dazed and having great difficulty concentrating. He had just finished his third drink. "Well, I'll tell ya', it takes a lot of money to get started. Those guitars alone probably cost $125.00."

"$125.00?" Thomas laughed. "Then they're good for shit! I never saw a decent guitar for less than $600. And the drums – at least a $1500, plus the amplifiers and a key board."

"Whew!" Jim whistled. "That kind of money, you could buy a good pick up!"

"Yeah, but a truck would cost you money, not make money. And besides if you made it big, you could buy any damn truck or car you wanted."

"Oh, wow!" the other three chorused. Their eyes were as big as saucers as visions of Ford trucks and Corvettes danced before them.

"What are you saying?" Dave demanded. "You think we could do it? Man, you're dreaming. Where would we get that kind of bread."

"From me!" Thomas smiled shrewdly. "I can get that much money from my old man or my sister. I'll outfit the band and you guys can pay me back out of our earnings."

"Us? In a band?" Jim cried. "You're off your rocker!"

"No, now listen. Jimmy, you could handle the drums. And Kevin, I could teach you the chords for the bass guitar, and

Davey could play lead. You're already pretty good. I can do the keyboard. We can all sing decently – at least as well as those clowns," he smirked, gesturing toward the band coming back onto the stage. "We could really do it, but we'd need something to really sell it," he said thoughtfully. "I know – that girl!"

"What girl?"

"That girl that hangs around the Pub all the time. She's tall and skinny with real long dark hair, about 22 or 23. And man, can that girl sing!"

They knew exactly who Thomas was talking about, and looked at him disapprovingly. "You mean Kitty McHale? Jeez, Thomas, she can sing but she's a drunk and a -- you know!"

"A whore? Slut?" Thomas volunteered, mocking his propriety. "Okay maybe she is, but she's still a great singer." But he could see by their faces that they were not convinced. The whole town knew that girl was trouble. "C'mon, she can really sing! And I'd be drunk too if I had all that talent and was stuck in a hick place like this!" He regretted it as soon as he said it. For once he was perceptive enough to realize that last statement was thoughtless, judging by his friends' fallen faces. "I mean, she probably had big dreams of being a star. Billy said she went out to California but it was a bust. She's humiliated and hurt, so she drinks a lot. So? She's an experienced performer with a band. She'd be perfect for us! Right?" They still weren't convinced, but he was confident enough for all of them. He'd find that girl and convince her to join their band. "Hey, you guys. I predict a year from now, it'll be us up there, playing our asses off!" For once, he had something to be excited about.

* * * * * *

When Annie and her sleepy crew pulled onto the yard that night, Mack headed down to Sonny's shed to go to sleep. He was already thinking that maybe he should have stayed in town. He could have gotten profoundly, totally drunk. But then he'd be sick in the morning and he already had enough to contend with. He stomped across the floor, slamming the door behind him.

279

Lunging for his bunk, he kicked off his shoe and threw it across the room.

"Ouch!" he howled when a sudden muscle spasm jolted his thigh muscles above the stump. "Goddamn it!"

Sonny leaped down from his bunk. "What are you trying to do? Straighten this knee? Christ, it's stiff as a board." He began kneading the tight muscles, but the painful spasms did not subside.

"I don't care!" cried Mack. "Just keep going!"

An half hour later, they both sat in a pool of their own sweat, grunting and gasping for air. They had managed to wring out a small degree of mobility from the stubborn knee.

"They have people trained for this kind of thing," Sonny muttered. "I'm sure there's a hellvalot better way than this."

"Yeah? So what?" Mack retorted, still having difficulty breathing. "The nearest therapy is Dubuque, and I'd have to go there four or five times a week. It'd take too long. They won't even talk about prosthesis until I can get this knee loosened up. C'mon, try it again."

They had more such sessions the next few days until they settled into a daily routine of doing it a twice a day and during the night if the spasms were bad. Mack became to rely on Sonny more than anyone he had never known. He wanted to be a whole person again, and Sonny was his only chance.

* * * * * *

The long, hot days of July slipped by quickly. There was always so much to do and never enough hours in the day to accomplish it all. Matthew was satisfied with the way things were going. Most evenings he'd take a ride down to the bottom and walk down the rows of corn. Often, he would think about Luke, how much he was missing. Matthew never sat down and wrote a letter to his son, but he mentioned things in passing to Annie, like, "Be sure to tell Luke we got the cultivating done and the fields look great!" or "I bet Luke'll get a kick out of old Bossie turning up pregnant. Guess she got out of the fence once too often." Annie wrote it all down faithfully, knowing her brother was hungry for any news about the farm. But she found that the sights and smells and the day to day happenings were hard to describe on paper.

Margaret was also having problems writing letters to Luke. She was afraid he might think them boring. She wrote just like she talked, the sentences meandering on, often whole paragraphs long. The letters should be casual, but not impersonal. Every letter was a struggle and many times she copied them over and over until they were just right. She signed off each letter with a "Sincerely yours," or "Take care." It was the safest way.

Luke's sixth week of boot camp would be the end of July. He never mentioned it in his letters, but soon there would be decisions made by him or for him regarding his future. Annie and Margaret both hoped desperately that he'd have some leave before the Army sent him someplace else.

Then the decisive letter came. It was very hot and even the window fans did nothing except blow around the hot, humid air. The boys were making hay and when they came in for dinner they resumed the month long argument with their father, demanding that the house should be at least partially air conditioned. It was impossible to sleep when the temperature barely dropped below 75 degrees. Even Annie thought the baby would less cranky if there was a cooler place to sleep. But their father showed no signs of relenting. He was sure that they'd be more miserable going in and out of a cooler place. Angrily, they all stomped out and went back to work with jugs of ice water.

The mail had gone unnoticed all that day. Annie thought of it at suppertime and immediately dispatched one of the boys after it. There was a large, manila envelope from Luke. It was a 8"x10", color portrait of him in his dress uniform. Annie gazed at it for a long time. His hair was short and his expression, firm and serious, so unlike him. Then she read the letter.

July 26, 1970

Dear Dad, Annie, and the rest,
Well, I made it. Graduation is this Friday. I didn't tell you because I wouldn't have any time off, and it's no big deal

anyway. There's certainly no sightseeing around here. Our own farm is nicer than anything down here.

    As I told you, we've been undergoing a lot of testing since I've been here. I guess the scores have a lot to do with determining where we go next after boot camp. We also made out "dream sheets" where we list what we'd chose for ourselves. Some guys said we should put what we really wanted third or fourth on the list because they never give you your first choice and rarely your second.

    Well then, I must be the exception because I got my first choice. I wanted helicopter gunnery training. I've been assigned to the 5th Infantry Division and will get my training at Ft. Polk in Louisiana. Me and the other guys will be leaving Saturday morning. I was hoping for some time off to   come home for at least a couple of days, but the Army says no.

    So, I guess my next letter will be coming from down there. I'll write once I get settled. Don't worry. I'm fine.

Love,

Luke

    Annie read the letter with tears streaming down her cheeks. What Luke was saying is that he volunteered for Viet Nam and the Army had obliged him. All her worst fears were being realized..

    Matthew read it, too, and understood what these short paragraphs meant to the life and future of his son. Without saying a word, he went outside and jumped into his pickup. Annie watched as the cloud of dust swirling after him as he went down the bottom road. She wondered what it would feel like to know that your son was going to war and it's your fault.

    Matthew was stunned by the fear that overwhelmed him as he read Luke's letter. He had been talking about Viet Nam for years, ever since Mack came of age. But now, Matthew's mind became filled with sights and sounds he had forgotten – the bombings and destruction, the bodies bobbing in the water on D-Day, and the visits to VA hospitals where young men laid injured and dying. Usually, he associated only pride and satisfaction with his tour of duty during WW II, but at that moment he only saw the blood and misery.

"Matthew," a voice broke into his tortured thoughts. It was Sonny. Matthew hadn't noticed him driving the tractor along the field roads. "I was checking the corn. There's no sign of that fungus they're talking about."

Matthew said nothing, but offered him a cigarette and lit one for himself. He sat down on the tailgate of his pickup and surveyed the acres of green stretched out before him. Sonny sat beside him, settling into the silence. These two had shared quiet moments like this many times before.

Sonny finished his cigarette and flicked the butt into the dirt. "I'll go on up and get started with the chores."

"Hey, Sonny," Matthew called, smiling. "You gonna come into town and have a drink with me?"

Sonny grinned, too. This was a longstanding joke between them. He gave his standard reply. "Nah, you do the drinkin', and I'll do the workin'."

Matthew turned and walked down a long row of corn. The tongue-like leaves licked his thighs. That damn fungus wouldn't dare invade his beautiful fields, he thought. His earlier fear and tension began to fade. With the help of God Almighty, Luke will come home to them well and whole. Everything was going to be fine.

Chapter 31

There are hot places in this world, like Africa or the Arizona desert, but there's no hot like an August day in the Midwest. At midday, there's no wind, and the humidity is so high, you can wring water out of the air. However, the farmers have to do much the same work whether it's a hundred degrees or ten degrees. As the sun slowly sinks in the western skies, a dusky haze settles over the land and an occasional breeze brings welcome relief from the relentless, exhaustive heat.

It was Saturday and Annie was in her garden picking tomatoes, having chosen to face the hordes of mosquitoes and weeds rather than the swarm of hungry males circling her kitchen. If they thought she was going to cook tonight, they were crazy. Sandwiches and chips were on the menu, and it was every man for himself. She could hear the baby crying, probably being ignored. She welcomed the quiet that settled across the place when the last tractor was shut down for the night and the relaxed laughter of her brothers heading toward the house floated across the yard. Everyone seemed to be in a good mood. She came around the corner of the house and found them all lounging on the back porch, spraying each other with shaken soda and beer cans.

"Well, boys," their father was saying, raising his beer can as though offering a toast. "The hay is finally done for the third and final time. We did everything we can in the fields. All we can do is sit back and let nature takes its course. Guess we'll do some more fencing and fix the barn-- "

"What?" Annie cried, stomping into their midst. "What about the roof on the house? And the yard, the orchard, the kitchen? You promised you'd work on my list of projects by mid-summer. Well?"

"Annie, c'mon," pleaded her father with mocked sincerity. "We've been working our tails off for months. We're finally caught up, and we're all in a great mood. Now, I promise, we'll take care of those things – honest."

"Ha!" she retorted. As far as she was concerned his promises didn't amount to a hill of beans, as Lori would say. And she also knew there wasn't a damned thing she could do about it. Everyone else knew it too, and they were laughing at her. Even Sonny was sitting on the porch rail, smiling and relaxed. She turned to go into the house, but then caught sight of Mack's bloody and dirty dressings.

"Mack! When's the last time you changed your dressing? It looks awful! It's gonna get more infected if you don't start taking better care of it," she scolded. "Get in the shower, and I'll put a fresh dressing on there. The rest of you, too – get your showers done. You guys would make those pigs smell like fresh flowers." She wrinkled up her nose making it clear she found them all offensive. They responded with a chorus of hoots and whistles.

"Well, Miss Winston," laughed Mathew. "You'd better take a shower yourself and put on your best jeans 'cause we're going into town and raise a little hell. And we all agree that you should come along -- that is, until you told us we stink!" he chided her good-naturedly.

Annie didn't need to be asked twice. She put the baby down and jumped in the shower, although there was barely enough water pressure to shampoo her hair. Every faucet in the house was running. She put on her tightest blue jeans and a cute, new blouse. She knew Sonny never joined them on such affairs, but she hoped he noticed when she skipped out the door, running for the truck.

* * * * * *

The Shannon Town Grill and Pub was a good place to go on a hot Saturday night. It was like most small town taverns – dark and smoky, a row of stools by the bar badly in need of re-upholstering. There was a pool table in the back, and a jute box and booths along the side wall. There were large lighted clocks behind the bar with the impressive Budweiser Clysdales and another with brilliant blue skies and waterfalls, with the words, "Hamns Sky Blue Waters". There were four different beers on tap and a bartender who rarely had to ask his customers which they wanted, and never the same person twice. Yes sir, the Pub was a good place to go on a hot, Saturday night.

Bill O'Reily was the proprietor of the place, third generation. His grandfather was one of the founders of the town. He could slip into a heavy brogue as easily as a hot knife cuts through butter. He was a bartender's bartender – always pleasant, always listening, but never put up with any trouble. The Pub was a place you could stop in with your kids, and Billy wanted to keep it that way. Yes sir, the Pub was a good place to go on a hot, Saturday night.

Billy was one of Matthew's favorite people. They both had been in the Navy during the war and were widowers with large families. Many times, late at night when the place was quiet, they'd sit and talk for hours about the green and grassy hills of

Ireland. Someday they'd go there together -- a pilgrimage. But tonight, there were no quiet, reflective talks. The place was packed, and music was so loud people could hardly talk to each other. Matthew put his arm around his pretty daughter and introduced her to Billy. Drinks were ordered, friendly insults were exchanged, the weather was dully noted, and good cheer was abundant. Matthew made his way toward the pool table and slapped down two quarters, signaling he would take on the winners of the present match. Sonny was drafted to be his partner. Yes sir, the Pub was a good place to be on a hot, Saturday night.

When the Winston's walked in, they were immediately greeted by several of their neighbors, most of whom would also be at Mass in the morning. Many people stopped to stare as Mack hobbled toward a back booth. It was true that the kid had acted like a snob when his family first came to town last spring, but people said he worked out in the fields and did as much as anyone else. Mack grinned amicably as he yelled cracks across the room to the Dobson boy. Nah, the kid was all right. He just had to get used to the way things were done around here. Yes sir, the Pub was a good place to go on a hot, Saturday night.

Annie enjoyed the attention shown her by a whole circle of men. She smiled and flirted a little, tapping her toe to a country tune blaring from the box. Marty McConnell even grabbed her and spun her around the floor a little, but there wasn't room so their dancing gave way to laughter. Yes sir, the Pub was a good place to go on a hot, Saturday night.

The atmosphere cooled for a moment when Tim Brady and his son came in. The word around town was that Tim, Jr. hasn't been the same since coming home from Vietnam. He could turn vicious for no reason, and he had smashed a bar stool through a window in a tavern in Crawleyville. But the Brady's were good people, and it wasn't the kid's fault. He had done his duty, and the community was proud of this young hulk of a man. He'd be all right after he was home for a while. An old friend patted him on the back and offered to buy him a drink. Yes sir, the Pub was a good place to go on a hot, Saturday night.

Annie thought she noticed Tim staring at her. Maybe it was

her imagination, so she decided just to ignore him. She moved to the back corner where her brothers were sitting. A few minutes later, Tim made his way toward them.

"Hello, there," he said. "How you folks doin' tonight?"

"Hey, we're doing fine," Mack responded. "Sure is nice to sit in the air conditioning, though. Man, it's been hot."

The friendly conversation continued, but Annie became more uncomfortable as Tim never took his eyes off her. He had a leering expression that frightened her.

"C'mon, honey," Tim insisted, "let's go to the bar and have a drink."

"Sorry, Tim," she said, "it's crowded over there. I'd rather stay here."

He jerked her to her feet and draped his arm around her shoulders. "I won't take no for an answer. Just one drink, that's all I'm asking."

"No, Tim, I don't want to. There's other girls over there. Why don't you ask one of them?"

"Damn little bitch," Tim cried. "You think you're too good to have a drink with me?"

"No, Tim, I'm -- well, I have to go to the little ladies' room, that's all."

She ran to the back of the room and ducked out the back door. It irritated her that neither of her brothers said a word to defend her. She felt hot and angry and decided she had enough fun for one night. It was time to go home. Unfortunately, they had all come together and she doubted anyone would want to take her home.

She walked around the side of the bar and noticed the phone booth across the street at the entrance to the riverside park. She found a dime in her pocket and phoned home. Sonny picked up on the second ring.

'Sonny, it's so crowded and everyone is getting sloshed. Can you come pick me up, please? I'll wait for you in the park."

"Okay," Sonny said. "I guess I can do that. I'll just tell John to watch things for a few minutes."

She was relieved he didn't argue or complain. She sat down at a bench near the river to wait for him. There was the gentle lapping of the water against the shore. The breeze kicked up at times, the trees rustling and swaying. The sky was dark. Perhaps the long awaited thunderstorm was on its way. She took off her shoes and buried her feet in the soft, cool sand.

Should she tell Sonny about her problems with Tim, she wondered? Wouldn't it be fun if he got a little angry or upset? She played the different scenarios in her mind and was so deeply in thought she didn't notice him drive up and park the truck.

"Annie?" he called, "Hey, you out here somewhere?"

"Over here. I'm sorry I didn't see you." She reached down and began to put on her shoes. To her great surprise, he lounged back again a tree and seemed in no hurry to leave. "Ain't like no New York river, is it," he said, gesturing toward the Mississippi.

"No, it certainly isn't." She was stunned that he actually initiated conversation. "I walked along the Hudson a thousand times, but it was never like this. There it's just geography, but here you feel like you own it, or it owns you," she mused. "My dad always talks about it like it's a person."

Sonny produced a knife from somewhere and started whittling on a piece of wood he found nearby. "You just gotta respect it, that's all. She can flow along smooth as silk, but she can turn on ya' quick, and whoosh – you can kiss it all good-bye." He smiled then, one of those half smiles that set Annie's heart racing.

"You sound like my dad. You understand the way he thinks a lot better than his own children, at least lately"

He bent over his work. "Nah, I think you're all doing fine."

"We haven't done too badly, have we, considering everything. But we never would have gotten this far if it wasn't for you." He shrugged his shoulders, looking embarrassed with the complement.

"I was just in the right place at the right time, I guess," he said. "I had nothing better to do. I did wonder why someone like your dad would try something like this. Guess I was curious."

They both laughed then, thinking of that night six months ago when Matthew came home bellowing about moving to a farm in Iowa. "Well, you know what they say," she smiled. "Money can't buy happiness. Daddy had everything, but he certainly wasn't happy, not like he is now. You don't seem like someone who cares about money. If you had all the money you wanted, what would you buy?"

He answered surprisingly fast. "A bike. Not a big road hog, but one with enough power to go on the highway or dirt." He stopped working then, and looked up, but not at her. There was a far away wistful glint in his eye that she had never seen before.

She could hardly breath. "Why Sonny, so you could leave?"

"No, just so I could be free. Just knowing I could go if I wanted to. That's better than staying someplace 'cause you got no way to leave." Their eyes met then, just for a moment. For Annie, it was as though time stood still.

"C'mon." He looked uncomfortable. "We'd better get home." He folded the knife and threw the wood aside. She didn't see what he had made.

"Okay, sure," she murmured. "I'll go inside to grab my purse and tell them I'm leaving." She hurried toward the bar. She could tell from the raucous noise emulating into the street that everyone in the bar was probably drunker than before. She walked inside, pushing her way through the throng toward her brothers' back booth. "I asked Sonny to come get me," she yelled over the roar. "I'm going home."

She turned to leave but Tim found her again and put his arm around her neck roughly. "Going home? Like hell. C'mon, babe," he slobbered. "Let's go have that drink."

"No, I don't want to, and don't call me babe," she retorted, ducking away from his arm. He was persistent and grabbed her again, his fingers resting on her breast. "Tim," she cried. "Let go of me!"

But he didn't. "Now listen, honey, don't get all high and mighty with me." His words were slurred and there was a snide sneer on his face. "Just cause you're the best looking bitch in here, don't mean--"

"Hey," howled Mack as he struggled to stand up. "You can't talk to my sister like that. Leave her alone!"

That seemed to be what Tim was waiting for. "Or what?

You're gonna need two legs to take me, and some guts, too. You ain't got neither, you sonofabitch!" He threw Annie aside and turned to face Mack. The place was suddenly quiet, everyone waiting to see what would happen next.

Tim's dad came across the room. "C'mon, son. Back off now."

"Back off? Why in the hell should I? If this here runt wants to try to prove somethin', let him try." He was sneering and his eyes were blazing.

"Now, Timmy," his father coaxed. "This man has no quarrel with you. Let's go home."

"No!" the young man thundered. "That'd make me a no good coward just like him!"

Annie had a terrible sinking feeling that Mr. Brady would not be able to influence his son. Andrew stood up at his brother's side, his face clearly showing he had no idea what to do. Annie became even more frightened. Perhaps she should talk to Tim herself, she thought. She started to approach when someone grabbed her and pushed her toward a back corner. It was Sonny. He moved quickly and stood between Timmy and Mack.

"You oughta listen to your dad," he said. "Let's all of us just call it night and go home." He turned away, motioning for Annie and her brothers to move toward the door. Mack hesitated, but then took his crutches and started to leave.

"Who the hell are you?" Tim roared.

"I'm Sonny. I work for the Winston's."

"So, you're gonna let this dumb, shit ass do your talkin'? That's alright. It'll be a better fight and a hell of a lot more fun."

"Mister, you can call me any names you want, but I ain't gonna fight ya'. The two adversaries were staring at each other as Sonny took little side steps, trying to get closer to the exit. "We're leaving," he said. He turned and walked toward the door.

Mr. Brady started to take his son's arm, but Tim pushed him away. He grabbed a pool cue off the table and followed Sonny, who turned around just as he heard Annie scream. Tim took the cue with fully extended arms and sliced it viciously across Sonny's midsection. Then with lightening speed, he whirled the stick over his head like a Medieval swordsman and hit Sonny again. The force sent Sonny wheeling across the floor, slamming him against the wall.

Several men circled Tim and tried to usher him out. Bellowing and screaming, he broke away, bulling his way toward Sonny. This time they tackled him to the floor and managed to get him out to his father's car.

Sonny was still on his feet, but doubled over, leaning heavily against the wall. He looked as though he wasn't breathing, but he waved everyone off as he struggled to regain his composure. Finally, he seemed to be breathing easier and tried to straighten a little.

The crowd was outraged. People were calling for someone to call the Sheriff. "Somethin's gotta be done about that guy. He's nuts!" they said.

"A doctor," Annie cried. "Someone get a doctor!"

"No," Sonny retorted, still barely able to speak. "Let's go home."

"The sheriff's coming!" Billie called. "He's gonna want to talk to you."

Sonny didn't argue, just started toward the door, unsupported. The rest followed except Matthew who volunteered to stay behind and talk to the sheriff. "I'll make sure they do something about that madman," he announced.

Sonny gingerly hoisted himself onto the truck seat and threw the keys at Andrew. No one could remember him ever doing that before. Annie tried to draw close so she could see how badly he was hurt, but he ignored her. "Just got the wind knocked out, that's all," he scowled.

"Huh," grunted Mack. "Looked like a hell of a kidney shot to me. We should probably take him to a doctor." Sonny snarled something that sounded like a definitive no. Annie remembered how uncomfortable he was that night in the hospital with Mack. She looked at his sweaty brow and his shallow, uneven breathing. Her instincts were to insist that they turn around and take him anyway, but even broken and bruised, no one argued with Sonny Jackson.

At home, he struggled to get out of the truck and walk down the hill toward his place just as it began raining. Annie followed at his heels, still asking questions, but he didn't answer. It took every ounce of concentration and strength to get inside his shed and somehow get onto his bunk. Mack reassured his sister he would watch Sonny closely. "Okay," she said, "but I'm waiting up for Pop. Maybe he can talk some sense into him."

Mack babbled on, but Sonny tuned him out. The throbbing in his belly was incredible. He laid very still, afraid to move, waiting for each successive wave of nausea to pass. All he needed was to puke right now, he thought. He loosened his belt, hoping for some relief from the terrific pressure. Mack finally turned off the light and got into bed, the vibrations knifing through Sonny like a burning bolt of hellfire. He gripped the sides of his mattress and tried to turn his mind away from the pain.

He remembered a kind of self-induced hypnosis that his grandfather had taught him. It had worked for him before. The trick was to concentrate on one small object, real or imagined, and push everything else out your mind. It was dark, and the wind from the storm seemed to be swirling all around him.

Concentrate. Concentrate.

But I can't, he screamed silently. *The chants, Grandfather – I can't remember the chants. Hold on. Concentrate. The small rock at the far end of the field – point the tractor toward it so the corn is planted in long, straight rows. Drive slow. Just keep the rows straight. Concentrate.*

A tremendous bolt of thunder and lightening cut through the night and permeated his body with a crashing spasm of pain. Oh God, he cried silently, there is really something wrong. He had been in pain before and had gotten through it on his own. I can get through this, he repeated over and over. *Get some rest. Just pass out.*

Chapter 32

Sonny had no awareness of time. He was cold, but his face was drenched with sweat. His shaking woke up Mack.

"Hey!" his roommate called out sleepily. "You still awake up there?" Mack hoisted himself out of bed and turned on the bedside lamp. He looked at Sonny, and what he saw jolted him awake. "Sonny!" he gasped. "My God!" Sonny's face was ashen, his hair pasted with sweat.

"Mack," Sonny whispered hoarsely. "Get that can thing they gave you at the hospital. I gotta take a piss – bad!"

"Yeah, sure, Sonny, right away." Mack scrambled to find the urinal. Sonny was hesitant to even move but he was hoping to relieve the terrific pressure in his gut. He used it clumsily and handed it back to Mack.

Mack switched on the light in the bathroom to empty it into the toilet. What he saw made him retch. Quickly, he put on his pants and boot.

"Mack," Sonny called weakly. "Where are you going?"

Ignoring Sonny's pleas, Mack hurried out the door and struggled up the hill to the house. He found Annie asleep on the couch and began shaking her awake. "Annie! Annie!" he cried. "Wake up! It's Sonny. He's hurt, worse than we thought!"

"Oh, Mack, he's not-- "

"No, he's still conscious, but he had to pee and it was pure blood! I saw it. He's shaking so bad, he woke me up."

"I'll take some blankets down to him," she said. "You go wake up Andrew and Johnny. See if Daddy's back yet. Hurry!"

It was a driving, cold rain now. She put her jacket over the blankets as she waded through the mud and rain. She climbed up on the chair so she could see him. For a moment, she thought he was dead, but then she could see his rapid, shallow breathing and his hands clasping the side of the bed. "Sonny," she whispered. "Sonny?"

"What are you doing here? I'm all right. Just leave me alone." She wasn't listening. She quickly spread out the layers of blankets over his trembling body.

By that time, the other boys were there. "What'll we do?" started Andrew. "Dad's not home yet. We could call the ambulance."

"In this storm? It would take too long," Mack cautioned. "I think we should get him into town ourselves. Goddamn it! We should have taken him in the first place."

"No," Sonny protested. "You ain't takin'-- "

"Just shut up!" Mack snapped. "You're bleeding inside. We're taking you to the hospital!" He moved around the bed, surveying the situation. "Andrew, you'd better go get the truck. John, Thomas, you're gonna have to haul him down from there."

"No!" Sonny screamed. "Don't move me!" His hands gripped even tighter.

"Mack, you can't," Annie gasped. "Just take him, bed and all. Don't hurt him anymore than you have to!"

They took out the bolts holding the beds together, and carefully lowered it. They tied ropes around him, covered him with rain ponchos, and carried him to the truck. Andrew drove with Mack acting as co-pilot. Annie got in the back to ride beside Sonny, yelling last minute instructions to John, who would be in charge of the household.

Jerking and jolting, they started down the road. Andrew leaned forward nervously over the wheel, having never quite mastered driving the truck's tricky clutch. Tonight, with the soft and muddy roads, it was more difficult than usual. They swerved and bumped their way through the night.

Annie crept close to Sonny, not knowing how to help him. Each jolt pierced him brutally. Sometimes, it looked as though he was screaming but no noise was coming out. Oh my God, she thought. He's bleeding to death right before my eyes. He could die! "Sonny, can you hear me? It's only a couple more miles to the highway. It'll be better then, okay?" Her hand crept underneath the blankets. He felt it and grasped it tightly.

"Annie," he cried "Tell them no junk – no pain shots. I don't need any! Promise me!"

"Yes, Sonny, I promise!" She didn't understand but she would have said anything to quiet him. She studied his breathing. It seemed to get more irregular. Go faster, go faster, she prayed.

"Just go to sleep, Sonny. Just rest!"

"I can't," he gasped. "I'm afraid if I do, I won't wake up."

Finally, they turned onto Third Street, swung up the hill toward the hospital, and pulled into the Emergency entrance. A swarm of nurses and doctors were there immediately. Someone moved Annie aside and they lifted him out. Possible ruptured kidney, someone said. His cries to be left alone were lost in the calls of the medical team.

"Let's get him off of this onto the stretcher. On the count of three. One... two... three..."

"Get X-ray up here, stat!"

"Lab is standing by, Doctor."

"Good, let's get a CBC, type and cross match for five units -- now!"

"Let's get two lines in. Cut off these clothes!"

Everything in their voices, their manner, said, "Hurry! Hurry!" The doors of the Emergency treatment room swung shut, leaving the little group of wet, worried Winston's to sit in the hallway. They delivered Sonny into the hands of these people so there was nothing more they could do except wait. Two men came out, carrying Sonny's bed frame and mattress. "They called us to come get this. We'll trash it, if that's okay," one of them said. It was soaked with blood and urine. Annie could not look at it.

At one point, they heard Sonny scream, "You're not puttin' that damn thing in me!"

Annie leaped to her feet. "What are they doing to him?" she cried.

A doctor who introduced himself as Dr. Rathburn came out and sat down by them. He asked some general questions about Sonny, who he was and information about his background. Of course, they knew very little. "Listen now," he started, "your man has been hurt very badly. He's bleeding internally. Both kidneys have been injured, one of them seriously. We can't be sure until we go in and look around."

"Doctor," Annie gasped, "what are they doing to him in there?"

"We have to put in a lot of tubes and things – one down his nose into his stomach to drain anything he ate or drank recently.

And," he hesitated, "we had to pass a catheter into his bladder to see how much he's bleeding. But your man is a real fighter – he should have passed out by now. They're giving him some sedation and finishing up the surgical prep. We've got to try to get him stable with some blood before we can do surgery."

Annie remembered what Sonny had said about not wanting any narcotics. She started to say something to the doctor, but she knew they had no choice. "I have to see him," she pressed. "Maybe I can get him to quiet down."

"Okay, miss. I'll tell the nurse to let you know when you can step in for just a minute." He walked back into the treatment room.

One of the nurses approached Dr. Rathburn. "Do we have any history on this kid?"

"Nah," Dr. Lamp shook his head. "The people who came in with him don't seem to know much either. He works for them. Apparently, he hooked up with them shortly before they moved here. Why?"

"We're having trouble starting the IV's. His antecubitals and ankles are like cement with scar tissue. Looks like he was a heavy user, but I don't think recently. I ordered a complete chemical screening just to be sure, alright?"

"Hmmmm," sighed the doctor. "Let me know if anything shows up. By the way, the young woman wants to see him for a couple minutes when he's cleaned up and prepped."

Annie began pacing nervously as the minutes dragged by. She became more and more anxious as staff people continued to pass back and forth. Then things seemed quiet, so she crept inside. There was a curtain drawn around Sonny's stretcher, but she could hear someone scolding him.

"Mr. Jackson, if you would just lie quietly, we could get this needle in. We wouldn't have to do this again if you hadn't pulled out the first one." Oh, Sonny, Annie thought, why must you fight them so? She peered around the curtain, but was not prepared for what she saw.

He was lying with his arms and legs strapped down. He was stripped with barely a towel thrown over his mid-section. There were tubes everywhere. He was thrashing around, making wild, throaty sounds. Annie was afraid she was going to be sick.

She backed away blindly, sending a table crashing to the floor. He saw her then. "Get her out of here!" he screamed.

She turned to rush out, his screams still ringing in her ears. She bolted past the boys and ran outdoors. Heavy, retching sobs came rushing out of her until she could hardly breath. Enough, she cried, enough!

Mack came to find her. "Billie brought Pop in," he said. "All the papers are signed and they're taking him down to surgery."

Annie wiped her face and steadied herself to go back inside. The elevator doors were closing just as she arrived. "He wouldn't even look at us," Andrew said. "We had to do this, didn't we?" They were all wondering if they had betrayed him somehow. Perhaps, he lived by a different creed – that it was better to die than submit to this. But there was nothing they could do now but wait and wonder.

* * * * * *

During the next few hours, Annie played it over and over in her mind. Just a short time ago, she and Sonny walked along the river. He had been relaxed and nonchalant, his eyes were soft and thoughtful, and the conversation, easy and unsolicited. She even remembered the way the moon glistened across his hair. We were close then, she thought, closer than we've ever been. Maybe that was the problem – maybe he had let down his defenses. He didn't want to fight that guy, and he had a knife. He could have used it, but he hadn't. The sight and sound of those vicious hits exploded in her mind over and over. It was all so unnecessary and stupid.

And here they were, just a few hours later. Sonny was totally subjugated and taken off to surgery. She could feel his hand clutching hers. She had touched him, brushed his hair aside. He seemed to need her, even if it was for just a few moments.

Matthew paced for a while, ranting about the absurdity of the situation, but he was speaking out of fear – fear that another person he loved might die. Everyone knew that if something

297

happened to Sonny, their father's dreams would die with him. Finally, Matthew sat down and fell asleep, his head falling back against the wall. They sat there, another long, silent vigil.

* * * * * *

Several miles away from them, in a farmhouse north of Shannon Town, another vigil was being kept. A woman sat at her kitchen table, wringing her hands – sometimes praying, sometimes weeping. Near dawn, she woke her husband and together, they went to their oldest son's bedroom. They awakened him and helped him dress. The three of them left together, their sleepy-eyed, baby-faced giant of a son, sitting quietly in the back seat. The expressions crossing between mother and father spoke volumes. He probably didn't even remember what had happened last night – he had nearly killed a man he didn't even know. Hadn't the doctors warned them? Were they wrong in wanting to try, thinking their love could make him well again? But he was a stranger to them now.

They headed west toward Iowa City, where the doctors and nurses at the Veterans' Hospital were waiting for them to deliver their son to them. They'd put him somewhere where he couldn't hurt anyone again. And, God willing, they'd find a way to soothe the rage inside their son so that someday he might return home to them.

* * * * * *

The night seemed to last forever. Annie's brothers dozed off at times so she was left alone with her fears. She thought of the nights and days she spent in the hospital, watching her mother waste away, but there was no violence or confusion associated with her death, not like this. She wondered if any of her brothers sensed that she cared for Sonny more than they knew. She was glad that Mack and Andrew decided to take Matthew home at daybreak.

A few minutes after they left, Annie felt someone touch her shoulder softly. It was Penny Lamp. "I heard about Sonny," she said. "I wondered if there was anything I can do."

"Penny, it's nice to see you," Annie cried.

"How's your brother?" Penny asked a little self-consciously. "My father says he hasn't seen him since he was discharged."

"Well," mused Annie, looking embarrassed, "I wish I could say he's fine, but I'd be lying. The incision still isn't healed – it keeps oozing and the dressings look awful. Sonny started working on his knee a few weeks ago – trying to get it straight." Her face clouded then. "I don't know who's going to take care of that now. Sonny's probably going to be here a long time and I –"

"Well, I'm going to my father's cottage by Shannon Town this morning. I could drive over there and see how he's doing."

"Oh, Penny, that would be great. Would you?"

Penny scooted off then, trying not to look too excited. She knew this was another traumatic ordeal for the Winston family, and she felt badly for them, but she was overjoyed at the prospect of seeing Mack again.

A weary Dr. Rathburn came to speak to Annie, his surgical garb soaked with sweat. The surgery had lasted six and half-hours. Taking a sip of coffee, he sat down beside her. His expression seemed guarded and grave.

"He made it through fairly well, Miss Winston, but there was extensive damage. That chap that hit him must have the strength of an ox. We had to remove his left kidney and his spleen, and there was damage to his other kidney and liver as well. He's going to be a very sick young man for a very long time. He'll be in intensive care for several days. The next few hours are critical. You look exhausted. Why don't you go home and get some rest."

"No, I want to stay." This time Sonny Jackson was not going to be alone.

* * * * * *

Penny's palms were sweating and her heart was racing as she drove toward Shannon Town that morning. That awful, empty feeling had lingered in the pit of her stomach since that day in

June when Mack Winston rolled down that corridor and out of her life, seemingly for good. But here she was, on her way to see him. What was she going to tell him? Just happened to be in the neighborhood, or maybe the truth, that she had seen Annie early this morning and asked about him. Either way, he might be mad as hell. She had no idea how he was going to react.

She went to the cottage. The lovely old place was as inviting and peaceful as ever. She went to the stables to say hello to her friends. Then she went for a long walk in the woods by the river. She had been away too long. By that time it was lunchtime, which wouldn't be a good time to barge in uninvited. If I keep putting it off, she thought, I'll lose my nerve all together. Finally, about 1:00, she got into her Jeep and drove to the Winston farm.

Chapter 33

Penny had known of the Weatherly place all her life. Her father had teased her with ghost stories about the house when she was a little girl. She was curious what it looked like now that real people were living there rather than Indian spirits. Actually, it still looks pretty awful, she thought as she turned into the long, rutted driveway.

Two little boys came running out to meet her before she even had a chance to turn off the engine. "Hi," she smiled. "I'm Penny Lamp. I was wondering if Matthew Winston is around this afternoon."

"Which one? There's two of them, ya' know," the older boy said matter-of-factly between licks of his Fudgesicle. "Do you man Senior or Junior?"

"Oh, it's Mack I'd like to see – your brother, I guess."

"Miss Lamp?" a deeper voice called out. It was Andrew. "Hi! Why did you , er – I mean, can I help you with something?"

"Hello, Andrew," she said, wishing she could get out from behind the wheel, but Andrew was leaning heavily against the door. "I was asking where Mack is."

"You're here to see Mack?" He appeared flushed with a

strange expression.

"I ran into Annie at the hospital and she mentioned that she was worried about Mack's dressings and exercises, now that Sonny is hurt." She peered at him closely. "Andrew," she said, "are you alright? Don't worry about Sonny. He'll be okay, really." Andrew didn't answer so she said, "So, could you tell me where I can find him?"

"Oh, sure. That's a good idea. He's down in the shed, er – that's what we call Sonny's quarters. Mack's been staying down there since – well, you know, his accident." He was stammering and looked very uncomfortable. "Is there anything I can do? Perhaps you should teach me the treatments and I could take over for awhile."

"Well, maybe, but I have to check things out first. I'm sure you all have enough to do already," she smiled, referring to the dish towel slung over his shoulder.

She walked across the yard in the direction of loud voices and paused at the screen door. Mack was stretched out on the plank floor while another boy, probably one of his brothers, knelt over him, his hands pushing on Mack's knee.

"Jeez, that's not what I mean, John," Mack was saying, grimacing. "Those are just spasms. Keep pushing. Sonny had it almost straight. You're just not pushing hard enough!" he cried, exasperated. "Oh, hell, just forget it!"

"I'm sorry, Mack," Johnny sputtered. "I was afraid I was hurting you. And look, it started bleeding again. And Annie's not-- "

"It's okay, John. Just go. I can change these dressings myself. Don't tell anyone, especially Pop, okay?" John charged out, nearly knocking Penny over, but Mack still didn't notice her. He was sitting in the middle of the floor, angry and frustrated. He threw his shoe across the room.

Quickly, before she lost her nerve, she stepped inside, letting the screen door slam. He looked up, ready to scream at whoever had the poor judgment to walk in, but then he saw her.

Penny was the first to speak. "Need some help?"

He stared at her for a moment. "Sure. I suppose your dad sent you, right?"

"No, he has no idea I came out here, although he did mention you didn't keep even one appointment." She squatted down to take a look. "My God, Mack!" she cried as she peeled off the old bandages. "It looks like raw hamburger, and its infected." She inspected it closely, horrified at what she saw. "And what were you trying to con your brother into doing?" As she spoke, she set to work trying to clean the wound the best she could with the small supply of peroxide and antiseptic she had in her purse.

"Sonny was working on it two or three times a day, trying to get this damn knee straightened. He'd just push like hell! It was going pretty well, too. Ouch! What are you doing?"

"You know what I'm doing," she retorted "How long has it been like this?"

"It was almost healed completely, but I fell on it and opened it up again. I know I should have gone to see your dad. It was stupid."

She did what she could, re-wrapped it with some fresh gauze, and put on a new ACE wrap she had brought along. She could not fathom why he hadn't followed through with the office appointments and therapies, but said nothing. "Well, are you ready?" she asked. "Let's see if we can get this thing straightened out." She bore down and kept pushing until the spasms finally lessened and achieved some extension of the joint. She did it again and again until neither of them could take any more. They sat silently for a few minutes, trying to catch their breath.

"I can't believe you're here," he said.

"I ran into Annie at the hospital and she said she would appreciate me looking in on you. I mean someone had -- you know, come out and see, er –" Her expression and her eyes were betraying her. This was no nurse-patient visit.

"Did you go riding this morning?" he asked.

"No, but I stopped by the stables. I haven't been able to spend much time out there – you know, with school and all." She still didn't look at him. Her chin rested on her knee as she traced the pattern of the quilt with her fingertip. Her long, black hair fell beautifully around her shoulders. If she had looked up, she would have seen him openly staring at her.

"You haven't been back there since my accident, have

you."

She got up and walked to the window in the far corner of the room. "I told you, I've real busy at school. I'd like to get better grades-- "

"Don't hand me that crap! You don't worry about grades. You've got the whole place eating out of your hand. And not because of your dad, either. You're good, really good."

"Oh yeah? Weren't you the one who called me a hard-hearted bitch?"

"Well, with some patients you have to be like that. You know, the difficult ones." They both smiled then. Penny came back and sat cross-legged across the end of his bed.

"Except for how awful the incision looks, you look like you're doing pretty well," she said, trying not to stare at his even more developed, tanned shoulders and chest muscles.

"I guess I am, but it was tough at first. I don't take anything for granted anymore. Things I thought I hated have turned out pretty good for me – like Sonny. I used to think he was the biggest jerk around, and I hated his guts. But he's the one who helped me the most. I couldn't sleep at night, so he rigged up the tractors so I could still drive 'em – ran my ass as hard as he could so I was dog tired at night. And he'd get up in the middle of the night to stretch it out if the spasms got real bad" His voice faded then. It was hard to imagine Sonny Jackson lying in a hospital bed.

"We had it all figured out, too," he continued. "We were going to work really hard on this thing so we'd, I mean, I'd be ready for my prosthesis by fall. It's gonna be rough – worse now with Sonny laid up. And there's so much work to do around here. I could sure do a hellvalot more with two legs."

"Hey, Mack, this is only August." She got up to retrieve his shoe. "I have three weeks vacation from school. I was planning on hanging around the cottage anyway. Why don't I leave this stuff here and come back tomorrow to change the dressings and do more therapy – I mean, if you want me to."

"Sure, that would be great, but it wouldn't be much of a vacation."

"That's okay," she assured him. "I have sort of a vested

interest in you, you know. I'd hate for one of my patients to have post-discharge complications. Makes me look bad." Her mind was racing, trying to think of something more to say. She was not rady for the visit to end, and she could tell he felt the same.

"Well, good. It's settled then," he said. "I'll see you tomorrow, right?"

"Yep, and like I said, I'll be staying at the cottage for awhile so I can come over anytime. Good-bye." She turned to walk back to her Jeep, knowing he was watching her. It had gone so much better than she expected. She had been there for only an half hour, but felt as though the earth had just shifted on its axis.

* * * * * *

The very words, "Intensive Care" elicit fear in anyone. Only patients who need round the clock one-on-one monitoring are put there. The sights and sounds of the menagerie of machines and equipment are frightening and intimidating. That is how Annie felt the first time she was ushered in to see Sonny. She had been told he was heavily sedated. When she saw him, lying there in the midst of all that technical jungle, she was glad he wasn't aware of any of it.

That first day, the usual ICU routine was strictly followed. She could see him ten minutes every two hours. All she could do was stand beside him, assuring herself that he was still breathing and then take a quick inventory of the tubes and things – which ones were the same or different. Of course, she didn't understand any of it except for the brief explanations offered by the nurses.

By nightfall, he began getting restless. Annie was told they were slowly decreasing the sedation. The second shift nurse let her sit by the bedside for longer periods. It seemed she had a soothing affect on him. Sometimes his eyes would flutter open, and he seemed to recognize her. The nurses kept his hands restrained. They heard about antics in Emergency, and they didn't want to take any chances.

He began running a dangerously high fever. It seemed to Annie that no one was surprised, as though they were expecting it. A cycle emerged of chills and trembling, then profuse sweating, followed by a short period of deep sleep until the chills began again. He would call out to persons unknown to her and say things she couldn't understand as though they were in another language. Time became a blur, and night became day and back to night again.

The second morning, Dr. Adams stopped by to see how Sonny was doing. He found Annie in the waiting room, pacing and wringing her hands. She looked physically and emotionally exhausted. "They keep telling me he's going to be alright," she said, "but he keeps running these high fevers. They're changing his sheets because he sweat so much. Could you go in there and find out what's taking so long?"

Dr. Adams stopped at the nurse's desk to glance at the chart. The curtains were drawn around Sonny's cubicle. "Sonny," one of the nurses was saying, "we're going to have to turn you so we can change these sheets, okay? Watch the NG tube. Oh, hello, Dr. Peters," she said, as the doctor stepped around the curtain.

The patient was carefully maneuvered on his side. "His incision looks good," one of the nurses said. "Good," being a relative term meaning that it was medically intact, but it looked hideous – a long cut around his torso, the skin pinched together with silvery staples.

As they worked, the sheet slipped off, exposing his backside. Dr. Peters noticed something that caught his breath. Across the top of Sonny's hips were strange, deep scars as though sliced by a knife. What startled Dr. Adams was that he remembered seeing them before. Just then, they turned Sonny onto his other side. The doctor studied the young man's face. His dark hair was matted with sweat, his eyes were wild with pain. Trembling, he clutched the side rail of his bed, staring back at Doc Peters through the bars. It seemed there was a flicker of recognition in Sonny's face, too.

The history on the chart was sketchy, nothing that would help the doctor remember when and where he had seen this young man before. He noted a paragraph on the doctor's admission note, telling of the scarred areas suggesting habitual drug abuse with needles. Dr. Adams was a patient man, and eventually he would piece the puzzle together. He said goodbye to Annie, giving her his standard lecture about resting herself.

* * * * * *

Finally, the second night, Sonny fell into a restful sleep. The medications had beaten his fevers, and Annie was told the worst was over. She sat at his bedside, watching him sleep until she, too, succumbed to her fatigue, resting her head on the foot of his bed so that the slightest movement would awaken her.

Hours later, she aroused to find him staring at her. "Sonny!" she cried, "you're awake."

Even though he was very weak, Sonny managed a fiery look in his eye. He pulled at the restraints holding his hands. He tried to speak, but the hoarse, crackling noises were inaudible. "Don't try to talk," she cautioned. "There was a tube down your throat so it's going to be sore for awhile."

"I can't...I can't breath!" He pulled at the straps around his wrists until finally he fell back onto his pillows, exhausted and frustrated. He laid motionless for a few moments, trying to summon what little strength he could. "I don't want you sittin' around here like this," he said. "Go home."

"No, Sonny. I have to stay here—"

"I don't want you here. Go home!" He didn't look at her as he spoke, so he didn't see the tears falling down her tired and worn face as bitter disbelief welled up inside her in dark clouds of anger.

"Fine!" she sputtered. "I don't care – handle this any way you want! To hell with you!" She left without saying a word to anyone.

In a few moments, she walked outdoors into the bright morning sunlight. She blinked her eyes, fighting the glare and the tears. An empty cab stood by so she jumped in and told the driver to head south. The driver did a quick double-take when she said she wanted to go to Shannon Town. "Here's $30. If that don't cover it, I have more!"

Then, as they were heading out of town, she had a sudden impulse. "Driver!" she called. "Take me to that little park on the

306

bluff by the Dubuque Monument. Do you know where the turnoff is?" The driver was looking at her even more strangely than before. "You can leave the meter running."

"Sure, lady, whatever you want. Stay for as long as you want." Soon, they turned into the gravel parking lot. The place was deserted this early in the morning. She followed the sidewalk to the tower of the stone, standing serenely on it lofty place. She could see why Sonny liked it here this time of day when everything glistened with the freshness of a new day. She stood very still to let the calm and peace of this place ebb over her.

Her mind began clearing a little, but as the hurt and anger receded, they were replaced with a hundred other emotions. She could feel Sonny's presence, the way he looked and acted that day when they were here together, the day she realized that she loved him. Love him? Did she dare use that word when there was so much fear and heartache, too? She started to cry again, turning her face to the cold, unfeeling stone. The man she loved had a wall around his heart as hard and high as this tower. She pounded her fist upon it as if it were her enemy – this heartless, faceless stone. How she hated it.

The sun was rising higher in the sky, a new day had began. Suddenly she felt lonely and a little afraid in this place. She pressed her hands against the stone one last time, wanting to make her peace with it. Then she hurried down the path and jumped into the taxi. She wanted to go home.

Chapter 34

Penny awakened at dawn. She had ridden Ol' Danny Boy, her father's horse, and then saddled up Molly, a beautiful chestnut mare she had helped deliver and train. The horse was unaccustomed to gravel roads, but Penny nudged her on. She had decided to ride over to the Winston place. She had gone over there three times, and each was better than the time before. They were becoming more at ease with each other, and she knew he was definitely interested in her.

She nudged her mount into an easy, graceful canter as they

turned into the driveway and trotted up the hill. Perfect! There he was, leaning against the fence by the barn. Was he watching for her, she wondered?

"Hi!" she called as she came to a stop near where he was standing. Grinning, he reached for the bridle, drawing them nearer. She smiled, too, as she threw him the reins and she jumped down.

"So, you're making house calls on horseback now, Miss Lamp?" He turned away, taking the crutches and headed toward the shed. He moved so well with them that she had trouble keeping up.

"Yeah, but I got off too soon. Slow down, will ya'? What are you doing – trying to impress me with your skill with those crutches?"

"Why not?" he retorted, grinning. "Weren't you trying to impress me when you came riding up just now?" She blushed as they smiled at each other.

Inside the shed, he moved to the middle room and lowered himself onto the floor. "How soon do you think I can get fitted for my new leg?"

"Mack, you ask me that same question everyday, and the answer is still the same. The stump has got to heal and you have to have full range of motion in this knee. They could never fit a prosthesis on this mess!"

"Well, come on! Isn't that what you're here for?" The smiles were gone now. His face had a look of total concentration as he steeled himself for what he knew lay ahead.

She removed the bloody dressing carefully. Actually, the incision looked a little better. It didn't seem to hurt as much, and there was less inflammation. She applied a couple of butterfly Band-Aids, and rewrapped it neatly. Then came the hard part. Taking a long, deep breath before she began, she watched his face as she worked. She had serious misgivings about this. She was no physical therapist. Mack gritted his teeth, trying to will his muscles to release and straighten. Finally, they were satisfied, and Penny collapsed onto the floor beside her patient.

Neither of them said anything for a while, and when they turned to look at one another, their faces were very close. Penny thought he might draw her near to kiss her, but he sat up. "A few more sessions like this," he said, "and I'll be ready by corn-pickin' time"

"It hurts like hell, doesn't it?"

"Yeah, well, you know what they say – no pain, no gain, right?" He hoisted himself onto a nearby chair and reached for her hands to pull her to her feet. She nearly came sailing into his lap. Clumsily, she regained her balance as they both laughed.

Just then, Andrew came to the door. In that single instant, he put it all together – the horse outside and Penny's long, black hair, plus her keen interest in Mack and all her questions. What a fool he was not to see it before. He wanted to turn around and leave, but he knew it would look strange if he said nothing. "Annie's back. She's cooking breakfast."

"Good!" Mack exclaimed. "Now we'll have some decent food around here again. Why don't you come on up and have some breakfast with us?"

They joined the noisy confusion of the busy kitchen. "So, what happened? Sonny kicked you out?" Mack teased his sister in his usual tactless way, grabbing a piece of toast as he walked by. "He must be better if he's giving orders. Annie, you remember Penny Lamp, my student nurse."

"Of course. Hi! It was really nice of you to look after Mack. It was pretty bad, wasn't it." Annie was juggling plates as she spoke. Penny came around the table to help.

"Yes, well, it's improving, I think. Who gets these eggs? Is this all the family, or did you invite the neighborhood in for breakfast."

"The one on the end, Peter, gets the eggs. And yes, these are all family, but only half of us. The one reading the cereal box is Danny. This is our little Joey and the baby, Becky. C'mon you guys, hurry up so I can get this cleaned up before the others come in."

The first shift was finished fifteen minutes later. Penny stayed to help stack dishes and set the table. Annie took this opportunity to ask the young student nurse questions about Sonny's condition and which tubes did what. Penny answered the best she could, trying to assure Annie that Sonny was going to be fine. Matthew came in with the older boys for their breakfast. There were introductions all around as Penny took a seat at the table.

She was a little apprehensive about seeing Matthew again, since their last meeting was not exactly cordial. Happily, Matthew did not seem to have any animosity toward their pretty young guest at all. "If they hadn't told me who you were, Miss Lamp, I wouldn't have recognized you," he said pleasantly. "Is that your horse parked out back?"

There were gasps and raised eyebrows around the table and surprised glances were exchanged as Mack's brothers realized who she was. "Oh," Thomas crowed at loud. "You must be the girl on the horse-" There was a definite disturbance under the table as Thomas received a not-so-gentle suggestion to shut up from Mack's good leg. Only Andrew was not smiling or participating in this newest family joke as he excused himself without eating.

Matthew started pumping Penny for medical insight as Annie had done earlier. Yes, she explained, losing a kidney is serious, but more important was the damage done to the other one. He'll have to be careful the rest of his life.

"Huh," Matthew grunted. "What about getting' back to work? How long will it take? We need him—bad!"

"Mr. Winston," Penny said sharply, "Sonny's incision is about fourteen inches long. All his lower abdominal muscles have been sliced open. Breathing will hurt like hell, much less lifting or sitting on a tractor. He'll be in the hospital for at least a month, maybe longer!" She stopped then, looking at the circle of somber faces. "Look, you won't be picking corn for at least eight or ten weeks, right?" she said, using a softer tone. "He'll be back by then – at least he can supervise. You guys can do it, right?"

"Supervise? Sonny?" Matthew cried. "You think he'll sit back and just watch while we're working? If he can walk, he'll be out there." The talk turned to farming then, and plans were made for the day. They had to work on fencing again. Annie said she planned on going to bed for a while. "Well," Penny said, "I should probably get going."

"No," Mack cried. "Why don't you come out with us? I'll

be driving the tractor all day, and you can ride along."

"For God's sake, Mack," his father blurted. "Why would a pretty young lady like this want to spend one of her few vacation days sittin' on a tractor?"

"No, no, I'd love to come. But I'll stay and help Annie finish up here first, okay?" Penny and Mack exchanged happy grins. They were both relieved that the first meting with the family had gone so well. John volunteered to unsaddle the horse and turned him out into the pasture. Hopefully, the fence would hold it, someone quipped. Penny was glad they were all making it easy for her to stay because she didn't want to leave.

Penny and Annie struck up a comfortable conversation as they worked in the quiet kitchen. Penny was aware of most of the family saga of how they came to live out here, but she wasn't sure about Sonny's part.

Annie half-smiled a little wistfully as she stood by the sink washing dishes for a few moments before she answered. She explained how he had helped rescue her father the night of the poker game, and then Matthew had asked him to come along to help them get started. "It's funny. None of us trusted him at first, except my father, of course. We thought he was so arrogant. But now I don't know what we'd do without him. If anything - - " Her voice faded then.

The kitchen was finished, so Annie offered to take her guest on a quick tour of the house. She apologized for the mess. "Whenever I'm gone, no one ever puts anything away."

"It's a beautiful house," Penny said as they ascended the stairs. "It has a lot of--" She was searching for the right word that wouldn't sound offensive.

"Possibilities?" Annie laughed. "Yes, I know. I've been saying that for months, but it's way down on the list of priorities. It's always, wait till the hay is done or the barn is fixed. I guess I should be grateful I have running water."

She led the way out onto the upstairs balcony. "Hey, boys!" Annie yelled to her brothers playing below. "I'm going to bed soon and you will have to watch Becky and Joey." She ignored the chorus of complaining and moaning that followed her announcement. "When you want to find the men, just follow the road around to the right. See? They shouldn't be too far. Tell them they'll have to eat cold sandwiches for lunch."

They went down the hallway toward Annie's room. She sighed as they passed rooms with unmade beds and clutter everywhere. "It's totally amazing to me how fast this place can fall apart," she said wearily.

"I'm utterly amazed, too!" Penny felt compelled to say. "I can't imagine trying to manage all this – all this responsibility!"

"It's just organization. I don't do all the work. I just have to make sure everyone does their share. I had no idea I could be such a bitch." Annie laughed.

"Do you ever—I mean, like, resent it? Having to deal with all this?"

"Sometimes, but I can't think of anything else I'd rather be doing. I didn't like college. I had no idea what I wanted or where I was going. I bet you knew for a long time that you wanted to be a nurse, right? You're so good at it."

"What is this?" Penny laughed. "A mutual admiration society? Yeah, I really like nursing, but I don't like school either. I just want to get it over with."

"Annie," a voice called from the hallway. "What about Joey? All he does is cry." Peter appeared, struggling with the boy.

"Well, Penny,' Annie said, sighing deeply. "I guess I'll take my bath now. Then me and this little guy will lay down together and take a nap."

Penny took her cue and went outside to find Mack. She felt excited and even more curious than before. She wanted to learn more about this family, especially son #1.

* * * * * *

There was a faint pinging on his window. Even before he was fully conscious, John knew what it was. He went to the window and saw Kenny standing on the yard below, his bike against the tree. He was ready to throw another stone when he saw Johnny's face.

"C'mon," Kenny whispered. "It's almost 5:30!"

312

John grabbed some clothes, shoes, and socks, and sprinted down stairs. Kenny, knowing the routine, already went into the kitchen and handed his friend a jug of juice as he headed outside. They took turns gulping it as John finished getting dressed.

"Haven't you heard of an alarm clock?" Kenny chided him. "This is the third time this week I had to come all the way over here and get your sorry ass out of bed!"

"I can't use the alarm clock 'cause Annie yells at me for waking up the whole household."

The two began stretching as they talked. "You ready? Let's go!" Kenny said, back-peddling toward the driveway. "How about to the old bridge and back. That's only five miles. We should be able to make that before your dad starts lookin' for ya."

So they began, loping along with long, evenly matched strides, their bare, bronzed backs glistened in the morning sun. "Well, it starts next week," Kenny said. "No sweat. We're in better shape than most of those pigs. Twice around the track and they're dead! Just wait till we start those drills in pads. Sure hope it cools down."

"I can't wait to get started. I can do those plays in my sleep, so I'm ready, right?"

"Right!"

They picked up the pace then and reached the bridge in record time, but instead of turning around, they jogged over it. "I feel real good this morning," Kenny said. "You wanna go the rest of the way around?"

"Sure, let's go," John smiled. That would add an extra two miles.

On they ran, past the cornfields and cows waiting to be milked, through the deep early morning shadows into the glare of the sun. It was sure to be another scorching hot, August day. Still harder they pushed, defying anything that would stand in their way or test their fates. They were young and strong and confident, motivated possibly beyond their capabilities.

They propped over the rim of the hill south of the McDuffy place. The house and barn were in sight. That was the cue to push even harder, straining to squeeze out that last ounce of will and energy, their fists clinched and their arms pumping hard with every stride. They eyed each other as friendly adversaries. They were natural competitors first, and best friends second. John passed the mailbox first.

They slowed to a stop, gasping for air. "I won!" John managed to gloat, sucking air furiously. "We're even – eighteen a piece."

"Hey!" his friend retorted. "You're the runner, I'm the quarterback, remember? You worry about these hands, and I'll worry about your legs. See? Watch?" He took the snap of the imaginary football and threw a terrific spiral into the waiting hands of his halfback, who swerved and spun his way through a slew of 300 pound defenders and danced his way into the end zone. As always, they had just scored the winning touchdown with less than three seconds left on the clock. "And don't forget," Kenny added. "When the reporters close in, don't forget to mention that your quarterback threw you an amazing pass!"

"Okay," John grinned, "I'll try to remember." They slapped each other on their backs and walked toward the house. There could hear activity around the place and Matthew was yelling.

"Sounds like the old man is already in a great mood," Kenny observed.

"Nah, don't worry about it. He never yells at me."

"Yeah? You sound pretty sure of yourself. How come?"

"I think he sorta wishes he was me – young and stuff. He had four bitchy sisters and a real wimpy father so he never got to do much physical stuff. Besides he knows that if I miss chores, I'll make up for it later. How you suppose I got these babies?" He flexed his arms to show off his bulging biceps.

"Get out of here!" Kenny howled as he retrieved his bike, ready to push off. "Maybe I'll come over Sunday afternoon, and we'll go over those plays one more time," he said.

"Hell," John smiled. "Maybe we'll make up a few of our own. See ya' in church." He watched as his friend headed toward the road, and then leaped up the stairs to put on some work clothes. He really felt good. That buzz he got from those runs with Kenny stayed with him sometimes for hours. He was buttoning up his shirt in the mirror, thinking about football practice starting soon, when a shrill voice penetrated his thoughts.

"You dumb jocks – you're all alike," Thomas sneered, but he left before Johnny had a chance to reply. Leave it to Thomas to try to spoil a perfectly good morning. He really detested his brother, but there was no time to argue now. Matthew never yelled at him yet for being late, but there was always a first time.

Chapter 35

The days following Sonny's accident went faster than Annie expected. There was so much to do. Matthew rather enjoyed being solely in charge of the place. Only John was excused from the long days of hard labor because football practice started mid-August. For him, it was a toss-up who was the hardest taskmaster – the coach or his father. Kenny hadn't exaggerated when he said it would be tough, no matter how in shape they were.

Annie concentrated on her garden. Her tomato crop was her pride and joy. She picked baskets of them everyday, and canned the ones they didn't eat, with a lot of help from her advisors, Ginny and Lori. Some of Annie's questions made them smile, even laugh, but they remained helpful and supportive. It proved to be an extremely successful venture for Annie. Soon, she had 54 quart of whole tomatoes in neat rows in the "fruit room", as she called her corner of the basement. Every jar was sealed, and she was certain that every jar was sterile and safe for eating, though she hated the thought of opening even one of her little beauties.

Penny came every day and began staying longer and longer. Mack's stump was healing nicely and the knee became more limber. He was hopeful that he would have his prosthesis by September. Penny took the rest of the family by storm, too. Only Andrew remained aloof. Annie noticed his resistance and asked him about it, but her twin refused to discuss it.

Annie had no idea there was a connection, but she knew how she felt when she saw Mack and Penny together. At dusk, they'd sit by the oak tree or on the porch swing, laughing and talking together. Often they'd hold hands or share a long, lingering kiss. Watching them made Annie want what they had, too. At night, when she heard their laughter through her open window, she'd thrust her pillow over her head and silent, painful tears would fall down her cheeks. It would never be like that for her and Sonny, she mourned, never in a million years.

She called the hospital once or twice everyday, and sometimes Dr. Adams would call with a progress report. Sonny was doing very well. He was being resentfully cooperative. The fact that he refused pain medication was astounding. He did everything that was asked of him and more. His recovery was faster than any of the staff expected. As soon as possible he was up walking in the hallways, dragging all his paraphernalia with him. The nurses reported that one by one, the hated tubes were removed. Not fast enough. Annie guessed.

* * * * * *

Summer drew to a close. That meant that once again, the large, yellow school bus made its slow, arduous route down the gravel roads. Many of its passengers, especially those from the Winston house, were less than enthusiastic about returning to the classroom.

Annie, on the other had, was relieved. Her home would once again have some semblance of quiet organization for at least a few hours a day. She usually had the house straightened by noon, and it stayed that way until the bus made its return trip. However, instead of reveling in the tranquility, she was restless and irritable. It became harder and harder to absorb herself in her work because of Sonny. She and the rest of the family had stayed away for two weeks now. One afternoon, just as she was thinking about going to the hospital to see him, the telephone rang.

"Hello," she said.

"Annie? This is Dr. Adams. I'm here at the hospital, and we were wondering if you've heard anything from Mr. Jackson this afternoon. He seems to have disappeared."

"Disappeared?" she gasped. "From the hospital?"

"Yes, I'm afraid so. He's been doing very well, but of course, we're concerned that he's apparently walked out. Perhaps he feels he's been co-operative long enough," he said with a laugh. As usual, the good doctor did not seem upset. "If he should contact you, please try to convince him to come back. In the mean time, I'll speak with his surgeon and discuss the situation. We may be able to discharge him this afternoon as soon as we check out a couple of things. It's much earlier than what we expected, but I'm sure Sonny would convalesce faster at home with you. You just get him back here, and I'll see what I can do. And Annie, when you see him – well, he's been through quite an ordeal. He'll be weak and won't look like you're used to seeing him."

What a dear man, she thought as she hung up the phone. He was trying to reassure her and prepare her for what she knew will probably be a shock. She knew he had lost weight and much of his strength, but she didn't care. "Home with you." That's what Dr. Peters said. Those words echoed through her over and over. And she was sure he was right, but first she had to find him.

She was sure she knew where he was, if he could go that far. She ran outside to find Mack and quickly explained the situation to him, asking him to stay with the little ones and listen for the phone. Then she ran to her car and drove toward Dubuque as fast as she dared. Her heart was racing, too. She was afraid for him, but glad she'd be seeing him soon.

She found the turn off to the Monument Park. As she turned the last bend of the road near the top of the hill, she spotted him. He had someone else's clothes on. The pants were so large he was holding them up with his hands. Obviously exhausted, he stopped every five or six feet, leaning over with his hands on his knees. She pulled up beside him. His face was a strange color and he looked like he might pass out, though she knew he wouldn't. When he looked up and recognized the car, he turned away and started walking again. She knew it was useless to ask him to get into the car, so she said nothing and followed him to the crest of the hill and into the parking lot.

She walked behind him as he staggered down the path to the stone monument. He sank down to his knees, gasping for breath. "I ain't goin' back to that hell hole! Don't even say it!"

She started to argue, but then thought better of it. She simply sat down on the grass and said nothing. He didn't seem real surprised that she found him. Perhaps, he expected it. She stole quick glances at him, aghast how gaunt and weak he was. She knew he was in a lot of pain, remembering how Penny had described the incision, saying that just breathing would be difficult. She wanted so badly to touch him, but she knew he'd never allow it.

"What were you doing?" she asked, trying not to sound reproachful.

"I didn't have no plan. I just had to get out of there." He spit the words, still having trouble breathing.

"Sonny, are you alright? You look--"

"Yeah, I know, I look like hell, but I'm still not goin' back," he cried. "That bitchin' nurse kept comin' in ever' fifteen minutes tellin' me to – Jesus Christ, what do they expect? They just took that damn tube out this morning. She said I had till 3:00 to go or she'd put it back in again. And I'm tellin' ya – no way I am goin' wait around for that!"

"They're just trying to do their job. You know a person can't go for hours without--"

"Don't start! I'd be alright if people would just leave me alone!" He struggled to his feet, indignant and embarrassed. He half-walked, half crawled to the other side of the monument. After a few minutes he spoke again, his voice stronger and calmer. "What did the old man say about all this? Look at me. I'm good for shit!"

She was appalled at his thinking. "He knows it'll be awhile before you throw a 60 pound bale around or drive a tractor for eighteen hours. The doctors said you were lucky to be alive." She walked around to where he was, wishing he would look up at her. "Sonny, why did you send me away?" she asked, almost whispering. "I could have been there for you, helped you. Why did you make me leave you there all alone?"

He didn't answer for a long time. "I have to handle things

my own way, alone." He moved away from her again.

She didn't understand, but she knew it was useless to press him. Sitting down cross-legged on the grass, she decided to change the mood by changing the subject. "Hey, you'll never guess who's our new hired hand. Did you meet the student nurse who took care of Mack? Penny Lamp, Dr. Lamp's daughter. Well, it turns out that she was his mystery lady, the girl on the horse. Anyway, she stopped by to check his stump, and now they're really close. She's been there everyday helping out. Mack seems happier than I've ever seen him. I can't believe how much he's changed this summer."

"I'll be damned. So his stump is doin' better?"

"Yeah, I guess so. Penny changes the bandages and does those stretching exercises like you were doing, and that's better, too. He wants to get his artificial leg as soon as possible. He's as anxious for harvest time as Dad is."

She stopped and glanced at him again. His face had the most peculiar expression of panic as he struggled to get to his feet. "Woaaaaa!" he cried as he rushed to the backside of the Monument into the bushes. He came back a few minutes later, looking supremely victorious. "Too bad Nurse What's-Her-Name missed it. But then, maybe she'd be disappointed…"

"Speaking of that," Annie started. "I think it's time to make a deal. Dr. Adams said he would talk to your surgeon about getting you discharged, but first you have to go back to the hospital."

"No, Annie, just take me back to the farm."

"I can't, Sonny, Dr. Adams said I should bring you back for an quick check-up," she insisted. "Now, let's go."

"No!"

"But Dr. Adams said he could arrange it."

"Adams? Why not Rathburn?"

"You'd better not complain. Most doctors would probably scream at you for your little stunt today. Dr. Adams is on you side."

"I'm fine. I made it all the way up here, didn't I?"

"That's just the problem. They have to check to see if you did any damage to yourself." But Sonny didn't move.

"Is there trouble between you and Dr. Adams?" she asked, trying hard to stay calm. "I can't imagine anyone disliking him. He's the gentlest, kindest man I've ever known."

"Okay, okay," he spat as he tried to stand up. "Just remember, if they try any stunts, I walked out of there once. I can do it again."

He got to his feet and managed to walk back to the car. She did not attempt to help him, as she knew he would never allow it. They drove back to the hospital in silence. They took the elevator to the second floor. There had been a changing of the guard at 3:00, Sonny's arch nemesis was off duty. Dr. Adams came to Sonny's room as soon as he was paged, carrying a suture removal kit and another package, which visibly upset the patient. The doctor turned to Annie and said, "There's a dietitian coming to talk with you about Sonny's special diet. Why don't you go to the nurse's station and wait for her. There's a few things I need to take care of anyway. And don't look so worried! I spoke with Rathbrun. If everything checks out, you take him home as soon as I'm finished." Telling the nurse he could handle things alone, he closed the door behind them.

"Okay, son," he said gently, "take off Mr. Wade's clothes, and we'll see if your little escapade did any damage."

Sonny paced on the other side of the bed. "Look, Doc, I'm fine. I had no trouble relieving myself as soon as I left this place, so I just want to go home."

"I realize you're anxious to go home, but I need to check you over."

"I've been checked over night and day for two weeks. I'm going home."

"Yes, Sonny, they tell me you've been a model patient, so just let me finish. It'll just take a few minutes. You're going to have to lie down here so I can examine you."

Sonny hesitated, but then laid down stiffly and allowed the doctor to proceed. Temperature, pulse, and blood pressure were fine. The incision was healing nicely. The remaining four stitches were quickly removed. "Now, turn over so I can see the back part of the incision." This time, Sonny did not move.

"It's fine, Doc. Just let me get out of here."

"Sonny, there's nothing back there I haven't seen before. I cannot discharge you until I finish this examination. Please, turn over."

Scowling, Sonny rolled over. The doctor moved his hand along the suture line, looking for tender spots or pockets of infection. But then, he touched the strange scars furrowed across the hips. Sonny turned back angrily and bolted upright, putting on the pin-stripped blue robe.

Dr. Adams said nothing for a long time, jotting notes in the chart and putting his things back in his black doctor's bag. "Sonny, have you heard of doctor-patient confidentiality? That means that anything that is said between us is held in the strictest confidence. Yes, it's true, I recognized you. I guess I'm getting old because it took me awhile to piece it together." He studied his patient for a few minutes but then continued.

"You seem very intent on keeping your past a secret, and that's fine with me. My main concern is the present. You seem to believe that you can walk out of there and this ordeal will be over. I wish it were that simple. There's going to be special diets, medicines, and follow-up exams with lab tests. I am certainly willing to take care of all that for you, but I can't if you insist on fighting me every step of the way."

Sonny stood staring out the window, but then turned to look at the doctor and allowed eye contact for the first time. "Okay, can I go now?"

"No, we're not finished yet," Dr. Adams said as he reached for the package. "I can't let you leave until you pass this last test. We need to check for residual, that is, to make sure that you emptied your bladder completely."

"You ain't stickin that damn tube back in me," Sonny cried, retreating to the far corner of the room.

"No, no, this is a different kind – it doesn't stay in. It'll just take a minute. C'mon, let's get it done so you can go home."

Annie paced in the hallway outside Sonny's room. She had already spoken at length with the dietitian and nurses about his diet and complications she should watch for. They discussed his medicines and their possible side effects. The door was still closed, and whatever Dr. Adams was doing was taking much longer than she expected. Maybe something was wrong.

Finally, the door swung open. Sonny was dressed, although his own clothes hung on him almost as badly as Mr. Wade's. Dr. Adams invited her in, wanting to talk to them both.

"I'm not going to waste my breath with a lot of rules and limitations," he began. "With most people I'd say, no lifting or stooping for several weeks, etc. But with you, Sonny, I'll simply say let your body be your guide. If you push yourself too hard, your body will punish you for a few days. The most important thing is not to forget your weekly check-ups in my office, okay?"

A nurse came with a wheelchair, but Sonny brushed past her and headed down the hallway. She had no choice but to follow behind them, pushing the empty chair.

When they arrived at home, Sonny stood for several minutes, looking around as though as he had been gone for years. Annie turned away, pretending not to notice. She was thankful that he was spared a rowdy welcoming committee.

He walked slowly down the hill toward his shed. His gut was throbbing and his legs felt like limp water hoses, but he walked erect. He knew Annie was watching. The place was dark. Good, he thought. If he had to face one more person tonight, he was going to puke.

They had done some renovating during his absence. The bare 2 x 4's were covered, and new beds and other furniture had been brought in. He sank against the doorway, reveling in the tranquility of being completely alone in the darkness. He thought of going to sleep immediately, but there was something he felt compelled to do first.

He flipped on the lights in the bathroom, ripping off his clothes as he went. He started the shower and stuck his head and shoulders into the warm stream of water even before he managed to stomp off his jeans. The water was as hot as he could tolerate, soothing his weak and sore muscles. It pierced the ragged edges of his incision, but he didn't care. He just wanted to feel clean.

He had seen a movie once about a woman who had been brutally raped, and she stood in a hot shower like this, hoping it would somehow wash away her rage and filth. He, too, felt violated. He tolerated those people touching and handling him in

322

ways he had never imagined. He closed his eyes tightly and shuddered, filled with an utter sense of self-condemnation.

Slowly the hot, hypnotic water quieted him and he was overcome by weariness. He fell against the wall and slowly sank to the floor. It was over, and it was time to get on with his life. With that realization, he turned off the water and crawled out. Moving gingerly, he managed to put on clean underwear and a T-shirt and make his way to bed.

Mack came in. "Sonny? Hey, are you alright?" he called. "My God, man, you look wasted." He waited for a response, but Sonny said nothing. He was already asleep.

Chapter 36

Sonny looked a little sheepish when he strolled into the kitchen the next morning at nearly 8:30. The boys had already left for school, and the rest of the family was sitting around the table enjoying a leisurely breakfast. He was greeted by a round of applause and mock cheering.

"Christ," laughed Matthew, "we were wondering if we should come check on you!"

"C'mon, give the guy a break," cried Mack. "Probably the first time he's had any sleep since he was unconscious. They never let you sleep in those places. They wake you up just to ask you if you're sleeping. Bet ya' can't wait for some honest-to-God home cooking – even Annie's!"

Sonny sat down and waited for the noisy teasing to die down. Then he said, "Well, how's everything been goin' around here? Hope ya' didn't screw things up too bad." There had been problems, and they made sure he knew he was missed. While they talked, Annie prepared his breakfast. It wasn't bacon and eggs like the others. She tried to place the plate and pile of pills in front of him discretely, but it did not go unnoticed by anyone.

"Oh, yuk!" Mack cried. "Toast without butter! Poached eggs! And all those pills!"

Annie fired a glare across the table. "The dietician explained that he has to eat this low-salt, low-fat stuff until they're sure he's completely healed. We can't take any chances, so why don't you just shut up!"

Matthew took the hint, and rousted everyone out. "Let's go. This place can't farm itself." Sonny watched them go, having no choice but to stay behind and eat his food, such as it was.

Annie felt awkward, moving around the kitchen trying to finish her morning routine. She could feel his eyes following her as she worked. She had prepared the baby's cereal and fruit, and sat down by Becky's high chair. Joey, who was lying on the floor, was more difficult to feed and would be taken care of later. His bowl was sitting on the counter.

The little boy's glee at seeing his friend was unmistakable. He giggled and purred as he managed to roll and squirm over to Sonny's chair. He seemed confused that Sonny didn't pick him up.

"Joey," Annie scolded, "you mustn't bother Sonny--"

She spoke too quickly. Sonny reached down and stiffly picked up the child, grimacing. He looked at the dish on the counter. Annie took the hint and retrieved it for him.

"What are you gonna do – about the boy, I mean," he asked bluntly.

"You mean about school? I don't know. There's no reason to rush into anything." Sonny's disapproving glace told her he disagreed with that rationale, but he said nothing. "Everything's been so hectic around here lately. All I have to do is call up that place and make an appointment. I should at least look the place over before I decide."

"Doc Adams said he made an appointment two weeks ago, and you cancelled at the last minute."

"What is this, you two ganging up on me? Yes, I cancelled. I had to register the boys for school and I was canning. Did I tell you I gave 54--"

"So, why don't you make another appointment?"

"Sonny, you don't understand. Everyone in this family knows how Mother felt about this. Shouldn't that count for something?"

Sonny did not answer immediately. He seemed to be mulling over what she said in his mind. "No, not really. She's not here, so you're left with the problem."

"You're talking like Joey's this huge burden that I should hand over to someone else because I can't handle it myself."

"No, all I'm saying is they can teach him things there." He turned away then, putting Joey back on the floor and standing up slowly. Neither of them said anything for a long time.

"Well, where is it?" he said finally.

"Where's what?"

"Your list. You have lists for everything. I'm sure you have a list of things you want done around here, right?"

"Sonny, no--"

"You've been harpin' about this stuff for months. Now's your chance."

Sonny, this is your first day home--"

"I ain't gonna jump on a goddamn tractor, but I ain't no invalid, either!" The screen door slammed before the last word was out of his mouth. She started to run after him, but then decided against it. He wouldn't listen anyway.

He was gone a long time, and she began to worry. She took the baby upstairs and scanned the yard from her window. She spotted him walking in the orchard, stopping frequently to study the scraggly trees. My God, she gasped, what is he doing?

Becky settled down quickly for her nap, so she put Joey in his wagon and pulled him across the yard to where Sonny was standing. He heard them coming, but did not acknowledge their presence. She followed him as he walked, his hands in his pockets and his expression grim. This had probably been a productive grove of trees at one time, but after years of neglect, they had gone to waste, a ticket of nearly barren trees.

"There's no way a little work out here is gonna get ya' bushels of cherries or apples next year," he warned. "It'll probably take three or five years to get this orchard in shape. If you ask me, we should just flatten it and start over with new trees." They had this discussion before. She knew he thought she was foolish about this, but she felt strongly about the new remaining links to the history of this place, and wanted the original trees to stay.

"Well, I guess you'd better get that little chain saw out of the shop. Oh hell, I'd better go with you. It probably needs gas."

Thankfully, Andrew materialized out of nowhere and volunteered to help. Soon, they were at work with Sonny hollering directions to Andrew over the whine of the chain saw. Utter frustration showed on his face. He was used to doing, not talking. He could have done it himself in a fourth of the time, but he had no choice but to be content with this for now.

By midday, the brush pile was higher than Annie, and they were barely started. Matthew and Mack joined them, and they had lunch sitting beneath one of the trees. Sonny sank down wearily, and once again the conversation turned to farming. The corn was turning, Matthew reported. He'd take Sonny down to the bottom in the pickup after supper,.

Mack kept looking down the driveway anxiously. "Hey! Over here," he called when Penny's Jeep came to a stop. She ran toward him and they gave each other a greeting kiss.

"Well, here I am, reporting for work," she grinned, enthusiastic as ever. "This is a fruit orchard, isn't it. My grandparents in Massachusetts have one. And grapes – you need a vineyard, too."

"Well," Annie said, "we don't know what we have back here for sure. Penny, this is our boss and general manager, Sonny, fresh from an engagement at your favorite institution." She noticed Penny's gasping stare, so she added, "Guess no one around here is big on long hospital stays."

"Well, anyway, I have some great news," Penny said.

"You've decided to quit school and move to the cottage permanently," Mack teased, giving her a quick squeeze.

"No, of course not, but I was talking to my father last night, and he says you can probably get your prosthesis in few more weeks. Isn't that great?"

"Hey, what's wrong? You tired of being seen with a one-legged gimp?" Mack teased.

"Yeah, ya' bum. Let's go change your dressing and do some therapy so we can get some work done." She took his hand and led him away, their eyes full of each other.

Andrew left shortly afterwards, wandering off the opposite direction. Matthew and Annie had things to do elsewhere, too, so

Sonny was left alone, still sitting beneath an apple tree. And there he stayed, sound asleep for most of the afternoon.

* * * * * *

If Sonny had a lot of pain or other difficulties, he never let on. He pushed himself to do a little more work each day. He ate the food and followed the other restrictions without complaint. He even endured the indignities of the weekly doctor's visits.

Annie was delighted to be able to cross some repairs off her list at long last. Sonny plastered the biggest holes, replaced bathroom fixtures, and added some much needed electrical outlets throughout the house. She hoped he would attempt some restoration of the old dining room table, but he scoffed at the suggestion. The fate of the baldy damaged, twelve foot oak table had been hotly debated on several occasions. Everyone thought it should be discarded, except Annie, who regarded it was a treasure worth salvaging. She covered it with a linen tablecloth and hoped that someday it would receive the attention she felt it deserved.

Things were changing as the green of the landscape turned gold and orange. Andrew packed up most of his belongings and moved into a small apartment off campus in Dubuque, but promised to come home on the weekends to help. Mack happily reminded him that he could catch a ride with Penny because she'd be coming out to the cottage every Friday.

Mack had several reasons to be happy these days. His relationship with Penny was great. He was getting along with his father better than he had in years. And he became a "whole man" again when he finally got his artificial leg. It seemed almost alien to everyone to see him walking somewhat clumsily with two legs instead of the crutches. It was strange for him also. In fact, he could move faster the old way, but he was determined to master it.

A hard transition for Annie was the brown van that came every morning at 7:30 to pick up Joey. She had gone alone to see the school and liked what she saw. It was a comprehensive program entailing all phases of daily life, including meals and an afternoon nap. The people were very kind. There were physical and speech therapists, as well as teachers trained to care for small children with special needs. They must have detected Annie's hesitancy because they stressed that the follow-up care at home was very important, and how they must all work together to help Joey fulfill his greatest potential.

Intellectually she understood, but emotionally it was very difficult. Sending him off that first day was one of the most difficult things she had ever done. She cried as he left. Joey fussed and clung to her, but after a few days he went gladly, which made Annie feel worse for some inexplicable reason.

* * * * * *

When football coaches talk about good running backs, they're likely to use words like acceleration, penetration, and finding the hole. He has to have good hands, intelligence, and be able to throw a block if necessary. A good running back can make a mediocre football team into a great one. A coach in a small, Class-C high school dreams of having a halfback with just a few of those qualities. One with several is a gift straight from the football gods. Or at least, that's what Coach Evans thought every time his team took the field. The new kid was really good, especially when teamed up with decent linemen and Kenny Beyers, a better than average quarterback. There was a bona fide feeling of optimism for the first time in many, many years.

The conditioning Johnny and Kenny had done over the summer paid off. If anything, the coach cautioned them not to push so hard. Their first game was a non-conference game against a neighboring larger school. Coach hated these games because they usually got trounced, which started the season badly.

This year it was a home game and the place was jammed. The coach sat in his office next to the locker room, listening to his team dressing. There was noisy excitement with profanities bouncing off the walls that would make their mother's blush. At the appointed time, he put out his cigarette and strode in to meet with his team.

Coach Evans's pre-game speech was anything but eloquent. "Listen up!" he called as he moved to the center of the room. "I don't have to tell you how important this game is. It sets the tone for the whole season. You guys have worked harder than any team I've ever coached. We have talent, enough to win a lot of games. And we have a lot of pride, so we're not gonna' roll over and play dead like they expect. So, c'mon, lets go out there and kick some ass!"

A rousing, ear-piercing yell punctuated the last statement, and was sustained all the way out of the building and onto the field. On the other side, the large visiting team did look intimidating as they strutted around arrogantly, assured of a seemingly easy victory.

The stands were filled on both sides of the field. High school football was a very big deal in small town Americana, and Shannon Town was no exception. The cheerleaders were leading hopeful cheers along the sidelines, and the band was gathering behind the goal post, waiting to make their entrance to play the traditional anthem.

John Winston was a bundle of nerves. He had already discreetly thrown up twice in the locker room, and was fighting the impulse to do it again. He knew that the coaches and his teammates were pinning their hopes on him, but he had his doubts.

"Hey, Rich Boy," Kenny teased. "Don't get so uptight. It's only the biggest game of your life!" John had no time to respond as the captains of the teams were called to mid-field for the coin toss. "Shannon Town as won the toss," the ref announced. "What's your pleasure, gentleman?" They elected to receive. Johnny and Kenny put on their helmets. It was time to play ball.

Separate special teams is not a luxury afforded to small school teams. Coach Evans sent Bobbie Simpson, the wide receiver, and John out to take the kick-off, hoping that one of them would turn the ball up field to secure decent field position for their first possession. John stood there, scarcely able to breathe. And then suddenly, he heard a faint, far-away whistle, and there it was, -- the ball, spiraling, spinning, plummeting toward him like a fiery comet dropping out of the sky. He could not catch it cleanly. It bounced against his chest where he smothered it, wrapping his arms around it. At the same instant, not because of any conscious effort on his part, he began to run.

First, right, then left, skipping away from one defender and then another. He had no sense of anything except movement—the momentum, the will to drive forward.

But then, there was a sharp jerking sensation at his ankles and he began to fall with a terrible weight upon him. His face was buried in the grass and mud. He couldn't move or breathe until at last he was able to roll over and the bright blaze of the field lights blinded him as he became aware of the thunderous crowd.

A man with a black brimmed cap leaned over him, looking at him expectantly. "Give me the ball, son," the man said. Hesitantly Johnny surrendered it to him. Kenny grabbed his hand and pulled him to his feet, ginning and cheering with the others crowded around, pressing, rejoicing, screaming. But it was the voice on the loud speaker who told John what happened. "Ball carrier #34, John Winston. 78 yard return. First and ten on the twelve yard line." Did he say 78 yards? Johnny peered down field to where he stood a few moments ago.

There was no time to digest what had just happened. Johnny huddled with his team, the play having been sent in from the coach. Kenny was to fake to John, step back into the pocket and dump the ball off to Bobbie. It worked nicely "10 yards on the play," the announcer cried. "The receiver, #84, Bob Simpson. First and goal on the two yard line." The crowds on both sides of the field were in a frenzy.

The next play was simple. Give the ball to John and let him run. He got nowhere. The whole defense was keying on #34. The coach called for a passing play again. The ball skipped out of Bobbie's hands. They were lucky it wasn't intercepted. Anxiously, the team huddled again. "C'mon you guys, we gotta bare down!" Kenny pressed as he waited for the play.

Ronny McNeal, one of the tight ends, reported to the huddle with the play. "Coach says, John, to the left." The Coach wanted to give the ball to his star and see if he could push it over the goal line, but everyone expected it, even the people in the stands.

"Hey, Johnny," Kenny whispered, pulling his friend aside as they broke the huddle. "Let's try a little razzle-dazzle reverse."

"The coach would kill us!" Johnny cried, wide-eyed and excited.

"What's he gonna do? Kick us off the team?" Kenny grinned. "C'mon, it'll work!" They had practiced it a thousand times on hot summer afternoons when they were bored with the same old plays. In their imaginary goal-line stands, it worked every time.

John lined up on the left flank, but at the last second, he went in motion and jumped to the other side. On the sidelines, the coach exploded. "What the hell!" he roared, throwing down his clipboard.

"22 – 24 – 26 – Hut!" Randy barked. Quickly, he served the ball to John, who danced around in the backfield as Kenny stepped around the mess of crushing bodies and streaked to the far corner of the end zone. Johnny hurled the ball his direction, but was decked before he could see what happened. "Touchdown!" the announcer screamed. The Shannon Town fans erupted into thunderous jubilation.

The boys stayed in for the point-after and subsequent kick-off. And when they did finally come to the sidelines, they kept their distance from the coach, whose face was as red as their opponents' uniforms. However, he sought them out, shouting over the crowd. "I'll see you in my office after the game!" he screamed. "And don't try any more stunts!"

Three hours later, it was over, and the statistics were impressive. Conference records were broken. Most Individual Rushing Yards: 142 yards, Most Yards Passing:186, Longest Kick-Off Return: 78 yards.

But they lost, 17 to 14.

However, that was difficult to tell by the way both teams and their fans acted. The red and white players hung their heads, knowing they were in for the verbal thrashing from their own coach. Luckily, they had pulled ahead in the closing seconds to avoid total embarrassment.

The Shannon Town crowd was ecstatic! Their bruised and muddied gladiators filed inside their locker room, whooping and slapping each other triumphantly. The coach called for silence and then stood there for several moments while he collected his thoughts. He was clearly emotional.

"Okay, you guys," he began, cradling the game ball in his huge hands, "I know it's been said that winning isn't everything – it's the only thing. And the guy who said that sure as hell was a better coach than I'll ever be. But if I coach another thirty years, there will never be another team or another game I'll be more proud of than this one tonight. It was a much larger team – hell, they still had guys on their bench with clean uniforms. I know they out-weighed us by a ton! But you guys never let up, you hung in there. They were lucky to get out of here with a win, and they know it. I said this game would set the tone for the whole season, and I'm tellin' you guys, I think we're in for a hellva season!" He was smiling, looking as though he was anxious to get on with in. "Okay, you animals, go out and have some fun cause Monday it starts all over again!"

They peeled off their layers of uniforms and pads, and headed for the showers, congratulating each other and making plans for post game activities.

"Yeah, man," one of them said, "I told Cathy I didn't want to make any plans until after the game cause maybe I wouldn't feel like doin' nothin'. But I'm tellin' ya' man, she'd better padlock her bra, cause I feel like a goddamn animal tonight!"

"I could tell by the grin on my old man's face when I made the last tackle he's gonna let me use the car," another one said.

"Well, at least I don't have to worry about doin' no studying this weekend. Coach would never flunk me in history now."

"I don't know, Boyd, you were pretty good, but not that good!"

"Ah, shit, get out of my face, Dunlevy!"

"Winston! Beyers! Need a ride? Ya' gonna scoop the loop with us?"

Kenny and John were dressing silently in the back corner. "Nah, no thanks, Boyd," Kenny said. "I got my dad's truck. And the coach wants to see us in his office."

"Well, then, maybe we'll catch you later, okay?"

"Yeah, sure." But the truth was they didn't feel like celebrating anyway. They really wanted to win that game, and didn't understand their teammates' attitude. They were so close.

A half hour later, they walked into the dark gym, the only light coming from the coach's office. A blue cloud of cigarette smoke floated into the hallway, and they could hear him talking on the phone, apparently being interviewed by the local newspaper. The boys waited restlessly. The adrenaline rush of the last three hours was evaporating, replaced by the aching muscles and throbbing joints that come from being buried by several 250-pound titans..

The coach hung up the phone and came out of his office. His huge shadow loomed across the gym floor. He stared at them, lighting another cigarette as he hoisted himself onto the bleachers. "You two really shocked me tonight," he began. "What surprised me the most is that I thought you understood that football is a team sport. You two hotshots can't go out there and win games by yourselves. That was quite a stunt you pulled tonight, and I'm sorry it worked. Now you might try something like that again. That's why we're having this little talk – to make sure you never attempt another unauthorized play like that again.

"But, Coach--"

"Don't you 'but, coach' me. You both have superior talent. We all know that. You also know that this team needs you to win. But you have the other guys busting their butts out there, and you got me. I am the coach! I call the plays, do you understand?"

"Yes, Coach," they mumbled, staring at the floor.

"Okay, then. Go out and have some fun. You deserve it."

They were dismissed. They shuffled toward the door.

"Hey, boys!" the coach called, "You really wanted to win, didn't you."

"Yeah!" they drawled back remorsefully.

"Good! Maybe next time you'll try a little harder," Coach grinned.

They did try harder, and each week they improved. It was contagious, as the whole team over-achieved on a weekly basis. Matthew was so proud of his son that he nearly burst whenever anyone mentioned it, which happened a lot. It proved to be an interesting diversion as the days of autumn slipped by.

Chapter 37

There was a distinct chill in the morning air by late September. Apple cider as 49 cents a gallon and the smell of burning leaves lingered in the breeze. It was an immensely satisfying time, full of energy and anticipation. And no one was happier than Matthew. The two new grain bins were ready for their first kernels of corn. The tractors were greased and ready for action. Three new bright green grain wagons were sitting on the yard. Every evening, Matthew walked down the long rows of turning corn and pick out a bulging ear, peel off the husks, and delight in the symmetrical lines of fat, yellow kernels of corn, and then hung it on a nail in the office. It was true what everyone said. This was going to be a bumper crop.

Matthew made arrangements for the Jameson outfit to pick the corn. They had three monstrous machines that moved through the fields, chewing up eight rows at a time, spitting out bushels of shelled corn at a tremendously efficient rate. Matthew fought the urge to invest in one of the $125,000 machines himself, and would have to be content to drive the grain wagons back and forth between the fields and the bins.

By the end of September, dark menacing clouds started rumbling in from the west, sometimes rolling past, but other times, bringing day-long rain showers. Picking had begun further south, and all the Winston's could do was wait their turn. Matthew became more concerned and irritable as the days passed. If the rain continued, his 320 acres of bottomland would become a marsh and the hill road, a giant mud slide, making it nearly impossible to get the corn out of the fields.

* * * * * *

October dawned cold and bleak. The gray cover was nearly constant now. Matthew's corn was ready, and he insisted that picking should start no later than the weekend. However, Mr. Jameson, who was equally frustrated with the mud and constant breakdowns, would give no assurances.

One Thursday morning near the end of the month, Matthew stood looking up at the steel gray skies and zipped up his jacket with a determined snap. Pulling his cap tightly over his ears, he finished the chores and then stomped into his office and dialed the Jameson place. His wife answered, saying the crew was finishing up a job over at Peosta today. Brushing aside breakfast, Matthew announced he was going to track the fellow down and get some answers.

"Oh, Lordy," Walt Jameson muttered when he noticed Matthew's pick up pulling onto the yard. "Like this day wasn't lousy enough already."

"Good morning," Matthew called. "Looks like you're done here. So my place is next, right?"

"No, I got another job over here at Cascade. It'd make more sense to do that job first before bringing the machines thirty miles to Shanny."

Matthew pressed harder. "The place by Cascade isn't bottom land."

"Well, still," Jameson sighed, "it'll be end of next week before we get over there. My guys are bone tired, and the machines need some maintenance."

"Ah, that's a bunch of bull!" Matthew argued. "They can rest later. All three of the combines seem to be working fine to me."

"Damn it, man! What difference does a couple of days make?"

Matthew had enough business experience to know it's counter productive to attempt to persuade someone after you've made them angry, so he decided to try another route. "Okay, then" Matthew said with much more restraint, "would you consider renting me your machines?"

"And who would drive them? I already told you, my boys need some time off. They've already worked 26 straight eighteen-hour days as it is."

"Don't worry. Me and my boys can handle it."

"Like hell!" Jameson exploded. "That's nearly $400,000 worth of machines. What makes you think that I would turn them over to you?" The inference was understood. He wasn't about to give his machines to untrained, inexperienced city snobs. These machines were his livelihood.

'I will guarantee to cover any loses or damages up to the full purchase price. You got a piece of paper? I'll write out a contract right now." Matthew grabbed a paper bag lying near by, ripped it open, and scribbled the contract. He ignored the fact that Walt Jameson was looking at him as though he was crazy.

"Okay," Jameson said as he put Matthew's contract in his pocket. "You got a deal. We'll be done here by noon. Then they'll be all yours."

Matthew went back into Peosta and called home. Annie listened to his instructions carefully. She was supposed to drive Sonny and Mack over there as soon as possible, and meet Matthew at the tavern. When she conveyed this information to the two young men, they exchanged worried glances.

"That's all he said," Annie said, "except it must be something big, because I'm supposed to get a hold of Andrew and tell him to come home as soon as possible."

"Well, then, I'll call Penny. She can give Andrew a ride after class."

They were less than enthused as they made their way toward the neighboring village. They found Matthew at the bar, drinking his lunch. Quickly, he explained his plan.

"It's true, you're really going to do it! You're nuts!" Mack wailed.

"We can do it. Sonny can teach us," retorted his father.

"Like hell, I can," Sonny cried. "I've never been in one of those things before! Why can't you just wait a couple of days and let the regular crew take care of it?"

"If we wait, it could all be lost! I'm not going to take that chance. OK, so you've never operated a combine before? You're gonna have to figure it out or just fake it. I'm not going back to Jameson and make a worse fool of myself than I already did. Now, c'mon, they're probably waiting for us by now."

They drove to where the crew was finishing the job. A couple of the men appeared to be working on one of the engines. Everyone looked curiously at the Winston's as they approached.

336

Sonny, who still looked gaunt and weak from his injury, sighed deeply as he outlined the plan. "Matthew, you'd better go talk to Jameson and stall for some time if you can. Mack, you stroll over and talk to those guys working on the engine and distract them while I climb up inside one of these suckers. I'll try to figure out how to run it. Annie, look over the map and find us a route home over the back roads. We'll all report back here in five minutes."

Annie felt like they should all grab hands and yell, "Break!" like they do in football huddles as they each went to their appointed positions. Fifteen minutes later, they were back in conference. Sonny told them the best he could how to drive these machines. They just needed to get home, and they'd figure out the rest of it later. Mack was mostly concerned with just climbing into the cab, not wanting to embarrass himself by falling. Sonny walked him over, giving him quiet encouragement until he was safely in his seat. Matthew took the lead, and at the speedy rate of five or six miles a hour, it would take the rest of the afternoon just to get home.

With a tip of his hat, Matthew turned the key. Although he was acting confident, he was shaken by the awful grinding of the gears until finally the machine lurched forward. The other two fell into line, and followed him off the yard. Annie was left to endure the snide comments of the Jameson men as she waited to take her place at the rear of the caravan. It was like three lumbering elephants in a circus parade, especially when traffic backed up behind them. Slowly, they made their way eastward.

It was early evening when they reached the farm. Andrew and Penny were waiting with the others. They all came running to see the sight, as one by one the monstrous machines turned into the driveway. Matthew waved as he drove by and headed down the bottom road. Mack slowed enough for Penny to jump up into the cab beside him, and the others climbed into the station wagon with Annie and followed them down the hill.

The machines lined up facing the field like tanks poised at the edge of a battleground. It was then that Matthew finally cut the engine and descended.

"Thank God," Annie cried, running to him. "I was afraid

that you would try to start tonight. It's almost dark."

"I would if I could," Matthew said disgustedly. "I'm not sure how to run the damned thing. What do you think, Sonny? You got it figured out?"

"Yeah, I think I got a fairly good idea," Sonny sighed, reaching for a cigarette. "It ain't too complicated, really. It's those two levers on the right..." They walked away toward the machine.

"Hey, look!" Mack shouted. "There he goes!"

As late as it was, as cold and tired as they felt, and as impossible as it was to explain, Annie felt a knot in her stomach as that awesome machine started down the rows of corn. The header dipped and its hungry threshing began with tremendous unleashed voracity. The once proud stalks of corn bowed before it and were delivered into the belly of the machine. It lunged forward hesitantly at first, but the man at the controls understood the power translated through the vibrating rods of steel and confidence swelled within him.

Even without seeing him, they knew he was grinning from ear to ear. They stood in the wake of the flattened rows, exalting their father as though he was a conquering hero. The sun was setting ahead of them so that the great, massive thing looked like a giant, dark shadow climbing into a blazing field of reds and yellows.

This was it – the harvest! The moment their father had been dreaming of all these months. They had done it – they had accomplished what no one thought they could. It had been so incredibly difficult—not only the work, but also the transition and emotional adjustment. And for what? They had asked themselves that question many times these past months, but now they were beginning to understand.

Annie reached down and squeezed a handful of soil and felt its gritty texture in her fingers. It wasn't dirt at all – it was heart and soul, blood and sweat. The each planted a piece of themselves in this place, and the roots had grown much deeper than any of them expected.

CHAPTER 38

The morning dawned gray and cold. Matthew, Mack, and Sonny mounted their machines just as the sun climbed over the eastern ridge. Everyone peered anxiously toward the ominous sky, trying to will the charcoal haze to turn blue. By noon it began to drizzle, but the machines rolled on, pausing only to empty their full hoppers of grain into the waiting wagons. Then Sonny's combine began to sputter and lose power. Frustrated, he jumped out of the cab and kicked the hapless machine. He took out his tool box and began working over the engine.

At sundown, Annie brought down a hot supper, but no one appeared interested. "I'm not hungry," Matthew insisted. "Just bring me more coffee."

Mack grabbed a sandwich as Penny anxiously crawled up to ride beside him. "C'mon, Mack," she cried. "You're bone tired. It's time to stop."

"Knock it off, Penny," Mack snapped. "If Pop wants to keep on going, so do I." He said nothing further. All of his senses were focused on keeping the machine crawling down the rows of corn as it swerved in the mud.

Earlier, Sonny had sent Annie to the house for a large dress box, from which he cut a makeshift gasket. It worked, and he drove his machine back on line. The uncertainty of the third combine and the threatening weather spurred them on. They turned on their overhead flood lights and kept going..

Near midnight, Annie climbed into the cab of Matthew's combine. "You gotta stop," she insisted. "Mack and Sonny need rest, and so do you." Reluctantly, he shut down his engine and signaled for the others to follow suit. They rode silently up the hill to the house and fell into their beds, barely stopping to undress.

The next morning, they awakened to the same steely, gray skies. It began raining soon after they crawled back into the machines. At first, it was a light sprinkle, but became harder as the morning wore on. Sonny's machine bogged down, and this time he did not attempt any repairs. He sent the ever-complaining

Thomas back to the house and took over his job. He knew the trip up the hill to the bins was becoming more difficult. The giant tractor wheels were beginning to slide, but he was able to coax the thing up the hill. If their luck held, they'd be done in a couple more hours.

Annie ran out of the house, a rain poncho draped over her shoulders. "I could drive the pickup down there so you have some place dry to get out of the rain," she said.

"That would be crazy!" Sonny cried. "All we need is another vehicle stuck down there!" He turned away.

The combines began to slide, but they pushed on. Even though it was midday, the floodlights were on as they watched for standing water between the rows. Turning the cumbersome machines at the end if the rows was becoming difficult. It was here that Mack swerved and sank into the mud. Sonny maneuvered his tractor into position to tow him out. Fifty more rounds – forty, thirty. Mack pulled his machine into line with Matthew to move down the last rows in tandem. Five more rounds, then three. Mack drove off to the side, letting his father finish it as he had began, solitary and triumphant.

There was no time for celebration as they turned their machines toward the road. Sonny climbed aboard the broken one, coaxing it to muster enough power to attempt the ascent. But the engine began to sputter as soon as he tried to accelerate. Matthew took over the controls to steer as Sonny towed it with the John Deere. They reached the yard and immediately turned around to go after Mack's. Once again the powerful green tractor was able to pull it up. Conditions deteriorated rapidly. The rain came down in sheets so that they could barely see fifty feet. After the second machine made it to the top, the men huddled for a quick conference. They were wet, cold, and nearly past caring, but they had to decide what to do next.

"We could leave it till tomorrow," Sonny said, peering up at the thunder clouds overhead, " but it might be worse."

"Yeah," agreed Matthew, " we should at least try."

The chains were attached and Sonny slowly accelerated his pet green machine, but there was still little response. The giant rear wheels spun furiously and produced little movement. The second tractor was hitched aside the first one. Together, they propelled the great sagging giant up the hill. Finally, all the motors were silenced. It was finished..

They sat in the kitchen, too tired to talk, much less eat or drink. Penny sat very close to Mack, feeling him tremble. She whispered something to him, then stood up and announced, "Mack's coming with me. He needs to rest."

"We all do!" Mack cried. "We have to finish the hill --"

"No, she's right, Mack," his father said. "Go with her so she can look after you. Besides, I think she wants you all to herself." He was smiling then, like an older and wiser man who remembers the impatience of new love. Mack got up laboriously, taking her hand as she led him toward the door. "And Mack," Matthew called, raising his beer can as though he was making a toast, "you were really great out there. We couldn't have done it without you. Your mother would be proud."

Mack smiled in recognition of his father's generous words. "Thanks, Pop," he murmured as he followed Penny out the door.

Matthew was as exhausted as everyone else, but excitement glowed in his face. He was a very happy man. "Remind me to have about twenty more loads of gravel dumped on that damn road next year," he said as he headed toward his office. "I sure as hell don't want this problem again." He sat down to drink to his success, but fell asleep almost immediately.

The other boys wondered off, too. Andrew sat drinking his coffee sullenly. "I do not understand why Mack should get any special praise," he blurted. "Hey, the rest of us were out there working our butts off, too, and Pop never said a word!"

"Andrew, honey," Annie said, "of course, you worked very hard, but-"

"Never mind. I'm going to shower and go to bed myself." He brushed her hand away and strode out of the room angrily.

After several attempts, Sonny managed to stand up. Knowing that Annie was watching him, he struggled to drag himself down to his shed and fell onto his bed.

* * * * * *

Hours later, when the house was quiet and everyone was asleep, Annie looked across the yard from her window. Sonny's place was dark with no smoke rising from the chimney. She prepared a tray of hot soup and coffee, and steeled herself for the confrontation she knew was coming.

She went in, groping in the darkness until she found the bathroom and flicked on the light. Just as she expected, Sonny was lying across the bed, his coat and boots still on. There was dried, caked mud everywhere, even on his face and hair. She crept close to him, watching him sleep. The familiar hard expression was fixed upon his face.

"Sonny," she whispered. "Wake up."

"Why? What's wrong?" he murmured.

"It's me, Annie. You've been asleep like this for hours."

His eye fluttered open "What the hell! You woke me to tell me I'm sleeping?" His voiced cracked then, breaking off in a raspy cough.

"Sonny, I want you to eat and take a shower. Look at you – you still have on your wet, muddy coat!"

"Who the hell cares! I'll clean up later, okay? Get out of here."

This time she was not going to be bullied. "I'm not leaving until you shower and eat!"

"No!"

"Yes, get up."

"Jesus! Forget it. Leave me alone."

"Sonny, you're a mess, and you're going to get sick if you don't take care of yourself." She began pulling off his coat.

He jerked his arm away from her, sitting up at the side of the bed. He started to argue further, but began coughing again. "All right, I'll take a damned shower, but you get out of here. I can take care of myself!" He staggered to the bathroom. She stripped the bed and changed the linens. As she worked, she remembered that first night they met. He had showered then, too, while she schemed to get him out of their lives. Here she was, eight months later, hoping for the opposite.

She realized then that the water had stopped running some time ago, but he didn't come out. She tapped at the door.

"Sonny, are you all right?"

"I'm fine," he grumbled, but he still did not come out.

"Sonny," she called again.

"Damn it, I'm waiting for you to leave!"

"Why? You haven't eaten or taken your pills. I'm not leaving!"

"For God's sake, Annie. Just go back to the house!"

"No! I'm not--"

"Jeez, I ain't used to no girls bein' down here. I got nothin' to put on!"

A fiendish smile crept across her face as she folded her arms and leaned against the door. "I'll give you something if you promise to do as I say." She opened the door a crack and threw in one of Mack's robes.

He came out, still mad and obviously very uncomfortable. "Don't you have enough to do without hovering over me?" he grunted. He sat down at the small corner table and began to eat. She busied herself around the room, adding wood to the fire in the stove and picking up dirty clothes. Finally, when she could think of nothing else to do, she sat down across the table from him. She could tell he was having difficulty swallowing. His cough was worse, and he looked flushed.

He knew she was inspecting him, and he did not like it. He threw down the spoon and glared at her. "I'm eating, all right! You can go now!"

"Why are you so angry? You all did an incredible job out there. Mack's leg was killing him, and you – my God, Sonny, you weren't ready for that."

"I'm fine!" He glanced at her then and saw the pained expression on her face. She was trying to hide her disappointment and remain casual, but he knew he had hurt her feelings. He saw it, but he didn't understand. What does she want from me, he thought. As she gathered the dishes, she inadvertently reached across him, and he was filled with the scent of her.

Her fragrance lingered after she left. It had a very unsettling effect on him, and he wanted to be rid of it. But it was everywhere, even on the clean sheets she had put upon his bed. As exhausted and sick as he felt, he did not sleep for a long time.

* * * * * *

Penny's plan was to keep Mack at the cottage until Sunday. He needed rest, and Matthew was right when he said she wanted him all to herself.

He showered and then stretched out across the bed as Penny changed the bloodied dressing. He was asleep by the time she was finished. She took a long leisurely bath and dressed in one of her mother's gowns. She stood in the darkness and slowly brushed her hair, watching him sleep in the firelight.

Maybe it was a mistake to bring him here. She had brought other boys here before and hadn't thought twice about it. Sex had been a casual thing for her since high school. She had never considered the morality of it. She thought of herself as an aggressive, independent woman who went after anything she wanted and usually got it.

What did she want this time, she wondered. She knew it was not simply sex, although she had fantasies about it. Sexual tension had been mounting between them for weeks, but neither had acted upon it. He had been with other girls, she was certain of that. But maybe this time he felt differently, too. These past several weeks were the happiest of her life. Yes, he was drop-dead gorgeous and charming, but he also was smart, sensitive, and funny with a certain worldly sophistication that she found very attractive. She crept up beside him and laid her head on his chest.

"Penny?" he murmured in his sleep.

"Yes, honey," she cooed, "I'm right here."

* * * * * *

Several hours later, she awakened when Mack cried out and bolted up in bed. He was trembling as Penny drew him close and tried to comfort him. "Mack, you're here with me, remember?" she whispered. "It's all right. You just had a bad dream."

"I'm sorry, I'm sorry." He pulled away from her and he sat up at the side of the bed, running his fingers through his hair.

344

"What happened? What are you dreaming about?"

"It's nothing, really, I just have these dreams sometimes."

"This has happened to you before?" She knelt in front of him, searching his face. "It must have been pretty awful. You were moaning and calling out."

"It's nothing, really--"

"Don't tell me it was nothing. I was here. I saw it."

"It's my brother, Luke," he began. "I keep having these dreams about him, but they always end they same – I find him with his legs blown off. Sometimes, we're in the jungle together, and there's bombs and gunfire. We get separated, and I find him laying there, covered with blood. Once I had a dream that I'm in this little white room with no windows or doors, no furniture, even. I wait and wait. Then I turn around, and there's Luke. He's sitting on the floor just staring at me in a pool of blood with no legs."

"Why do you think Luke blames you? He enlisted of his own free will."

"Because of me. He never would have done it if it weren't for me!"

"Because of the accident?"

"That's part of it, but these last three years I pulled every trick in the book. I wasn't going. No way. I dropped every name, wrote letters and forged my father's signature. I even slept with girls just so they'd let me cheat at school. If I flunked out, I'd get drafted for sure."

"Everyone knows this war is insane."

"I know, that's what I kept telling myself. When that draft notice came, I thought, man, that's it. My ass is gone! Then this happened – freaky, goddamn accident. What the hell was I doing out there with a gun? I was just being arrogant and so fucking dumb! And then, Luke goes off and enlists. He thought he was saving face – for me, for my dad, for all of us! He's just a kid – just a nice, quiet kid who never hurt anyone in his life. It should have been me."

"Why you, or anyone, for that matter?"

"If I just would have gone, by the time Luke turns 20 or 21, the whole thing will probably be over." He got up as he spoke, steadying himself on the table. "Guess I'm not doing as well as you thought."

"Why would you say that? You've come so far."

"Cause I'm not that same self-absorbed jerk I was before? Too bad I had to lose half my leg in the process." He sank back onto the side of the bed. "You know what the worse part is? It's so damned inconvenient. I have to pre-think everything. I mean, a goddamn flight of stairs scares the hell out of me. And it's so ugly. I mean, you're a nurse so you see this kind of thing all the time, but as a woman, don't you see how hideous it is?"

"Don't do this," she whispered, reaching for him. "A leg is just bone and muscle. Why are you pushing me away?"

"I don't want to, but --"

"But why?" she pressed.

"Look at you. You can have any guy you want. Why do you care about me? Is it because you feel sorry for me?"

"How can you say that?" She reached for him, and this time, he did not turn away. She kissed him on the cheek. "Don't be so afraid."

He kissed her hard and long and caressed her soft, velvet skin where her gown slipped off her shoulders. "You are so beautiful," he murmured. "In the middle of the craziness, you make me feel so good." They sank back onto the bed, and he began unbuttoning her gown. She held him tighter, electrified by each touch. He could feel her heart racing. "I don't know if we should do this. Maybe--"

"Don't stop," she gasped. "Just love me."

Those three words were all that was needed to open the flood gates as weeks of pent up passion were unleashed. He wanted to satisfy her in a way she had ever known before. Each movement was tender and sensual, each caress slow and caring. Together they soared to a place that was the fulfillment of every desire. The passion built magnificently until the moment of splendid explosion that left them blissfully exhausted but yearning for more. And when they finally slept, they were wrapped in each other's arms, hoping to keep the feeling of sublime happiness from evaporating. They wanted to wake up with it, carry it with them. They hoped it would last forever.

* * * * * *

They slept late. Mack hadn't stayed in bed until 11:00 since leaving New York, and it felt great. That was her plan all along – no chores, no worries, nothing, "except me," she added, smiling playfully. They were both starved, so they cooked a huge breakfast and ate sitting on the porch. It was a warm, autumn day, complementing their exaltation from their night of love-making.

Penny skipped out to the stable and soon appeared with two horses. "Mack!" she called. "Come on out here."

He took one look and ducked back inside, but it was hard to refuse her anything on such a day. She teased and cajoled until finally he said he'd try. He hadn't been riding since he was a boy at summer camp, when he hadn't liked it much. He followed her lead across the open pastures and exploring the woods by the river. They made love in a pile of leaves, and again that night by the fire. The clouds and the rain came back, but would have been unnoticed except for the soft symphony it played on the cottage roof.

Chapter 39

Sonny got up for chores that morning, but appeared to be moving slower than usual. He only nodded when Matthew admitted he was stiff and sore. After breakfast, they cranked up the two functional combines and finished the 80 acres of hill ground. The bins were full and the job was done.

"I can't wait to see Jamison's face when he shows up here bright and early Monday morning," Matthew grinned as they sat down. "Hey, I'm going into town to celebrate. Who wants to go along?"

No one seemed too interested. Andrew had studying to do, and Sonny said nothing as he sat eating supper. He would have liked to skip eating altogether, but Annie would have badgered him about it. His raspy cough was getting worse, and it still felt like he had a watermelon sitting on his gut He ate enough to satisfy his watchful, self-appointed nurse. He didn't sleep very well that night either.

Annie wanted the customary Sunday dinner to be extra special as a sort of early Thanksgiving to celebrate their harvest. Mack and Penny arrived in time to eat with the family. They were smiling and holding hands, hardly taking their eyes off each other.

"Well, at least Mack looks refreshed," Annie remarked as she dished up the vegetables.

"Personally, I think it's disgusting," hissed Andrew, picking up the dinner rolls. "Why did they have to go off by themselves anyway." Annie was about to say if he had to ask, he was more naïve than she had imagined, but he stomped out before she had a chance.

Even if Andrew was irritable, it did not hamper the festivities. As usual during this time of year, the talk centered around football. Shannon Town High had won another game last Friday night, and Matthew promised he'd never miss another game the rest of the season. John mentioned that one of his teammates had invited him and Kenny to go to an University of Iowa game next week.

"The Hawkeye's aren't having much of a season, but I'd like to see a game," he said. "Maybe I'll go to college there and play football."

"At Iowa?" retorted his father. "Nah, Notre Dame. Imagine how proud your mother would be if one of her boys went to college there. Talk about football – they're trouncing everyone. Should go undefeated. What's the name of that quarterback, er--"

"Theisman – Joe Theisman," answered John. "Yeah, he is really good."

"Doesn't sound very Irish to me," interjected one of the little boys. "Thought you had to be Irish to got to school there."

"No, Danny," Matthew said as everyone laughed. "You just have to love football."

"Wonder who's gonna draft him? Maybe the Jets," John said a little wistfully. "They were supposed to have a good year, but Namath already went down. There goes their season right down the drain."

"It starts with the quarterback," Matthew said. "How about Balanda in Oakland – he kicks and he's a hellva quarterback! Maybe your friend Kenny could be like him someday."

"I don't think so," Annie quipped. "He's too nice of a guy. You know those jocks – egotistical and cocky. I don't want him to turn out like that."

"You mean, have him be like John? Yeah, you're right, Kenny's too nice of a kid for that," Mack teased, for which he promptly received a bun planted between the eyes.

The talk went on, everyone lingering around Annie's old table long after dessert, except Sonny who ate a little and got up to leave. "I gotta work on one of the combines," he said.

Later, Annie stood at the kitchen window and watched him work in the cold drizzle. "The last thing he needs is to spend another day in the rain," she murmured to no one in particular.

Annie was not the only one who noticed that Sonny was even more non-communicative than usual. Penny asked Mack about it as they were walking toward her Jeep. "Maybe he's mad that I took you for those two days," Penny said. "I know Andrew was."

"Yeah, I noticed Andrew was a little peeved, but Sonny don't care. Sometimes I think the less people around here, the better he likes it. Besides, I don't care if the whole damn family is mad. It was great. When are you gonna steal me away again?"

Andrew stood by as they said one of their lengthy good-byes. It was all he could do to control his rage. Mack had done it – defiled her, added her to his long list of sexual conquests. The thought of it sickened him. He'll hurt her, he thought, just like every other woman who's ever been foolish enough to become involved with him. Finally, Penny called that she was ready to leave.

Mack watched them leave, and then turned his attention toward Sonny, who was still working on the broken combine. "Hey, you need any help?" Mack called.

"Nah, I'm just tinkering," Sonny replied without looking up. "I just thought if I could fix this piece of junk then the old man could really tell Jamison to cram it."

"That'd be great!" Mack chuckled. "Can you do it?"

"Yeah, I think I got it. They weren't lying when they said these things needed some maintenance. As soon as I figure out how to put it back together, I'll see if it runs."

Mack was no mechanical wizard, but was an able assistant. Together they worked until Sonny slammed down the engine cover, jumped into the cab, and turned the key. It started. "Well, I hope it runs long enough for them to drive it off the yard." Sonny grinned, obviously pleased. But his usual serious, glum demeanor quickly returned as he began picking up his tools. "Guess we'd better get goin' on the chores," he said.

"Ah, screw it, man. Me and the boys can handle it tonight."

"Hell! What's goin' on around here! Your sister's following me around, shovin' food and pills in my face. The old man says I should lay off for awhile. Just leave me alone and let me do my work."

"Okay, okay! Why are you getting so damn mad? You didn't care when I took off for a couple of days, did you? I was bone-tired, and I'm not ashamed to admit it." Mack followed Sonny to the tool shed, not willing to drop the subject. "C'mon, you got time for a cup of coffee? I'm buyin'."

Sonny was about to fire back an angry response, but broke into a long coughing spell instead. They warmed themselves at the wood burner stove while they waited for the coffee to get hot. "What you need is some cough medicine, Sonny Boy," Mack quipped as he produced a flask of whiskey.

Sonny said nothing as he drank it down. Mack reached over to re-fill his cup. "The trouble with you, Sonny, is that you do not know how to relax. Not me, man. Wow, do I know how to relax!" He reclined back, smiling.

"Yeah, right," Sonny scoffed. "She's a fine lady, but I have no idea what the hell she sees in you!" They both laughed then, which started Sonny coughing again.

"Whoa, there, buddy, you need another dose of cough syrup." Mack poured another generous dose of whiskey into Sonny's coffee mug. "I don't understand what she sees in me either, but I sure do like what I see in her. I cannot believe I had to come to this God forsaken place to find her. But here I am, just as happy as a pig in shit. I thought I'd be packin' by now. But I'm not going nowhere. No sir, not me!" He drank down his drink and poured another. "I cannot believe we actually did it! Here's to us." He hoisted his cup, and for a moment, their eyes met. They had come a long way, in the work they had accomplished and the unlikely, trusting relationship they had forged.

Sonny shrugged his shoulders wearily, drained his cup, and reached for his coat. "Man, I told ya', me and the boys can do the damn chores tonight!" Mack cried.

"And I said, forget that shit," Sonny retorted. "What'll the old man say if I can't do my work?"

"Is that what this is all about? You think if you ain't busting your ass eighteen hours a day, the old man is gonna can you? My God, that is the stupidest thing I have ever heard. Besides, you taught us good. We can struggle along without you every once in a while."

"Yeah, I know," Sonny murmured. "Now you guys know as much as I do. I guess I did what I was hired to do – get you started."

Mack stared at him, even more dumbfounded than before. "Look, you dumb shit, we've been through a hellvalot. That counts for something, don't it? Just try to leave, you sonofabitch. Just try it! Get used to it, Sonny boy, you're stuck with us – the whole damn mess!" He took his coat, too, and together they stepped through the door.

Twilight had fallen, and a thick blanket of mist enveloped the landscape. Shrouded by the shimmering stillness, the house looked like a mystic hilltop castle in a fairytale. The subtle odor of burning wood lingered in the air, and there was a soft inviting beacon shining from the kitchen window. The boys, who appeared like dark, shadowy figures trudging across the yard, were heading toward the house having finished another day's work.

"See, I told ya," Mack whispered, as though not wanting to disturb the quiet. "You taught us good. They managed without both of us. C'mon, let's go have supper."

He walked toward the house, too, but Sonny held back. Leave this place? The mud, the work, the run-down buildings, the people. No, not likely.

Chapter 40

Since entering the mainstream of busy campus life at the University, Margaret McDuffy had far less time to agonize over every sentence in her letters to Luke. Between hurrying off to classes in far-flung buildings and long hours of studying, she still managed to write some every day, though she worried that her letters were too self-absorbed. His letters were shorter and less personal, and he never mentioned Vietnam. She didn't either, even though talk of the war surrounded her at every turn.

The confusion and turmoil of Vietnam seemed suffocating at times. The semester began a few days after the bombing of a building at the University of Wisconsin in Madison, which was just a couple of hundred miles from Iowa City and a Big 10 Conference rival. Margaret stayed away from the large organized, anti-war demonstrations and the war bashing session's in dormitory rooms and hallways. Though few of her fellow students approved of the radical activities such as the bombings and sabotage, most vented their utter mistrust of governmental agencies and their increasing presence on campus. ROTC headquarters and laboratories used for government purposes were especially despised. In some instances, the administrations' answer to the insurgencies was more armed guards and troops which, of course, only heightened the already turbulent situations.

The constant state of tension was just one of the things that bewildered the innocent, young girl from Shannon Town, Iowa. She knew everything was going to be different, but she didn't expect to be so frightened and overwhelmed. And she certainly never would have guessed that she'd be homesick, but she was. She longed for the little mundane things she thought she detested. Living in a dormitory was more difficult than she imagined – so many strangers and only one bathroom for thirty girls. The food was awful, and the water tasted horrible. She decided this would be a good time to begin that diet she had always thought about but never started. She forced herself to try that new soft drink, Tab, a diet pop with no calories. There were no more excuses, no Aunt Betty to blame. This was the new beginning she had longed for, so why was she so damned scared?

It didn't help that her roommate was having an equally hard time. They got off to a horrible start. Their first meeting as assigned roommates had gone very badly. Margaret arrived at their room first. Once unpacked, she couldn't wait for Aunt Betty to leave. Over and over, Margaret promised never to stay out late or walk alone after dark. She swore she'd be careful never to sit on a dirty toilet seat or wear other girls' clothes. The elder Mrs. Duffy was eventually satisfied and left, but not until she mortified her granddaughter by shouting back to her across the crowded corridor to remember to line dry her bra's. "They'll last a lot longer," she called. And then, finally, she was gone.

Margaret flung into action, digging out of a paper bag of things she had carefully hidden in one of those awful goulashes her aunt insisted she bring. First, she shaved her legs. Luckily, she also had a box of Band-Aides because she needed several of them – one on each ankle, two on her right shin, and one on her left knee. Then she tried to apply make-up. However, without her glasses she found it nearly impossible. The lipstick kept smearing and the mascara was running. It was then that her roommate, Cindy, and her parents arrived. The room was cluttered and smelled like an Avon factory because of a broken bottle of cologne buried somewhere in Margaret's luggage.

Margaret excused herself and rushed to the bathroom. She hid there for several minutes, and when she slipped back into their room, she was surprised to find Cindy already alone. They began unpacking, barely speaking. Actually, Margaret thought as she stole quick glances at her roommate, this girl was no princess either. She had hoped to room with a gorgeous girl who could teach her about make-up and things, but Cindy was very plain with frizzy, recently permed hair, and dark glasses a lot like Margaret's. She must have been crying because her eyes were swollen and red. Damn, Margaret thought, here it is – one of the most momentous days of my life and I'm stuck with a crybaby.

Things did not improve during the next few days. They seldom spoke, each keeping to themselves as though there was an invisible line down the center of the room. Not only was Margaret having difficulty interacting with Cindy, but with everyone in general. The classes were huge and impersonal. She resented that the other students seemed so at ease, laughing and talking with each other as they hurried off to the next class. Margaret felt as though she was in a constant state of confusion, and she hated it.

One afternoon, Cindy came back from class and found Maggie holding Luke's picture with tears glistening in her eyes. "Is that your boyfriend?" she asked shyly.

Margaret was tempted to say yes, that they were madly in love and practically engaged, but why lie? "Well, sort of," she began. "He's a boy who just moved into our neighborhood last March. He was so nice to me. He even took me to the prom."

"And you're just crazy about him, aren't you. I have three older sisters so I recognize the symptoms."

"Yeah, I guess I am, but I'm afraid the feelings are not mutual."

"He gave you this picture, didn't he? A 8x10, even. That means something' right? Where is he now? Did he go away to school?"

"No -- well, sort of. He enlisted in the Army, and he's in training in Louisiana But I haven't told anyone – I mean, no one around here. I don't want to get into any stupid arguments about the war and everything."

Cindy stared at the smiling, handsome face in the picture. "Are you worried – about him being in the Army, I mean? One of my sister's husbands was in Nam. He's been back for two years. He came through it all right, but sometimes he has the strangest look on his face. 'Course, I thought he was strange before he went over there," she giggled.

They talked late that night, finding that they shared many hopes and fears. The next morning, Margaret wrote a quick note.

Dear Luke,

After weeks of barely speaking, Cindy, and I finally had a good talk – for several hours, in fact. I think I really like her. She comes from a huge family like you and according to her, all her sisters are very beautiful and she's the ugly duckling of her family. She's very shy and goes around apologizing for things that aren't her fault. Maybe some of my tactless bluntness will rub off on her. Anyway, it's nice having someone to talk to again now that you're so far away.

The fall colors are just beginning to turn here. There's a huge sugar maple outside my window that's absolutely gorgeous. Wish I could paint like you. I'd draw it and send it to you. I suppose there's not much fall colors by you.

Aunt Betty called again last night. I think she really misses me and wants me to come home for the weekend. I told her I have too much studying, but I'm just not ready to go home. I don't have the hang of this place yet. And I'm NOT going home until I have it conquered. Does that make any sense? I have to admit, I do feel better today than any other day so far.

Well, gotta go. Professor Pinhead just walked in for another two hours of lecture about Pavlov's dogs. Great!

Anyway, you take care,
Maggie

There was much more she could have told him – how she and Cindy decided to experiment with makeup, different clothes, and hair styles. They both wanted contact lenses, and they even practiced walking and talking differently. With renewed vigor and dedication, they vowed to change their image and strive for a new sophistication befitting co-eds. They had wonderful plans, and now neither would have to struggle alone.

However, Margaret did not feel comfortable confiding all this to Luke. A girl just does not tell the man of her dreams all the particulars of how she plans to become more attractive. She was so afraid that he would be ship out to some far off place without her seeing him again. He might meet someone new and forget about her altogether. That's why the letters were so important.

Luke did write every four or five days, except during those long periods when he said he was "away." She assumed that meant some kind of field training – maneuvers, they called it in the movies. When she asked him why he didn't talk more about his new life, he explained in one of his letters:

Maggie, I know you're curious about what I'm doing down here but there's not much to tell. Actually, it's boring as hell. Writing these letters is a way for me to get away from all this – like an escape. It's like going back to a nicer time before the Army. There's no color here and there's rules for everything. Thank God, this won't last forever.

His training at Ft. Polk was nearly over. He knew that large groups of men were no longer being shipped overseas to Nam. In keeping with the presidential decree that those numbers should be drastically cut, only replacements for the killed and wounded were being sent. There was a general sense of relief among his fellow trainees. His own test scores were high, as were his accuracy numbers at the shooting ranges. Most of the others sneered at him for trying so hard.

Many of the instructors were obnoxious, swaggering lifer's who had already completed their tours of duty in Vietnam. Sgt. Will Garrett, a gunnery instructor, was different. His unflappable, impersonal manner exuded military precision. They said he had been to Nam twice and had a chest full of metals that he never wore. Beyond that, no one knew anything about him. He was always alone, and seemed to prefer it that way,

One late afternoon, Luke and his group were finishing up a class on the firing range. Dismantling and cleaning their guns quickly, the class dispersed. Luke was the last to finish and was still squatting on the ground when he became aware of Sgt. Garrett standing nearby, staring at him.

"I see on your record that you enlisted and you're from Iowa. You don't talk or act like no country boy," he said.

"Well," Luke stammered, leaping to his feet, " my family moved there last spring."

"From where?"

"New York City, Sergeant."

Knowing that this was not a friendly conversation, Luke stood awkwardly, waiting for the Sergeant to make his point. It came soon enough. "What the hell are you doin' here? You probably got a nice family back home, and a cute, freckle-faced, virgin girlfriend waitin' for you to be done with this shit. So why are you tryin' so hard?"

He stood with his hands on his hips, staring at the young private and jerking a toothpick back and forth in his mouth. "Only the top two or three of your class will be shipped over. If you're not damned careful, you're gonna be one of them." Sergeant Garrett took Luke's rifle, examined it, and handed it back. "I've been there twice. I ain't gonna tell ya' that it's no place for a kid like you 'cause that'll just piss you off and make ya' try harder. But I am gonna say this – Nam ain't like you think. It's not about patriotism or bravery or any of that crap. It's about coverin' your ass and getting out of there alive. If you're goin' over there to be some kind of hero, you're going for all the wrong reasons. Only heroes I ever knew were dead ones."

The Sergeant clicked his heels together and stood at attention for a moment, saluting crisply. And then he was gone, leaving the young soldier to contemplate what he had said. Luke appreciated the Sergeant's attempt at dissuading him, but it changed nothing. The chain of events that would send him to Vietnam had been set into motion a long time ago.

Chapter 41

It was a cold, Tuesday afternoon. There was just one more day of classes before Thanksgiving break. Margaret and Cindy skipped supper and made popcorn instead. They read somewhere that popcorn could be eaten while dieting because it was filling and low calorie, except for the salt and butter they piled on "for flavoring." Cindy sat at her well-organized desk while Margaret lay sprawled on her bed, finishing a letter to Luke. She was so deeply engaged in her writing that she didn't hear the floor telephone ring in the hallway.

"Margaret!" Cindy called. "The phone – it's for you."

Margaret ran down the hallway with all her fingers and toes crossed. Oh please, she prayed, just this once, let it be Luke instead of Aunt Betty.

"Hello?"

"Maggie? Hi! It's Luke."

She could scarcely breathe, much less speak.

"Maggie?" he said again. "Are you there? It's me. Can you hear me?"

"Yes, Luke, I can hear you fine. I'm just surprised, that's all," she cried. Then a sudden fear swept over her. "Are you all right? Is there anything wrong?"

"Everything's fine. I got your letter this morning, and you mentioned you had four days off for Thanksgiving. I was wondering if you might want to come down here. I have four days leave so I thought maybe you could fly down here – tonight."

Margaret was so stunned she was speechless again. Go down there? How could she arrange it? "C'mon, Maggie. I know you're probably shocked as hell, and I should have called sooner. But what about that stuff you told me about wanting to see the world – here's your chance. C'mon, let's do it."

"Well, I suppose I could figure something out to tell Aunt Betty. Cindy could cover for me. But what about a flight? I bet everything's booked." Her voice began to quiver as the excitement began to build.

"Really? You think you could swing it? About the flight – don't worry. I've already checked. There's one leaving Iowa City at 7:10 to Chicago. From there you go to St. Louis, and then to Leesville. There'll be some long stopovers, but that's the best they can do. So?"

He was waiting for an answer. She had never done anything like that in her life, much less by herself. But he really wanted her to come. She could hear it in his voice. She drew a long deep breath, and said, "Sure, I'd love to come, Luke. But you'll be there to meet me, won't you? I mean no matter what time I get there, right?"

"Are you kidding? Of course, I'll be there. Don't you

358

worry."

He's really excited about seeing me, Margaret's heart sang gleefully – me, he asked me. "Oh Luke, this is so terrific. I can't wait to see you. I'll be there by morning. Bye."

As she hung up the phone, she became aware that a group of her dorm mates were gathered around her, grinning and squealing.

"I'm going to Louisiana!" Margaret cried. "He wants me to go down there – tonight! In three hours! I have to get packed, and call the airport! Oh God, my hair!"

"I can call the airport," volunteered one of the girls.

"And I'll call one of my friends who lives off campus. He has a car. I'll ask to borrow it so we can take you to the airport," said another.

"What are ya' gonna do with your hair?"

"What are ya' gonna wear?"

"I bet it's warm down there. You can't wear a wool skirt and a sweater."

"I have a nice culottes outfit."

"And I have some nice cotton slacks that would probably fit you."

The next two hours, the whole third floor was a flurry of activity, getting Margaret ready for her big adventure. Someone's blouse went nicely with someone else's skirt. Jewelry, scarves, and all matter of accessories were assembled. Her hair was carefully shampooed, cream-rinsed, conditioned, dried, teased, curled, styled, and sprayed by committee. Even her nails received careful attention. The perfect shade of polish was borrowed from a friend of a friend on the second floor. Finally, it was time for her to leave.

Margaret stood in front of the mirror as Cindy paced nearby. "You worry too much," Margaret scolded, noticing her roommate's turned up, wrinkled nose, which was a sign she was disapproving of something. "If we just stick to our plan, everything should be fine."

"How could you lie to your aunt like that? You're spending the weekend at my house? She'll probably call my house, looking for you. What'll my folks think when they hear me lying through my teeth?"

"No, now listen," Margaret insisted. "This plan is fool-proof. I'll call her Thursday morning, and tell her we're going to church and then to one of your relatives for dinner. She thinks we're working on some project together for school, so I'll tell her we're spending all day Friday and Saturday at the library. There is a library in Mason City, isn't there? She won't suspect a thing. Besides, she can't call you because I won't give her the phone number. So stop worrying!" She reached for Kathy Hutchinson's jacket and Mary Stern's matching purse. "How do I look? I can't wait till he sees me in contacts. God, I hope I don't lose one. I'll just die!"

"Margaret, what about – you know, sleeping arrangements? I mean, are you gonna – you know."

Margaret knew exactly what she was asking. She had been wondering about that herself. Since moving into the dorm and sharing all night bull sessions with the more worldly co-ed's, her curiosity about sex had greatly increased. "I don't know. I guess I'll know the answer to that question when I get back." She gave her roommate a big hug. "Just keep your fingers crossed, OK? This just has to be perfect!"

She arrived at the airport in plenty of time for nervous pacing and worrying. There was a million things that could go wrong. What if he wasn't there? What if she missed one of her connecting flights? He didn't even know for sure she got her ticket. This was so crazy, but wasn't this what she always dreamed of – jet-set romance, late night rendezvous. She trembled with excitement.

However, her first experience of world travel was hardly glamorous. The small, prop commuter airplane she boarded in Iowa City made three more stops before it finally touched down in Chicago. Seven hours later, after long layovers in the O' Hare and St. Louis airports, she finally boarded another small commuter plane for the last leg of her journey to Leesville. By this time her skirt was wrinkled, her hair fell limply around her shoulders, and smudged make-up streaked down her cheeks. Feeling alone and frightened, she began to cry weary, silent tears. It wasn't supposed to be like this, she sobbed.

A stewardess with a nice smile tried to comfort her, encouraging her to rest by promising to awaken her when they reached Leesville. Margaret allowed herself to succumb to her profound fatigue and slept. Almost in an instant, the stewardess was gently shaking her, saying the other passengers had already disembarked. Margaret startled awake quickly, praying that Luke was nearby. She cringed as she passed a small mirror in the passageway, but there was nothing she could do about that now. She just wanted to see Luke.

She stepped outside and dragged her bags down the stairs across the tarmac toward the small airport lobby. The place was nearly deserted, the other passengers having already scattered. For an instant, she was afraid that he wasn't there, but then she spotted him. He was sound asleep in one of those plastic, straight-back airport seats, his uniform wrinkled and unkempt. She smiled, thinking what a fine pair they made. She sat near him, watching him sleep for a few moments, until his head jerked and he stirred.

"Luke," she whispered. "It's me. I'm here – finally." His eyes opened slowly, like a little boy waking from a nap.

"Maggie? Oh, God, I'm so glad to see you!" He hugged her and smiled broadly. "C'mon, lets get out of here." He put his arm around her shoulders and led her outside toward a little Ford Mustang parked in the lot across the street. "Well? Do you like it?" he grinned. "I had to try three rental agencies before I could find one – a convertible, I mean. It's not a big Harley, but it has sort of the same effect."

Margaret had no idea what he was talking about but could see he was excited about his plans for their weekend. As soon as they were seated in the car, Luke produced a map and opened it for her inspection. "See?" he said. "Here we are – Leesville. We'll take Highway 10 southeast and some of these little side roads to Bunkie – can you believe they named a town 'Bunkie'? Anyway, we'll just keep goin' east till we get to the river. I can't wait to see it again! I bet it looks different down here," He chatted away until he noticed Margaret's fallen face.

"Hey, what's wrong?" he asked. "I thought you'd be really happy about this!" He sounded almost angry. She couldn't look at him, afraid that she was going to embarrass them both by crying.

"I just assumed we'd go into camp," she stammered. "You know, Ft. Polk. You've been telling me about this place for months, and I want to see it."

"But Maggie, why would you care about seeing that place? It's just a bunch of buildings – rows and rows of them. I thought we'd --" His voice trailed off with disappointment ringing in his voice.

Maggie sank against her door, and neither of them said anything for several minutes. "Why would you care about seeing that place?" he asked again, this time turning to her for an answer.

"Because – because, I don't know where to put you – in my mind, I mean, when I think of you down here. And don't you have friends?"

"No, not really – I mean, I've gotten to know a couple of guys, but --"

"Is it because you're ashamed of me?"

"Heck, no! Why would you say a thing like that? That's not it at all. You look great – you finally got your contacts, aye?" He smiled at her then, that sweet half grin that she missed so much. "I'm sick of this place, Maggie. I thought we'd have this great adventure. Look! I went to four music stores last night to find this. The last guy wanted to close but I made him keep looking." He took a 8-track cassette out of a bag and pushed it into the player. "Listen!

Lookin' for adventure on the open highway.
Lookin' for adventure whatever comes my way
Born to be wild!
Born to be wild!

The raw, cutting lyrics and throbbing guitar accompaniment burst into their uncomfortable silence like a heralded Alleluia chorus. It was so loud that Maggie didn't have to say anything. It was obvious he put a lot of effort and planning into this – the music, the convertible, New Orleans. The references were unmistakable. This was to be their very own

Easy Rider adventure. She smiled her approval.

Luke was not much interested in sight-seeing as they drove through the Louisiana countryside. He pushed on, driving east toward the Mississippi. The warm sun beat down, warming and relaxing them, as they passed one small town after another and endless miles of farm, woods, and rolling hills.

Finally, in a small town called Morganza, they stood on the banks of the Mississippi. Luke was right when he said it wouldn't look the same as back home. The area was very flat where the wide, muddy river meandered through the cotton and sugar beet fields. They saw several tows with barges and two large dredging units battling the endless tide of silt that threatened to occlude the channel.

Luke sank onto the grassy hillside and stared at the sight for a long time. Margaret stood back and didn't disturb him. It was his river, his moment. Finally, he stirred. "Guess we'd better start thinking about making some arrangements for the night. And food. My God! I haven't fed you all day. And look at this uniform. I gotta get some other clothes – blue jeans would be great. And underwear," he cried, not noticing that she blushed slightly. "Some real, honest-to-God, regular underwear." His face was radiating with enthusiasm. He grabbed her hand, and they ran back to the car. What followed was a whirlwind shopping spree and a wonderful supper at a small café.

Back on the highway, they headed further south for a few more miles until they came to a crossroads. He stopped at a stop sign, peering both directions and checking his watch. "If we go left, there's a bridge across the river which takes us to US 61. Yep! The same one that goes through Dubuque. It's a four lane most of the way to New Orleans. To the right are some little state highways, but none of them go very close to the river either. So, I guess we should head across the river and maybe find some back roads."

Maggie just smiled. "You don't fool me. I know what you want – to see the sunset across the river."

He laughed, too. He had been found out. He turned east and soon, they were driving across the beautiful, expansive river. He turned onto the yard of a neatly trimmed homestead and jumped out before Maggie had a chance to ask him what he was doing.

Luke knocked on the door, straightening his tie as he waited. A pleasant looking, middle-aged woman came to the door. A few minutes later, she pointed down a pasture road. Luke jumped back into the car and drove down a little dirt road. "They were nice people," he said. "Too bad I had to lie to them. Well, it wasn't exactly a lie – I am a poor soldier boy, a long way from home. But if one of them calls you Mrs. Winston, try not to choke or anything."

"You told them what?" Maggie cried. "And could you please tell me what we're doing. Looking at a sunset or what?"

"Oh, didn't I tell you, I brought along some camping. Hey, we're real, honest-to-God 'easy riders', aren't we?"

"Well, just remember what happened to those men when they camped. One guy got his head bashed in."

"Not to worry. That's why I still have on my uniform. These people love us military types. They're very patriotic, and they love the money the Pentagon spends down here." By that time, they rounded a little hilltop and came within full view of the river. "Ain't she pretty?" he whistled.

As though in honor of this special occasion, they were treated to a breath-taking, gorgeous sunset. The slowly sinking, scarlet orb made a golden pathway across the shimmering waters until it disappeared behind the hillside on the other side. The trees were gently swaying, and there was cattle grazing in the pastures near the water's edge. Luke grabbed his sketch pad and began working quickly in the fading light.

He brought a tent, but since it was a warm, clear night, he didn't set it up. Rather, he laid out two sleeping bags and motioned for her to have a seat. Sitting by the fire, gazing at the distant river in the moonlight, reminded her of their Camelot night. That was six months ago, and Margaret still wasn't sure how he felt about her. How would she react if he suggested anything intimate, and how would she feel if he didn't? The day had been wonderful, but except for that joyous hug at the airport, there was hardly a passing kiss.

He stretched out and looked up at the stars. There was a

million points of light in the Milky Way and the moon was full and bright. "Just remember," he murmured. "Wherever we are, no matter how far apart, the moon and the stars are the same." She laid down, too, wondering why he had said that. She wanted to ask him, but he was already asleep.

* * * * * *

The next three days were a magical whirlwind of fun and adventure. They packed up their stuff Thursday morning and stopped by the farmhouse to say thank you. The farm couple convinced them to stay and have dinner with them. Their married children were all coming with their families, so Luke and Margaret stayed to enjoy the festivities – Thanksgiving, Louisiana- style. Mrs Lasance filled the table with turkey with cornbread dressing, red beans and rice, gumbo, and a fabulous array of vegetables and fruit salads, topped off with generous slices of pecan pie. Amid the festivities, Margaret remembered to call her aunt, who was curt and obviously angry.

That afternoon, they drove down to New Orleans. They walked hand in hand through the French Quarter, having a late dinner at a romantic, sidewalk café. They checked into a motel that night, both of them thankful for a shower and soft beds. Once again, they fell asleep, exhausted but happy.

On Friday, they explored the city, even found one of those above ground cemeteries, like in the movie. They felt uneasy there, so they didn't stay very long. Saturday, they got back in the car, and traveled south again. They found a highway that followed the main channel of the river through the delta. He drove along happily at first, but he became more distracted the further they drove. Finally, when they drove as far south as they could go, he took out a pair of binoculars and climbed onto the roof of the car. He could see the brown, muddy waters of the river churning into the deep, blue sea.

Luke stood mesmerized by sight. "It's nothin'!" he cried.

"What?"

"The river. Look at it. It's nothin'."

He said the words with so much anger and contempt that

Margaret was frightened. "What do you mean? Why are you so mad?"

"It all gets swallowed up by the ocean."

"Of course, it does. But—"

"Don't you see? We thought it was so big and powerful. It's nothing." Tears began streaming down his cheeks. "It's all so--" His face was dark with anger and frustration as he appeared to be searching for the right words. But then he abruptly turned and began to run, disappearing into the brush.

"Luke!" she called. "Come back!" She was crying, too, feeling confused and afraid for him. He didn't come back so there was nothing for her to do but return to the car and wait.

At nightfall, he emerged from the timber, his face, arms, and hands scratched and bleeding from the weeds and mosquito bites. His face looked pinched and tortured. "I'm sorry," he mumbled, as he started the car.

"Luke, why did you take off like that?" she demanded. "What aren't you telling me?" He stared ahead and kept driving without speaking.

He drove for hours. She fell asleep as they traveled into the night. She awakened, realizing they were stopped in a rest stop along the highway. Luke was leaning against a tree, staring at the sunrise in the eastern sky. She got out of the car and stood beside him. There was a cigarette dangling from his mouth, a sad and pained expression across his face

"I'm shipping out to Nam tomorrow," he said.

She was swept over by a sudden wave of nausea and her knees began to buckle. She would have fallen if he hadn't caught her. "I'm sorry, I'm sorry," he whispered, holding her tightly with his face pressed against hers. "I should have told you right away, but I couldn't say the words. I'm sorry, I'm sorry."

She tried to pull away from him, but he wouldn't let her. With her free arm she began punching and hitting him "Why are you doing this? Why?"

"You act like I have a choice. I'm in the goddamn Army, remember? Just eleven months, and I'll be back, I swear! Next year, we'll have Thanksgiving at home together."

His words sounded hollow and meaningless. He couldn't

promise those things, no one could. Too much of what was happening was out of their control.

They drove on with very few words being spoke between them. The hot sun beat down upon them, but there was still a chill in the air. They arrived at the airport, and sat in the parking lot where their adventure had began just a few days earlier.

Luke picked up the *Easy Rider* 8-track and handed it to her. "Here, you can take this home with you, if you want."

"Thanks, I'd like that." They didn't look each other.

"You're not sorry you came, are you?"

"God, no! Why would you think that? It was great, wasn't it?"

"Sure, except – I shouldn't have ran off like that. I'm sorry I scared you." He looked at his watch. "I guess we'd better get you checked in."

"Luke," she whispered, "I love you."

He hesitated for a moment, but then continued getting out of the car.

"Did you hear me? I said I love you."

"Maggie, don't say anything you might regret later."

"Regret? You know I'm crazy about you, and now you're leaving, so I had to say it. Don't be mad, okay?"

He smiled then, that slow, gentle smile that she knew so well. "I'm not mad, Maggie. And I know what you're wanting to hear, but I can't say it. It wouldn't be right."

"Why?"

"I'm going away for a long time. I don't want you to think that I expect you to put your life on hold while I'm gone. You're gonna meet other boys who'll see how terrific you are."

"No, Luke, there's no one like you."

"Like me? I'm just the boy who gave you your first kiss. There's gonna be lots of others, Maggie. You'll see."

No, she wanted to scream, there will never be anyone for me except you. But she didn't want to spend their last remaining moments together arguing, so she said, "We have a date for next Thanksgiving, right?"

"Sure." He smiled. "Hopefully, Annie's cooking will improve by then." He took her luggage, and turned toward the

367

airport. He expected her to follow, but she couldn't move. "Maggie," he called, "we have to go or you'll miss your flight."

"Well, that wouldn't be so bad, would it? I could stay until tomorrow. Please, Luke, let me stay with you a little longer," she pleaded.

"I have to be back on base in an hour," he said, sounding absurdly calm and logical. "Maggie," he whispered, taking her into his arms, "I know you're scared. So am I, but I'm gonna be all right, I promise. I'm sorry I got you involved in this mess."

"Oh, no," she cried, trying to smile through her tears. "Don't ever say that. I'm going to miss you terribly, but that's still better than not knowing you at all." He kissed her one last time, and then, she had to go.

A few minutes later, she took her seat at the back of the small commuter plane and began sobbing again. Why did he have to go, she cried bitterly. This was not his war. She felt betrayed, not by him, but by the cruel fates who had given her the miracle of love, and now threatened to take it away.

Chapter 42

Somehow, as the weeks and months slipped by, Annie realized that she stopped counting Luke when she reached for a stack of plates, and she no longer scolded Thomas when he scattered his things all over Luke's bed. She could actually go for hours, a whole morning or afternoon, without thinking of him. The fear that once gripped her heart was gone. Luke was safely tucked away in Louisiana. His letters were filled with humorous descriptions of the land and the people down there. The war was a world away. In mid-October, President Nixon had announced that 40,000 more troops will be withdrawn by Christmas. The South Vietnamese were going to have to fight this war themselves. Luke would be home for Christmas. Everything was going to be all right.

A few days after Thanksgiving, Annie was in the kitchen making cookies when she noticed the mailman's blue pickup. She checked the timer and decided she had time to run to the box.

She grabbed her heavy sweater and wrapped it tightly around her shoulders. It was cold, but the skies were a brilliant blue. The wind was toying with the few remaining leaves left lying about. She walked quickly, not wanting to subject herself to more ridicule for making another batch of burnt cookies.

As she hurried down the lane, she heard Ol' Mr. Gruder, their tom turkey, gobbling in the barnyard. She chuckled a little, thinking how fortunate he was to still be among the living, considering he was slated to be the main course at their Thanksgiving dinner. Matthew brought him last spring with the other livestock, intending to fatten him all summer. But he became a pet and not even Matthew could bring himself to carry out the execution. The story had been carefully chronicled in a long letter to Luke, which he should have received by now. She was anxious to hear about his Thanksgiving away from the family, and she expected an apology for why he didn't call.

She reached inside the mailbox and shuffled through the bundle of bills and junk mail until she spotted Luke's handwriting. She tore the envelope open, trembling from the cold.

Dear Dad, Annie and all,

Happy Thanksgiving! Guess I should have called. Sorry. I have a little trouble imagining my sister cooking a turkey with all the trimmings, but I suppose anything's possible.

"Ha!" she retorted out loud. "My Thanksgiving meal was very good, thank you very much!" She continued reading.

I spent the day with a friend and ate dinner with a local family. It was very nice, but it was 81 degrees and Mrs. Lasance didn't make dressing with those little water chestnuts like Cook used to do. But it was great having some real food.

I don't mean to shock you, but I have some big news. By the time you receive this I'll be on my way to . .

Annie stopped mid-stride and clutched the pages against her heart, gasping for breath. "My God!" she screamed. "No!"

She sank to her knees onto the cold, pitiless ground. The pages of his letter slipped from her hand, and she stared up at them as they floated upward. They seemed eerily distorted as the ghostly white papers soared higher and higher toward the gleaming blue skies, fluttering silently in slow motion. She was conscious of nothing else.

When or how she came to be sitting in the kitchen, she had no idea. She gradually became aware of voices calling her name. Slowly, the fog lifted and she looked up to see her father standing over her, looking concerned and confused. She felt the pages of Luke's letter pressed in her hand. They must have flown back to her, or perhaps she had retrieved them.

Matthew gently took the letter from her. He sighed deeply. "So, they shipped him out." Annie starred at him. He appeared shaken, but there was none of the grief or horror that she wanted to see. "By the way you screamed, I thought maybe he was dead!" he added.

"He might as well be," she mumbled.

"Damn it, Ann," Mack cried, "Why did you say that? Not everyone who goes over there gets killed."

"Mack's right," their father said. "There's no reason to expect the worse. He's a gunner on a goddamn helicopter – he's not on the ground. Nah, he'll be fine." Anne knew he was trying to sound reassuring, but he failed miserably. He turned to retreat to his office.

Mack stayed, pacing and casting quick glances at his sister. "Damn it, Annie," he blurted finally. "Don't do this."

"Do what? How should I act? Like you and Dad?"

"Oh, I get it! You blame me? And Pop, too – is that it? It's our fault they packed him off to the fucking war?" He spat the words with gut-wrenching self-incrimination, but Annie showed no sympathy. He, too, went away to suffer alone in another part of the house.

She thought she was alone until she saw Sonny begin moving around the room. He took the burnt cookies out of the oven and threw them outside. Then he brought a afghan from the living room, draped it around her trembling shoulders, and left the room without saying a word.

She pulled the woolen blanket tighter and sat alone in the quiet. Maybe she should feel guilty for lashing out at Mack like that, but she didn't. Once again, each of them retreated deep into the shadows of their own private despair.

It was only when Andrew arrived later that night that she was able to talk about any of it. John called him and he rushed home to be with the family. He and his twin climbed up to the attic room, the refuge he had shared with Luke. His easel still stood in the corner.

Andrew stacked some books and picked up an empty wine bottle. For the first time, the room seemed dark and sinister. "Luke and I spent many happy hours up here," he mused, "but we rarely spoke." He stood back in the shadows, his cigarette making a faint, flickering glow in the dusky veil that had fallen across his face.

And then, as though he had just thought of something momentous, he walked quickly to the small corner closet. "Look, he left them here," he said, pulling out several canvas paintings and sketch pads. "I don't know why I didn't think of these before. Look at them, they're beautiful!" They leafed through the pages of drawings, many of them of the same thing – the sunrise over the valley. "No mater how good I thought they were, he was never satisfied. See, these are the ones he did when we first came last spring, before the leaves came out. This must be the last one he did before he left," His voice faltered then, clearing his throat. He put Luke's things down and stepped over to the rough, plank table where he had studied while his brother painted. "Why are we doing this, Annie. This is not a wake. Luke would have a fit if he saw us acting like this."

"I keep thinking about that boy who hit Sonny in the Pub – his face and those eyes. They said he was a nice guy before he enlisted, came from a good family. He wasn't wounded or anything. Something happens to these boys when they go over there. And now our Luke is there, in the middle of it. Oh God, how could this happen?" She fell into her brother's arms and sobbed.

"C'mon, Ann. No use making yourself sick over this. What about the kids? They're so scared." Slowly, her sobs begin to subside.

"I understand what you're saying, Andrew," she said. "But I don't know how I can possibly help them understand something I don't understand myself."

"Where's Mack?" Andrew asked in that strange, hollow voice he used sometimes. "Penny called a little while ago. John told her no one knew where he was or when he'd be back. I bet she's going crazy wondering what's going on out here. If he really cared for her, he would have told her right away."

Annie wiped her tears and murmured, "I wonder if Luke has any idea the profound effect this has on us."

"Probably not. He always underestimated his value to this family. He'll be all right. He just has to be."

Annie mustered a hopeful smile at her twin, and turned to go back downstairs. "We just have to remember to trust in God and keep him in our prayers," Andrew called after her.

Annie knew he was trying to sound hopeful, and that he'd leave in a few minutes to go back to school to retreat into the safe haven of his little apartment and his books. She envied him this respite. His schoolwork demanded nothing of him except his time and his thoughts. She did not have that luxury. Recognizable noises were filtering up from all parts of the house. A faucet was left running somewhere, and music was blaring from another corner of the house. Someone was yelling that the baby needed changing. It reminded her that life goes on, regardless of crises and heartache.

* * * * * *

Later in the week, Penny began to worry. She hadn't been able to get a hold of Mack. He never came to the phone or returned her calls. He was avoiding her for some reason. She wanted to know what was wrong, and she had something very important to tell him.

This sudden break in communication baffled her. Their relationship had been going so smoothly. With her classes and his work on the farm, they both had very full, busy lives, but they lived for Friday's. The minute she pulled onto the yard, he'd be there, waiting with open arms. They spent the days on the farm. She put on blue jeans and boots, and worked side by side with him and the other Winston's. They spent their nights at the cabin, enraptured in hours of sweet, wonderful passion. She had never known a more romantic or devoted lover, and she cared for him more than she thought possible.

After another night of sitting by the phone with no word from Mack, she decided to drive out to the farm the next afternoon after class. She arrived at dusk, but there was no open arms waiting for her. There was only the yapping of the dogs and the eerie silence that falls over a farm at sundown. Someone emerged from the barn and began walking toward her. Instinctively, she knew it wasn't Mack – there was no telltale limp or staggered step. It was Thomas. "He's down in the barn," he called curtly, not bothering with any amenities.

She hurried toward the barn and stepped inside, calling, "Mack! Where are you?"

"Penny? I'm up here," he answered from above in the hay mow. "What the hell are you doing here tonight? Why didn't you call?"

"I did, several times. Didn't they tell you?" She climbed up the ladder and found him sitting on a pile of bales. "I was worried about you. What's wrong, honey," she murmured, stroking his cheek.

He didn't answer for a long time. He just looked away, fumbling with a long shaft of straw. "I tried calling you a couple of times, but I just can't talk to anyone about this."

"Not even me? God, now you have me really scared!" She searched his face and recognized the anguished scowl. "It's Luke, isn't it," she whispered.

"Yeah, it happened. He shipped out to Nam."

"You must have known this was possible. I'm sure he'll come through this okay."

"You don't know that. He could get killed over there."

"Why do you insist on thinking the worst?"

"How do you expect me to feel, especially since it's --"

"Since it's your fault? That's what you think? God, Mack, don't do this to yourself."

373

"What am I doing? Worrying? Getting mad? Damn right, I am. You don't understand because you never knew him. I cannot imagine him pointing a gun and shooting people. I'm telling you, he's just not that kind of a kid."

"Oh, and I suppose you are. If it was you, it'd be real easy for you, wouldn't it."

"If I had to, to stay alive."

"And don't you think Luke will, too? He's not going over there to get killed. Yes, he's a good and decent kid. Well, wars have always been fought by nice young men."

"Vietnam is not the same. I'm so sick of people comparing it to any other war. This is a war we can't win. My brother is over there for nothing." His voice choked off then and he turned away. After a long, uncomfortable silence, he said, "Look, I guess it's gonna take some time but I have to work my way through this alone."

"Are you telling me to leave?" she gasped.

"Well, it's getting late and obviously I'm not fit to be around." He reached out to take her hand but she turned and started down the ladder. "Hey, you're pissed off at me? Jesus, you think you could be a little understanding?"

He followed her to the Jeep. She said nothing as she climbed in.

"I'll see you this weekend, right?" Mack asked. "We'll talk, okay?"

"Yeah, sure," she said curtly. She slammed the door, and roared down the driveway.

Mack was startled by her attitude and angered that she seemed incapable of understanding how traumatic this was for him and his family. He was even more shocked when she called the next evening to tell him that she couldn't come for the weekend.

"Why?" he demanded.

"My mother thinks I haven't been spending any time at the house lately. And it's true. I mean, I haven't been home for a weekend in a long time."

"But, Penny, we need to talk about some things. I don't think you understand --"

"Look, you said you need some time to sort some things out yourself, so here's your chance. And I have a huge test next week that I have to study for, so I'll see you later, okay?"

"You're worried about school and your parents at a time like this? Fine!" He slammed down the phone.

But the more he thought about it, the less sense it made. He decided to drive into town Friday night and insist that they talk. Besides, he wanted some time away from the house. Everyone was so irritable since Luke's letter, especially his father, who was drinking more. And Mack couldn't stand looking at his sister's pained face. He was convinced the fear and anger he saw in her eyes were directed toward him.

CHAPTER 43

Mrs. Lamp answered the door, scowling at the intrusion Mack stood awkwardly until he recovered his voice. "Mrs. Lamp? I'm Matthew Winston, Penny's friend. Could I see her please?"

Her glare said he didn't need to introduce himself. She looked him over from head to toe and then nodded for him to step inside. She stared at his legs as though she was trying to guess which foot was the prosthesis.

"Well, Mr. Winston, I'm afraid you have been misinformed. My daughter is not here. She called to speak to her father, but he's still at the hospital, even at this late hour. I have no idea where she is. Penelope, as you probably know, is a very independent, high spirited young woman. She pretty much does what she pleases, whether it upsets me or not." The insinuation was unmistakable. It was obvious that she did not approve of their relationship. "Actually, I'm rather surprised you don't know where she is – she certainly spends more time with you than her own family." With that, he was dismissed.

Now Mack was really confused. Why would she lie to him like that? He drove to the dorm, but her Jeep was not in the parking lot. He went in and introduced himself to Mrs. Finch, the housemother. She was less than cordial. "I believe she checked

375

out for the weekend. Our girls know that we have strict regulations about signing in and out so that we are aware of their whereabouts, especially for overnights," she said as she propelled herself in her roller chair over to the small file cabinet at the other end of the desk. "However, Miss Lamp pretty much does as she pleases with little regard for our rules."

"So, did she sign out this time? Where did she say she was going?" Mack demanded.

"I'm sorry, but that's privileged information. I cannot tell just anyone who walks off the street where my girls are."

"I told you, I'm Penny's boyfriend. I need to talk to her. Just tell me where she is."

"Young man, I do not appreciate your tone. I said I cannot help you."

"Fine then, I guess I'll just have to sit here and wait till she shows up."

"You can't do that. She may not be back until Sunday. You're going to have to leave. Perhaps I should call Security."

"Okay, okay! Don't freak out! I just want to talk to my girlfriend, that's all. Is Jenny, her roommate, here? Maybe she'd know."

"She's not here either," a voice chimed in from behind him. He turned to see a pretty young woman, apparently another of Penny's classmates, standing nearby. She was smiling, jumping up on the desk and crossing her shapely legs. "Jenny and a bunch of girls went out for pizza. Maybe Penny went along. I'd be glad to come with you to help you find them."

"No, that's all right," he said, stealing a quick glance at her legs. "I'm sure I can find them. Penny's Jeep is pretty easy to spot."

"Yeah," the girl retorted, her smile fading. "Guess there aren't too many people who get pretty, shinny Jeeps for birthday presents, are there."

Mack retreated back to the truck. He was getting a whole different picture of his lover. Not that other people's opinions mattered much to him, but he wondered about all this resentment toward her, especially since he thought she was very near perfect.

He checked the parking lots of every pizza place he could

think of, even a bowling alley and a few taverns. Finally, he drove back to the dorm, but the Jeep still wasn't there and the doors were locked. The house mother sneered at him from behind her desk.

Angry and frustrated, he headed home. He was driving too fast as he swerved around the curves on the gravel road when he was seized by the clear, indisputable truth of where she was. He slammed on the brakes and turned into the driveway of Lamp's cottage. He stormed to the door and began pounding loudly.

"Open this goddamn door," he screamed. "I'll break it down if you don't let me in."

"All right. You don't have to yell." She opened the door.

"What the hell do you think you're doing? You tell me you're at your parents, so I drove into town and looked like an idiot in front of your mother. She has no idea where you are, so I went to the dorm, had a scream session with the old biddy housemother. Some girl said you might be out with your friends for pizza, so I drove past every damned joint in town.. And you were here the whole time? Jesus, Penny, if you didn't want to see me, you could have just told me instead of lying!"

"That's right, I didn't want to see you, but I couldn't think of a good way to tell you."

"What the hell is going on? I don't need this shit right now. I pour my guts out to you, and you pull this stupid disappearing act?"

"I know, I'm sorry," she pleaded. "I just need some time."

"What? All of a sudden we're spending too much time together? Since when? You know, everywhere I went tonight, I heard the same thing. You're a high and mighty, Miss Independence. You do whatever you want, to hell with rules or any consideration for anyone." He backed away from her. "How can you say you need time away from me? I thought we couldn't get enough of each other. But maybe it wasn't that way for you."

"Honey, I'm sorry. I didn't mean to hurt you like this. I know you're going through a tough stretch right now, but I needed some time, that's all. Maybe we're getting too serious too fast."

"Too serious? My God, I used that line with dozens of girls

and then laughed my ass off. I guess we're two of a kind, aren't we." He grabbed her arms and shook her with every word. "How could I get serious about you? You're a spoiled, pampered little bitch who plays with people like dolls and throws them away when you're tired of them."

"Mack! You're hurting me," she cried.

The sight of her pinched, sobbing face only made him more angry, so he flung her across the room and went to the door. "When you decide you want to play again, look me up, but I can't guarantee I'll still be around." He slammed the door and left.

Penny ran after him. "Mack! Come back. Don't leave like this." Mack didn't stop or even acknowledge her. She went back inside and flinched when she heard him peel away. "Oh God, I should have told him the truth!"

The next day, Penny found herself staring down the lane and stayed close to the phone. She prayed he would come or call, but he didn't. She paced, she fretted, she fumed, she cried, until finally she decided the best thing to do was just to confront him outright and tell him truth. Should she beg him to take her back? She bristled at that notion.

She never begged for anything in her life, and it was difficult contemplating doing it now, but she knew one of them had to take the first step. She took her jacket and marched to her Jeep. He had probably cooled down by now, and was ready for a conciliation. She would go to him and say she was sorry. Hopefully, he'd listen.

* * * * * *

The farm was quiet. As Penny pulled onto the yard, she noticed Andrew's little black Ford parked by the house. He had bought it a few weeks ago right after the harvest. Penny guessed he didn't like being dependent on her for rides any more. She approached the house and saw through the window that Annie was sitting between the table and high chair, looking tired and worn. She was barking orders to Peter and Danny as she fed the baby and tried to coax Joey to eat a little more. She stopped mid-sentence when Penny came to the door. Penny couldn't tell from

378

her expression if she was glad to see her or not.

"Hello, Annie," Penny called, trying to sound cordial.

"Hi, yourself," Annie replied. "I was wondering when you'd come. I knew you'd give in before he did." Her tone was not very sympathetic.

"He's pretty mad. I thought he might be ready to talk, or at least listen."

Annie shoveled another spoonful into Becky's mouth. "Well, we haven't said more than ten words to each other all week so I have no idea what he's thinking. I do know he looks miserable, but then everyone does." She took the dishes to the sink. Her shoulders were slumped and she looked old beyond her years. "He went with Daddy into town. I'm sure they're both in fine shape by now. Daddy's been drinking too much all week, ever since --" Her voice trailed off then, and she began to wash the dishes.

Just then Andrew walked in. "Hey, Penny," he said.

"I'm gonna put the baby down." Annie took the Becky and headed upstairs.

"Did I come in the middle of something?" Andrew went to the refrigerator and poured himself some milk.

"No, not really. I was just telling Ann that Mack and I are not exactly on speaking terms right now, and I'm not sure why."

"I'm not surprised. Mack's been acting like an ass all week. This is not about him, ya' know. He's not the one who got sent off to some stupid war."

"Yes, but Mack blames himself. He feels awful about this."

"He feels guilty? Maybe he should."

Penny was shocked. "He's not responsible for what the Army did."

"Of course not, but why do you think Luke enlisted in the first place? You don't know what it's like been like these past two or three years. Mack never cared about a damn thing except himself."

"But Andrew, he's your brother, too," Penny said, almost whispering. What was he saying? That's he'd rather have Mack in Vietnam? "Maybe Mack never cared about anything before, but he does now. And nobody feels more rotten about Luke than he does."

"I know one thing. He's been at the bar for two hours so he's probably smashed by now. No use trying to talk to him. Why don't we go back to Dubuque and have dinner?"

"No, Andrew, I need to talk to Mack."

"But why? He's irrational when he drinks. C'mon, let's go for a pizza."

"I'm sorry, I can't. I'm not hungry anyway. Maybe some other time, okay?" She turned to leave. "I have to make things right with Mack."

* * * * * *

Penny walked into the tavern and saw him. He was sitting at the bar with Chris McGraw, a boy she knew. The place was quiet for a Saturday night, but it was early. She knew he saw her but ignored her, laughing at some obnoxious joke. She called his name, aware that everyone was watching. He didn't acknowledge her, so she called him again.

"Yeah?" he sneered, without turning around to look at her. "What do you want?"

"Mack, we have to talk."

"About what? Shall we reminisce about those cozy evenings of bliss in your bungalow, our private little love nest? Hey, meet my ol' drinkin' buddy, Chris. Oh, yeah, you already know each other, don't you. Funny thing, we were just talking about you. Kinda like comparing notes."

"Mack, what are you--"

"Chris, here, tells me that we're just two of a long list of men you took to your little hideaway. Seems like you got tired of him, too. I must have the record – I lasted the longest. But then, I haven't met all your lovers."

She was reeling, gasping for breath. She saw Matthew approaching, so she wanted to get out of there before anyone else said anything. "You bastard!" she hissed, the unspeakable repulsion burning in her eyes. Then she ran out.

"Ya' know, you ought to talk to Billy Tyler," Chris was saying drunkenly. "Miss High and Mighty was seeing him--"

"Oh, shut up!" Mack exploded. He had enough. He stood

up, nearly falling. Two glasses crashed to the floor, and his stool fell against the bar.

"Mack," Matthew said, coming up quickly to catch him. But he pushed his father aside, staggered back to corner booth and waved at the bartender to bring him another drink. And there he sat until Matthew helped him to the truck and delivered him home.

* * * * * *

Mack felt miserable the next morning – his head was pounding, even his hair ached. He stayed in bed all day, barely able to drag himself out to help with the evening chores.

The next morning was worse. His body didn't hurt any more so there was no shield against the pain in his heart. How could he have done that to her in front of all those people? Who was he to ridicule her for having other lovers. He had behaved the same way back East. He had really done it this time, he chided himself, messed up the one good thing he ever had.

Penny was not faring much better. She missed classes Monday and Tuesday. Early Wednesday morning, Jenny found her roommate doubled over the toilet, vomiting.

"You know, there's pills you can take for this sort of thing," she offered off-handedly.

"For the flu? Nah! I'll be all right."

"You're sticking with that flu story? Well, it is the strangest flu I've ever seen. You look like hell every morning, but by afternoon you're the picture of health – positively glowing, in fact."

Penny froze momentarily. She had been found out, the one thing she had been hoping to avoid. "Well, don't worry," she said, trying to sound careless and detached. "I'm gonna get the cure for this flu this weekend." She leaned over the sink and splashed water on her face.

"What? I don't believe it!" Jenny cried. Then remembering to lower her voice, she said, "How can you do that? You can't just go to the corner drugstore and get an abortion." She whispered the last word as though it was some vulgar word.

"God, what would your mother say if she knew."

"She's arranging it. She met Mack and was not impressed. There's no school Friday. We're supposed to spend the day in a clinic or doctor's office, right? Well, good ol' Mom put in a call to some gynecologist friend of hers from college and arranged it like that." She snapped her fingers in her friend's face. Jenny turned paler by the moment.

"I don't care what your Mom or anyone else says, what about Mack? Doesn't he have a say in all this?" she implored. "You haven't even told him, have you, I don't get it! You find a really terrific guy and fall madly in love. You've been floating around here for months, practically sickening at times. And then you find out you're pregnant, and right way you want to get rid of it? You're crazy – certifiable!"

"Hey, he got rid of me! Not the other way around. I tried to tell him the truth, but he never gave me a chance."

"But, Penny, have you thought this through? Never mind. It's useless to try to convince Penny Lamp of anything. Do what you want."

Penny packed her overnight bag that night. She was flying to Chicago alone in the morning and have the procedure early Friday morning. It would be listed on the surgery schedule as a D&C. The doctor could write "menstrual abnormalities" on her history and physical, no questions asked. It would all be taken care of very efficiently. She had no idea how she'd feel afterwards. She'd just have to cope with it somehow, and Mack must never know.

Chapter 44

Thursday night, Annie wondered into the barn. She was curious why Danny and Peter brought in half as many eggs as usual that night. The answer was not difficult to ascertain. There were shells lying about with several egg yolk stains on the wall. "I'm sorry," she cooed to the birds sitting serenely on their nests. "I'll make sure this doesn't happen again." Just then she noticed Mack sticking his head in the door, but leaving just as quickly.

"Mack!" she called. "C'mon. Are things so bad between us that we can't even be in the same hen house together?" She laughed.

"Us – in a hen house," he said, shaking his head. "If those lovely Fifth Avenue ladies could see us now."

"Or Aunt Esther," she giggled. "They just don't know what they're missing, do they."

"No, I guess not. What happened in here anyway?"

"That's why I'm here. I was wondering why the egg basket was half empty tonight. I was just consoling the ladyships."

"Are you gonna tell Dad?"

"No, I'll just make sure they get it cleaned up before he sees this. He's been so -- well, you know, irritable." The laughter was gone just that quickly.

"Yeah, I know."

"Seems to me, he's not the only one who's been acting pretty surly lately. I was hoping Penny might be able to help you. I was sure she wanted to work things out."

"When did you talk to her?"

"Saturday night – you know, the night you and Daddy went into town early. She looked as bad as you have lately. Didn't she find you?"

"Oh, yeah, she found me, but I was an ass and said some really rotten things. I don't think she'll ever speak to me again."

"I can't believe that. You were probably pretty drunk by the time she got there. And she knows how bad – I mean, I'm sure she'd understand that you're upset about Luke if you'd just give her a chance."

"I don't know. I treated her really bad – in front of a lot of people. And I wasn't that drunk. I knew what I was doing."

"So, what are you going to do?"

"Well, I guess it's my turn to find her and try to talk to her. I've known for a long time, but I guess I was scared." Annie knew he was afraid she'd push him away. Rejection. That was a word Annie thought would never be used in the same sentence as her oldest brother. She crossed her fingers as she watched him walk across the yard.

* * * * * *

Mack contemplated calling first to make sure Penny was there before he drove all the way into town. He even dialed the number twice, but hung up both times. She probably wouldn't come to the phone anyway. No, he'd have to go and possibly sit there all night. Sooner or later, she'd come out.

He pulled into the dorm parking lot in record time. His heart sank when he saw the Jeep was not there. Maybe her father or one of her friends was using it, so he decided to check anyway. This was Thursday night, so she couldn't be gone for long. There were strict rules about weekday curfews here.

Mrs. Finch was sitting on guard duty at her desk. It was obvious by her expression that she had not forgotten him either.

"Can I help you?" she asked in her best matronly voice.

He was about to yell that she knew exactly what he wanted, but he restrained himself and very calmly stated his business.

"She's not here – checked out for the weekend," she snapped.

"But this is Thursday. How can she be gone already?"

"Well, I'm not sure. Several of the other seniors have left."

"Oh, damn it anyway!" he groaned, more to himself than anything.

But the lady across the counter was not amused. "Young man!" she retorted tersely. "I will thank you to remember that this is a residence hall for young ladies, and you must reframe from using that kind of language as long as you are a visitor here."

But Mack wasn't listening. Out of the corner of his eye, he noticed Jenny coming down the stairs, but she spun around quickly when he saw him. Mack sprang after her, which greatly alarmed Mrs. Finch, who followed in hot pursuit.

"Jenny," Mack called. "Wait up. Tell me what the hell is going on around here!"

"Young man!" cried the indignant Mrs. Finch. "You must leave now."

"I am not moving one inch until she tells me where Penny

is!"

"Linda! Call security," Mrs. Finch countered. "Tell them there's a lunatic running around the hallway in the women's dormitory!"

"No, no," Jenny broke in. "C'mon, Mack, I'll go downstairs with you. He won't cause any more trouble, Mrs. Finch, really."

He followed her, and peace was restored. Jenny suggested they talk outside, since Mrs. Finch's daggered stares were not very conducive to meaningful dialogue.

"Okay, so where is she?" Mack pressed. "Is there something wrong?""

"You should talk to her."

"How can I if I don't know where she is?" Jenny's tone and serious manner perplexed Mack even more.

"A lot of seniors are gone for this weekend because we have a special assignment for tomorrow. We're supposed to spend the day in a clinic or doctor's office. Well, Penny's certainly doing that!" She hesitated, taking a deep breath. "She went to Chicago. He mother knows a doctor there, a gynecologist? She's having a D&C." She watched his face closely to see if any of this was penetrating.

"Cancer? My God, she has cancer!" he exploded, his face draining of color. "My mother – my mom died – she had a female--"

"God, no! The surgery she's having to scrap the uterus, to get rid of anything that's in there? Do you know what I'm saying?"

If he looked pale before, he was totally dumbstruck now. He understood perfectly. He had heard whisperings of girls having that done back in New York. "She's pregnant," he murmured, looking as though someone had kicked him in the gut. "My God, that's what she was trying to tell me. She's pregnant with my baby." He was barely able to grasp he meaning of the words. But he disbelief quickly gave way to anger. "It's my kid, isn't it?"

"Of course, it is. She's crazy about you."

"Well, then why didn't she tell me?"

385

"She wanted to, but then something happened – didn't you get some bad news or something? You ended up fighting, so she never had a chance."

"She should have made me listen!"

"Yeah, right. Then she'd always wonder if she trapped you into something you didn't really want. You could end up hating each other. What took you so long to come around anyway?" It was a fair question, but that was all in the past. Right now all he was concerned about was stopping her.

"When's the appointment? How much time do I have? And what's the name of the sonofabithchin' quack doctor?"

Jenny provided the name of the hospital, but didn't know the name of the hotel where she was staying. "Good luck," she called as he rushed off. "I hope you get there in time."

"Thanks, Jenny. Don't worry, I will!" He peeled out of the packing lot, drove across the bridge into Illinois and headed toward Chicago, driving through the countryside at breakneck speeds. He left Dubuque at 8:15, and reached Chicago before midnight. He checked a phone book to find the address of the hospital and asked a gas attendant for directions.

"How the hell would I know if there's any hotels close to that hospital?" the kid retorted. "Do I look like somebody who stays in fancy hotels in downtown Chicago?"

Mack found the hospital, parked the truck, and began walking to area hotels. He asked the desk clerks to check over and over again for her name or her mother's mane. He even showed them her picture, but most of them had just come on duty and couldn't help him. He asked bellhops and waitresses in lobby coffee shops. Discouraged and exhausted, he returned to the truck and parked by the main entrance of the hospital. The lump in his throat was getting bigger. He was becoming more and more afraid. What if he never found her? He might never get the chance to tell her how much he loved her and wanted this baby. "I have to find her in time," he said over and over. "I just have to."

* * * * * *

Slowly, Mack returned to consciousness. It was daylight, and the streets were alive with honking, clattering city noises. My God, what time is it, he wondered as he jerked himself upright. 8:45. Jesus! Maybe he was too late!

He sprang out of the truck and darted across the busy street. He stepped in front of a line of people at the information desk. "Excuse me," he said. "I'm looking for someone. She's supposed to have surgery this morning and I have to stop it!"

"Sir," retorted the woman, "Slow down. I cannot understand you."

"It's Miss Penelope Lamp. She's a patient. Just tell me where I can find her." He hop-scotched from one foot to the other while she checked her files. "Hurry! This surgery is a mistake. I have to stop her!"

"I cannot imagine any of our fine doctors scheduling a surgery that is not necessary. According to this list, her procedure is already underway. But there's a waiting room --"

"Surgery! Where is it? Maybe it's not too late!" She pointed down the hallway, and Mack began running before she could finish the directions.

"Day Surgery! Where is it?" he asked someone dressed in white. He would listen long enough to get pointed in the right direction, and then ask another and another until he was directed into a small waiting area. Not bothering to ask the gray-smocked lady at the desk, he burst through the door that said, "No Entrance." It was the recovery area. The shocked staff gasped as he ran from stretcher to stretcher. She wasn't there.

"Can someone help me?" he cried. "I need to find Penelope Lamp. She's having surgery, but I have to stop it!" There was no quick response, so he turned and fled down a short corridor he hoped would lead to surgery. This time he didn't get very far. As soon as he stepped through the swinging doors, surgical personnel wrestled him to the floor.

"Call Security!" someone yelled. "Drag him out of here!"

"Don't you know you're endangering people's lives by being in here?"

"Can't ya' read? It says 'KEEP OUT'."

"Okay, okay," Mack said, realizing he was out-numbered. "I'll go peacefully, but I have to talk to someone about stopping a surgery!"

"Who in the hell do you think you are, trying to stop an operation?"

"It's my baby that gonna get flushed down the drain. Abortions are still illegal last time I checked." That got everyone's attention. "My girlfriend's pregnant, and she's in here for some kind of surgery to get rid of it."

"Let him up." A middle-aged woman pushed through the crowd. "I'm the head nurse. Please step into my office. Someone get him a gown and a hat. Now lets see if we can get to the bottom of this." She went to her desk and began looking on some lists. Mack looked at the clock. 9:04.

"Thank you for helping me," he said "I'm not usually like this. I just wanted to stop her, that's all. A thing like this probably don't take too long."

The nurse, who looked as though nothing shocked her any more, signaled him to follow her as she led him through a maze of corridors to a small corner cubicle, stepping aside for him to go inside alone.

Mack heard quiet sobbing as he stepped around the curtain. He knew instantly it was Penny. He held her as she cried.

"I couldn't do it," she sobbed. "I thought I could, but I just couldn't. They gave me my pre-op, and everything was set to go, but I just couldn't go through with it. Oh, Mack, I'm sorry. I'm so sorry!"

Mack could hardly believe what he was hearing. Their baby was alive.

"Excuse me," a burley voice broke in. "I'm Dr. Simpkin, the sur--"

"Get away from us, you bastard," Mack cried. "What the hell kind of doctor are you." He swept her up in his arms, wrapped her trembling body in blankets he took from the laundry cart, and carried her back down the corridors and out into the street. "Which hotel?" he asked as he lifted her into the truck.

He carried her into the lobby, pausing only long enough to get a key at the desk and dispatching a boy back to the hospital to retrieve her things.

He laid her on the bed and crawled in beside her.

"Why didn't you tell me?" were the first words he whispered. He hated himself for saying it, but there it was. "I mean, you love me, too, don't you?"

"Of course, I do. But you were – we were both so--"

"I know, I know. I said some terrible things. I'm sorry, I didn't mean any of it." He kissed her cheeks, forehead, even her nose.

"I didn't know what to do, so when my mother suggested this, I just went along with it. I almost made the biggest mistake of my life." She buried her face in his chest.

"Okay then, what are we going to do?"

"I dunno – guess we could eat. I'm starved!"

He gazed down at her, stunned at that last remark, but she began giggling and soon they were rolling and romping beneath the great mound of blankets. The pink returned to her cheeks, and the flimsy hospital gown slipped off her shoulders. "You are so beautiful," he said as he drew her near. She unbuttoned his shirt and unzipped his jeans as he cast off her gown. He lowered himself over her and penetrated her carefully. "Is this alright? What about the baby?" he murmured.

"No, no. It's fine. God, don't stop now." They made love with the satisfying familiarity of knowing the most intimate desires of a lover. It was different than before, fueled by the intensity that comes from the promise of commitment.

Just as they were sinking into the delicious afterglow of their love making, the phone rang. "God, it's my mother," Penny moaned. It rang several times until it finally went silent.

"Jesus, what is she gonna say when she finds out we're married. I mean, you are going to marry me, aren't you?"

She brushed away a tear before she spoke. "I will, if you're sure that's what you want. I just don't want you to feel obligated – you know, trapped."

He looked into her eyes and summoned as much passion and emotion as he could. Taking her hand, he said, "I have never wanted anything more in my life. I love you. I think we should get married right away. Having a quickie Justice of the Peace thing would be fine with me if it's all right with you"

"I just want you, me, and this baby." The tears flowed freely now.

"I was so scared -- afraid I might lose you and the baby. I really want this baby – ya' know, my kid, our kid." Timidly, he cupped his hand over her belly. "I was so afraid I wouldn't be able to find the words to make you understand how much I want this baby, but as it turned out, I didn't have to."

They kissed then, smiling at each other through their tears. "Do you suppose it'll always be like this, Mack, loving each other so much that you could just burst?"

"Yes, it will, I promise – for better, for worse, for richer, for poorer--"

"In sickness and in health, till death do us part--"

"I'll love you and keep you forever and ever."

"And nothing will part us, so help us God."

* * * * * *

Now that the promises were made, there was still the matter of making it legally binding. Stopping first at the hospital for blood tests, they hurried to the courthouse and got their marriage license. They strolled down Michigan Avenue and enjoyed the spectacular Christmas decorations. They stopped at a jewelers and bought simple gold wedding bands. Penny ducked into a boutique and picked out a new dress, insisting that Mack not see it.

"It's not a real wedding dress, but it is white," she said, biting her lip nervously. "Is that okay?"

He did not hesitate a second before he answered. "What we have is as new and pure as any there ever was. Yes, it definitely should be white."

They stopped at several shops, but they spent the most time in the baby store, amazed and awed by the tiny clothes and accessories. They bought miniature moccasins and a mobile for their baby's crib.

For dinner, they ordered room service of expensive lobster, calling it their rehearsal dinner. They retired to the bed, telling each other they should enjoy their last night of sin because tomorrow it would be legal, but, they hoped, not necessarily less enjoyable.

The next morning, they checked out of the hotel, charging the whole thing to her mother's credit card. It was her wedding present, they laughed. They drove to Galena, Illinois, a small picturesque village a few miles away from Dubuque. The Justice of the Peace and his wife kindly let Penny slip into a bedroom to put on her wedding dress. No groom ever thought his bride was more beautiful as she stepped up to stand beside him, dressed in lace and taffeta. Five minutes later, they became man and wife.

They found a homey, rustic inn with a café nearby. They ordered dinner, but barely touched their meals before they raced back to their room. He swept her up in his arms and carried her across the threshold. They found that sex after marriage was every bit as wonderful as it was before.

CHAPTER 45

In the cold light of day, reality began to settle in and the happy couple faced some rather daunting problems. The first was waiting for them in Dubuque. They found Dr. and Mrs. Lamp sitting at the dining room table, having a leisurely Sunday brunch.

"Penelope!" her mother exclaimed when she looked up and saw them standing there. "I didn't hear--"

"Mother, Daddy," Penny broke in quickly. "You remember Matthew Winston."

"Well, yes, of course," Dr. Lamp said, rising to shake Mack's hand. "How are you?"

Mack cleared his throat and croaked, "I'm fine, sir."

"We got married yesterday," Penny blurted. "Here's the certificate – it's all legal."

"Oh, my God," cried Mrs. Lamp, clutching her heart. "What about the baby?"

"Baby – what baby?" exclaimed Dr. Lamp.

"I'm pregnant, Daddy – about two months. I told Mother, and she arranged for me to see some doctor friend in Chicago."

"Burt Simpkin?" demanded her father, sounding more angry by the second.

"But I couldn't go through with it. And then Mack found me and we talked and decided to get married. So we did."

"Oh, merciful heavens!" gasped Mrs. Lamp, collapsing onto her chair.

"You're pregnant -- with his baby? And your mother knew?" Dr. Lamp exploded.

"But, Dennis, we knew how upset you'd -- "

"Shut up, Lorena!"

"What about an annulment? You could--"

"I said, shut up! For heaven's sake, she's pregnant with our grandchild. And you, young lady, do you love him, or did you get married because --"

"No, Daddy, we really do love each other, and we both want this baby." She hugged her father.

As they left a few minutes later, they could hear Penny's mother wailing how she didn't know how she would explain this to her friends at the Club. The worst was over.

They headed out of town toward the farm. "I wonder what Miss Adamson is going to say when I tell her I'm married AND pregnant," Penny wondered out loud. "Luckily, the baby's not due until July and my graduation is in May."

Mack looked at her incredulously. "Graduation?"

"She'll be shocked, but there's not a damned thing she can do about it."

"Wouldn't it be better if you stayed home?"

"I can't believe you're saying this. It's a proven fact that expectant mothers who stay busy and involved in their careers, or, as in my case, school, have much easier pregnancies and deliveries. Don't look so shocked, Mack. You must have known I wasn't going to sit at home just because I'm pregnant."

"That's the way it was for my mother – yours, too, probably. Besides, why do you care? You as much as told me you started on a whim!"

"God, Mack. You of all people should know how serious I am about my career. You were a patient of mine. You know I'm good, damned good!"

"Career? It's a career?"

"Of course, it is. Why wouldn't it be?"

"But what about the farm? All the fun we had this summer, working together. Isn't that important, too? And besides, Dubuque is thirty miles away. How the hell are you going to commute back and forth everyday, especially with you being pregnant and winter coming?"

"So, we're living on the farm? You decided that all by yourself?"

"Where would I live – your goddamn dormitory?"

"Don't be an ass, Mack!"

By this time they were both red-faced and angry. Mack looked as though he was ready to explode. Penny sat with her arms folded, her body wedged against her door as far from her new husband as possible.

"I do understand – about you graduating. I don't know what I was thinking. I'm sorry."

"I know. I'm sorry, too. And of course you'd assume we'd live on the farm – or at least close to it. We could live in the cottage."

Mack shot a quick cautionary frown. They rode the rest of the way in silence.

They walked into the front door just as two bodies went whizzing past. Someone was obviously mad at someone. Annie was yelling from the kitchen for everyone to be quiet because she finally got the baby asleep. Matthew and Sonny could be heard "discussing" something in the office. Penny shot a reproachful you-want-to-live-here? look at Mack, but he ignored her and made a loud announcement that reverberated the through the entire house.

"Everyone!" he called. "Come down here. And cut out the moaning. You'll want to hear this – honest!" He waited until the entire family assembled and motioned for quiet. "Pop, Annie, everyone, I'd like you to meet the new Mrs. Matthew Winston." No one said anything, so Mack went on quickly. "We got married – yesterday. See!" He waved Penny's hand around so that everyone could see her ring. "And there's more – we're pregnant – I mean, Penny is. Well? Don't everyone congratulate us at once."

Annie recovered first. "Yes, of course – it's wonderful," she stammered. "It's just that we're surprised because – well, you've been fighting, remember?"

"I know," Mack grinned. "But boy, do we know how to make up." Everyone laughed and surrounded them with hugs and kisses.

"You did the right thing, son," Matthew said, embracing them both. "Welcome to the family, Penny. I wish Mack's mother was here."

"C'mon, everyone," Annie called. "Dinner is almost ready. Let's get the table ready."

There was a flurry of noisy, happy activity as the table cloth was spread and the plates and silverware laid out. Mack and Penny followed Annie out to the kitchen.

"Mack's room is fairly large – it'll be OK for now – until the baby comes," Annie said.

"Yeah, we were just talking about that," Mack said, smirking at his new bride. "It'll be all right for now, but we'll get our own place after she finishes school."

"School?" Annie echoed.

"Yes," Mack retorted. "Since she's this close, she definitely should finish, don't you think?"

"Well sure, I guess so," Annie agreed. "But what about the drive – you know, drive into Dubuque every day? Isn't that going to be hard?"

"Nah," Penny replied. "I'll probably end up spending some nights in the dorm, especially if I have early calls. I've driven back and forth a lot in the past, so I can handle it."

"So, we have a plan," Mack whispered. "This married stuff isn't so hard, is it."

Later, as Penny put the rolls on the table, she noticed Andrew leaving through the front door, suitcase in hand. "Andrew," she called, rushing after him. "Where are you going? Dinner's almost ready. Aren't you going to stay and celebrate with us?" Her voice sounded like sweet singing, but it stabbed Andrew brutally through the heart. He turned away, not wanting to look upon her beautiful, radiant face.

"Well, I would, but I want to get to the library before it closes."

"Oh, c'mon Andrew, won't you stay?" she coaxed, playfully pulling off his backpack and scarf.

"Really," he said, swallowing hard, "I have to get a book for this paper I'm writing." He reached for his things and clumsily gave his new sister-in-law a kiss on the cheek. "Congratulations, Penny. I hope you'll be very happy." He tried to say the words with some conviction, but knew he failed miserably.

"You are happy for us, aren't you, Andrew?" she asked.

"Yes, of course. I'm just surprised, that's all." He whispered the words, nearly choking.

"I know it's shock for everyone, but isn't it wonderful?"

"Sure," he murmured, managing to smile. "Anyway, like I said, I have to go. Explain it to Annie if she asks, okay?" He escaped out the door.

He stepped out into the cool, December air, gasping for air. He ran to his car and drove away quickly. His heart was pounding so hard, he thought it would burst. It was finished. The sweet, secret fantasies he had been dreaming these past months were shattered, replaced by immeasurable guilt. He was in love with his brother's wife.

Chapter 46

Monday, Dec 7

Dear Luke,

I have some wonderful news. Mack eloped with Penny. Really! And they're going to have a baby. Mack a father? Pretty scary, isn't it. She's the best thing that ever happened to him, and they're madly in love. They're going to live here on the farm for now, and get a place of their own later. I can't wait for you to meet her. I know you'll like her a lot. The whole family is crazy about her. Of course, if you had come home for a few days before you shipped out, you could have met her already. I really wish you would have. We all miss you so much. And we can't help but worry. Peter and Danny have a calendar with the days marked off – it's 349 more days until you come home. None of us are going to be all right until you're back safe and sound.

Well, Christmas is only two and a half weeks away. I still have so much to do. We already sent off a package, so watch for it. I hope it gets there in time. Daddy thought we could find a nice tree in the timber. He and the little boys went out weeks ago and found one they liked. But when it came time to cut it down, they began talking about how pretty it was with the snow. And then a couple of squirrels came scurrying out from beneath it.

Anyway, you guessed it, they left the tree and phoned Giles and Miss Grace to send the decorations from the attic, especially Mother's artificial tree. It looks wonderful in the foyer. (Covers up a lot of the holes in the plaster.) Do you remember when Daddy ordered that tree for her? She hated the idea of cutting trees, too, especially since we like such big ones.

We decorated it the best we could, but it doesn't seem the same without her – without you, either. It needs your artistic touch, I think. It snowed about three inches last night. I wish you could see it. Guess we'll have to get some sleds for the boys for Christmas.

I'd better sign off – I'm trying my hand at Christmas candy this afternoon. Ginny gave me the recipe. Wish me luck. If it turns out decently, I'll send some to you and hide the rest so there's some left for the holidays. I miss you. Take care.

Love,
Annie

Annie folded the letter and kissed it before she surrendered it to its envelope. It was hard to write letters to him. She never told him how much she hated that he was over there, and how his going was making everyone crazy. Annie wondered what Luke would think when he heard that Mack was blissfully happy, while he was stuck in the middle of a war.

As she did every night, she crept to her window to look across the yard at Sonny's shack. As usual, even though it was late, his lights were still on. He had been working late into the night even more that usual these past few weeks. No doubt her father had started some project that Sonny needed to finish. She pulled the afghan tightly around her shoulders. It was the same one Sonny had given her that day Luke's letter came. She had taken it to her room and used it every night since. It was her comfort, her solace. She remembered the way he touched her then, trying to help her the only way he knew how.

When she thought of him, she wanted to use the word "love", but it just didn't seem right. Sometimes she'd try whispering, "I love you, Sonny Jackson," but the words seemed wrong. When a person says they love someone, she thought, they're expecting something back. She had no illusions of that happening. He was as distant and reclusive as ever. It was the rest of them who changed. They no longer mistook his quiet resiliency and preference for solitude as insufferable arrogance or lack of emotion. She didn't understood him fully yet, but she was no longer afraid that he was incapable of caring. He showed so much tenderness when dealing with Joey, but more importantly, there was his love for the land. The reverence and extraordinary devotion he felt for this place was a special bond between him and her father. Annie took comfort in that because she knew he would never leave.

Now that their first Christmas on the farm was approaching, she wondered what it meant to him and if he had family somewhere. She wanted so badly to give him a perfect gift – something small and personal. Matthew had brought him a tremendous gift, but that was from him. At least she had been able to tell her father what Sonny wanted. She couldn't wait until he saw it. He would know right away it was her suggestion.

She turned to her lists. So much to do and so little time. She wanted to make this Christmas special even though Mother was gone and Luke was thousands of miles away. That was all the more reason to work hard and make it as wonderful as possible.

* * * * * *

It was Christmas Eve, and Matthew stood in he doorway, waving as his family drove off the yard to go to 6:00 Mass. It was a tradition started years ago when Mack, Annie, and Andrew were small. Matthew couldn't wait until Christmas morning for his excited children to open their presents, so he told them he had to stay home and help Santa Claus, just in case he came early.

He had been dreading this night for weeks. This, like so many things in his life, was intertwined with memories of Kathleen. She had been the very embodiment of the spirit of this holy time, and when she died, he was sure she had taken Christmas with her. He missed her so much he still ached for her, remembering how beautiful she looked when she sat by the tree, dispensing gifts along with dozens of hugs and kisses. But life goes on, and now that Christmas was here, he turned his attention to the tasks at hand. He moved about the house, gathering presents from various hiding places, piling them in giant heaps under the tree.

The house was filled with the pungent aroma of spices and the evergreen branches across the mantle. The drab, old house looked spectacularly festive. He walked through the dinning room, pausing to sample Annie's cookies and candies. He was surprised how good they were. In the kitchen he spotted one of her lists hanging above the sink, everything was crossed off except eggnog, so he busied himself making it with the recipe laying on the counter.

He checked the clock. They'd be back in a half hour. Feeling rather ill at ease alone in the quiet house, he went out to check the stock. It was very cold, so they had put the cattle in the barn. They stood quietly, munching on their hay, droopy-eyed and contented. There were a couple of chickens roosting in the rafters overhead, and the old black cat lay in the corner, grooming herself. Matthew surveyed the scene, satisfied that all was well.

As he turned away, it occurred to him that this must have been what it was like two thousand years ago when the Christ child was born in a stable. He inhaled deeply, absorbing the barn smells he loved – the animals, the hay and the oats, the damp wood, the dusty air. What better aroma could there be to greet the son of God when he took his first breath. A bright star had shone that first Christmas night. Matthew stepped outside and gazed into the heavens. There were thousands of bright diamonds shining in the clear winter sky.

Sonny called to him from his shed. He needed help carrying packages up to the house, one in particular. Matthew complied, grinning at the thought of all the surprises to which he was privy. He waited while Sonny retrieved several clumsily wrapped gifts hidden in his closet. He was not smiling, looking even more grim than usual.

The prospect of spending Christmas Eve with the Winston's in the big house seemed rather daunting to him, but he knew he was expected. The younger boys had gleefully hinted that there were several presents for him under the tree, making him feel manipulated into participating in the gift ritual. The giving and receiving of presents was alien to him, and he found himself worrying that his crude offerings would not be suitable for the Winston's. The one he had worked on the hardest was under a blanket in the corner. Matthew helped him carry it to the house, taking it upstairs to Annie's room.

They heard the cars pull onto the yard, so they hurried downstairs. The boys came running in and gasped at the magnificent sight. The old house was transformed into a glittering Christmas wonderland with the tree and presents, the roaring fire, and the boughs of holly on the worn, creaky banister.

Sonny reached for Joey. Annie recognized this maneuver – he'd take care of the little boy all evening to shield himself from the rest of the family. She also noticed that he was wearing the sweater she had bought him weeks ago when she had gone on a shopping spree for winter clothing for the family. The rows of knitted deer were of particular meaning because of their arguments about his deer hunting.

Annie started upstairs to change Becky, but Johnny quickly volunteered. And later, when she wanted to go to her room to get her camera, Danny said he'd get it. She never suspected a thing.

As dictated by tradition, first a family portrait had to be taken in front of the tree. Sonny said he'd take it, but everyone loudly vetoed that idea, shouting that he had to be in the picture, too. The camera was set up on the tripod and the timer set. Three pictures had to be taken, just to be sure.

After that was accomplished, an uncomfortable silence fell upon the room. "What's this?" Penny murmured. "I expected a wild, noisy dash for the gifts." Mack didn't answer her, looking as uneasy as the rest of the family.

Their father stepped forward, clearing his throat as though he was about to make a speech. "I know what you're all thinking," he began. "It seems almost unthinkable that your mother and Luke aren't here with us. But if you think back, last Christmas was really rough, too. Mother was in the hospital, and we knew--" His voice faltered but then a slow smile began to spread across his face, and he continued. "Christmas was very special to your mother, and I know she'd never want us sitting around her tree, sad and unhappy. And I'm sure Luke would say the same thing. Now, come on, let's open these presents!"

"But, Pop," Danny said. "What about Mother's song."

"Well, son," Matthew murmured, "your mother's not--"

"Thomas can sing it," Annie interrupted, "He did last year. Mother asked him, remember?"

Matthew stepped aside and motioned for his fifth son to come forward. Thomas hesitated, probably disappointed that his father didn't think of it himself. But he said nothing and in a clear, rich tenor voice he began to sing the lovely words of *Ave Maria*, motioning for the others to hum the chords as Mother had taught them.

And then, as if to lift the pall that befallen them, Mack began to chant, "Killeen! Killeen!" and the others joined in until their father returned to center stage. "Okay, you asked for it!" he cried, the twinkle having returned to his eye. "Here it goes!" He launched into his rendition of *Christmas in Killeen*. It had begun many years ago as a joke for his wife and became part of the Christmas tradition. The celebration was once again filled with jubilation.

At long last, they turned their attention to the presents. Soon there was a growing mound of paper and ribbons as all the gifts, which had taken months to carefully select and wrap, were dismantled in a matter of moments. Delighted squeals rang out like Christmas chimes and merriment abounded everywhere.

Everyone was especially excited about the presents from Luke. Each was thoughtful and sentimental – a book for Andrew, matching engraved ID bracelets for Mack and Penny, perfume for Annie. There was even a little blanket set for the unborn Winston. Annie noted that each of her brothers received beautiful, hand-sewn, deerskin wallets or gloves from Sonny, but there was nothing for her. It was probably her own fault, she thought. She had made such a huge issue of her opposition to deer hunting, but couldn't he have thought of something else? He did appear appreciative of the flannel shirts and work gloves from her.

When it was time to clean up, Annie announced it was time for the baby to go to bed. Annie passed her around for hugs and kisses, and then started upstairs.

"Here," her father said. "I'll change the baby. Why don't you model the new gown and robe set I gave you." He followed her up the stairs and motioned for the others to come, too, as Annie stepped into her room to change.

Just as she became aware of the hushed giggling in the hallway, she saw the large covered object in the corner. The card said, "Merry Christmas from Daddy and Sonny." Her father and brothers came busting through the door when they heard her surprised gasp, excited at the unveiling of the closely guarded surprise. She slowly pulled off the cover and cried when she recognized the old troddle, Singer sewing machine that she had rescued from the garbage pile during their first days on the farm. The gorgeous cheery wood was beautifully polished, and the intricate, engraved moldings were restored. It was wonderful. Only Sonny would have had the patience to refinish something so beautifully.

"Open it! Open it!" everyone cried.

She lifted the hinged cover and miraculously, a shiny new machine popped up where the old, broken one had been. She began to cry, hugging her father and searching for Sonny in the throng, but he wasn't there. She led the way back downstairs. He was still in sitting in the chair, holding the sleeping boy. She would have liked to say more, but she simply thanked him for the spectacular gift, hoping he noticed the tears of joy streaking down her cheek.

There was another wave of excitement filtering through the group. "Now Sonny! Now Sonny!" they cried. It was his turn to look stunned. Someone slipped Joey off his lap as Matthew handed him one last gift.

"What is this?" he asked. "A motorcycle helmet?"

"Yes! Yes!" they screamed as the crowd's momentum carried him to the front door just as it swung open. There it was – a sleek, shiny new bike. He reached out and stroked it reverently. He mounted it and saddled the monstrous machine as someone handed him a coat and gloves. Thrusting his whole body down hard on the starter rod, he grinned when the machine's roar exploded into the night air. He revved the throttle a couple of times and then took off. Annie and the others stood on the porch, watching him circling the house, fish-tailing through the snow until he disappeared down the road toward town.

When everyone returned inside the house, Annie lingered a few moments longer. How she would have love to jump on the seat and ride with him into the night. She could imagine her arms clasped around his waist, her face buried in his back as the biting cold wind whipped against them. Wherever he was going, she sighed, I want to go, too.

* * * * * *

It was already late, but most of the family stayed downstairs for a long time. They gathered around Thomas and his small electric piano and sang carols, sipping eggnog and snacking on Annie's goodies. Matthew sat back and surveyed the happy scene. It was a very happy Christmas, much better than he expected. He could feel Kathleen's spirit in the that room with them that night, and he was sure she was pleased.

He couldn't help noticing how lovely Penny looked tonight as she stood smiling with her husband's arms wrapped around her. She wore a green velvet dress that draped around the small, barely discernible mound below her waist. She exuded such life and happiness. She seemed to embrace each day with tremendous vitality and energy. Yes, Mathew thought, coming here was a very good idea. Everything was working out better than he planned.

Andrew was watching the newlyweds, too. What his father perceived to be Mack's newfound contentment and happiness, Andrew viewed as arrogance. Who else could carelessly shoot off his own foot and come out of the ordeal with the most beautiful woman in the whole world? And what's more, Mack now had the respect and adoration of a father who couldn't stand him before all this happened.

Andrew loathed the way his brother smiled at his bride, touching her obscenely when he thought no one was watching. Such outright lust was indecent. And what about this pregnancy? No one, not even Annie or their father, had said one word of disapproval concerning their immoral behavior. If Mother was alive, what would she say, he wondered. Of course, if she was still alive, everything would be so different. Then Mack would have never met Penny and he would have gone on with his crude, womanizing ways. Andrew thought about the way things used to be. He wished he was still at school back East, his ideals firmly entrenched. And no Penny. He watched her move, the way she tilted her head so provocatively without even being aware of it. Perhaps the sharp stab he felt in his heart each time he looked at her was better than never having known her at all. At least there was still hope, he found himself thinking. My God, he chided himself, what was he hoping for? She's a married woman! His own thoughts were so despicable that he turned away from the festivities and ran upstairs to the sanctity of his own bedroom.

* * * * * *

One by one, everyone went to bed except Annie. She moved around the house, picking up dirty dishes and turning off lights. She started to unplug the tree but she couldn't. It was so beautiful, glittering in the peaceful. darkened house. There was still a good fire, so she curled up on the couch, trying to think of an excuse for being up when Sonny came in after his ride. She fell asleep.

Sonny put the bike in the shed and wiped it down gently.

403

His fingers, toes, and most of the rest of his body had lost their feeling, but he didn't care. He had such a feeling of exhilaration, he could hardly contain his excitement. Never had he received such a magnificent gift. There were still some lights on in the big house, so he decided to go up to have a cup of coffee.

He walked in the front door, wondering why everyone had gone to bed and left the tree lights on. As he bent to turn them off, he noticed Annie asleep in the living room. She was wearing the pretty lavender gown and robe her father had given her, and she was smiling as she slept.

"Hey." He nudged her awake. "I'm back. I didn't crash or anything. It was great! Really great!"

"I guess you liked it then, huh," she grinned. "My God, you look positively – happy."

"Yeah, well, I guess you'd better go to bed. I have a feeling those brothers of yours are gonna wake up bright and early."

"Yes, I guess so. Christmas isn't over. Ya' know, 'the stockings were hung by the chimney with care in hopes that Santa will soon be here'."

"More presents?"

"They're just little things. Daddy just wants them to wake up with more surprises. It's his fault we open presents on Christmas Eve, anyway. Years ago he started telling us that New York was Santa's first stop so we got our stuff early. Truth was he was the one who couldn't wait. My mother used to say the reason Daddy never minded her always being pregnant was because kids are so much fun at Christmas. Like tonight – wasn't it terrific?"

"Yeah, it was great! Never really saw anything like it before. I'll turn off the lights and stroke down the fire. You can go to bed."

She reached out and touched his hand for a fleeting moment. It was still freezing cold. "Sonny, why don't you sleep here tonight," she said, as she walked to the closet and brought out piles of blankets and pillows. "You're probably still cold from your ride, so why don't you stay here and sleep by the fire where it's warm." He seemed to hesitate so she added. "It's

Christmas Eve."

"Okay. Sure. I guess that'd be all right."

"Good," she murmured. "Well, good night then." She turned and escaped upstairs.

Annie couldn't sleep, excited with Sonny's easy manner. Dare she hope this might be the turning point she wanted so desperately? No, probably not, she thought, but it could be the beginning. She was glad he experienced this night with her family so that he had a better understanding of how wonderful things like this can be.

December 28, 1970

Dear Luke,

I'm sorry I haven't written a letter in a few days. Everything has been such a blur around here. I'm afraid if I tell you how wonderful Christmas was, you'll feel terrible. We missed you so much, and Mother, too. Couldn't help but think of her constantly. You would really be pleased at my first attempt at a Christmas dinner. True, it wasn't exactly duck in wine sauce like Cook used to make, but it was pretty darned good – ham, sweet potatoes. Well, enough of that. It's not really fair to rattle on about home cooking when you're 10,000 miles away.

Ginny and Ben joined us for dinner. I thought they'd probably have some other commitment, but they jumped at the invitation. Danny and Peter were especially pleased. They brought gifts so I was glad we had some for them. Ginny gave me some books on gardening and canning. She's such a dear. I don't know what I'd do without her. Charlie, Lori, and the kids came out. Lori was so happy when I invited them. I guess they always spent Christmas Eve AND Christmas Day with her mother-in-law, so she was "tickled to death" to spend the day out here. She told Charlie he could spend the day with his mother if he wanted, but her and the kids were coming here. She said they wouldn't have much of a Christmas if it wasn't for us. She's sure we saved them from going under.

And guess who else stopped by – Margaret McDuffy. I think she really misses you. Daddy says he's seen her walking in the woods every time she's home from school. I'm always afraid all the noise and confusion in this house will bother her since she's an only child and used to the quiet. But I think she enjoys it here.

Everyone was so happy with the wonderful gifts you sent. I love my perfume. Daddy was absolutely speechless with the terrific wood carving of the farmer. I tried to get Margaret to tell me what you sent her, but she wouldn't tell. I'm dying to find out what it was.

Mack and Penny had a nice first Christmas together, I guess. Unfortunately, they were obligated to spend most of Christmas Day with her parents, especially since her sisters and their families were there, too. Mack says they're a bunch of stuck up so-and-so's. That's pretty funny coming from him, isn't it? He gets along fine with Dr. Lamp, but not with Penny's mother. I don't know what happened, but I think Mack and Penny had a whale of an argument on the way home. They fight, but, but they get over it pretty fast.

We had more snow the day after Christmas. The boys love it. They have been ice skating on Ben's pond. We'll probably have the traditional Winston New Years Bowl Game. I bet you're real sorry you're missing that, right? Ha, Ha! Just like Andrew would love to get out of it. He's sure been in an awful mood lately. I used to think Thomas was bad!

I hope your Christmas wasn't too awful. Take care.

Love ya',
Annie

December 31, 1970

Dear Luke,

It's New Year's Eve, and I'm here all alone – except for a 6-pack. Don't worry. I won't drink it all tonight. I had to sneak it up to my room cause if Aunt Betty found out, she'd skin me alive, especially since I'm drinking alone. (She says that's a sure sign of an alcoholic.) But I'm not because in my mind, you're sitting here. too. Here's to you. Cheers!

I went over to your house on Christmas Day. There was quite a houseful and the boys were wild. They're really great kids. I love going over there. Everyone was pleased the gifts you sent them. She wanted to know what you gave me, but I didn't tell her. I could have – I wasn't embarrassed or anything. I just want to keep it to myself a while longer. I hope my present got to you in one piece. I packed it as well as I could.

We've gone to Mass so many times since I've been home that my knees are sore. I think Aunt Betty is trying to make up for the times she knows I miss when I'm at school. (She's determined to save my soul from damnation, I guess.) The church really is beautiful, though. When you walk in, you smell the evergreen, the incense, and the candles all blend together. There's a huge tree on one side of the alter. (Miss McCracken wanted it out of her front yard anyway.) There's a beautiful nativity scene in front of it and candles in every window. I look at the star on top of the tree and find myself wondering if there really is a God. Why would He let there be wars? Christmas is supposed to be a time of great joy and hope, but I just don't feel it anymore. I told God that if he really wants me to be a believer, then he'd better bring you home safe and sound soon. It's probably sinful to lay down conditions like that but I can't help it. You're supposed to have faith and accept that there's a reason for everything, but it's so hard. Sometimes I find myself questioning if He hears my prayers anyway. But then, I start to feel so alone and insignificant, and even more afraid.

I'm getting pretty deep, aren't I. It's probably the beer talking. Besides, I'm serious by nature. Everyone always says that about me. I don't think questioning things like this is a bad thing anyway, do you? It's part of growing up, maturing, right? That's what they say, but I don't understand why there has to be all this confusion and turmoil, do you? I'm going to bed. Good night.

Hey! It's the next morning now. Happy 1971! We are leaving for church soon, but I did run down to your special place, Luke. It's gorgeous! There's a beautiful shroud of snow over everything, untouched except some rabbit tracks. I hated to disturb anything. The trees looks so noble, standing there holding up all that snow. The skies are clear blue. I did take some pictures. I'll mail them to you soon.

Only 19 more days until school starts. I can hardly wait. Time goes so much faster when I'm buried under tons of *homework. Let's concentrate on how wonderful this new year will be. It's the year you'll come home. We'll have beer together next New Year's Eve!*

Luke, I love the necklace. Thank you.

Love,

Maggie

Chapter 47

Annie clutched the steering wheel so tightly that her hands hurt. She knew she was driving too fast for the road conditions but she didn't care. She pressed on, but eased up on the accelerator when she felt her wheels sliding. I'd better not have an accident, she thought, or I'll never hear the end of it. Both her father and Sonny told her not to go, but she didn't listen. It snowed another six inches overnight, which was blowing and drifting across the road. School was cancelled again. It was the middle of March and the boys already had at least 10 snow days. She was sick of winter. The sight of snow nauseated her.

On the car seat next to her were two piles of letters from Luke. The largest pile was tied up in a yellow ribbon and contained his letters from early December until early February. These were the "good" letters, the ones filled with humorous, light hearted stories and descriptions of the people and the area where he lived. He sent drawings and sketches which Annie guessed were designed to put the family at ease and calm their fears. He talked a lot about being homesick and counting the days until he came home. These letters were so much like Luke, it was as though he speaking to them. There were 29 letters in that pile, counting the letters he had written to Danny and Peter. She had read them so many times that she had memorized most of them.

> *You guys asked a lot of questions. I'll try to answer them as best I can. The reason there was geese in some of my drawings is because we have quite a large flock of them in camp. They're our "watch geese." You know how noisy chickens and turkeys are? Well, geese are REALLY loud, so if some strangers*

are trying to sneak up on our compound, or camp, they squawk like crazy. One of the best jobs is to take care of the geese. I'm a new guy here, so I don't get to, except I like to talk to them and I do give them some treats sometimes. They are very fond of Annie's cookies. (But don't tell her I said that, OK?)

The other, smaller pile were the letters that started coming a few weeks ago. These were the ones that came after the frightening weeks in February when no letters came at all. The family knew that Luke's unit was involved in the Laos campaign. It was lead story on every newscast for weeks. The South Vietnamese Army launched a massive assault along the Ho Chin Minh Trail to cut off the supply routes. The President succumbed to legislative and public pressure and stipulated that no US grounds forces could take part. However, the ARVN received "air support." Those two simple words made Annie's heart turn cold. Air support meant helicopters and that meant Luke.

When Luke started writing again, his letters had a different tone and emphasis. The language was terse and angry. First week of March, he wrote:

Dear Annie,

This is going to be quick. I got 9 letters today -- first mail call we've had in a long time. So I haven't written in a while, but it sure as hell wasn't my fault. I'm not going to tell you what's going on over here, cause they'll probably trash it anyway. It's not like it's a deep dark secret. You probably know more from reading the newspapers than I do.

Like I said, I'm fine. But I have to go. I'll write more later.

Luke

Annie knew her brother was changing and was frightened for him. Matthew said she read too much into those letters, but there was a terrible feeling of dread that deepened with every passing day. There was only one other person that would understand and that was Margaret. Annie called her and suggested that they meet at the little café on Highway 151 that was midway between Dubuque and Iowa City. She wanted Margaret to read the letters, and she wondered if Margaret would share hers, too.

She parked beside Margaret's old Buick. There was no mistaking it for anyone else's, especially since there were Iowa Hawkeye decals all over the back window. Annie rushed inside and found Margaret seated in a booth in the far corner of the restaurant. Her eyes were swollen and red. Annie reached across the table to hold her cold, trembling hands.

"I got a letter this morning," she cried. "Hanson's dead." Annie knew that Mike Waters and Greg Hanson were Luke's best friends in Nam. Margaret handed the letter to Annie.

March 10, 1971

Dear Maggie,

Things have not settled down around here. I'm tired, but I thought I should try to write. Like I said, this has been a rough 6 weeks.

Hanson's dead. Jesus, I can't believe he's gone. Don't know why I'm so shocked. What did I think? I'd go through 11 or 12 months of war without anyone I knew dying? That's nuts!

He was from Denver. He talked about the mountains, and we talked about snow all the time. He loved to hike and ski. He had a wife and a little kid waiting for him there. Now that little boy will never know what a great dad he had. He loved kids -- he told his wife he wanted a whole bunch. Maybe that's why he died the way he did. There was a Vietnamese village close to the border that was bombed by mistake. We were sent in to rescue as many civilians as we could. We got there too late. The whole valley was in flames. But Hanson said he heard something so he ran in there. He came out with a little baby in his arms -- his shirt and pants were on fire, but he just kept running. It was the bravest thing I ever saw. We took him to the hospital but he never made it. So far, the baby is doing OK, I guess.

You know what really makes me mad? This My Lai thing. We have reporters with us all the time, and they always want to talk about it. Christ, that thing happened years ago! And just because those guys reacted that way doesn't mean we all would. When the Chaplain did the service with our unit before they loaded Hanson's coffin, he read something to us. It's from the military laws or something, I guess. He gave me a copy. It goes:

> *Men who take up arms against one another in a public war do not cease on this account to be moral beings, responsible to one another, and God.*

I didn't know there was a rule like that, and neither did Hanson. It's like the Chaplain said -- he didn't need a law to tell him how to act. He did the decent thing. The people back home think we're baby killers! Who in the hell do they think they are? They're not here. They don't know anything. We're just a bunch of guys trying to get through this and go home.
> *I have to go.*
> *Luke*

Annie wept as she read it, too. Her heart broke for her brother, that he would have to hurt like that and be so alone. "Poor Luke!" she whispered.

"All I know is--" Margaret wiped the tears and sighed. "All I can think about is thank God, it wasn't Luke. Isn't that despicable? I'm glad someone else is dead." Her shoulders heaved with deep, anguished tears.

"He mentioned that Mai Lai thing in my letters a couple of times, too. Here, read this." She handed it to Margaret to read.

Have you been following the My Lai trial in the papers? The reporters that hang around our unit ask us about it all the time. I heard they found Calley guilty of killing 21 people instead of 102. We heard the verdict touched off demonstrations like crazy. I guess people thought he should have been convicted of more. Others felt he was the fall guy and his charges should have been dropped like they were for superiors, especially since he claimed he was following orders. We don't talk about it much here. But I guess it makes us mad that people back there think they know about it when they don't – they can't unless they're here. Some of the guys are scared to go home. They don't want to

411

be treated like that – that's crazy. I mean, what the hell? The whole thing just pisses me off.

"Doesn't sound like Luke, does it," Annie said. "You can just feel all the anger and tension. And now Hanson is dead? What are you going to say when you write back to him?"

"I know one thing, we can't harp on him about not writing. I think it makes him mad, like we're putting pressure on him. He has enough to worry about, right?" Tears started to flow again. "It's just that I get so scared when there's no letter in several days. I'm always so damned afraid."

"Yes, you're right, Margaret. We gotta lay off the guilt trip. He knows we live for his letters and I'm sure he writes as often as he can." Annie picked up the pile of so-called happy letters and flipped through them until she found one in particular. "Here, read this. It's such a great letter. It'll make you feel better."

Jan. 21, 1971

Dear Peter and Danny,

It was great getting your letters and sketches. You guys are getting better and better. I have all your pictures taped up on the walls around my bunk, even on ceiling, so when I lie down, I can look up at them. Anything you send me from home makes me feel a lot better.

So you liked the pictures of my bird, or helicopter. It's called a HUEY because it's a HD-ID, so they call it HUEY for short. And you're right, it does look sort of like the Baby Huey cartoon. The word "Sophie" is written on the front because the pilot, Lieutenant Leonard, named her that. He told me the helicopter reminded him of his Grandma Sophie -- she has sort of a wide bottom, I guess. He loves his grandmother a lot and thinks calling his bird "Sophie" brings him luck. I'm a door gunner. I stand by my gun at the big opening on the side. I have one side, and my friend, Timmy Waters, has the other. Our helicopter can carry ten or eleven other guys besides the crew. That's mostly what we do, pick up and drop off personnel. I don't know why they're called "grunts". No, they don't grunt all the time. They're foot soldiers, the guys who have to go into the jungle and

412

fight this war. Us guys in the helicopters just provide the taxi service.

As for your other questions, yes, I'm scared sometimes. It's all right to be afraid once in a while. And yes, I do go to Mass here. There's a priest who's stationed right here in our camp. He doesn't have a church, and sometimes the alter is a barrel or a crate, but the words and the prayers are all the same. I have my Rosary with me that Mother gave me at my first Communion. I feel better if I have it in my pocket, even when I'm up in my helicopter.

So, boys, keep those letters and drawings coming. I have a calendar, too, where I mark off the days until I get to go home. I can't wait! Take care and study hard. Behave and try not to drive Annie crazy!

Love you guys!
Luke

Margaret smiled through her tears. "You're right, that was a great letter. Sounds so much like him, doesn't it? Trying to make everyone else feel better." She bit her lip then as she swirled the ice in her water glass. "I didn't bring mine. I could have, I guess, but --"

"That's okay, Margaret. I didn't think you would. The letters he writes us are more like community property. They get passed around and everyone reads them. I'm very glad he has you – you know, a girlfriend."

"You think of me as his girlfriend, Annie?"

"Well, sure. That's what you are, right? I meant to tell you, you look fabulous. You lost more weight and your hair is so pretty. I can't wait for Luke to come home and see what a beautiful young woman you've become."

Margaret blushed. "I can't wait either. He told me to date other guys, and believe it or not, I've been asked. It makes me feel good – you know, to get asked out, but I can't. I just want Luke to come home safe and whole and --"

"And be the same, sweet kid. Margaret, do you think that's possible? Can a person see the things he's seen and not be changed?"

413

"I don't know. I pray for that every day. But then, sometimes I think I don't care about that. Just as long as he comes back, we can fix the rest later."

The two young women sat for two hours, talking and passing Luke's letters back and forth. It began snowing again and they knew they should each start for home.

"We'll do this again, all right?" Annie said as she put on her coat and scarf. "I feel a lot better, don't you?"

They walked arm in arm to the cars, pausing to peer up at the snow as it brushed past their faces. "Luke loves the snow," Margaret murmured. "I hope we have an early snowstorm next year at Thanksgiving. I can't wait."

"Personally, I'm sick of the snow and I'm ready for spring." They gave each other reassuring hugs and headed out in opposite directions.

Later that night, when the house was quiet, Annie wrote the letter she had composed in her head during the drive back home that afternoon. She decided not to tell him that she spent the afternoon with Margaret or say anything about his friend, Hanson's death.

March 19, 1971

Dear Luke,

We got two letters yesterday. Thank you for that. The mailman turned into the driveway and delivered them to the backdoor. Just as we expected, there wasn't too much specific information, but I know the censors would black it out anyway. We all sat down to watch Nixon's press conference last week. He says the campaign is a tremendous success. All I care about is that you're safe.

OK, enough of that. I'll change the subject. It's hard to believe that we've been living here for a year. The baby was a tiny infant when we arrived, and now she's walking and getting into things. She constantly pulls all my pots and pans out of the cupboard. "My pots and pans". I couldn't imagine saying that 12 months ago. Our lives have really changed, but none more than yours. 261 more days until you'll be home, having Thanksgiving dinner with us.

414

There's still a lot of snow on the ground. Daddy doesn't seem as restless about getting started with the farming this year. Sonny says it's not going to be nearly as hard. However, he and Mack are pretty nervous because Daddy's talking about renting the Gibson place this year. Jake says he's too old to keep working that hard. Daddy hasn't made up his mind yet -- that is, he hasn't got the others convinced yet.

I stop by church almost every day. I pray and light a candle -- not just for you, but for all the boys over there. I know there are people there that you care about very deeply, and I worry about them, too. Mostly I pray for this madness to be over soon. Please be careful.

Love,
Annie

Chapter 48

April finally arrived. The long, cold winter was slowly lessening its grip. The family gathered for a Sunday dinner. There was a huge ham in the oven with baked yams and candied apples. An upbeat atmosphere prevailed, and Annie was sure they were going to have a wonderful day.

She would have liked Margaret McDuffy to join the family gathering. They spoke almost daily, especially since neither of them heard from Luke in nearly two weeks. They both realized that he had grown tired of their hysteria during these lapses of mail, so they were trying to remain calm and continued writing casual letters.

Since Ginny hadn't been out of her house for weeks because of the weather, Annie invited them to join the family for dinner. Annie was trying one of Ginny's recipes for pineapple salad, so she wanted her mentor to be there to judge it firsthand. Upon arrival, Ginny was wheeled into the kitchen to chat with Annie and Penny in the kitchen. And as usual, the conversation centered around babies.

"I had both of mine at home," Ginny said. "That's the way we did it back then. No one thought anything of it. But I had a doctor there both times, and help for a while afterwards because, in those days, you were in bed for at least two weeks, sometimes longer."

"Whew!" Penny exclaimed, "Now you're lucky if you get to stay in bed for a couple of hours. Get 'em up and moving, that's the motto nowadays. Of course, we don't send mothers home to do field work or milking."

"Who says!" retorted Mack, who had ambled into sample the cooking. "No lazy life for you once the kid comes. Slop those pigs! Milk those cows!"

"Milkin', aye!" Penny cried, giving her husband a friendly jab in the ribs. "Yeah, I'll be milking all right, but there's only enough for one."

"Oh, yeah?" Mack grinned, eying his wife's quite enlarged bust. "I don't know about that. I think there might be enough for twins, maybe more!"

The conversation moved into the dinning room, where the dilapidated old table was covered by a freshly pressed tablecloth, napkins, and a floral centerpiece.

"Whew!" whistled Johnny, along with several others. "Look at this! The table looks great, Annie!"

Mack laughed and said, "When you say the blessing, Pop, be sure to ask the good Lord to keep this thing standing for one more meal."

"Hey," Matthew exclaimed, "I'm waitin' for this thing to collapse so we can throw it out in the junk pile like we should have when we first got here."

Annie smiled and withstood their good-natured kidding. True, it was battered seemingly beyond repair, but she was intrigued by the table as part of the history of the house. "Perhaps someday someone who is quite good at woodworking will take time out from his other more important work to fix this old thing so at least we won't have to worry that it will stand safely." She wasn't looking at Sonny, but everyone knew to whom she was speaking.

"Sure," her father laughed, "like he has nothing else to do."

The conversation moved on to other things, such as baseball's spring training.

"My God, John," Matthew howled. "Just because you're a Midwesterner now, you're gonna turn your back on the Mets?"

"Yep," Jake quipped, pressing the napkin tucked in his collar to his lips. "The boy got smart. He's a Cubbie fan now."

"The Cubs?" Matthew cried. "I thought Mets' fans were supposed to hate the Cubs. Tom Seaver is still there. Who you gonna root for when they come to Wrigley?

"I don't know," Johnny said with a grin. "Maybe some sucker will drive me and Kenny to Chicago for a game. I'll figure out who I'll root for once I get there."

"If you're gonna go to a game, go see the Pirates," Mack chimed in. "They're gonna take it all this year." That remark was met with a chorus of boo's. "You'll see. Come World Series time, it'll be the Pirates and the Orioles. They got the Robinson boys and Davie Johnson. And pitching! Baltimore always has great pitching. That Palmer kid should be great this year!"

And so it went, the usual dinnertime chatter of a predominantly male household, until someone called out, "Where's the rolls?"

"Oh, darn!" Annie exclaimed, rushing back to the kitchen.

"Forgot again?" they all chorused.

The buns were burnt to a crisp. Luckily, they hadn't started smelling badly, and she had more in the freezer. Annie took the cookie sheet of blackened bread out the side door to throw the evidence in the snow where the dogs were sure to devour them before anyone knew.

Just as she was turning to go back inside, something caught her eye. There was a car turning slowly into the driveway. She saw it was a dark green sedan with official-looking lettering stenciled on the side. She let the pan drop as she clasped her hands across her chest, gasping for air.

"He's dead!" she screamed. "Oh, my God, he's dead!"

* * * * * *

417

Three days earlier, there was talk about baseball around the table in the mess hall of Luke's unit, too, but he wasn't listening.

He was trying to eat, but the unappetizing stench of the grease and the sweating bodies around him made him push his plate away. He looked across the table at his buddy, Tim, who wasn't eating either. He sat hunched over a cup of coffee he hadn't touched. His face was drawn and gaunt, his eyes were troubled and frightened.

"Man, what is the matter with you?" Luke murmured, not wanting to draw attention to themselves. "You look like shit!" His friend didn't answer. Luke became aware of the loud conversation at the other end of the table.

"Lord Almighty, yes!" someone said. "Them black brothers are gonna run their asses off in Baltimore. Frank and Brooks, ain't it? Brooks! What kind of name is that?"

"It sure as hell ain't 'Books'." Luke recognized the voice without looking up. It was Krowloski, the hulking big man who controlled the camp even though he was only a private. "Everybody knows those colored boys can play ball, but they sure as hell can't read." Again, there was uproarious, mocking laughter, seemingly directed toward Tim and Luke. "But at least they're honest Niggers. They don't try to be something they ain't."

This man was the meanest, ugliest person Luke had ever seen. He was wearing a dirty cap over his stringy unwashed hair, his face dark and bearded. His Army blouse looked more like an open vest with the sleeves and buttons ripped off. He wore several strands of beads and medallions around his neck. His unkempt, bedraggled appearance would have been forbidden earlier in the war, but now was commonplace in the fragmented Army of 1971. He stared at Tim and Luke as he spoke, no longer laughing.

Luke was confused and angry enough to challenge him and demand an explanation for his inferred accusations. He was sick of their ignorant bigotry and constant racial ranting. But before he could react, Tim jumped up from his seat, his hands clinched at his sides and the muscles of his face twisted and quivering. There was silence for a moment as everyone waited to see if Tim would challenge the disagreeable giant, but he stormed out amid loud heckling and jeers. Luke went after him.

Tim took long, enraged strides across the compound so that Luke had difficulty catching up with him. "Jesus Christ!" Luke cried, running up to his friend and turning him around roughly. "Now you tell me what the hell is going on with those animals there, and what the fuck it has to do with us!"

But Tim shook off Luke's hold, and bolted away. Again, Luke followed him. "God damn it! You tell me right now, cause somehow I'm in the middle of this, and I don't have any fucking idea why!" He was screaming even louder now, but then he noticed a group of Blacks nearby who were casting menacing glares their direction. Tim returned their cold stares, but then turned to lead Luke away to a quiet, more private place. He squatted down close to the ground and lit a cigarette. He drew in a couple of long draws.

"You're right, you are involved," he said. "You are the worst kind of filth to those guys back there." He raised his eyes to meet Luke's. "Yeah, man, you're a Nigger-lover."

Tim's tone and cold unflinching eyes frightened Luke. He heard the words, but he couldn't absorb their meaning. Tim continued. "Look, remember last week when the Red Cross came here looking for blood donors. Well, the Sarg told Krolowski to go through the files to find guys with whatever blood type they were looking for. And guess what little tidbit he found in mine? See this black, curly hair. Yeah, I know, it drives chicks crazy. I got it from my mother's side of the family."

"What?"

"Don't ya' get it, man?"

"Get what?"

"My grandmother was Black."

"So?"

"What the hell do you think those guys were talkin' about back there?"

"But – but," Luke stammered, "why didn't you tell me?"

"Why the hell should I? Jeez! It's bad enough here without getting into that shit! We were doing fine – kept to ourselves, did our job. I didn't think anyone would find out."

"Why didn't you just lie to the recruiter? What's the big deal anyway. I mean you don't look... you know, Black."

"I couldn't. Everybody in the county knew anyway. Where I come from, if you're a fourth Black or all Black, you're a Nigger, and they don't take kindly to anybody lying about that kind of thing. Besides, my mama – I just couldn't, that's all!" The anger was gone from his voice, replaced by desperation. "I mean, who the hell cares anyway? Truman desegregated the Army twenty years ago, right? What war are we fightin' here, anyway? The freakin' Civil War? Oh, Lordy, I can't sleep. I can't eat. I am a dead man, you hear me? I am dead!"

Luke's mind was racing. "No, now listen, we'll go out today, and when we get back we'll go to the Sergeant. We can ask to get reassigned."

"Oh, shit man, you're not thinking straight. Go to the Sarg? Oh, sure, right. You know goddamn well Krolowski has the Sarg in his hip pocket. Krol is his pipeline, man! Where do you think he gets his stuff? Nobody fucks with Krolowski. Nobody!"

The call was sounding in the compound. "Hey, we'll think of something, Tim. C'mon, we gotta go."

* * * * * *

Helicopters were the Jeeps of this war, even though in many ways they failed to provide the advantage hoped for by the American strategists. Helicopters were noisy and could not penetrate the dense, jungle terrain so "landing zones" had to be cleared, eliminating any element of surprise. There was the constant danger that a secured LZ might be sabotaged on a return trip. The helicopters were of little use for reconnaissance because the enemy usually moved at night or underground, impossible to locate from the air. Luke was assigned to a Bell HD-ID, a pot-bellied flying transport for supplies and personnel. His job as a door gunner was to supply peripheral vision for the pilot and protection for the ground forces.

Luke and Tim knew the routine well. They retrieved their guns from the munitions hut, mounted them on the turrets, loaded the ammunition, and waited for orders to move out. Gently, the helicopter lifted and headed west over a rim of low, rounded hills, across bombed and barren valleys, past thousand year-old villages and roadways that were no more. As usual, the ride seemed somewhat refreshing, almost relaxing, but became much more tense when they crossed the muddy waters of the Anamneses River into Laos. They began hearing the sounds of war – the gunfire and explosions, the jets thundering overhead.

As they had done dozens of times since the Laotian campaign began, they touched down in a small LZ near the front and immediately encountered enemy fire. Luke fired his gun into the surrounding bush while the ARVN troops scurried to retrieve the boxes of supplies, and then hastily loaded the bodies of the dead and wounded. The South Vietnamese were running for their lives, being pushed back toward their own border.

From his lofty position as a gunner on a helicopter, Luke never looked directly into the faces of the enemy. But he did see the grim expressions of the casualties as daily they were loaded into the cargo bay of his chopper. In the beginning, Luke had tried to aid and comfort them – he'd turn their heads if they vomited, tighten their dressings or cover protruding bones. But eventually, the endless flow of the mangled bodies eroded his senses and so now, he adverted his eyes, not wanting to look at them any more. Then one would cough or cry out, and he'd turn to stare at them, laying bleeding and dying at his feet. There was no peace, no honor, no answers in their faces, only fear and pain.

Their first run had gone as usual. They delivered 7 wounded to the hospital and 5 bodies to the ARVN morgue, loaded more boxes of ammunition at the munitions depot, and headed back. This time, the South Vietnamese were more panicked. The dead and wounded were left lying in the mud as the supplies were flung to the ground, and twenty or thirty terrorized troops began fighting for a space, desperate to escape the ensuing enemy. A pistol carrying officer arrived on the scene, and order was restored.

Fifty feet away, by a tree at the edge of the clearing, Luke watched as a young, frightened soldier put his rifle into his own shoulder and pulled the trigger. Luke called to the pilot to wait as he helped pull the injured man on board. Their eyes met for a moment as the soldier slumped to the floor, reeling from the pain and loss of blood. Having no desire to be this man's judge nor his redeemer, Luke felt strangely unaffected and detached. He turned away, and did not look at him again.

Back at the base, other helicopter crews were reporting similar frantic receptions, and many were hesitant to return for their third and final run of the day. The pilot and co-pilot of Luke's bird sat briefly with other pilots, arguing about the best way to handle this volatile situation. Finally, Lt. Leonard threw down his cigarette and walked resolutely toward his chopper, motioning for Luke and the rest of the crew to follow.

"Krolowski!" he yelled across the compound, "you're coming with me! Grab a couple extra rifles. Our orders are to evacuate the wounded – period! Let someone else worry about those other poor sonofabitches!"

Krolowski grinned as he reached for rifles and extra clips and climbed on board. "Hey, Pretty Boy!" he called toward Luke. "Don't you feel better, now that ol' Krol is here?"

Luke returned Krolowski's sneers with an hostile scowl. He despised it when they called him that. "Pretty Boy" denoted the soft, effeminate characterization that he hated. It had started soon after he arrived when his bunkmates discovered he liked to draw. The situation became worse when he refused to accompany them to visit the Vietnamese whores in the boom-boom rooms in a nearby village. His slender features and small hands made him easy prey for their teasing, and no matter how he conducted himself in the field, their opinion of him never changed.

Their aircraft began getting pelted with bullets a couple of miles away from the landing zone. Luke and Tim were astonished by Krolowski's glee as he returned fire, screaming, "Take this, you bastards!" Even before the helicopter touched down, they were besieged by dozens of frantic ARVN soldiers. Screaming obscenities, Krolowski sprayed a round of bullets over their heads. And when that failed to deter them, he began thrusting the butt end of his rifle at their heads, sending several of them sprawling to the ground.

"Let's get the hell out of here!" shrieked Lt. Leonard.

A barrage of gunfire broke out from a small knoll behind them, and several South Vietnamese were hit, their bodies strewn in and around the helicopter. Luke had been pushed away from his gun and could not return fire.

Krolowski began throwing bodies aside, screaming, "Go! Go!" but the helicopter barely lifted, pitching up and down due to the excessive weight.

Panicked and more afraid than he had ever been since arriving in Vietnam, Luke peered frantically across the cargo bay, searching for Tim. He had been hit and was holding his arm. And at that same moment, Krolowski saw it, too. Just as the helicopter began to climb, Krolowski lunged toward Tim, grabbed him savagely, and flung him out of the door.

"Jesus, no!" Luke screamed. "What the hell are you doing?" Horrified, he looked down and saw his friend get up, stumbling toward them, dazed and afraid. "Lieutenant! Waters is down there! We gotta get him!" Whether it was because the Lieutenant heard his pleas or because of the added weight of several South Vietnamese dangling from both runners, the helicopter suddenly careened downward so that Luke was able to jump off and began running toward his friend. The sounds of the rapid gunfire, the frenzied screaming of the Vietnamese, and the thunderous pounding of his own heart reverberated through his being like a thousand firecrackers exploding in his brain. Without consideration of logic or forethought of strategy, he bolted across the clearing, hurdling over bodies and darting from side to side to dodge the bullets as he ran. Just as he was nearly close enough to touch Tim, he heard two soft, hollow thuds, like pennies being dropped into a wishing well.

"Oh, my God!" he screamed as he saw the blood spurting from Tim's chest. Luke cradled his friend in his arms as they fell to the ground together.

"Hang on, Timmy, hang on!" he cried. "I'm gonna get you out of here, I swear!" He began dragging Tim toward the helicopter. " Just hang on!"

But then, Luke looked up and saw something that stopped his blood cold. Krolowski's hulking body was standing across the doorway. Luke could see his yellow-toothed sneer from across the clearing. "Lieutenant," Krol called, "everything's secure back here. Take off!"

In that same instant, more shots rang out. Luke was aware of a vague, hot sensation in his legs and he knew he was hit. Helplessly, he watched as the helicopter sprang toward the sky, melting into the bright sunlight. Luke laid on the ground beneath his dead comrade looking up toward the skies, which were suddenly clear and still.

Somewhere, from the deep recesses of his mind, he heard Sergeant O'Brien's voice calling to him. "What are you doing?" the voice said. "I told you, don't try to be no hero. Only heroes I ever knew were dead ones!"

"Yeah, Sarg, I know," Luke whispered, "but I didn't know what else to do."

Chapter 49

Thirty years ago, during World War II, the town always knew when one of their native sons had fallen because the somber and grim-faced Mr. Beasley could be seen wheeling his dilapidated, old bicycle through the streets. He was the postman and the telegraph operator, so the job of delivering the dreaded messages from the War Department fell to him. Although technology had made tremendous advances since then, it was still true that news of any magnitude as well as meaningless gossip still traveled most expeditiously by that tried and true system of word of mouth.

The appearance of two Army officers stopping at the Sinclair station to ask directions to the Winston place had the telephone wires buzzing. It would have been much too presumptuous to call the Winston house directly, so it was suggested that Ginny Gibson would be a likely source of information. An old friend of Ginny's, Edna Wheeler, was appointed inquisitor. She called the Gibson's just before suppertime. "Everyone is so worried," she said. "My goodness, I hope nothing terrible has happened to that nice young man."

"Yes, they did receive some news today," Ginny said. "But

it could have been worse. Luke is officially listed as 'Missing in Action'. They think he's still alive, at least."

"Oh, my goodness. How terrible. So how is the family doing?"

"Well, they're doing just as well as you'd expect," Ginny responded tersely. "Me and Ben stayed for awhile but then we slipped away. We didn't want to intrude at a time like this. I hope the rest of the town will have the good sense to do likewise."

She wanted to get off the line but Mrs. Wheeler persisted. "Did anyone call Betty McDuffy? Her niece and that boy are sweethearts, aren't they?"

"Yes, they're friends but I'm sure one of the Winston's called over there. Oh, my goodness, the hamburger is burning. I have to get off the phone. Good bye." She was exhausted and did not want to discuss the sad affair any further. Ben pushed her back to the table where her Bible laid open to Psalms.

I will lift up mine eyes to the hills, from whence cometh my help. My help cometh from the Lord, who made heaven and earth.

She knew these words as well as she knew her own name. She had turned to them many times in her life. She thought of Annie and her family. They were plunged into the depths of such sorrow that Ginny was afraid for them. She understood their anger, too. In one, brief conversation, their hopes and dreams had vanished.

Ginny, as well as everyone in that room that day, would never forget the events that unfolded before them. They were sitting around Annie's dinning room table, eating and chatting away when they heard her scream. Through the window they saw the car stop in front of the house and the two officers approach the house slowly, as though marching to some silent cadence. They knocked on the front door, but no one moved until Matthew rose stiffly from his chair to usher them into the dinning room.

"Mr. Winston," one of the officers began, "I am Captain Lewis, and this is my driver, Sergeant Curtis. I have the unwelcome task of notifying you that your son has been reported missing in action." He hesitated to clear his throat, but his expression did not change nor did he appear affected by the horror-stricken gasps of the young woman slumping into her brother's arms. "However, I have been authorized to inform you that your son was alive when last seen, and there is a possibility that he was captured, so --"

"--he's a prisoner of war," Matthew finished the sentence. He turned and stumbled out of the room.

"But Mr. Winston," Captain Lewis called after him, "you should know that your son left the safety of his helicopter to aid a friend." The Captain spoke the words expectantly, but Matthew did not respond. They heard the office door slam closed, where he would most likely barricade himself the rest of the day.

Andrew was the only one who was able to speak. "Are you – or they – absolutely certain? Is anyone looking for him? How will we know if he's safe, if he's – you know, alive?"

Captain Lewis had well-rehearsed responses to their questions. This was not the first time he had been called upon to participate in these conversations. He explained the procedures in simple terms. "I would like to assure you that your family will receive regular communiqués from the Pentagon. This is the business card of the liaison officer. Feel free to call him at any time with any questions. You also need to know that you should expect delivery of Private Winston's trunk and personal items within the next few weeks." He spoke in subdued, even tones, being somewhat reassuring without being overly hopeful. "The Army," he said, sounding very official and military-like, "as well as the United States government, will do everything within their power to bring all pressures to bare to secure the safety of Private Winston." And then they left. It had all been said in less than ten minutes. The family sat at the table, numb and shocked, not knowing what to say or do. Only Annie seemed able to pour out her grief openly. Ginny opened her arms to her and held her as she wept.

"I believed him!" she sobbed. "He said he'd be fine, that I shouldn't worry!" Ginny said nothing, allowing the distraught girl to lay her head in her lap until Annie was calm enough to go upstairs, saying she had to check the baby. The rest of the family had wandered off to other parts of the house by that time, except Danny and Peter, who waited patiently for their time with Ginny. They drew near as soon as Annie left.

Later that night, as Ginny sat in her kitchen with her Bible, she worried about the boys. In the morning, she would call and tell them she needed help with something. She planned to keep them busy for a while, and then they would talk over milk and cookies. She knew they had questions, and she thanked God for putting her on this earth at this time in this place to comfort and reassure them as best she could.

* * * * * *

Margaret McDuffy returned to her dorm room after an early afternoon stroll. Unable to concentrate on her studying, she had gone for a walk along the river, feeling miserable and lonely for Luke and angry that time was passing so slowly. Her roommate, Cindy, acknowledged her entrance by scowling disapprovingly. "You look absolutely frozen!" she hissed. "I told you to take a hat and mittens!"

"Oh, I know," Margaret responded off-handedly. "It's really cold for April. Maybe it'll snow just one more time."

"McDuffy!" a voice broke into her melancholy. "You have a phone call! Long distance!"

Margaret was startled. Who could be calling her? Annie Winston had just called just two days ago and she spoke with her aunt this morning. She wouldn't call again unless there was kind of emergency. Margaret hurried to pick up the receiver.

"Margaret, this is your Aunt Betty." She started every phone call that way, as if Margaret could mistake her shrill, commanding voice for anyone else. "Annie Winston just called. They were having dinner and--"

"Yes, I know. Annie called and asked if I was coming home this weekend."

"Well, honey, listen." There was a long pause. "While they were having dinner, two officers – two Army officers—came to talk to Mr. Winston."

"Army officers? Came to see Luke's father? My God,

427

what did they want? What did they say? Is he dead?" She was screaming.

"Honey, he's not dead, or at least they don't think he is. He's listed as missing in action. They think maybe he was captured."

"MIA? Captured?" The awful words escaped her lips, wrenched from deep within her. She dropped the phone and ran to get her car keys.

Without a conscious plan, she turned her car onto Highway 1, heading north. The drive home takes two hours normally, but she nudged the execrator faster and faster, passing other vehicles recklessly at times. She stared straight ahead, not crying, no hysterics, just pressing homeward. She'd deal with all of this when she got home.

Betty McDuffy paced the kitchen floor. Cindy had come on the line after Margaret dropped it and said that her niece had rushed in for her keys and ran out without even bothering to take her coat. Cindy promised to call if she heard anything. Was she coming here, Mrs. McDuffy wondered. Her heart broke for her niece. Margaret worshiped that boy. He was the first one who ever paid any attention to her, and she was counting the days until he came back, sleeping with his picture under her pillow. Although it was true that Luke had done wonders for Margaret's self-confidence, Betty had cautioned her to "not put all her eggs in one basket". But Margaret never listened.

And now this. Yes, it was devastating, but Betty had a little speech prepared. She would tell Margaret not to give up hope, that she should go on with her life. The busier she was, the better she'd feel.

Betty didn't hear the car pull up, so she was startled when Margaret came busting through the door. She was shivering. The heater in the old Buick didn't work very well anymore. Margaret grabbed her heavy choring parka and slipped some boots over her shoes. Without saying a word, she turned and was gone. Betty stood at the window and watched her disappear into the woods.

There was still patches of snow in the dark shadows of the timber. Margaret drudged on, sometimes slipping on the steep inclines. Once she fell and slid several feet, but picked herself up

428

and kept going. Further down the trail, she fell again and scrapped her knee on a jagged rock camouflaged under a thin venire of snow. It hurt and it was then that angry tears began welling up in her eyes. She struggled on, sometimes crawling, sometimes running, pushing toward Luke's special place.

She pulled herself onto the familiar rocky perch. Wrapping her arms around herself, she began rocking back and forth, sobbing and calling his name. Her mind was flooded with the sound of his laughter and the words he used when he talked about this spot – his hopes, his dreams. "Please don't die. Please! Come home!" she screamed to the treetops. And she prayed to the God she had been taught to trust. "Please, God, give him the strength. and courage to endure whatever lay ahead.

The stone was cold and unrelenting, and she derived no comfort or hope in this place. She thought she would, so the emptiness that settled deep inside her was all the more frightening. But then, she felt something lightly touching her face. She looked up and saw showers of snowflakes dancing all around her. She stood up and held her arms out wide, lifting her face skyward and opening her mouth to taste the snow and be a part of it. The snow filled the hollow places in her heart, and she began to feel glimmers of hope. Oh, thank you, God, her heart sang. Thank you for reminding me to believe. Luke was all right, she knew it.

Dusk settled across the land, and the finality of it did not frighten her, but cemented her resolve. Her aunt would be worried, so she should go home. She lingered for a moment, whispering the words she had given to this place.

In short there's simply not
A more congenial spot
For happily ever aftering
Than here in Camelot

* * * * * *

429

Her aunt was dumbfounded when Margaret came back to the kitchen for her supper that night and announced calmly that she was going back to Iowa City. "I don't want to miss any classes," she said. There was no sign of the hysterics Mrs. Duffy expected.

Margaret drove back to Iowa City that night through the dark countryside accompanied by a few lingering snowflakes. She did not cry, but felt calm and confident, empowered by the covenant she had made with God that afternoon. She was determined to never tell anyone about the snow. Its meaning would be too difficult to explain. She wanted it to remain a secret to keep close to her heart to carry her through the long, hard months she was certain lay ahead.

Chapter 50

Difficult as it was to cope with this latest family crisis, it was amazing that time continued to grind on. The worst part of this was not knowing anything. Was Luke dead, was he hurt? What happens to POW's, and was it reasonable to hope that he might actually be all right and come home? The family felt like they were on a deserted island, guilt-ridden and miserable, cut off from the rest of the world.

They each seemed to have their own methods of dealing with their fears and anger. Their father became much more of a recluse, and said very little to anyone. Andrew stayed in town, studying, and the other boys each found solace in their own special places, but seldom with each other. It was Mack who seemed particularly despondent and inconsolable. Penny tried to comfort him, but he turned away to his own private hell. Many nights, he didn't even come to bed. He'd sit up, watching the news and doze off on the couch.

One morning Penny came wondering into the kitchen, and asked, "Did Mack have his breakfast yet?"

"No, I haven't seen him today," Annie replied curtly. "All I know is when I came downstairs this morning, the TV was still on, but he wasn't around. As usual, he's off on his own somewhere."

Penny understood the tone and in part agreed with it, but right now she was worried. Where could he be? She dressed and went outside. Matthew came walking across the yard, obviously upset about something.

"Where's that damn husband of yours?" he demanded. "He took my truck without saying a word. I gotta get into town!"

Now Penny was even more perplexed. She drove to school, but paid little attention during her classes. She was afraid for Mack, but angry, too. She stopped off at Andrew's apartment after class, wanting to vent her feelings to someone before she exploded. She had done this before when she and Mack were arguing or having some difficulty. She found Andrew to be a good listener and sympathetic friend.

Other members of the family began worrying when Mack did not return by the next morning. They called the Sheriff's office and area hospitals to see if there had been any accidents. Penny checked her family's cottage three or four times a day, thinking that he might have retreated there to spend some time alone, but there was no trace of him anywhere. Finally on the third day, Friday, there was a quick, cryptic phone call. Unfortunately, Penny wasn't at home to take the call.

John happened to answer the phone. "All he said was to tell Penny that he's fine and that he'd be back on Monday or Tuesday. He'd explain everything when he got home."

Penny was relieved, but her rage mounted with every passing day. She stayed home from school on Monday, pacing and looking out the front window every few minutes. Dusk fell across the land, and still no Mack. As the family sat down to supper, Annie thought about scolding Penny that she needed to eat because of her baby, but knew it would be useless so she said nothing. Three times, lights were seen coming down the road, but each time the car passed on by. Penny was nearly inconsolable. Andrew, who had come home that evening, tried to comfort and reassure her, but she refused to listen. She continued to pace in the foyer.

The little boys were sent to bed so that house grew even more quiet. Annie and Andrew sat at the dinning room table, slowly stirring cups of tea. Matthew was in his office. Even Sonny sat in the kitchen, waiting. 9 o'clock, 10 o'clock. No Mack.

Then, shortly before midnight, the truck pulled into the driveway. Penny said nothing, but everyone knew Mack was back by the way she threw the door open and ran outside. Rather than blasting him with the severe tongue-lashing everyone expected, she ran into his arms crying.

"Oh, honey, I'm so sorry," he repeated over and over. He half carried her back to the house. They all went into the living room and gathered around the warm fire.

Matthew was the first to speak. "Where were you?" he demanded, his voice strained and cracked. "You had us half worried to death!"

Mack hesitated before he answered. He was haggard-looking, dirty and unshaven, and appeared to be wearing the same clothes he wore when he left nearly a week ago.

"I'm sorry, Pop" he said. "I went to Washington, DC."

"What? Why?" they all chorused.

"I was watching the news, not really paying much attention as usual, when I noticed they were talking about some rally going on in DC and--"

"So? There's always some rally out there?" Andrew cried.

"Yeah, I know, but this one was different. That's what caught my attention because it was a gathering of Vietnam Vets. See, there's this organization – called the V.V.A.W. It's the Vietnam Vets Against War. A few Vets organized it and it's caught on like wildfire. I guess in February they held these meetings, or hearings, in Detroit. They called them the "Winter Soldier Investigations". They were hoping to get some publicity and tell people what really is happening over there. But nobody paid much attention. I mean, I didn't hear about it, did you? So they put together this rally in Washington, DC. It started a week ago Saturday, but the press didn't cover it at first. But it got bigger and bigger, and I heard about it on the news, like I said. I thought maybe these guys could help us, so I got in the truck and drove over there."

"Help us? Help us how?" Andrew retorted, anger still

dripping from his voice. "What did you think, that one of them would know where Luke was or what happened to him? That's the most ludicrous thing I've ever heard."

"No, I just had so many questions. We all do, don't we? Haven't you wondered what it was really like over there? The goddamn Army hasn't told us anything. These guys were there! They just want people to pay attention to what they have to say, and I wanted to listen. No government bullshit or stupid propaganda – the truth!" He paused then and searched each somber face around him. It occurred to him that the other members of his family might not share his quest for realities. But no one argued so he continued.

"I wasn't sure what I was going to do once I got there, but as it turned out, it was easy. All I had to do was go to the Mall by the Capital Building, and there they were, hundreds of them, and more coming every day. They weren't violent or militant, they just wanted to get their point across. The police didn't hassle us, but they announced over loud speakers that it was against the law for them to camp overnight, and we should leave. But we didn't. No one was sleeping anyway. Well, some dozed off after awhile, but mostly, people just sat around and talked. I found guys that were on helicopter crews like Luke, one of them was from Iowa, too. They hated it over there – they all did."

"But what do they think happened to Luke?" Annie pressed.

"They said they heard from guys that were still over there that the whole campaign was a mess. The South Vietnamese got their asses whipped! Our chopper crews were supposed to be there only for support and transport, but they were constantly caught in the middle, and a lot of them went down. I heard that by the time this thing was nearly over, when a helicopter landed in a hot spot in Laos, they were overran with ARVN soldiers wanting to get out of there. They'd hang on the runners, and then the helicopters were so heavy that they couldn't clear the trees, so those men were cut to shreds." He hated being so graphic, but he felt they needed to know. As distasteful as this was, these were the kinds of things their brother had seen on a daily basis.

"But Mack, what did they say about the chances of Luke

being alive?" Matthew demanded.

"They said it could have gone down a lot of different ways. The area was overran by the enemy and it's impossible to hide from those devils, so he probably was taken prisoner. What did they did to him depends on whether Luke was severely wounded or not." He studied his sister's face before he proceeded. Better she would know the truth, he decided. "See, the Viet Cong are on the move all the time. If he was hurt so seriously that he couldn't keep up, they'd, well, they'd..." His voice trailed off then, knowing that they were not ready to hear that the bastards would have shot Luke on the spot. "If not, well, they take their prisoners with them. There's been reports of jungle camps with POW's. Some of them eventually get handed over to higher authorities and end up in prisons in Hanoi. There's four or five hundred Americans in those places already – most of them are Naval and Air Force. They don't know too much about these places, only rumors. There's been a few guys released when the North Vietnamese want to make a show of good faith. But the government doesn't release details because they don't want to make it worse for the guys who are still there." He could have told them the stories he heard about the torture and unimaginable, filthy living conditions, but he didn't. There was no reason for them to know any of that.

"The best thing that could happen for us is his name will appear on one of those lists that Hanoi releases from time to time. Then we'll know for sure, and when there is a POW exchange at the end of the war, he'll come home. Of course, that doesn't mean that it couldn't still happen even if his name isn't listed. It's just a little more likely, that's all."

"These guys sat there and answered every question I had. They were incredible, really. And you know what else? They took me along to meetings with Senators and Congressmen. I met Harold Hughes. He's the Senator from Iowa. He was very sympathetic. He wants this war to be over, too. There was this guy, Lt. John Kerry. He was their main spokesman. He made the most tremendous speech before the Senate Foreign Relations Committee. I was there. He said this war is wrong! It has to be stopped! There were men dying over there for nothing. Their group, this VVAW, is going to keep up pressure, but they want to work within the system to stop this thing."

"And then on Friday, the most incredible thing happened. The Police heard that they were going to try to get in to see the Supreme Court to ask them to declare this war illegal. But there were barricades across the steps with armed police. The Vets stopped and while some of the leaders were trying to decide what they should do, all of a sudden, out of the crowd, came a medal. Someone threw it onto the steps. Then there was another and another. Purple Hearts, combat ribbons, everything. There was even some World War II vets and guys from Korea. One by one, they came to the barricade and threw over their stuff. It was so quiet, all you could hear was those medals hitting the cement stairs. Then they'd turn and walk away. It was like they were going up to the Communion rail at Mass."

"The grand finale was a big march yesterday. 200,000 people marched down Pennsylvania Avenue. It was orderly and calm, but we carried a message – this damn war has to end! Nixon cannot be so stupid as to think that Hanoi is going to hand over any of their POW's until we get the hell out of there."

"But what about Luke?" Annie asked, nearly whispering.

"It means we're not alone. There's a lot of people, some very powerful people, who are working hard to end this war so Luke can come home. I got the name of this group called the Committee of Liaison With Families of Servicemen Detained in North Vietnam. They gave me all kinds of information. For instance, Annie, you should keep writing Luke. They say it helps the family and sometimes, letters and packages get through. And they have lobbyists in Washington and contacts at the Pentagon. I guess they have ways of finding out information that the government won't tell us. There's a woman right here in Iowa who will be our contact person. I gave her our address and phone number. We have a right to know, don't you think?"

He looked long and hard into his wife's face before he continued. God, she was beautiful, even now as she gazed at him with tired, weary eyes. He wondered if she fully understood the amazing transformation he had undergone during these past tumultuous days. Out of the chaos and uncertainty, he had found his soul. This newfound sense of purpose that filled him with passion and strength, displacing years of apathy and lethargy, was sure to cost them, and he wanted her to understand. He chose his next few words very carefully.

"The most important thing I learned," he said, "is that there are things people like us can do. We do not have to sit by helplessly. I have lists of people that I am going to write and call on the phone. I'll make more trips back to Washington. I will be in their faces morning, noon, and night. I will never let them forget the name of Luke Gregory Winston."

* * * * * *

Annie sat at her little desk in her room. It was very late, and the house was quiet. She pulled the afghan Sonny had given her around her shoulders. And just as she had dozens of other times, she took out a pen and paper and began to write.

Tuesday, April 26th, 1971

Dear Luke,

How are you? I have no idea if you will get this letter, but I shall write it and mail it anyway.

At long last, the weather is warmer. The long, hard winter is over. It rained yesterday, so no one could work in the fields again today. The river is behaving herself for now, but everyone expects we'll have some flooding this year. Two years in a row with no floods is unlikely. Yesterday, when the boys got off the bus, wading through the mud, they looked up and saw an especially beautiful rainbow. Danny came running to the house to take me outside so I could look at it. The colors were so clear, I wanted to reach out and touch it.

The family is fine although very worried about you. We pray every day for your safe return. I believe He is watching over you. There must be a God, because He gave us this family, this land, and that rainbow. I love you,

Annie

Chapter 51

As promised, Luke's trunk was delivered three weeks later. It sat in the corner of the foyer for days without anyone opening it or talking about it. But then, Margaret came by one quiet morning when she knew Annie would be alone and asked to see it. Together, she and Annie unlocked it and began looking through Luke's personal things. They both felt uncomfortable as though they were invading his privacy, but they pressed on, hoping this would help them to somehow feel closer to him. There was three, neatly organized bundles of letters. One large pile, tied in a red ribbon, were from Annie and another with letters from Margaret, bound in blue. The third was a miscellaneous group with letters from his brothers, several from Ginny, and even some from Father Fritz. There was even an unfinished letter in his tablet, but neither were strong enough at that moment to read it.

It was obvious that Luke had done quite a lot of sketching. They flipped through the pages of several pads – drawings of home, the places he missed the most. There were some scenes of Nam, such as sunny, tranquil meadows with grass hut villages and children playing. But there were also vivid sketches of crashed helicopters and fiery hilltops, men lying on the ground bleeding, their mouths open wide as though they were screaming. Horrified, Annie and Margaret looked at them, realizing the contempt and fear he must have felt when he drew them.

Margaret's cheeks pinked a little when they uncovered 8" x 10" of the two of them in New Orleans. If Annie noticed the strange surroundings, she said nothing. There were other pictures, too, of the family mostly, with his Bible, a prayer book, and empty Rosary case. Annie was surprised to find books on log cabin building and general carpentry, even some wood-working magazines. "He's going to build a log cabin down in his favorite place in the woods," Margaret explained. And in the bottom of the trunk, wrapped very carefully, was a small snowball. Margaret shook it slowly, staring at the tiny white flakes cascading down upon the miniature house barn.

"I gave this to him at Christmas," she whispered. "He always loved the snow." Annie closed the lid sharply. There were tears streaming down her face as she turned away. When she could speak, she said, "Look, I think you should have this – I mean, take care of it until Luke gets home. I don't want to divide it up or anything. I think we should leave it just like this for him, okay?"

"But Annie, what about your father?"

"He'll never look in there. It's been sitting here for days and no one's even touched it. I thought I'd have the boys take it upstairs to the attic, but now I think you should have it. Please, take it, and take good care of it. Really."

They carried it out to Margaret's car. "I guess I'm not handling this very well," Annie said. "Neither is anyone else. We're all stumbling around, scared and miserable, but no one's talking about it much. And I just cry all the time, which probably doesn't help much," she sighed, drying her eyes on her apron. "How about you? How are you doing?"

Margaret hesitated before she answered. "At first, I didn't believe it – I mean, how could God let this happen to him? But then, I remembered how determined he is to come home. I just know somehow he'll get through this." She smiled and accepted a warm, sisterly hug from Annie.

It was a good idea for Margaret to take the trunk, Annie thought as she walked back to the house. She's the only one strong enough to handle it.

"I gave it to Margaret," Annie announced at supper that night. "The trunk – Luke's trunk." They received this bit of new the same as everything else, silently and sullenly, so Annie went on. "None of you seemed interested in opening it, so we did, together this afternoon. She seemed to handle it a lot better than I did, so I told her just to take it."

They all stared down at their plates awkwardly. They knew what she meant; Annie had cried and Margaret hadn't.

John was the only one to speak. "Well, what was in it?" he asked.

Annie got up and cleared away some dishes. "Just some letters and pictures, of us mostly. He did a lot of drawing – there's several sketchpads. And a pile of magazines about woodworking and house building. I guess he wants to build a log

438

cabin when he gets back home. Margaret says he has a spot picked out. He's taken her there several times. I guess they're quite close – I mean, he never told any of us that stuff." She felt compelled to validate her decision. "Anyway, I did it – guess it was sorta spur of the moment." No one objected, so she went back to the sink to finish the dishes.

Mack headed toward the door, glancing over his shoulder at his wife as he took his coat. Recognizing her expression of apprehension and alarm, he looked away. God, he thought, I hate doing this to her. This should be one of the happiest times of their lives. She could be one of those glowing, pampered mothers-to-be, not worried and haggard like she looked tonight. He wanted to reach out and hold her, reassure her that everything was going to be all right. And talk to her – if only he could explain it, make her understand. He had tried, but didn't have the words.

But then she stood up and reached for her own coat. "I need some fresh air myself," she said. "Can I keep you company?" He smiled and took her hand, leading her out the door.

The others scattered, too, so Matthew found himself sitting alone. The meal had been shortened by Annie's abrupt announcement. Annie watched him as she moved around the room, wondering if he would say anything. He looked so much older than he did a couple of years ago. She remembered how handsome he looked the day of her and Andrew's high school graduation. She still had the picture on her dresser – Mama and Pop posing with them, smiling that proud way parents always do on such occasions. She sighed and went back to her dishes, wondering if it would ever be like that again.

* * * * * *

It was unusually warm for May. There wasn't a cloud in the sky, so Annie decided to hang out the wash. The sun felt warm and comforting on her face as she worked, pinning dozens of sheets, shirts, and jeans on the clothesline Sonny had strung for her across the front yard. As though an answer to her prayers, spring had brought renewed hope and resilience, and a small

439

glimmer of optimism.

Becky frolicked nearby, being entertained by a baby kitten. She giggled when the long shafts of grass tickled her nose. Annie squatted beside her for quick hugs and kisses. The baby was so beautiful. Mother would be so proud.

She went back to work, pausing from time to time to glance at her rows of tulips and daffodils blooming by the house. She was thrilled that they actually came up after the particularly hard winter. She smiled as she remembered how Sonny teased her for her impatience, but then came bolting into the kitchen to tell her the first sprouts had appeared.

The mailman stopped at her box. She missed that rush of excitement she used to feel when he came by. There were no more letters coming from her brother now, only an occasional so-called "update" from the Army, which were actually pieces of worthless propaganda with no substantive information. True to his word, Mack was able to procure more facts than would have otherwise been available to them. He poured himself into the enterprise with such intense drive and persistence that it was difficult not to get swept up by his enthusiasm. He strung extensions for the phone and electrical cords up to one of the small rooms on the third floor. He typed dozens of letters and made numerous phone calls all over the country. Penny seemed to tolerate his crusading well, pleased that he had immersed himself in this worthwhile endeavor which snapped him out of his earlier destructive depression.

It was her father who seemed to be still languishing in the isoltion of his own grief and misery. She was afraid he was unable, or perhaps unwilling, to deal with things. Certainly, there was the uncertainty regarding his third son, but she sensed there was more to it than that. Sometimes she would notice the strangest expression cross her father's face – a look of such confusion and pain, like a small child who cannot understand the harsh complexities in the world around them. World War II vets discarding their medals and ribbons, the massacre of innocent civilians, combat units fighting more among themselves more than against the enemy. These things were incomprehensible to him, and certainly did not fit the neatly packaged ideals by which he had lived his life all these years. Annie understood his anguish, but she still resented it. He had behaved this way after Mother died, when his family needed strength and guidance from him, not isolation and drunkenness.

Annie didn't notice the long, black sedan pulling into the driveway until a loud, persistent honk invaded her serenity. It seemed the car sank in the low spot of the driveway, and its occupants were not all happy about the situation. Annie yelled at Danny and Peter to get the men. Annie chuckled a little at the high-pitched wails of strong indignation disseminating from the stranded vehicle. She guessed they were merely lost and were coming to ask directions. But then, from somewhere in the deep recesses of her mind, a thought surfaced that there was something recognizable about this particular screaming. Oh no, she moaned, it can't be.

But then came the horrifying conclusive shriek. " Ann Marie Elizabeth Winston! Come here this instant!" The words pierced the air like a sword thrust through the heart. It was unmistakably, undeniably, Aunt Esther.

Just then Matthew appeared and he heard it, too. "Oh, my God," he muttered as he waded through the mud toward the sunken sedan. Scarcely believing his eyes and ears, he peered inside, pressing his face and palms against the window. He must have looked like a lunatic – dirty, sweaty, and unshaven. The two elderly ladies, speechless and shaken, clung to each other in the back seat of their sunken ship.

But it was only a momentary lapse, as Esther was not one to scare easily. She looked more closely at the distorted face in the window. "Matthew, is that you? Well, for heaven's sake, don't just stand there. Get us out of here! Now!"

"Esther, Gert? What the hell—Just stay there. We'll get your car out in a few minutes, unless you'd like to climb out of there, and walk in this mud. Annie!" he called. "It's your aunts, Esther and Gertrude. You'd better put some water on for tea."

The car was pulled safely to the top of the hill, and Matthew swung open the door, inviting his two rather portly sisters to disembark. Totally disgusted, Esther hesitated but then proceeded to walk through the mud toward the house in their

$300 Italian shoes.

"You know, of course, this is a rental car," she sputtered. "You know they'll make us pay for any damages. What a God forsaken place! You live here? Thank goodness, mother and father are not alive to see this."

Matthew took his two sisters in the back way, inviting them to clean up a bit at the back sink. Annie was already panicking in the kitchen. She had been working outside all day, so there were piles of dirty dishes, soiled clothes heaped in the corner, and mud tracked across the floor. All of this did not pass without comment from her Aunt Esther.

"Matthew!" she shrieked. "What kind of help do you have here? I've never seen a house in such deplorable state!"

"Huh, humm." Matthew cleared his throat. "Well, you see, we don't have any hired help. It simply isn't done that way out here. We do the work ourselves." Aunt Esther appeared close to fainting. "Annie, why don't you get your aunts something cool to drink."

"Oh, yes," crowed Aunt Gertrude, "a glass of cold water would be lovely." Without thinking, Annie quickly got two glasses of water from the faucet. That was a terrible mistake. As soon as the two women peered down into their glasses and saw the filmy, clay-colored water, they began shrieking at the tops of their lungs.

"Now, now, Esther, Gertrude. Calm down. No, it is not poison. It's well water, which contains a lot of iron and minerals. Actually, it's very good for you. Why don't you two ladies come into our living room."

Of course, as luck would have it, the pitted and unsightly dinning room table was not hidden beneath a cloth, but covered by Peter's latest science project. Nobody understood it, but it smelled awful. The aunts said nothing, but the look of disgust on their faces was telling enough. Much to everyone's relief, the living room was fairly presentable.

Aunt Esther was, as usual, not at a loss for words. "Matthew," she started, "I cannot tell you how upset we were to hear about – oh, what is that boy's name – the one who likes to draw all the time. I was over at your house the other day, and your servants were in an absolute tizzy. I mean, that old Nanny was blubbering like she had lost her best friend. Good heavens, Luke is a soldier and missing? Well, I assured her there must be some mistake!"

"No, Esther, it's true," Matthew said. "I called them last week after we were notified. They've known him all his life, so I knew they'd want to know."

"Well!" she shrieked. "That dear boy is our flesh and blood. When were you going to tell us? And how could you let this happen anyway? Eunice Iverson's grandson was supposed to go, but she called Judge – oh, what's is that man's name. Anyway, it's done all the time, that is, in the civilized world." She glanced around the room disapprovingly. "Lord only knows how one manages such things here."

"But, Esther." Matthew's teeth were clinched and chin quivered as he struggled mightily to control his temper. "Luke made it perfectly clear that this is what he wanted to do, and I didn't want to interfere. You know how I feel about such things."

"Oh, yes I certainly do! It broke Father's heart when you ran off like that! He said--"

Just then the front door flung open, and in stomped Mack and Penny. Both appeared red-faced and angry.

"Listen, you egotistical, arrogant, selfish sonofabitch!" Penny fired furiously. "Since when do you tell me what I may or may not do. I'm a big girl now and--"

"Yeah, you sure are! You're as big as a house with my kid!" Mack retorted. Just then he turned to see there were guests. "Aunt Esther!" he exclaimed.

"Junior?" Esther blurted, equally dumbfounded. She was staring at Penny, scanning the young woman's profile.

Matthew interceded, saying, "Ladies, this is my daughter-in-law, Penelope. Penny, these are two of my sisters, Esther and Gertrude, unexpected visitors from back East."

"I had no idea there is to be an addition to the family," Esther whined. "But then, it seems we're learning a great deal on this little impromptu visit."

Matthew was just about to retort something snide, but he was interrupted by Danny and Peter running into the room, juggling little Joey between them. "Annie! Annie!" they cried.

"Joey's nose is bleeding again!" Peter wailed.

"But it ain't our fault!" Danny added. "We didn't do nothing to 'im! It just started gushin' again!"

"I know! I know! Hush now," Annie hissed, gathering the little boy in her arms and trying to quiet his excited cries. She started to usher the three boys out, but Aunt Esther's shrill clamor stopped her in her tracks.

"My God! Look at that poor pathetic child! He's covered with blood!" she cried. "Matthew, shouldn't you call for help? They do have ambulances out here, don't they?"

"This is no emergency," Penny said in her best, professional voice, throwing off her coat so that the visitors could see her uniform. "He hasn't lost much blood, and it's happened before. We know how to handle it."

Penny meant to sound reassuring, but of course, it backfired. "This has happened before?" Esther cried. "Has he seen a specialist?"

"Esther!" Matthew bellowed. "This is not the wilderness! There are good doctors here. I know it's not New York City, but if I wanted to live there, I would have stayed, right?"

"Well, then, why did you leave? You turned your back on everything you've ever known – your family, your job, your responsibilities!" Esther was pacing now, huffing and pulling like a volcano. "I'm glad I came out here to see this for myself, because I never would have believed it. I thought it would be distressing, but this is much, much worse than I expected. But what I cannot possibly comprehend is how you, in good conscious, can subject these poor, defenseless children to such an unhealthy, deplorable place? You obviously have no regard for their safety or well-being."

"What the hell do you care about my kids? You never did before. For Christ's sake, you can't even remember their names!"

"I am shocked! How dare you raise your voice and shout obscenities in our presence. Have you lost all sense of decorum? Of course, I have always cared about your beautiful children. We have all been sick with worry about them since you disappeared after the passing of your dear wife."

"Oh, bullshit! You never approved of my marriage to Kathleen. Didn't you think we knew that? But it didn't matter to us, and it doesn't matter what you think of our new home. We're doing very nicely thank you, and besides, it's none of your damned busines."

"Oh, isn't it? You can shout your vulgarities all you want, but I know the truth. If things are going so well, why are you constantly needing more money? You've sunk a fortune into this dump. And what's more, your children probably don't even know that you're sacrificing their birthright for—for this!" She finished with a grand flourish of smug self-righteousness.

"Esther!" Matthew hissed with a warning glare.

"Oh, yes" She turned to address her nieces and nephews. "You probably have no idea that your father has been taking large amounts of money from your trust funds – money that was set aside by your grandfather to assure all of you the security and comfort you deserve! And what's more, I have copies of several checks written on the company accounts – a business to which you have contributed nothing for months!"

"I have done nothing illegal," Matthew countered, red-faced and indignant.

"No? Well, perhaps we should just see about that. I think its only fair to tell you that we have consulted an attorney."

"About what?"

"To end your association with our family, most especially the business – make sure you can't get your hands on any more of our money – that is, the company's money. If you're so determined to separate yourself from us, then I, er—we, feel it should be a total severance – financially and otherwise."

"Oh, you'd love that, wouldn't you, Esther. At long last, you could run the whole damn thing. Fine! Take it, it's yours. Give me the papers. I'll sign them! Just get the hell out of our home!"

"Oh, Matthew, I only want what's best for us all! This is breaking my heart. I think you've gone quite mad." she cried. She opened her purse, dug out a silk hanky and wiped her tearless eyes. "I am sorry to have to say this but I really believe it's necessary to intercede in behalf of your children. I think I should sue for custody of your minor children."

A loud, audible gasp echoed across the room. This was unbelievably brazen, even for Aunt Esther. All eyes were on Matthew, waiting for his response. He appeared shocked and speechless, so Mack stepped forward quickly. "Aunt Esther, perhaps you mean well, but--"

"My dear boy," his aunt interrupted, sounding condescending. "One can only imagine the horror you have endured since your father dragged you out here. But don't you worry. There's nothing a good lawyer can't handle." She stared pointedly at Penny as she spoke. "Do not despair, my dears. I will attend to this situation with the utmost haste. Come Gertrude, we should be going. I cannot leave this vile place fast enough!" She picked up her purse and gloves, and then marched across the room to stand in front of her brother. "Matthew, do not make the mistake of taking me lightly. These are no idle threats. You'd better get a lawyer – a good one." She turned to walk out, with Gertrude close behind.

The driver, caked with mud up to his knees, was just unhooking the chain with which Sonny had pulled him out of the mud. Esther started barking orders at him the moment she stepped onto the porch. "For heaven's sake, don't just stand there. How do you hope to get us away from this despicable place without some kind of assistance? Obviously, we'll have to be pulled. Look at that awful mud all over the car! The rental agency will probably charge us extra! Gertrude, could you please hurry!"

The ladies climbed into their muddied auto, Esther still shouting orders. "For heaven's sake, step on it! Don't you know how to drive?"

446

Chapter 52

Annie told the little boys to go play outside. Matthew stood speechless in the living room until he stirred and turned to retreat to his office, but Mack blocked his path. "Where in the hell do you think you're going?" he demanded. "Don't you think we deserve some kind of explanation?"

Matthew met his gaze for a moment, and then stepped around him and walked away. Mack motioned for them to follow as they all filed into his office behind him, surrounding their father with sullen faces.

"Well?" Matthew cried, "you must have known I was spending a hellvalot of money. Jesus, I had to pay nearly a quarter million dollars just in back taxes alone! And then there was the upkeep, taxes, and salaries for the house back East. C'mon, where did you think I was getting all that money?" But his children's faces were not softening, so he continued. "My personal account of ready cash went dry last fall – Yeah, that's right, last fall! Most of my money is invested in the company and not easy to access. So I wrote some checks on the business account, but then Aberrantly said that the office was giving him grief about it, so I didn't want to do that anymore. I am sure that this place can eventually support this family, but in the mean time, we needed more money! So I started drawing money out of the trust funds. As executor I am legally able to do that. And besides, I thought once this place started making money, I'd pay the money back and no one would be the wiser." His voice sounded strained and desperate. "Don't you see? The survival of this place is important to all of us."

His children stood speechless, until Mack, always the most volatile, exploded. "My God, I can't believe you did this! How could you be so stupid? Didn't you realize you'd get caught? They're gonna say you're insane, and maybe they're right!"

"Mack!" Annie cried. "Screaming isn't going to help. We're just surprised, Pop. You should have told us."

"I don't understand," Andrew said, looking perplexed and fearful. "Are we broke? What about school?"

"For Christ sake, Andrew," Mack admonished him. "Is

that all you ever care about? Your precious, goddamn school? What about this--"

"No, that's all right, Andrew," Matthew broke in. "I never touched any of your accounts, just the six younger ones."

"You sure took a lot for granted," blasted Mack. "We could have gone bust out here. Where would we go, what would we do? What were--"

"Oh stop it!" Annie screamed, putting her hands over her ears. "Who cares about the damn money! Didn't you hear what Aunt Esther said? She wants to take the kids!" Close to tears, she ran out of the room.

Her father went to the door and called after her. "Don't you worry, honey. I would never allow that to happen – never! I can take care of my sisters!" He was trying to sound resolute, but he was trembling and running his fingers through his hair. He opened another beer without realizing that he had hardly touched the first one. He slumped down into his chair.

"Ah, come on," Mack said. "Let's get the hell out of here!"

"Yeah, sure," Matthew agreed, clearing his throat and sitting erect in his chair. "Why don't you fellas get the chores started. I think I'll try getting in touch with Abernathy and clue him in on my sister's latest scheme. He can out-maneuver any legal beagles she can hire." He sounded upbeat and cheerful, but no one was listening.

Matthew never came out of his office all afternoon. Annie heard him arguing with someone on the phone. She went upstairs so she wouldn't have to listen. She rocked the baby and read her a story, trying to distract herself from the fear and anger burning in her stomach. Her thoughts kept returning her to her father. For the first time in her life, she couldn't trust him to be in control of things. She put Becky to bed and went outside to weed her flowers, but the happy, carefree enthusiasm of spring had evaporated.

By supper time, Matthew was passed out on the couch in his office, which was probably best for everyone. No one wanted any more scenes. Annie was very short-tempered with the boys, irritated by their whining and fighting. She sent them all to their rooms early that night. Mack took Penny, who looked ill and exhausted, for a long drive, and Andrew sulked away, too. Thankfully, Annie found herself alone as she worked quietly in the kitchen.

She lingered as long as possible, listening for familiar footsteps as she cleaned. Sonny hadn't come in for supper, so she knew he'd stop by later. She was anxious to hear his thoughts about the day's events so she sat down at the table to wait for him

"Oh, Sonny," she cried when she saw him at the back door. "I put a plate in the oven for you. I can heat it up if you want." He said nothing as he took the plate of cold food and sat down at the table.

After several bites, he said evenly, "Well, the old man got himself in some hot water, didn't he."

"Yeah, he sure did," she mused, relaxing when she saw that he was willing to talk. "He was on the phone all afternoon with his hotshot lawyer, but it didn't sound like it went very well."

"So, what does Andrew and Mack think?"

"Mack was mad as hell, as usual, and Andrew took his normal, quiet, wait-and-see approach. Guess they're pretty worried."

"About the money?"

"Well, yeah, that's part of it. I mean, we've never had to think about it before. And we have no idea how bad it is because Daddy isn't saying much, which just makes it worse."

"Yeah, well, the way you folks are used to living – I guess I'd worry, too. Man, I never saw anyone go through money like that. Christ! I tried telling him to take it a little easy."

Annie smiled inwardly, remembering how convinced they were that Sonny would try to steal them blind. "I guess that's why I'm so mad!" she said. "He should have budgeted the money better and not get Aunt Esther so upset. She can be so mean sometimes. Should have seen her when she came walking into this house. She's not kidding when she say's she'll take him to court."

"C'mon, Annie, they can't split up a family, take away a man's children, without more proof than a lot of baloney from some shriveled up old biddy."

Annie giggled as that was the best description of her Aunt

Esther she had ever heard. "Well, just think about it. If you heard about some fifty year old man from a wealthy family who suddenly uprooted his family of ten children to live in some broken down place like this – what would you think?"

Sonny was smiling, too. "Well, maybe the idea is a little crazy, but not the man." He got up and immediately reached for his coat. Annie's heart sank, disappointed that he was leaving. But instead, he turned to her, still smiling. "I'm gonna go out and have my last cigarette. It's a real pretty night. Why don't you come out. It might clear your head." It was the invitation Annie had wanted for months. She hoped she didn't jump up too quickly.

He led the way to the rocky place. There was moonlight, but they could have found their way in total darkness. Annie sat down on one of the large tree trunks while Sonny lounged nearby. There were faint whiffs of smoke from his cigarette. He gazed out at the valley, bathed in silvery moonlight.

"I can understand it, though," he said. "People leave money to their children, and mostly they just piss it away. But if you have land -- land like this -- well, this is something you can fight for."

The words were simple. Annie embraced them as though they were her lifeline, and she loved him even more for having said them. He had done this before – other late night talks when he reminded her she could affect changes in her life, sometimes scolding her for acting like the perpetual victim. Quick tears glistened in her eyes, not because of sadness but because of the utter relief that comes from empowerment.

Annie searched for something more to say so he wouldn't leave. She trembled as the branches danced in the cool breeze overhead. She was reminded of the story Mrs. McDuffy had told about this place. "Do you believe in spirits? I mean, do you believe that poor Indian haunts this land?"

He inhaled deeply on his cigarette before he answered. "I don't know. Doesn't really matter, does it?"

"Well, it sort of makes me feel like we're trespassing, like none of this really belongs to us. We're just borrowing it for a while, that's all." Sonny said nothing so she continued. "After all, wasn't he just trying to do the same thing as my father? Wanting to give this land to generations of his own people?"

"This place belongs to your father, and that's all that's important," Sonny said. It was obvious that he was not given to sentimentality about the people who walked this land before.

They talked about other things – the upcoming growing season, Joey's progress in school, all the work that needed to be done. Later they each went their own way into the darkness, but for Annie, the night wasn't nearly as black as it was before.

Sunday, May 17, 197

Dear Luke,

You'll never guess who showed up on our doorstep – Aunt Esther and Aunt Gert. Yes, honest to God. Talk about a shock. As luck would have it, the house was even messier than usual and of course, they were appalled. We probably shouldn't have kept it a secret in the first place.

Spring is everywhere. I love this time of year. My garden is over half planted and will be better than ever. Dad and the others have most of the planting done on the hill, but the bottom is still too wet so they can't work down there yet. Pop is crabby. There's nothing he'd rather do than to be down

there planting. Sonny and Mack are ready, too, but Mack has other things on his mind. Penny's going to have that baby in just a few more weeks, and they're both very anxious. We all are!

Luke, I keep writing these letters, praying that somehow you'll get them – just one even. Have faith and hope. This will be over one day, and you will come home to us. We all love you very much, and think of you constantly.

Love,
Annie

CHAPTER 53

Penny's last day of class was that next Wednesday. Graduation was on Friday night, six weeks before her due date. Mack drove into town to pick her up, wondering if she might want to celebrate with a nice dinner in town., but she slumped into the seat wearily. She had done it – finished it! She had taken most of her finals standing up because she could not tolerate sitting down for very long. On this, her last day of clinical's, she had been mercifully assigned to cleaning and stocking the shelves in the med room, probably because her pinched, fatigued expression was not exactly what sick patients needed to see.

She was aware of the hoopla and merry-making going on around her as she closed the car door. The trees were draped with toilet paper streamers and the other seniors were dancing and laughing, popping Champaign bottles and following the tradition of tearing their student uniforms to shreds – at least as much as was deemed decent by the watchful nuns and school administrators.

She sank into the seat of Annie's car, which was the only one in which she still fit, and said, "Oh, God, I am so glad that's over. I didn't think I'd make it. Oh honey, just take me home, okay? And don't scold me. I know you said I should just stay home today."

Actually, he was proud of his wife, fat ankles and all. He admired her tenacity, and resolved to pamper and spoil her thoroughly from now on. He had been dwelling on all the negative circumstances of their lives for so long that he was glad to focus on his wife and unborn child. He was just so anxious for the baby to be born. He longed to hold it in his arms and know that everything was fine. And he wanted Penny to be her old self again.

Friday evening, Penny dressed for the graduation and stared at herself in the mirror. Her nurse's maternity uniform wasn't stylish or pretty like the ones the other girls were wearing. She quickly reminded herself that she got herself into this predicament, so she'd better just shut up and make the best of it. Mack gallantly knelled on one knee to put on her new, white shoes, since she had lost sight of her feet several weeks ago. As they descended the stairs toward the throng of well-wishers who would accompany them to the ceremony, someone playfully hummed, *Here she comes, Miss America.* Penny identified the culprit as John, whom she gave a kidding jab. She knew this should be one of the happiest nights of her life, but she just wanted to get it over.

Dr. and Mrs. Lamp met them on the stairs outside the church. Her father was beaming with pride, but her mother looked totally aghast. At least her daughter would be graduating as a "Winston", which was important, considering her obvious delicate condition.

The graduates marched in alphabetically and settled in their pews for the long, arduous ceremony. Soon after she sat down, Penny became nauseated. Well into the commencement speech delivered by a well known proctologist, she began noticing that the cramping sensation was occurring intermittently. She rested her hand on her belly and felt a spasm. Could these be contractions? That's impossible, she thought. She had six, maybe seven, more weeks to go. She tried to put such a preposterous notion out of her head, but soon it became apparent she was definitely in labor. She did not want to disrupt the service. She could imagine her mother's face if she stood up and ran out of the church. No, she could handle this for a little while longer. She concentrated on the breathing, trying to be as inconspicuous as possible. But gradually, the others around her became aware of what was happening, and word was passed down the rows of her classmates.

They reached the end of the service when the names were to be called and each graduate would receive their class pen and diploma. And as luck would have it, "Winston" was near the end. At last, it was her row's turn to stand and take their position by the podium. Penny thought it would help to stand up, but then, as she waited, she began to feel warm and dizzy, and there was a trickle of dampness between her legs. Oh God, she prayed, no gushers.

Her fellow graduates noticed the look of sheer panic on her face, and word was sent down the line. One by one they nudged

453

each other to hurry. They began walking so fast that Sr. Agatha barely had time to read the names. She cast a quick reproachful glare toward the young ladies, as if to say, "This in NOT the way we practiced it!" Finally she read, "Mrs. Penelope Lamp Winston". Penny waddled up the stairs, pressing her thighs close together and hoping desperately that she wasn't leaving a trail of amniotic fluid behind her. She grabbed her diploma and school pen and waved off the rose and kiss she was supposed to get from the class sponsor. She turned and began running down the center aisle, frantically searching for Mack's face in the crowd. He leaped from his seat, stopping on several toes as he headed down a long row of shocked spectators. Clasping hands, they fled together, hardly noticing the applause that crescendoed into a hearty cheer, probably more for the young couple running out of the door than the other members of the class of '71 they left in their wake.

Mack tried to remain calm, but his heart was pounding in his throat. He wanted to say something reassuring as he helped his wife into the car, but he was nearly paralyzed with fear. It was too soon. However, Penny seemed fairly calm. "The keys, hon," she said, "you can't start the car without the keys." He had crawled into the driver's seat, gripped the steering wheel, and turned to look over his shoulder to back out of the parking space without starting the car.

They shot up Third St. hill to the hospital and pulled into the Emergency entrance. He was supposed to leave his wife with a nurse who would take her to the maternity ward while he completed the admission procedure downstairs. But he stood frozen in the middle of the corridor, even after she had been wheeled away, until someone tapped him on the shoulder and reminded him that he had left his car in the middle of the driveway with the door open and the motor still running.

Later, when the preliminaries were completed, he was ushered into his wife's room. She began crying and reached out her arms to him, trembling and frightened. He had only seen her like this once before – that day in Chicago when she nearly aborted their baby. He held her hand tightly, saying, "This is all my fault. All the tension and strain, never being there for you

454

when you needed me."

"What about me, Mack? I had to graduate, didn't I," she sobbed. "This baby just has to be all right, just has to."

"Hey," he whispered, taking her face in his hands, "my little sister was born eight weeks early, and look how beautiful and healthy she is. Our baby will be fine – look at his parents. We're both fighters, aren't we?"

"Yeah," she smiled through her tears. "Too much, sometimes." Then a contraction swept over her, and her face became pinched with pain. A nurse announced that things were "moving along quickly." The doctor was on his way.

Mack watched helplessly. This was not the way they had practiced. There was no time for breathing techniques, focus spots, or gentle backrubs between pains. Their baby was coming, whether they were ready or not.

Twenty minutes later after admission, the doctor arrived and Penny was moved into the delivery room. Mack was escorted into the changing room. He rushed to join her, uniformed in his green surgical garb and mask. He insisted he wanted to do this, but inwardly his stomach was rolling. Please God, he prayed, don't let me be sick. His trembling fingers crept beneath the covers to touch her hand, but he was quickly reminded to not touch anything. His wife was draped in a green shroud, her legs up in those awful stirrups. She had already began pushing. Sweat glistened across her forehead as she strained with every ounce of strength. She recognized him then, a fleeting smile crossed her face. But just that quickly, she was seized by another contraction. She called out his name, half yelling and half grunting. Then there was a sniping sound of the episiotomy and a spray of blood across the doctor's chest. For a moment, the room began spinning as Mack nearly vomited, but he heard the doctor calling his name.

"Mack, why don't you step around here and look over my shoulder," he said sounding absurdly calm and matter-of-fact about such a tremendous event. "Your baby is almost here. Just one more push, Penny," he called. "It's almost over. Push! Push! You're doing great!" One of the nurses led Mack through the maze of equipment and got up in place just in time to hear the doctor exclaim, "That's it! Here it comes!"

And just that quickly, it happened. First there were tufts of wet, cheesy hair and then a whole head. The nose and mouth were quickly cleared and the placement of the cord checked. And then, before Mack had a chance to breathe, out slipped a grayish, purplish body with little feet already kicking defiantly. Later he would be told he cried, but he had no recollection of himself or anything else except staring open-mouthed at that beautiful baby that had just miraculously dropped into their lives.

"Mack!" Penny called. "Say something! Is it a boy?"

"No, but how about a beautiful baby girl, Penny," the doctor said as he quickly passed the small bundle over to a nurse. "She's very tiny, of course. I'm guessing about 4 pounds, but she looks healthy – her color is good and she's breathing well on her own. I've called Dr. Gilliam to see her right away. He's a pediatrician who specializes in preemies. They're waiting for her upstairs." There was no time for holding or touching. Penny reached out her empty arms as the baby was whisked away.

Penny began sobbing as Mack held her and tried to comfort her, but he was frightened, too. One of the nurses gave her some kind of sedative, and Mack stayed with her until she had quieted. As she was being attended to in the recovery room, Mack went out to where several of his family, along with Dr. and Mrs. Lamp, were waiting.

"It's a girl!" he proclaimed, trying to sound happy and joyous. "She's small – my God, she's so little and--" His voice choked then, unable to conceal his anguish. He had never felt anything like this before in his life – his child, their child. He had seen her breathe, move, even heard her cry. He had seen the tiny toes and clinched fists. Never had he known such joy and so much despair.

"Son, believe me, I know just how you feel," Matthew said, "I'm sure she's going to be all right. Your sister was premature and look at her now."

"I know, Pop. Penny and I were talking about that before. But – I mean, four pounds? She's so little."

"Now, Mack," Dr. Lamp interjected, "Chuck Gilliam is here, right? He's excellent with preemies. Was she breathing on her own?"

456

"Yeah."

"Was she crying?"

"Yeah."

"See? C'mon, try to relax. My God, a baby girl. I'm a grandfather again!" he cried. He was beaming while his wife remained restrained and cool.

There were more questions – how's Penny and did she have a rough time? Did the baby have hair and all her fingers and toes? Mack talked with them a few minutes, but then excused himself to go back by his wife. He went to her bedside, and found her crying. He held her for a long time as they waited for information about their daughter. What was taking so long? Finally, word came down that the baby was doing well, and all preliminary indications were that she was going to be fine. They both cried then.

"You are so beautiful," he murmured between kisses. "Our daughter is so beautiful! My God, this is the most incredible thing that's ever happened to me – to us. A baby girl, a baby girl!"

Chapter 54

Penny was told to rest between the endless checks and examinations as the nurses attended to her post-partum needs. Finally, she was permitted up in a wheelchair so that she and Mack would visit their baby. She was sleeping in her incubator, a plastic nest of tubes and paraphernalia. They crept up beside her and put their hands through the portholes to touch her. Her skin was so incredibly soft. She responded by yawning and squiggling a little, delighting her parents beyond belief. Mack and Penny were told that she was doing well, and the next 24 to 48 hours would be the most crucial.

Penny tried to sleep, but she was filled with the panic and dread that comes with knowing too much. She could list several complications that occur with pre-maturity, and she worried that the closest neonatal intensive care was in Iowa City. Trust. That was the word her father and others used repeatedly. Trust that the baby was in good hands, trust that the staff knows what they're doing. Even though she tried hard not to frighten him, Mack could sense her apprehension. Together they suffered those first, tormented hours, heartened only by the sight of that tiny chest heaving up and down and the reassuring beeps and buzzes of the menagerie of machinery. Finally, they abandoned all hope of resting and spent most of the day entrenched near their daughter. Penny began to relax and believe that her baby was going to be all right.

* * * * * *

Penny was discharged two days later and accepted her mother's invitation to stay in town so that she could be near the baby. Mack agreed, but was not pleased with his mother-in-law's smug attitude and noted that same invitation was not extended to him. He drove home alone. This was not the way he imagined it – the two of them coming home with their baby to an excited welcoming committee of Winston's. Oh well, that would happen soon enough. And he planned to spend as much time with his wife and child as possible. Besides, his brother lived in town and could keep Penny company.

Andrew couldn't have been happier with this arrangement. He was taking a light load of classes that summer and had plenty of free time to chauffer Penny back and forth to the hospital while Mack was busy working on the farm. Andrew loved to watch her with the baby and told her often that she was going to be a wonderful mother. He was able to witness many intimate moments such as when Penny was allowed to hold and feed her baby for the first time. Mack came into town as often as possible, but Andrew made himself as invaluable to Penny as he dared. He was overjoyed to see that old sparkle return to her eyes as daily the baby became stronger. Every ounce of weight she gained was reason for rejoicing.

All the Winston's, particularly Matthew, were thrilled that Penny and Mack named their baby girl Kathleen. Waiting for the baby's homecoming was a pleasant distraction from the turmoil that was engulfing all other facets of their lives. There had been no substantive word from the Army since the arrival of Luke's trunk. The climate on the home front was becoming more stormy, too. Matthew had long, sometimes loud, conversations with his lawyers, saying little to his family. But they sensed that Aunt Esther had followed through with her threats and Matthew was in the fight of his life. The more he insisted he could handle it on his own, the more frightened Annie and the others became.

* * * * * *

Annie was sitting in the kitchen one afternoon, looking through a box of old and dear baby things, when the phone rang. The woman introduced herself as a cashier at the J.C. Penny's store in Dubuque. "Miss Winston," she said, "I am calling you because a check you wrote on the 12th of this month was returned due to insufficient funds. We were hoping you could come into the store and take care of this as soon as possible."

"My goodness!" Annie gasped. "Insufficient funds? Returned? I'm sorry, I--" She had no idea what this woman was talking about.

"Miss Winston," the voice droned, "your check bounced because there was no money in your account. You need to come here with the cash to cover the check, plus processing fees, of course."

My God, what's next? How is this possible? She mumbled something, assuring the woman that she would attend to this immediately. She took her jacket and ran outside to search for her father. She found him working on some machinery behind the barn.

"Dad!" she cried, "I just got a call that a check I wrote didn't clear – it bounced! How could that happen?"

Matthew picked up a wrench and continued with his work. He did not appear surprised, but he didn't look at her either. "It happened because you always take checks out of the book and never write anything on the stubs," he said matter-of-factly.

"So?" she demanded. "I never have. No one told me I had to. So what happened?"

"You already know what happened," he retorted, still not

looking at her. "The goddamn check bounced because there was not enough money in the goddamn bank!" He paused in his work then and turned to meet her stare. "Look, honey, there's no reason to be upset. It happens to people all the time. I'll take care of it, all right?"

"No reason to be upset?" she cried. "I am very upset. I don't care if it happens to other people, it never happened to me. You should have been honest enough to tell us what the hell is really going on. I've been spending money because I had no idea I wasn't supposed to! Why are you treating us like this? You want us to be mature, responsible adults, but at the first sign of trouble you treat us like babies!" She stomped her feet, acting a little childish even as she spoke, but she didn't care. She was incensed. and embarrassed. Never in her life could she imagine such a thing happening.

Mack had come when he heard the yelling and stood at the door long enough to hear the end of the discussion. "She's right, Pop. We're smart enough to figure out there's trouble here, and we have a right to know what's going on. It concerns all of us, not just you," he said, glaring at his father.

Matthew seemed visibly affected by this unexpected confrontation, but did not speak. He put the wrenches into the toolbox and turned to walk away.

"Hey!" Mack cried after him. "Haven't you been listening? Why in the hell won't you talk to us?"

"I will, I promise," Matthew said, still walking away. "As soon as I get some things sorted out, I'll lay the whole thing out for you – all of you."

Mack picked up a piece of wood and slammed it on the ground. "Jeez, I never thought I'd have to worry about money. And now I have a wife and child to take care of. It's worse not knowing what in the hell is going on."

"Yeah, I know," agreed Annie. "We don't even know if Aunt Esther has started litigations. If we had some idea what we're dealing with, we could plan out strategy, get ready for the fight?"

"Fight? Strategy?" Mack frowned. "You make it sound like a war."

"It is. We can't let this family be torn apart, can we? We're going to have to match wits with Aunt Esther and her high powered lawyers. We can't let her win!" She remembered Sonny's words that night on the bluff in the darkness. "Everything's been such a mess for so long, but this time we can do something about it!"

Her words rang with optimism, and she hoped her brother would take it to heart. After all, he was right. This was an important time of his life. He had a family of his own, already feeling the burden of pressures coming from every direction. It was difficult for all of them to enjoy the good things when their future seemed to be so uncertain. There might be some tough decisions to make soon. What if their father would be forced to go back East and fight Aunt Esther in court? Who would go, and who would stay? What was going to happen to this family?

Friday, June 29, 1971

Dear Luke,

I have wonderful news. Little Katie is ready to come home. It's been four long weeks, but she has finally gained enough weight so that she can leave the hospital. Oh, Luke, she's so beautiful! I can't wait for you to see her. She has dark hair, just like Mama. I've been thinking a lot about her these past weeks. She'd be so happy! Not only that she has a granddaughter, but she'd be so pleased how Mack has matured and handled all these responsibilities.

Otherwise, everything is fine here. The bottom is finally planted, thank God. And school is out. I hope it gives you strength to know that we're here – all of us together, waiting for you to come home. Home, this land, this farm. Do not despair, Luke. This will all be over soon, and you will come back home where you belong.

Our prayers are with you.
Love,
Annie

* * * * * *

461

The big day finally arrived. Mack drove to the hospital full of excitement and joy that his family was coming home. So what if the rest of the world was screwed up, he didn't care. He was determined to not let anything spoil this day. So many times he had watched the ritual from the window of the brownstone, as his father – chest puffed out, a proud smile across his face, assisted mother and child out of the car and up the front stairs.

When he arrived at the nursery he was disappointed to see Penny's parents. But today, he could even face his mother-in-law with a smile. He could, that is, until she began insisting that Penny and the baby should stay with them for at least a few days. "The farm was just too far away and the roads too primitive," she said. "And who will take care of you and the baby? I already hired a nurse to stay with you at our house."

"Now, just wait, I--" Mack stammered. He had been patient and understanding about her staying in town since the baby was born, but not this.

"Now, Loretta," Dr. Lamp interceded. "Don't you think Penny has been away from home long enough? There's plenty of people out there to look after them. Mack will be there. I'm sure they'll be fine!" Mrs. Lamp seemed quieted, though less than gracious, and said nothing more.

The proud parents stood back as the nurse dressed the infant in her own little pink, frilly outfit, taking dozens of pictures to capture the moment for the posterity. And then they left for home. The baby fussed, but Penny simply unbuttoned her blouse and put the baby to her breast. "Well, at least we'll never have to warm bottles," she mused. Katie sucked for a few moments and then went back to sleep. Her parents talked quietly as they rode along.

"Do you believe we're whispering?" Mack chuckled. "You know there will never be a moment's peace where we're going. I think that was one of the things your mother was objecting to."

"Never mind my mother. Babies adjust to noise if they're exposed to it. I missed all that noise myself. It'll be good to get home."

Most of the family was assembled on the front porch, waiting for the first glimpse of the Jeep coming down the road.

Annie was upstairs, putting finishing touches on the nursery – or rather, the corner of Mack and Penny's bedroom which was to be the baby's domain. All the baby things, old and new, were laundered and put away in the new white dresser. Annie wondered how much Penny would need her, or allow her, to help with the baby. She was experienced at taking care of other women's babies.

There were shouts of excitement filtering up the stairs. Annie ran downstairs and gave her sister-in-law a quick hug and pleaded to hold the baby. Penny smiled her consent and Annie took the small bundle in her arms, happy tears running down her cheeks. She didn't hold the baby for long as Matthew muscled his way through the throng and took her, dirty hands and all.

A hush fell over the group as they followed him into the house. They watched spellbound as the layers of wrappings were peeled away. Becky stood on her tip-toes at her father's knees, looking at the little dolly sleeping on his lap. Even Sonny was a little awestruck as he watched from a distance. He slipped out the side door, not seen again until late that night. Annie knew his gift was doing twice the work so that Mack was free to spend the day with Penny and the baby.

Annie went into the kitchen and finished lunch. She made some soup, prepared a tray for Katie's tired parents, and took it upstairs. Penny was settled into bed, and Mack longed nearby. Annie crept in, feelings as though she was intruding in some quiet, intimate moment.

"I'm sorry," Annie apologized. "I thought maybe you were hungry."

"Oh Annie, it looks delicious. I'm starved!" Penny cried. "Breast feeding is wonderful. I can eat and eat, but nothing has a chance to turn into fat. But poor Mack – he'll never have the chance to experience the joy of 2 AM feedings, right honey?" she laughed.

But he wasn't listening – he was gazing off into space, deep in his own thoughts. And by the look on his face, they weren't happy ones.

"Honey," Penny called. "Why so intense?"

Mack didn't answer at first. He didn't want to spoil their

happiness. "Oh, it was nothing, really," he sighed. "I've been thinking about Mother a lot today. I think she'd finally be proud of me."

"Oh, Mack," Annie said, "I was thinking about her, too. But you make it sound like she was never proud of you before. That's not true. She thought you were – well, a little free-spirited, that's all." They all laughed then. Annie could vividly recall overhearing Mother and Daddy's sometimes heated debates regarding their oldest son's lifestyle and behavior. "But you're right, Mack," she added, peering into the crib where her little niece was sleeping. "She'd be so happy with this little darling."

She turned to smile at her big brother then, but saw a shadow of despair crossing his face. Penny saw it, too. "And Luke," he said bitterly. "I wonder what he'd say."

"Oh, Mack!" Penny cried. "Why do you do this?" She sounded angry and frustrated. "This is one of the most wonderful days of our lives. We'll remember this day always, like the day you found me in Chicago and the day we got married. But you can't let yourself be happy. For God's sake, can't you forget your guilt for one day?"

"But Penny," Mack began, "he's my brother. Why shouldn't I think about him?"

"Worry about him, sure, but--" Penny adjusted the blankets and turned over the pillow. "I know, honey, and I'm sorry for snapping at you. It's just that I hate seeing you so sad on such a happy day."

"I am happy, really happy," Mack said, reaching to give her a giant hug. "I don't want anything to spoil this day either."

Annie cleared her throat to remind them they had company. She wanted to make a quick exit and let them have their privacy. She was so glad it hadn't blown up into one of their patented fights. "Well, you guys, enjoy your lunch and get some rest, okay?" She was side-stepping toward the door.

"Oh, Annie, don't rush off. I'm sorry if we embarrassed you." Penny laughed. "I mean, we always talk like this to each other, but not usually in front of anyone."

The phone rang and someone called Mack to the phone. He excused himself to take it downstairs so he wouldn't disturb his sleeping angel. Annie and Penny chatted awhile longer, until Annie was summonsed to the settle an argument at the other end of the hallway.

Chapter 55

Penny drifted off asleep for a few minutes, and when she awakened, she wondered what was keeping her wayward husband so long. She trekked into the hallway, and was astonished to see him retrieving a suitcase he had just put away an hour earlier.

"Mack," she said, "what are you doing? We just put it away."

He cleared his throat, looking a little like the cat that had swallowed the canary. "Honey," he began, "that was Jack Morganston on the phone from DC. There's something big going on out there this weekend, and they—"

"What?" Penny exploded. "What in the hell are your talking about?

"Honey, I'm sorry, I really am, but – "

"No, this is just nonsense! Why do you have to go?"

"They're trying to put a big rally together. There's a busload ready to go, but they need someone to drive."

"I don't give a damn what they need! Did you tell them you brought your new little baby home today?"

"Yes, I explained all that, but Penny, this is really big. The Senate is voting on the McGovern-Hatfield bill on Saturday. Don't you see? If it passes Nixon will be mandated to bring all American servicemen home by the first of the year. The war would be over!"

"But Mack, why do you have to be there?"

"Luke would be home soon if this passes – maybe by Christmas!"

"I heard you! I understand! I just don't see why you have to be there!"

"I just do! I'm sorry, Penny. I'll be back in three or four days. I'm driving down to Davenport tonight and meeting them there. If I drive all night, we can get there in time for the big rally

465

on the Mall tomorrow afternoon." He had began this conversation with a soft, conciliatory or hopeful tone, but it was no use. She did not understand, and he did not have the words or the time to explain it. He turned to leave, pausing to kiss her tear-streaked cheek. "I love you, but I have to do this." Then he was gone.

* * * * * *

After Mack left, a dark cloak of despair covered the house and swallowed the happiness that surrounded them when Katie came home from the hospital. Mack's family, who had lauded Mack's maturity and sense of responsibility, now shook their heads in disbelief.

"I understand the importance of the McGovern-Hatfield legislation," Annie said at the supper table that night, "but I can't believe he left like that." "What was he thinking?" Andrew cried, sounding equally incensed, but inwardly, he was overjoyed. If Mack continued on this present course, Penny was sure to tire of him, and Andrew planned to remain close to help her pick up the pieces when their marriage was over.

Penny was very quiet those days as she concentrated all her energy and time on her child. Annie tried to help as much as possible, but Penny seemed to prefer privacy. She lied to her mother during her twice daily phone calls. Everything was fine, Penny said. Not surprisingly, considering all the turmoil and anger that surrounded her, little Katie was fussy and colicky. Annie could hear her muffled cries at night, but Penny seemed so annoyed with the whole family that she was not open to help from anyone.

Mack didn't call once the entire time he was gone. The family heard the results of the Congressional vote on the news. The McGovern-Hatfield Amendment was narrowly defeated in the Senate on Tuesday, the 16th, by the vote of 55 to 42. The next day, the House also turned it down. The anti-war forces vowed they could continue to fight for their cause. They returned to their buses and caravans to make the long trip back home..

Annie cried after hearing the news on TV. She had almost allowed herself to believe that Luke might come home yet this

466

year and Mack would be vindicated if he came home victorious. But neither was true, and sadness once again poured over her.

Mack came home late Thursday night. He shuffled into the kitchen, looking defeated and shaken as well as dirty and unshaven. He lifted his dark, sullen eyes wearily at Annie for just a moment and then turned to trudge upstairs. His sister was afraid for him, afraid that Penny might turn on him with the rancor and anger that had accumulated during these past 5 days. Annie crept up the stairs behind him, listening for Penny's acrimony. But there was none. Penny welcomed her warrior back home with comforting arms and forgiving whispers. A quiet hush fell across the house.

* * * * * *

It did not last very long. After the temporary diversion of Mack's absence, everyone was waiting for Matthew to call a meeting and tell the truth about their financial situation at long last. It happened the next Sunday, minutes after the family returned home from Mass. Andrew came home for the weekend and waited along with the rest of the family.

Matthew stopped briefly in the kitchen to drink a much needed cup of hot coffee and announced, "We'll talk in a little while." He went to his office, where he had slept and ate the past two days, and immediately began dialing the telephone. Annie moved around the kitchen, putting lunch on the table for anyone who cared to eat. Worried glances passed between the older siblings, knowing that whatever their father had to say to them, it was not good news.

Finally, Matthew opened the door and called for them to come in. He sat down wearily, shuffling through a pile of papers, not looking at any of them as they walked in. Sonny took his customary place behind Matthew's chair.. Annie was reminded of the phrase "seated at the right hand of the Father." Sonny never had much to say, but he always positioned himself close at hand in a protective posture.

They waited for what seemed an eternity for Matthew to begin. Finally, he cleared his throat and began speaking.

"Abernathy says we have to go back to New York. That goddamn sister of mine has a judge ready to issue some kind of paper demanding I show up in court to defend myself and the decisions I've made for this family. In the mean time, she has frozen all my assets. I had hoped that all this could be settled amicably out of court, but that woman is as stubborn as they come. She is determined to ruin me!"

"And while the court decides whether I'm a fit parent or a not, all minor children must be brought back into their jurisdiction until this thing is settled. So, I have no choice." He looked pained and drawn as he spoke, sounding as though he was pleading his case with his own children. "I can beat this thing, I know I can. I had hoped to spare all of you from more heartache, but I couldn't. It'll be over soon, I promise. After all, " he said with a faint grin, "I have to be back by corn pickin' time, right?"

"You bet, Pop," Mack cried, sounding surprisingly confident and upbeat. "Hey, we're gonna have a hell of a crop this year! Better than last!"

"I don't know, son," Matthew sighed. "There's an awful lot of work left for two men to do. It took all of us working night and day last year."

"You mean three, don't you, Pop? I'll be here, too," Andrew interjected, trying very hard to mimic his brother's assuring words. "At least I can drive one of those confounded tractors now." He looked pale and shaken.

"No, Andrew," his father said. "I could never ask you to do that. I thought you were going to school this summer to finish up your degree."

"You're not asking me, Pop. I'm volunteering. They'll need all the help they can get, so why shouldn't it be me?"

"Ok then, thanks Andrew. You'll be a great help."

They stood silent again, not knowing what to say until Annie gave voice to the one remaining unspoken question. "When will we leave?" she asked.

Matthew sighed deeply before answering. "Well, honey, I guess we ought to leave next weekend. I have some preliminary meetings the beginning of next week." He started to turn away, but then seemed to remember something he wanted to say.

"Mack, I was wondering – I mean, if it could be arranged – the baptism, I mean. I was hoping that you and Penny could arrange it before we leave. You'd like that, too, wouldn't you, Annie?" Once again, they were stunned. The Sacraments and other rituals of the Church never seemed that important to their father. Before Mack could respond, Matthew turned and strode outdoors.

They followed him onto the back porch toward the rocky place. They stood looking out upon the land as they had that day they arrived. Today, the skies were a brilliant blue and the treetops swayed in the lazy afternoon breezes. There was a hush of inexplicable tranquility that comes with simplicity.

"Don't worry, Pop," Mack murmured. "We'll take care of things around here till you get back. You go back there and kick some ass."

Matthew did not answer and walked away, his head bowed and shoulders sagging. His children wondered if he was up for the fight that awaited him.

The baby could be heard crying through the open window, so Mack hurried up the back stairs to be with his wife and child. He was, no doubt, anxious to relate these latest developments to Penny.

Annie watched Sonny closely, trying to detect any emotion or clues of what he was thinking. She hoped for some trace of sadness that she and the others would be leaving soon. But, as usual, his expression showed nothing. He picked up his tools and assembled materials and began climbing the stairs. He was going to fix the gapping hole in the window frame in Annie's bedroom. Considering how long it had needed fixing, it was ironic that he was going to repair it now when it has just been announced that she was leaving. She followed him, pretending to busy herself in Becky's room for a few minutes until she came out and sat nearby while he worked. The warm sun felt soothing on her face, and she was comfortable with his silence, watching him.

"Hey, nobody died or nothin'," he said. "It just ain't goin' the way the old man planned, that's all."

"Yeah, I know. We'll just go back East for a couple of months. It'll be all right." But she didn't sound convinced.

"Won't it be nice to go back?" he asked as he tore away the

469

rotted wood.

"Not really. I'm going to miss all this – even this crummy, rundown old house. But I'll tell you what I'll miss the most," she sighed, wishing she could tell him the truth. "The sunrises – I come out here early and watch the sun come up. Each sunrise is more gorgeous than the next. When winter came, I just hated that this dumb wall was here. I wish there was a giant window here so I could curl up in my nice warm bed and never miss a one." She looked over at him then and saw that he was staring at her with the most peculiar expression. But he turned away and continued to work in silence. She wished he would say something – some little phrase so that she'd know he didn't want her to go or that he'd miss her. Just a look – a nod, a quick, telling glance.

"I patched it up as best I could. Shouldn't leak as bad," he said, but then he hesitated for just a moment. "Ya' know," he said, "sometimes you go away from a place for a while, it just makes it that much better when you get back." He left then, having said more than was his custom. But Annie knew there was much more that he hadn't said. Things like, don't sit around whining about something you cannot change. Life goes on, things change, but the important things stay the same.

There wasn't much time for anyone to sit around feeling sorry for themselves. Packing was almost as difficult as when they left New York. There were so many decisions to make – what to take, what to leave. While it was true that they were not heading into the unknown, they didn't know for how long or what was going to happen to them. Matthew pushed himself from early dawn to very late. He wanted to get as much done as possible before leaving.

Sometimes, late at night when he couldn't sleep, he drove down to the bottom. He turned off the motor and lights, and just sit in the quiet. The dark, freshly worked fields glistened in the moonlight. The planting was finished, but there was still so much to do. Now, more than ever, this land and this crop meant everything to him. Money. Money to support his family. If everything went the way he expected back East, he would be returning here with his family to make this their permanent home, his fortune reduced to nothing more than this land. It was useless to re-evaluate the wisdom or validity of that decision now. It was too late to change anything, not that he wanted to. But what about his family? It surprised him a little that they seemed unanimously supportive.

Even Mack, who had been dragged here, kicking and screaming, eagerly agreed to stay and work the place. He promised he would work very hard, and Matthew was grateful, but also felt twinges of resentment. His son was so young and vital, with his beautiful wife and child, with a whole lifetime ahead of him. Matthew felt very old and tired. He was getting cheated out of a whole summertime of his dream. These were thoughts he could think only in the stillness of the night. He couldn't express these things to anyone because it sounded so ungrateful. He just didn't want to leave, that's all.

Chapter 56

Their exodus was planned for early Saturday afternoon. By late Friday night, everything was mostly packed. Sonny came into the kitchen for his usual late night cup of coffee. He smiled when he noticed Annie's lists carefully laid out on the counter. It was going to be strange not having her around – all of them, but especially her. He lingered, wondering if she'd come down.

Annie heard him moving around downstairs. For a moment, she thought about going down. There were a million excuses she could use, but she knew he liked drinking that last cup of the day in solitude. She wondered what he was thinking. Maybe he was glad they were leaving. No little ones to get underfoot. No Matthew to second guess him every step of the way. And no me.

She punched her pillow and pulled her covers tightly around her shoulders. He probably never thought much about me at all, she thought wearily. What is it they say? Absence makes the heart grow fonder? If only that were true.

* * * * * *

Breakfast was quiet. There were the usual scrabbles here and there, such as why was Peter allowed to take a suitcase of books when Thomas was told to leave his music and guitar in his room. He scowled as usual. He seemed surprised when his buddies drove on the yard to bid him farewell. They were a somber group. There would be no gigs this summer. Their leader was leaving. Kenny came by for an early morning jog with John, who had begged to stay behind with Andrew and Mack. Unfortunately, he was a minor and listed in the court order. Besides, his father told him he would need his support in court to plead his case.

The chores were finished. Matthews lingered as long as possible, giving last minute directions and discussing ideas he had. There was so much he had hoped to accomplish this summer. Finally, he had no choice but to shower, change, and get ready to leave. Annie noted with disappointment that Sonny did not do likewise.

Father Fritz gladly consented to have the baptism that morning. The "Little Princess," as her father called her, was beautifully dressed in the well-worn family, baptismal gown. Annie thought of Mother, knowing how happy she would have been. Daddy was right to ask to do this before they left. It was good for them to be all together one last time, gathered at the alter to welcome Kathleen's namesake into the Church. Annie thought Andrew must be thinking the same thing, judging by the pale, pained expression on her twin's face.

No one could have guessed the extent of anguish and sorrow reverberating through his whole being as he knelt in church that morning, waiting to take his place beside his brother and wife to become the godfather of their baby. He wondered if he could go through with it. Surely the God that knew what was in his heart would not look down favorably on such a deceitful hypocrisy. What if his sinfulness would somehow be reflected on his innocent child? No, a just and benevolent God could never allow such a thing to happen.

The services began. The sacred and revered oaths were taken. "Are you ready to help the parent of this child in their duties as Christian parents?" the priest asked. With great solemnity, Mack and Penny answered that they were.

Little Katie slept through most of it, even when the oil was anointed upon her chest and the drops of precious water were sprinkled upon her head. "Kathleen Elizabeth, I baptize you in the name of the Father, and of the Son, and of the Holy Spirit," Father proclaimed.

"God is light; in Him there is no darkness," was the response, and even as Annie said it, her heart was touched by such a feeling of gladness and hope, as though God was reaching down from the heavens and touching her with His hand. Her heart had been filled with so much sorrow for so long that she forgot that she believed there was a God who watches over things. Happy, rejoicing tears fell down here cheeks as she stared at the baby in her arms.

The service ended with the blessing. Father Fritz seemed to put emphasis upon every word, sensing their special meaning to this family which was about to be spilt apart with so much uncertainty. "May God continue to pour out His blessings upon these sons and daughters," he said with out-stretched arms. "May he make them always faithful members of his Holy Church. May He send His peace upon all who are gathered here, in Christ Jesus our Lord. Amen.

Pictures were taken as the family lingered for a few minutes in the sanctuary, waiting to leave for the airport until the last possible minute. Annie slipped away to place a boutique of flowers from her own garden at the Blessed Virgin's alter. She lit a candle, as she had done every day since they had gotten word of Luke's capture. How she wished he was here today. "Holy Mother," she whispered, "please pray for us that these troubles will be over soon so that this family will once again be together. Protect Luke and keep him safe."

She was delighted and relieved to find Sonny leaning against one of the giant oak trees in the churchyard when they came outside. Taking Joey into his arms, he said, "C'mon, you'd better hurry or you'll miss your flight." There were hugs and kisses for Ben and Ginny, who put her hanky to her eyes more than once. Lori and Andy were there, too. He looked pale and grim while Lori seemed drawn and red-faced. Annie knew things were not going well for them, marriage-wise as well as their business, especially since the store's biggest customer was going back East to face financial ruin. Annie would love to slip way for a cup of coffee and compare miseries, but there was no time.

The Dubuque County Airport was very small, offering commuter service to the larger airports. The little DC 9 they took to Chicago was smaller than the private jets Matthew once chartered for afternoon jaunts to Boston or Atlanta.

When their flight was called, there was another round of quick hugs and kisses, everyone telling each other not to worry because they would be back together soon. Annie reached forJoey but the boy was clinging to Sonny's neck like a frightened baby opossum. "Come now, Joey, we have to go," Annie coaxed. "We get to ride on an airplane." But he was not convinced.

Then Sonny began to whisper something in his ear. Not even Annie could hear what he was saying. But the boy broke out in a broad smile, happily allowing himself to be handed over to his sister. Sonny and Annie's eyes met briefly during the exchange.

"You take care," he said. "You're gonna have your hands full, but you can handle it."

"I hope so. At least the time will go fast." She boarded, not wanting him to see her cry.

Annie and her brothers gazed out the little windows of the plane as they ascended into the clouds. "There's the river," someone cried. That lazy, old river, Annie thought. It will still be there when we get back – the town, the farm. Those things are forever. That's why it was all worth fighting for.

* * * * * *

The ride back to the farm was very somber and subdued for the four who were left behind. It was almost spooky when they walked into the house. The baby was sleeping so Penny took her upstairs. Andrew made some coffee. They sat around the table, listening to the pot percolating when they heard the baby cry.

They were all startled – the sound that filtered down sounded so strange. None of them had ever heard it so clearly before. When Penny went upstairs, her footsteps echoed through the hallway like a tomb.

"God, this is ridiculous," Sonny said, hoisting himself out of the chair. "I'm gonna go change. Let's get some work done."

"Me, too," echoed Mack, thankful for the distraction. "There's still plenty of daylight, and we sure as hell have enough to do."

They needed to work on the fences, which were patched and the patches were patched. But the persistent pigs and cattle kept getting out anyway. An electric fence had never been used because there had always the little boys running around so Matthew never wanted to risk it. But that reason no longer existed, so maybe this was a good time to string it up.

They were discussing this and other issues as they trudged back into the kitchen that evening for supper. There were decisions to be made, but they were hesitant to finalize anything without Matthew.

"I know there's so a lot to be done out there," Mack said with a sweeping motion to encompass the barnyard. "But what about the house and yard? If there's a trial, it probably won't start for weeks or months. Aunt Esther and her big shot lawyers might come back for more pictures to show how bad it still looks. Well then, we ought to try to fix it up and quick. Might go a long way in proving we have a decent place to live."

"But there's so much," Andrew moaned. "Aluminum siding, a new roof, landscaping. Plus the farming?"

"I know, but it's up to us," Mack countered. "Of course, there's one thing we haven't talked about yet – money. I know we're not used to worrying about that, but we have to now. What we do largely depends on how much money we have to work with."

"There's our trust funds," Andrew suggested, looking very dejected at the prospect of his school money being used for paint and windows. "Annie told me last night we could use hers for anything we needed. Between the three of us we have 80 or 90 thousand, right?"

Mack did not notice his wife's sudden change in expression. Although she and Mack had never discussed it, she assumed that the money was for their future – theirs and the baby. But it was worthless to fight about it. She was tired of playing the devil's advocate all the time.

She was still thinking about all this later when she went for a stroll at sundown. She was startled to find Sonny crawling around in Annie's flower beds, weeding and planting some small sets of petunias and marigolds Annie had bought but never planted.

"So, Annie's flowers aren't going to go to waste after all," she said. "They were looking so pathetic, I thought Annie must have thrown them out."

"Nothing' else to do," he said without looking up "I figured I might as well put 'em in."

"I'd be glad to help."

"Nah, I'm almost done. You'd better go back inside before the 'skeeters eat you alive."

Penny wasn't surprised at the brush-off. They had never been very comfortable around each other. He wasn't rude or anything, but they rarely talked. Perhaps all that would change this summer, she guessed. She knew it would take all four of them working hard together to pull off this monumental task. Wouldn't Annie be amazed to see Sonny planting her flowers. Penny thought of herself as being fairly perceptive and she was aware of some special chemistry between Sonny and her sister-in-law, although un-acted upon by either party. Any kind of attraction that was unexpressed by word or touch was unthinkable to her, so she wondered if her intuition might be wrong in this case. But still, watching this rather crude man kneeling in Annie's flower beds must mean something.

Penny surveyed the scene around her. Even shrouded in the shadowy, twilight mist, this place looked decrepit. No wonder Matthew's snotty sisters decided to take legal action after one look at this house. She had even questioned the wisdom of bringing her own child into such a place, although she'd never admit it to her mother. But, for better or worse, this was the home her husband had chosen for them. She knew him to be a fairly realistic and materialistic man, so why was he so drawn here? She knew the answer even before she asked herself the question. It was the challenge, his own ego and fear of failure, and the land. She reminded herself that she loved this place, too—she had fallen in love with him here.

And what about this other man? Why was he laboring over these wilted little flowers? She felt compelled to pick it up and began watering the tender seedlings. Sonny must have noticed, but said nothing. Silently they toiled until it was done and each went their own way, knowing there was nothing more they could do but wait and see if the morning dew and sunlight would work their magic. Then, perhaps, there would be lovely, flowering beds of color for Annie when she returned home.

* * * * * *

Sunday morning, Mack and Penny dutifully went off to Mass with their newly baptized baby with Andrew. Sonny was well accustomed to the eerie Sunday morning silence and usually welcomed it. But today it felt unnatural. Matthew was not there, playing hooky from church and happy to drive down to the bottom just to sit and gaze at the fields.

Sonny found himself sitting on the old gazebo, staring back at the ramshackle house. There was so much work to be done. He walked around the house, pausing to check rotten wood that needed replacing and window frames barely intact. The flowers hadn't improved much overnight – they were more pathetic looking in the sunlight.

He wandered into the kitchen and poured himself a cup of coffee. The cracked, gray walls and the dilapidated cabinets and shelving were unchanged since those first days on the farm when he had made them barely functional. There just wasn't any time. He agreed with the decision to concentrate on the exterior. He pushed through the swinging door into the dinning room. Penny cleared the table and put the cloth in the wash last night. The old table stood naked with it's many cracks and scars. He smiled as he remembered Annie's insistence that this had once been a handsome piece of furniture in its day. But stripped of its deceptive covering, it stood as a silent testimony to the gross defects of this house. Sonny stroked the rough and blemished surface. Perhaps it could be restored.

Many hours later, when the others trekked off to bed, the muffled sounds of sandpaper and hand tools echoed through the house as Sonny worked on the table. No one asked why he was attempting such a monumental task. He wouldn't have answered them anyway.

* * * * * *

From the first moment they re-entered the brownstone, the situation between the Winston's and their household employees was difficult. Upon arrival, Giles approached Matthew, saying, "I've made inquiries at one of the agencies about hiring more household staff. I should think we'll need a cook and an upstairs maid who could also serve dinner."

"No, Giles," Matthew said. "Annie will cook the meals and we can put the food on the table ourselves. The money situation around here has changed drastically."

"Yes, sir, I understand. Can I get you some coffee or a cup of tea perhaps?"

"No, Giles, I just want a cold beer. I can get it." Matthew was bent over some papers sent over from his lawyer's office so he didn't notice the look of hurt and confusion on his butler's face.

Miss Grace could barely contain her dismay when she discovered the baby wore disposable diapers and was put to bed with her bottle.

"I know, Grace," Annie said. "You and mother never did it that way. But it's so easy. I just lay her down with it and in a few minutes, she's asleep."

"Yes, well, she's well over a year old so she needs to be weaned immediately."

It was very difficult for both Giles and Miss Grace to accept the Winston's new found independence. Since no one's roles were clearly defined, they seemed to be stepping over one another. Giles was appalled at the way Annie, Matthew, and the boys hung around the kitchen, making sandwiches and snacks all hours of night and day. The biggest mistake he and Grace made was assuming that the children would be anxious to come back to the "more civilized" New York City.

Of course, nothing was further from the truth. The were all so homesick they had trouble sleeping. The days were even worse. There were glaring troublesome things that they had never noticed before. The constant noise and confusion seemed deafening to them now. The people on the streets seemed to move around with blank, uncaring expressions. Even the air bothered them – sometimes they felt as though they couldn't breathe. There was light and darkness, but the sun, moon, and the stars had vanished so their days had no rhythm. They felt like lonely transients in a place they had once called home.

Boredom was their worst enemy. They struggled constantly to find ways to fill the terrible void of uselessness. John's priority was trying to keep in shape, but he found jogging alone on the crowded sidewalks and parkways was frustrating. His running seemed laborious and tedious rather than exhilarating like it was back home. Thomas seemed to be having the easiest time renewing old acquaintances, sometimes staying out too late for a sixteen year old boy. Annie tried to reprimand him but lacked any authority. Matthew as too pre-occupied to take any parental measures.

Matthew spent everyday huddled with Abernathy, planning their strategy. A few days after arrival, a courier arrived with several boxes of personal items from Matthew's office. He realized that in order to bring this conflict to a swift acceptable end, the first step was to terminate his association with Winston Ship Builders, Inc.

The second order of business was to amend his potentially criminal difficulties with the missing trust fund money. Thankfully, the D.A.'s office did not seem inclined to press charges as long as he made arrangements to repay the money quickly. His only option was to sell off a large percentage of his remaining shares of the company. He hoped distancing himself from the family business would appease Aunt Esther, but she seemed even more determined to have her day in court.

Matthew became irritable and depressed as the days and weeks dragged on. Unfortunately, these emotions brought on excessive drinking, which only made his mood worse. He nearly missed an important meeting with his sisters and both corps of lawyers because of an awful hangover. And then he became incensed when Abernathy had the nerve to tell him that the next time he was in such a state, they'd all be better off if he would stay in bed.

Annie was having an equally hard time, and the irony of the situation did not escape her. There were so many times during their time on the farm when she longed to have carefree hours with no chores, no demands, no responsibilities. But she, too, found idleness monotonous. Because of their financial problems, she couldn't amuse herself with shopping. She had kept a few hundred dollars out of her trust fund when she closed it out and sent the money to Andrew and Mack. But she felt guilty indulging herself in anything frivolous. In fact, she didn't spend any of it, so she kept it hidden in a sock in her dresser.

She tried contacting some of her old friends, but no one seemed interested in associating with her anymore. Feeling further alienated, she stopped calling them. She sent long letters to Lori, Penny, and Ginny, often times the words smudged by her tears. She told them how much she missed them, but really her heart ached for Sonny – the sight and touch of him, even the smell. She lived everyday in the state of panic, worrying what would happen if somehow, unbelievably, the judge's decision would not go her father's way. What then? How could she leave her little sisters and brothers behind to go back to the farm? How could she leave them, but how could she live in this place without Sonny? The judgment had to go their way. It just had to.

Matthew and Annie found excuses to call the farm frequently. Penny usually answered the phone. They were working so hard, she said. Annie was disappointed that even at 9 o'clock at night, Sonny was seldom in the house.

One day she impulsively called Cousin Millie to ask her to meet for lunch. Millie had gone back to Ireland soon after the Winston's departure west and had just recently returned to New York for her tour of duty. She was more than a little curious about the invitation. She was extremely surprised when her young cousin wanted to talk about Ireland. In all the years she had been associated with this family, none of Kathleen's children had ever shown much interest in her homeland. But from the moment they say down in the little pub on First Avenue, it was obvious to Millie that Annie had undergone an amazing transformation since they had last spoken.

Annie wanted to hear about everything – Millie's children and family, her home and village, the green meadows and the heather that bloomed on the hillside. Millie told funny stories about their parish priest who traveled around the community scolding anyone who missed Mass, and the old widow who came to the Pub to drink ale from the same glass sitting on the same spot every afternoon for as long as Millie could remember. Widow O'Clarke would drink the last sip promptly at 3:30, turn the glass over saying she needed "to rest her eyes for a wee moment," and take a two hour nap, snoring like a field hand. Annie laughed so hard she had tears running down her cheeks.

"How can you stand it?" Annie cried, all traces of laughter disappearing from her face. "All the honking and screaming, all the people. How can you stand coming here to such a noisy, dirty place?"

"Oh, my dear, it isn't such an awful place," Millie cooed. "You had a good life when you lived here before. Your mother loved Ireland, to be sure, but a person can get used to anything if you're surrounded by the ones you love. Like they say, home is where the heart is." She studied the lovely young woman sitting across the table who looked so distressed and heartsick. She recognized that look. "Your heart just belongs somewhere else, that's all. Just remember, honey, there is a God who takes care of such things. If it's meant to be, then your dreams will come true. I'm sure of it."

"Just take one day at a time, right?" Annie smiled, remembering Ginny's often repeated favorite phrase. "The world will just keep on turning, and things will take care of themselves."

Mille and Annie spent a pleasant afternoon together. Annie described the farm – the valley, the drafty old house, and all the work. Though Millie had some difficulty picturing Annie and her brothers tending livestock or driving tractors, she was convinced of Annie's sincerity and newfound maturity. Many times these past months, Millie had worried about Kathleen's family, wondering how they were coping with such a tremendous loss and overwhelming sadness. But that day, when they hugged each other and went their separate ways, Millie knew she would worry no longer. Annie and her brothers stumbled upon direction in their lives and found their souls.

June 18, 1971

Dear Luke,

If you receive this letter and see the return address, you must be terribly confused. Yes, we're back in New York, but it's only temporary. Dad had some legal loose ends to tie up, and was getting nowhere over the phone, so we decided it was time to come back here for a while. We're going to pack up the house and put in on the market. It's foolish to keep it. We need to break our ties with this place, once and for all. This isn't home anymore. I miss the farm terribly. It must be so difficult for you.

Walking into this house was really strange. Everything is exactly as we left it, as though time was frozen and waiting for someone to snap his fingers and start it again. Giles and Nanny Grace were so glad to see us. Nanny moved back into her little room off the nursery, anxious to look after Becky.

We're hoping that to get this all done in a relatively short time. We are all very anxious to get back to the farm. Imagine us saying that 18 months ago, but it's true. This place is a house, but it's not our home.

Love, as always,
Annie

Chapter 57

A court date was at long last set – Monday, August 2nd. Abernathy became a fixture around the brownstone, telling Matthew and the children, even Danny and Peter, that they were his only case. He explained that he would call each of them before the judge and ask them where they wanted to live. "When the other lawyers ask their questions, just tell the truth," he said, "but think about what you're going to say." He elected not to coach them or spoon-feed answers to them, saying that it would be better for them to say things spontaneously in their own words. Matthew will be the main witness, taking the stand in his own defense.

During the two weeks preceding the court hearings, there was a court-ordered psychologist who came to the house to interview each member of the family. As nerve-racking as this was, it proved to be a good training ground for what was to come.

Annie watched her father as the days dragged on. He looked so haggard and tired. The ordeal took an awful toll on him. He looked so much older than he did three summers ago. Mother was still alive, and they had vacationed in upstate New York that summer, together one last time before Annie, Andrew and Mack went to college. Her parents were so happy, so full of life and love for each other. Was that really only three years ago?

* * * * * *

During the week before court, Annie made sure everyone's suits were cleaned and their shoes polished. She wanted the family to look as neat and civilized as possible. Sunday night, she put everyone to bed early, tucking each one with a good luck kiss and hug. "Try not to worry," she said as they said their prayers and settled in for a long, restless night.

Matthew sat in the darkness at the head of the dining room table. One of his children was missing. Thomas had left the house Saturday afternoon and had not returned or bothered to call. Matthew considered his fourth son to be cause for concern. Thomas had never tried to hide his contempt for their life on the farm. How would he answer the lawyers' questions? Matthew was determined to wait however long it took for his wayward son to return.

Several hours later, Thomas came home. Even in the dim light, Matthew saw that he was swaggering drunkenly. Only when his father cleared his throat did the boy realize that he was not alone. "What's the matter, Pop," he sneered. "You ain't

483

finished your bottle yet?"

Matthew turned over his empty, dry glass and stared at his son. "No, I'm not emptying any bottles tonight. As you may recall, we have a big day tomorrow."

"Yeah, sure," Thomas grumbled as he turned to walk away.

"Thomas!" Matthew cried. "Where are you going? We have to talk."

"About what?"

"Well, for one thing, where have you been for the last two days?"

"Not that you really care, but this guy, Richie let me sit in with his band. Remember, I told you about him – no, wait. I tried to tell you about him, but you weren't interested so--" Again, he turned to walk away.

"What do you mean, I wasn't interested. This is the first time I ever heard any mention of this Richie fellow."

"That's a bunch of bull. He has a band playing at a bar downtown, and he needed a drummer. Oh, screw it anyway! I told you about this at dinner a few weeks ago, but I knew you weren't paying any attention."

"Why would he let a 16 year old play at a bar? What is this guy thinking?"

"He thinks I'm good, that's what! He knows I want my own band someday, so he's showing me the ropes."

"That's not all he's showing you. My God, look at you! You're drunk or high or both. I do not approve. I don't want you hanging around this guy any more."

"Oh, go to hell!"

"What did you say? How dare you talk to me like this!"

"Why not. Look in a fuckin' mirror, why don't ya'. Like father, like son, right?"

"If your mother were alive--"

"Well, she's not, is she. If she was, none of this bullshit would be happening. So why don't you cut the crap and tell me why you stayed up for me tonight."

"What do you mean?"

"You wanna know what I'm gonna say when I testify, don't you?"

"Son, I just--"

"I said, cut the bullshit! You're afraid I'm gonna blow everything right out of the water, aren't you. And I could. I could tell them about the leaky roof, how the toilets don't flush half the time, how you work us like slaves, keep us home from school to work in the goddamn fields."

"That's not true--"

"It is if I say it is! I can be very convincing. I can make that stupid farm of yours sound like a hell hole!"

"Why would you do that? Do you really hate it that much?" Matthew was trembling, his voice sounding hallow and scared.

"Well, that depends." Thomas seemed to enjoy watching his father squirm. "What is it worth to you for me to walk in there and make it sound like a goddamn paradise."

"What is it worth? What do you mean?"

"I mean, I'm open to negotiations."

Matthew slumped into the chair. "Negotiations? Are you trying to blackmail me?"

"Blackmail? That sounds a little harsh, doesn't it? I just mean that I want certain concessions. It's a win-win situation, don't you agree?" His father said nothing, so Thomas continued, speaking in a quiet, but demanding tone. "You see, I have plans, too. I could accomplish them a lot more easily here in New York, but I guess I could be convinced to sacrifice my own happiness. I'll go back to that house of horrors, but it's going to cost you."

"You mean money? I don't --"

"Money, Well, an extra $100 or so every week wouldn't hurt. I was talking more than that before. Of course, with your present financial difficulties, you won't keep that shoe box full of cash in your closet anymore."

"You were stealing --"

"Stealing? There you go using those vile words again. You mean, like taking money from your own company or your children's trust funds? That kind of stealing? Anyway, my terms aren't really about money."

"Terms?"

"You see, maybe I could tolerate living in that God

forsaken place if I didn't have to get up at the crack of dawn and do those goddamn chores. And that stupid school! I'm a musician! Why do I have to go to school?"

"Thomas, you're talking nonsense. How could you explain not doing chores and dropping out of school. Everyone would--"

"I don't give a rat's ass what anyone else thinks. Besides, you'll be doing the explaining, so figure out something to say, because that's my deal." He hoisted himself onto the table, leering down at his father with that same cocky sneer. "And when we go back there, if you suddenly develop a bad case of amnesia, I'm warning you, I will bring you down. I will destroy everything you hold dear. And believe me, I can do it." He stared deep into his father's eyes, and then, satisfied that his words achieved the desired effect, he got up and sauntered out of the room. "Good night, Daddy."

Matthew was left alone in the darkness to contemplate his state of affairs. He tried to muster righteous indignation over his son's audacity, but lacked the energy or the inclination. Although he was shocked by Thomas' mean spirited insolence, Matthew chastised himself for allowing himself to be so easily manipulated. Sitting in the quiet, having been forced to face the demons that haunted the shadows of his days and nights, he realized that he would sell his soul to the devil to insure a favorable outcome in court. Perhaps, he already had.

* * * * * *

For once they were not late. Annie and her brothers paraded somberly into the court, promptly at 9:45 AM, as directed by Mr. Abernathy. Annie had fussed over each of them, applying the proper amounts of spit and polish. Although the boys squirmed in their high buttoned shirts and neckties, they seemed to sense the seriousness of the situation and endured these hardships silently. Even Thomas seemed agreeable and marched into the courtroom with the rest of the family. However, Annie noticed a disagreeable glance between Thomas and her father, who was sitting at the table talking with Abernathy in hushed tones.

Court was called to order, and the case of "Winston vs. Winston" began. The matter before the court was the question of custody of six minor children. Aunt Esther's head lawyer, Mr. Gerald Levison, stood to begin his opening statement. He stepped out from behind his table, buttoning his $3000 Italian suit coat with an air of great importance.

"A father has no greater responsibility than the welfare of his children," he began. "A good father foregoes any personal desires and understands that riding off to joust at windmills is not a particularly worthwhile endeavor, especially when it compromises the safety and well-being of his children. Matthew Macalister Winston was a respected member of the business community and CEO of his family's successful, 86 year old company, The Winston Ship Building Co. He sat on the board of directors of a large, international banking conglomerate and served as a chairman of various foundations and charitable concerns. And befitting his position and immense wealth, he and his family moved in New York's more renown social circles."

"Then suddenly that all changed. In January of 1970, he announced that he was taking his family for an extended vacation. Known to be despondent over his wife's death, none of his friends or family were surprised. It seemed logical that he might do such a thing. Months passed. His sisters, with whom Mr. Winston has always been close, began to worry. There were no letters, no phone calls. His sisters, Esther, Gertrude, Ruth, and Eunice, became increasingly anxious about the whereabouts of their missing brother and his ten children. Esther began investigating and asking questions. And to her utter astonishment, she discovered that her brother and his family were living on a farm – not just any farm, but a dilapidated, ramshackle place in a tiny farming community in eastern Iowa. And even more shocking was the revelation that Mr. Winston was withdrawing funds from the business accounts here in New York. In fact, according to our records, which were verified by certified accountants, Mr. Winston managed to pilfer the total sum of $780,450 from the company's account during the past 18 months." There was a loud, collective gasp that echoed throughout the courtroom. Even Judge Graham, although attempting to remain stoic, appeared affected by that incredible announcement. Annie, John, and the others were likewise stunned.

"Furthermore," the esteemed attorney, Mr. Levison, continued, "it has also been determined and further verified by accountants, that Mr. Winston chose to take many thousand more dollars from his children's trust funds. These funds were generously stipulated by the children's grandparents to be held in reserve to ensure that each of them could begin their adult lives unencumbered by financial worries or unnecessary burdens. Without regard for his own children's welfare or long-term happiness, Mr. Winston helped himself to these funds."

"And what did he do with all that money? Did he bring in carpenters to build a suitable residence to keep his family safe and warm? A roof over their heads that would not leak and keep out the cold? Suitable plumbing, electrical service, carpeting for the floor or nice furniture? No, he did not."

"Did he hire staff to help in the fields? To help his young daughter with the daunting task of running the household? The laundry? The cooking and cleaning? To help take care of his infant daughter? No, he did not."

"Rather, he took his children away from a lovely, upscale home here in New York City where there was never fewer than five household servants to take care of his family's needs. He took them to live in a run-down house which had been deserted for years and is, still to this day, barely inhabitable. And furthermore, this once caring and loving father forced his own children to work eighteen hours a day in the fields."

"Your Honor, it is therefore understandable and, I think, very generous, of Esther Winston to come forward and partition the court for guardianship of these six minor children. After we present our evidence, we are confident that you will concur with this request." Mr. Levison surveyed the courtroom with an air of supreme confidence as he sat down. His client was also smiling with a smug, tight lipped sneer.

Then it was Mr. Abernathy's turn. Annie bit her lip anxiously. Perhaps her father had used poor judgment when asking him to represent them in such an important case. After all, Abernathy was a corporate attorney, much more at ease with contract disputes and labor issues than such a sensitive civil case. But Matthew had insisted that he would stick with Abernathy, whom he valued as a trusted friend as well as his attorney.

Abernathy cleared his throat, squared his shoulders, and after a quick glance at his client, he began. "Your Honor, I can understand why anyone hearing this story for the first time might find it somewhat unbelievable. I must confess, I had moments of consternation when my client first confided in me his intentions to relocate his entire family. Because of my 20 some years of association with the Winston family, I knew that Matthew was overwrought with grief at the death of his beautiful wife, Kathleen. So when he told me that he was going to make this move, I counseled him not to make such a drastic decision so hastily. As usual, when Matthew Winston makes up his mind to do something, he moved quickly and decisively. A week later they were gone."

"But, the fact remains, that this man has the right to do what he wants as long as it does not jeopardize the health or well-being of his children. The Winston children are here in court today. Do they look mal-nourished to you or in poor health? Do they appear tortured or mistreated in any way? No, they do not. They are here to testify in their father's behalf. Each one will testify that they support his decision, and are very anxious to go back home."

"Home. What a simplistic but yet, complicated word. Webster says that a home is: *the place or structure where one lives; an environment or haven of shelter, happiness and love.* For Webster to use the word 'love' in the definition of home, it must be an important component. A home is not only walls and a roof, but a sanctuary. It is the responsibility of a father to ensure that the home he provides for his family has an abundance of all those things."

"The crux of this case hinges on whether Matthew Winston is crazy. His sister and Mr. Levison would have us believe that anyone who leaves the lap of luxury to live and work on a farm must be insane. And because Mr. Winston asks his children to somehow exist without servants and luxury, he must be nuts. Well, guess what. I washed dishes when I was a kid. I put away my own laundry, and I baby-sat my little brothers and sisters. I've had a job since I was 14. Did I enjoy these things? No, not always, but I knew they were expected of me. So, does that mean that since this was the life my parents provided for me they were unfit parents? Was my father crazy when he made me get up at 4:30 and do my paper route? Was my well being in jeopardy because we didn't live in high society? No, I don't think so."

"It is our inalienable right, guaranteed by our Constitution, to live the life we want. Mr. Winston is luckier than most because he actually had a choice. Most of the people who live on farms and small town all over America, don't have a choice. But even if they did, I'm not sure any of them would give up their lifestyle, because, believe it or not, there are millions of people who live across this vast country who actually enjoy their lives and wouldn't trade a minute of it for all the high priced caviar on 5th Avenue. Thank you."

Robert Abernathy had not spoken with the refined eloquence of Mr. Levison or used the well-placed, dramatic pauses, but his voice had rang with conviction that money cannot buy. Annie breathed a deep sigh of relief. They had won the first round.

Chapter 58

The Plaintiff's presentation took only two days. Aunt Gertrude, nervous and fidgety as ever, took the stand first. She described in great, gut-wrenching detail the deplorable condition of the house in which they found her brother's family living. She told of her horror when confronted with the unkempt kitchen and the filmy, red water. She used adjectives like "unsanitary", "squalor", and "madness" very convincingly, sometimes weeping and looking very distraught. She pleaded with the court to grant custody of these "poor unfortunate children" to her sister, Esther, that they might live in the safety and comfort they deserved.

Then it was Abernathy's turn. "Apart from the rather primitive surroundings of Matthew's farm, did the children appear unhappy, malnourished, or unclothed?" he asked. "Did any of them ask to go back to New York? Did they indicate they were being mistreated in any way?"

"Well, no," Gertrude said, "but we weren't there long enough to speak privately with the children."

"Oh, you weren't? Approximately, how long were you there?"

"About half an hour."

"Did you see their bedrooms? Did you have a meal with them?"

"Gracious, no! Eat at that house? Never!"

"Okay, then, since the Winston children have been back in New York, how much time have you spent with them?"

"Well, none actually."

"Perhaps you were advised to stay away from them for now?"

"No."

"You say you worried incessantly about them while they gone, so I would imagine that you were very anxious to spend some time with them."

"Well, yes, I was, but you see, I haven't spent summers in the City for years. My husband and I summer at our place on Long Island. The heat here is just intolerable."

"But yet you say you will help you sister with the rearing of these children as much as possible, correct?"

"Well, yes."

"This place on Long Island, does it have several bedrooms? Surely you would invite your nieces and nephews to summer with you, especially since summers are so *intolerable* here in New York."

Gertrude looked frustrated and glanced at her sister for guidance. "I don't know. You see my husband, Mr. Simmons, has a delicate heart condition. That's why we never had children of our own," she whined.

The witness was excused.

Next Mr. Levison called Peter Carlson, Esther's private detective, to the stand. Several poster-sized pictures he had taken were admitted as evidence. Of course, they looked as appalling as Gertrude had described. The mud, the weeds, the rundown buildings and ramshackle house were all there in living color. Annie and her brothers could barely breathe, afraid that the photos would have a disastrous effect, particularly since Abernathy had no questions for him.

The witness was excused.

Mr. Levison's last witness was Aunt Esther. She took the stand, clutching her lace hanky. "I have taken this action against my own brother with great reluctance and trepidation," she said with a deep heaving sigh. "I have always thought my brother was a wonderful father, and this ordeal is breaking my heart. I just cannot understand how Matthew could have subjected his poor children to such misery."

"And what about the money? After all, if the farm was capable of supporting the family, why did Matthew need to abscond with so much? And now that he has signed papers relinquishing all ties with the company and no longer had access to those funds, how was he going to subsist and meet the needs of such a large family? Well, my goodness! The entire situation seems totally hopeless, doesn't it?" Aunt Esther turned and addressed that question directly to the judge, who appeared unmoved. Mr. Levison thanked her for her candor, returned to his table, and turned the floor over to Abernathy.

"Miss Winston," Abernathy asked, "have you ever been married?"

"Yes, twice."

"And divorced twice, I assume?"

"Well, yes. I'm sorry to say that neither of my choices were good matches and we were, each time, incompatible."

"I'm sorry. You will, then, if awarded custody, be in effect, a single parent of six children?"

"Yes, but I can afford servants such as a nanny, so that I wouldn't exactly be raising them alone. I've always loved children and am looking forward to this opportunity."

"Do you have any idea how much noise six children make?"

"Well, yes, I have some idea--"

"Do you? I wonder. How large is your home? Is there a park nearby?"

"Mr. Abernathy, if you would allow me to answer your questions, I would tell you that I am presently residing in an apartment. Of course, I would have to move if the children are awarded to me. It would be quite a sacrifice, one which I am willing to make."

"Miss Winston, are you aware that these children were baptized Roman Catholic and would expect to continue in that faith?"

"Yes, I am aware of that. It would be difficult but I--"

"Have you ever had a close relationship with any of these children?"

"How could I when their father scurried them away?"

"Yes, but that was only for the last 18 months. I'm talking about before? Did you ever have a close, personal relationship with any of these children?"

"I love them--"

"Miss Winston, John Winston plays football. Do you know what position he plays?"

"No, but--"

"Are you aware that football is played in rain or snow. His father believe it's important to never miss a game? Don't you agree?"

"I don't--"

"Thomas plays several instruments. He likes to practice them all the time, especially the drums. I suppose you would not find that objectionable?"

"Well, no. I--"

"Are you aware that Peter and Danny have pets? They could probably get along without their pet lamb and pigs, but I'm sure that if they were to live here permanently, they would insist that their three dogs would reside with them. How would you feel about that?"

"I've never had any pets before, so--"

"Miss Winston, the baby, Becky, is eighteen months old. Do you know which immunizations are needed for toddlers?"

"No, but there are doctors who can provide such information."

"When would you begin potty-training? And have you ever

changed a diaper?"

"No, of course not, but--"

"Miss Winston, are you aware that young Joseph has special needs and is likely to be that way for the rest of his life?"

"But there are places – nurses and doctors that --"

"You mean, you would institutionalize him? Why, Miss Winston? Does having a handicapped child not fit into your high society lifestyle?"

Mr. Levison threw down his pen, and jumped to his feet. "Objection! He's badgering the witness!"

"Withdrawn!" Abernathy paced for a few minutes, and when he spoke again it was with a noticeably calmer tone of voice. "Miss Winston, you say you are very fond of your brother, true?"

"Of course."

"And very fond of his children?"

"Yes. We wouldn't be having these proceedings if I weren't."

"I understand you were very fond of your father?"

"Yes. I adored him. We had a very special relationship. But what does that have to do with any of this? He passed away nearly 26 years ago."

"Miss Winston, isn't it true that many times these past few weeks you have scolded Matthew by saying, 'Matthew, what would Father say if he could see you now!' What do you think he would say if he were still alive to see what has happened to Matthew and his family?"

"Well!" Aunt Esther shrieked. "He would be aghast! But then, Matthew has been doing things to shock my father since the day he was born."

"They never got along?"

"No, never!"

"Since you were so close with your father, you blamed your brother whenever he and your father disagreed, correct?"

"Of course. Matthew disobeyed my father repeatedly. If Father said black, Matthew said white. My father said, stay away from the war and attend to your responsibilities here, Matthew sneaked away and enlisted anyway."

"Yes, and your family wanted him to marry into a nice, Fifth Avenue family, and what did he do? He married a poor, Catholic girl from Ireland. How did that make you feel?"

"Oh, I loved Kathleen. She was beautiful and gracious. We objected only because we felt his marriage might interfere with his obligations here. The only reason Matthew took over the business was because my father became ill, and my mother begged him to come home – from the war, that is."

"So Matthew never was happy about running the business?"

"No, not really. You'd think that being the CEO of a major, multi-million dollar corporation was a hardship. I mean, my goodness, some people would kill for a chance like that!"

"Would you?"

"Would I what?"

"Kill for a chance like that?"

"Mr. Abernathy, I have no idea what you mean. Back then, women were not afforded those kinds of opportunities. But I have always felt that I have a very good head for business."

"Did you try to secure a leadership role after Matthew left?"

"No, I couldn't. It was too late – the business has grown and things are so technical."

"Is that why you're so angry with your brother? He had position, wealth, and prestige, and he squandered it away, betraying your father's memory?"

"Yes, that's exactly how I feel. My grandfather and his father were dock workers in Liverpool when they decided to come to America. They made our company one of the best in the world. How could my brother turn his back on everything they worked so hard to create? This company is our birthright. Apparently, that means nothing to my brother."

"So you feel betrayed?"

"Yes, of course, I do. He has ten children – eight sons! They should be here, learning the business, ready to take over the helm when it's time for their generation to assume control. They should be here, not in some God-forsaken hole in the ground in the middle of nowhere. They belong here!" Her hands were clinched tightly and pounding on the arms of the chair as she spoke. Abernathy had succeeded in exposing the real reason for her outrage.

The witness was excused.

Annie was the first one called to the witness stand for the defense. She was asked to tell in her own words how it felt to leave their home and move to the farm. What was the place like and how did she manage without servants? She spoke as clearly and un-emotionally as possible. She ended by saying, "A neighbor of ours, Mrs. Ginny Gibson, has lived on a farm all her life. She told me once that if a person has no work to do, they have no reason to get up in the morning. When I lived here in New York, I had no reason to get up in the morning – no usefulness, no direction. Now I do, and it makes me feel good about myself."

"Annie, why do you think your father was eager to leave New York and move his entire family to such a place?"

"Objection!" Mr. Levison cried. "Question calls for conjecture."

"I'll rephrase the question, Your Honor. Annie, based on the conversations with your father, can you explain your father's rationale for moving his family to Iowa?"

"Yes, I can. For as long as I can remember, all of us kids knew that my father had yearnings to farm. He always said that the time he spent in Ireland Mother's family farm was one of the happiest times of his life. He would go to the country every chance he had. But after my mother died, he didn't care about anything any more. He had been away from the office throughout her long illness and discovered that they really didn't need him there as much as he thought. And when the farm sort of fell into his lap, he jumped at the opportunity. It was his chance for a fresh start, to build something that was his own. The farm is his legacy now. I would have gone to the moon with him if there was a chance that my father would feel alive again. And he does."

"You lived on the farm for over a year. By your own admission, it was very, very hard. But you're anxious to return there. Why?"

"My brothers and I moved there because of our father. But

we stayed there because we found the thing that was missing in our lives, too – a sense of purpose and accomplishment that we had never known before. The farm is our home, and we belong there."

Mr. Levison approached the witness. "Miss Winston, can you honestly tell this court that this farm is a safe and healthy environment for your brothers and sister?"

"Yes, of course. Like Mr. Abernathy said, there are millions of children who live on farms, and they're perfectly fine."

"But don't these other farms have decent housing?"

"Our house may not be the Ritz, but we're comfortable."

"Isn't it true that your brother, Matthew Jr. was seriously injured as a result of a gunshot wound? In fact, his leg was amputated, wasn't it?"

"Yes, but that was a terrible accident. He tripped and--"

"Does your father usually allow your brothers to run around the woods with guns?"

"No, of course not. That was an isolated incident --"

"That's all. No further questions." The witness was excused.

A parade of young Winston's followed, each asked if they like living on the farm. If given the choice would they return there or stay in New York? Their answers were an unanimous endorsement of farm living. They were all homesick and wanted to go home as soon as possible. Danny told the court about his dog and pet lamb. Peter described the woods and what it's like to wake up in the morning to see deer standing at the edge of the yard. John told the court that he liked the chores and hard work because it kept him physically fit. He also described the leadership role he had assumed on his sports' teams which he was sure would help him in his adult life. The air is cleaner there, he said. It's a healthier place to live. Mr. Levison asked each one if they had been coached what to say when they were on the witness stand, trying devilishly hard to get them to admit they were saying what their father wanted them to say.

He tried this tactic on John who looked him straight in the eye and said, "Mr. Levison, I am fifteen years old and smart enough to make up my own mind about things. One thing that living on a farm really teaches you is to be independent. You have to be able to think for yourself and figure out a way to get things done. It's not always easy, but when it's done, you feel real proud. And that's a good feeling."

The witness was excused.

Thomas took the stand. There were well-concealed undercurrents of nervousness among the Winston's. No one was exactly sure how he would respond to the questions.

Abernathy began by asking him questions about his music and what opportunities existed to utilize these talents while living in a small town like Shannon Town. "Well, Shannon Town is no Lincoln Center," Thomas said, "but it's not totally void of culture either." When asked if he minded the farm work, he surprised his siblings by saying the work there wasn't that hard. He looked directly at his father while he spoke. His tone was smug and condescending at times, but on the whole his testimony seemed believable and credible. The Winston's slowly began to relax as his testimony unfolded unscathed.

Abernathy's last question was why he wanted to return to the farm. A slow, snide grin spread across Thomas's face as though he was enjoying a private joke. "Well, you see, my brothers and I have learned that it's better to be a large frog in a small pond than a teeny, weenie tadpole in a huge pond."

The witness was excused.

The trial, or hearing as Abernathy called it, was nearing completion. Matthew was the only remaining witness. The stage was set for his testimony. He seemed strangely serene and calm that morning. He even joked and laughed at breakfast. His confidence was contagious, so they all felt hopeful as they dressed and made their way down to the courtroom for what they hoped would be the final time. He took the stand and smiled at his children confidently. This case was his to win or lose.

The first question asked was the most obvious one. "Matthew, can you tell this court why you moved your family?"

Matthew answered in a calm, unwavering voice. "As my daughter told you, I have always been interested in farming. It was sort of a hobby of mine, but never took it very seriously. My life here in New York was fine as long as my wife, Kathleen, was alive. But when she died, nothing was the same. I thought it was time to make a change."

"You sister's attorney has attempted to convince this court that you were so grief-stricken that you acted irrationally. What would you say to that?"

"My wife and I had a wonderful life together. Her and the kids were my whole world – the only thing that made going to that office every day bearable. Yes, it's true, her death was a terrible loss. There was an emptiness that nearly destroyed me – maybe all of us. I couldn't go on like that much longer."

"Were you drinking excessively during that time – that is, the three months between your wife's death and your decision to move?"

"Yes, I was drinking, but alcohol is supposed to make you numb, but it didn't help. And it never affected my judgment. Then this miracle happened. The farm was a chance of a lifetime, an answer to my prayers. I felt very strongly that moving out there was the best thing for my family."

"Why do you say that?"

Matthew hesitated before answering, gathering his words carefully. This had to be the definite statement – something that would make everyone understand. "I was never an ambitious man. Everything I ever had was given to me – wealth, position, everything. I tried to do my best, to contribute – I owed that much to my father. Kathleen understood – family means everything to an Irishman. But after she died, I realized I had been fooling myself. I was a 52 year old man without any idea who I was or what I wanted. I had never done an honest day's work in my life. I have ten wonderful children, and as a father, I'm supposed to give them a sense of direction and self-confidence. I realized I had given them nothing except possessions that I had never earned."

"So when I came home with that deed and told my children we were moving, they thought I was crazy, too, especially the older ones. But then something totally unexpected happened. They fell in love with the place themselves. We made it through those first miserable months in that old, rundown house, until harvest time. My oldest son, Mack – the most obnoxious, spoiled kid you'd ever want to meet, worked along side the rest of us. There's 420 acres of land that we planted and tended ourselves. It was back-breaking work, but never was a father more proud of his family. We did it together. Mack is back there with a baby of his own. There's a new birthright now, something that we're building for ourselves together."

His words echoed around the room like hallowed words whispered in church. His unflattering conviction and forthright candor were compelling. "Me and tens of thousands other men have fought in wars to preserve our freedom. The freedom of choice is the most basic of all freedoms. Just because I've chosen a new lifestyle doesn't make me crazy. Stubborn? Yes. Determined? Yes. My children are still the most important thing in my life, and I feel like I've given them so much more than I ever could have before. I'm talking about dignity and self worth, and the understanding that you don't look down on someone just because they have a little dirt under their fingernails."

"I'm sorry, Esther, if you think I've betrayed the family. Yes, I have eight sons and it's reasonable to assume at least one of them was destined to take my place at the company. Maybe it will still happen. This company will be here long after all of us are gone. I don't expect all my children to become farmers. What they do with their lives is up to them. But at least they'll understand that everything in life is not just given to them. They have to work and go after what they want. The best things in life are earned."

Matthew paused then and reached for his wallet. He took out a small, carefully folded piece of paper and turned toward the judge to explain. "I have a son who is Missing in Action in Vietnam. His name is Luke. We pray everyday for his safe return. When I feel full of grief and despair over his welfare, I take out this letter he sent me months ago before he shipped out. I'd like to read it.

Dear Dad,

I feel so bad that I missed the first 4ᵗʰ of July in Shannon Town. Sounds like everyone had a great time. Annie wrote that Independence Day has a whole new meaning for her since I enlisted. I don't know why. It shouldn't. Other people's brothers and sons have been doing this for 200 years.

I want you to know that I miss home -- the farm. The way it smells and tastes, the way the dawn spreads across the valley, and how the stars look at night. I want to thank you for giving that to me. And when I think of home, that's what I dream of. You were right to bring us there. I'm proud of you, Dad, and I miss you very much.

Love,
Luke

I know why my son wrote this to me. He was always very perceptive and intuitive about people's feelings. He knew there would be times when I doubted myself and the decision I made. And he also knew that if anything happened to him, I would be consumed with guilt. So he wrote these few, simple words to absolve me of my culpability and reassure me that he, at least, understood my decision and motives. The farm is his home, and with God's help, he will come home to us again."

* * * * * *

"Mack! We're coming home!....Yes, the day after tomorrow...I guess the judge must have thought the whole things was ridiculous because he recessed for lunch and came back with a judgment in our favor. . . . . Should have heard your father on the witness stand. He was absolutely eloquent...Thank God, it's over!"

Matthew took the receiver from Annie's hand. "Let me talk," he demanded, still grinning from ear to ear. "Son?...Yes, it's over...Yeah, I know, the whole thing was a farce, but you know your Aunt Esther. Listen, Mack, did you get those back 20 acres cleaned up? ...No? Well, what the hell have you been doing?...Well, never mind, the old man's coming home! It's August. We got plenty of time yet! OK, here's Annie. She's jumping up and down here...Don't talk too long. Long distance calls cost money, ya' know. Here's your sister."

"Mack, we'll come in at 3:05 your time," Annie cried. "I know, I can't wait either...But there's so much to do. The real estate people are coming tomorrow, and the moving company Friday morning...See ya' all then. Give the baby a big kiss from all of us! Bye!" She hung up the phone and joined the celebration. This was one of the happiest days of their lives.

* * * * * *

Late Saturday night, Matthew sat alone in the darkness in the small sitting room next to the master bedroom. It was difficult to absorb the reality that this would be the last time he would ever sit here. The fireplace was dark, and most of the furnishings were packed. His finger crept along several of the scratches and etchings on the small table that sat next to his chair. It was like a map of their family history – one gash from John's ice skate and another from when Danny's airplane knocked over the lamp. There were several cigarette burns, most of them from those long nights when he slept in his chair when Kathleen was so sick he couldn't even lie next to her in their bed. He could still feel her touch, even her smell – the perfume she always wore – hear her laughter and that soft, soothing way she spoke. Oh, how he needed her. If she was here, what would she be saying? The same thing that she had said the last time the spoke – go after your dream. Make it happen.

Now it was time to close this chapter of his life. He was selling the house – he needed the money. He was leaving this room behind, but he was comforted by the thought that the sweet memories would stay with him always. He felt no guilt about abandoning this place. Kathleen had given her blessings long ago.

August 11, 1971

Dear Luke,

Well, this is it – our last night in this house. Everything is packed and we're ready to go. I can picture how everything will look back home – Mother's dishes in the buffet, the books in the library. I can't wait.

All your things from your room have been carefully packed. There's probably a lot of things you forgot about, like your little statue collection and the signed Rockwell print. It will all be waiting for you when you come back home.

What a wonderful word, home. Daddy read a letter to us that you sent him a year ago when you were still in Louisiana. He keeps it in his wallet. I think it makes him feel close to you. Anyway, I love the way you describe home. Anyone reading that letter would understand why the farm is home to us now.

The next time I write it will be from my own little desk in my room back there. I can't wait to see the sunrise, and the stars and the moon again. Everything will be perfect as soon as you're home, too. We pray for you every day.

Love,

Annie

CHAPTER 59

They came down the steps from the airplane to brilliant, blue skies and the green and golden world they had missed so much. Mack, Penny, and Andrew came running the instant they emerged from the plane. Sonny sauntered out casually, separated from the rest, but he was grinning as wide as anyone. Annie wanted to run to him and throw her arms around him but she restrained herself. There was the old bus, washed and polished, still the only vehicle that would hold them all. Soon they were on their way home.

It was a noisy trip. The boys were asking a thousand questions. Were there any new calves? How were the puppies and the lambs? Mack, Penny, and Andrew were red-faced and excited, too, as though they were dying to tell them something.

But all the begging and cajoling would not break their resolve. Even Sonny looked like the cat that ate the canary, grasping the steering wheel so tightly that his knuckles turned white. They turned the last corner, honking as they buzzed past the Gibson's place. They could see the trees that lined the north side of the yard, then the barn and the corn cribs. Finally, there was the house. Sonny stopped at the entrance of the driveway so that everyone could get the full effect.

Everyone gasped. The sprawling old house was now a glistening white jewel, crowning the hill. It was trimmed with jade green shutters, a new roof, aluminum windows and screen doors. The yard was groomed with flowers everywhere.

"There's a pond! There's a pond!" the boys screamed. Below the house, the troublesome low spot in the driveway was now the top of a raised, earthen dam for a large pond. Its blue waters shimmered with the reflection of the handsome house. At the far end of the pond stood the immense weeping willow tree which had shaded dozens of sheep or cattle where it stood alone in the middle of the small pasture. Now it gracefully draped its long leafy fingers over the water, serene and regal, the perfect accent for the breath taking picture.

One of the boys opened the door and everyone poured out, reminiscent of when they had waded through the mud toward the house when they first arrived on that cold, frightful day in last spring. Just like she did the first time, Annie sat staring until someone took her hand to pull her along.

"C'mon, Annie," Penny cried, "you have to see the back, too."

There were even more wonderful surprises waiting for her as she rounded the corner of the house. The whole back verandah was screened, and the little gazebo was fixed and painted, surrounded by more flowers. Annie felt Sonny's eyes watching her, studying her for her reaction. He caught her gaze and looked upward, hoping she would follow. She did. This time she let out a little scream.

"Oh, Sonny," she cried, "my window. You put in my window." She dashed up the back stairs into her room. There it was, just like she had dreamed it would be someday. A huge picture window had been installed opposite her bed. Now she'd be able to awaken to wonderful sunrises every morning without even getting out of bed. She ran out to the balcony and smiled down at them, still crying.

"It was Sonny's idea, " Mack called. "But don't be disappointed when you walk through the house. We fixed up the outside but not the inside--"

"Except the dining room," Penny exclaimed. "C'mon down. You have to see this."

Mack was right when he said not much interior work had been done. The holes in the plaster, creaky steps, and unpainted walls were unchanged. She didn't care. She skipped down the stairway into the foyer, anxious to see what other fantastic wonders awaited her. She got her answer soon enough.

The broken down, dilapidated table was now a beautiful, richly finished piece of furniture. All the cuts and gashes were gone, replaced by a polished surface of resplendent oak.

"It was all Sonny!" Penny cried, clasping her hands with excitement. "I think he had a lot of nervous energy. Every time he had a couple spare minutes, he'd be working in here. We all told him he was nuts, but he just kept at it. Isn't it fantastic?"

Annie ran into the kitchen to tell Sonny of her tremendous appreciation, but she was stopped in her tracks by sober uneasiness hanging in the room. She looked at her father. His jaw was set, his eyes were full of anger and bitterness. She was confused. Mack and Andrew looked equally perplexed with disappointment stinging in the faces. Matthew cast them a parting glare as he walked out the back door, across the porch into the office.

"Honey, what happened," Penny asked her husband. "Wasn't he pleased?"

"Apparently not," Mack retorted. "He didn't say two words about the house and yard. Only thing he said was the fields have weeds and he's pissed that we sold some of the stock."

"Didn't you tell him we couldn't do two or three hours of chores every morning and night. It was too much. What did he expect from us?"

Mack turned and stared out the window. "I tried to tell him

that we wanted to get the place fixed up in case they came back taking more pictures. We even took some pictures ourselves. We were going to send them to use but the trial was over too fast. " He motioned toward the large manila envelope stamped and sealed lying on the kitchen table.

"What you did is wonderful," Annie declared. "I don't know how you managed it all." She watched Sonny. He had an equally pained expression. "It's wonderful, it really is."

"Well, don't look too close," Mack muttered. The corners of his mouth began twitching into a grin. "Just wait till the old man sees that the barns are only painted on the sides facing the road. The other three still look like shit."

Everyone laughed and the shroud of disappointment lifted. Just then they noticed the clatter as the boys care clamoring down the stairs with swim suits and towels, announcing they were going swimming. Mack and Penny decided to play lifeguard and walked out arm in arm. Annie turned to say something to Sonny, but he had disappeared. Annie knew he had retreated into the solace of finding some work to do. She busied herself with unpacking and settling down the baby, glancing out the windows a hundred times as she moved through the house, hoping for a glimpse of him.

Annie hurried to get supper on the table. She was disappointed when Sonny didn't come out to eat with the rest of the family. Everyone in the house settled down and a hush fell across the land as the sun slowly set. She wondered onto the back balcony to soak up the quiet and noticed someone sitting in the shadows at rocky place. She knew at once it was Sonny by the stooped silhouette straddling the tree trunk. She ran down the stairs and arrived at the rocky place breathless without trying to mask her happiness to find him alone like this. He appeared a little startled, which surprised her because his sixth sense usually prevented that. She said nothing, wanting to first assess his mood and demeanor. He appeared unusually meditative and pained. She guessed he was frustrated over her father's attitude.

"The place looks great, Sonny," she began. "You got so much done in a short amount of time. It's amazing." She wanted to reach out and comfort him, but she couldn't. "Penny said you were like a crazy man, that you hardly took time to eat or sleep."

He was embarrassed, but she didn't stop. "And you saved my table. God, Sonny, I knew it could be beautiful, but it's better than I ever dreamed. And my flowers and the window. Thank you."

"Well, Jeez, I had to do something. It was so damned quiet around here." He leaned back against the tree with his arms crossed across his chest.

She was relieved to see a smile steal across his face. "You missed us, didn't you. I know we're a lot of trouble, but – God, it's just so good to be home." He put his arms down and leaned forward. She took this as an invitation to move closer and was thrilled when he did not move away. "I'm sorry about my father, Sonny. I know it seems like he doesn't appreciate everything that you accomplished, but he does. He's just disappointed, that's all. Coming home on the plane, he showed me a list of things he wanted to get done around here. You did a lot of it already. He probably just feel like you don't need him as much as he thought, that's all."

"I know. It was just so much easier to get stuff done around here without so many – you know, so many people." The moment was comfortable and warm, but he seemed to be avoiding looking at her. Then their eyes met for just a moment. He reached out to stroke her cheek and kissed her.

It was sweet and soft, like a young boy's first kiss, but she wanted more. She could scarcely breathe as he drew her near and kissed her again. Her arms slipped around his shoulders, pressing him closer.

Suddenly, he jerked away and the spell was broken. She was startled by the angry expression on his face. He started to walk away without saying a word, but she moved to block his escape. "Sonny! Don't you just walk away. Why are you so mad?"

"Look," he said without looking at her, "I'm sorry. Just go to the house and forget it."

"Forget it? Why? It seems like I've -- Sonny, stop. For God's sake, look at me! We didn't do anything wrong!"

"Just go to the house." He moved her firmly to the side and walked off.

"Oh-h-h-h-h!" she screamed, wishing she had something to

throw at him. She ran upstairs, threw herself across her bed, and cried harder than ever before. First she was angry and beat her pillow with her fist. Then the hurt crept in. Loving someone like Sonny Jackson must be the hardest, most frustrating kind of love possible, she moaned. It just wasn't fair.

Sonny rushed inside his shed without turning on the lights. He stood at the window and watched her run toward the house. Even without seeing her face, he knew she was crying and he hated himself for that. How could he have done something so stupid? It was just a kiss, but he knew it meant much more to her. He had managed to suppress any show of emotion so far. But tonight – her shimmering hair flowing in the breeze and her luscious, inviting lips. Never again, he chided himself. There would be too many questions.

* * * * * *

There had been other mornings where Annie listened half-heartedly as she lingered in bed. But today she awakened in full anticipation of it and eagerly strained to hear and identify each sound. It was wonderful to be surrounded once more by the faint, melodic little noises that floated through her open window like a soft, carefully orchestrated serenade

The birds were the most conspicuous, each with their own distinctive song. The robins with their tuneful chirping, the blue jays with their sassy chattering, and the invasive, irreverent cawing of the pesky crows. The maple tree which stood guard outside her window was a variable factory of sounds – the industrious squirrels scurrying from branch to branch, a woodpecker jack-hammering for his breakfast, and, of course, the soothing whisper of the rustling leaves stirred by a gentle breeze. And down by the pond, there was a deep-throated frog croaking in harmony with the constant chirp of the crickets.

From the barnyard, she could hear the distant bleating of the sheep, the busy-body cackling of the chickens, and the un-elegant grunting of the pigs. There was the clapping of the small, metal doors of the feeders and the banging of an unlatched gate. Somewhere off in the distance was the soft whining of a

508

neighbor's tractor, already at work, and the humming of rapidly moving traffic on the highway two miles away. From down the hallway came the rhythmic sounds of her father's deep snoring, augmented by the dizzy buzzing of flies circling outside her window screen.

All of this was deliciously woven together by the brightening hues of pastels appearing across the eastern skies and the touch of the fresh, crisp linens on her bed. It all fit – the rich tapestry of wonderful sights, sounds, and smells. She laid there, rejoicing in it all, remembering those familiar words: *"God is in His heavens, and all is well."*

Then there were stirrings in the old house – Mack's alarm could be heard from the other end of the hallway, the sounds of running water and a toilet flushing. It was time to get up and get to work if they were going to make it to 9 o'clock Mass. This Sunday was likely to be like all the others – the rushing, the arguing, the mild hysteria that accompanies getting this many people ready. But today, at least, it would be music to her ears.

* * * * * *

Danny and Peter had rushed down the road to see Ginny and Jake shortly after arriving home but Annie was not able to steal a way for a visit until Sunday afternoon. She loved driving her own car again, even welcoming the swirl of dust that followed her down the gravel road. Her friend, Lori Bean's old station wagon was already on the yard. Bolting through the back door, she was greeted by the wonderful aroma of Ginny's kitchen – still warm, freshly baked cookies, coffee percolating on the counter, and the camphor ointments Ginny used on her aching legs. Overjoyed, Annie hugged them both so hard she was afraid she might hurt them. They laughed and listened eagerly as Annie recounted the events of the past two months. When Annie pressed Lori with questions of how her summer was going, her friend smiled thinly and said there would be plenty of time to talk about all that later, now that Annie was home. The two fondly embraced each other again. "Yes," Annie sighed happily. "I'm finally home."

Chapter 60

The delirious euphoria Annie and her brothers felt upon their arrival home did not last very long. An ominous cloud of dread spread over them as soon as they realized that their father's foul mood was not temporary. Matthew grumbled at anyone who glanced his direction so everyone ran the other way when they saw him coming. Mack and Andrew could hardly contain their bitter disappointment with their father's attitude. Penny was the only one who voiced her resentment, over the glaring objections of her husband. She did not understand everyone's hesitance to confront Matthew about his apparent lack of gratitude and good manners. More than once, she and her father-in-law traded barbs across the kitchen table. He would come in, complaining about the weeds or an assigned task not done to his satisfaction, and she would snarl right back. "Everyone's doing the best they can," she hissed. "Perhaps the boys would do better if they had more supervision." That comment was an obvious reference to the increase of Matthew's drinking and a decrease in his own workload.

The climate within the kitchen was dark and angry at times as well. It started almost immediately when Annie reached for some dish or cooking utensil, only to find that her kitchen had been totally rearranged during her absence. At first, Penny apologized, saying that cooking for the four of them did not require most of the larger items so she put them up, out of her way. Annie found it aggravating to constantly have to hunt for everything she needed, often slamming doors and muttering obscenities under her breath. Penny responded by staying out of the kitchen, leaving both of them resentful and wounded, too stubborn to admit they missed those long girl talks they used to have while cooking and cleaning together. Somehow everything had changed.

The most puzzling thing of all was Thomas. He never got out of bed before 10 am, seldom did any work, and disappeared off the yard for hours at a time. To make matters worse, his behavior was completely unchallenged by his father. Every time someone would complain to Matthew, he'd mutter something nonsensical and walk away. Seemingly, Thomas was untouchable, and no one understood why.

The hot, dog days of the summer dragged on. The only one who seemed truly happy was John. He and his friend, Kenny, resumed their early morning workouts and were deliriously happy when football practice began in mid-August. This was their senior year and their last football season to wear the green and white SHS, and they wanted to make the most of it. The whole community was happily anticipating a championship season, their hopes riding on their star quarterback and halfback.

The two were inseparable, often staying overnight at each other's home. Unbeknown to these two athletes, their activates were being watched intently by Thomas. Often at night, Thomas crept down the hallway, opening the door to John's room and watched the two of them sleep. He grinned ruefully and whispered, "Sleep now, boys, while you can."

* * * * * *

The news from Washington and Southeast Asia was nearly non-existent. After years of nightly casualty reports and vivid descriptions of battles and massive campaigns, the lack of substantive information was maddening. There were rumors that the peace talks in Paris stalled while awaiting the outcome of the political battles in South Vietnam. Walter Cronkite lead off the 6:00 news with stories of the suspected contrived free election in South Vietnam, whereas all of the President Thieu's opposition were mysteriously dropping out of the race. Annie and her family knew that any political maneuvering in South Vietnam had a direct effect on when and how the war would end. It was also noted that on August 6th, the last of the 4th Battalion left Vietnam for home. This was the first unit deployed to the area back in 1965 when the nightmare began. The South Vietnam Army were said to have successfully driven into Cambodia and cut off a Communist supply route through Pnompenh, but Annie didn't believe it. The inadequacies of the supposedly well-trained ARVN units cost her brother his freedom, so she had no illusions of their effectiveness. Besides, if they were still fighting, the war was no closer to being over than before.

Annie fought hard not to let the frustration crush her. She tried to call upon the warmth and rapture of that golden moment with Sonny when he kissed her and held her in his arms, but it was gone. Maybe it hadn't happened at all, just a mirage that had evaporated in the summer sun, gone forever.

* * * * * *

Not one to sit around while everything crumbled around her, Penny began to formulate an escape plan. She considered the atmosphere at the Winston house to be unhealthy and she wanted out. Finding something close and appealing was her only chance of convincing her husband that they needed a place of their own. And of course, money was a major issue.

After weeks of searching and secretive negotiations, she was ready to reveal her proposal. Even the unveiling was carefully planned. One Sunday afternoon, she saddled up Mr. Phipps and Goldie and brought them around to the side kitchen door. She called Mack out. "C'mon, hon, let's go for a ride. Annie will watch the baby for us, won't you, Annie," she cooed, smiling provocatively.

Knowing how these rides usually ended, he jumped into the saddle and followed her down the lane. He didn't even notice that she was not taking them on their usual route down the bottom road into the timber. He always rode Goldie because she followed Mr. Phipps as blindly as Mack followed Penny. They chatted as they rode along, passing fields of golden corn and beans, ripening beneath the brilliant skies of blue. This was a good idea, Mack thought. He needed to spend less time fixating on things over which he had no control and concentrate on his family. Penny looked as beautiful now as last summer when she was his mystery lady, galloping into his heart atop her magnificent steed.

They headed south and then turned right at the crossroads, climbing onto the high, rocky land that lay west of their farm. And then, seemingly unexpectedly, she turned into the yard of an old country school. Mack noticed this place before. It was littered with garbage and the weeds were as tall as the horses' backs. The red-brick building had not been occupied in over twenty years when one-room schools were phased out of use. Across the door, and old, faded signboard still hung, reading: "Pleasant View Township Schoolhouse #1."

Penny nudged Mr. Phelps forward, wading through the weeds and debris to the steps. She jumped off her horse, beaming happily. "Well, what do you think of this place?" she blurted. Mack had no idea how to respond, sitting dumbstruck atop his horse. She produced a key from her pocket and opened the door. She disappeared inside so that Mack had no recourse but to follow.

The windows were boarded so that narrow beams of sunlight were emitted, where tiny bits of dust danced in the light, giving an illusion of motion to the dark and lifeless room. The desks, blackboards, and bookshelves had been taken away so that cavernous, high-ceiling room stood vacant and silent,. Penny's footsteps echoed softly as she moved around the room. Feeling compelled to whisper, she turned to Mack and murmured, "I think this place has definite possibilities."

"Possibilities for what? A warehouse, a grain bin? What?"

"No, I think –" She hesitated, knowing that she had to chose her words carefully. "I think this could make a nice house – like a big ol' one-room log cabin or something." She could see disbelief and confusion mounting in her husband's face, so she hurried on. "Mack, I know it doesn't look like much right now, but it's a well-constructed, brick building that's been standing for at least fifty or sixty years, so I'll bet it would last for at least another half a century." She took a deep breath and exhaled slowly. "It's the only place for sale around here for miles and miles – you want to stay close to your family, right? Mrs. Miller would sell the 240 acres on this side of the road. It's hilly and rocky, only about 100 acres are tillable. But there's enough pasture to support a good sized herd of cattle. And it's cheap -- $125 an acre. That's only $30,000 for the whole place. It would be ours, Mack, our own farm."

Mack could see the earnest intensity and anticipation

illuminating from her face, but he could not grasp what she was saying. "Our own farm? How?"

"If we have 20% down – that's $6,000, and my dad would co-sign a loan for the rest."

"Your father? Christ, Penny, what are you saying? Where in the hell are we going to live? In here?"

"Yes, here. Okay, so it looks bad, but it's better than your house was when you first got here, isn't it?"

"Penny, there's no plumbing, no nothing!"

"Neither did your house."

"It would cost $1000's of dollars to make this place livable."

"So? You have $22,450 left in your trust fund."

"What"

"We're married aren't we? I looked your last statement."

"That money's our nest egg, for emergencies—for our future."

"Future? What in the hell do you think I'm talking about? This is our future? It's our chance to build something together – you, me and Katie. You're pouring every ounce of blood and sweat you have into your father's place. For what? When everything's said and done, it's still his farm. My God, look at the way he's been acting since he came back. He didn't appreciate anything we did – not one thing. He's always surly and irritable."

"Things are tense because of everything that's going on right now."

"Why do you keep making excuses for him? I want out of there. You deserve better. If you work that hard, do it for yourself. Do it for us."

"But Penny, this is such a huge step. We'd have to fix this place up, start a herd – my God, it would take every cent we have."

"I know it's a lot, Mack, but isn't this what you want? Why shouldn't you be the boss of your own place, make decisions for yourself?"

"What if I don't know enough? I'm new at this. What if we get in way over our heads, and lose everything?"

"You wouldn't be doing this alone, Mack. I'll be here every step of the way. And there's Sonny, your brothers, even your father. I'm sure he would gladly give you his opinion about everything." They laughed then, their foreheads touching as they grasped each other's hands.

Their minds began racing, and words spilled out faster. "Winter's coming soon, so we'd have to get this place ready fast," Penny said.

"We can buy this lot now, and take over the farm in March. That'd give us some time to look at livestock and begin buying in the spring."

"We could put the kitchen over there and the living room there. We could have one of those breakfast bars separating them."

"We could put up one of those pole barns. They don't cost a lot."

"We don't have to buy a lot of new furniture, at least not right away. But we're going to have to buy appliances. We could buy used ones, I suppose."

"Sure we could."

"Sure we could do what?"

"Build a barn."

"Build a barn?"

"Yes, we'll need a barn."

"I thought we were talking about the house – furniture and appliances. I'll have to cook, right? And wash your dirty, smelly clothes?"

"Absolutely," Mack smiled as he took her into his arms. "My loving wife will meet me at the door every night after a hard day's work, peel off my filthy, God-awful clothes and-"

"You mean like this?" she cooed, unbuttoning his shirt.

"Yes," he whispered, doing the same to her blouse.

They christened their new home with their love-making, invigorated with new hopefulness. This was a whole new beginning for them, and they felt more optimistic and unshackled than they had in a very long time.

* * * * * *

515

The Winston clan received the news with indifference. "I'll still be here to help on the farm when needed," Mack said, "but it's was time for me and Penny to strike out on our own." They outlined their plans, not mentioning the fact that Penny's father was going to co-sign their mortgage. No one said anything at first. Matthew listened, then left the room abruptly without responding.

"Well, I'll help as much as I can," Sonny said.

"Thanks, man," Mack said. "You know I can't do it without you."

All Ann could muster was a polite, "That's wonderful," but her head was swimming. She was not prepared for further fragmentation of the family. The pretense of a happy, well-adjusted family was evaporating. Penny's absence meant that Annie was back to taking care of eight people by herself, while her sister-in-law was off caring for her little family of three. Turning to the sink to attack a pile of dirty dishes, she brushed back angry tears. She understood their decision. Who wouldn't jump at the chance to get out of this place? Sometimes Annie imagined what it would be like to go off with Sonny in a little house of their own somewhere – quiet and unencumbered, just concentrating on each other. But she knew that would never happen. They were both tied forever to this family and this land. She resented that Mack and Penny were able to separate themselves so easily.

* * * * * *

Once the decision was made, Penny and Mack began to work quickly to make their place habitable. However, unlike when work began on the big house, finances were a constant concern. Luckily, Sonny was able to do most of the technical work so that electricity and plumbing were installed. Penny worked night and day, doing what she could alone while the men worked elsewhere. After a quick supper, they were back at it, working late into the night. Everyone helped as much as they could. Matthew stopped by occasionally, never helping but muttering unsolicited advice.

Considering that Penny was raised in the lap of luxury, she was amazingly frugal. She purchased used appliances, carpet remnants, and scoured her mother's attic for boxes of forgotten drapes, curtains, and furnishings. She scrubbed, painted and wall-papered with ravenous zeal. Her proficiency with a hammer and screwdriver were remarkable. Three and a half weeks after she first proposed the idea to Mack, they packed up Katie's crib, toys, highchair, and their own belongings and moved out for good. Their house was barely habitable, but they didn't seem to care.

The large bedroom at the end of the hallway did not stay vacant for long. A large scale shake-up in bedroom assignments ensued. Unceremoniously removing the flowery wall paper, Thomas moved into Penny and Mack's old room without bothering to consult anyone, saying that he lived in Luke's "memorial museum" long enough. Andrew, who seemed to be stopping by much less frequently these days moved his few remaining belongings into the third floor room which he had shared with Luke those long ago quiet evenings.

Penny's joyful optimism that things would vastly improve after their change of residence was short lived. As with everything these days, it all came down to money. They didn't have any. How could they when they had no income? Mack dutifully went off each morning to work with his father, for which he did not receive any pay. Both he and Penny agreed they would not use the trust fund for ordinary living expenses. The situation was grim.

Once again, Penny was determined to find a solution by using her own resources. The answer seemed fairly straight-forward to her. After all, she was a registered nurse, capable of earning a considerable amount of money. Then, thankfully, a wonderful opportunity fell into her lap as though it was pre-ordained. At least, that's the way it seemed to her, but she was sure her husband would not agree. Once again, she had to choose her words carefully.

She decided she would tell Mack one night at supper. They sat at their small kitchen table, eating fried eggs and toast for the third time that week. Mack brought eggs home each night and

Penny had baked bread early that morning before the summer heat became intolerable. Mack pushed the food around his plate. He was hungry, but not for this particular fare.

"Mack," she began. "I took Katie to Doc Peters for her check-up today. Guess what? His office nurse, Helen Carson, is retiring."

"Hmmm," Mack murmured, not really caring to engage in idle chit chat. He looked tired and despondent.

"They're looking for someone to take her place." Mack's head jerked up and his fork fell onto his plate with a loud clang. She had his full attention now. "He asked if I was interested in the job."

"Interested? Don't try to bullshit me, Penny!" he cried, leaping from his chair. "You probably already told him that you'd take the job, right?" She didn't answer but her imploring, earnest eyes confirmed his worst fears. "Jesus, Penny, I'm such a piss poor provider that my wife has to go to work?"

"That's not what I meant."

"Then what? Explain to me why you think you have to work!"

"It's not your fault we don't have any money. You refuse to ask your father to be paid for the work you do over there."

"OK, then, I'll go over there right now and ask him."

"No, you won't. You don't want to give him the satisfaction of seeing you come begging to him. Isn't this a better idea?"

"No, it is not!"

"Mack, what choice do we have? The utility bills are going to be coming in soon. We already used more of the trust fund than we expected. We need stuff for the house. Christ, we need groceries!"

"You think I don't know that? I'll figure this out. I'll get money somehow."

"You stupid jerk! Why in the hell is this any more your problem than mine? Why do you have to take care of this?"

"Penny, just listen—"

"No, you listen! I am a registered nurse, or at least I will be as soon as I get my State Boards results. You know better than anyone how much my profession means to me. What did you think? I would never work! Why in the hell did I bother graduating? It's only part-time. Doc Peter's office in Shanny is only open on Tuesday's and Thursday's."

"What about Katie? My sister can't baby-sit her."

"I realize that!" she retorted. "Helen said she'd love to take Katie when I'm at the office – we'll trade places. And I'm sure my mother would love to watch her when I'm at the hospital."

"Why in the hell would you have to go to the hospital?"

"Only every once in awhile. I'll go on rounds with him sometimes, for dressing changes and things. You know how busy the staff nurses are there. I could learn so much!"

He said nothing for a few moments, his eyes filled with unmistakable hurt. "I thought you liked our life together here. I liked coming here for lunch or stopping by for a quick cup of coffee. I like having you...near. I'm sorry if that sounds selfish, but I liked it like that."

"I know what you're saying, but --" How could she make him understand that she wanted to get up in the morning and have more to think about than cooking, cleaning, and laundry. She didn't have to. He said it for her.

"This is more about you wanting to work than the money, isn't it. You're just itching to get out there, aren't you."

She leaped into his arms, smothering him with joyous hugs and kisses. Never had she loved him more than at that moment. She adored him for understanding and for not making her explain it. She felt certain that everything was going to be fine!

* * * * * *

Finally, Penny was doing something of which her mother approved. Mrs. Lamp even insisted that she take her daughter shopping for new uniforms and shoes. Considering their financial situation, Penny did not object. She couldn't wait to get to work.

She found quickly that her own anti-establishment personality fit in perfectly with the causal, unregimented atmosphere of her new job. That didn't mean that there were no challenges – there was a wide range of diseases to diagnosis, medicines to dispense, and gashes and cuts to suture and bandage. The confidence that the community had in Doc Peter was well founded. The kind and devoted doctor was immensely knowledgeable and proficient. Penny was more and more impressed each time she worked with him. Helen, equally accomplished, stayed on to orient the eager new office nurse. The dilemma regarding Katie was easily solved when Doc Peters suggested Penny bring her young daughter into the office with her which allowed Penny the luxury of slipping away to nurse her baby when needed. Katie slept in one of the examination rooms while they worked.

As Penny's life took a turn for the better, the rest of the family had no such luck. The hot days of August wore on as the boys anxiously looked forward to the beginning of school.

September 2, 1971

Dear Luke,

At long last, the SHS football team had began their season, and they won! Of course, your brother was the star – scored 21 of the total 35 points. He plays some position of defense, too – cornerback, I think, whatever the heck that is. Anyway, he did very well. I wish you could see him play. Mr. Hornick, one of the fathers, is filming the games on his movie camera, so John will be anxious to borrow the films and the projector to show them to you. They're expected to go undefeated.

It's hot for September. Your brothers are cooking in school, but no one seems to mind. Monday is Labor Day. We're not doing anything special. That was never one of your father's favorite holidays anyway, especially since he never seemed to be able to please the union workers at the factory, remember? Thank God, he doesn't have to worry about any of that anymore.

The corn is starting to turn. Daddy drives down to the bottom every day and walks down the rows. Another month, it will be picking time again. Oh, Luke, I wish you were here. Nothing will be complete; nothing will be all right until you're here with us. You are constantly in our thoughts and prayers.

Love,

Annie

CHAPTER 61

"Where's Pop?" Andrew asked as he came into the kitchen. As was his habit, he came home on Saturday afternoon to check the family and do some laundry before heading back to Dubuque later that night.

"He went down to the bottom," Annie said. "I guess the only thing that makes him happy these days is walking the rows, checking the crop. At least if he's down there, he's not yelling at everyone up here." She turned back to the stove and stirred a pot of chili. It was late September and cold enough for soup.

"He's still so crabby?" Andrew mused. "God, when is he goin' get over it – if we can ever figure out what set him off in the first place."

"Well, Thomas isn't helping much. Maybe you could talk to him."

"He won't listen to me any more than anyone else."

"He's gotta listen to someone. Daddy just ignores him, even when he refuses to get up for school or comes home at two or three in the morning. I don't get it. If that was any of you other boys, he'd be riding your butts like crazy. Thomas don't seem to care what anyone says or thinks. His music, his band --that's his new family, the only thing he cares about."

"Is he still hanging around that girl – what's her name?"

"Kitty McHale. Yes, Thomas is her new pet. She's at least ten years older than him, but they're practically inseparable. He was so happy when he convinced her to listen to him play and join his band. He thinks with her singing they actually have a shot at making it big."

"Isn't she living with that guy – the one that everyone says is a drug dealer?"

"Curtis Peet. Yeah, she sure does. This whole town thinks he's the devil incarnate. Everything bad around here gets blamed on him, especially drugs. He's enough to make mothers grab their children and cross to the other side of the street. And our brother hangs around with that guy? My God."

"Well, I'll try to talk to Thomas, but I'm not making any

521

promises. I gotta get back to town tonight."

Annie shrugged her shoulder in response. Just like with so many other things these days, more problems but no solutions, questions without answers.

* * * * * *

As the weather began to change and the countryside began to ease into the golden time of autumn, she found countless other things occupy her mind. Like the busy little squirrels filling their nests with nuts, it was a time to harvest the fruits of their labor and store it carefully away for the hard winter ahead. She was glad to immerse herself in the long days of work, concentrating on canning recipes instead of obsessive worry about Luke or her father or the thousand other concerns. Another pleasant diversion was gazing out the kitchen window and watching Sonny work on the yard, stubbornly attempting to fix broken equipment or mending fences. Since that night when he had unexpectedly kissed her, he was more ill at ease with her and they seldom spoke. She was content to watch him from afar, dreaming of the day when there would be something more.

There would be no dramatic harvest this year. The Jameson outfit had been contracted for the combining, and Matthew would have to be content to wait his turn like everyone else. He didn't like it, but he was powerless to pull off any kind of wild, unbelievable stunt like last year. He winced at the thought of how arrogantly he had written out that cardboard contract with Walt Jameson – he agreed to pay the purchase price of the machines if anything happened. He'd be the laughing stock of the whole town in he tried that now. People were already jeering and making jokes about him behind his back. He had stolen his own children's money to try to turn that run-down, God-forsaken place into a thriving farm. They thought of him as an eccentric millionaire before but now he was just a pathetic fool. This year, Jameson had humiliated him by insisting he put down a cash deposit. All Matthew could do was sit back and wait, hoping that Mother Nature would cooperate. It was a humbling experience for this once wealthy man. Now he was a simple farmer, no better than anyone else.

There was another important difference between last year and this. They desperately needed money. Bills were mounting and major purchases were put off until they sold the crop, which meant Matthew might be forced to sell early before the grain prices went up. Every day at noon, Matthew took his dinner into his office, turned on the radio, and listened to the grain prices. He hoped they would nudge upward by early November, but that seemed doubtful because by all accounts, this was going to be another bumper crop.

The one thing that made Matthew smile was sitting in the stands at John's football games. The whole team played sensationally, but John was spectacular. He was on target to break every school record on the books. His friend, Kenny, was also having a banner year as quarterback. They were the talk of town. His son's accomplishments on the football field was the one reason Matthew Winston still had to hold his head high and accept congratulatory slaps on the back from his drinking buddies at the Pub.

If Matthew's pride in John was sky-rocketing, he had another son that was giving him nothing but grief. Thomas' antics became the number one topic of conversations around town. Well-intentioned parents made it very clear to Matthew that he should keep Thomas away from their sons and daughters. Matthew once got into a brawl at the tavern that began when Jim Mather's drunken father began threatening Mathew to keep his "fuckin', doped-up, no good kid" away from his son. Matthew never told anyone about the incident at home, but word of it soon reached other members of the family. Annie heard about it from Lori and flew into a terrible rage. She had no idea why Matthew tolerated Thomas's behavior, but she had enough.

Annie made up her mind to confront the both of them as soon as possible. It was high time Thomas got back into school and forget all the music nonsense. And she expected her father to back her up on this. She would insist.

* * * * * *

The opportunity for this planned confrontation came one morning when Matthew came into the kitchen for a mid-morning coffee break just as Thomas ambled in, blurry-eyed and obviously hung over. Annie began her much rehearsed speech. "Good, I'm glad you're both here. I have something to say. Daddy, I heard some talk that you got into a fight at the Pub the other night with Jim Mathers father because he wants you to keep Thomas away from his son." She was standing at the kitchen table, clutching the upright posts of one of the chairs.

Matthew glared at her angrily. "Not now, Ann. The cattle got out--"

"I'm sorry, Dad, but if we don't settle this now, when will we? Everyone's asking why he isn't in school. I've been getting calls from teachers, councilors, and even Mr. Moore, the music teacher." Thomas interjected a loud, snooty hoot at the mention of that name, but Annie ignored it and went on. "I have no idea how things got to this point, and I don't care. It has to stop. I want him in school – now!"

"But Annie, what good would that do? He's not going to apply himself." Matthew retorted.

"Yeah, that's for sure," Thomas sneered.

"So? Then make him! Ground him, take away his privileges. If he doesn't get decent grades, then no music, no band."

"Like hell! I'd like to see you try that one!" Thomas cried.

"What?" Annie shrieked. "How dare you talk to him like that. Daddy, do something with him."

"Like what," Matthew said wearily.

"There's got to be something! Look at him – he's been drinking, maybe even using drugs. He's a mess – he never works, treats everyone around here like shit! Comes and goes whenever he pleases."

"What do you want me to do, Annie, tie him up in the barn?"

"I cannot believe your attitude about this, Daddy! Why do you tolerate this from a smart ass, punk kid?"

"I know he's not doing so well right now.," Matthew said, slumping back into a chair, "but I keep hoping he'll wise up and re-join the human race. He's been raised to know right from wrong. He'll come around."

"Hey! What am I, pork sausage?" Thomas cried. "Quit talking about me like I'm a stick of furniture. Can't I say anything?"

"Oh, shut up, Thomas!" Annie blasted. "You haven't had anything decent to say in months, you asshole!"

"Annie—"

"I don't care! That's what he is! What about the other boys, Peter and Danny? They see him walking around here like this. How long before they try it? I don't blame Mr. Mathers for not wanting him around his son."

"Bubba Mathers is a no good, boozing, trashy sonofabitch who has no business saying anything to me," cried Matthew, much more animated than before. "I told you. There's nothing I can do, short of kicking him out. I can't do that. He's only 16—"

"That's exactly my point. He's still a minor. You have guardianship of him. I've been doing some checking. There's a facility in Iowa City for juvenile addicts and—"

"Addicts! I'm not no fucking addict!"

"The hell you're not! All Daddy has to do is sign some papers, and he can put you away in there so fast your head would spin."

"And how the fuck are they going to make me stay?"

"Hey, Thomas, I got news for you. These places have three hundred pound guards and nice padded rooms."

"You bitch, you wouldn't dare!"

"Oh, yeah? Just—"

"Stop it, both of you," Matthew shouted, leaping up from his chair. "I've had enough. It seems I was wrong. There is something I can do." He turned to face his son for the first time. "But that sounds a little drastic, doesn't it, Thomas? Perhaps you'd like to reconsider some of your choices."

"Oh, like hell I would—"

"I'm not asking much, just that you get up and go to school. You can ease back into the choring routine later. All I want is for you to come home at a decent hour and go to school everyday. Could you do that?"

525

The two were glaring at each other, their eyes locked on one another as though in deadly combat. "No, Father dear, I see no reason why I should bother with that pathetic, ridiculous hole in the ground they call a school. I believe I've expressed my feelings about that once before, remember?"

"Yes, I remember us talking about it briefly a while ago, but I think it's time you stop acting like a spoiled, pampered brat and get back to school. What was the name of that place?"

Annie watched the two combatants closely. Apparently there was some history between them that precipitated Thomas's odd behavior. She waited breathlessly to see what would happen next.

"You both can go straight to hell," Thomas hissed quietly. "Try it, and see what happens."

"Son, I'm not asking for anything outrageous. Just go to school and show this town that you are not some evil fiend."

"Oh, I'll show them all right," Thomas muttered. He sighed deeply, never taking his eyes off his father, and continued. "Okay, I'll go to the damn school. I have some unfinished business there anyway. But remember, Father dear, this was your idea."

With that, he turned and sauntered out of the room. Even though he had made a major concession, he still moved with an air of disdain that made Annie shudder. She turned to talk more with her father but he, too, was gone. Standing alone, staring at their empty chairs, she had a frightening feeling that this situation was far from resolved.

* * * * * *

Just as he promised, Thomas came downstairs in time to board the bus for school. His brothers gasped, but they said nothing.

"Thomas, why didn't you tell John you needed a ride," Annie called as they hurried out the door. John drove to school every day in an old beat up Ford Mustang purchased for him by his father. "I'm sure you could have ridden along with him."

"No way," Thomas snarled. "Who wants to get up that

early."

The explanation sounded reasonable to Annie, so she never mentioned it again. She knew these two intensely disliked each other, so why push it.

John barely acknowledged his brother's sudden appearance at school. He was keenly aware of Thomas's reputation around the community so he wanted to distance himself as much as possible. Besides, he had far more important issues. Homecoming was in ten days which he regarded as the single most important event of his short life. Not only was this the biggest game of his career, but he had been elected by his team to be one of the official escorts for the Homecoming Court, considered to be an immensely prestigious honor. Annie smiled at the meticulous way he had gotten his suit dry-cleaned and shoes shined. Perhaps he was beginning to notice girls after all.

Chapter 62

John did not realize that something insidious was slowly engulfing his world until a few days later. The team was in the locker room after a long, hard practice. John was basking in that inner, exhilarating buzz he always got after one of these gut-busting, full-out workouts. He and Kenny showered leisurely, joking about poor passes and missed tackles. As they dressed they made plans for the evening, discussing stopping by the Pub for supper and then going over to Kenny's house to finish their homework. Slowly, they became aware that everyone was staring at them, and the usually noisy room was very quiet.

"Hey, guys, what's up?" John chided, tying his sneakers. "C'mon, it was a good practice. We're gonna' kill those suckers Friday night, right?" He threw a wet towel at Thompson, the huge, usually jovial center who looked away without responding. "Hey, Thompson, what's going on?" John pressed, thoroughly confused by everyone's behavior.

It was only when John and Kenny pushed open the door to leave that someone spoke. "Sweet dreams, boys," a voice from the back of the room called. "Don't let the bed-bugs bite." The words were accompanied by a not so subtle chorus of stifled snickering. John glanced over his shoulders, wondering who had said it and what it meant. He and Kenny discussed it over French fries and burgers and decided that perhaps a few of the guys were jealous because it was widely known that college scouts would be at Friday's game, looking primarily at them. They agreed it was just one of those petty things that would pass quickly.

But the odd behavior continued the next day. At school, other students stopped and stared at them when they walked down the hall. The hurtful sneers were nothing compared to practice. As co-captains of the team, they were supposed to lead calisthenics. Kenny called everyone to line up, but everyone turned their back, milling around disdainfully. After several more attempts, order was not restored until the coach finally looked up from his clipboard and barked at them to get started. Even then, the jumping jacks and stretches were completed haphazardly, each player moving at their own pace, refusing to follow John and Kenny's lead.

Coach Evans wanted to work on some new blocking schemes. He knew the next opponent had scouted them well, so he wanted to use some different alignments. Time and time again they tried it. "No, no, no." he screamed exasperated. "This is a running play off the left side. For God's sake, open up a goddamn hole. Winston, what the hell are you doing? You're running up the backs of your own blockers! Let's try this again!"

It was true, John was getting tangled up in his own linesmen. No one was moving. At the end of every play, he was hammered viciously to the ground, a fact not missed by their coach. "Jesus Christ, guys! What the hell is going on? Defense, this is a walk through – you don't have to kill him. And leave the quarterback alone! I never called for any blitzing! Lets try this again!"

They did try it again, over and over, but nothing seemed to be working. Totally enraged, the coach ended the practice early. Bruised and battered, John and Kenny limped back to the locker room and received the same silent treatment as the day before.

With great uneasiness, they dressed for practice the next

day. The stares were getting increasingly more contemptuous, and the boys did not have a clue what was wrong. They lingered in the locker room until the coach finally called them out. "Winston, Beyers, get your asses out here," the coach roared.

They resumed practice where they had left off the day before with no better results. The team's savage treatment of John and Kenny continued. Becoming unhinged, Coach Evans began stomping around screaming and cussing at the top of his lungs. "Jesus fucking Christ," he roared. "I am trying to get you people ready for the biggest game of the year. What the hell are you doing? Gilliam, McGiver – you two don't tackle in games like you're slamming Winston! He's your teammate, for Christ sake. Get over here. I need to have a little talk with you two and maybe figure out what the hell is going on around here this week!"

Begrudgingly, the two young men followed the coach over to the side for a private conversation. John and Kenny watched keenly as their teammates stood silently, shaking their heads and shrugging their shoulders without ever looking at the coach. He was seemingly asking them questions as he would pause expectantly at times and became angrier when neither one answered.

Finally, after an apparent severe blistering, Dick Gilliam, who was known for his short temper, blasted something back, throwing his helmet onto the ground. Whatever he said had infuriated the Coach. "That is the biggest bunch of bullshit I have ever heard!" the Coach exclaimed as he waved the two back in line, his face purple with utter exasperation. He called his two hapless assistants over, gave them instructions to carry on the practice with more drills. The he turned abruptly and stomped back to his office, leaving John and Kenny dumbfounded as to what Gilliam had said.

Later that night, John stormed into the house. Annie, Matthew, and the others who were sitting around the dinning room table having supper, watched open-mouthed as the usually pleasant John bolted upstairs. The loud slam of his door echoed through the house.

"Wonder what that was all about," wondered Matthew.

"He's usually in a great mood close to a big game. Jeez, I hope he didn't get hurt at practice." He got up quickly from the table and followed his son.

No one noticed that Thomas also went upstairs. He crept close to John's room, trying to hear what was being said.

"What do you mean, something's wrong with the team?" he heard his father cry.

"I don't know, Pop, but everyone's acting crazy!" John said, sounding though as he was close to tears."

"Crazy, like how?"

"They won't talk to me and Kenny, and they're beatin' the shit out of us every time they get a chance – tackled me so hard they tore my helmet off!"

"What the hell? They're just jealous – they know you and Kenny have college scouts coming to watch you the rest of the season."

"That's what me and Kenny thought, too, but that's not it. It's like we suddenly got the plague. Somethin' bad is going on, really bad!"

"I'll call the coach. He's got to stop this – the big game is in two days."

"No, don't do that. He'll get to the bottom of this – he has to. The guys listen to him. He'll straighten this out, okay?"

"Well, if you say so, but if things don't improve soon, I'm gonna call him, you hear?"

"Okay, Pop. Don't worry. It'll be alright."

"You hungry? Why don't you come down and have some supper."

"Nah, I got a lot of homework to do."

"But son, you gotta keep up your strength."

"I know. I'll be fine."

Thomas knew his father would be coming out soon, but he didn't move away from the door. Matthew almost ran into him as he stepped out of the room. "What's wrong with Johnny Boy," Thomas chirped sarcastically. "Got a severe case of jock rash?"

Matthew stared at his son intently for a few moments until his expression changed as though something suddenly became very clear to him. "It's you – you're behind all this!" he cried.

"What did you do? What did you say to turn everyone against your brother!" He grabbed Thomas around the throat as he spoke, but Thomas's sardonic sneer did not fade.

"Watch it, Father," he scoffed. "Physical abuse of one's children is punishable by law."

"Really? At least I'd get the satisfaction of beating the hell out of you, once and for all."

"Ah, ah, ah – that would not be smart. This town already thinks you're certifiable. Just think what they'd say if you get your ass hauled off to jail."

"I don't give a shit what anyone thinks--"

"Yes you do! Reputation is everything to you, especially when it comes to John."

"And up till now he had a terrific reputation. And you can't stand that, can you. What did you do to screw that up? Tell me now!" He was holding tighter but Thomas did not back down from his father's loathsome stare. If anything, he seemed to be enjoying it.

"Go to hell. I'm not going to tell you a thing. It's much more fun letting it come out a little at a time, don't you think?"

"Why are you doing this? How can you--"

"Why are you so shocked? I told you if you didn't keep our little deal, I would destroy everything you hold dear. Remember?"

"But Thomas--"

"Hey, a deal's a deal, and you screwed it up, not me. It wasn't my idea to go back to that God forsaken hell hole school."

"But, you're only 16 years old. People were beginning to talk. I--"

"See, there's that reputation thing again. Too bad you didn't think about your precious reputation before you started shooting off your mouth about schools and padded cells. This is your fault, not mine."

"My fault!"

"Yes, your fault. With all your experience in business, I thought you'd understand what happens when someone welches on a contract. And don't try to make it up to me! It's too late. There's nothing you can do now." With that he pushed

Matthew's hands aside and swaggered away. Matthew had a sickening feeling in his heart that whatever Thomas had done, it was going to have catastrophic results.

* * * * * *

The next day, John entered the locker room with renewed resolve, having decided during a long sleepless night that he would not permit this foolishness to continue. He was determined to find the truth. He dressed quickly and slammed the metal locker door shut. He surveyed the room, hoping to find someone looking at him so that he could address that person directly. But he was unable to catch anyone's eye so he trotted out to the field.

The Thursday's before a game were always light practices, no contact, no hitting. Once again Coach Evans called for a walk-through of the new plays he was trying to implement, however unsuccessfully so far. Kenny set up behind the center, barked out the cadence. He took the ball, and just as he was ready to hand the ball off to Johnny, one of the huge defensive linesmen, Kyle Kaufman, came through and sent both Kenny and John sprawling.

"What's the matter, boys." he scowled. "Isn't this the way you do it at home? Or is Winston supposed to be on top!"

At first what he was saying didn't penetrate, but then it suddenly became clear what had been happening these past few days. John jumped up and angrily bulldozed into the stomach of the sneering giant.

"What the fuck are you saying?" John stammered. "You think we're--" He couldn't say it. He had never uttered the words gay, fag, or homosexual before in his life. Kaufman flung him back to the turf, but John bounced up and went after him again. Kenny jumped in and a small fight ensued until the coach moved in quickly to intercede.

"Break it up, boys! Now!" he roared. "Kaufman, you jerk. Why couldn't you just keep your mouth shut!"

"No!" John cried. "I'm glad he said it. At least we know what the hell is going on with these guys!"

"Oh, yeah?" Coach Evans scowled. "So now what? Tomorrow is the game. Tomorrow! You have got to put al of this stupid shit out of your minds! Now listen up. Anyone tries a stupid stunt like Kaufman's and you're benched, including the game tomorrow. Do you understand?"

John's head was swirling, but he tried hard to concentrate and get through the practice. Later, back in the locker room, no one said much as they dressed. The traditional pep rally, complete with a huge bonfire and screaming cheerleaders, was scheduled for that night. Johnny did not want to go, but he would look more guilty if he didn't make an appearance. He and Kenny didn't speak and left separately.

John survived the pep rally and the next day at school, barely able to stomach walking through the corridors and sitting in his classes, feeling as though he was caught in a terrible nightmare. Everything appeared distorted and warped. He and Kenny avoided each other all day. The whole school seemed subdued and nervous. The juicy gossip about the school's two star athletes had run its course, and the realization of what this meant regarding the game began to settle in.

Normally on game day, John and his teammates gathered in the locker room after school to hang out until it was time to get dressed. But John fled in his car, driving around until he had to go back. As it had been all week, the room was uncharacteristically quiet. John kept thinking that he should make a statement, like an apology or some kind of appeal. Everything they had worked for was about to go down the drain unless someone did something. He knew the only one who could stop this team from self-destructing was Coach Evans.

Shortly before game time, Coach slammed the door hard as he strode into the room, getting everyone's attention. They could tell from his face he had something to say. He cleared his throat and began.

"Gentlemen, listen up. There's something we have to clear up before we go out on that field. You guys know me pretty well. I'm your coach and it's my job to teach you to play the game of football. But my responsibilities do not stop there. The lessons that I have tried to teach you go a lot further that that. My hope is that many of the things you've learned here will stay with you for the rest of your lives. How many times have I stood here and told you that this is a team – that we play as a team, we win or lose as a team. We depend on each other. That's what it means to be part of a team."

"I've been very proud of you guys. You've learned your lessons well – or at least I thought you had. But these past few days there's been a disease creepin' into this locker room that's trying to destroy us – destroy our dreams, our goals. Somehow the rumor got started that two of our guys are fags. Personally, I think it's a bunch of bullshit, but you big, macho 200 pound lumps of manhood decided to believe it. All of a sudden, everything changed even though neither of these guys did one damned thing that would suggest in any way that they're guilty of anything. Did anyone of you defend them? Did you bother to ask them if it's true? You guys know each other better than you know anyone. You've been in the trenches together, been hurt, played in the mud, the rain and sleet and cold together. You're teammates, yes, but you're supposed to be friends, and in my book that has to account for something."

"You guys know that we're on the verge of something special here. You're young, and your lives are just starting – you'll have tons of big days ahead of you like getting' married and having children, but I'm telling you no matter where you go or what you do, you'll carry this with you always. This is your championship season. And years from now, when you think about how hard you worked and fought for this, I want you to remember, you did it as a team."

"You all have friends n' family out there – hell, the whole damned town is here tonight. They're wondering what's gonna happen, how are you guys gonna react to all this crap. Everyone knows this is gonna be a tough game. They were conference champs last year. But not this year. This is our year. We are gonna go out there and kick their asses. Defense? You are going to bare down like never before. I don't wanna see no missed tackles, no forty-yard completions down field. No! You are gonna hold 'em! Offense! We are going to march down that field like a finely-oiled machine. I don't want to see no 3rd n' long's. I don't want to see any blue jerseys even close to my quarterback." He stood with hands on his hips, surveying his team intently. His face was red, his jaw was set, and his voice had a slight quiver. Suddenly he raised his fists. "Are we gonna win this game?" he bellowed.

"Yeah!" they chorused weakly.

"What!"

"Yeah!" they cried louder.

"What?"

"Yeah!" they screamed as they jumped onto their feet and ran out of the room, sustaining the roar until they thundered onto the playing field.

From the opening play on, it seemed all the players had taken the coach's words to heart as they played harder than ever before. By half-time they were ahead 21 to nothing. Two hours later, they returned to the locker room, loudly celebrating a crushing victory, 35 to 0. John Winston rushed for 158 yards and three touchdowns, and the quarterback, Ken Beyer, connected on 21 of 29 passes. Everyone showered quickly and put on their suits and ties for the dance. The coach was right – this was one of the greatest nights of their lives.

October 16, 1971

Dear Luke,

I pray, as always, that this reaches you. Autumn is in full swing here. The colors are gorgeous. The whole yard is covered by a carpet of gold and red leaves. Some people rake their lawns and you can smell the leaves burning, but we don't. It's so much work and I like the way it looks anyway. Danny and Peter did make a huge pile together the other day just so the baby could jump into it. She's so cute. When she giggles, it makes everyone else feel better. You just can't help but smile no matter what's going on otherwise.

The corn picking is almost finished. The yield should be pretty good, but not as good as last year. That was special in a lot of ways. Poor Daddy can only drive the tractor with the grain wagons up and down the hill as Jameson and his crew do the rest. It's not nearly as exciting, but we can use a little less excitement around here.

John's football team is doing well. Undefeated so far.

535

*He has college scouts looking at him. Pop is so proud. We're
also very happy with the progress little Joey is making this year at
school. He has a tiny walker, which he pushes around the house.
Can you believe it? Sonny was right when he pushed me to get
him in that school. You and Andrew said the same thing. I even
think Mother would be pleased.*

*So, take heart. I hope this nightmare will end soon
and you will be home with us. We love you, and pray for your
safe return.*

Love,
Annie

CHAPTER 63

John began to relax as his high school football career
wound down. He and Kenny rarely spoke. At least the team
continued to pull together as they moved toward their ultimate
goal – an undefeated season. But the rest of the students and
community did not forget so easily. Yes, they said, it was
impossible to fathom that such masculine, virile young men could
possibly be gay. But on the other hand, there were rumors that
Rock Hudson was a homosexual If it was true, then anyone could
be. Homosexuality was one of the mysterious, taboo subjects that
was never openly discussed. After all, it was a sin and every
mother's worst fear.

There was a great celebration after their last game. They
had totally annihilated their opponent, and everyone was
confident that they would be named #1 of the Class C high
schools of the state by the UPI sports' writers. Several of the
players gathered at Coach Evans' house, waiting for the early
edition of the *Des Moines Register and Tribune* to be delivered.
Since there was no post-season championship play-offs, their
destiny now laid in the hands of the Iowa sports' writers. When
the paper finally arrived, there was a loud whoop that exploded
throughout the room when the headline was read. "Power House
Shannon Town High Named #1." They had done it.

Later, John headed toward home, but he wasn't ready for

this night to end. He felt compelled to drive down to the creek bridge, the one which had served as the finish line for dozens of early morning races with Kenny. John wasn't surprised to see his friend's red, Chevy pick-up already there. The two of had not spoken in days. Here, in the middle of the night on a deserted country road, perhaps it was safe.

"Hey, man," John called softly.

"Hey," Kenny replied.

"That was some game, aye?"

"Yeah, it sure was – quite a game."

"Hellva season. I hate to see it end, don't you?"

"Yep, I sure do."

"Did you see Gilliam? Jesus! He nearly took off that tailback's head!"

"God, he had 5 sacks. Great game – that was a great game."

"It sure was – a really great game." They sat silently for a few minutes, each staring straight ahead. Then John passed over the can of 7-Up he was drinking.

"Is this straight pop," Kenny chided, "or does it got a little extra in it?"

"Nah, it's straight. I don't need nothing' extra, man. I'm already higher than a kite."

"Yeah, me, too. It's a great feeling, ain't it?"

"Yep, it sure is – best feeling in the world. We're number one in the whole damn state! Football is the greatest game in the world."

"That's for damned sure."

"That's all we did, you know – just love of the game. Why does anyone have to make something dirty out of that?"

"I don't know, man, I do not know."

"It's not over, you know? Maybe the guys on the team are okay with this shit, but the rest of the town won't let it die. We could go out there and win a hundred football games, but they won't forget."

"Yeah, I know," Kenny drawled, sighing deeply.

"Hell with 'em anyway. A few more months we'll be out of this place, playing big time football at college. I bet those scouts got a eyeful tonight." John paused for a few minutes, waiting for an enthusiastic response from his friend, but Kenny said nothing. "I think the phone's gonna start ringing off the wall pretty soon." Still Kenny said nothing. "Hey, man, we're gonna get scholarships. We're gonna be Iowa Hawkeye's just like we dreamed, right?"

"I don't know, man. I think that was more your dream than mine."

"Bullshit! How many times did we talk about it – right here, on this bridge!"

"No, Winston, you talked. I mostly listened."

"What?" John cried, jumping out of the car. "It's this dumb fag stuff, ain't it. Is that why you suddenly don't want to go to college with me?"

"No, it ain't that shit."

"Kenny, I don't know how that crap got started. If I knew I'd rip the jerk's head off. It don't meant nothin'!"

"I'm tellin' ya', that ain't it."

"Listen. We'll show this town. I'll screw some cheerleader and then everyone'll forget it!"

"No, John, that's not it."

"You know very damned well I get a hard-on every time I look at Jeannine McPherson. We both do!"

"John, you ain't listening. My not going to college has nothin' to do with any of that. Listen. I don't want to go to college. I hate school. The idea of 4 or 5 more years of sitting in class makes my skin crawl. Besides, if some college coach would consider offering me a scholarship, he'd look at my grades and keep right on going."

"What the hell are you talking about. Your grades are fine."

"No, they're not. 2.2's do not get big time college scholarships. Besides, I got other plans. I'm gonna work with my dad. He'll probably make me his partner. I like working' with him. I don't mind getting' my hands dirty--"

"Well, neither do I!"

"John, listen. You got a great future ahead of you. But high school quarterbacks are a dime a dozen--"

"That's bullshit! You're good, Kenny, you're really good!"

"That's because you made me look good. I just stand in the pocket and hand the ball off to you."

"You were 18 of 24 tonight, Kenny – you passed for 232 yards. That's fantastic for a high school quarterback."

"It's good, but it ain't nothin' special. Look, John, we're a bunch of small town country boys having a lot of fun playing football. It's like the coach said. I'll remember this as some of the best times of my life."

"You love football, Kenny, as much as me. You taught me everything I know about playing this game."

"Now who's talking bullshit," Kenny said, smiling. "What you have is a God-given talent. Nobody taught you that. You can go through a hole where there ain't one. You got the best hands of anyone I've ever seen, and you play smart. You're in, buddy. You are in! And I'm happy for ya', man. I'll come watch ya' play, but I am staying right here where I belong."

"What if none of this had happened – all this talk about you and me. I bet you wouldn't be saying any of this."

"No, I'm telling you, that's not it. It's just the way it is – honest."

But John was not convinced. As far as he was concerned, who ever had created this cruel coax had just cost him the best friend he ever had.

* * * * * *

The next morning, John sulked into the kitchen, still brooding angrily. Matthew and Mack were sitting at the table for a late breakfast, warming themselves with coffee. Thomas shuffled in, surly and annoyed as usual. Annie was busy feeding Becky and Joey.

"Hey, Johnny," Matthew crowed proudly, holding up the sports' section of the paper. "You should be on top of the world. You did it. #1, right?"

"Yeah, I know," John scowled. "Most of the team stayed at Coach Evan's house till it came out. We weren't really surprised."

"That's what I love," sneered Thomas. "He's so modest and humble."

"What a season," Matthew continued, ignoring Thomas's remark. "Everyone's talking about it. They never saw anything like it before."

"Yep, it's only a manner of days now before scholarship offers start coming in by the dozens, right Johnny?" quipped Mack, who was grinning just as proudly as his father.

"Yeah, sure," muttered John, who was obviously anything but happy.

"Now, c'mon, son," Matthew cajoled. "You're not still upset about this other business, are you? That's all blown over anyway. You're a hero around here." John said nothing as his father chatted on. "How about Kenny? He must be happy, too. You two are the heart and soul of that team."

"He's probably waiting for colleges to call, too, right?" Annie asked as she brought her father another cup of coffee.

"Yeah, that's what I thought, but try telling him," John spat bitterly.

"What do you mean, John?" Thomas sneered. "I thought you two were all set to ride off into the sunset – together, of course." Everyone in the room glared at him, but he continued. "Very together, if you know what I mean."

"Thomas, stop it!" Annie hissed hotly. "I'll have none of that hateful, vile talk in this house. I thought all of that would have died down by now."

"Well, it hasn't, and I don't think it ever will," John retorted. "And now Kenny's decided he's not going to college. He says it has nothing to do with everything going on right now, but I know it does! If I ever catch the sonofabitch that started --" John glanced up at his father for reaffirmation of his anger and saw something in one quick moment that made everything clear for the first time. Matthew and Thomas were staring at each other, and the inference was unmistakable. "It was you!" John said slowly. Louder and more angry, he said it again. "It was you!"

"What?" chorused the others in the room. "Who?"

540

John stood up and slowly circled Thomas's chair, whose smirk never changed. He seemed to be deriving pleasure as the little scene played out. "It was Thomas! When he went back to school, all the trouble began."

"Oh, no, John," Annie cried, "you must be mistaken. He would never--" Then she saw it too, and knew at once John was right. "My God, Thomas, why would you do such a terrible thing!"

"Why? Ask him." Thomas smirked, gesturing toward Matthew.

"What the hell does Pop have to do with this?" Mack demanded, also jumping up from his chair.

"It's quite simple. We had a deal, and he welched on it," Thomas said, shrugging his shoulders arrogantly.

"So you're justified in causing all this havoc, Thomas?" Matthew hissed, his fists clenched and his jaw quivering. "Is that what you're saying?"

"Hey, man, let the chips fall."

"What deal? What are you saying?" cried Annie.

"It was just a little gentlemen's agreement we hammered out in New York last summer. I agreed to go into that courtroom and say exactly what he wanted, and in return I was to receive certain – concessions, I guess you'd say. I kept up my end of the bargain. We're here, aren't we? But part of the deal was I'd never have to set foot in that God awful school again. I told him if he tried to make me, I'd destroy everything he held dear."

"What the hell do I have to do with this?" John demanded.

"Think about it. -- you're his golden boy, his pride and joy. You had the whole damn town kissing your feet – but not anymore."

John lunged at him, but Mack quickly blocked his way. John angrily broke his hold and grabbed Thomas, shaking and slapping him until Matthew and Mack separated them. Annie began crying and screaming. "Oh, my God, how can this be happening to us," she cried, as she sank to the floor.

"You sonofabitch!" John shrieked. "How could you do this to me?"

"It wasn't that hard," Thomas retorted, seemingly

unaffected by his brother straining to get at him again.

"Thomas, this is a family! Why would you try to destroy your own brother like this?" demanded Mack.

"If only Mother was alive," moaned Annie. "None of this would ever happen."

"She's not alive, is she!" Thomas screamed, suddenly enraged and red-faced. "And whose fault is that?"

"Fault?" Mack said. "It's no one's 'fault'."

"That's what everyone says, but I know better!"

"Thomas, what in the hell are you talking about?" Matthew cried. "Cancer is never anyone's fault!"

"The hell it isn't!" Thomas spat. "You filthy – it was your fault!"

"Thomas!" Annie gasped.

"No, let him finish," Matthew stammered. "You believe I killed your mother?"

"You would never leave her alone. You had to have her – every night. Sometimes I'd sit outside your bedroom and hear you groping all over her like a goddamn animal."

"Your mother and I loved each other very much. You know that!"

"Really? I know she had 10 babies in about 20 years. My God, she was pregnant all the time. Why couldn't you just leave her alone?"

"Sex is a natural thing between two people who love--"

"Just shut up! You can say anything you want, but I know the truth! You crushed her! You wouldn't leave her alone."

"Thomas --"

"I said shut up! What was it, your fucking, macho pride? You had to have all these God awful kids?"

"Your mother never believed in birth control. She --"

"Wasn't 5 or 6 enough? You should have left her alone! But no, not you. She had another kid, then another and another. She didn't have enough time for the ones she had! And then, at the end, there she was, pregnant again – why in the hell didn't she get rid of it – then maybe she'd still be alive! You should have convinced her! It was up to you! It was your goddamn fault anyway! Don't you see? He killed her!"

542

His words pierced the air like hot arrows. Annie gathered the baby into her arms as if to shield her from such harsh, cutting cruelty. Matthew stood like stone for a few moments, trying to control himself until finally he grabbed Thomas by the scruff of his neck. "How dare you stand here and say something so idiotic. I did not kill her. How could I? I loved her more than life itself. Don't you think I thought about this? I've been over and over it since the day she died. But I know I had nothing to do with her death – nothing."

"Oh, yeah? Well, you can live in your little fantasy world all you want, but I know the truth – your selfishness, your arrogance, your masochistic filthy raping of her every chance you got – you killed her!" He knocked his father's hands away and strode out of the room..

"Daddy," Annie cried, reaching for him, "don't listen to him."

But Matthew pushed her hand away and bolted for his office. Old scars were ripped open and familiar heartaches resurfaced.

* * * * * *

Thomas left that night. He packed up a few clothes and his guitars and skulked out of the house after midnight. Annie heard him but did nothing to impede his departure. She heard the car door slam and the clatter of Curtis Peet's old Pontiac as it pealed off the yard. Good riddance, she thought, but then cried into her pillow as she had hundreds of times before.

Chapter 64

The weather gradually cooled and the winds never seemed to quiet as time swirled around them in an never-ending cycle of endless days of work and nights of sleepless heartache. A few days after Thomas left, Annie went into his room and begrudgingly began cleaning. Tears of bitter resentment welled in her eyes as she made his bed and organized piles of records and sheet music. She closed the door and paused to study the other door that was seemingly permanently closed across the hall. Luke's room. It seemed as though this house was being engulfed by closed doors.

She was surprised to find herself wondering about Thomas, although she had vowed that she wouldn't. As much as she despised and hated him for all the horrendous trouble he brought into their house, she often woke in the middle of the night and worried about him. Was he sleeping and eating properly? How badly was he embroiled in the so called "drug culture"? And if he got himself into trouble, who would he call? Dad? Never. Mack and Penny, or Andrew? Who was there for him if he really needed someone? She thought she was relieved when he left, but she hated not knowing where he was.

Annie dreaded the holidays as never before. As Thanksgiving approached, she tried to plan the meal and make preparations but she just couldn't. This was when Luke was supposed to be home. He wrote many times in his letters that he wanted all the traditional dishes, especially mashed potatoes and Jell-O. He wanted bowls and bowls of red Jell-O. Annie knew she should be calling Margaret to see how she was doing, but she couldn't do that either. She was falling deeper and deeper into a pit of destructive depression. Some days, getting out of bed was nearly impossible.

* * * * * *

Danny ran down the stairs into the kitchen and poured a bowl of cereal, knowing that the bus was due any time. He was already wearing his winter coat at the table, which did not go unnoticed.

"Hey, Danny." Peter called sarcastically. "What's that shirt you're wearing?" But Annie, who was standing at the counter with her back to them, slumped and distracted, didn't seem to hear him so Peter tried again. "Since when do you wear a Cub Scouts shirt?"

"What?" Annie said, arousing slightly and turning to face them.

544

"Yeah, look. He has one of those stupid uniform shirts on."

"What?" Annie murmured. "Danny, show me what you're wearing." Begrudgingly, the boy unzipped his coat to reveal the dark blue shirt, the creases from the packing still visible. The small, triangular patches were pinned above the left pocket, crooked and ill-placed. "Where did you get it?" Annie demanded.

Danny stared into his cereal bowl as he answered. "Mrs. Andrews, our den leader, got if for me. She said she knew you were busy so she bought it." There was a loud, impatient blast from the horn of the school bus. Danny got up quickly, zipped up his coat emphatically as he took his school bag. "Don't worry about picking me up after Scouts," he mumbled, still not looking at her. "Mrs. Andrews will drop me off after the meeting. You always forget anyway."

Annie stood at the kitchen door and watched her brothers scamper onboard the bus. How eager they were to leave, she thought. Slowly she turned to survey the room. No wonder. Dirty dishes were stacked everywhere and there was an undeniable stench lingering in the air. Tears began to stream down her face and her whole body began to shake. "Oh, my God!" she cried. "What's happening to me? To this family?" That poor little boy, she sobbed. He feels so neglected and sad. And it was solely her fault. She resolved to do better and began washing the dishes. But then Becky came downstairs, dragging her blanket and demanding breakfast. After she ate, Annie changed her and laid down on the sofa to watch her play. Annie relished the frequent hugs and kisses. Becky was her lifeline, her only joy.

After lunch she took the toddler upstairs and rocked her asleep. She was still sitting in the rocking chair when the boys came home from school. She listened as they rummaged around the kitchen, trying to find something to eat. Once again, silent, tormented tears streamed down her cheek, but she did not move.

* * * * * *

545

Thanksgiving was now only a week away, and Annie had made no preparations. Ginny understood the situation and invited the Winston family to eat dinner at her house. Her relatives were coming, so she suggested they combine forces. Annie accepted knowing that Ginny saw the sadness in her little brothers' faces and wanted to help.

Annie and Becky went to help Ginny cook and clean. The women chatted as they rolled out the pie crust and peeled the apples. Ginny's kitchen was a safe haven for Annie, a place where she could bare her soul. Ginny never let her blame God for the tragedies in life. God never willed things to happen, she said, but was always there to help you get through it.

When Annie complained about Thomas and the havoc he had caused his own family, Ginny had a surprising response. "That poor boy," she said.

"How can you say that? He's the one who did such despicable things. Why would anyone feel sorry for him?"

"I learned a long time ago that when someone dies, the one thing people feel more than anything else is guilt. He feels bad for being mad at your mother, and he's taking it out on all of you."

"Mother was the only one on this earth that Thomas ever loved. He wasn't mad at her. He adored her. She was a wonderful mother to all of us."

"I'm sure she was. That's why he has so much anger and guilt twisted up inside of him."

Annie had enormous difficulty trying to pity her conniving brother, but small shreds of what Ginny said began to seep into her consciousness, however hard she tried to repel it.

The Thanksgiving dinner was wonderful. Ginny beamed happily as platters of turkey and bowls of vegetables and salads were passed until everyone's plates were over-flowing. Annie had a good time in spite of her herself. She stayed to help until all of Ginny's best dishes were tucked away in the buffets until another feast. She knew what was waiting for her at home.

The house was dark with no poignant smells of holiday cooking lingering in the air or leftovers sat on the counter. Although Ginny had insisted that Annie take home several plastic containers of food, it wasn't the same. She felt like a coward –

surely she could have forced herself to cook a meal for her family. This was still a family, wasn't it? She wasn't sure any more.

If Thanksgiving had been difficult, Christmas was going to be impossible. In early December, the little boys began asking about the tree and decorations. Shouldn't they make out their lists, and what about shopping? Annie mumbled some trite excuses until finally they stopped asking, which was even worse. This had always been a Christmas family, and Annie wanted desperately to feel that magical rapture again, but it was gone. She wondered if it would ever return.

One night, a few days before Christmas, Annie went to bed early. The house was in total disarray with piles of greasy dishes in the sink and clutter scattered in every room. Unable to face it and angry that she had to, she went to her bedroom and closed the door. She tossed and turned in bed, unable to sleep.

And then the phone rang. She glanced at the clock. It was 1:10 AM. Panicked, she picked up the receiver quickly, feeling certain it was some bad news about Thomas. "Hello?" she cried. "Who is this?"

There was a lot of static on the line, but she heard a voice. "Hello? Hello? Can you hear me? Is this Ann Winston?"

"Yes, this is she?"

"Hello. I'm Sergeant John W. Howell, United States Army."

"Yes?"

"Ma'am, I'm sorry this is so late, but I wanted to call you right away. I'm calling from the Philippines. I was just released by the North Vietnamese – me and two other guys. Maybe you read about it in the news."

"What? You were a POW? Did you see my brother?" The words tumbled out so quickly that she could hardly breathe.

"Yes, I did. That's why I'm calling. There were 17 of us held together in a camp in Laos. Us three promised the other guys we'd make these calls as soon as we could."

"Oh, my God!" she screamed joyously, barely aware that Matthew and the others had encircled her.

"Sergeant, is my brother alright?"

"Yes, he's doing fairly well. Did you know he was shot –

in the legs – both of 'em. But they took decent care of him and he's been walking better. He told me not to tell ya' but I thought you should know. He's a tough kid."

"Yes, yes, but how is he doing otherwise – how are his spirits?"

"Well, I guess you'd say he's doing all right -- 'bout like the rest of us. He sure likes to draw. He's even did some drawings of the guards for extra stuff, like food. All he talks about is home, and the log cabin he's gonna build when he gets back to the World."

"How come – I mean, how did they decide who – I mean, I'm happy for you that you're out, but --"

"How did they decide who they wanted to release? Well, I don't really know. It was just for show with the peace talks and this being Christmas and all. I guess the three of us look pretty good. We're pretty healthy looking."

"Are you saying my brother looks bad?"

"No, no, I ain't saying that, exactly. Things are getting better for all the men. They were fixin' to move all the guys to Hanoi."

"Hanoi? Is that a good thing? What about --"

"Miss Winston, I'm not sure what I'm suppose to say, okay?"

"But Sergeant, I --"

"I'm sorry, but I have more calls to make. I'll call again, after I get home."

"Yes, of course, thank you. We really appreciate it. I'll be sure to tell Luke that you kept your promise."

"Thank you, ma'am. And Merry Christmas!"

"Yes, Merry Christmas to you, too. Good bye." She held the receiver close to her heart, crying jubilant, thankful tears. "Yes, Merry Christmas," she whispered again.

"Well, what did he say?" everyone chimed. "Is he all right?"

"Yes, the man who called was in a POW camp with Luke. He and two others were released, and they're calling the families of the other 14 still captive. He said Luke's doing okay. He's drawing and talking about home."

Everyone cheered and hugged each other, jumping up and down. They used words like "miracle" and "happy", words they hadn't used for a long time.

Annie called Mack and Penny. Annie didn't tell them that Luke had been shot in the legs. "They let those three go because of Christmas. Isn't that wonderful?" she exclaimed. "Doesn't that mean that maybe they're not so bad. They understand about things like Christmas and families?"

"Sure, Annie," Mack said. "This is great news. There only thing that could make it better is Luke on the other end of that phone. Next Christmas, Annie, next Christmas."

"Yes, I bet you're right. I'm certain of it!" Annie hung up the phone and quickly called Andrew, receiving the same joyous response. She wanted to call Margaret, but the dorm phones were turned off at 10 o'clock. Annie would call her in the morning. Then she threw her robe around her shoulders, wanting to run to Sonny's shack to tell him. But when she flew down the stairs, she found him already in the kitchen, plugging in the coffee pot. "Oh, Sonny, you're here!" she cried. "How did you know?"

"I noticed the lights. I figured something was going on."

"Oh, yes," she exclaimed breathlessly. "I have such wonderful news. Another POW called who knows Luke. They were together. He's alive! He's all right!" Sonny grinned and for an instant, her impulse was to run to him and throw her arms around him. But the rest of the family poured into the room, everyone talking excitedly at once.

"Oh my God, Christmas is almost here!" Annie cried, pacing around the room frantically. "I have so much to do!"

* * * * * *

She didn't waste any time getting started. By the time the boys got home from school the next day, the house was clean and ready for decorating. Mother's tree and ornaments were brought from the attic and everyone happily set about completing the pleasant task by bedtime. The light-hearted chatter was reminiscent of the other years, and Annie could not stop smiling. Even Matthew helped, first putting on the lights and then supervising the placement of the ornaments. He sipped hot cider, not beer.

No one complained that there was not the limitless money this year. If anything, it made shopping more challenging and more meaningful. Gifts were items people needed. Annie bought many flannel shirts, warm hats and mittens, and new coveralls. She hinted that she needed new frying pans and dishes for the kitchen.

On Christmas Eve, when the family attended Mass, she knelt by the candle stands to pray. Margaret crept up beside her, her tears glistening in the flickering lights "This time next year, he'll be home," Annie said.

"I am so thankful that at least we know he's alive," Margaret whispered. "I prayed so hard for this, but I wish . . ."

"I know, Margaret. We just have to be patient, but now, at least, we won't be so afraid."

Several hours later, when the gifts were opened and the house began to quiet, Annie slipped into the kitchen and dialed the telephone. Lori had said that she had seen Jim Mathers in town with his mother. He was Annie's only hope of getting information about Thomas. She wondered how her call might be received. "Hell, Mrs. Mathers? This is Ann Winston. I'm sorry to bother you, but could I speak with Jimmy for just a moment?"

Mrs. Mathers smothered the receiver against her chest, but Annie could still hear her muffled words. "Jim, it's Aunt Lizzie. She wants to talk to you."

"Hello?" he said.

"Jim, this is Thomas' sister, Ann. Tell your mother thank you for allowing you to speak with me. I know how she must feel about my family. I'm so glad you're home, safe and sound. Can you tell me where Thomas is?"

"He told me not to talk to any of you."

"Yes, I know, but it's Christmas. We miss him – really. I just need to know that he's safe and well."

"Yeah, sure, he's all right. They got a gig at some club in Chicago. It's not much, but the way they're packin' 'em in, it won't be long before they get a bigger one. At least, that's what Thomas keeps saying."

550

"Is he with Kitty and Curtis Peet?"

"Sure, she's singin' real good, and Curtis is the manager for the band. They just didn't have nothing for me to do, so I came back home. Thomas said he'll call me as soon as they need a bigger band."

"Why don't you stay home with your family. Would that be better?"

Jim didn't respond at first. "No, ma'am," he said finally. "I'd rather be with Thomas. Look, I'd better go, all right?"

"But we have presents for him under the tree. Can't you tell me where he is, please?"

"Thomas would skin me alive if he found out I said anything to you. My dad's looking at me kind of weird. I gotta go." The line went dead.

Annie slowly returned the receiver to the cradle, fiercely fighting back the tears. This had been a wonderful day and she didn't want to let any despair creep inside.

"So, what did he say?" a voice quietly broke into her solitude. It was Sonny. "You called Jim Mathers, right?"

Annie began fussing with dirty dishes, without looking at him. "I heard he was in town," she said. "I just thought he might know something about Thomas. I know we've practically disowned him, but --"

"But you're worried about him, I know. Did Jim tell you anything?"

"No, not much. I guess they're playing in a small club in Chicago."

"I could find Thomas if you really wanted me to, but why?"

"He's a minor. We could go to the police. They'd send him home."

"Annie, you could haul his ass home a hundred times, but it wouldn't make no difference. He'd just take off again."

"Why? Because he hates us so much?" she whispered, close to tears.

"He'd say it was because of that, but it's the drugs. He's hooked on the stuff and that's all he cares about."

"Are you sure? Do you really think it's that bad with

551

him?"

"Oh, yeah, it's bad. I know the look. He'd sell his soul for a hit of coke."

"Oh, Sonny, how is that possible? How could someone from our family get involved with that?"

"It can happen to anyone – good families, bad families, rich people, poor people. It don't matter."

"What can we do? He needs to be home with us. But then, he'd just keep blaming us, wouldn't he?"

"He's got a lot of hate in him right now, but that don't mean it'll always be there. Maybe he'll work things through and show up on your doorstep one of these days." Annie knew the possibility of that was pretty remote, but she appreciated Sonny saying it. "See, he's got something a lot of people like him don't have – a home and family to come back to. As long as he knows that, he's got a chance. Did Jim say anything else?"

"Not much. Apparently, Thomas told him not to."

"Do you blame him? Jim would never want to do anything to piss off his only friend. He thinks Thomas is his ticket out."

"I've heard things were bad for him at home."

"I don't think you get that many bruises from being clumsy. And that's only what we can see – there's probably more under those flannel shirts he wears all the time."

Annie shuddered at the thought of a father beating his own son. And she had seen Mrs. Mathers in town with cut lips and black eyes. "If the whole town knows he hurts his own family, why doesn't anyone do anything?" she wondered at loud.

"That's the way it is everywhere. Not just here."

Annie couldn't help but wonder how he knew so much about such things, but she didn't press him. She saw that pervasive sadness in him before. But like tonight, it seemed too private and far removed to ask him about it. Someday he would tell her about his life, but not yet.

Trying to shake off the melancholy, she said, "Hey, this is Christmas Eve. We're supposed to be happy. It's not like last year, is it. No expensive presents."

"Does that bother you?"

"No, not at all. That phone call made this the best

552

Christmas ever. The only thing that would make it better is Luke actually coming home. And Thomas, too." She sighed.

There was a scratch at the door. "I guess ol' Mutt wants some Christmas goodies, too," Sonny grinned as he grabbed some sausage and cheese off the counter. He stepped outside and gave the treats to his dog, petting and stroking her fondly. Annie came out, too, gazing up at the cold night sky. There was no moon, only a dark canopy of clouds. An occasional snowflake drifted by.

"We're supposed to get a couple of inches of snow overnight," she mused. "Whenever it snows like this, I think of Luke. He loved the snow."

"Yeah, well, there'll be plenty when he comes back. After every summer and fall, comes winter. Nothing can to stop it."

Those simple words were strangely comforting. She said them over and over in her mind. The perpetual cyclic certainty of nature reassured her that human dramas come and go, but the earth is forever.

Christmas Eve, 1971

Dear Luke,

Merry Christmas! As I wrote all week, your friend Sergeant Howell, gave us the best Christmas present possible when he called. I should have asked him if you ever received my letters, but I didn't think of it. I have a million questions for him. I'm hoping he'll call again soon. He sounded very nice on the phone.

It's snowing, Luke – soft little flakes floating by. I know why you love the snow. It covers up all the mud and bare ground and makes everything look so clean and elegant. You will have your snow again, Luke. Some things change, but nature never does. This family, this home, and this land will be here for you when you return. Take heart and know that we are praying for you every day. We will have the best Christmas ever when you come home, even if it's in the middle of July. Don't know where we'll get the snow, but we'll think of something.

I love you, Luke. God Bless!
Annie

Chapter 65

As 1972 began, Annie felt certain that Luke's ordeal would soon be over. "President Nixon's said that he would bring 70,000 more troops home by May," she announced one evening at supper. Mack and Penny were over with the baby to celebrate Becky's second birthday.

Her older brother did not share her optimism. "If you ask me, he's just doing it so he can get re-elected in November. The Democrats better come up with someone who can beat him – or at least scare him."

"Who's that going to be?" Matthew asked, grinning slightly. "George Wallace?"

"Can you believe that bigot actually has his name in some of the primaries?" Penny said as she wiped up spilled milk on the high chair tray.

"I can," her husband said, frowning. "All he's doing is causing us bad press and scaring the hell out of most people – everyone except Nixon. He probably loves it."

"How's the McGovern headquarters coming along in Dubuque, Mack?" Annie asked. But she regretted it as soon as she said it as she noticed the dagger glares exchanged between her brother and his wife. She should have known it was a sensitive subject considering how angry Penny was that Mack was spending more time in the office at Dubuque than at home, running his farm.

Annie attempted to ask her about it later when the two women were in the kitchen washing dishes. "I guess Mack is putting in a lot of hours, trying to get the McGovern campaign up and running in Dubuque."

"Why should you be sorry, Annie?" Penny said, sounding irritated. "It's just that he has so much work to do at home, especially now." She bit her tongue and looked away, as though she nearly let a secret slip.

"Especially now? What does that mean?" Annie demanded.

"I'm pregnant again. Can you believe it? Those damned pills. I thought they were supposed to be 99.99% effective. Just my luck. "

Annie surmised this was a time for sympathy, not joy. It was obvious that her sister-in-law was not happy about this unexpected news.

"It couldn't have happened at a worse time." Penny began scrubbing the stove top furiously. "I love my job, and we just put in the foundation for the new barn. We're signing the mortgage in March. Jeez! This is a fine time for him to be gone all the time." Just as Annie was recovering from Penny's announcement, she got another shock a few minutes later when the adults were sitting around the living room watching Becky tear open her presents.

"Pop," Andrew said, looking unusually serious even for him. "I'm not going to the seminary next fall. I don't want to leave the area until Luke is home, so I thought I'd take some more classes at the University."

"In what?" Matthew cried. "How many more classes are there?"

Andrew cleared his throat and hesitated before he continued. "Well, I thought I'd take some business courses." This news was met with a round of stunned gasps. "I got interested in finance when I took over the books for the farm. You know I'm good at it, Pop. You don't have any angry creditors calling you anymore or bounced checks, right?" No one said anything, so he continued. "I'm not saying I won't go to seminary eventually, just not now."

"Well, this certainly is a night for announcements," Annie said later when she was back in the kitchen with Penny. "Andrew really caught me off guard. He's talked about the priesthood ever since I can remember."

Penny put the ice cream in the freezer and covered up the left over cake. "Actually, he hasn't mentioned it in a while. He told me about this business school thing last week."

"Really?"

"He made supper for me and Katie last Friday. Mack was gone, of course. Andrew called me and said he had made lasagna."

"He cooks? I had no idea."

"He asks us over fairly often – when he knows Mack is gone. He has baby-sat for me a few times, too. Sometimes we watch old movies, but mostly we just talk. I bitch about Mack all the time. He's a wonderful listener. "

"He is? I mean, are we talking about the same person? He always seems to busy to talk about my stuff."

"You're not mad, are you?"

"Of curse not. I thinks it's great you have someone to talk to. I know I haven't been there for you lately. I'm sorry."

"No, it's not that. It's just nice to have a quiet place to vent your worries, that's all."

Annie bent over the sink and began rinsing the dishes. Actually she did feel a little jealous. She had no idea Andrew was so attentive to his brother's wife and child. She made a mental note to speak to him next time he was around, which might not be for weeks. He seemed to be spending less and less time around his family. She should call her twin more often and include him in the family's activities. I need a good listener, too, she thought.

* * * * * *

Matthew hung up the phone disgustedly. "Damn vultures!" he muttered. "Why don't they leave us alone?"

"I know, Pop," Annie said. "That's the fourth reporter that's called today."

"This guy wanted to know if he could set up his cameras and film our reaction to Nixon's speech tonight."

"Do you really think Nixon will have any earth-shattering announcements? I mean, I've had my hopes up so many times before. Mack still thinks he's playing election year politics, but it's only January."

"Well, we'll see what the man has to say, and there sure as hell aren't going to be any TV cameras within 5 miles of this house – if I can help it!"

At 7 PM, Nixon took to the airwaves to announce that there had been secret, on-going meetings in some undisclosed place near Paris for several months. He "regrettably" acknowledged that the negotiators had reached an impasse. Apparently, the main

556

sticking point was the all important "mutual with drawl" by both the U.S. and North Vietnamese armies. Furthermore, Nixon proposed free, multi-party elections should be held throughout Vietnam since the North Vietnamese had long maintained that the majority of the people in South Vietnam would not be in favor of the government currently in power. Nixon claimed he was bringing this information to the American people because he considered it vital that the country stand firmly united in forcing these demands.

"He never said one word about the POW's," Annie said.

"Hey, look," John cried. "There's Mack. He's on TV."

Mack stood on his front porch and faced the hordes of reporters camped on his front yard. He looked dazed and somewhat bewildered.

"What did ya' think of Nixon's speech?" someone asked.

"Frankly, I believe it's just party politics as usual. He knows the Democrats are complaining that he's not doing enough to stop the war. So he thinks this will shut 'em up."

"Do you think it will?"

"In order to get re-elected, Nixon needs to have the American people believe that is doing everything possible to end this war. He's trying to keep the public opinion in this country from eroding even further. The North Vietnamese could use that as an advantage at the bargaining table." He paused briefly, but then looked squarely into the camera and said, "Frankly, I'm surprised to hear of these meetings. I have several reliable contacts in Washington, and none of them knew anything about this. Do I think it's good? Sure, but in such an open, public society as ours, how did they keep this under wraps for so long? Nixon's people must be very good at keeping secrets."

* * * * * *

There was less snow that winter than the one before, but the entire Midwest was thrust into a deep freeze from December until the end of February. Annie fought hard to keep from plunging into the deep depression she has endured before Christmas. She tried to get up every morning with lists of things to accomplish, and then labored hard to complete them. Danny and Peter seemed to keep her at arms length as though they expected her to suddenly slip back into her old ways. She realized then how much she had hurt them and resolved to work hard to win back their trust.

Matthew was quiet. He drank less and seemed more accessible to his children. He never openly criticized Mack's plunge into politics which was interpreted as some measure of approval, although he never condemned the war or the president. It was mostly through his and Sonny's efforts that Mack's barn was finished before the first of March. On the day of the official signing of the mortgage of Mack and Penny's farm, Matthew broke open bottles of Champaign, proclaiming his tremendous joy and pride that on this, the second anniversary of the Winston family's pilgrimage West. His oldest son was now a farmer and a land owner.

Annie dreaded the spring. Although she had managed to postpone it as long as possible, the doctors at the Chicago Rehabilitation Center wanted to do surgery on Joey. The ligaments in the back of his ankles needed to be released or lengthened so that he could walk more normally.

"I think you're doing the right thing, Annie," Mathew said. "Look how much he's changed already." It was true, the little boy had undergone an amazing transformation during the past year and a half. He commando-crawled from one room to the next with as much curiosity as any five year old child. His receptive language skills had sky-rocketed and his expressive abilities were emerging.

"But, Daddy," she said, "Chicago is so far away, and he'll have so much pain. He'll never understand."

"He's a little boy who won't even remember it in a few weeks. I'll drive you to the hospital and stay with you till you're settled. I can't stay, but if he gets real bad, you call and one of us will come, I promise."

Matthew drove them to Chicago on Sunday afternoon. Still uncomfortable with the child, he signed the surgical consents and left an hour after Joey was admitted. The surgery was early the next morning. Joey whimpered when he was not allowed to eat and howled when he was given the pre-operative shot. Mercifully, they only had to wait a few minutes before they took him into surgery. Annie could hear him screaming as they rolled him down the long corridor.

"The surgery went well," the surgeon announced two hours later. "As I told you, he has casts on both his legs. That bar will keep his legs in a spread-eagle position. I want as much extension as possible. He will be like this for six to eight weeks, but you can take him home in a couple days. The nurses can give him medications if he gets too uncomfortable." It sounded so simple.

Joey slept for most of the afternoon, but later that evening the anesthesia wore off and he began to cry inconsolably. "It's horrible," Annie cried to her father on the phone later that night. "They tied down his hands because he pulled the IV out twice. My God, none of the medicine seems to be working."

"Well, then tell the nurse to give him more!" her father commanded. "There's got to be something they can give him, right?" Feeling worse than before she called, she trudged back to her brother's bedside and braced herself for what she knew would be a long, miserable night.

But then, at midnight, one of the nurses came in and said, "Security just called, Miss Winston. It seems that there is a young man insisting that he be allowed to come up to see the boy. I believe they said his name is--"

"Sonny Jackson. Tell them to let him come up."

A few minutes later, Sonny strode into the room and went straight to Joey's bedside. He flung off the straps on the little boys wrists and picked up the whimpering child. Annie helped him prop up the heavy casts with pillows and then covered them both up with blankets.

"Okay now, little man," Sonny said. "Just settle down." Fifteen minutes later, the boy was asleep.

Annie crept to her cot, confident that everything was under control. She laid there, watching them for a few minutes. The boy's face was snuggled beneath Sonny's strong, angular chin. As she drifted off to sleep, she imagined that she was in Joey's place, held by those wonderful arms and feeling his breath upon her cheek.

* * * * * *

Sonny stayed in Chicago the entire four days of Joey's hospitalization. Annie was thrilled to have him to herself without countless distractions. The boy was a model patient after Sonny's arrival, loving all the attention showered on him. They played his favorite games and read his *Poky Little Puppy* book so many times that they could recite it verbatim. Joey scribbled on sheets of paper and presented them to Annie and Sonny as masterpieces. There was one which Annie labeled as "Joey and Sonny Playing in the Snow, alluding to that day Sonny took the boy outside during their trip West. Sonny carefully folded the paper and tucked it in his pocket.

"I wonder how Daddy is handling everything at home," Annie laughed. It was nearly midnight on the third day. Joey was asleep and the room was blissfully quiet.

"I think he can handle the cattle and the chores better than those boys." They both laughed then, imagining Matthew making breakfast and sending his sons off to school.

"I wonder how Mack and Penny are doing?" Annie said. "Things are pretty rocky over there."

"Yeah, well, the whole damned world is so screwed up."

"That's a pretty intense statement, Sonny."

"I don't like Nixon or the war any better than Mack does. They're making such a big deal that he went to China, the first president to do that shit. No one else wanted to go. He's probably making some back room deal with those Communists, too."

"So, you think Mack is doing the right thing? I can't believe howhe's transformed himself into this activist. Andrew, maybe, but not Mack."

"Yeah, well, from where I sit, the changes are good. He's not such an asshole any more."

Annie went to the window and gazed out over the Chicago skyline. "Thomas is out there somewhere. I can't imagine him turning his back on his family to live in such a cold, horrid place."

"Yeah, well, who knows? Maybe he's not as bad off as you think." He said nothing more and lounged back in the recliner and closed his eyes as though he was going to sleep.

Annie could not sleep. She knew their retreat would soon

be over because Joey was due to be discharged the next afternoon. These few days were wonderful and she was sorry to see it end. She crept close to him and kissed him lightly on the cheek. She wished he would wake up and acknowledge her touch, but he never moved. He'd probably get angry and they'd argue. But then at least she could ask him why he kept her at arm's length when she was certain that he had feelings for her. She longed for a kiss or an embrace – anything. Familiar bangs of frustration enveloped her as she allowed herself to imagine holding him in her arms and feeling his body against hers. "Someday," she whispered, "when all this trouble is over, we'll be together. I know it.

An hour later, Annie woke up when the night nurse came in to check on Joey. She was startled to see that Sonny was gone. There was a note on the bedside table that said, "Be back in the morning." At first she was frightened that maybe he had been awake when she kissed him and sensed her frustration. But then she realized what he was doing – looking for Thomas. She laid down again and soon fell back asleep. If anyone could find her brother, it was Sonny.

* * * * * *

Sonny never said whether he was able to find any information about Thomas or if he spoke to him. When Annie awakened the next morning, he was sleeping in the recliner. By noon, they were on their way home. Joey laid comfortably on a throne of pillows in the back seat, babbling and demanding attention. When they got home, Sonny carried Joey into the house and then headed outside. Annie stood at her kitchen window and watched him stride across the yard. She smiled, remembering the moment she crept up to him and kissed him while he was sleeping. Someday, she wouldn't have to wait for him to be asleep to show how she really felt. She knew that was the one hope that would sustain her through whatever laid ahead.

Chapter 66

Any hope that the war in Vietnam would be over soon was crushed when the Winston's awakened Easter morning, March 30, to open the paper and find a screaming headline that announced North Vietnam's invasion into the South. Thought to be as disastrous as the Tet offensive in '68, the "Easter offensive" was to be the first real test of Nixon's Vietnamization policy. American forces were so depleted that the ARVN would have to fight this battle themselves.

After weeks of fierce fighting, the North Vietnamese controlled a large portion of territory south of DMZ. They captured several provincial capitols in the highlands and were coming dangerously close to Saigon. All would have been lost quickly if not for the ceaseless US air support. Nixon was so angry with North Vietnam's outrageous conduct this late in the peace process that he ordered retaliatory bombing of Hanoi. Annie wept with fear that her brother might have endured more than a year of imprisonment only to be killed by bombs from his own country.

This time, there was little civilian unrest or public outcry. There was no half million marchers demonstrating at the Capitol. Instead, there was more emphasis on the political process, and Mack appeared intent to be apart of that.

One morning, Annie came downstairs to find her older brother sleeping on the sofa. "I went to a Democratic party meeting last night," he explained. "I'm going to be a delegate at the National Convention. She didn't like the idea much, I guess."

"Why?'

"The money. Delegates have to pay their own wy, and she says we can't afford it."

"Well, can you?"

"No, not really. But there are ways to do it as cheap as possible. I really want to do this and she won't try to understand."

* * * * * *

562

As April and May passed, the upcoming presidential election became the number one topic of conversation everywhere. McGovern and Humphrey became the front-runners for the Democratic nomination as Muskie slipped out of contention and quit as an active candidate. The biggest surprise of all was the unexpected surge by George Wallace, which ended when he was shot and seriously wounded on May 15th. Although Mack deplored the viciousness of such an attack, he was more certain than ever that McGovern was on the verge of victory. As the convention drew closer, he found himself sleeping on the sofa more often as the rift between him and his wife widened. Penny's pregnancy was barely mentioned.

John graduated from high school the end of May, still hailed as a hero. He looked so handsome in the green cap and gown, his National Honors Society sash around his neck. The humiliation and innuendo from last fall were at last behind him. At least he was not burdened by the threat of world events as Luke had been on his graduation day two years ago, Annie thought as she watched John cross the stage and receive his diploma. It was expected that the draft would be ended by the time he turned nineteen. His future was secure. In the fall he will start college at the University of Iowa. Annie knew her father would proudly follow Hawkeye football as he had John's high school career. In four or five years, John would marry a nice girl and get a job coaching in some small town like Coach Evans. At least, one of her brothers was happy and fulfilled.

As summer wore on, Penny and Mack barely spoke, and if they did, it would soon escalate into a bitter argument. Mack chose to deal with the situation by staying away for longer and longer periods, plunging himself into his campaign work

The "Stop McGovern" movement was building in the old-line segment of the Democratic party. Mack could not understand the mentality, especially since Mc Govern won decisively in the last round of primaries. He was clearly the people's choice and was only 210 votes short of first ballot nomination.

"Mc Govern will never beat Nixon," Matthew said onE day at dinner.

"Why does everyone say that?" Mack retorted, cutting his slice of ham with vicious slashes. "This is not all about Vietnam any more. McGovern has made good proposals regarding domestic issues, too. He has a solid platform if people would just listen."

Matthew reached for another slice of bread. "People are hearing him alright, Mack, especially when he says things like cutting $31 billion dollars from the defense budget. Where does he get these ideas? And all this trouble with the California and Illinois candidates. He can't manage his own party, much less the whole county."

Mack did not reply. It was true that the party scrabbling made daily headlines as the Credential's Committee took away dozens of McGovern votes in California, while alleging that the pro-McGovern, Daley machine had deprived the people of Cook County fair representation in Chicago. The Democratic party was in total chaos, and Mack couldn't wait to get in the middle of it.

* * * * * *

The Convention was scheduled to begin Sunday, July 9th in Miami. Mack planned to leave Friday morning with some other delegates from the area. There was a stack of unopened bills on the counter. He hoped the creditors would hold off until he returned. There was barely enough money for the trip, but he planned to be as frugal as possible by skipping meals and sleeping on the floor of a friend's hotel room.

He walked the perimeter of the pastures to check the fencing, knowing how enraged Penny became when the cattle got out when he was gone. He watched the four remaining pregnant cows closely, praying they would deliver before he left, but none of them did. Friday morning, he came to the kitchen table wearing traveling clothes with his suitcase in hand. His wife did not acknowledge him as she rushed around the room, trying to feed Katie and get ready for work.

He sat down with a bowl of cereal and said, "Those last four haven't gone yet. I checked them again this morning. They could go any time."

Penny bristled at the sound of his voice. "Why in the hell are you telling me? Talk to Sonny or your father."

"I did. I just thought you should know, that's all."

Neither of them said anything more until Penny picked up Katie to leave. Mack stood up and tried to give the baby a kiss, but Penny whisked her away. "Damn it, Penny!" Mack cried. "You can be such a bitch sometimes. I can't even give my own daughter a kiss?"

"She doesn't need another fucking good bye kiss from you!" Penny spat. "What she needs is a father who stays home and provides for her welfare."

"Oh, yeah? And who's the one taking her to a goddamn baby-sitter."

"Don't even start. If I wasn't working, we wouldn't have anything. I'm hoping they don't turn off the electricity before my next paycheck."

"But, Penny, this is important. I have--"

"I know all that. I've heard it a hundred times. Just go." She left then without looking back. He watched them drive away and vowed he would make this up to both of them. He took his suitcase and waited on the front porch for his ride. Soon, he too, was gone.

* * * * * *

They made it down to Miami in less than 24 hours, driving straight through the night. The five delegates from northeastern Iowa were excited to be apart of the loud, raucous atmosphere surrounding the convention. The main topic of conversation was the question of the Chicago and California delegates, which was the first piece of business on the agenda. It would largely determine the course and tone of the convention.

Mack arrived at the convention hall early, waiting for the door to open to begin what he imagined to be one of the most momentous occasions of his life. He was trembling with electrified anticipation. He was not alone. Many of those standing around him were also young and impatient, most of whom Mack assumed were amateurs like him.

They were not disappointed. When the doors flung open, Mack waded through the sea of delegates to find the Iowa section, located near the rear of the hall. Rumors swept across the floor like wind across the sand. It was believed that if the California and Illinois votes went to McGovern, Humphrey and Muskie would withdraw their names from the race, which would give the convention a more focused look of solidarity. Everyone was aware of the television cameras panning the convention floor. The country was watching.

After hours of long-winded speeches and boring technical explanations, the first vote on the California question was taken. The Iowa delegation had poled its members earlier. They, along with the majority, voted to return the seats to the McGovern people. With great fanfare and thunderous applause, the 151 delegates were triumphantly ushered into the hall.

Hours later, after more political maneuvering and grand standing, the complex Illinois issue still was not put to a vote. Mack grew restless and began wondering the floor. He saw for himself that what the national press was saying about this convention was true. There were more young people, women, and minority delegates than any other convention in history. He studied the faces in the crowd. There were more of the long-haired, hippie types than the more traditional suit and tie middle aged men. Everyone was talking, seemingly at once, and no one appeared to be listening. The chairman was banging his gavel, ordering silence so the second vote could begin. Many of the delegates were grinning and wringing their hands with lusty anticipation.

The votes was taken, and the red-faced Mayor Daley and his 34 delegates were escorted off the floor while Jesse Jackson led his group in to take their place. The convention erupted into a spontaneous victorious clamor. Once again, the vanguard of the Democratic party had been defeated. Mack felt as though he should join in the rebel-rousing, but he felt nauseated and dizzy. He pushed his way through the sea of dancing and screaming delegates to an exit and burst outside.

He leaned over with his hands on his knees and sucked in several, quick deep breaths as though he was suffocating. But the humid, Miami air was stale and oppressively hot. Mack peeled off his shirt and hurried back to the hotel. Even though it was 2 AM, he needed to call home. He wanted to hear Penny's voice and apologize, but the recording told him that the phone was disconnected. "Oh, my God!" he cried at loud. "She's going to be so pissed when I get home."

He did not sleep well, tossing and turning all night. He got up early, went outside and bought a roll and coffee from a sidewalk vendor. He tried calling home again, hoping something had changed, but it didn't. Throngs of convention goers were everywhere, chatting about yesterday's victories and the scheduled events of the day. Humphrey and Muskie were sure to concede failure and release their delegates to the McGovern camp. Mack sometimes stopped and listened for a few minutes, amazed at the gloating and arrogance. Twice on the way through the hotel lobby, someone grabbed his arm and drew him into a group of delegates, introducing him as "the young man whose brother is a POW in Vietnam." Both times this announcement was met with knowing nods of condolences. Mack murmured something and moved on quickly.

At the elevator, there was another group talking. "Have you noticed there are no Kennedy's here?" a young woman said. She was wearing sunglasses even though the corridor was dimly lit. "Or Johnson people, either. Even Meany stayed away. You know, George Meany, head of the CIO-AFL."

"Really? I hadn't noticed," chimed in another, a twenty-something man with long, straight hair and a dangling earring which swung as he shook his head. "The Democrats have always had labor in their hip pocket. McGovern had better talk to him fast. We need those votes—"

"And their money," another voice said. It was a girl with a head band across her forehead with a peace symbol embossed across the front. "I can't imagine a Democrat winning without the labor vote."

"Yeah, but we have Shirley Chisholm." This was said by an older man standing at the back, looking ridiculous in his Hawaiian shirt and plaid Bermuda shorts. "We have to have the Black vote, or we don't have a chance."

Mack stood back and listened to the exchange of Democratic rhetoric. He had met Shirley Chisholm once at a rally. She was a strikingly beautiful, charismatic Congresswoman from Texas and the first black woman to ever run as a national candidate, a testament to her extraordinary strength and courage. The fact that she was being regarded as a token Negro vote-getter for the Democrats was infuriating.

He entered the Convention Hall at mid-morning, just after the expected announcements of the Humphrey and Muskie withdrawals had been made. The delegates thundered their approval.. They were impatient to get down to the real business of the Convention -- to officially nominate their candidate, even though that was not scheduled until the next day. First the party platform had to be hammered out, which was sure to be another late night, hard-fought battle between the McGovern people and the party regulars.

As the day wore on, all the speeches, the haggling, the cheering, the booing, and the endless, constant buzz that enveloped Mack became increasingly indistinguishable and meaningless. Once again, he roamed the floor, searching for reason and sanity. There was no decorum, no quiet, no control. He found himself at the front of the hall, staring disbelievingly at a group of long-haired, poorly dressed, bare-footed men and women, sitting in a circle on a large rug placed squarely in front of the podium. He looked up to see a large television camera aimed squarely at this absurd display. No wonder no one's taking us seriously, he brooded angrily. Suddenly, he felt miserable and deflated. It was as though he was standing in the middle of a snake pit, swallowed up by chaos and confusion. He hated it and began pushing his way toward an exit. He wanted to go home.

He stopped briefly to call the hotel and leave a message at the desk that he was leaving and to give his vote to an alternate. He didn't have enough money for a taxi so he wandered the streets of downtown Miami until a policeman pointed out which bus would take him to the Greyhound Station. He had enough money to get to Chicago. He would have to hitch-hike the rest of the way, but he didn't care. He just wanted to go home.

Chapter 67

The day that Mack left, Penny and Katie had supper with her parents and returned home late. It started raining earlier that afternoon, a slow, steady rain that the weatherman on the radio said was going to hang around throughout much of the weekend. When she pulled into the driveway, she immediately noticed that there was no light coming from the kitchen window and the large yard light by the barn was not on either. Her heart sank as she realized that the electric company must have turned off their power again for non-payment.

She thought about turning around and heading back to her parents, but she imagined how smug and condescending her mother would look. She carried her sleeping baby into the house and opened the windows on the east and north sides of the house and felt refreshed by the cool, damp mist that brushed over her. She sat down in her rocking chair to rest her weary feet and would have dozed off if it wasn't for a persistent braying she heard from the nearby pasture. Her eyes suddenly flashed opened as she realized that when she left the yard this morning, the herd had been grazing in the south pasture.

"Damn it!" she muttered angrily. "They're out again! Old lady Becker will have a fit if they get in her garden again!" She went to the phone to call Sonny, but the deafening silence on the receiver told her that it was cut off, too.

Penny checked the baby to make sure she was asleep and then grabbed a lantern and rain poncho, and headed out. Struggling through the storm and darkness, she finally located the source of the sound she had heard before. She herded the cattle into the barn lot, counting them as they waddled in. 25 ... 26 ... 27 ... 28. There were two missing. She had noticed two of the cows were still heavily pregnant. Mack had said four were still undelivered. She wondered if the missing two were out there in labor somewhere and had gone off by themselves.

Tired and irritated, she went back to search for the missing two.

She found them standing in a ravine about a quarter mile

from the house. Both were obviously in labor, their bellies and back haunches intermittently spasming with pains. There was some blood mixed in the rain water puddled around one of them, and she seemed to be breathing rapidly.

"You stupid, Goddamn animals!" she screamed. "Why do you always do this at the worst time possible?" She considered going to the Winston's for help, but she doubted there was time. She and Mack could ill afford to lose even one cow or their calves. Their survival was vital for their financial future.

Taking a long, deep breath, she preformed the distasteful job of sticking her arm down the birth canal. She identified what she thought was the butt of the unborn calf. Just like humans, it was better if a calf fetus presents head first. She had assisted Sonny and Mack in a difficult birth like this last spring so she knew that this calf would probably be still born. The cord was wrapped around ifs neck and there was nothing she could do about it. The important thing now was to save the cow.

Penny reached in again, grabbed the baby's tail, and pulled with all her might. "C'mon!" she screamed, "you stupid bitch! Help! Push!" But it was no use. If a grown man could not do this alone, how could she expect to do it? Frantically, she devised a plan. Running back to the house she started up the tractor and drove it back to the two cows. She managed to tie a rope around one of the baby's hooves. Slowly nudging the tractor forward, the baby was expelled. It laid motionless and Penny could see it was dead. Within moments, the afterbirth was delivered and the bleeding seemed to decrease. The mother cow nudged her baby, trying to make it stand up. Annie then turned her attention to the other cow.

She was surprised to see one new born calf lying in the mud beside the cow, which was obviously still experiencing a great deal of distress. "My God, she's having twins!" Penny exclaimed, furious with the cow for having the ill graces to do this on such a night.

She examined her as she had the first, this time finding a small hoof and a nose midway down the birth canal. Penny turned her attention to the first born calf, lying half dead at her mother's side. She decided to gamble on mother nature. Herding the first cow into the barn, she carried the tiny calf into the barn. She tried to introduce the tit to the newborn, squeezing small drops into its mouth, begging it to drink. The cow stamped her feet and seemed to move away at first, but then quieted, allowing Penny to work with the baby. It drank enough to sustain itself. Penny covered it with some blankets and laid it in the hay to sleep. She returned to the pasture, already exhausted and shivering in the cold.

She found the cow in hard labor. For at least another hour or more, Penny worked with her, pulling as hard as she could to facilitate a faster delivery. Finally, just as she was about to give up, the baby appeared. Amazingly, it appeared as though it would survive, but Penny wanted to get them inside. Crying and screaming, she whipped and kicked the poor, exhausted animal to herd it toward the barn. Just as the dark skies were beginning to show lighter hues of gray, Penny scooped up the baby, trudging and stumbling through the mud and praying for enough strength to make it this one last time.

Wearily, she sank down onto the floor and watched as the new baby began to nurse. Its mother began cleaning it with her long, sandpaper tongue. Penny smiled as the other calf didn't seem to take much notice of her own mother as she snuggled at the feet of her foster parent. It appeared as though both calves and mothers were going to be fine. Penny would have liked just to lie there and sleep for awhile, but she remembered her own child who would be waking soon.

Struggling to her feet, she turned to walk toward the house. A few feet from the door, she was suddenly hit with a sharp, stabbing pain in her abdomen. She doubled over and she fell to the ground. "Oh, my God!" she cried. "My baby!" Knowing she had to get inside the house, she tried to stand up, but the pain was unbelievable. Half crawling, she managed to get inside. Pulling off her wet, muddy, and blood soaked clothes, she stuffed towels between her legs. There was nothing she could do but lie on the bathroom floor, decimated by each successive wave of pain.

She knew her baby was only six and a half months along, so the chances of it surviving such an early delivery was unlikely, especially out here alone, with no help or facilities. She prayed fervently that someone would come and find her, but the hours passed agonizingly slowly with no one in sight. Katie crept out of bed, confused and crying for breakfast. Penny was able to reach inside the cupboard and reached a box of dry cereal. The baby whimpered and fussed throughout the long morning, until finally she curled up on the floor near her mother and slept. Penny had covered herself with a table cloth so that the little girl could not see the bright, red blood draining life out of her.

Clinching her fists and trying valiantly to keep from screaming, she continued on through torturous, long hours of labor. Finally, at 3: 15 in the afternoon, she delivered a tiny baby boy. She knew the moment she touched him that her son was already dead. Wrapping him in a small hand towel, she held him close and wept gut-wrenching, distraught tears with what little strength she had left. Then she laid down, so tired and full of grief that she wondered if she might die right here on the spot. But she saw Katie lying nearby and crept close. Holding both her children, she passed out.

* * * * * *

Andrew tried calling Penny Saturday morning and threw the receiver down angrily when he realized her phone was disconnected again. His first impulse was to drop everything and drive out there, knowing that his cowardly brother had left town again. But he thought better of it, not wanting to crowd her. Besides, it work to Andrew's benefit if Penny had enough time to get really angry at her husband. But, unable to fight the temptation any longer, he picked up her favorite pizza for dinner and headed toward Shanny.

Rehearsing several casual greetings and valid excuses whey he was dropping by uninvited, he drove toward her place, still wondering if he should just forget it and go back to Dubuque. It was still raining, and the dark, menacing skies only served to make him more uncomfortable.

He pulled into her driveway, happy to see the Jeep parked outside. He could hear Katie crying so he assumed that Penny was busy with the fussy child and let himself in. He sensed there was something wrong the moment he entered. The place was eerily dark, and there was a hideous odor in the air. He followed the sound of the baby's cry toward the kitchen.

"Oh, my God!" Penny was lying on the floor covered with blood, still cradling the little bundle in her arms. "Oh, my God!" he said again. Was she dead? No, he touched her and she responded slightly. What should he do? There was no phone to call for help. He usually wasn't very good in these situations, but he knew he had to move quickly. He wrapped Penny in some blankets and carried her to his car. Then he went back for Katie. Hurry, you fool, he admonished himself. Hurry, or she might die!

He was thankful to deliver her alive to the Emergency Room at Mercy Hospital. He sat in the waiting room with Katie whimpering in his rms. He was aware he should make phone calls to the families, but he couldn't move. He wasn't even aware that he was crying until he felt the tears running down his cheeks. I saved her, he said over and over in his mind, I saved her. If it weren't for me she would have died and it would have been Mack's fault! Now she'll hate him for sure and want nothing more to do with him. He killed her baby!

Apparently, someone on staff in the ER called Dr. Lamp because within minutes he and his wife came running down the corridor. Mrs. Lamp was hysterical. "I want to see my daughter," she yelled. "Dennis, tell them we have to see her right away."

"Lorena, it would do neither her or you any good to go in there right now," Dr. Lamp said, trying to sound rational and calm although anyone could see that he was as upset as his wife. "Andrew, is that you? Did you bring them here?" He picked up his granddaughter and cradled her in his arms.

"I didn't know what to do," Andrew mumbled, his arms wrapped around his stomach as he rocked back and forth.. "She was lying there, covered with blood. I thought she was dead!"

"My God, why didn't she call someone?" Mrs. Lamp shrieked.

"The phone -- there was no phone."

"Oh, yes, I tried to call her this morning. It was disconnected, wasn't it. I should have driven right out there and made her and Katie come into town for the weekend. That damned, no-good husband of hers-- "

"Lorena! Stop it!" Dr. Lamp demanded. "This is not the time for any of that. Did you contact Mack?" he said turning to Andrew again. "She'll need surgery. He should be here."

"I don't know where he is. Maybe Penny does, but I don't."

"What kind of an idiot goes off and leaves his pregnant wife with no phone, no electricity, and runs off to God knows where!" Mrs. Lamp wailed.

"You know he's at the Democratic National Convention." Dr. Lamp snapped angrily. "We just don't know which hotel."

"I don't care if he's having dinner at the goddamn White House!" Mrs. Lamp cried. "If you ask me, this is all his fault."

"I know you're upset," Dr. Lamp said, his voice quivering. "We all are. This is just not the time to start laying blame." He turned to Andrew again. "Why don't you call home? Perhaps one of them knows where he's staying."

Andrew did not want to call, but he knew he had no choice. He didn't want Annie and the others crowding into this room, crying and wringing their hands. He was sure one of them would say, "Poor Mack!" and he simply couldn't bear to hear it. And how would he explain his tremendous grief and desperate worrying? What would he do if someone figured out how much he loved her?

It didn't take long for an entourage of Winston's to arrive. Mrs. Lamp was barely civil toward them, especially when they acknowledged that when they called the number Mack had given them, they were told he had already checked out and no one knew where he was. Both families stood a tense vigil throughout the long night. Thankfully, the surgeon was able to clean out the uterus and control the bleeding without performing a hysterectomy.

"Penny should recover just fine," he said. "She's had four units of blood, so she's pinking up nicely. I'm hopeful that she will be able to get pregnant again and carry the pregnancy full term." He explained that she had suffered what is called, "placenta abrupto." For whatever reason, the placenta tore away from the wall of the uterus. "Saving the baby in those situations is very difficult," he sighed. "He probably died before she delivered him."

"My poor girl," wept Mrs. Lamp. "And that poor baby."

Annie watched Andrew throughout the evening. Everyone was worried, but he seemed noticeably distraught. Perhaps he was upset having been the one to come upon the bloody scene. He never handled that kind of thing very well. Maybe he felt badly for Mack. She moved closer to her twin to console him.

"Andrew, she's going to be all right. Didn't you hear what the doctor said? I feel bad for Mack, too. I wish we could call him."

When she said those last words, he visibly bristled. "Why would you feel bad for him? This is all his fault. He can go straight to hell for all I care."

Annie was stunned. "What are you saying? This wasn't his fault."

"Yes, it was! She begged him not to go. They've been fighting about it for weeks. If he stayed home and paid his damn bills, at least she could have called for help. I can't stand to think of her lying there all alone and --" He stopped then, realizing he already said too much. Annie was looking at him so strangely. "I mean, she could have died." He moved away then, and avoided her the rest of the time they were at the hospital together.

* * * * * *

In the morning, when everyone was assured Penny was going to be all right, he tried to sound reasonable as he refused to go home. Even Mrs. Lamp, having seen her daughter, was content to go home for a short nap and bathe. But Andrew stubbornly refused to leave.

"I'll catch a quick shower and eat something later," he said. "I'll stay until her mother gets back. I don't want her to be alone, all right?"

They left then, and he sat on a chair at the side of the bed. She looked so pale and vulnerable. She hadn't spoken much since she had regained consciousness, only asked a few medical questions and worried about Katie. She didn't mention Mack even once, Andrew noticed. He was sure this was finally going to be the end of their marriage. There was no way she would ever forgive him for this.

"Penny?" he whispered. "I'm going to stay with you, I promise."

She smiled a little, and then turned away to sleep. She's depressed, he thought. I can help her deal with this if she just lets me. I'll make her realize that she can trust me. I would never hurt her like he did.

He kept his promise and rarely left her bedside. He worried about her state of mine. There was an impenetrable sadness on her face that was heart breaking. Not even her father was able to make her smile, although he was the only one she allowed to hold and comfort her. She didn't want to deal with her mother at all, asking Mrs. Lamp to concentrate on little Katie instead.

Penny insisted that no one tell her mother that she would be discharged Wednesday morning. Andrew's spirits soared when she asked him to take her home that day. He would have ample chance to talk to her alone. He had rehearsed over and over what he was going to say.

He began as they drove toward Shannon Town. "Penny, I was wondering if you would like to come stay with me for a few days. We can pick up some things from home, but you don't intend to stay there, do you?"

She didn't answer at first. Her stony, vacant stare was still in place. "I don't know what I'm going to do," she murmured. "I haven't thought about it."

"I'd be glad to help you pack, whatever I can do to help."

"I know, Andrew. You're a wonderful friend."

That word "friend" cut through him like a knife. "A friend?' he said sharply. "Is that how you think of me?"

"Well, yes. Maybe more -- a brother?" There was confusion ringing in her voice so he decided to drop it. She was too weak to process any of this. There would be time later to tell her how he felt. They drove the rest of the way in silence.

Chapter 68

Thankfully, Annie had gone to the house and cleaned everything up before they arrived. Andrew took Penny's hand and led her slowly inside. As she entered the front door, she looked more panicked than he had ever seen her.

"Penny, just sit down," Andrew said, steering toward her rocking chair. "I'll pack some things for you and Katie, and we'll go back to my place, okay?"

She said nothing, so he took that to mean she agreed. He filled suitcases, scornfully pushing aside any reminders of his brother's existence in this house. His hands were trembling. This was it. His dream was coming true.

He heard someone come in. Thinking it was probably Annie. Andrew went out to face his twin, determined not to let anyone change Penny's mind.

It was Mack. He was standing there, looking more disheveled than he usually did when he returned from these trips. He was leaning heavily against the door sill, obviously exhausted. "Where's Penny?"

"She's -- I mean, I thought she was sitting in her rocking chair over there." But the chair was empty.

"Honey?" Mack called, wondering through the house searching for her. "I'm home."

"I don't think – well, I'm sure, she don't want to see you right now."

"What? Of course, she wants to see me! What's going on around here?" He went to refrigerator, and was immediately met by the overpowering stench of rotting food. "Oh, I get it! She's pissed because of the phone and electrical."

"No, Mack, its more than that -- a lot more!"

"Like what? Just spill it. What in the hell is going on around here?"

"There was trouble while you were gone. Penny was alone here with no phone or anything. She was bleeding-- "

"Was it the baby? What happened?" His face suddenly

paled, and once again he went from room to room, searching for his wife, this time more frantically. Then saw the suitcases. "What's going on here?"

"I picked her up at the hospital this morning and now she's going to stay by me." He said those words as resolutely as he could muster. He was ready for a fight, even a physical one if it came to that.

"What in the hell are you talking about? Penny, honey? Where are you? It's Mack! I'm home!"

"Don't you get it?" Andrew barked, following him. "She was in the hospital for three days, and she never asked for you once. This was all your fault. None of this would have happened if you wouldn't have been such a inconsiderate, selfish jerk! She's through with you!"

"What the fuck are you saying?"

"Your baby, you asshole. She lost it. She delivered it, lying on this goddamn floor, all alone. I found her, covered in blood. If it weren't for me, she would have died!"

"Oh, thank God, you got here in time. The baby? It's dead?"

"Yes, you sonofabitch! You left her here all alone with a baby and another one on the way. No phone. No electricity."

"I know, I know," Mack cried. "but everything was fine when I left. I thought everything would hold until I got back!"

"Well, you thought wrong! How could you be so stupid? You say you love her, and you let something like this happen? It's over – finally. You never loved her, not like she deserves! Not like I could!" The words came tumbling out like water overflowing a bucket. The truth that had been choking him for all this time was finally extricated from deep within his soul. He squared his shoulders and braced himself for what the fight he was sure would follow.

Mack stood motionless for a few moments as though trying to absorb his brother's words and decipher their meaning. Then, he turned away and waved his hand as though to dismiss the whole idiotic incident. He stormed out of the house. He found her standing by the pasture fence. "Penny," he called.

Andrew hurried after him and hissed, "She doesn't want to

see you. I told you, she's through with you!"

"She is my wife, and I have to speak to her."

"Just leave her the hell alone!" Andrew cried, trying to grab his brother. But Mack pushed him aside, and approached his wife.

"I'm home."

Andrew could barely breathe as he waited for her response. His whole life, his very being, hinged on these next few seconds. She didn't turn to look at them, standing statuesquely with her beautiful hair flowing in the wind. "Look," she murmured, "there's the two calves that were born that night."

"What night, Penny?" Mack asked.

"Friday night. I came home late. It was storming. The fence was down, and 1 found those two having trouble. I knew I had to help, like you and Sonny did that time. Remember how Sonny said these things always happen at the worst possible time?"

"Sure I remember, but why didn't you get help?"

"I didn't think there was any time. I thought I could handle it," she said, tears beginning to stream down her face. "I always think 1 can handle everything."

"I should have been here. You were right! I didn't need to go. My being there didn't amount to a pile of shit!"

"What?" she whispered.

"There was all this excitement, like we were going to change the world or something. But once I got there, all I wanted was to come home." He stepped toward her, reaching out to touch her, but then pulled his hand back. "I finally understand I don't need to take care of the world. I just need to take care of things here."

She had appeared unmoved and unaffected until he said those last words. Her head tilted ever so slightly and her expression softened just enough that he moved close to her and gathered her up as she collapsed into his arms.

"I'm so sorry, Penny. I'm so sorry." She said nothing, just wrapped herself around him, burying her face in his chest.

"But, Penny," Andrew gasped as they walked past him. "What about-- " It was hopeless. Neither of them acknowledged him in any way.

Andrew jumped into his car and peeled away. Barely able to see because of his rage, he raced down the road and didn't notice the approaching car until it was too late. It was Annie. They swerved to miss each other and Andrew's car spun out of control, coming to a stop in the ditch. Annie ran to him quickly. "Andrew," she cried. "Are you okay?"

"Sure, I'm fine!' he howled, jerking open the door so he could get out.

"Well, what's wrong then?" she demanded. "Is Penny alright? I was just coming over to see if she needed any help."

"Oh, she's fine, just fine, now that the Boy Wonder is back." Sarcasm and frustration was dripping from every word.

"Mack's home? But the convention isn't even over yet."

"Yeah, well, he left early, I guess! And just like always, the whole damned world stops turning the minute that jerk shows up!" He was yelling now, but he didn't care. "He is such an asshole. Why can't she see that?"

"She loves him, Andrew. She always has, from the moment they first laid eyes on each other, I think."

"Why? What is so fucking special about that creep? What the hell is there about him that women just fall at his feet, especially her. No matter how many times he hurts her, she never sees he's no good for her?"

"They're married."

"So what? They fight all the time."

"They're both very strong-willed people. They argue, but that doesn't mean it's not a good marriage."

Andrew sank down onto the edge of the road. "I know, but Annie, I could -- I mean, I want to --" The words stuck in his throat. It was very difficult to articulate sensations and emotions that have been buried for so long. "I could love her the way she deserves."

Annie understood for the first time the depth of his anguish. She was more astonished that he was capable of that kind of passion than the scandalous nature of his betrayal. "How long have you felt this way?"

"From the first moment I saw her, that day she was taking care of Mack I didn't know she was his 'mystery lady'. I just knew

580

that she was the most incredibly beautiful girl I had ever seen. I started having these fantasies that I would call her up and casually ask her out. But then she and Mack got involved, and there was nothing I could do."

"But Andrew, they got married and had a child! Didn't you realize -- "

"That I didn't have a prayer? Sure I knew, but I kept hoping."

"For what? They'd get a divorce?" There was a slight accusatory tone in those words that she regretted as soon as she spoke. "I'm sorry, but -- "

"I know what you're saying. I hated myself, but I couldn't stop. I felt glad when he hurt her because I thought she'd turn to me. Me! We started spending more time together. Every time she was mad at him, she'd come to me. She'd sit for hours and complain about him, but she always took him back. But this time -- man, I thought she was finally through with him. She was going to stay at my place for awhile."

"Really? She said that?"

"Well, she -- I mean, when I suggested it, she didn't say no."

"Does she know? How you feel, I mean?"

"No, I don't think so, unless Mack tells her. If I only would have been a little faster! I almost had everything packed." He picked up a stone and threw it across the road. "And ya' know what? As soon as she swooned into his arms, it was like I was the invisible man. I had just told him that I was in love with his wife, and he just pushes me aside like I'm nothing I thought he'd hit me or something but he didn't even -- " His words trailed off then but she knew what he meant. Not being taken seriously was the worst insult of all.

They sat there on the edge of the road silently for a few minutes until Annie said, "What are you going to do now?"

"I sure as hell am not gonna be a priest!" he hissed sarcastically.

Annie gave him a sisterly nudge. "C'mon, Andrew, your life isn't over. I know you'll never be a priest because -- well, not because you're this terrible sinner or anything, but because now you know what it's like to love someone. And there's someone out there who will love you like Penny loves Mack."

She meant for her words to comfort him, but he wasn't ready to accept the finality of the situation. He wanted to sulk away and lick his wounds in private. Annie stood and watched him drive away, wondering how many more scars and schisms this family could withstand.

CHAPTER 69

"Hey, Mack," Matthew said as his oldest son sauntered into the kitchen. "You were right. It's only August, and already the Democrats are self-destructing."

"I know, Pop. I heard it on the news. McGovern is dum ing Eagleton. Poor guy. No one heard of him before McGovern picked him, and now the press is crucifying him."

"Well, McGovern's the one you oughta feel sorry for. Kennedy should have taken it, or even Humphrey. He's screwed now."

"That stuff they're saying about Eagleton isn't even true," Mack said as he poured himself some coffee. "Well, the part about seeing a psychiatrist is – I mean, so the guy went to a specialist. Big deal. But these allegations of driving drunk are just trumped up charges. Nixon's people probably started all of that."

"Well, welcome to the wonderful world of politics, son." Matthew glanced at his son and smiled. These political conversations with Mack never ceased to amaze him. They never argued any more, but debated like any two concerned citizens. "So, who's he gonna pick now?"

"Well, the word is he's chosen Sergeant Shriver."

"Really? I didn't hear anything about him."

"Well, Pop, I have my sources." They both laughed then, appreciating the irony of that statement. "It makes sense though. He's the next best thing to a Kennedy since he married one, and he got the Peace Corps up and running. McGovern thinks the public will go for him."

"What do you think?"

"I don't think he has a snow ball's chance in hell." Mack put his coffee cup in the sink and walked toward the door.

"Hey, Mack, there's an article in here about you. I guess these local reporters still want to know your opinion. Says you declined comment."

"Nah, I promised Penny I'm done with that shit. No more tilting at windmills. I just want this damned war to be over and my brother back home where he belongs."

"We all want that, son." Matthew folded the paper and followed Mack outside, who was heading toward the Jeep.

"Where you off to?"

"I'm gonna pick up Penny and we're going into town. The baby's headstone is ready." He said nothing more as he started the engine and headed down the driveway. Matthew watched until the curl of dust disappeared over the horizon. He shuddered as he remembered the small white coffin being lowered into the ground in the small cemetery behind the church. Penny had picked out a small white headstone with an engraving of a baby calf above the name. Matthew McAllister Winston IV.

As Matthew turned to go back to work, he paused to ponder about his second son. Andrew was conspicuously absent at the funeral. He hadn't offered much of an explanation. He simply said he had this trip back East planned for weeks and couldn't change it now. He still wasn't back. Matthew assumed it had something to do with the priesthood. Andrew had put it off for years now. He hadn't talked about it in months, so why the rush now? Matthew headed toward the barn and made a mental note to speak to his son as soon as he came home.

* * * * * *

Penny and Mack kept to themselves after their baby's funeral, working their farm together and helping each other through a difficult time. Penny made Mack promise that the two calves that she had helped deliver that rainy night would never be sold under any circumstances. Both calves were females. Penny fitted each with a collar with engraved names befitting their personalities: Stormy and Sweetness.

Mack and Andrew did not see each other again until late August. St. Patrick's was having a huge festival as a fund-raiser for the new roof. The church grounds were transformed into a country fair atmosphere, featuring children's games, a beer tent, fabulous food, non-stop bingo, and live music. The Winston's attended enthusiastically, volunteering in several areas. This was going to be fun!

The grand finale was the Sunday afternoon tug-a-rope. The rules were that each team must be composed of blood relatives with at least one female. Matthew eagerly signed up his family and named his team – himself, Sonny, Mack, John and Annie. Andrew, a committeeman and an organizer to the affair, said nothing when his name was omitted.

That morning, the family assembled on the yard. "Where's Sonny?" Matthew barked, eager to get started. "We need him for our team."

"Did you tell him that?" Mack asked as he tightened the seat belt on Katie's car seat. "He never goes to town, especially since that guy nearly killed him, remember?"

"That was two years ago. He should be over that by now."

Just then Annie emerged from the house and bolted past him. "You looking for Sonny? He's not coming. He says he's not a blood relative anyway."

Matthew threw his cap onto the ground. "Now, what are we gonna do!"

"We gotta get someone else," John pressed. "Peter?"

"Nah! Are you nuts? Look at the size of the other teams. We're not doing this to get embarrassed."

"What about Andrew?" Penny suggested. "Just because he's on the committee doesn't mean he can't be on our team, right?"

"Andrew?" Mack hissed. "Why him? Isn't there anyone else?"

"Like who?" Matthew countered. "We have no choice." He climbed into the truck and turned the key. "Let's go."

John was dispensed to find Andrew as soon as they arrived at the festival. They appeared just as their name was called for the first round. It was obvious that he was no more excited about this than Mack was. However, Matthew didn't give him a chance to refuse. "It's about time! Let's go!" he commanded, handing everyone a pair of gloves.

Andrew and Mack eyed each other ruefully. "What's the matter, Andrew," Mack spat. "You afraid you might actually sweat?"

"I sweat all the time, but I also use my brain. You should try it sometime."

As the teams assembled for the first round of competition, good natured heckling and name-calling abound. Teams were drawn from a hat for pairing. Matthew was delighted when he drew the Bishops, a neighboring farm family he knew from the Pub.

"Hey, Winston," George Bishop called across the field. "You sure you wanna do this? You're playing with the big boys now."

"What big boys – I don't see no big boys," Matthew jeered. The crowd howled their approval.

"I'm man enough, all right," Andrew retorted, throwing down his clipboard and rolling up his sleeves. "Let's do it!"

They took their positions by the rope. Matthew insisted on taking the anchor spot at the end. Next was John and then Andrew. Annie had the unenviable position of being between her two feuding brothers. They dug in, as did their opponents, and when the whistle blew, they bared down with every ounce of their strength. The red handkerchief in the middle was stationary for several seconds as neither team would give and inch. But then, slowly, it began to move toward the Winston side.

"Pull! Pull!" Matthew screamed. They somehow managed to take small steps backwards until the flag passed the marker, and the Bishops came tumbling to the ground on the Winston's side. Mr. Bishop offered a congratulatory handshake, complaining that two of his boys had eaten too much fried chicken just prior to the contest.

"I have to get back," Andrew said, adjusting his shirt and wiping his brow.

"Don't be too long," his father commanded. "We'll go again in about a half hour, so get back here fast!"

"Yeah, Andrew," jeered Mack. "Don't get so excited judging the quilting contest that you forget to come back, ya' hear?"

"Mack!" his wife reproached him playfully. "Why are you so mean to him? Let's all go get something cold to drink. I was getting hot just watching you guys."

"Like all hot and bothered?" Mack teased, obviously for his brother's benefit.

"No, now you stop that, Mack. C'mon Andrew, come sit with us," Penny coaxed, her long, bare arms wrapped around her husband's shoulders.

"Nah, Mack's right. I have some stuff to do, but I will be back."

The Winston's opponent in the semi-final round was Joe Kennedy's family – two sons, niece and one nephew. He had met with Matthew between matches over beers and a friendly wager was made.

"Don't screw this up for us," Mack said so only Andrew and Annie could hear him.

"Just worry about yourself," Andrew replied, taking his place at the rope. The whistle blew, and both sides were straining so fiercely that their bodies were nearly parallel with the ground. The red flag had started to float towards the Kennedy's side when suddenly one of them grabbed his shoulder and began to wail in extreme pain. The Winston's won by default. Big Joe looked disgusted, but recovered in time to extend his hand. Matthew took it, but then gestured he was waiting for something more. Joe good-naturedly reached for his wallet. The two of them went off together as Matthew suggested they throw the money in the donation basket, which was conveniently placed in the beer tent.

Annie watched her father anxiously. His face was so red, and he was sweating profusely. Meanwhile, her two brothers were glaring at each other with utter contempt again.

"You almost lost that one for us, you stupid weakling!" Mack cried.

"You think you're so tough, don't you!" Andrew countered.

"I'm a man all right, man enough for --"

"Man enough for what?"

"That's enough!" Annie said, stepping between them. "People are starting to stare.

"Then tell this stupid sonofabitch --" Mack was saying, but stopped when Penny approached them.

"Hey, you guys, that was great," she gushed. "I took a look at that guy's shoulder. I think he dislocated it. Can you believe that?"

"Did you guys notice Dad? His face was so red," Annie asked.

"I'm sure he's fine," Penny said, sounding unconcerned. "It's really hot out here, and this whole thing is pretty intense, don't you think?"

"Yeah," John laughed, "your face was pretty red, too."

"I know, but he's in the beer tent again," Annie worried.

"That's okay, and even if it weren't, who gonna tell your father not to drink?" Penny replied. "C'mon, Mack. Let's go find your dad and see if we can convince him to drink some water -- for the good of the team, right?   "Annie's right, this is not the time for this," Mack muttered.

"Fine. Then just leave me alone."

* * * * * *

As luck would have it, they were facing the Jamison's in the championship round. The prospect of beating Walt Jamison had given this friendly little competition a whole different meaning for Mathew. Jamison had ridiculed Matthew all over town after the Winston's financial problems became public knowledge.

"I really want this," Matthew said as he huddled his team. "We can beat these guys."

"I don't know, Pop. They look awful big to me," Andrew said.

"You're gonna wimp out before we begin?" Mack quipped sarcastically.

"No, I just said--"

"Andrew's right," Annie cut in nervously. "Look at the

size of those guys! And Karla Jamison is as big as some of her brothers."

"They're big all right, but we can beat 'em," John boasted confidently.

"How? They beat both those other teams in less than 30 seconds," Annie countered. "They're more powerful than anyone we've faced so far." "Yeah, around the middle," Matthew retorted. "Look at those guts. Now look, they've been winning with a big initial jerk. So if we can just dig in and hold 'em, those fat sonofabitches won't be able to last," Matthew strategized. "Now, come on! We can do this!"

Both teams took their places on the line. The whistle blew, and as predicted, the Jamison's gave a mighty tug that nearly sent the Winston's over the marker for a quick defeat. But they somehow hung on and stopped the flag a few inches short of the post. It hung there, suspended for a few minutes. The crowd roared as neither side gave in, and very slowly, the Winston's were actually beginning to regain some of their lost ground in painful, minuscule increments. Annie was nearing collapse, but she hung on as her father and the others groaned and strained as each agonizing moment passed.

But then, her feet became tangled up with Andrew's and they tumbled to the ground. With one mighty pull, the Jamison's ended it quickly. Matthew looked on resentfully as the Walt Jamison was awarded the trophy. Matthew limped off to lick his wounds over another cold can of beer.

Andrew and Mack squatted on the ground where they had fallen. "You goddamn jerk," Mack spat. "You lost this for us."

"I did not," Andrew exclaimed angrily. "I was--"

"Andrew's right," Annie cried. "It was my fault. I lost my footing--"

"Just stop it, Annie," Andrew cried. "You can talk till you're blue in the face and he won't believe you. Go ahead, think what you want." He got up and walked away, but Mack caught him and jerked him around roughly.

"How's this? I think you're a no good, fuckin' asshole who--"

"No, not here," Annie pleaded, trying to get between them.

"She's right. Let's go take care of this somewhere else," Mack snarled.

"Fine with me. Let's go."

"Good. Annie, go find Penny and keep her busy for awhile. This shouldn't take more than a few seconds." With that, they marched off.

It was difficult finding a private place in the middle of a festival., so they crossed the parking lot towards the high school and went behind the concession stand by the football field. They turned to face each other. Mack's hands were tightly fisted and began to encircle Andrew like a boxer in the ring. "Okay, let's have it. Tell me why you tried to steal my wife away from me."

"I didn't have to try very hard. You nearly gave her away."

"How in the hell can you say that? You think you're the only smart one in this family, so I can't have convictions?"

"You jackass – just because you're wallowing in your own guilt, don't try blaming this on me!"

"At least I tried to do something. You didn't even care."

"You stupid sonofabitch!" Andrew screamed. "You know I care – I care a lot. But that doesn't mean I have to go gallivanting across the country. You deserved to lose everything for being so idiotic." He lunged toward Mack.

This time, Mack swung and connected with a savage jab that sent Andrew reeling. "Idiotic, aye? I'll show you idiotic." He began punching Andrew mercilessly until finally Andrew was able to grab a handful of his hair and backed him away. He landed one punch, and this time it was Mack who went sprawling in the dirt.

"I don't care if you don't agree with what I did," Mack exclaimed, jumping to his feet. "This is not about politics. This is about you and my wife."

"Somebody had to take care of her. You had something so perfect and you were ready to piss it all away."

"I was not and you know it. It's just the same as always. You always wanted what you can't have. You always wanted to be me."

"You arrogant ass! Why in the hell would I want to be like you -- you insufferable, pig-headed jerk. You never once gave a damn about anyone except yourself." They went at it again, wrestling and rolling around on the ground, punching and scratching each other until the extraordinary physical events of that afternoon caught up with them and their punches became powerless, glancing blows. Finally, they could do nothing but sit on the ground, hurting and exhausted, but still very angry.

Andrew picked up a handful of dirt and flung it across the field. "Damn it, Mack, you act like I wanted this to happen, but I didn't."

"I don't know nothing about anything! I wasn't doing nothing wrong – I wasn't out there drinkin' and whorin'. I didn't leave my family behind for days at a time because I didn't care about them."

"You sure acted like it sometimes."

"Fuck you. Maybe it was guilt. I know that's what Penny thinks. I thought I was doing the right thing. I really did."

Andrew had no sarcastic reply for such sincerity. He heard it before, but never believed it. He picked up another handful of dirt and threw it. "Maybe you were doing what you thought was right, but you ignored the damage it was doing to Penny and Katie. She came crying to me all the time – you'd leave her behind with no money, no nothing. You'd go days without calling home. You were such a jerk!"

"I know. I told her I was sorry, but --" His voice trailed off. "I'm gonna make it up to her somehow, I swear it. But Andrew, she is my wife – my wife! What the hell did you think you were doing?"

Andrew didn't answer at first, trying to find the words to explain it. "I didn't mean for any of it to happen – it just did. I hated myself, but I couldn't help it"

This time it was Mack who threw a fistful of dirt across the field. "Well, you must have done a damn good job of keeping how you felt a secret 'cause she doesn't have any idea. I was afraid for a while that she had feelings for you, too, but she don't – except like a friend or a brother. And I don't want to louse that up for her, so I didn't say anything."

"Yeah, I know. I didn't think you would."

"So, what are you gonna do now?"

"I'm moving back East?"

"What?"

"I have it all worked out with Aunt Esther. I haven't said anything to anyone else yet, but I'm going to be a junior executive in the company."

"My God, I can't believe it! You're gonna be a big time business man? What about the family? You leaving would break Annie's heart."

"I'm not done at school until spring, and I told Aunt Esther I won't leave until Luke's back."

"Why are you doing this? Because of me and Penny?"

"No, for once this is not about you," Andrew blurted tersely. "This is about me, and what I want!"

"Well, what exactly do you want?"

"I want it all – everything."

"Like what?"

"Everything that Pop had with Mother – like you and Penny. I want the beautiful wife, the sex, the family, the success, the money – I want all of it."

"Wow," whistled Mack, "but do you have to go back East to find it?"

"Why not? I'm good at business, and why scratch around looking for a job when Aunt Esther will give me anything I want on a silver platter."

"I just can't picture it, that's all. All those year's of seeing Pop in that office. I just can't – you know."

"Yeah, I know. You just can't picture me there, can you. Well, I want it, and I aim to have it. If there's one thing I learned from all this – if you want something you have to go after it. And there's something else I learned, too."

"Yeah? Like what?"

"The next time I see a pretty girl, I'm not going to hang around daydreaming."

They both smiled then and got up, dusted themselves off, and started back toward the churchyard.

* * * * * *

Only Annie was aware of the drama that had unfolded that afternoon and was happy it was over. Her brothers apparently reached some kind of understanding, as they were more civil toward each other now than in months.

She was shocked when Andrew announced he was planning to pursue a career in business elsewhere, perhaps New York. He promised he would not leave the area as long as Luke's whereabouts and welfare was unknown. His hope, as well as everyone else's, was that Nixon would keep his campaign promise and end the war before the election. Annie was already beginning to plan the family's Christmas celebration, certain that they would all be together.

Although she understood his motives, it was difficult for her to imagine Andrew moving away. She was already having difficulty coping with John being away at college. Another room was empty, another door closed.

Chapter 70

As the weeks of fall slipped by, Matthew and the boys were busy in the fields. The harvest was finished by mid-October. Mack's corn crib and hay mow were full, too, so he and Penny approached the coming winter confident that there was plenty of food for their herd. Their relationship seemed stronger than ever. Mack kept his promise and was a devoted husband and father. He worked hard to make their farm a success.

Annie loved autumn. It was a time of triumph and fulfillment. Her garden had turned out better than she had hoped, and the orchard had produced moderate amounts of apples and pears. She spent hundreds of happy hours laboring over a hot stove, cooking and canning until the shelves of her fruit room were over-flowing with dozens of jars of tomatoes, pickles, beets, fruits and relishes. But a vast store of food for the winter was not the only thing that had her smiling. She and Sonny were becoming closer. Late night meetings at the rocky place were common place during warm weather. And now that the days were shorter and cooler, they lingered over coffee at the kitchen table.

But she longed for more.

Whether it was frustration that her relationship with Sonny had not progressed any further, or because she just felt like having a good time, she accepted Mike Holmes' invitation to attend Homecoming. John and the other seniors from last year's championship team were going to be honored at halftime, so several of the Winston's planned to attend.

A few days before the big event, Annie announced her plans at the supper table. For the first time since they moved here, she needed to hire a babysitter and wondered if anyone had any ideas. A few names were discussed, but everyone knew it would be difficult to find anyone on such a big night.

"I can watch the kids for you," Sonny said. Annie watched him to see if there was a hint of jealousy. She was disappointed that there wasn't.

"But, Sonny," Matthew countered, "are you sure you wouldn't like to come? You've never been to a game, and hell, they're a lot of fun. John will be the man of the hour!"

"Nah," Sonny replied, sounding disinterested. "You guys go and have a good time." And that was the end of it.

Friday night, Annie dressed the little ones in their pajamas early. She only had about twenty minutes to take her hair out of the rollers, apply her makeup, and get dressed in one of her cutest sweater outfits. She was barely finished when she heard Sonny answer the door. She skipped down the stairs, fully aware that all her curves were bouncing the right way. Sonny tried to look away, but Annie knew he was watching her as closely as her date. Mike helped her with her coat and whisked her out the door. "Don't wait up!" Annie sang out, but she knew he would.

* * * * * *

Several hours later, she returned through that same door, giggling and giddy. As she had several times that evening, she playfully reminded Mike to keep his hands where they belonged. He wanted to stay, but Annie insisted it was time to call it a night. She permitted one long and noisy kiss so that he'd finally leave. She closed the door behind him and turned to investigate the light coming from the office.

Just as she suspected, it was Sonny, reading from one of those farm magazines he liked so much. She sauntered in, blatantly showing her drunkenness as she threw her coat on the floor. One look at her flushed face, unsteady gait, and impish grin, it was easy to tell she was smashed.

Totally uninhibited, she plopped down on the desk in front of him, crossing her shapely legs to take off her boots, knowing full well that her skirt barely covered the tops of her panty hose. "Whew!" she exclaimed, "those people sure do know how to have a good time at football games! Those little wineskin thingies – oh my! I wasn't cold at all. But not to worry, I had everything under perfect control – well, almost." She giggled as she held up the tails of her blouse which were sticking out from under her sweater.

Sonny stood up abruptly. "Okay, I think you'd better have some coffee and some aspirin, or you'll be sick as a dog in the mornin'."

" 'Sick as a dog!' I never understood why people say that, do you? Dogs don't get sick. Have you ever seen a sick dog?" She was trying to stand up, but nothing seemed to move the way it should. She nearly fell, but he caught her and helped her onto the sofa. He left to get her some coffee, but when he returned she was gone.

He found her outside, lying on the porch swing. "I needed some fresh air," she said.

"C'mon, Annie, it's cold out here. You're gonna get sick-"

"As a dog?" She giggled. "I want to stay out here."

"Okay, but drink this."

"This is a switch," she said between sips. "You taking care of me! I always want to take care of you, but you make it so damned hard! Why do you do that, Sonny Jackson?" He didn't answer as he struggled to wrap her up in the blanket. She knocked his hand and the hot coffee spilled down her chest.

"Jesus, you're gonna get burned!" He unbuttered her sweater and quickly peeled it off. "Okay, that's it!" he cried, picking her up. "I'm taking you to bed."

"Oh, yes, take me." She threw her arms around him as they

began climbing the stairs to her bedroom. She began to unabashedly kiss his neck and face. Without responding, but not resisting either, he carried her into her room and laid her on the bed.

"No, don't go," she purred. She unfastened her bra and flung it aside. He didn't move, staring at her supple, beckoning flesh. She took his hand and drew it to her breast. "Sonny, stay with me," she whispered. Unable to refuse her, he laid down next to her and caressed her. Trembling with excitement and anticipation, she moaned expectantly as he touched her, held her, wanted her. Suddenly, a deep, anguished, throaty cry escaped his lips as he pushed away and stood up.

"Where are you going? Stay here with me."

"No, I can't."

"Why? Please, Sonny, don't go." He said nothing as he covered her up and stepped away from the bed. She seemed to give up then, her arms falling limp at her sides. She smiled as though she was having a wonderful dream. Shaken and still aroused, he sank weakly into the chair next her bed.

* * * * * *

She awakened to the usual Saturday morning clatter, but even the simple task of opening her throbbing eyelids was impossible. So this is a hangover, she thought wearily, as she struggled into the shower. Even the gentle spray of the water on her skin was painful, but she hoped it would make her feel better. It didn't. In fact, standing upright that long was excruciating. She noticed her clothes from last night were strewn around the room. It was then she remembered some of the distorted events of last night. She had to talk to Sonny.

Downstairs, she was greeted with a round of noisy heckling. She tried to drown out the agonizing racket by putting her hands over her ears, but it didn't help. Smelling the pungent odor of bacon and eggs cooking, she was afraid she was going to be sick so she opted to go outside, having the good judgment to grab a pair of sunglasses before she stepped out into the glaring sunlight.

Matthew emerged from one of the buildings. "Hey," he called, smirking, "How ya' doin'? You sure looked like you were having a good time."

"Yeah, well, if this comes with having a good time, I'll pass," she winced, rubbing her throbbing temples. "Pop, have you seen Sonny?"

"Sure, he was up with the crack of dawn. He's crabby as hell, but won't say why. I think he's down in his shed."

She found him sitting by the stove, leaning back in an old, creaky chair and sipping a cup of coffee. Since her gait was less than graceful, he had to know she came to his door, but he didn't turn to look at her.

"Hey, I could use some of that." He poured her a cup, still not looking at her. They sat silently for a few minutes, Annie's head beginning to clear as she drank. "At least it's quiet down here," she said. "They were having so much fun watching me suffer. I guess I had a little too much to drink last night."

"Yeah, I noticed," was all he said.

He's making this too difficult, she thought. "About last night, I'm sorry."

He rocked his chair abruptly upright and slammed his cup onto the top of the stove. Reaching for his jacket, he stood and moved toward the door.

"Sonny, I'm sorry. I just remember little snatches of things, but I do know that nothing happened. My virginity is intact," she said, sounding disappointed. "And don't worry, I'm not going to make a habit of getting drunk and trying to seduce you. It'll never happen again until--" She sighed deeply before she continued. "Until we're both ready."

"I know that's what you want, but it can't happen--ever."

"Why?"

"It just can't."

"Why? Tell me!"

"Look, just drop it, alright?"

"Why do you always shut me out? Don't you trust me?"

He reached for the door handle. "I don't know what to say to make you understand. It's never gonna be the way you want."

"No, don't say that!" she cried. She stepped in front of him

596

and searched his face. His expression was grim and fixed. She knew it was useless to discuss this any further. "Look, we have to talk, but not when I feel like I'm about to pass out. I gotta get some aspirin. I'll see you later, okay?" He didn't look at her or answer, so she left.

Coming across the yard, she saw Dr. Adam's black sedan pull into the driveway. "Making house calls?" she called as he stepped out of his car.

"Well, I just decided to do some fishing this afternoon. Not too many of these nice days left, ya' know. Matthew says I have an open invitation to fish whenever I feel like it. By the way, is he around?"

"I think he's in the house, Doc. They're making bacon and eggs. Your welcome to have my share." She retched at the thought of eating.

"Thanks, Annie. I might have a cup of coffee. Is there anything I can do for you while I'm in the neighborhood? You look a little peeked."

"Other than the fact my head is about to explode and my mouth is full of cotton, I'm fine." They walked into the house together. She stayed vertical long enough to put Peter in charge and went back to bed.

Later, when the doctor walked back toward his car, he spied Sonny ducking around the corner. Dr. Adams called him over, and Sonny begrudgingly complied.

"Say, Sonny, I haven't seen you in a long time. Everything all right?"

"Sure. I'm fine. Why you hanging around here, anyway."

"I needed to talk to Matthew, that's all."

"Why? He ain't sick, is he?"

"Well, if he was, I couldn't discuss it with you. Patient-doctor confidentiality, remember?" He got back in his car and left. Matthew never told anyone what they had talked about that day, and no one asked.

* * * * * *

On October 26, the usually austere and unemotional Henry Kissinger appeared pleased and optimistic at a White House press conference. He announced that during the preceding weeks, he and Le Duc Tho, North Vietnam's chief negotiator, had hammered out a nine step peace plan. "Peace is at hand!" he said, beaming victoriously. He predicted that one more Paris session was all that was needed to end this terrible ordeal. There was jubilation in the Winston household. It was nearly over.

Kissinger was wrong. Even after Richard Nixon won the election by an unprecedented landslide on November 7, there was no news of peace. Kissinger and Tho met again in late November and again in mid-December. On December 16, a much more subdued and cautious Kissinger held another press conference. "We will not be blackmailed into an agreement!" he proclaimed.

The Winston family had no idea what that meant, except that their hopes of Luke being home by Christmas were fading. Later that night, as the family gathered to finish the last of the Christmas decorations, it was suggested that they would make a pact that these decorations would stay lighted until Luke came home. They put up more lights outside than ever before. The trees, the porch, even the flagpole were adorned with thousands of lights. Matthew climbed high on the roof and hung a six foot star, which was never turned off during the long, heart-breaking weeks that followed.

* * * * * *

This was the most difficult Christmas since mother's death. Annie wanted badly to make the holidays special for the little ones, but it was hard to hide her disappointment. Many of the presents remained unopened, saying they'd wait until everyone was home. There was a large mound of gifts for Luke, and some for Thomas, too. A whole year had passed without hearing anything from him. Annie wondered if his time away had healed some of the heartaches. There was so much left unspoken and unfinished. Annie longed for the day when their family would be together again.

CHAPTER 71

As 1972 ended, the Winston's were horrified when President Nixon ordered resumption of massive bombing in North Vietnam. Heavy damage and civilian casualties were inflicted upon the enemy until Nixon finally suspended the air raids on New Year's Eve. Kissinger was to meet again with Tho on January 8th. Nixon proclaimed he wanted peace with dignity, but the Winston's just wanted it to end.

The first three weeks of January were like a roller coaster ride. Some days the news was hopeful, but often the outlook seemed very bleak. It was a chess game between two worthy, but stubborn, adversaries.

And then, the announcement they had been waiting for finally came. On Saturday, January 27, 1973, the peace settlement was signed. Annie called Margaret, and they cried for an hour on the phone.

At 6 PM, church bells everywhere across the country rang in unison to signal the end of a very dark, ugly period of American history. It was a misty, eerily quiet night when the Winston's gathered on the front porch. They could hear the faint choir of chimes floating across the heavy, damp air from the bell towers of three churches of Shannon Town. They embraced each other and wept. It was over. It was finally over.

* * * * * *

The war supposedly ended, but the political sparing was far from finished. The POW's served as the chief bargaining tool. There were reports of frequent cease-fire violations and "procedural difficulties." The Winston's, who waited impatiently by the TV and radio nearly 24 hours a day, became more frightened than ever. What if he didn't come home? Annie had a reoccurring nightmare of Luke waiting to board an airplane, but the door closes in front of him and he is left standing alone.

By mid-February, the news became even more disturbing. The implementation committees were arguing more than ever, and the U.S. announced that the troops and weapons withdrawal were stopping until more progress could be made at the bargaining table. On Tuesday night, February 27, one month to the day when bells announcing peace had rang out that foggy night, Matthew sat glumly in front of the television. It was like a thousand other nights. The boys were fighting, and Annie was scolding them for not doing their homework. As usual, Matthew yelled for quiet so he could hear the news.

Howard K. Smith opened the newscast with the day's lead story:

"This morning the State Department released a communiqué from North Vietnam that there would be no release of US prisoners until conditions of the cease-fire were implemented. In response, President Nixon ordered Secretary of State, Bill Rogers, to stay away from the International Conference in Vietnam until release arrangements were completed. In the meantime, minesweeping of Haophong harbor and withdrawal of US troops from South Vietnam have stopped once again."

Matthew shot his empty beer can across the room, hitting the defenseless TV screen. "Who in the hell do they think they are," he cried, "playing with our boys like that. Will someone please get the damned phone?"

Annie heard it ring, but was in the middle of making gravy and assumed one of the boys would answer it, since in all likelihood it was for one of them. Muttering angrily, she turned off the burner and picked up the receiver. "Hello!" she said roughly.

"Yes, this is an overseas operator. You have a collect call from the Philippines. Will you accept the charges?"

"My God," Annie cried. "Yes! Yes! Of course! Luke? Is that you?"

"Annie!" said the hoarse, trembling voice at the other end. "It's me!"

She tried to answer but no words came as tears streamed down her face. Matthew took the phone from her hand. "Luke? This is your father. Are you okay? My God, Luke, when are you coming home?"

"Dad, I'm fine, really. I guess we'll be coming into some Air Force base in California in a few days, maybe the weekend! They told us to tell our families that they will give you details as soon as possible. There's a bunch of other guys waiting to use the phone, so I gotta go, okay? I'll see you soon. Bye, Dad." And then the phone went dead.

Matthew hung up the phone slowly, but then a smile crept across his face until he exploded into a loud, joyous scream! "He's coming home! He's coming home!" There was great rejoicing – hugging, dancing, screaming – the greatest joy a family can know. One who was nearly lost, was coming home.

* * * * * *

Matthew and Annie took a flight to San Francisco on Thursday morning. The Army sent a car to the airport to pick them up, the same kind of dark sedan that pulled onto their yard that day, nearly two years ago. They and several other POW families were installed at a nearby hotel. Friday and Saturday mornings they waited in long lines to see if Luke's name was listed with the probable arrivals, but he wasn't.

Annie's prayers, like her dreams, were haunted by the faces of the men, mostly Naval and Air Force pilots, who arrived the two two days. Annie and her father watched on television as the frail, emaciated men with hollow, dark eyes stepped off the planes. Matthew and Annie consoled each other that these men were held five or six years, much longer than Luke. He was not an officer tortured for information. He wouldn't look so bad.

Sunday, Matthew went to the base early, but Annie went to Mass at a nearby church. She recognized other family members. They grasped each other's hands and whispered the sacred words of "Our Father". The Communion lines moved slowly as each paused at the alter for a prayer of hope that this would be the day their loved ones would at last come home.

When the Mass ended, as Annie knelled to light a candle, she felt someone's hand reach for hers in the near darkness. She looked up to see her father's face, tears flowing freely. Clinched in his hand were two passes that would admit them to the disembarking area. Luke was coming home today.

They made their way like refugees traveling to a new place. They waited in lines again to have their names checked off at the all-powerful, all-knowing lists. When someone was turned away, a terrible jolt reverberated up and down the line.

"My son is Lucas Gregory Winston. I'm Matthew Winston, and this is my daughter, Anne Marie Winston" They held out there I.D.'s. The young man with the clipboard looked at the sheet and nodded. They boarded a bus that took them to a far corner of the base.

There was more waiting. Matthew took a sleeping child from an exhausted mother. "He's never seen her. I wanted her to be here," she said. A slow steady rain began to fall. Overcoats were pulled tighter. Strangers offered to share umbrellas. Finally, uniformed dignitaries began to assemble. There was an Army band warming up. People stared anxiously at the row of ambulances lined up across the tarmac. The crowd pressed forward. "There it is!" came the cry. The first plane appeared, dropping out of the clouds.

As though in slow motion, the plane touched down and taxied to the designated spot. The stairs were rolled into place and the door swung open. Dressed in hospital garb, the men, many of them bandaged and needing assistance to walk, began to disembark, each saluting as they stepped off into the waiting arms of loved ones. The lump in Annie's throat was getting so large it nearly choked her. Luke wasn't there, but another plane was circling overhead.

The scene was repeated when the second one pulled into view. More broken and bandaged men came down the stairs. There were even a few being unloaded in wheelchairs and stretchers.

Matthew and Annie saw him at the same moment. They ran to him with open arms, screaming and crying, then kissing and hugging him. Luke didn't speak. He wept silent tears, his eyes closed. He was very weak, leaning heavily on his crutches. An attendant appeared to help him board the bus. He hobbled to a seat, smiling when Annie sat down next to him. Sitting there, she really looked at him for the first time, inspecting his face. They held hands, but his felt cold and rough. His lips were dry and cracked, his head was shaved, and eyes were cold and distant. There were what appeared to be scabs from insect bites on his face, but most of him was covered by pajamas and a robe stamped "US Army". What other marks and scars were hidden, Annie wondered.

Upon arrived at the base hospital, Luke was admitted to a large, open ward with several other men with the same eyes, same frightened stares, and surrounded by bewildered loved ones. Annie and Matthew sat nearby, not knowing what to say or do.

The drizzle fell all evening. The fog rolled in off the ocean. The families were invited to share the evening meal. It was served in a huge dining room with red, white, and blue streamers everywhere. This was meant to be a celebration, but the crowd was subdued. Luke was brought downstairs in a wheelchair. His legs were wrapped in bandages, but he offered no details. The food was delicious, but he just picked at it. Annie and Matthew tried to make small talk about home and his family.

Just as they were running out of things to say, Luke put down his fork and looked up at them. "Tell me about the farm, Pop – that first harvest." A slow, little grin perked up the edges of his mouth, and he looked more like his old self than at any other time that day.

Matthew was a little startled at first. "Well, you know you're asking about my favorite subject," he said with a wide smile. "Didn't anyone write you about it? Man, it was great." He leaned back in his chair and lit up a cigarette like he was sitting on a bar stool at the Pub. He described it all from beginning to end -- Jameson and the cardboard contract, that triumphant first round, the long, hard days in the rain, the mud slides on the hill road. His embellished version made it sound even more dramatic.

They talked so long they weren't even aware that the room was nearly empty. An orderly came by and insisted that it was time to take Private Winston upstairs. Annie gave him a quick kiss, and Matthew patted him reassuringly on the shoulder.

"We can talk more in the morning," Matthew called. "I can't wait to get you home where you belong, son. You'll be home in time for planting."

"Do you really think so, Dad?" Annie asked as they left for their hotel.

"Of course, I do," Matthew retorted. "He's knocked up a bit, but there's nothing that going home can't cure."

* * * * * *

The doctors they talked to the next afternoon described a different prognosis. The surgeon was very concerned about both Luke's legs. His wound in his right calf was open and draining. He recommended surgery to debris and close it. The bone in his left upper leg had healed wrong so that leg was shorter than the other. This, too, could be fixed with an operation. Luke would need months of physical therapy even though it was likely he would never be able to walk normally again. The psychiatrist who had spoken briefly with Luke wanted him to undergo extensive counseling. "Turning these boys out on their own before they are ready might seriously jeopardize their mental well-being and their ability to re-enter society successfully," the doctor said.

Matthew disagreed. "All that boy needs is to come home. We tried talking to him about things, but the only thing he's interested in is the farm."

"He's looking for a distraction," the psychiatrist said. "I sense that he's dealing with a lot of guilt. He needs time to work through this. You need to understand that he's changed."

"Look," Matthew said, "I can see he's changed. We expected that, but he's not crazy. You guys patch him up and get him ready to come home as soon as possible. I'm telling you, he needs to go home." Embarrassed by the tears welling up in his eyes, he stormed out. Annie murmured apologies and followed him.

"Annie," he cried, "I'm telling you, we got to get him out of here as soon as possible. The only place he can find himself is home. If these people keep telling him he's crazy, he'll start believing it"

* * * * * *

Annie only stayed a few days. She could tell from the daily telephone conversations that the household was in chaos, and she was needed at home. Matthew, however, had no intentions of leaving without his son.

Luke's surgery was labeled successful. The loss of muscle mass in the right calf was termed "problematic" but at least the wound was cleaned and closed. They said he needed more surgery on the left thigh as well. Matthew stayed at the hospital from morning until dark every day, sometimes talking, sometimes sitting in silence for hours. Luke never mentioned anything about the last two years. On days when he was communicative, he talked about home. Gradually, Matthew told him about some significant events, such as the problems with Aunt Esther and how he cut all ties with the business so that the farm was now their sole means of support. He talked about John's accomplishments, but didn't mention anything about Thomas's abrupt departure. Luke seemed interested in hearing about Mack's anti-war activities. He smiled, saying it was hard to imagine his brother as a political activist.

One morning the ward was a buzz. There was a general coming to present medals. Those who could, stood at attention as the entourage of officers moved through the ward. Medal's of Valor and Meritorious Conduct and Purple Hearts were dispensed with full military fanfare. More than a few quietly wept. Others wanted to know when the Army was going to give them their past wages. When the General approached Luke's bed, he appeared detached and unemotional, and said nothing as the General gave him all three medals. Matthew, who stood close by beaming with pride, was very surprised by his son's reaction, telling the general he had just undergone surgery and was not feeling well. Luke said nothing the rest of the day.

The next morning when Matthew entered the ward, he was shocked to see Luke's bed empty and stripped. "They transferred him during the night to another ward," one of the orderlies said. "You'd better check at the desk." Stunned and fearing the worst, Mathew demanded to know what happened, especially when the staff seemed evasive. One of the nurses took him aside and explained that Luke had attempted suicide during the night and was taken to the psych unit.

Matthew's fear and anger mounted as he climbed the stairs to the seventh floor. He remembered vividly Annie standing in the kitchen, crying and demanding that he call the recruiter. My God, he thought, sinking down onto the stairs, this is all my fault. How could he have let this happen to his own son?

There was an element of anger, too. Why couldn't his boy be stronger? He talked about home all the time, so why wasn't he trying harder to get out of here? The other men didn't appear to be affected like this. Some had already been discharged home. Tears sprang to Matthew's eyes. Maybe he should let the doctors have their way and go home. No, they'd give Luke more pills, keep him sedated. They didn't care about him. Matthew stood up, dried his eyes, and straightened his clothes. He had to see his son.

The door was locked. A male nurse admitted him, appearing very bothered and harried. "Oh, yeah," he said, "he's the new admit. I think he's sitting in the day room. He didn't eat his breakfast. He says he don't want any visitors, but they all say that. Tell him to eat."

Matthew found Luke sitting alone, his head bowed, perhaps staring at the bandages around his wrists. Matthew crept close to him, not at all sure what he should say. Luke sensed his presence and said, "Why are you here, Pop? Didn't they tell you I don't want to see you?" His voice was quiet with more sadness than anger. "Why don't you go home?"

"I'm waiting for you, so we can go home together. Everyone's waiting."

The boy sat motionless for several minutes, trembling slightly and still not looking at his father. "I'm not ready," he murmured.

"I know, son. Not right now, but --"

"No, Pop, I mean it may be a long time. Don't they need you back home?"

"No, damn it, I'm not leaving here without you! Those damned doctors tell me I should go, too, but I'm not going

606

anywhere. Not yet! How in the hell can they know my own son better than I do?"

"What makes you think you know me?"

"I know you a lot better than you think," Mathew retorted. "Maybe we were never that close, but I was so happy with the way you took to the farm. You loved it there. I can still see it in your face when you talk it."

Luke wheeled his chair to the window and did not look at his father. "I don't understand," Matthew pressed. "Why don't you want to come home? Are you mad at me?'

"No. Why would you say that?"

"Because it's my fault that you enlisted, isn't it? All that talk about the goddamn war. That was all for Mack! He was the one I wanted to enlist. I thought it would help him grow up. Not you, Luke. I didn't want it to be you."

"Why? Didn't you think I could handle it?"

"No, that's not it. You were so young, barely eighteen. But, it's over and you survived. You have more guts than anyone I've ever known. But you need to come home now and get back to work. Men have been doing that since the beginning of time – coming home from wars and going back to the fields. You'll feel the black dirt between your fingers, plant the seeds, and watch them grow. Your life isn't over." He searched Luke's face to see if anything he had said made any difference, but Luke's expression and demeanor remained unchanged. "Get some rest. I'll be back later." He turned to leave, but then hesitated at the door. "You're a decorated hero, Luke. I'm so proud of you."

Matthew went into town and walked around for hours. He had a quick supper at a stand-up counter, and then took a taxi back to the base. He was totally unprepared for what he found when he stepped into Luke's room.

The doctor called it a form of catatonia. As though frozen or paralyzed, Luke did not respond to anything. The doctors stuck needles into his body and he didn't even blink. It was like he had turned inside himself and shut out everything else. Perhaps it wouldn't last very long, the doctors said.

"Can he hear anything?" Matthew asked.

"We're not sure," the doctor said.

Matthew hardly left his son's bedside, talking and reading to him, but there was no reaction. They started an IV and put a tube into his bladder for elimination. Therapists exercised his joints to keep them limber. Finally, heartbroken and frustrated, Matthew told his son good-bye and left for home.

Chapter 72

Annie was inconsolable "What did you say to him?" she blasted her father. "Maybe I should go back."

"It's no use," Matthew said. "He'll wake up when he's ready."

Margaret was also crushed. Her first impulse was to rush to him, too. She wanted to believe that he was like Snow White, waiting for a kiss from his true love, but she wasn't sure she meant anything to him anymore. They had spoken on the phone, but his voice had sounded flat and unemotional. There was nothing to do but pray and wait.

Never, in the years since her mother's death, had Annie known such sadness. Perhaps she had been foolish and unrealistic to think that Luke's homecoming would be as simple as stepping off an airplane. She kept thinking about Tim Brady, the young man who had gone crazy and nearly killed Sonny that night in the bar. He was still bothered by psychotic episodes and was in and out of the VA hospital.

They called the hospital daily, but the news was always the same. March slipped away, and when April arrived, the weather fit the mood. It seemed as though it rained everyday. The river was already full and overflowing down south. Everyone agreed this was going to be a terrible spring.

After being home for several weeks without any improvement in Luke's condition, Matthew announced he was going back "If he don't snap out of this soon, he never will! If nothing else, I want him transferred to the VA in Iowa City so at least he'll be close."

That evening, Matthew walked down to the bottom. The road was too muddy to drive, so he waded through the muck and mire until he arrived at the wide expanse of the fields. Even after three years, he was still overwhelmed by the rush of pride and power he derived from this land. He pushed on to his favorite spot by the river, which was bank full and churning menacingly. Matthew sat down and watched it, hypnotized by its movement and strength.

He rubbed his left arm. It was hurting like the devil, especially after the exhausting walk. Doc Adams had been prodding him for months to come back to the office for more tests. Matthew took one of the tiny white pills out of his pocket, placed it under his tongue, and waited for the sudden headache and hot flashes that came when the medicine began to be absorbed into his body. He waited for his head to clear and the pain to subside, and then he began to pray.

"God, by some unbelievable miracle, you brought me to this place. And I have thanked you for it every day since. I've tried to live my life the best I could. I know I've made mistakes along the way, and I'm sorry. I should have done better. But I'm asking you, please, don't make my son pay for my mistakes. He never would have gone to that war if it wasn't for me." He sighed deeply and tightly clasped his hands before he continued. "You've given me so much, so maybe I have no right to ask for anything else. But God, please, bring my boy home. I would gladly give my life for my son. Give him back his soul, God, give him back his heart."

He looked skyward and realized the winds, which had been swirling the clouds around, suddenly calmed, and there was a small hole in the gray, overcast western skies. The golden sun shone through for just an instant before the seam closed again. Matthew was washed over by a higher power.

The next morning, Annie drove him to the airport and he was gone.

* * * * * *

Matthew had decided to have a very resolute, no nonsense attitude with the hospital authorities. One way or another, his son was coming home. With wide, purposeful steps he walked onto

609

the unit. One of the nurses called out to him as he strode past the nurse's station. "Mr. Winston," she cried. "Dr. Brietzman wants to talk to you." Matthew ignored her plea and went to Luke's room. He stopped short and gasped with shock. Luke was sitting up, and the orderly was feeding him.

He met his father's gaze evenly. He still had that sorrowful look in his eyes, but Matthew didn't care. He gathered his son in his arms and held him for a long time. His prayers have been answered.

The doctors said there was no explanation for what had happened. Last evening, Luke suddenly began to respond. He hadn't spoken yet, but they were sure he would.

Days passed and Luke began to find his way back. At first he spoke only two or three word phrases, but gradually began meaningful dialogue. He had no in-depth conversations with his father, but did have long, closed door sessions with his psychiatrist. He worked very hard at physical therapy, too, although he fatigued very easily.

One night, three weeks after Matthew returned to California, they sat in the lounge, eating ice cream. Luke was very quiet, but Matthew had the distinct impression the boy had something on his mind. He was wearing the blue jeans and shirt that Annie had brought for him from home. "Luke," Matthew said, "you sure look good."

"Yeah, it feels good – to put on real clothes, I mean," he said, smiling. "Dad, I'm sorry for putting you and the family through all this. I don't know why I checked out like that."

"Oh, Luke, don't --"

"Just let me finish, okay? That day I got those medals, remember? I don't know if you can understand this, but I didn't want them. The doctor said he had seen that kind of reaction before in other guys. It's like I feel guilty for being alive when others like Hanson and Timmy didn't make it." He paused to compose himself, but he clearly wanted to go on. "You'd think I'd be happy to go home. It's just – I'm scared. That seems unbelievable cause – I mean, thinking about home was the only thing that kept me from going nuts." His voice broke off again, but he continued. "It's just that I made so many promises to people – like Annie and Margaret and the boys. I promised them I could get through this and be fine. But I'm not, Pop. And when they see me, they'll know."

"You think they'll be disappointed? We know what you've gone through is bound to change a person. We're just so thankful you're back. The rest will take care of itself."

Luke smiled at his father then. "I hope so, Pop," he said, inhaling deeply, "cause I told the doctors I want to go home as soon as possible."

Matthew jumped up and let out a yell that echoed down the quiet corridors. At long last, things were finally starting to fall into place.

* * * * * *

Matthew did not tell anyone at home of Luke's decision until he talked to the doctors. It took some convincing, but they finally agreed that he could go, for at least a visit. His doctors made a referral to staff at VA Hospital in Iowa City, where he could go for follow up care. They settled on a release date of Sunday, April 16th. Matthew was finally able to call home and announce they were coming home in less than a week.

Annie, Mack, and the other boys were amazed how quickly the news spread around town. It seemed that the whole community was intent on marking the occasion in grand fashion. By Friday, there was a flag hanging from every flagpole and store window, and the little bandstand in the park was wrapped in red, white, and blue bunting. The local American Legion, Post 208, was breaking out the old uniforms and planning a ceremony in full military regalia. The Winston's were not all sure that Luke would be able to handle so much attention, but they were powerless to stop it. Their brother was the closest thing to a local war hero, and everyone was intent on making the most of it.

Annie and her family were busy getting ready for the big homecoming, too. She wanted the house as clean and nice as it could possibly be. True to their vow, the Christmas tree and all the decorations were still in place. Annie planned a huge Thanksgiving-type feast that was going to be the best meal her brother had ever eaten. The most uncertain ingredient in all these wonderful plans was the weather. It was unseasonably cold for April and the persistent rain was getting monotonous.

After supper on Friday night, when Annie finally let her brothers relax and stop cleaning, she realized she hadn't seen Sonny all afternoon. "Oh, yeah," John explained, "he told me to tell you that he had something to take care of. He'll be back Sunday for sure."

"Well, that's just terrific," Annie retorted. "He sure picks a fine time to take off. Where in the heck do you think he went?" She was hurt that Sonny would leave when she needed him the most. In situations like this, he could get twice as much done in half as much time as anyone else. What in the world was so important that he had to leave now? She was even more angry when he didn't return Saturday or Sunday morning. Where was he?

* * * * * *

The plane was due to arrive at 12:30. Annie frantically fussed over her cooking, getting everyone dressed in their Saturday best, and getting the whole crew to the airport on time. They all assembled at the appointed time in the foyer for the last minute inspection. This was the day they had all prayed for so long, but yet they were frightened. Mack didn't say much, but Annie could tell he was very apprehensive.

When the Winston's arrived at the airport in their infamous half bus, which was still the only vehicle that could hold them all, they were shocked to see the crowd of people gathered. Young and old alike huddled in the troublesome drizzle, waiting for the guest of honor to arrive. American flags were everywhere as well as hand made signs, saying things like, "Welcome Home!" and "We're proud of you, Luke!" There was a great cheer when the plane finally landed.

Luke saw it all from the window and had a look of terror on his face. "Don't worry, Luke," his father said. "Don't blame them for wanting to make a fuss. A lot of these people have been praying for this day for a long time. It'll probably die down soon enough."

The other passengers disembarked first. "I'll get the wheelchair, son," Matthew said as the last passenger left.

"No, Dad, I'll walk." Luke rose to his feet and leaned heavily on the seats as he made his way toward the door. The roar of applause rose as he slowly managed to climb down the stairs. He was engulfed by his family, all of them hugging, kissing, and crying. Luke was utterly amazed by everything. Becky was so big. Katie was so beautiful. Joey looked terrific. Everyone grew so much. "Oh, my God!" he exclaimed over and over.

They boarded their yellow chariot and drove toward Shannon Town. With sirens and flashing lights from the Sheriff's escort, they made their way down the Great River Road. They passed strangers standing on their porches waving and cheering. Cars stopped to let them pass. The last mile leading into town, the roadsides were packed with honking cars and applauding throngs of people. The bus stopped at the riverside park and Luke slowly made his way through the crowd toward the bandstand, smiling and shaking hands.

He did seem to be searching the crowd for one, familiar face. "She's waiting for you at the house," Annie told him. He grinned his approval.

On the stage, were Mayor Strong, Father Fritz, and the American Legion dignitaries. Luke, leaning heavily on his crutches, moved awkwardly up the stairs as the crowd roared. The wind had begun to whip even stronger as dark, menacing clouds churned overhead.

The ceremony began with the high school band playing the "Star Spangled Banner" and the American Legion Commander lead the Pledge of Alliance. Father Fritz offered a short opening prayer of thanksgiving.

Then Mayor Strong, on behalf of the entire community, welcomed the young man home. "According to what I've been reading and hearing in the press, it seems that many of the young men and women returning from Vietnam are not being welcomed home. Well, we are not gathered here to necessarily honor the war, but to honor one of our own who did what he had to do with dignity and grace. We all appreciate his sacrifice and that of his family. We want him to know that he can hold his head up high because we are all very proud of him. Welcome home, Luke," he said, beaming and extending his hand.

There was another thunderous ovation as the guest of honor moved tentatively toward the microphone. He hesitated for a few minutes. It was clear that he was trying to check his emotions and decide what he was going to say. The crowd waited patiently for him to begin.

"Mayor Strong, Fr. Fritz, and all of you who came out in such terrible weather, I can't tell you how happy I am to see you all. Like the mayor said, I know my brother soldiers are being laughed at and spit on as they walk down the streets of other towns. I honestly didn't know what to expect. This is so much better than I ever dared hope. I just want you to know that I did the best I could and I never did anything that would bring shame on me, my family, or this community. I am just so happy to be home. Sometimes I thought this day would never come. Thank you for coming." He waved and stepped back.

The crowd cheered as Luke descended the stairs just as the rain began to fall harder. They dispersed quickly and ran to their cars. For the Winston's, it was time to take their hero home, gather around the supper table with a few close friends, and give thanks for miracles.

CHAPTER 73

The ride home felt strange to everyone. It was the same curvy, gravel road they had all traveled a thousand times. But today they looked at is as Luke did, as though they were seeing the woods, hills, and green meadows for the first time in years. He didn't say much, just stared out the window and looked amazed. He leaned forward anxiously when they turned onto their road and smiled when he noticed Matthew's star shining from high on the top of the house. The old bus swerved and bumped its way past the tree line as the house, barns, and buildings came into view.

"Oh, my God! The house, the pond, the yard!" Luke stood

to stare at the monstrous old house on the hill, drenched in rain and framed by wind swept trees and colorless skies. "It's beautiful!" he cried as he climbed down the bus steps. He didn't go into the house, but headed toward the rocky place. There laid the land and water as far as he could see. Luke stood motionless as he gazed upon it, his face shining with exultation.

"See, I told you," Matthew whispered to his daughter. "All he needed was to come home."

"Come on, Luke." Annie took her brother's arm. "You've got the rest of your life to look a this." He turned away and followed them into the house.

"The truck's back," John said as they climbed the back stairs. "Sonny must be home."

Annie pushed ahead of the others, ran into the kitchen, and found Sonny drinking coffee at the kitchen table. There was another lanky, bearded young man whom she didn't recognize. She looked at him again and cried, "My God, Thomas!" She hugged him even though it was like embracing a fence post as he did not respond in any way. His brothers slapped him on the back and welcomed him home. Only John and Matthew hung back from the crowd.

"Good to see you, son," Matthew said. The words sounded sincere but his face showed concern. John said nothing.

There was awkward silence until Annie said. "C'mon, you guys, we have a surprise for you in the foyer." There it was, the Christmas tree, beautifully aglow and surrounded by piles of brightly wrapped presents. "We decided to wait to have Christmas, until we were together again, no matter how long it took." She looked pointedly at Thomas, hoping that he would realize that his family wanted him home, too.

Amide the squealing and laughter, Matthew shouted, "Oh, no, not now. We've waited this long, we can wait a little longer. We have guests coming.

"Luke," Annie whispered, "I think there's someone in the living room who's very anxious to see you."

Margaret had imagined this moment a million times. In her dreams, they would smile and run to each other across the room to embrace and kiss passionately. But now that the moment finally arrived, she stood by the fire, wringing her hands and trying to calm her nerves. Her mind was racing. Did she have on too much make up? Would he think she was pretty? She had tried on every article of clothing she owned and settled on a red velvet dress which she hoped accented her trim figure and long, shimmering hair. Around her neck was the necklace he had sent her that first Christmas.

When they turned to face each other, she could tell by the way he looked at her that the ensemble had the desired affect. "Say something so I know it's you." Luke smiled at her broadly. "You look so different."

"I do?"

"I guess you--" But before he could finish his sentence, he was surrounded by guests and their momentum carried him away. Margaret busied herself tending the fire, hoping no one noticed she was crying. Their reunion lasted only a few seconds and they didn't even touch. She chided herself for being so upset since she should have expected that kind of reception with so many people around. She slipped away from the house, praying that he would eventually come looking for her in their special place.

Luke scarcely had time to talk with anyone. Ginny Gibson took his hand and pressed it tightly for a moment. Old Ben slapped him on the back, joking about how skinny Luke was and how he needed some good farm cooking. Andy and Lori Bean were their with their children, along with Fr. Fritz and others. He tried to be congenial with everyone even though he was becoming weary and emotionally spent.

Dinner was served shortly. Luke was concerned when Margaret did not join them at the table. He was sure he had hurt her feelings and he wanted to go find her. But he also knew he would disappoint his sister if he didn't stay at the dinner table with the family and guests. Annie beamed as she served Luke's favorite things, including the cherry Jell-O and heaps of mashed potatoes he had asked for in his letters.

His brothers began telling tales of their childhood. "Yeah," cried John, "I was always taking the fall for you guys. Remember when someone ate all the frosting off that stupid cake. Cook was flying around that kitchen, waving those fat arms of hers."

"Yeah, I remember." Andrew spooned heaps of green bean casserole onto his plate. "Dad didn't care but he had to do something 'cause she was so mad. So we told you to take the blame cause Mom and Pop wouldn't do nothing'. Then you got grounded for two weeks!"

"You should have known better. They grounded us all the time!" Annie said, laughing. "What about the time Mack got grounded for a whole month because he refused to wear that angel garb in the Christmas pageant."

"It was worth it! I wasn't gonna wear no damn white dress!" Mack quipped. "Mother was so mad!"

"Angel clothes would have been out of character anyway," Luke said, setting off gales of laughter.

"And don't think your mother and I didn't know you were sneaking down the rain gutter," Matthew chimed in. "You're lucky you didn't break your neck."

It was wonderful teasing each other like this again and recalling such happy times, especially since it made Luke feel less like the center of attention. He said the food was wonderful, but he didn't eat much. "I'm sorry, Annie," he said. "I guess with all the excitement, I --"

"That's all right, Luke." She took his plate. "I think Luke needs to go upstairs and change out of that stuffy uniform," she announced loudly, allowing her brother a graceful exit.

A few minutes later, he hobbled down the back stairs and found Annie chatting with Penny and Lori Bean. He was wearing a winter coat and his sister knew immediately where he was going. "Go ahead, Luke. Go find her." Annie reached for a woolen scarf and wrapped it around his neck. He kissed her on the cheek and rushed out the door.

His legs were already throbbing so he had no idea how he was going to make his way down the rutted terrain of the bottom road. But there was Sonny, leaning against the small John Deer tractor, smoking a cigarette. "Hey, kid," Sonny called. "How ya doin'?" He waited until Luke hobbled closer. "Look, I concocted this contraption for Mack when he was laid up. Do you think you remember how to drive one of these things?"

"Sure," Luke cried as he hoisted himself up onto the seat.

Sonny explained the hand controls.

"And here's a flashlight," Sonny said as he stepped back. Luke waved his appreciation and then took off, jerking along as he nearly killed the engine when he released the clutch prematurely.

He drove down the bottom road slowly. The light from the tractor's headlight shed a eerie flickering beacon that seemed to be swallowed up by the dark surroundings. Luke was concentrating so hard on not getting stuck in the muddy tracks that he was nearly to the bottom before he realized that he must have missed the path. He managed to turn around and head back up which was even more difficult. He began to feel disoriented and panicked.

He spotted the large stone near the entrance to the path and climbed down from the seat. This was going to be the hardest part. He inhaled deeply and waded into the woods. The spiny, bare branches of the brush slapped his legs and arms as he labored to use his crutches while shining the flashlight on the path ahead. Anger and frustration began to build until he felt as though he couldn't breath. It wasn't supposed to be like this. For three years he had imagined this moment, thinking he could navigate this trail blindfolded. But the darkness and cold engulfed him so completely that he was afraid he was lost.

The path sloped downward and the wet stony walkway was as slippery as ice. He lost his footing and started to fall. He managed to keep his balance, but the flashlight slipped from his hand and rolled into the brush. He tried to retrieve it, but he couldn't maneuver low enough to reach it. Hot, stinging tears sprang to his eyes. Unable to see, he toppled over and rolled down into the ravine. "Jesus!" he cried out loud. "Jesus fucking Christ!"

Then she was there. His eyes were still blinded, but he felt her arms embracing him and helping him to his feet. They struggled down the hill, across the little bridge, and arrived at the clearing where a chaise lounge was sitting by a roaring fire. He slumped onto the seat as she covered him with a thick sleeping bag and wrapped her arms around him. Neither of them said anything for several minutes. He was cold and the pain in his legs was so excruciating it eclipsed everything else until he gradually began to feel her warmth wash over him.

"It wasn't like you pictured it, was it," he murmured. "If you weren't here to drag my sorry ass--"

"Shhh, Luke, it's alright. You're here now. That's all that's important."

"I thought so, too, but now I'm not so sure."

"What do you mean?"

"Jesus! It was just so hard -- I mean . ." He started to say that he felt embarrassed that she found him crawling through the woods, blubbering like a baby, but he didn't want to upset her more and he didn't want her pity. "Did you come down here often?" he asked.

She hesitated before she answered. "Sure, sometimes. I mean, you said-"

"I wouldn't have taken you here if I didn't want you to come." He noticed a tarp covering some box-like shapes at the edge of the clearing. "What's all that?" he asked.

"Oh, that. Just some stuff." She got up and removed the tarp to reveal a large wooden crate and a trunk. Annie opened one which was filled with more blankets and flashlights, and there was aluminum cans shining in the light. "What's that? Beer? Good girl!" he said, grinning. She handed one to him and opened one for herself. "Is that my Army trunk?" Margaret dragged it over to where he was sitting. He opened carefully. Everything was the way he left it. He picked up his writing tablet and found the last, unfinished letter. Soberly, he skimmed over it.

"....They're having trouble handling their guilt because, somehow this is their fault? Jesus Christ, you should read their letters! I shouldn't be here. It's all right for someone else's brother or son to be here, but not me? Not their fair-haired golden boy with the artist's hands. How terrible this must be for a someone like me! They're right. I see things – really see things. I try to shut my eyes and not see anything,   but I can't. Shit! The pictures I could draw! I wish I couldn't. I wish I never picked up a fucking pencil and drew anything in my life!
I am not going to mail this letter. I should . . ."

"God!" he muttered. "I forgot about this. I should have ripped it up and threw it away."

"No one else saw it, Luke. After the trunk was delivered, none of your family could bring themselves to open it. So one day, Annie and I did. She was pretty upset, so she asked me to take care of it. I decided to keep it down here. I added the letters you sent me, too, so I'd sit and read them over and over. It helped me feel – you know, closer."

"I'm sorry,"

"For what?"

"That I didn't listen to you. You said--"

"There's no reason to go over all of that now," she murmured. He could feel her eyes watching him, searching for clues of what he was thinking.

"You have a lot of questions, don't you. I can't talk about it – not yet."

"I know. Annie told me the doctors said we weren't supposed to press you to talk about anything you didn't want to."

"So, they gave instructions, huh? How to act? What to say? That's great. No wonder everyone's walking around on egg shells. It's not like I'm going to break apart or anything. Christ."

"No one wants to say the wrong thing, that's all."

He was embarrassed for raising his voice. Of course, everyone was nervous. So was he. "It wasn't that bad."

"I'm just glad you made it home, that's all."

"Really, it wasn't like you think. The worst problem was boredom. It drove us crazy. Nothing to read. Nothing to do, especially me since I couldn't do much work because of my legs. The guards and the people from the village asked me to do drawings sometimes. They brought little scraps of paper so I sketched some portraits. Even the commandant of the camp asked me to draw his children. But I still had a lot of free time, so I built my cabin three times – in my head. Piece by piece, nail by nail. I imagined walking along the bluff, down by the river, looking for logs. I used an ax – no chain saw. Took me days of searching and hacking until finally I had 82 logs. 82 – that's how many I figured I need. I sorted them – long ones for the front and back, and shorter ones for the sides. My cabin is 36' by 22'. Good size, don't you think?" He looked down at his hands. "I guess it must sound pretty stupid, huh?"

"No, Luke, go on. I want to hear!" she coaxed

"It was like a math puzzle. Every nail took 6 strikes with a hammer, and each section of a board took five nails. So, I'd count $1 - 2 - 3 - 4 - 5 - 6$, then $2 - 2 - 3 - 4 - 5 - 6$, $3 - 2 - 3 - 4 - 5 - 6$, like that. I'd have to concentrate to remember how far along I was. Every log, every board, every door and window, the floors and the walls. The last time I built it, it took me almost a year." He turned to look at her then, to see if anything he was saying made any sense. "Do you see what I mean? I built it in my mind. I could see it so clearly. I knew I'd make it home – I knew I'd make it back to this spot." Their faces were very close, and he could see tears shining again.

"And you did," she whispered. "That's all I wanted."

"Annie said that you were incredible through all this. She said she couldn't believe how strong you were."

"When Aunt Betty called to tell me that you were reported missing, I drove home and ran here as fast as I could. It was cold, like now. I was so mad at God, and then it began to snow. I knew then that somehow you would come home to me. I knew it." She took his hand, pressed it to her lips.

He sighed deeply as he withdrew his hand. "You waited for me all this time, and look at me. I'm a mess, Maggie."

"But Luke, you're back home now, safe and sound. We can fix this, I know we can." She buried her face in his chest. She felt his arms around her. They were thin and sinewy with no strength or warmth.

And then, they saw it at the same instant. There were snow flakes swirling in the wind. "My God, it's snowing – in April? That's not possible, is it?" Luke cried.

They were like excited children, hugging and crying. "Everything's going to be fine," Maggie said. "I know it."

* * * * * *

Annie worked in the kitchen, singing to herself. She turned on the radio to get a weather report. They predicted major accumulations for the next two days. This was going to be the largest and latest snow storm of recorded history. By the time their guests left, several inches had already fallen. It did look pretty, she thought as she paused to look out her window. She wondered where Luke and Margaret were.

Remembering she had other concerns, she put down her dish towel and went looking for Thomas. He had remained aloof and uncommunicative throughout the evening. She found him upstairs in his room, looking through stacks of records.

She rapped on his door and let herself in when he didn't answer. "We haven't had a chance to talk. How are you?"

"I'm okay," he muttered.

"I'm really happy to see you."

"Oh, yeah, I bet you are," he drawled sarcastically.

"No, really. I was very worried about you. I'm glad you're home."

"I wanted to see Luke. I guess I'll stay a couple of days, but that's it."

"But, Thomas," she cried, "things are a lot better now. You look so thin. My cooking has really improved, you know. Can't you stay?" she begged. He shrugged his shoulders and said nothing. She pressed on. "Did Jim tell you I spoke with him a few times when he was home?"

"Oh, so that's how Sonny tracked me down," he shot back roughly.

"Don't blame Jim. He never said much at all, except to let me know you were alive. I don't know how Sonny found you, but I'm glad he did. I was so worried, I --"

"Okay, I get it. Maybe I'll call every once in awhile from now on, but don't hold your breath."

She left then, realizing that nothing had changed. She decided to wait for Sonny. He had gone out about an hour ago to check the stock. Finally, about 11:30, he came in, tired and wet. She had a cup of coffee ready for him by the time he took off his coat and boots. As was his custom, he sat silently until he drank several sips and lit a cigarette.

"I tried to talk to Thomas tonight. He says he's leaving right away. I was hoping he'd stay for awhile."

"Nah, I don't think so. They were between gigs this week, but if they get a booking, he'll go. If you should have seen that place – I mean --"

"What? The place where he was living? Was it really bad?" she gasped.

"Well, I'll tell you, this house looks like the Ritz compared to that flop house. Anyway, as soon as he heard Luke was coming home, I didn't have to twist his arm." He sipped his coffee. "Luke's not back?"

"No, not yet. I guess they have some special place down in the woods."

"Yeah, I know. It's a nice place."

She went to the counter to pour another cup. "Can you believe this snow? It doesn't look like it's going to stop any time soon. I'd better get out the candles and the flashlights in case we lose power." She knew the drill well. Losing power during storms was a routine event.

"Is Mack home?" Sonny asked. "They drove into Dubuque after dinner. Did they get home?"

Annie picked up the phone. "It's dead." She went to the basement and brought up buckets to fill with water. If they lost electricity, the pump wouldn't work, and she hated melting snow to wash dishes.

"Well," Sonny sighed, "I'll go over to their place tomorrow afternoon and check their herd if they don't make it back." He got up to leave.

"No, don't go. It's so cold, and what if Luke doesn't come home soon? I might need you." He followed her into the living room and sank onto the couch wearily.

She stoked the fire and sat down next to him. "Thanks for bringing Thomas home. Who knows, if we can keep the peace around here, maybe he'll stay longer than he thinks."

"No one's going anywhere in this weather, that's for sure."

"I hope Luke and Margaret are okay."

"If they're not back in a couple of hours, I'll go look for them."

"I know." She got blankets from the closet, handed one to him, and took the other for herself. She curled up on the sofa near him and was delighted when he did not pull away. They stared at the dancing flames, listening to the crackling fire and the howling storm outside. Annie relished the sublime feeling of contentment that washed over her. Her family was together again and she was in love with a man who could seemingly quiet the winds and conquer any storm. Finally, there was reason for hope.

* * * * * *

Luke and Margaret came in a couple of hours later, soaking wet and exhausted but giddy and laughing.

"Can you believe this snow?" Luke cried. "Isn't it fantastic?"

"Well, maybe you think so." Annie pulled off his wet coat. "You're both ice cold. Let's get you into bed. The phones are out so you can't call home, Margaret. Won't your aunt be worried?"

"Probably more mad than worried," Margaret giggled. "But I'm twenty years old. What is she gonna do? Ground me?"

"C'mon, lets go upstairs." Annie led the way into the foyer. "Good night, Sonny." She would have liked to stay, but she was tired and needed to sleep. But tonight, as she drifted off asleep, she smiled, no longer filled with dread. The wind serenaded her dreams of snowy white castles and marshmallow fields.

Chapter 74

It snowed throughout the next day. Schools and businesses were closed across the upper Midwest. The electricity went out during the night at the Winston farm, but they managed to get the morning chores done by noon. Later that afternoon, Annie noticed Sonny pushing his bike out of the barn. She threw on her coat and mittens as she struggled through the drifted snow toward him. "Where are you going?" she screamed over the howling wind.

"I can get to Mack's place on the bike. I have to check his stock."

"Are you crazy? What about using a tractor?"

"I think this will work better." He mounted the bike and thrust down on the starter. "I told Matthew I probably won't be home till tomorrow."

She jumped on behind him and wrapped her arms around him. "I'm going with you."

"The hell you are! I'm not going to take you out in this storm!"

"If it's not safe for me, then it's not safe for you either."

"That's nuts! Get off!"

She buried her face in his shoulder and clasped her hands tighter.

"Get the hell back to the house! We could get stuck out there!"

"So why are you going? Besides, I'll put more traction on the back of this thing. Just shut up and lets go!"

"You better get back in the house and tell someone you're leaving."

"Oh, no. I'm not getting off of this bike. Besides, John is looking out the kitchen window." She waved toward the house. "Let's go."

He hesitated for a few moments, but then roared off. They got stuck once, so Sonny pushed it backwards and took a running jump at the three foot snow drift. They were both nearly frozen by the time they pulled into Mack's driveway.

"Get in the house," Sonny instructed her sternly.

"Let's get this done so we can both get out of the storm. C'mon."

Struggling through waist high drifts, they opened the barn door and herded the cattle inside which were huddled nearby. There were eighteen cows plus several calves. "Damn stupid animals." Sonny slammed his fist against the barn wall. "There's twelve more out there somewhere." They climbed aboard Mack's tractor and drove through the pasture, peering through the driving snow to find stragglers. They found them in small groups of two or three, some with small, bewildered calves. Sometimes Annie jumped down to slap or kick the animals to get them moving. It was dark by the time they closed the barn door for the last time.

"Go to the house now," he commanded. "I'll be up in a few minutes." This time she did not argue. She was never so cold in all her life. She was happy to sit by the fire until she thawed enough to be able search Penny's closets and find a warm robe. She was lounging by the fire, toweling her hair, when Sonny came in.

He turned abruptly, as though hoping she hadn't noticed him. "Sonny! What's wrong?" She pulled off his coat and steered him toward the fire. "Come in here and warm up." She knelt to pull off his boots. The awkwardness of the situation had not escaped her either. Here they were, alone and isolated in a cabin in a storm. She busied herself heating water for coffee on the fire, not knowing what to say.

Sonny sat in silence for several minutes and then said, "You were great out there."

"Thanks," she replied, smiling. "I liked being out there with you. It was tough, though, wasn't it? You're right, cows are really stupid." She laughed then, but Sonny's expression never changed. He said nothing, looking absurdly tense, so she went on. "I laid out some dry clothes. Why don't you go change?"

He cleared his throat. "I thought--well, you know, I thought I'd take some blankets and sleep in the barn."

"Don't be ridiculous."

"No, I just think I'd better stay out--"

"No, absolutely not." She steered him toward the bedroom. "Now, put on some dry clothes while I heat up some soup."

Annie thought she knew all his expressions and what they meant, but this was one she had never seen before. His dark eyes flashed around the room and his lips were pressed tightly together as though he felt trapped. His shoulders sagged as he reluctantly did what he was told and soon appeared wearing Mack's oversized sweat clothes. He took his soup and sat down at the table across the room from where Annie was curled up by the fire.

"There's seven pregnant cows yet, ya' know. They could go any time."

"They're inside and none of them appear to be in active labor, right? If Mack was here, would he be down there sleeping with the cows?" She crossed the room to sit next to him. "God, listen to me. I can't believe I know anything about this. My friends at the sorority house should see me now."

"Do you miss it, all of the society stuff?"

"No, not at all. I thought you knew how much I love my life now."

"Well, yeah, but I wondered if--you know, maybe--"

"No, Sonny, I'm very happy here. I want to spend the rest of my life here – with you."

"Annie, don't --"

"Don't what? Say something like, I love you. Don't touch you like this." She stroked his arm softly with her fingertips. He flinched as though he'd been struck and quickly pulled away. Undeterred, she continued. "Sonny, for three years we've lived in a crazy world that didn't make much sense most of the time, but you were always the one, sane part of my life that made me happy in spite of everything. You gave me hope. You made me feel safe."

"So, you think just because I can take care of things, that – I mean. That can't be --"

"Love? Yes, it is. You can't say it, but I see it in you all the time. Why do you always hide from your feelings?"

"If you knew me, really knew me, you wouldn't ask that question."

"You keep saying that. Why don't you just tell me?"

He turned away. "I can't. I just can't." He got up, staggered across the room, and slumped down in Mack's over-stuffed chair. She followed him, determined not to let this moment slip away.

"Don't you trust me?" She kneeled at his feet and gazed up at him.

"You know that's not it. I --"

"Then what?"

"I just can't."

Unchecked tears began to fall, and he reached out to brush them aside. She melted at his touch and put her small hand over his to keep him from pulling away. "Sonny, what are we going to do?" She kissed him with all the passion that had been building for months.

He held her in his arms for a few moments, but then pushed her aside. "This is wrong. We can't do this."

She walked toward the fire and stared at it for a few moments until she turned toward him again, her tear stained face glowing in the faint light. "I don't know what's right or wrong any more. I only know what I feel. I love you, Sonny, and you love me, too." She untied her robe and let it fall to the floor. She stood before him, naked and unafraid. "I can't wait any longer."

He tried to look away, but all logic was cast aside. He swept her into his arms and laid next to her on the bed. He tried to go slowly, but the frenzied desire in him was overpowering and devoured them both. It was over too quickly and when he collapsed beside her, he saw a look of confusion and expectation on her face. He was aroused again, driven by his desire to satisfy her. Carefully and tenderly he led her to a place of wonderful, sensual fulfillment, letting her touch his secret places and experience an ecstasy that surpassed her fantasies. Finally, they slept.

* * * * * *

She awakened slowly, letting consciousness flow over her gradually, frightened the dream would evaporate in the cold light of day. But he was there, sitting fully clothed in the chair, watching her. Afraid of what he might say, she rushed to him and said, "Please, Sonny, don't say this was a mistake. Please."

"I don't want to, but --" His voice failed him then. He got up and walked toward the door. "Look, I have to talk to your dad first. There are things I need to tell him. I owe him that much, all right?"

"Oh, yes," she cried. "When? When are you going to talk to him?"

"Well, soon, I guess, when things settle down, all right?"

"Don't look so scared. It can't be anything that bad. Just say it and get it out in the open. And don't take too long. I want more nights like this."

She hoped for a last kiss, but he turned away, buttoning his coat and pulling his cap over his ears. "I have to check the stock and get you back. You clean up here, and be ready to go in an hour." She knew what he was saying. Neither of them wanted any clues of their love making to remain behind. This had been one of the most defining few hours of her life and she wanted to savor the sheer wonder of it a while longer without opening it up to scrutiny.

The sun shone brilliantly and the roads were partially cleared. She clasped her arms around him tightly, relishing his touch and wondering how long it would be before she would feel his heart pounding again. Not long, she prayed. Please, not long.

Chapter 75

Mack and Penny pulled into the driveway just as Annie and Sonny arrived. "Hey," Mack called, "isn't it a little chilly for a bike ride?"

"Nah," Annie said, jumping off the bike. "It's perfect weather for it." She was watching Sonny out of the corner of her eye. He was grimacing, looking ill at ease. "It was the only way we had to get over to your place and check your herd. It's fine, by the way."

"What? You two went to our place? When? Last night?" Penny peered at them with a gleeful grin. Annie knew that any hope of keeping their secret already vanished. Penny and Mack exchanged knowing looks.

Sonny turned to escape to the barnyard when suddenly he stopped in his tracks. "Did you hear that?"

"Hear what?" Mack retorted, still chuckling.

"No, listen," Sonny cried, holding his hands up for silence. "I thought I heard something that sounded like an explosion."

"Really? Are you sure?"

Sonny ran toward the tall fir trees which occluded the Gibson's yard from view. "Look, something's on fire over there. I bet he was trying to light that damn heater on the water trough. I've been telling him for two years that thing is dangerous!" He ran toward his bike with Mack close behind. "Tell the old man to get help! Try the CB in the pickup if the phone is out! C'mon,

Mack, let's go!"

When they pulled onto the yard, they ran toward Ben's barn, already engulfed in flames. Fighting the smoke and heat, they fought their way inside and found the old man huddled in the corner, his face and hands badly burned.

Once outside, Sonny laid his hand on the old man's chest to make sure he was still breathing. "Stay with him! Pile snow on his burns!" He ran back inside to save the livestock. Kicking open the burning doors, he slapped and hollered at the frightened animals to drive out as many of them as possible until he was nearly overcome with smoke. Mathew, Annie, and Penny came running across the yard just as Sonny staggered out. "I think I got most of them," he cried, coughing and choking. "I couldn't really see!"

Sheriff Wilkerson's truck pulled onto the yard. "I was at an accident on the highway when the call came through. They're gonna try to send a fire truck, but the ambulance is already heading into Dubuque with the--" He stopped mid sentence and stared at Sonny, who was still bent over trying to catch his breath. "Who's this?" he asked.

"Why, this is Sonny Jackson, of course," Mathew retorted. "You mean you never met each other? Anyway, what's the plan?"

Penny knelt over the unconscious man, checking his pulse. "Well, since there's no ambulance, Mack and I will take him to the hospital. We've got to hurry. He's already shocky."

Everyone was so concerned about Ben that no one noticed how the sheriff continued to stare at Sonny, or how Sonny turned abruptly away and seemed to bury his face in his coat. He nearly slipped on the icy incline as he dashed across the yard toward the machine shed where Ben's ancient tractor was stored. He jumped up on the seat and turned the starter It grinded stubbornly. "C'mon, you piece of shit, start," he screamed.

"Sonny," Matthew called. "What are you trying to do?"

"I want to get some rope strung across to the pond so we can haul the fire hoses down there! The barn is done for, but maybe they can save some of the other buildings and the house! Damn! This thing won't start!" He jumped down. Off in the distance, there was the faint cry of the fire truck. "Here! Tie off

630

one end of this and I'll walk it down to the pond." He began wading through waist high drifts toward the small pond in the back pasture. In spite of the storm and cold, the pond was unfrozen. Sonny got to the water's edge just as the fire truck pulled onto the yard.

The volunteer firemen understood what he was trying to do. They tied their hose onto his rope and signaled for him to begin pulling. He strained to drag it toward him. Slipping and sliding on the shoreline, he fell into the water twice, but he persisted until finally he plunged the hose into the pond. The signal was given and water began spraying over the fire and adjacent buildings.

In the house, Ginny kept Annie busy preparing coffee and sandwiches. Showing no outward signs of fear, Ginny focused on the needs of the men who were sure to start trailing in as soon as the danger had passed. As the other neighbor ladies arrived to help, Ginny instructed them to bring piles of blankets and quilts, knowing the men would be cold and wet.

Danny and Peter came scampering in, throwing their little arms around Ginny's neck. Annie began to scold them for interfering, but it was apparent that Ginny was comforted by their presence.

"Oh, Ginny," Danny cried, "we were so scared and.--"

"The closer we got, the bigger the fire got." Peter finished his sentence.

"But they got the cows out. They're all over the yard." Danny held Ginny's hand. "We can help Ben herd 'em into the lot."

"Where's Ben? Is he out there with the other men?"

"Maybe we should go help him, ya' think?"

Ginny reached for her hanky from her bosom and pressed it to her lips. "They took Ben to the hospital, boys. He has some burns on his face and hands, but they say it didn't look too bad. Penny's with him, so I'm sure he'll be okay."

Annie was touched by the looks of panic and horror on her little brothers' faces. "Don't worry boys. We should hear something soon."

"But his heart!" Danny stammered. "Do they know 'bout

his pressure?"

"Yeah, his blood pressure," corrected Peter. "He takes two little white pills every day. They'd better not forget to give 'em to him!"

"And what about you, Ginny. Who's gonna take care of you till Ben gets home?"

"Don't you worry," said one of the ladies standing nearby. "We'll take turns staying with her until Ben is his old self again."

"Do they know where everything is?" whispered Danny, leaning closely to Ginny's ear. "How about the big cans of coffee in the upstairs closet or the foot tub in the basement. We know where all that stuff is. Couldn't we stay 'n help just in case you need us?"

"It's up to Ginny," Annie said.

"Well, sure." Ginny was smiling now. "Maybe you could even sleep over a couple of nights. You could sleep on the floor in the living room if you want." She wiped her eyes as she welcomed their hugs. What are neighbors for, she would have said if she could speak, but no words would come.

* * * * * *

It was nearly two hours before the volunteer firemen began coming in shifts for food and coffee. They reported that the fire was completely out and the other buildings were bathed in sheets of icy water. Ginny sat in her kitchen table, graciously offering second and third helpings of refreshments as well as heart felt thanks for all they had done. She approached the whole situation pragmatically. "It could have been so much worse," she said over and over. "Thank goodness you got here in time."

Matthew came in, shadowed by Sheriff Wilkerson. "Looks like you lost three or four head of cattle," Matthew explained to Ginny. "Most of the fencing is destroyed, so the boys are gonna take the herd down to our place for now."

Annie anxiously watched Sonny from the porch window as he moved about, still organizing and directing traffic. "Sonny needs to come inside. He must be freezing out there." She put on her jacket to go outside to talk to him.

"Yeah, that kid is something else," the sheriff said, reaching for a sandwich. "You're right, Matthew. I can't believe I never laid eyes on him the entire time you've been here. How is that possible?"

"He don't go into town much – never goes to the Pup. Guess your paths just never crossed." He glanced at the sheriff and was stunned by the intense look of concentration on the lawman's face. "It's no big deal, is it?"

"Nah. It's just one of those things, except--"

"What?"

"No, it's nothing."

The phone rang. It was Penny calling from the hospital. The news about Ben was good. There were some third degree burns, but the doctors said his prognosis was excellent.

The volunteers drove the fire truck off the yard just after sundown. A quietness settled across the place that seemed startling so soon after so much anxious activity. Annie stayed with Ginny to help clean the kitchen, knowing that her friend would not rest until everything was washed and put back in its place. Danny and Peter amazed her with their familiarity of the house. They scampered about, chatting incessantly as they helped put things away. Although Mrs. Jenkins, Ginny's widowed cousin, was staying overnight, Ginny welcomed the company as the boys made their beds on the living room floor.

"I think they're already asleep," said Annie in a hushed voice. "How about you, Ginny. You must be exhausted."

Ginny sighed deeply in response to that question, but then smiled broadly. "It could have been much worse," she said again. "You go on now and call someone to pick you up."

Annie called her father. "Dad will right over," she said, but then noticed the old lady reaching for her well-worn Bible from its place on the buffet. Annie crept close to her. "You're tired, Ginny. I can read to you for a few minutes if you'd like."

"Oh my, yes. My eyes are very tired." She took off her glasses and folded her hands as though in prayer.

"What shall I read? Something in Psalms?" Annie knew these were some of Ginny's favorite passages.

"Not tonight. I was thinking about a little part of

Ecclesiastes that was read at our wedding." Her wrinkled, gentle hands turned the pages. She pointed to the verses and then closed her eyes as Annie began to read.

Two are better than one, because they have good reward for their toil. And if they fall, one will lift the other; but woe is he who is alone when he falls and has not another to lift him up.

Again, if two lie together, they are warm; but how can one be warm alone? And though a man might prevail against one who is alone, two will withstand him. A threefold cord is not easily broken.

She finished reading just as a horn sounded outside. "He'll be alright, Gin. He's a pretty tough old bird, ya' know." Annie kissed her on the cheek.

"I know, but I don't just don't like sleeping alone."

Annie turned to leave but then stopped suddenly. "But Ginny, why does it say a threefold cord?" she asked. "Who's the third person?"

"I used to wonder that myself," Ginny said quietly. "But I decided it must be God. It's his grace and power that binds two people together. Without Him, we are nothing." Annie smiled and left then, knowing that she had just been given a wonderful lesson in strength, love, and faith.

"Mack and Sonny fell asleep on the couch two seconds after they walked in," Matthew said, "but Penny convinced Mack to go home with her. Sonny hasn't moved a muscle since he got back. He pulled off quite a stunt today." There was genuine admiration ringing in his voice. "Say, wasn't that strange the way the Sheriff acted this afternoon? He kept looking at Sonny."

"Really? I didn't notice." She rushed into the house and felt Sonny's forehead. "I hate to wake him, but he can't sleep like this all night," she sighed. "He hates it when I fuss over him like this."

"C'mon, I'll help you." Matthew nudged and badgered Sonny until finally he got up and staggered into the office to take a shower. Annie had a bed ready for him when he reappeared. She wanted him to take some cough medicine to help him sleep, but he waved her off. "I'll be fine," he mumbled, collapsing on the couch. "I just need some sleep."

She squeezed his hand for a moment, then covered him up. *Two are warmer than one,* it said in the Bible. Such simple, beautiful words. It only she could lay with him and keep him warm – not for just one night, but forever.

* * * * * *

Matthew was not the only one who thought what Sonny did that day at the Gibson place was heroic. The next morning, while they were sitting in the kitchen having a second cup of coffee, there was a knock at the door.

"Good morning." A young man stood at the back door, pressing his glasses back on his nose. "I'm Morton McDonald, a reporter for the *Dubuque Telegraph Herald* You know, the daily newspaper? I was supposed to cover the fire at your neighbor's house yesterday, but I got there too late – on account of the bad roads, my car overheating halfway here, and then getting lost. But be that as it may, I was able to talk with some folks and they indicated that I should speak with a…" he hesitated as he checked his notes, "a Mr. Sonny Jackson. That's who is pictured here, correct?" He took out some 8 x 10 pictures of Sonny with burned remains of Ben's barn in the background. "Could I speak with him, please? It'll only be a minute."

Sonny seemed momentarily stunned, but then became agitated. "What the hell are you talking about? All we did is help our neighbor. Anyone would have done the same thing. It sure as hell don't rate no pictures in no damn newspaper." With that he stormed out the back door.

If he had stayed a moment longer, he would have heard Mr. McDonald explain the story and pictures were already in this morning's paper, but he was looking for the human interest angle, since Luke had just come home and all. Annie excused herself and went after Sonny, leaving Matthew to explain that Sonny was very tired and not feeling well.

Annie found Sonny on the back porch, his hands on his hips and breathing rapidly. Annie could hear a wet raspy rattle in his chest. She touched his shoulder timidly and said, "C'mon, Sonny. Come, inside. I'll make you--"

"For Christ sake!" he muttered. "I'm not going back in there."

"Daddy is talking to him in the kitchen. We could go in through the office and I'll bring you another cup of coffee."

"I had enough. I've got work to do." With that, he walked away, leaving her to wonder if she would ever understand him. She thought about following him, but intuitively she knew it was better to let him cool off alone.

Later that afternoon she tried to insist that he go into town to see Doc Adams, but of course, he refused. They never talked about the fire. A week later, when Ben came home from the hospital, Sonny found an excuse to skip the celebration. He missed Ginny's homemade pies and cakes and Ben's comic stories of his stay at the hospital. He also missed Jake's announcement that he was retiring from active farming and then produced a prewritten Bill of Sale, signing his herd over to the Winston's for rock bottom prices.

"Guess it shouldn't have been such a surprise," Matthew said that night as he recounted the story to Sonny over a late night cup of coffee. "I know a lot of people thought they were way past their prime a long time ago. Their relatives are constantly trying to get them into the old folks home in town."

"Yes, but they'll never move," Annie insisted. "Ben was born in that house, and it would take a hurricane to get him out of there. It's just lucky for them that we happened to be standing on the yard that morning when you heard that explosion, Sonny. I mean, what if something happened to Ben? Ginny would have no way of getting help."

Sonny said nothing, but the next morning he disappeared off the yard without any explanation and appeared on the Gibson's yard late that afternoon with a strange cargo. He asked the speechless Ben to call Matthew to get some of the boys to help unload.

"A bell?" they all said. "Why a bell?" There it sat,

swaddled in ropes holding it upright in the back of the pickup. About three feet high, it appeared to be a very old, rusted cast iron bell with a grooved wheel attached on one side.

Sonny explained his intentions. "We'll put it outside the kitchen window and attach the rope where Ginny can reach it. If she ever needs to call for help, and she can't get to the phone or it's out, she can ring the bell and we'll know to come. She can even ring for Ben if she needs help."

"Where did you find it?" someone asked.

"It's been at the junkyard for years. No one knows for sure, but it might be the ol' school bell from your place, Mack." The bell was rusted and definitely needed some work, but it rang loud and true. It became routine for the boys to ring the bell three times to signal Annie that they arrived safe and sound whenever they visited. Ginny said it was one of the greatest gifts anyone had ever given her.

Chapter 76

Mack sat in the kitchen. He told his father that he needed an extra cup of coffee, but actually he was hoping to catch a quiet moment to speak with Luke. The two of them had not been alone since his brother came home.

Mack shifted in his chair. It was warmer today, and the windows were open. Annie's yellow gingham curtains stirred in the breeze. His sisters had gone into town for groceries and the boys were in school. Sitting in this house when it was this quiet was unsettling. Mack wished his brother would wake up.

Then he heard Luke's shuffling, uneven footsteps in the upstairs hallway and start down the back stairs. Luke froze on the stairs for a moment when he saw Mack sitting there.

"Hey!" Mack jumped up quickly, so fast that his chair fell behind him. Maybe this wasn't such a good idea after all, he thought. Too late to escape now. "How about some breakfast or maybe some coffee?"

Luke shook his head no as he hobbled over to the table. Mack studied him. His face was flushed and sunken, and his clothes were disheveled as though he had just fought a battle in them.

"Bad night?" Mack asked, trying to sound casual.

"Yeah, I guess." Luke shifted in the chair, looking uneasy and self conscious.

"Man, I can remember nights like that – couldn't sleep for shit!" Mack hesitated then and swirled his coffee cup around a couple of times. "Not that – I mean, I didn't have it that bad, not like--"

"Like I do? Why would I have it any worse than you? Jesus, you lost half your leg." Luke spat the words with choked emotion that seemed to come from deep inside of him.

Mack was startled and didn't know how to respond. "No, I meant – well, I thought--" They sat silently for several minutes, neither of them looking at the other. To Mack, his brother's words and demeanor were stark confirmation of what he had feared these past months. Luke's posture and tone of voice seemed to scream resentment. Mack wondered if he should leave.

Then Luke seemed to relax as he slumped down further in his chair. "Besides, I might lose mine, too, you know."

"Really? Why now -- after all this time, I mean."

"Doctors said if it doesn't heal this time and gets infected again, they should amputate."

"Wow, that stinks."

"Does it? I mean, wouldn't it hurt less? Shit! It's like a knife every time I take a step."

Mack got up and rummaged through the cupboard until he found a bag of Oreo cookies. He was stalling for time, trying to decide if he should tell the truth. If he lied, the kid would come back later and ask him why he hadn't been straight with him. "Ever hear of phantom pain?"

"Yeah, I heard a couple of guys talking about it at the hospital, but I thought they were just talking shit."

"Believe me, it's not shit." Mack poured two glasses of milk and placed the Oreo's in the middle of the table. "The brain doesn't know that the leg is gone. The nerves are still programmed to receive messages from a foot that's not even there any more. I swear to God, it fucks with your mind worse than you can imagine."

"No shit? It's pretty bad, huh?"

"Yeah, man, my heel burns or a toe itches – still, after nearly three years. Sometimes, my calf still hurts. It's the craziest thing." Mack dipped a cookie and dropped it into his mouth. "But then, it's nothing that a couple a beers won't cure." They both laughed then, harder than the joke deserved.

"Hells, bells! I just as well keep the damned thing," Luke said, still laughing. He ate two cookies and wiped the milk dripping down his chin. Then he looked more sober again and said, "It's just that I feel so useless."

"Yeah, well, you need to check yourself into the Sonny Jackson Rehab Clinic. He'll whip you into shape real quick. For me the nights were the worst. Everything hurt twice as much and I couldn't sleep. So Sonny put me to work driving the tractor and ran my ass around here until I was dead tired every night. You'll see, as soon as the weather clears, he'll get you out there."

"Hell, Mack, that would be great except – I mean, I had such big plans. I spent the last three years planning this cabin I want to build. Now I can't even walk good enough to get back there."

"Go to plan B. Don't walk. We'll make you a road, or – hell, ride a horse. Penny will loan you one of hers."

"Except I'd need a fucking ladder to get on and off!" Luke grinned again as he dunked another cookie.

Mack was grateful for his brother's improved mood, but there were still things that needed to be said. He stared at his empty milk glass and cleared his throat. "I don't know if anyone told you, but I campaigned against the war."

"I know. Pop told me -- Annie, too. So?

"Well, I thought maybe you'd be pissed. But when I was marching in those rallies, it wasn't against you or--"

"Jesus, what the hell do you have to apologize for? I can't stand all the guilt-- you, Pop, even Annie, Andrew. I see it every time I look at you. Why do think this is your fault?"

"Cause you never would have signed up if it weren't for me. Pop could have stopped you, but he didn't. You almost died out there."

"But I didn't. And even if I had, you didn't shoot me. Pop didn't force me to enlist. What I did, I did on my own. I wish to hell you would just get over it." He stood up and looked as though he would have stormed out of the room except a sharp spasm of pain sent him reeling back into the chair. "Anyway, all that shit Pop told us about patriotism and everything -- he was right. Standing at attention in formation, saluting the flag, it gives you such a rush. It's the guns and the war I could have done without." He smiled again, evidently intending for that last line to be funny.

Mack obliged him by laughing. "You know Pop was saying all of that for my benefit, right?"

"Yeah, I know. He wanted you to grow up. I think you did just fine without the Army." He popped the last cookie into his mouth. "Speaking of Pop, what the hell is going on with Thomas? No one is telling me anything."

"Him and Pop got into it so he left. He was gone for over a year. No one heard a word from him until Sonny brought him back here."

"What happened?"

"He got pissed off at the old man, so he made up some vicious rumors about John to get back at Pop."

"What kind of rumors?"

"It got all over town that John and his friend, Kenny, are fags. Right in the middle of their last football season together. It was quite the scandal."

"That little shit. Why was he mad at Pop? He must have been pretty sore about something."

"He thought – or thinks – Pop had something to do with Mother's death. It's stupid, I know, but that's what he said." Mack stood up and put the glasses into the sink and then turned toward the door. "You can probably tell, things are still a little cool between Thomas and Pop. John, too." He re-adjusted his cap as he opened the door. "Well, I gotta get to work. Hey, do you need a ride down to the VA Hospital in Iowa city? You never did get your license, did you?"

"Nope! But Margaret is going to take me. She wants to show me around campus anyway."

"Hummm. I see."

Luke shot the wadded up Oreo wrapper across the room. "Just get back to work."

Mack laughed as he ducked out the door and headed toward the barn. That had gone well, better than he expected.

Luke sat at the table a few minutes longer and wondered what he should do next. Maybe he was the one who could patch things up between Thomas and his father. He took his medicine bottle out of his pocket and threw two more pain pills into his mouth before he started the ordeal of going back upstairs. He stopped at Thomas' door and listened for any noise or activity. Don't be stupid, he chided himself. It's only 10:30. Thomas would not be awake yet unless someone dragged him out of bed. He knocked and opened the door.

Thomas was sleeping so soundly that there was barely any discernable chest movement. Luke had seen guys back in Nam sleep like that, after they had smoked or shot up. He had recognized the glazed, stared eyed expression in Thomas a couple of times when he came downstairs to raid the refrigerator late at night. Luke sat down on the edge of the bed and began shaking his brother awake. "Thomas, Thomas. Wake up."

"What the fuck?" Thomas slapped Luke's hand away and rolled over.

"Thomas, wake up. It's Luke. We gotta talk."

"The hell we do. Get out of here, man."

"No, I won't, not till we talk. I want to know what's going on between you and Pop."

"Go ask him. I'm sure he'd be glad to tell you what a screw up I am."

"No, I'm talking to you. Why did you leave like that?"

Thomas laid motionless for a few minutes and then turned back to face his brother. "We were both pissed off at each other, so I left, alright?"

"I have no idea what happened, but I do know one thing. Mother would never approve of this. In fact, she'd hate it."

"But she's not here, is she. That's the whole point. And don't get all Catholic on me and start talking about heaven and shit."

"Do you think you were the only one who was angry when

Mother died. We all were. Maybe you can't bring yourself to be mad at her, so you're taking it out on Pop."

"You've spending too much time with psychiatrists, man. I don't need any of your psycho mumbo, jumbo shit. Get the hell out of here."

"No." Luke was prepared to stand his ground.

"I said, get out. Now."

"I said, no."

"What the hell is it to you anyway?"

"Cause the whole time I was gone, I had this vision, this idea, of all of you at home together, and all I wanted is just to get back – here, to my family."

"And you did? So, what's the big deal?"

"They were happy to see you, too, you know."

"No, they weren't. You're the prodigal son, not me."

"Why do you say that?"

"Have you seen Pop say more than two words to me? Or John? They're both treating me like I got the plague."

"I haven't seen you talk to them, either."

"Why should I? What's the big deal, anyway."

"Cause I want you to stay, that's what. You know, all my life, I thought Pop didn't approve of me. It took me nearly getting killed to find out that was never true. I think that's the way it is between you and him, isn't it."

"You and I are nothing the same."

"I don't want to argue with you. I thought everyone was acting weird around here because of me, but I think it has a lot to do with you, too."

"I don't give a rat's ass what anyone around here thinks. All I know is I'm waiting for my guy to snag a booking, and I am out of here. I might even go back to New York. If I see Aunt Esther, I'll be sure to give her your regards." He turned away again and pulled the blankets up around his chin.

Luke knew he had been dismissed, but he did not leave. "Thomas, I know this rundown old house is not exactly the Taj Mahal, but I have a feeling that you've been places and seen things that make it seem pretty nice to be back. I think if you'd give Pop a chance, you might find out he's not near as mad as you thought. C'mon, I'm asking you to stay around here for awhile. Please."

Surprised, Thomas glanced back at his brother. "Whatever. I said I'm not going anywhere, not now."

"I need some help getting my cabin started. I gotta look for some logs. You want to come along sometime?"

"Yeah, sure, that's just what I wanna do – tromp around the woods in the mud and weeds. Sounds like fun."

Luke smiled as he stood up and started toward the door. "See ya," he called as left. Tomorrow he would try again. He didn't make it home to come back to a family that was splintered and angry. He would have to fix this.

Chapter 77

April slipped away on a flood of never ending rain. It just never seemed to stop. The river was misbehaving badly with massive flooding from Cairo, Illinois, to the Twin Cities.

Annie hoped that since things were finally starting to settle down that someday very soon Sonny was going to have that talk with her father. But both of them were brooding and short-tempered, which Annie attributed to the rain and flooding. There would be no planting this spring. The entire season was washed out. Annie began to fear that nothing had changed between her and Sonny, as if their wonderful night of love making had never happened at all.

Luke seemed to be doing well. The only thing he seemed to care about was building his cabin. He was aching to get started, but the mud and lingering pain in his legs kept him in the house. Penny began coming over every morning and headed upstairs to Luke's room, carrying her bag of dressings and ointments. She was the embodiment of professionalism as she did not divulge any medical information. What scars and wounds laid under his baggy blue jeans were not known to anyone except her.

One day, she and Mack saddled up two horses and called Luke outside. "C'mon, go to the front porch. You can jump into the saddle from the top step." Luke eagerly swung onboard. He and Mack went out together the first time. After that it was either Margaret or Thomas.

They left for hours at a time, lumbering through the timber to search for the perfect trees. Many of the neighbors, such as Miss McDuffy and the Gibson's, had given Luke permission to look through their woods, so some days they traveled miles from home. He brought along a spray can of red paint so that he could mark the chosen trees and then recorded each one meticulously on his map. He returned at night, grinning from ear to ear with more color coming back to his cheeks every day.

One day, he and Margaret were searching through the woods when Margaret noticed a field of violets and Dutchman's britches wild flowers. She climbed down from her horse and began to pick a boutique. She was humming softly as she knelt, surrounded by the purple and white flowers. But then she became aware that Luke was staring at her.

"What?" she said, the edges of her mouth peaked in a cute grin.

"Oh, I just realized something."

"Realized what?"

"You know all that stuff I said, that I didn't expect you to wait for me and how you should date other guys?"

Maggie wrapped her flowers in her jacket and hoisted herself back onto her mount. "Yes, I remember."

"Well, I just realized that all those thousands of times I imagined myself in these woods – well, you were always there, like you are now." He nudged his horse forward and pulled up close to her, facing her. He leaned over and kissed her. It was tender and loving, but much more passionate than before. "I'm glad you didn't listen to me," he said.

* * * * * *

The weather refused to improve as each day brought more rain and flooding. Sonny seemed more distant and withdrawn as the days went by. He rarely spoke to her. Worried glances were exchanged between him and her father, but neither of them said anything. At first she thought it must have something to do with her, but it was something else. Annie had assumed that all the turmoil that engulfed their family for the last three years would be put to rest once her brothers were home. But there seemed to be as much apprehension and dread as ever, and she had no idea why. Her hopes that someday soon Sonny was going to have that talk with her father began to fade.

One night Luke came to the supper table and announced happily that he had found the 84 trees he needed. "Every one of them is marked and I'm ready to begin cutting them down. The only thing I need now is a draft horse."

"What? Why?" they all chorused.

"Yes, I'm going to use a horse to drag the logs to my building site. Penny's horses aren't trained to do that sort of thing, but I think that's a better idea than a tractor, right?"

"Sure," Matthew said, "I guess you could get in there easier with a horse, and it wouldn't tear up the woods as much. I bet you could find one for sale in the Sunday paper. There's ads in there from all over."

A few days later, Luke and Margret borrowed Dr. Lamp's trailer and left for Missouri to pick up his horse. He seemed so excited. Annie waved good bye as they pulled off the yard. She was so happy that for Luke, at least, things were looking up.

* * * * * *

The day that Luke and Margaret were supposed to return from their horse buying trip began like any other Saturday. It was raining, but the chores were done early, and most of the family gathered in the kitchen for a late breakfast. Annie noticed that her father was unusually irritable. She knew he wasn't sleeping well, presumably because of the flooding. "Hell," he muttered. "I can't stand all this racket. I'm going into town."

"It's only 9:30 in the morning," Annie cried. "Boys, go upstairs and play so your dad can have some peace and quiet." But he was already out the door. Annie stood at the window and watched as he headed toward his pickup. His shoulders were slumped and he appeared tired. She wished this could be a happy time for him. His family was doing well, their finances were stable, and the outlook looked good. She was pleased that he stopped drinking so heavily the past few months and his severe mood swings had lessened. She hoped that this was just a momentary setback which would improve with the weather.

* * * * * *

"Hey, Billie!" Matthew walked into the Pub and took his usual place. A beer was poured and waiting on the bar before he got settled onto his stool.

"Matthew! Kinda early, ain't it?" Billie pulled the lever on the tap and poured his friend another.

"Oh, hell, this blasted rain! I'm so sick of this shit." Matthew downed the second one.

Just then Matthew became aware of someone walking up behind him. "Yeah, everyone is. At least you own your farm free and clear." It was Sheriff Wilkerson. Matthew did not turn around or respond. The Sheriff must have been sitting in one of the back booths. If Matthew had seen him, he wouldn't have stayed. Ever since the Gibson fire, the Sheriff made Matthew feel uncomfortable. Twice he had pulled onto the yard at home and asked to speak with Sonny. Matthew lied both times and said he was gone. Sonny did not verbally acknowledge his mistrust of the sheriff, but Mathew had a feeling that there was going to be trouble.

"Some of these fella's are gonna lose their places if they don't get a crop in this year," Sheriff Wilkerson drawled.

"Yeah, I guess I can be thankful I don't have to worry about that."

"How's Luke doing?" Billie asked. "I haven't seen him since he got back."

"He's been busy," Matthew reached for a pretzel. "He wants to build his cabin. He's got a spot all picked out down in the timber somewhere."

"Well then, I guess it's good you fetched him home, right?"

"Hell, yes. I knew he didn't need to sit around no damn hospital. Stupid doctors. They were giving him pills all day long. I knew if they kept him in there much longer, he'd never come out. I know my own boys."

"That's good to hear, Matthew. I think he's going to be all right, don't you?"

"He's not crazy, that's for sure."

"Not like that Brady kid." Sheriff Wilkerson settled onto the stool next to Matthew. "Remember that night that he took after Sonny? My God, he--"

"Hey, Sonny Jackson!" Billie exclaimed. His face looked like he had just come to a startling realization. "That's who I was trying to think of."

"What the hell are you talking about, Billie?" Matthew asked.

"It's probably nothing, but last night I was looking through this box of stuff that Mildred McFay dropped off here the other day. I'm on the homecoming committee that's trying to put this here book together on the history of Shanny. Anyway, she thought we might be interested in looking through this stuff of her mother's."

"So what? What's that got to do with Sonny?"

"This stuff went way back. There were several newspaper articles from the early 1900's. I come across this bunch of clippings about your place, Matthew. There was a picture of that poor Indian they hung. You know the story, don't ya'? Anyway, I looked at the picture, and I swear to God, it gave me the creeps and I didn't know why. I just figured it out. That man was a dead ringer for Sonny."

"Really?" Sheriff Wilkerson asked. "I'd like to take a look."

"Oh, come on," Matthew retorted. "That's crazy."

"I'm not kidding," Billie insisted. "You don't believe me, do ya' I'm gonna go home and get that stuff so you can see for yourself. Watch the bar. I'll be right back." He hung up his apron and disappeared out the back door.

Matthew sat with both elbows on the bar and swirled the few drops of beer left in the bottom of his glass. He had no idea where all of this was leading, but he had a bad feeling in his gut.

"Well, Matthew, it's interesting that I ran into you this morning, cause I was thinking about driving out to your place this afternoon," began the sheriff.

"Really? What for?"

"You know I got a bee up my butt about your man, Sonny. You know, I never forget a face, and I know I've seen that kid before somewhere."

"Well, Sheriff, I don't know how that's possible. He came out here with me from New York. So exactly when do you think you've seen him?"

"New York, huh."

"Yes, I was in a pretty bad scrape with some fella's and Sonny jumped in and saved my life. I hired him on the spot, and I haven't regretted it since."

"Just happened to be in the right place at the right time, right?"

"Guess so, but lucky for me he was there. I tell you what, he's smart and works hard. He's a good man."

"Did it ever occur to you that Sonny Jackson is not his real name?"

"No, why should I?"

"Well, I ran his name through the system and nothing showed up – no driver's license, no nothing. You don't suppose he's been driving all over the state of Iowa without so much as a valid driver's license, do ya'?"

"That's why you've been asking to see him?"

Just then Billie returned and began spreading several newspaper clippings on the bar, including the story of the Gibson's fire. He laid Sonny's picture next to the yellowed, older pages Billie had talked about. Matthew stared at them dumbstruck. The resemblance was uncanny.

"My God!" Sheriff Stone exclaimed. "You're right! Look at that, will you?" He began reading the article out loud.

"... Jack Blackstone was brought in for questioning as the chief suspect in the theft of several cattle from area farms. Mr. Blackstone continued to plead his innocence and insisted that Sheriff McNaugty produce evidence, of which there was none. He was eventually released, but before he left he berated the sheriff for what he termed as false imprisonment. As he exited the

Courthouse, he was quoted as saying, "I know what you are trying to do. You want me and my family to leave and never come back. Even if I do as you want, this is not finished. This place belongs to my people, and my spirit will never rest until my sons, or my son's sons, return to claim this land. No matter what happens, it will still belong to me."

As Matthew listened, a cold chill settled over him. "This is the Indian they hung at my place? Where's the story about that?" He began shuffling through the stack of old tattered papers.

"C'mon, Matthew." Billie flung his bar towel over his shoulder. "You can't write about a lynching in the paper, not even back then."

"Don't you think it's strange that their names are kind of similar?" Sheriff asked, staring at the pictures. "Do you think there's any connection? Says here that these people were from a reservation in Kansas. Guess his wife and children must have went back there afterwards, right?"

Matthew did not answer. He was trying to appear calm, but inwardly his head was starting to spin. Sonny said he was born in Kansas, and every time he mentioned it, there was always a bitterness in his voice that Matthew never understood.

"Holy shit!" the Sheriff exclaimed. "I just figured it out. I did see that kid before. Billie, you remember about five or six years ago when that bunch of wild kids took over the Weatherly place? We got a tip that some of them kids were in bad shape, so me and Doc Adams went out there with a squad to make the bust. We carted that whole bunch of dope fiends off to jail. Crazy sonofabitches. And your man Sonny was one of 'em.

"I'll be damned," Billie cried. "How is that possible?"

"What do ya' mean, how is that possible? That kid is probably a relative, right?" The sheriff looked giddy as he reached for the phone "I wonder if he did time? I thought they sent all of them kids off to prison at Ft. Madison. It's easy enough to check. Hey, Mildred," he called into the phone, "go check the file on Jack Blackstone. I arrested him in July '66. Yeah, I'll wait." He put his hand over the receiver. "Billie, get me a Coke, will you? I'm dry as bone."

649

Matthew sat frozen on the stool, his hands grasping the edge of the bar. He felt like someone had just kicked him in the groin. He tried to argue that none of this made any sense, but in his heart he knew it did.

"Born, May 25, 1949. Okay, what else? . . . . . A detention center? He ran away when he was fifteen? . . . . . . Yeah, well he was older than that when I had him. . . . If there's a parole violation, check if there's still an active warrant. . . . There is? That dumb sonofabitch has been living in my county all this time . . . What's that, you say? A fire? Where? . . . Oh, hell. You'd better ring the alarm." He threw the receiver back on its holder. "There's a fire out at the Hanson place."

The siren at the firehouse began to wail, calling volunteer firemen from stores and farms all over the township. "I gotta, go, Matthew, but I want your word that you're not going to say anything to that kid of yours. I want your word." He was back peddling out the door as he spoke, a cautionary finger wagging in Matthew's direction. "I'll be out there as soon as I can, but you tell him to stay put. Otherwise I'll arrest you for conspiracy to commit a crime. I want your word, now Matthew, your word."

Matthew stumbled to his pickup. He had to get home, but found it was difficult to drive. There was a familiar ache in his left arm and a heaviness across his chest that was suffocating. The news articles, the pictures, the sheriff's snide expression. Drugs. Prison. The words exploded in his head until he could hardly see. *My son, or my son's sons*, was what the Indian said. Matthew had to get home.

Chapter 78

Annie peered out the kitchen window. Luke and Margaret should be back by now. She decided to look for Sonny. He and Peter went out to one of the furrowing sheds earlier because one of the sows was having trouble. Annie made some sandwiches and headed out, throwing a rain coat over the tray. She was as sick of this rain as everyone else.

She found Peter sitting in the shed, smiling proudly over

the sow with her eight suckling's. "Sonny let me help birth the babies," he cried. "And see that little tiny one on the end? He's the runt, and Sonny says I'm supposed to watch 'em to make sure he gets a tit. If he don't eat soon, Sonny says I'll have to bottle feed him. And if I do a good job he gets big and fat, I can take him to the county fair. Ain't that somethin'?" The boy was talking so fast that he could hardly breathe. Annie congratulated him on his newfound fatherhood and reminded him there is no crabbier mother than a sow. Giving her brother some sandwiches and a soda, she left to go find Sonny.

Peter said he was in the barn, so she headed down there. "Sonny!" she called stepping inside. "Are you in there?"

"Yeah, in the back."

She could hear hammering. "What are you doing?"

"I'm trying to get a stall ready for Luke's horse. I don't think he has any idea how much trouble he's let himself in for, buying that damn thing. Give me a good tractor any time."

"Why didn't you say anything when he was talking about it?"

"Ah, hell, he was going to do it anyway, so what's the use. I just hope it comes with all the gear, especially a harness." Annie offered him a sandwich and hoisted herself up on the old trough. She loved to watch him work. She was going to scold him about going to see Doc Peters about his persistent cough, but before she had a chance she heard someone pull up on the yard.

"Maybe that's Luke and Margaret," she cried. But looked out the window and was surprised to see her father pull onto the yard. "Wow! That was quick. I didn't think he'd be home for hours." She opened the door and called, "Pop, we're down here." She noticed right away that his gait was uneven. "My God," she groaned. "How did he get drunk that fast?"

"Sonny?" Matthew slammed the barn door shut as he stepped inside. "We need to talk right away." His face was ashen and he wouldn't look at his daughter. She was frightened.

"Pop, what's wrong?"

"Ann Marie, go to the house. Sonny and I have to talk."

"But, Pop, there's nothing you can't--"

"Annie, go to the house like he says." Sonny turned to face

651

her father, his eyes fixed and cold. "Go!" She flinched at that word. It was only one syllable but it shot through her like a sword. She fled to the house.

Sonny was the first to break the stare as he stooped to pick up his tools.

"I was in town just now, talking to Billie. Sheriff Wilkerson was there, too," Matthew began in a hushed, restrained tone. "Did you know that the past few weeks, ever since the fire, he's had this feeling he knew you from somewhere. Well, he got it all figured out – just now, while we were talking."

Sonny froze for a moment but then went on working. He said nothing so Matthew continued. "He says your real name is Jack Blackstone, the same as that poor devil that was hung 70 some years ago. Is that true?" Again, Sonny did not respond. "All this time you were living here, working with me, you --- It was no accident that you were there that night at the bar, was it? Why didn't you tell me?" Still Sonny said nothing as he headed toward the door.

"You gutless asshole," Matthew cried. "We worked together for three hard years and now, when I ask you to tell me the truth, you walk away?"

"What do you want me to say?"

"I want you to tell me how your great-grandfather vowed that someday his children or his children's children would take this place back. Is that what you were doing? Trying to take this place from me?"

"No. Why would I do that? I just wanted to live here, that's all." He took a few more steps and said, "I have to get out of here."

"If this place is so important to you, how can you just walk away?"

"I don't have much choice, do I?"

"Yes, you do. I can help you. Sonny, there's a goddamn warrant out for your arrest. The Sheriff is probably on his way out here right now. Stay here and we'll help you fight this. We'll get a good lawyer and argue it in court."

"Like hell. You can't do nothing. I have to go."

"Go where?"

652

"Somewhere. Anywhere. I am not going back to prison."

"You're gonna turn your back on this place? That's bullshit! We can fight this thing. I can help you. What are you afraid of?"

"I'm not afraid of nothin', except-- I have to leave."

"What about Annie? I'm not blind. I've seen what's been going on between you two for months? You're going to leave her behind, too?"

"I told her that there things from my past. Look, if I go away now, she'll never have to know."

"God damn it! If you care about her, you'll stay and fight."

Sonny said nothing, but walked out the door and headed across the yard.

"Do not walk away from me," Matthew screamed. "You come back here, right now!" But Sonny kept walking, and disappeared into his shack.

Matthew staggered out the door. He couldn't breathe and the feeling in his chest was worse. He saw Annie and Luke, who had just arrived home moments earlier, running toward him. Annie was already crying.

"Pop, what's going on," Luke called.

"Where is he?" Annie asked, pushing in behind her father. "Sonny?" she called. "Where are you?"

"He's leaving, Ann."

'What?"

"He's over in his shack packing right now."

"What did you say to him? What's wrong?"

"For Christ's sake, nothing." He looked at his daughter's face, pinched with fear. He brushed past them and headed for the truck. Not wanting to argue any more, he headed down the bottom road. He did not intend to be here when Sonny rode away.

Annie ran to Sonny's shed, but the door was locked She began to beat upon it with both fists. "Sonny! Let me in! Please tell me what's happening." She stopped only when Luke compelled her to go into the house for a while to let things calm down.

Someone must have summonsed Mack because soon the Jeep came roaring up the driveway. "What the hell happened?"

he yelled as he burst into the kitchen. "Where's Pop?'

"He jumped in the truck and headed down the bottom road," Luke said. "And he didn't look good. His face was gray and his breathing was bad."

"He can't go down there," Mack exclaimed. "He's probably already stuck. We'd better go check. Where's Sonny? He can drive the tractor."

"He's leaving," Annie murmured. "Pop said he's getting his stuff packed to leave."

"What the hell?" Mack roared. "What's going on around here? I'll talk to him. Don't worry, Annie, but first we gotta go get Pop."

* * * * * *

Mack was right. Matthew didn't get very far before the front tires of his truck became mired in the deep mud. He reached for the bottle of whiskey he kept hidden under the seat and gulped it down without taking a breath. He reached for his bottle of Nitroglycerin, but remembered he had forgotten to take it along this morning.

The pressure in his chest became worse and he felt so hot. He needed some air, so he got out and began stumbling toward the bottom. He was filled with an overpowering need to see it. He made his way to where the flood waters covered the road.

He fell to his knees. "That goddamn Sonny. I can't believe he's going to walk away." He laid down and felt refreshed by the cool rain splashing on his face. He rolled over, struggled to his feet, and wadded along the water's edge. He could feel the submerged corn stalks grab his feet. He stretched out his arms and cried, "If he don't want to fight for this, well then, to hell with him. I don't need him." But then he began to shake with anguished sobs. "This was ours, his and mine. I've got to talk to him – make him understand." He fell again, choking and gasping from the tremendous pain. "Oh, God," he whispered, "what's happening to me?"

* * * * * *

654

Mack tried to talk to Sonny. "C'mon," he called, banging on the door. "We gotta go look for Pop. He's probably stuck so we thought we'd drive the tractor down there. You wanna come?" There was no answer, but Sonny's bike was still parked outside, so Mack knew he was still there. "Listen, you dumb shit. I do not know what the hell is going on around here, but you stay put till we get the old man up the hill. You hear me? Do not leave."

He drove the tractor to the back door.. "I guess he's not gonna come. We'll worry about that later." Annie and Luke climbed onboard and they started down the hill.

They found their father lying in the mud, barely conscious.

"Hang on, Pop!" Mack was the first to reach him. "We'll get you back up the hill. We need the wagon." He started back up the hill.

Annie sank down beside her father and lifted his head into her lap, clutching his ice cold hand. Matthew's breathing was shallow, and there was a frightening gray pall across his face. She began rubbing his arms and hands, trying to coax warmth back into them. "Just hang on, Pop. We're gonna get you back to the house as fast as we can."

Mack made it back to the yard in record time. He saw Sonny straddle his bike, preparing to take off.

"Sonny wait. It's Pop. We found him passed out down in the mud and water. He looks real bad. Help me get the wagon."

Sonny dropped the bike, ran across the yard to the flatbed hay wagon, and lifted the tongue so that Mack could back the tractor into place. They stopped at the house long enough to tell Thomas to call the doctor and find Andrew. They rushed back down the hill. "We gotta get you back to the house," Mack said.

"No, no," Matthew murmured. "Just let me lie here. Please. Where's Luke? Don't worry about him any more, Annie, he's going to be fine." His eyes fluttered open for a moment and saw Sonny. "You're still here? You hear that?" Off in the distance there was a siren wailing. "You'd better get the hell out of here. But if you go . . ." He collapsed back into Annie's lap, his fingers squeezing a fistful of mud. His breathing slowed and then there was no movement at all.

"No!" Annie cried, shaking him. "Daddy, wake up! Mack, do something!"

"He's gone, Annie," Mack whispered.. "It's over."

"No! That's can't be!" She glared at Sonny. "You did this, you and your damn secrets! You heard him. He said go! Get the hell away from us!"

"I'm sorry. I never wanted . . ." Sonny stumbled backwards, slipping and falling in the mud. "I'm sorry!" He disappeared into the timber.

They laid their father's body upon the wagon and started back toward the house. Doc Peters arrived just as Penny and the ambulance, now a hearse, pulled onto the yard. The gentle, country doctor made a brief examination where Matthew laid and signed the death certificate. Then they took him away.

* * * * * *

Sonny came up the hill through the woods, staggering over the uneven terrain parallel with the wagon. He sobbed for the first time since he was a little boy. The old man was dead, and just like Annie said, the truth was what killed him. "Everything I touch turns to shit," he muttered through clinched teeth. "I should have left long ago."

He slipped into his shed unnoticed, stood in dark silence at the window and watched as they loaded Matthew's body into the hearse. He saw Annie being helped into the house, her body limp with grief. He slipped out the window and pushed his bike around the back of the barn. Following the ruts of tractor tracks to make sure the nubbed tires were not leaving a telltale trail, he left through the pasture gate and headed into the woods where he planned to hide until the Sheriff came and left. He stared at the big house on the hill. It stood immense and proud against the harsh, dark skies, defying anyone or anything to intrude upon its dominion. He could not see the bottom because of the curtain of trees, but every detail was etched in his mind. Everything that mattered to him was here, but now he was leaving it all behind.

* * * * * *

Annie, Mack, Penny and the others trudged into the kitchen with Doc Adams. "What happened here?" the doctor asked.

"All I know is that Pop came home from town and went straight to Sonny," Mack began. "They talked for a few minutes, and then he got in his truck and tried to drive down the bottom road. He got stuck and then walked the rest of the way. That's where we found him."

"It has something to do with Sonny," Annie sobbed. "Pop told him to leave."

Just then there was a knock at the door. It was Billy. "I heard in town that they needed the ambulance out here for Matthew," he gasped. "He's dead? But I just saw him — just this morning in the bar. What happened?"

"He had a massive heart attack, Billy," the doctor explained.

"I knew he was upset, but my God! I showed him some old newspaper clippings. There was stuff about this place, and a picture of the Indian that they hung way back. I wanted him to see how much that guy looked like Sonny."

"Who looked like Sonny? The dead Indian?" Mack's shock was mirrored in the faces of the other Winston's sitting around the table.

"Turns out he's some relative or something, probably a great-grandson."

"His lies broke my father's heart," Annie cried. "That's what killed him."

"I doubt that, Annie," Doc Peters said. "He had a very serious heart condition, but he wouldn't let us tell you. He had been having chest pains for months now. I warned him that he had better change his ways or it'd kill him. "

"Did you know about this?" Mack was glaring at his wife.

"Yes, she did," Doc Peters replied. "But she is bound by the same rules of confidentiality that I am."

"I'm sorry, honey, but your dad made a point of asking me not to say anything. All of you were so worried about Luke. I did stay after him about his medicines. Maybe I should have done more." Penny reached for her husband's hand. "What's that?"

657

There was the sounds of fast approaching sirens. Three sheriff's squad cars pulled onto the yard.

The Winston's watched from the kitchen windows as Sheriff Wilkerson strode across the yard toward Sonny's shed, his hand resting on his holster. "Spread out, men," he called with a frightening menacing tone. He walked inside Sonny's place and soon reappeared. "Look in every building on the place, but I'm sure he's gone." He went to his car to call in the APB and then headed toward the house.

He knocked briefly and then came inside. "I passed the hearse on my way out here. I am very sorry for your loss, but right now I need to find your man, Sonny. There's an warrant for his arrest."

"Warrant for what?" Mack's voice cracked as he spat the words.

"Parole jumping. It seems Sonny felt it unnecessary to check in with his parole office even once after his release from prison."

"What are you talking about? Sonny was in prison?" Luke exclaimed.

"Yes, he was. And for the record, his name is Jack Blackstone. I knew the second I laid eyes on him the day of the fire that I had seen him before. I figured it out this morning. He was in this area in the summer of '67. That guy from Chicago owned this place then, and his kid took over this house with a bunch of his hippie drugged out friends. I called Doc Adams to come with me when we raided the place. I knew those kids would need some medical attention. I was right. We sent two of them to Mercy in ambulances – one almost died from a drug overdose. We did strip searches on all of them, supervised by the doctor, of course. And that's when we saw him -- this skinny, messed up kid with terrible scars across his butt. He was in real bad shape, too – strung out on heroine."

"You knew him from before, Dr. Adams?" Annie gasped. "Why didn't you tell us."

"I couldn't, Ann. You know doctors are bound by patient-doctor confidentiality. I recognized him at the hospital, not so much from his face as those scars. When he was in the emergency

658

room, they ran tests. There was no trace of any drugs. And later I ran more tests. He's a different person. He never went back to the way he was before. I just wish that he had been able to trust someone with the truth so he wouldn't be in this trouble now."

CHAPTER 79

That night Annie tried to rest, but found herself wandering through the house, standing beside the beds of her sleeping brothers and sister. She had no more tears to cry, but derived comfort from looking at their faces.

Each time she returned to her room, she crept up to her window and stared across the yard at the dark place where Sonny should be. Where did he go? How could she find him to say she was sorry? She tried to shut out the deafening echo of everything she has heard today. Sonny had so many secrets. She now understood that it was no accident that he came to be with them, but was that the only reason he stayed?

At sunrise, she gave up trying to sleep. She dressed and was on her way down to make coffee when she thought she heard someone in the kitchen. "Sonny?" she called. "Is that you? You came back!" But it was Mack, not Sonny, standing by the sink.

"Sorry, kid," he said. "It's just me. I thought I'd get a early start on the chores. I mean somebody's gotta do it, right?"

"Yeah, sure," she murmured as she poured herself a cup of coffee.

Within a few moments, Luke and Andrew came downstairs. They, too, headed for the coffee pot and sank down on the kitchen chairs, saying nothing. The hot steam that rose from the cups offered scant comfort in the early morning gloom.

Mack cleared his throat and shifted in his seat as though he was preparing to make an announcement. "Look," he said, "since we're all together, there's something I want to show you. C'mon, follow me." They stepped outside into the stillness of the new day. The rain had stopped during the night, and the sun was rising in full view, conspicuous in its glare after so many days of rain. Mack led them across the yard past the barn to small field of hill ground sandwiched between the barnyard and the timber.

"Pop took me here once. He said him and Sonny stumbled across it once when the cows got out, but I'm betting Sonny knew it was here all along. See?" He pointed at a stone-covered rectangular area at the crest of the hill. "Pop said this was probably the grave site of the Indian they hung. It stands to reason that he was buried here somewhere. They sure as hell wouldn't have buried him in the cemetery in town, and his wife couldn't take him back to the reservation."

They stood staring at the grave for several minutes.

"Anyway," Mack murmured, "I think Pop showed this to me because he wanted to be buried here, too. It's a nice place, don't you think?" It was very peaceful. The valley and river laid in full view. There were birds making lazy circles overhead, and white and purple wildflowers grew nearby.

"Sure," Andrew agreed. "And I think we should bring Mama here, too. He would want her with him, right? I'll` talk to Abernathy to get the proper papers filed. I'll call Aunt Esther, too." They all shook their heads in agreement. It was reassuring to have someone willing to manage such things. Andrew went into town to speak with the undertaker and Father Fritz, and then boarded an airplane for New York.

Later that day, when she needed a respite from the incessant phone calls of condolences and the sad, hallow stares of her grief-stricken siblings, Annie returned to the quiet hilltop. She sank onto her knees and began to cry. "I'm sorry," she sobbed out loud, calling to the spirit of the man buried there. "You probably think we have no business being here, but my father loved this place, too. And now this place belongs to us – our generation – us and Sonny. I swear I will find him and bring him home. I promise."

* * * * * *

660

Making arrangements for the funeral and burial of her father was the most difficult thing Annie and her brothers had ever done. She had no idea there were so many decisions to be made. Andrew took care of most of it before he left, but Annie had to pick out a suit and tie, and there was the music to choose and the scriptures. As a veteran, there should be a flag over his coffin, Mr. Jensen, the undertaker said. What about the playing of Taps and a 21 gun salute? They worked their way through the process until everything was set.

The boys worked at the gravesite from early morning until late at night the two days before the funeral. It was mowed and a white picket fence was built. Andrew came home late Sunday night, accompanying Kathleen's coffin on the plane with the four bereaved aunts in tow. Annie had dreaded their arrival, but even Aunt Esther seemed intent to be on her best behavior.

The wake was Monday night. Most of the town turned out. Annie, Andrew, Mack, Penny, and the others stood in a receiving line at the doorway of the chapel in the funeral home, and murmured their appreciation of everyone's kind wishes and condolences. Yes, they said, he was too young. Yes, it was a blessing he went so quickly. No, he didn't suffer.

Later that night, after the younger ones were put to bed, the older Winston's assembled around Annie's kitchen table, munching on a platter of cookies dropped off by the Rosary Society ladies. Little was said, but no one wanted to go to bed either. Even Thomas sat with them. He hadn't said a word to anyone this whole time.

Annie gently slid her arm around his shoulders and said, "I'm so glad you're still here, Thomas. Thank God you didn't leave right away."

"Sure," he muttered, "I'd hate to miss all this fun." Annie sank back into her chair, rebuked by his sarcasm. Thomas wandered away from the table and disappeared upstairs.

"You know," Penny said, "I was hoping this time it might be different."

"Who, Thomas?" Mack retorted. "He's always like that."

"No, I mean the rest of you. Whenever something tragic happens in this family, you turn away instead of helping each

661

other. When we got word of your capture, Luke, you should have seen these people. For Christ sake, this is a time for you to help each other. Don't you know how?" Penny grabbed Mack's hand and reached for Luke's hand, too. "Doesn't anyone have anything to say?"

"Well," John said tentatively, "I was thinking how Pop would have laughed when Roger Greeley came in there tonight, drunk as a skunk." There was a smattering of giggles.

"Yeah," Mack added. "I think he was pissed we weren't serving food."

"And did you see Mayor Strong's face when Andrew told him we were burying Pop out here instead of the cemetery in town?" Luke retorted. "Jeez! He looked insulted or something."

"Even old Mr. McGruder was there," Andrew said. "I thought maybe he was going to pull out a pen and a paper napkin and try to sell us something." They laughed remembering that day he had appeared on their yard with a truck full of livestock.

"God, Sonny was so mad!" John said, but then looked afraid to have mentioned his name.

"I know," Annie said, smiling. "Remember that first gallon of milk? We could hardly drink it."

On it went, more stories, more remembrances. They talked half the night. Annie enjoyed it as much as anyone but suddenly she felt sick and excused herself. Penny found her leaning over the toilet, vomiting.

"I don't know what came over me." Annie mumbled, embarrassed and surprised. "I think I've only thrown up once before in my life."

"Don't worry," Penny cooed in her best nurse voice. "It's pretty understandable, considering everything you've gone through lately. C'mon, I'll draw you a bath."

The warm water did feel soothing, but it did not relieve her nausea. "You do look a little green," Penny observed as she helped her sister-in-law dress and get into bed. "Do you get sick with your periods? Maybe your hormones are screwed up. That happens sometimes when there's a lot of stress."

"Nah," Annie replied, dismissing that explanation. "I take after my mother – as regular as --" She stopped short and looked suddenly very panicked. "Now that I think about it --" Her voice trailed off again. "Oh my God, I'm late. I mean --"

"I know exactly what you mean," Penny smiled. "The people in maternity are already marking the middle of January on their calendars. Nine months after that big snow storm, we're going to have a huge baby boom."

"No, you don't understand. Me and Sonny, we only --"

"Did it once? It only takes once, my dear. Didn't you take precautions?"

"It was so spontaneous, so -- it was my first time," she said, embarrassed at her own inexperience. "And now I'm pregnant?"

"Yeah, probably, but you need to come in and have tests to make sure. And Annie, there's a lot to consider. Abortion is legal now."

"Oh, no! I would never do that. It just makes it more important to find Sonny."

"Well, you can't do anything right now. You'd better get some sleep. You're going to have a long, hard day tomorrow." Penny stood up and turned off the light. She hesitated at the door. "Annie," she called, "I should have known better than to mention an abortion. I'm sorry."

She closed the door and left Annie alone in the darkness to toss and turn with gut-retching dread. Even if they found Sonny, there were still the fact that he was wanted by the law. We'll just have to find him first and worry about the rest later.

* * * * * *

Penny was correct when she said the day of Matthew's funeral would be a long, difficult one. The Mass was well attended. Father Fitz held a beautiful service. The choir sang, the prayers were repeated, and the blessings given. Kneeling in the front pew of the church that day, the notion that their father was actually dead was still inconceivable to the Winston children. They were supposed to pray for their father's immortal soul, but mostly they prayed to have him back.

They climbed inside their cars and slowly followed the hearses that bore their parents' bodies to the farm. Their sons had dug the holes themselves that early morning. The cars that followed them made a caravan a mile long.

"Pop would be proud," Andrew said.

"I just hope we have enough food," Annie worried. "These people expect to be fed."

They turned down the driveway, through the pasture, and around the side of the field toward the waiting cemetery. Matthew's pall bearers, Billie, Mr. Strong, Andy Bean, and the others from the Pub, bore Matthew's coffin up the grassy slope while Kathleen's sons carried hers. The rich, mahogany coffins were carefully placed side by side, glistening under the clear, welcoming skies. Annie clutched the flag that had draped her father's coffin, trembling as each round of shots cracked the air. And then it was finished.

The on-lookers began to move back to their cars, as Billie and the others helped lower the coffins and put the lids on the vaults. Then Mack politely asked them to go, saying that the family would finish themselves. Slowly, gently they began to spade the dirt. No one spoke until it was done. The boys stood back and surveyed their handiwork.

"This is good," Andrew said. "Pop would be happy, don't you think?"

"I guess we should go back to the house," Annie murmured. "We've left our guests unattended long enough."

One by one, they started to turn away, but then they noticed Luke, the spade still in his hands. He was trembling as unchecked tears streamed down his face. His anxious siblings drew near again and waited for him to speak.

"Maybe it's better this way. He'll never have to know," he said.

"Know what?" Andrew asked.

"That it wasn't his fault that everything went bad for me in Nam. I know he blamed himself, but he shouldn't have. He didn't know how much things had changed – that the things he believed weren't true any more."

"What do you mean, Luke?"

He bit his lip, hesitating before he spoke. "Pop thought it was a righteous war. Maybe it was in the beginning, but not when

I got there. And the thing is --" he paused and drew a long, deep breath before he continued. "The thing is, I wasn't captured because of anything that made any sense. You see, this guy – one of the guys in our unit --" Luke inhaled deeply again. "He found out my friend, Tim, lied about being part Black. That asshole just threw him out of the helicopter like a piece of garbage. I tried to help, but I got shot. They just left us there!" He fell to his knees as anguished sobs shook his entire body. "They just left us there," he said again.

"Pop kept talking about the North Vietnamese 'bastards' who did this to me. Hell, they could have shot me on the spot. They usually did when they found someone as shot up as me. You know what saved me? They found my sketch pad in my pocket. I guess there was drawings of the Vietnamese children around the camp." He shook his head in disbelief. "Can you believe that? They took me to their village and the officer asked me to draw his portrait. I could barely see, but I stroked his face on a scrap of paper. Wouldn't Pop laugh if he knew the thing that saved me was the fact I can draw."

"Did they hurt you?" Margaret asked.

"Hell, they didn't have to. I was all shot up. There was no medicine, no food. The others worked in the fields every day, but I couldn't walk, so I drew pictures of the guards' children or wives. I was in bad shape. I still can't believe I didn't die."

"But Luke, you didn't," Mack said. "You're home now."

"For what? So I could help bury my father?"

"Just remember how much he loved you, Luke," Annie whispered. "Don't punish yourself. Pop would never want that." She paused while her brother struggled to compose himself. "Anyway, we should go."

One by one, they broke away and headed toward the house. When Margaret and Luke were alone, she asked, "Why didn't you tell me?"

"I couldn't. I mean, what good does it do?"

"I don't understand."

"Look at you. You're mad as hell, aren't you?"

"Of course, I am."

"So now, every time someone mentions the word Vietnam,

this is what you're going to remember, isn't it?"

"Probably, but --"

"See? People think that we were all a bunch of assholes, but guys like Tim and Hanson were decent people, and they're not coming back," he cried. "Krolowski was such an idiot – a racist, fat pig. He killed Tim – not the Cong or the North Vietnamese. He did! And I will never forget that ugly fucking sneer of his. But I don't want all of us to be lumped together with people like him."

"You're not," she whispered. "Not to me. But Luke, you can't carry this all by yourself. That's not fair. No wonder you --"

"Shut down? You're afraid I'll do that again?"

"Secrets do that to a person, don't they?" She reached up and touched his sweaty brow, beginning to cry. "I'm so afraid for you. I don't want to lose you again, Luke. I just want--."

"I know what you want – you want me to be like I was before. I can't. Don't you see? I'm just faking it, Maggie. I talk to people, act normal, but it's not real. I'm so twisted up inside I just want to smash something!" He raised his clinched fists above his head. "It was all for nothing! Tim and Hanson died for nothing! I sat rotting in that goddamn hole for two years for nothing. Every step I take is like a knife sticking in this fucking leg, and for what? I try to separate myself from it – I try to tell myself just to let it go, but I can't."

"It's too soon. You've got to give yourself some time. But I think you're doing the right thing, working hard every day. Little by little, things will get better. I really believe that."

They huddled on the hilltop, their arms wrapped around each other. Gradually, he calmed, but the shadow of deep sadness still cast a desperate pall across his face.

"Look at the river and the land out there," she murmured. "It'll never go away. I'm glad your father lived long enough to bring you home, Luke. This is the only place where you can find yourself again."

"That's what Pop said. Guess he was a pretty smart man." He kissed her and took her hand to stand up. "C'mon, let's go down to the clearing. I don't want to go back to the house."

He picked up his uniform jacket. The metals and ribbons

shimmered in the noon day sun. He stared at them for a moment and then picked up a spade and began digging in the loose dirt of his father's grave. Maggie saw what he intended to do, picked up the other spade, and together they dug a hole several feet deep. Pausing to finger each metal one by one, he flung his jacket into the hole and began covering it up.

When they were finished, Luke stood silently for a few moments. "There they are, Pop," he said. "I never wanted them anyway." He put his arm around Maggie's shoulder and together they walked away.

Chapter 80

Annie was relieved to be able to fuss over the food and beverages for her guests. She preferred that over having to make small talk about her father's death. It was gratifying to see that Matthew was well-liked in the community, but there were others who came simply out of morbid curiosity. Annie had managed to make the place look somewhat presentable. Thankfully, the weather cooperated and people were able to sit outside in the backyard. Aunt Esther and her sisters were gracious as they were introduced to Matthew's friends. She even told Annie that the house looked nice, and the food was very good. However, Annie was very relieved when they left to go back to New York.

Later that night, Mack and Penny tossed and turned in their bed. It had been a difficult day, and even though they were exhausted, they could not sleep.

"What ya' thinking about, Penny?" Mack asked.

She didn't answer at first, but rolled over and put her arms around his neck. He saw she was crying. "You were right, Mack," she whispered.

"About what?"

"About the damn war! Today, when Luke was talking, I kept thinking how many times you tried to tell me how wrong it was, but I didn't listen."

He stroked the fleshy, soft part of her upper arm and

thought of all the times he laid in this bed when she angrily turned away from him. On those nights he had doubted himself as guilt was his constant companion. "I know it was hard on you, and I'm sorry." He hugged her then and kissed her forehead. "It was so much worse than I ever thought. I can't imagine how Luke could carry all that around and not say anything. Jesus! I just wish there was something more I could do."

"Do what you do best, Mack."

"What?"

"Why didn't you tell me people have been talking to you about running for the state legislature?"

He was stunned. "Who told you?"

"I ran into Amos Owens' wife at the hospital. She asked me if there was a chance you might reconsider your decision to run."

"I promised you, Penny. I told you I would stay here and take care of you and Katie. How can I--"

"How can you not? You said yourself that our generation has got to take a more active role in the decision making. Besides, you're good at politics – that's what Mrs. Owens said anyway. However, I think she's more enamored with your cute butt than your political views." She giggled as she jabbed him in the ribs. "People listen to you. I think you should do it."

"I didn't think there was a chance in a million that you'd even consider this," he gasped.

"It was Luke. You were right when you said he's a nice kid. The war was wrong. People have been saying that for a long time, but the demonstrations and sit-ins just scared people. You need to work within the system. The state legislature sounds like a good place to begin."

"What about the farm? We're just beginning to get our finances on an even keel."

"Luke wants to help us."

"What? You talked to him about this?"

"No, he mentioned it one day when I was changing his dressings. He said he heard we were having money problems and he wondered how you'd respond if he asked you about becoming a partner. He has a lot of money from back pay and he hasn't touched a penny of his trust fund."

"I don't want to take his money."

"He has a good idea, actually. He wants to buy the 120 acres next to our place and enlarge the herd. He wants to help you work the place. He can take care of things when you're in Des Moines. I think it would work, don't you?"

"Just imagine what my dad would say – me and politics."

"I know something else that would have please your father," she purred seductively. "Another grandchild. I'm ready, Mack. What do you think?"

"I think my parents would definitely approve. Why do you think they had ten kids?" He slipped his hand under her gown.

"I didn't mean we had to start right now, tonight," she chided him.

"You're right. I'm too tired anyway." He sighed deeply.

"Mack, I think we should bring our baby home. I want him buried here with your mom and dad."

"Sure, Penny. I'd like that, too. We'll talk to Fr. Fritz right away." Neither of them said anything for several minutes. "And you know, when our kids carry me to the top of the hill like we did my father today," Mack murmured, "I hope they say that I was a good man and a good father."

"They will, Mack. They will."

* * * * * *

The next morning, Annie and Penny went into town together to see Doc Adams. The test confirmed what they suspected. The doctor examined her and set her due date at January 15th. "Does he know?" the doctor asked as he took Annie's hand to pull her up to a sitting position.

"No, he left before I found out myself, but I'm sure how he'll take the news."

"Why?"

"I think he'll probably be upset or mad. I mean, we had plenty of chances to sleep together. And it wasn't that I didn't try, but he always stopped. I think he thought because of his past he should never. . ." Her voice trailed off as she struggled to explain Sonny's feelings. "There's so much I didn't understand before, like the way he tried to stay away from you. He knew you'd recognize him."

"I know. He never trusted me."

"I think he has trouble trusting anyone," Annie sighed, "or otherwise he would have told us all of this a long time ago."

* * * * * *

The next few agonizing days grounded on slowly as the likelihood of finding Sonny or the chances that he might return on his own, dwindled. She couldn't eat, couldn't sleep.

On Saturday morning, May 12th, Annie stood staring out the kitchen window as her brothers gathered around the breakfast table.

"Look a this," Andrew said from behind the newspaper. "They're going to have the ceremony today."

"I still can't believe that they actually dug up 200 year old graves and separated their bones," Mack retorted.

"I guess they didn't want no stinking Indian buried in that grave," Andrew said sarcastically.

"What did you say?" Annie cried, turning around quickly.

"I said I guess they didn't want no stinking Indian buried in that grave. Of course, I was being --"

"I know. I know. What ceremony is today?" she pressed.

"The one when the bones of the two Indians will be buried near Dubuque's monument. They separated them last year --"

"I know. Sonny told me about it. He'll be there. I know he will," she cried as she reached for her car keys.

"Annie, where are you going?" they called after her.

"To find Sonny." She ran to her car and drove toward Dubuque as fast as she dared. When she turned onto the gravel road leading toward the park, she was amazed how many people were there. She had to park near the bottom of the long, steep hill and began the long hike to the top. Near the entrance of the park, there was a group of Native Americans sitting in a large circle, chanting and beating drums while others danced in full Indian dress. Even though she couldn't understand the words, Annie

670

thought the haunting music sounded sorrowful and dispirited. She paused respectfully while searching the faces in the throng for Sonny.

And then she saw him, standing at the back of the crowd, that hard expression affixed upon his face. He appeared to be in a trance as he nodded his head with the beat of the music. Annie was relieved, but also frightened. Now that she found him, what should she say? She began practicing scenario's as she made her way through the crowd.

Then, as though he was struck, he startled to attention. Annie thought he must have noticed her, but then realized that his attention was focused in the other direction. Two deputy sheriffs were making their way toward him from the other side. He vaulted over a crowd of people sitting nearby and ran toward the timber. The deputies called after him, "Hey, you. Stop!" One even pulled his gun, but was quickly reprimanded. "Too many people," the other one said. They chased Sonny toward the bluff. Finding no paths and the brush too thick to penetrate, he cut back across the road, but there was no place to run.

He was wrestled to the ground as one deputy shouted, "Spread 'em!" Sonny was being handcuffed just as Annie arrived, breathless and panicked.

"Why are you doing this?" She tried to get closer, but one of the deputies held her back. Sonny turned to look at her. There was mud on his face, and blood trickled down his cheek. His eyes were dark and full of rage as they pulled him to his feet.

"Look, lady," said one of the deputies, "there's been a warrant out on this guy for more than five years. He has three and a half years left on his prison sentence plus whatever else they add on. He ain't gonna see the light of day for a long, long time." He yanked Sonny's arm and started to lead him through the crowd.

"No, Sonny, no!" Annie cried. "You're not going back to prison. We'll get a lawyer." She tried to get past the deputies, but she could do nothing but watch as they shoved him into the back of a squad car. "Where are you taking him?" she called as the car peeled away. She had no idea where the jail was. An onlooker said the jail was downtown, near the courthouse. She rushed to her car and tried to weave through the throng of people. "Get out of my way!" she screamed. "Let me through!" Everything was taking too long.

She stopped for a moment at a phone booth to call home. "I found him," she exclaimed, not even sure who picked up the phone. "They arrested him. Tell Andrew to call a lawyer right away. I'll wait at the jail."

She soon learned there had been no reason to hurry. She was forced to wait over an hour in the outer area of the jail while they "processed" Sonny. She detested this place and hated that Sonny had to spend even an hour here. Finally, an uniformed office approached her.

"I'm sorry, miss," he said in a flat, emotionless voice, "but he doesn't want to see you."

"Oh, no, there must be some mistake. Did you tell him who I am? I'm Ann Winston. I'm sure he'll see me. Ask him again."

"I already told him that, but he said to tell you to go home. He don't want no visitors."

There was nothing to do but leave. Broken hearted, she turned to go. "But, Officer," she called s she hesitated at the door, "tell him I'll be back tomorrow. Tell him."

Driving home was difficult as she tried to see through a veil of tears. If the judicial system made things hard, his own stubbornness was even worse, but she wasn't surprised. His pride was the only thing he had left.

CHAPTER 81

Sonny didn't remember much from that night six years ago when he was arrested the first time. He was so wasted that everything was a blur. But this time there were no chemicals to dull the sensations of handing over his personal effects and then getting finger-printed and photographed. He was taken to his cell.

A resolute look of desperation must have shown upon his face because the deputy took Sonny's belt and even his shoelaces. "There's more than one way to fly the coop," the Deputy sneered. "I already had one kid do that, and it ain't gonna happen again, not on my watch." With that, he slammed the door. Sonny shuddered as the echo reverberated through the barren place.

The smell was the same. He remembered the stale odor more than anything else. It was like this was a dead place with no air. He wrapped himself up in the rough, woolen blanket and climbed onto the bunk. He studied the design of the cement blocks of the wall, like stair steps going nowhere. There was no color, only different shades of gray. He got up and paced. If there was only something to do. All his life he dealt with things by burying himself in activity. Don't think, just work. Break something, build something, plant something, fix something. He grabbed the bars with his hands. Nothing. No movement. No sound. I can't do this! I can't. He wasn't even sure if he cried those words out loud or did they only echo in his mind. He collapsed against the wall and sank to the floor.

The only way he survived before was the drugs. He sold his soul to anyone with money and connections to keep the stuff coming. Here, he was alone. His mind was bombarded with a thousand memories of how his life had been – the smell of coffee in the kitchen, the long straight rows of corn in the fields, and the way she touched him the night they made love.

His fists were clinched so tightly that they began to spasm with pain. He trembled from the cold, but yet his gut and chest were fire hot. Waves of nausea swept over him. He retched and would have vomited if there had been anything in his stomach. The loud pounding of his heart began to dissolve into the sound of the drums. The chants engulfed him and lifted him back to the clearing where the elders sat, their faces grim as the sang the sacred words. Freeze your mind. Concentrate. Concentrate.

Grandfather, why do the sun and moon never touch?

My boy, their love for us is greater than it is for each other. Grandfather Sun gives us life as he gives us light. Grandmother Moon gives us harmony and marks the seasons as she smiles to us in the night. Grandfather Sun makes the path across the sky and she follows.

Grandfather, where does the wind come from?

673

The wind is the song of the sky. All things must bow before it. It commands the clouds to bring us rain and spreads life across the land as seeds float upon the breeze The wind reminds us that the most powerful things are often unseen.

But Grandfather, where does the wind start and where does it end?

The wind is like all things in nature – there is no beginning or an end. The wind teaches us that the cycle of things around us is never still. The rivers comes from the clouds, and the clouds are born from the water. There is no stillness or there is death.

If stillness is death, Sonny called to the spirits of his ancestors, then am I to die in this place?

Each man chooses his own path and his own destiny. The bear chooses to sleep in winter because he choose life, not death.

Sonny remembered then the maddening way his grandfather answered his questions. The riddles were lessons and the lessons were always more riddles. Sonny sat in the cold, colorless place and pondered these things for the first time in many years.

* * * * * *

Annie drove onto the yard, exhausted and angry that no lawyer had arrived at the jail. Mack and Penny, Luke and Margaret, Andrew, and John were sitting around the kitchen table waiting for her. "Where was the goddamn lawyer? I said get one right away!"

"We did," Mack said. "He just called. He must have gotten there right after you left. He said Sonny refused to meet with him. But there's a hearing later this month, so at least he won't get shipped back to Ft. Madison right away. There's a chance Sonny can beat this thing, but he has to talk to the lawyer."

"He wouldn't see me either," Annie cried. "My God, what are we going to do if he won't co-operate with any of this? Everything is so screwed up. Who is he? I can't even remember to call him by his real name. Maybe I really never knew him at all?"

Penny reached for her hand. "A person's name means nothing. The parts of him that matter are still the same. Maybe he'll see you tomorrow."

But he wouldn't. Not the next day, or any other. Annie drove to the jail every afternoon, and each time the officer came back with the same message. "He says go home, and don't come here anymore." One time, just as she turned to leave, the officer hesitated and added, "Miss, I can't make him see you, but I wish I could. Maybe you could talk some sense into him. He's not eating or even drinking. He just sits there, cross-legged on his bunk like he's in a trance or something. We took away his belt and shoelaces because we're --" He didn't finish the sentence because the meaning was clear.

Annie called Penny at work and asked Dr. Adams to visit Sonny. She knew what he was trying to do, and she was not about to let that happen.

* * * * * *

Dr. Adams visited the day Sonny marked his two week anniversary of being in jail. "This is a visitor you can't refuse, " the deputy said.

"What do you mean, I can't refuse. Hey, get him out of here."

But the doctor was not deterred. "You're wrong, Sonny. I could get these deputies in here to hold you down, but I'd rather not. C'mon, let me see how you're doing."

Sonny didn't move. "Hell, no! I still have rights, don't I?"

"Shut up in there!" the deputy called. "Just be quiet and let the doctor check you over. Your cough is keeping everyone awake around here."

"It'll just take a few minutes." the doctor coaxed.

Defeated, the prisoner complied.

The doctor started as he always did, working from the top down – eyes, ears, nose, and throat. He took out his stethoscope and instructed Sonny to take deep breaths. "They tell me you haven't been eating or drinking since you've been here."

"Says who, Annie?"

"She's been here every day. She's very worried about --"

"Tell her to stay the hell away. I'll go back to prison and do my time, and that'll be it."

"Annie and the others want to help you get out of this mess, so you can go back home."

"Home? That's not my home! For Christ sake, can't they get it through their thick skulls that I'm not getting out of here?"

"So you can slowly kill yourself instead?"

"What?"

"Isn't that what you're doing? You've been here two weeks and already you've lost ten pounds, you have pneumonia and a severe bladder infection. You're not eating or drinking."

"You got it all wrong, Doc. I've tried to eat – I just can't. Even the water tastes like shit!" Dr. Adams began to draw up some injections from a vial of milky white vial medicine. "What's that?" Sonny demanded.

"I can't be sure that you're going to take any oral antibiotics that I'm going to prescribe, so I'll load you up with these shots, with or without you co-operation."

"Okay, but you can't go running to Annie or Penny and tell 'em anything." Dr. Adams agreed and told Sonny he'd be back in a couple of days to check on him.

* * * * * *

Mack and the boys planted the hill ground, but otherwise there was not much to do. The bottom was still covered with flood water and the time for planting passed as May turned into June.

Annie's daily bouts of morning sickness were bothersome, but she usually felt better by noon which was when she made her trips into Dubuque to try to see Sonny. She was afraid if she

676

stopped coming he would think she had given up and stopped caring.

Mr. Freedman, their lawyer, was building a strong case, even without the co-operation of his stubborn client. His case centered around proving that Sonny had turned his life around, so a return to prison was unnecessary. Dr. Adams agreed to testify, not only as a character witness, but also as Sonny's physician with clinical evidence that he had been drug-free for over three years.

"We need another witness--perhaps a priest or some leader of the community," Mr. Freedman said one day as they discussed the case around the kitchen table.

"I have no idea who that would be," Mack said. "Sonny had never socialized with anyone in town, always stayed close to the farm."

"What about ol' Ben?" Andrew suggested.

"Yeah," Mack agreed. "He's a little hard of hearing and he might go off on some tangent, but Sonny saved his life the day of the fire."

Mr. Freedman seemed satisfied and decided he'd pay the elderly couple a visit. Old Ben Gibson might be just what they needed to pull this off.

* * * * * *

On the day of his hearing, the deputy took Sonny to the shower and directed him to put on the dress shirt and pants Annie had brought for him. He refused, climbing onto his bed naked and defiant, "If you want me in court, I'll go like this."

Court was called to order and the charges read. "And where is the defendant?" the judge asked tersely. There was an uneasy silence until one of the deputies spoke up. "Excuse me, Your Honor, but the defendant is ill and under a doctor's care. He is unable to appear in court." The Judge seemed somewhat annoyed, and asked if council for either side wished to reconvene at a later time when the defendant could appear.

"No," Mr. Freedman said quickly. "He wasn't going to testify in his own behalf anyway. Mr. Blackstone's health is not likely to improve soon."

"I hope this is not an attempt by the defense council to win sympathy from this court," the judge said, "because I guarantee you, that will not work."

"No, Your Honor, I assure you that is not our intention. I will call Mr. Blackstone's physician to testify during these proceedings so you can ask about his medical condition yourself if you'd like."

The DA, Mr. Daley, shrugged his indifference so the judge said, "Very well. The defendant is excused."

"The situation seems clear to me," Mr. Daley said in his opening statement. "The defendant should have been returned to prison as soon as he was arrested."

Mr. Freedman countered with lists of precedents, but the judge cut him off abruptly. "I am hoping to conclude this hearing today. Call your first witness"

Mr. Daley presented records from Sonny's original hearing and the standing arrest warrant. "I'm not going to waste the Court's time in calling any witnesses," he said. "The documentation speaks for itself."

The defense began its case. Mack was the first witness called. He described how Sonny was instrumental to the welfare of the family during the past three years. He described Sonny as honest and hard-working, and emphasized the importance of Sonny's return. "We rely on him for everything, especially now that my father has died. His return is vital to the survival of our farm and our family."

The only question Mr. Daley had for the witness was, "Now that you've learned of Mr. Blackstone's past, are you somewhat apprehensive about having him around the children?"

"Not at all. He never gave us any reason to worry before, so why should we now?"

"My next witness is Benjamin Gibson." Mr. Freedman announced.

Ben approached the stand as casual as if he were walking down the lane to fetch the mail on a summer's day. Mindful of the judge's edict that these proceedings end quickly, Mr. Freedman tried to keep Ben on the subject at hand. He was asked about the fire. "That was right after that big storm, ya' know. It could have been much worse. They took me to the hospital," he said to the judge. "See these scars on my face. The doctor said--"

"Mr. Gibson," Mr. Freedman interrupted, "has Sonny Blackstone been a good neighbor to you these past three years?"

"Oh, he sure was. People were telling me and my misses that we're too old to live out there any more. Ginny is in a wheelchair, and I ain't getting' no younger, ya' know. What if something happened to me and she couldn't get to the phone? It could happen. Our phone service gets knocked out anytime a little wind comes through there."

"Ben, you were telling us what kind of neighbor Sonny has been."

"I was getting to that. One day he comes on the yard with this big old school bell. He put it outside the window and strings it up so Ginny could reach it. That's a damned good idea, don't ya' think?" Once again he turned to speak directly to the judge.

"Well, yes," Judge O'Brien agreed hesitantly, "that's a very good idea."

"Sonny don't say much, ya' know. But he's smart and a real hard worker, too. The Winston's never would have made it if it weren't for him."

Mr. Daley began to question him. "Now that Mr. Blackstone's history has come to light, have your feelings changed about having him as a neighbor?"

The answer was emphatic. "No sir! I don't give a damn about any of that. Why should I? Why in the hell don't ya' just leave 'im alone. He ain't hurtin' nobody!" There were no further questions.

The last defense witness was Dr. Adams. "Is it true," Mr. Freedman asked the witness, "that you were present at Sonny Jackson's original arrest?"

"Yes, I was. It was August of 1966. I accompanied Sheriff Wilkerson to a raid at the Weatherly place. He expected there might be some medical difficulties because of the illegal drugs. He was correct in that assumption. There were two heroine overdoses, and others who were seriously under the influence, including Mr. Jackson, er – Mr. Blackstone."

"How is it that you remembered him so vividly?"

"He was quite young, probably 16 or 17 years old, and he had very unusual scars across his lower hips and back that I'll never forget. He was sent off with the rest of the group. As it says in court records, he pleaded guilty and was sent to prison."

"When did you see him again?"

"He was gravely injured in the summer of 1970. I was astonished when I recognized him."

"Was he screened for any drug use?"

"Yes, he was. The nurses had alerted the doctors in the emergency room of the very noticeable scaring from mainlining, or frequent needle use, so they ran a full drug panel. Everything was negative. In fact, considering the serious surgery he underwent at that time, it was quite remarkable that Sonny used far less narcotic analgesics than normal."

"Is there any proof to substantiate the fact that Mr. Jackson has been drug free?"

"Yes, there is. Each time he came to see me for follow up care, I ran tests on his blood and urine. Happily, I can report that all tests were negative."

"In your opinion, Doctor, would incarcerating this man serve any purpose?"

"Objection!" Mr. Daley exclaimed, jumping up from his chair. "The doctor's opinion of this manner is irrelevant."

"No," the judge said, "I'd like to hear what Dr. Adams thinks."

"Well, I'll say this. An addiction like that is very difficult to overcome. I would say that Sonny has managed to arrive at the desired results. He never hurt anyone except himself. He was not imprisoned for any act of violence. I cannot, in all honesty, see any reason to put this young man back in prison."

"Thank you, Dr. Adams. Your witness," Mr. Freedman said, yielding to his learned colleague at the prosecution table.

Mr. Daley did not rise immediately. Everyone in the room realized he thought the entire ordeal was merely a formality and had thus far had not presented much more than a token attempt of prosecuting his case. "Dr. Adams, how did Mr. Blackstone receive these serious wounds in August of 1970?"

"He received a vicious hit from a young man in a bar with a pool cue. Sonny had one kidney removed and sustained damage to the other."

"Why was such an upstanding citizen in a bar room brawl?"

"Well, it wasn't really a fight. The man hit Sonny when his back was turned. He was walking away because he refused to fight."

"Well, then, er--" Mr. Daley bristled and cleared his throat loudly. "Dr. Adams, isn't it true that it's possible to continue to use drugs and hide it, even from his doctor?"

"No, because he never had any idea I was running those tests in the first place. I did it just to satisfy my own curiosity."

"Curiosity? Because it's likely that this young man will return to his former habits?"

"It's impossible to predict something like that. I am a simple, country doctor. I don't have degrees in psychiatry, only my instincts which tell me that if you leave him alone, in an environment in which he can control and contribute, chances are he'll be fine"

"Yes, well," Mr. Daley pouted, obviously disappointed with the results from that line of questioningly. "No further questions."

"Well, ladies and gentlemen," the judge said, "if neither side has no more witnesses, let's press on with the closing statements and get this done today. Let's be brief, gentlemen."

Mr. Daley did not even stand up. He said simply, "I believe the record on this matter speaks for itself. I believe this man should be remanded over to the authorities and returned to prison as soon as possible. To not do so would make a mockery of this court, which sentenced him correctly in the first place. Thank you."

Mr. Freedman rose from his seat and made a longer and more ingenuous statement. "Your Honor, no one in this court is arguing that Mr. Blackstone did not deserve the sentence he received six years ago. It is also indisputable that when he walked out of Ft. Madison Federal Prison, he had no intention of cooperating with the parole mandate. However, I think we have demonstrated that Sonny Jack Blackstone has managed to became a productive member of society, and is no longer a threat to himself or anyone else. He has achieved the goal of rehabilitation. It costs on average $48.00 a day of tax payer's money to house a prisoner. If Mr. Blackstone serves the remainder of his three and a half year sentence, it will cost at least $59,645. I believe that money could be put to a much better use. I submit his sentence should be commuted, leaving this whole ugly chapter where it belongs – in the past. Thank you."

There was a short recess, and when the judge returned, he said simply, "I order that Sonny Blackstone's sentence be commuted to time served. Good luck to all of you. Court dismissed." Annie cried with happy excitement for the first time in weeks. A major obstacle had been overcome, but she knew the most difficult part still lay ahead – convincing Sonny to stay.

CHAPTER 82

Dr. Adams suggested that the Winston's go home, and he would bring Sonny out to the farm as soon as he was released. Sonny glared at the doctor when he appeared at the cell door. He was still sitting on his bed, covered with only a blanket having refused to get dressed all day. "I ain't taking no more of your damn shots. All I can do in here is sit, and thanks to you, I can't even do that." But his voice cracked as he lapsed into a lengthy coughing spell.

"Just relax," Doc Adams said. "I'm not here to give you any more shots, although I dare say you could use some. I'm here to take you out of here. You're free to go, Sonny. The judge dropped all charges." He paused for a few moments to allow what he was saying to sink in. "C'mon, Sonny, I'm gonna take you home."

The doctor reached out to put his hand on Sonny's shoulder, but he flinched and moved away. "I can't go back there."

"They just want to talk to you. Besides, you'll need your bike to leave, won't you?"

"How'd they do it, anyway?" Sonny asked as they were heading out of town. "They tell the judge what a fine, upstanding citizen I am?"

"Yes, something like that," the doctor said, smiling. "Your lawyer simply made a case around the fact that it would serve no purpose for you to serve the remainder of your sentence. You were arrested on drug charges, and that's no longer an issue."

"How do you know? Hell, I could have been snortin' cocaine or dropping speed this whole time. Just cause I ain't shootin' up no more don't mean nothing."

"Sonny, I'm a doctor. I ran tests and they were always negative. I would think you'd be proud that you got yourself off all that junk. How did you do it, anyway? Did the drug rehab program in prison work for you?"

Sonny laughed at that last comment. "Are you kidding, Doc? Let me tell you something. The only way to get off that stuff is cold turkey. I just decided I had to get out from under it, and I did." It was a simple statement, but the doctor knew such things were never that easy. However, Sonny appeared uncomfortable discussing it, so they rode the rest of the way in silence.

They turned into the driveway. The house was dark, except the kitchen lights. Doc Adams handed him a small bag as he got out of the car. "Here's some medicines to take for your cough," the doctor said. "Then I won't have to give you anymore shots."

"Don't think you have to worry about that, Doc, cause I ain't hanging around, that's for sure." He started to close the door, but then turned and said stiffly, "Thanks – thanks for everything."

He climbed the two steps to the side door and looked through the screen door for a few moments. They were all there – Mack, Penny, Andrew, Luke, and of course, Annie. As soon as she heard his footsteps, she had jumped up and busied herself at the sink.

He walked in and was washed over by the smells and sensations he had tried not to think about while he was away. There was coffee percolating on the counter, the lingering odors of supper, the warmth and easiness that had always been a part of this room.

Andrew was the first to speak. "Hey, man, it's good to see you."

Sonny brushed past him. The hook where his bike keys hung was empty. "I want my keys. Just give 'em to me, and I'll be out of here."

"Don't you think we need to talk?" Andrew asked.

"There's nothin' to talk about. Just give 'em to me. The bike is mine, ain't it?"

"Of course, it is. But Sonny, it's dark and you're not feeling well. What's the hurry? At least stay overnight."

"No, I'm fine. I just want to go – now. Give me the keys."

"How can you just leave?" Mack flung the bike keys onto the table. "After everything we've been through,? Give us a chance to say we're sorry."

"Sorry for what? Sorry that the old man found out the truth and now he's dead?"

For the first time Annie came forward to speak. "It wasn't your fault, Sonny. He was sick for a long time and didn't tell us."

"Besides," Andrew said, "that's all behind us now. C'mon, Sonny, this is your home."

"My home? This was never my home. I was just the hired hand."

"You know that was never true. Look, here's the deed to 160 acres. It's in your name."

Sonny took the paper and slowly read it. He recognized Matthew's signature. But then he wadded it up and threw it onto the floor. "I just want the keys to my bike!"

"Oh, bullshit, Sonny!" Mack jumped up from his seat. "You just can't face us 'cause now we know about your past – the drugs, prison., all of it."

"Get out of my way, and let me go," Sonny snarled.

Mack stood his ground and would not let Sonny pass. "How can you just leave like this? You want us to say you're no good to us any more? That'd make it real easy, wouldn't it. Okay, sure, I understand."

"You understand, huh?" Sonny snarled. "Understand what? You don't know shit."

"Okay," Mack replied, "then tell us."

Sonny began to pace without looking at anyone. His fists were clinched and his face was dark with anger. "Okay, here it is. Your mother died in childbirth, right? Well, so did mine, but it wasn't in no nice, clean hospital. She wasn't sick. Just pregnant and married to the biggest asshole there ever was. There we were, in the middle of nowhere in winter, and my old man decided to go on a two-week drinking binge. And when her time came, man, I didn't know what to do. I just watched her and that little baby bleed to death, or freeze to death, I don't know which."

"After she died, my old man didn't have her to kick around anymore, so he beat me. That went on until some dude did me a favor and killed the sonofabitch in a tavern somewhere. So, they gave me to my grandpa. He'd sit for hours and talk about how he wanted to get this place back. He was just a little boy when he watched his father hang, and he never got over it. Talk – that's all he ever did. I loved that old man, but he talked too much."

"And then one day, they told me he had cancer. He begged me to take him home so he could die in his own bed. But I was too young to take care of him, so he just wasted away until he finally died, too."

"And what do they do with 12 year old Indian boys with no family? They put them in foster homes. And there's plenty of those on the reservation because it's easy money. They put me by this fat ol' pig who liked having us boys keep her company at night. Yes sir, I took my turn keepin' that bitch happy." He was staring at Annie as he talked, and when she began to cry, he walked quickly around the table, grabbed her shoulders, and began to shake her. "You wanted to know the truth, so here it is! Are you listening?"

"But see, I didn't like it, so I kept running away, and they kept catching me. I went from one stinking home to another. But then one of my dear old, foster daddy's introduced me to a whole other way of bustin' loose. You light up or take a pill, sit back and start flying. It was beautiful, man. Just rip off some old lady's purse, and you could buy anything you wanted after Daddy got his cut. The only problem was, I wasn't very good at it. The juvie judge and I were on a first name basis. But after a while it seemed real clear that I showed no signs of redemption, so he decided society would be better off if they put me in one of those juvenile homes – those cozy little places with high, barbed wire fences and bars on the windows. Didn't take me long to figure out that I didn't like that place neither, so I split."

"And this time they didn't catch me, cause I was smart and left the county. I was free, but didn't know what to do or where to go, so I just headed out and found this place. Grandpa showed me on a map hundreds of times. But when I got here, it was nothin' like he said. Instead of the land of milk and honey, I found this rundown, broken place with this bunch of rich, hippie freaks. It was great – all the free dope I wanted as long as I went along with their sick gang bangs. Jeez, do you Ivy Leaguers even know what that is? It's a lot of fun – bunch of spaced out, stinkin' gorks, slimmin' all over each other --"

"Sonny, stop it." Annie cried. "Why are you doing this?"

"Why? Because you all said you wanted the truth, right? Well, let me tell you that was a great summer. Right here, in this house. They introduced me to new pleasures, like heroine and LSD. There I was, living in this house like I promised my poor ol' grand pappy, only I was so strung out, I couldn't remember how to piss, much less anything else."

"But good things can't last forever, right? The Sheriff and his boys came riding in here like the Lone Ranger and rounded us all up. The strip search wasn't hard, though, cause we were mostly naked anyway. Good ol' Doc Adams was there, too. Bet he already told you – hell, he probably told the whole courtroom today how he recognized me. I guess my ass must have made quite an impression on him. I bet he never seen scars like the ones my daddy left me with." His voice cracked then and his shoulders slumped for just a moment. But then he pulled himself erect and continued, punctuating his next words with pointed clarity.

"Anyway, we all pleaded guilty and were sent to the federal pen at Ft. Madison. We were given the drug rehab routine, which was a joke. Besides, it didn't take me long to learn how things worked in there. Just like anywhere else, you show respect to the ones with the power, the guys who control everything inside those walls, even the guards. They could have anything they wanted and were more than willing to share, especially with the junkies like me. All us little guys had to do was keep those bastards happy."

"I was in there for 18 months – a real model prisoner. I was given parole the first time my name came up. I walked out of there with nothing except the name of my parole officer in one hand and a list of drug contacts in the other. But I couldn't do it anymore. I just started walking and never stopped until I got here. I laid down in the grass out there behind the house, used my last hit, and decided that was enough. That was it! No more!"

"I stayed here that summer. Hid mostly – ate squirrel and fish, even stole some vegetables out of Gibson's garden. By the time fall came, I decided it was time to do something about getting this place. I hated to see it so empty and tore up. So, I found the guy in Chicago and learned he lost the deed to some other mob guy in New York. I followed the trail, and that's how I ended up being at Gonatelli's poker game that night. I was waiting for him to make a mistake, and he did. He laid down a straight against Matthew's full house."

"I followed the old man into the street that night. I didn't know what I was going to do. I mean, there was this guy in a tuxedo with a shit load of money. Why would a guy like that give a rip about a farm in the middle of nowhere? I guess I would have talked to him or maybe mugged him, but Gonatelli's goons beat me to it. I ended up helping him and jeez! I thought he was nuts. He started blabbing about moving his family out here. I didn't think there was anyway you'd last more than a couple of months. I was gonna just play along until you got tired of it and be here to take it off your hands."

"Things didn't work out like I figured, but that's okay. You're in good shape here. I taught you all I know, and I faked most of that. I don't belong here anymore." Without looking at anyone, he stepped toward the door, but then stopped mid-stride. "Thanks for getting me out of jail," he said, reaching for the keys Mack had thrown on the table. And then, he was gone.

Annie reached down and picked up the deed Sonny had thrown onto the floor. "I don't care about any of that. I can't lose him!" But then she slumped against the door frame. "What if I can't make him understand?"

Andrew stood up and put his arms around her trembling shoulders. "Don't let him walk away like this. Tell him we all need him, but not nearly as much as he needs us." Annie kissed her twin and went out into the night.

* * * * * *

Sonny didn't waste any time. He went to the feed shed, grabbed two burlap bags of oats, and dumped them out on the floor. He hurried back to his shed and began emptying his dresser drawers. He came across the picture Joey had drawn while he was at the hospital after his surgery. For a fleeting moment he wondered what Joey would say when the boy realized his friend was gone, but then he wadded up the drawing and threw it aside.

"It's easy to throw away a piece of paper, Sonny," Annie's voice broke in, "but what about people? What about us? Can you throw us away, too?"

"There is no 'us', Annie." He did not look at her.

"Yes, there is and you know it. And what's so terrible about that? Why can't you have happiness or love? Love, Sonny – you can't even say the word."

He picked up his bags and began to walk away. "Let it go, Annie, just let it go."

"Why the hell should I?" She grabbed him and flung him around to face her. "None of that stuff matters – it doesn't change anything. I know you tried to make it sound as vulgar and disgusting as possible so--"

"I didn't try to make it sound vulgar or disgusting – that's just the way it was. And I sure as hell don't need your pity--"

"Pity? You're right. You feel sorry enough for yourself."

"Oh, that's what you think? I don't need this shit! And I sure as hell don't need you!" He brushed past her and headed for the door.

"Like hell you don't," she cried. "I'm your last chance. What do you think is going to happen to you if you walk out of here? You need me, all right, but what you need more than anything is this place, this farm. Why do you think you kept coming back here? If you leave, you'll end up crawling into some hole and die. Why are you giving up without a fight?"

"A fight? Who or what am I supposed to fight? How can I fight to hold onto something I never had in the first place?"

"What about this?" She held up the deed to the 160 acres. "This is yours, damn it." He turned away and stepped closer to the door. "Sonny, you can't go. You can't. Please." She tried to hold him back, but he threw her aside and she fell onto the floor..

"Stop it," he cried. "I have to go." He picked up his bags again and headed for the door.

Desperate, heart-broken tears streamed down her face. She crouched on the floor, wrapped her arms around herself, and began rocking back and forth. "If you leave, you should know everything you're leaving – everything. I'm pregnant, Sonny."

He froze for a few moments, but then dropped the bags, turned, and lunged toward her. "You're going to get rid of it. You hear me? Get rid of it!" He grabbed her and shook her hard. "You get an abortion!"

"You're hurting me, Sonny," she winced. "I would never do that, never. This baby is mine, too, and I want it even if you don't!" She struggled to free herself from his grip, but she couldn't.

"Weren't you listening to me before? That was no fairy tale. I'm talkin' heroine, coke, LSD. And what about those filthy sluts and – No, get rid of it – right away! There's gonna be something wrong with it."

"Sonny, listen to me. I've seen Doc Adams. He said everything is fine."

"He don't know shit! He can't look inside you and see this baby!"

"There are tests. We did some already, and we can do more when I'm further along."

"No, Annie, this is wrong! I didn't want this to happen. I should have left after--"

"When we nearly made love the first time? If you left, you would have ripped my heart out of my chest. I love you, and I love this baby."

"This should have never happened. I'm telling you, this is no good." He brushed her away and picked up his bags again.

"What are you doing?" she screamed.

"The biggest favor I can do for you is just walk out of here."

"Why? What are you afraid of? We belong here – together. Why can't you see that?"

"You don't know what you're saying. You're so damn confident – like everything is all worked out, like we're going to have this perfect life. It won't be like that."

"Why not? These last three years were the happiest years of your life."

"But it was all built around a lie!"

"No, it wasn't. I read that newspaper article. Your great-grandfather said someday this place would belong to his sons or his sons' sons. You are here. I'm here. This was meant to be."

He let the bags slip from his hands as he sank onto the floor. "But what about the rest of it? I don't know how to be a husband or a father. What if I can't give you what you need? People like me – we never learned how to…"

"To love? You think you don't know how to love? Oh, Sonny, you show it every time we talk or smile across the table. What about Joey, and the way you taught Peter how to bottle feed that runt pig and tied those knots in Danny's Cub Scout book." She held him in her arms and kissed him, but confusion and fear still showed in his eyes. "It's like the way you feel about this place. I couldn't understand it at first – how could anyone get so emotional about a pile of dirt and rocks, but that showed me you were capable of caring You gotta trust me, Sonny, and trust yourself. We're gonna be fine!" She kissed him again, but then he swept her into his arms and held her so tightly she could scarcely breathe.

"If you marry me, I'll take good care of you and our baby. I swear it."

They held each other on the cold, cement floor until Annie became aware that he was trembling. She led him to his bed and piled all the blankets she could find. As she crept in beside him, she murmured a familiar phrase.

"What did you say?" he asked.

"It's something from the Bible that Ginny taught me. It says, 'If two lie together, they are warm. How can one be warm who sleeps alone?' I'll keep you warm, Sonny, I promise."

Gradually, Sonny's shivering lessened and his breathing became easier. She assumed that he would sleep, but he began to talk. He told Annie about his family. "My mother was beautiful. The thing I remember about her the most was her eyes – sad, dark ones. She was slender and always carried herself so erect and proud which used to piss off my old man. He hated being an Indian and never let her speak the language or practice the old ways."

"Everything I know about my people came from my grandfather. I remembered a lot of the chants and stories when I was in jail. My people are the Mesquakie. It means the 'Red Earth People'. The name 'Fox' was given to them by the White Man and they hate it. They were always getting pushed around, chased off their lands by the bigger tribes, like the Iroquois. Then the French pushed them across the Mississippi in the 1600's. They lived here, on the west side of the river, for about a hundred years."

Sonny's voice sang with more emotion than she had ever heard from him before. As he spoke, he emerged from the shadows and was revealed to her as a person with dimension and texture, and she fell in love with him all over again. He talked of how his people had been forced off the land in Eastern Iowa and forcibly moved to a worthless tract of land in Kansas in the 1840's. There were no rivers or woods there, only endless prairies and skies. In order to obtain the money promised to them by the U.S. Army, the Mesquakie had to attend the Christian churches and send their children to government schools. The people suffered terribly, especially when small pox spread through the villages. It was then that many of the Mesquakie decided to secretly save their money and buy back their lands between the Iowa River and the Mississippi.

"My family stayed behind for a long time until my great-grandfather and two other young men had enough money to break away and buy some land, too. They wanted the piece of land they called 'place of the shinning stone' because of the way the rocky place shines in the morning sun. They believed that this place had strong medicine and would make their hearts strong again. Instead, it was a disaster." Sonny sighed deeply as he finished. There was a sadness and frustration that spilled over from generation to generation.

"You'll have a lot to tell," Annie whispered.

"What?"

"To our children – you'll have a lot to teach them."

"I guess so," he said. She could feel him smiling in the darkness until he finally slept.

CHAPTER 83

"Annie, it's after seven o'clock. Wake up."

"God! I'd better go see what's going on up at the house." She was thrilled when he leaned over and kissed her.

He reached for his boots. "I'll see about the chores."

Mack came walking across the yard just as Sonny stepped outside. He had two cups of coffee and motioned for Sonny to join him at the rocky place. "God!" Mack exclaimed as they neared, "I can't stand all that racket this early in the morning. I don't know how Annie does it."

They sipped their coffee, watching the crows and hawks circling over the flooded waters in the bottom which looked more like a peaceful Minnesota lake than a river bottom It would have been a pretty sight except both men knew there should be a rows of foot high corn down there, not water.

"I guess we're gonna get married," Sonny blurted. "I mean, if it's all right – I mean, you're the head of the family now, right?"

"Good. That's what we were all hoping for, you know." Mack slapped his future brother-in-law on the back. "You had us a little scared last night. But when your bike was still parked over there this morning, I figured you were staying. My sister can be very persuasive when she wants something. And Sonny Boy, she's had her sights on you for quite awhile."

"Did you know she's pregnant?"

"Yeah, Penny told me a while back. That's not the only reason you're staying, is it?"

Sonny plucked out a long reed of grass and chewed on it for a while. "Nah, but I can't believe you don't have a problem with this after everything – you know, everything I said."

"You know what they say about throwing stones and glass houses. I nearly fucked up my life with drinking and womanizing, and I was born into a great family. I know you'll take care of her and your baby, and that's all I care about. She's crazy about ya', man."

Just then, Annie, Penny, Andrew, Luke, and Margaret came out to join them. Penny went straight to Sonny and gave him a big hug. "Congratulations!" she exclaimed. "Finally, we have some good news around here!"

Peter called from the house that Mr. Freedman was on the phone. The lighthearted atmosphere disappeared. "I'll take it," Andrew groaned.

"What's going on?" Sonny studied the solemn faces surrounding him.

"He's pushing us to get some legal stuff done," Mack explained. "He wants us to make a decision about guardianship of the kids. I guess he knows his stuff. He got your ass out of jail, didn't he?"

"What do you have to decide?"

"We gotta make sure everything is wrapped up all neat and tidy so Aunt Esther won't try to swoop down and try to take the kids again."

"So?" Sonny shrugged, reaching down to pick up another blade of grass, "The guy knows his shit, so what's the problem?"

No one said anything at first, as quick, cautious glances passed between them. "The kids have to have legal guardians," Mack explained. "What if Joey needs surgery or the kids need consents signed for school? Since you and Annie are getting married soon, it makes sense that you two should be guardians."

Sonny sprang from his perch. "Are you out of your damned minds? That lawyer ain't no miracle worker. You want him to ask some judge to give custody of five children to a guy

693

with my record? It'll never happen."

Andrew rejoined the group. "He wants to come out this afternoon. He says he can't stall Social Services much longer."

"C'mon, Sonny," retorted Penny. "We realize this is a tremendous responsibility, but Mack and I will be close by."

"Wouldn't it be better for you and Mack be their guardians?"

"We talked about that," Mack said, "but that's not what the kids need. Annie has mothered these kids for three years and done a damned good job. Penny has a career and has her hands full with Katie. We're settled into our own place. This is where the kids belong."

"Sonny," Annie cried, "the judge set you free because you deserved it. Anyone who looks at the facts will see that. No one loves the kids more than we do. We can do this, I know we can."

Sonny turned to look at her and the others. "Well, I guess, we could talk to the lawyer and see what he has to say. But if he says he don't think this will work, we'll have to come up with something else, all right?" The others nodded. "Anyway, this farm won't work itself. Ain't there some work to do?"

Sonny started off toward the barnyard when Annie said, "Wait. There's something I want you to see." She led him around the back of the barn, through the back field, to the little cemetery.

Sonny stared at the new gravestones. "God, I miss him," he said.

"I know, Sonny, I do, too. But every time I come here, I feel such a sense of peace. We wanted to put a marker by your great-grandfather's grave, too, but we didn't know if there's...you know, rules or customs. We thought we should wait and ask you. It wasn't hard to have my mother brought here. You could have your grandfather moved here, too. Would you like that?"

Sonny didn't respond, so she continued. "We'll be buried here, too – you, me, Mack and Penny, Andrew– we all will, I guess. It's pretty up here, don't you think?"

"This is going so fast, Annie," he exclaimed. "Twenty four hours ago I was sitting in jail, thinking I was done for. And then you tell me you're pregnant and we're getting married. And now this guardianship thing?"

694

"We have to. There's no choice really. That's a bunch of pretty terrific kids. We can do this."

He gazed at her then, standing so erect and proud like a beautiful princess with a magnificent kingdom at her feet. He envied her strength and conviction. He took her in his arms and kissed her. "I love you," he whispered.

She took his face in her hands and smiled deep into his eyes. "I've been waiting to hear those words. Next time, don't make me wait so long, okay?"

* * * * * *

Mr. Freedman came promptly at 2:00. He reached out to shake Sonny's hand, saying he was glad to see his ex-client under happier circumstances. He seemed genuine and friendly enough, but still Sonny didn't trust these lawyer types. They went in the house and sat around the table to talk, but Sonny preferred to stand back in his usual corner.

"Well," Mack began, "we all agree that Annie and Sonny should be the legal guardians. They're engaged and will live here in this house, so they're the logical choice."

"As I told you before," Mr. Freedman said in his best lawyer voice, "the ultimate decision will be made by a judge. He will largely base his decision on an in-depth report completed by a court-appointed social worker."

Sonny sighed deeply, turned his back to the group, and stared out the window. The inference of that statement was obvious to everyone in the room. "Mr. Freedman," Annie spoke up, "what you're trying to say is that with Sonny's record, a judge might be hesitant to award guardianship. Well, we all discussed it and decided that this is the best way."

"Well, if that's what you want, then I suggest we go full steam ahead. You'd better get married as soon as possible. As soon as you set a date, I'll file the preliminary petitions at the court-house."

There was still one question that needed to be asked. Luke said it out loud. "What happens if the judge says no? I don't want to think about it, but we have to cover all the bases, right?"

"Basically, the judge can award custody to anyone he wants. Granted, the options are rather limited, especially since there's so many of them and there's no other relatives living in this jurisdiction. He might look elsewhere, like your relatives back East. Mack and Penny are a little more established as a married couple, but of course, they have a separate residence. I suppose we do have to consider the possibility of foster homes."

"No!" Sonny blasted as he sprang across the room. "No way are those kids goin' to no damn foster home. Just do your job like Annie said and tell that social worker she can come out here any time she wants – night or day. We got nothin' to hide!" He punctuated his demands by slamming the door behind him as he walked out. The others disbanded as well.

Since the meeting was obviously concluded, Mr. Freedman began to pack up his briefcase as Thomas sauntered into the kitchen, having just awakened at 2:45 in the afternoon. "Hey, man," he sneered sarcastically, "how's it hanging?"

"Mr. Freedman," Annie said nervously, "this is one of my brothers, Thomas." She was embarrassed because her brother was obviously hung over or high and had the foul stench of one who hadn't bathed lately. The lawyer openly stared, but said nothing.

Annie followed him out to the car. "We should have warned you about Thomas. He's our problem child – has been for several years."

"Well, he could be a real big problem now. We don't need any more issues than we already have. You say that you and Sonny can handle this family. You'd better start with him."

Annie rushed back into the kitchen just as Thomas was heading back upstairs. "You asshole!" she cried. "Why did you have to come in here like that! You knew we were having a meeting with the lawyer today!"

"Yeah, right. How in the hell was I supposed to know that?"

"Oh, I forgot! You just sleep here occasionally but never have meaningful conversations with anyone. You don't even take a bath, for Christ sake! You reek!"

"Ah, Sis, that's so sweet! I didn't know you cared!"

"You arrogant, self-centered sonofabitch! We have one of the toughest fights imaginable in front of us, and you act like this?"

"Oh, poor baby! Do tell. What's going on in your humdrum, middle class existence?"

"Isn't it obvious? Sonny and I are going to court to try to get guardianship of all you kids. Otherwise, they'll pack everyone back to Aunt Esther or worse, foster homes! That man is our lawyer. And guess what he said after seeing you for thirty seconds! You're a problem – a very big problem!"

"I don't need no goddamn guardian!"

"This isn't about you, Thomas. It's about the other kids. If they find out we have a drugged out, deadbeat brother that cannot be controlled, then maybe they think we can't handle anything. They'll try to split up the family!"

She began to cry, but he showed no pity. "Oh tisk, tisk! They ain't gonna do that. Besides, maybe we could work out a little deal like I did with Pop. I could go into court and lie through my teeth. I'll say that next to the Virgin Mary, you're the best little mommy there ever was! And Boy Wonder out there! Well, who cares if he has a police record a mile long and the personality of a wet blanket!"

"Don't you dare insult Sonny! At least he's here when we need him! Not like you -- you just hide in a bottle or escape to la la land with your drugs."

"Oh, I get it. You want me to leave? Just disappear? Out of sight, out of mind, right?"

"That's not what I said! You put us through hell the other time you left. I thought I'd be relieved to have you gone, but it wasn't that way at all. I was worried sick about you. If you were in trouble, who would you turn to?"

"It sure the fuck wasn't anyone here," he said with cold, unfeeling eyes.

"Then you're a fool. We're your family, and whether you realize it or not, in the end, we're the only ones you can count on. Those so-called friends of yours will come and go, but we're right here! Why can't you see that?"

He turned to walk away. "If this is all we got, then we're in deep shit!"

Annie had a very unsettled feeling the rest of the day. She knew there had to be a decision made whether to ignore him or try to fix it. Thankfully, she did not have to make that decision alone. She brought it up that night when she and Sonny were sitting with Penny and Mack on the back porch.

"I've been going crazy all day," she cried, "but then I kept wondering if maybe I'm making too big a deal out of this – he'll be eighteen in a few months and besides, Daddy couldn't control him either, so why should we try?"

"But Annie," Mack said, "this could blow up in our faces when we go to court. The whole town knows he's a druggie. What if they bring it up? Maybe we should make a deal with him like he said – just pay him to get out of town."

"Mack!" his wife retorted. "I can't believe you said that! He has a real problem – a life threatening problem! People die from drug addictions! Maybe we could have him locked up in one of those drug rehab places?"

"I thought of that," Annie said. "I even called that place in Chicago this afternoon. In the first place, there's a waiting list a mile long, and it's very expensive."

"I know what I'd do," Sonny said quietly. "Get him off this stuff as soon as possible."

"How, Sonny?"

"Just take keep somewhere until he's off it."

"You mean cold turkey?"

"Yeah. It works better than those fancy detox centers. You get that sick, you're less likely to go back on it."

"I don't know, Sonny," Penny responded, sounding very professional. "It's risky and not always effective. I could call Doc Adams and--"

"I could do it. It takes about 48 to 72 hours." No one said anything, so he went on. "Where is he now?"

"He left right after we talked. Who knows when he'll show up again."

"The best place to find him is at his supplier. That's Curtis Peet, right? How about it, Mack? We'll wait for him to show up over at Curtis' place, and then I'll take it from there." As usual, no one argued. They headed out.

"Man, Annie, when that guy decides to do something, he doesn't waste any time, does he?" Penny exclaimed.

"I know, and I love it."

CHAPTER 84

Sonny drove the car into a field and parked it in the brush. They walked the last quarter mile and hid behind the garage where they had a full view of the both entrances to the rundown, shabby house. There was nothing do to but wait.

The house was quiet and dark even though the Joe's dilapidated Pontiac was parked out front. An hour later, they were shocked to see Janet Evans, the coach's wife, drive up. She walked up to the front door and knocked several times before she resorted to yelling and kicking. A light went on in the rear of the house, and someone came to the door.

"Hey, what do ya' think! I got all day?" she cried. "Give me my stuff!"

Curtis looked around anxiously. "Good God, woman! You want to tell the whole damn neighborhood?" He motioned for her to step inside. She reappeared as she zipped her purse and thrust money into Curtis' fist. She left without saying another word.

After she left Curtis and Kitty started arguing. It was sounded as though it was a continuation of a long-standing discussion. "I told you, I don't mind you selling the stuff to adults," Kitty said, "but not the kids."

"Since when do you give a shit about a bunch of spoiled brats?" Curtis yelled. "Don't get all high and mighty on me, missy!"

"I'm not! I just don't like it, that's all, especially the boy."

"You mean Thomas? Don't waste your time worrying about that dumb bastard, unless you got a thing for young boys?"

"No, Joe, that ain't it."

"It better not be, bitch! I'm keeping my eye on you two,

you know. We got that gig tomorrow night in town, and then I think we should split! You're ready for the big Apple. Would ya' like that, baby, go to New York?"

"I don't know. Eddie. My dad would be real upset if I leave again."

"You saying you don't want to go with me? I say we're leaving, so we're leaving." There was more yelling. Eddy slapped her a couple of times, and they began to run from room to room.

"Right out of *Better Homes and Gardens*, aren't they?" Mack sneered..

Then things were quiet and time dragged by slowly. About 12:30, Sonny noticed a small light bobbing up and down as it came nearer. It must be a bicycle lamp, Sonny thought as he shook Mack awake. It was Thomas riding on the handlebars of Jimmy's bicycle.

"Thomas, you just oughta forget it," Jimmy said. "As soon as Curtis finds out you ain't got no money, he'll turn you down flat. Let's go!"

Thomas knocked on the door. "Yeah? I'll tell him I can sneak back in my house later and get some dough. He'll give me a fix, I know he will. Besides, tomorrow is our big gig. He won't let me crash tonight."

"Well, boys," Curtis called out cordially as he opened the door. "C'mon in here. What can I do for ya'?"

"My sister and I had this big fight so I had to leave the house before I had a chance to nab some cash. I can't get any until everyone's down for the night. But you know I'm good for it! I really need it bad, man. You know, one of those specials you've been giving me lately." There was a thinly masked hint of desperation in his tone.

"Hmmm," Curtis sighed. "So you're getting some heat at home, aye?"

"Yeah, I think it's time to clear out of there. My sister's a nag, and I hate bein' around those jerks. But right now, I need some stuff real bad."

"Well, I'll tell you what. We're getting paid $500 for that gig tomorrow night. I'll give you some stuff and take it out of your share. How's that?"

Thomas mumbled his agreement as he rolled up his sleeve. Curtis prepared the stuff as he chatted. "Too bad about the money, though kid, cause me and Kitty were plannin' on hittin' the road tomorrow right after the show. If you don't have no money, you can't go – what with expenses and all."

"He can have my share," Tommy said. "Then he could go, right?"

"Your share?" Curtis sneered. "What the hell are ya' talkin' about?"

Thomas was trembling as Curtis handed him the dripping syringe. He thrust the needle in, and the reaction was immediate. Sonny watched through the window and clinched his teeth as he remembered the warm, tingling sensation as the stuff begins to pulsate through the veins.

"Okay, kid, get out of here!" Curtis said, dismissing them with a wave of his hand.

"Couldn't we stay here tonight?" Thomas mumbled. "I don't want to go back there."

"No way, kid. Get out of here! Me and Kitty got plans to make."

"You're gonna leave, Joe?"

"I said we were, didn't I."

"What about the band? We gotta have Kitty. And what will she do without us?"

"Kitty can always catch on with another group. I'm tired, kid. Get out of here."

"But, if you leave, where can I get the stuff?"

"Don't worry, kid. I'll check around and give ya' a couple of names tomorrow night. Go home and get some sleep. You look like shit!"

As soon as the bike started past them, Sonny and Mack each grabbed one of the boys, putting their hands over their mouths so they couldn't alert anyone in the house.

"Come along, Thomas," Sonny hissed. "We're taking you home." He put the car in neutral and it rolled down the hill, away from the house.

Thomas began to complain, but Mack cut him off cold.

"Just shut up. We're taking you home. What about you, Jim? Is it safe for you to go home?"

"Yeah, sure. Drop me off on the corner."

When they got home, Thomas jumped out of the car and started toward the house. "Not so fast, kid!" Sonny commanded, grabbing him by the arm. "Everybody's asleep in there, and I don't want you to bother them. You're gonna stay with me tonight." He pushed Thomas in the direction of the shed.

"Oh, wow! What a punishment! Anything but that! Give me the electric chair, please!" He turned and jeered defiantly in his jailer's face.

Sonny shoved the boy through the door. "Now, buddy boy, let's have some facts. How long have you been main-lining? How often do you need it? And what do you take in between to get by?"

"Man, you really know about this shit, don't ya', Mr. Big Shot Jackson, or whatever the hell your real name is. You know what they say. Once a junkie, always a junkie! Just get the hell out of my face!"

Sonny responded by jerking Thomas across the room and shoved him against the wall. He took Thomas's arm and pushed up his sleeve, exposing the needle marks. "You can stand here and insult me all you want. But sooner or later, I'm gonna find out the truth because all I have to do is sit back and let it happen." He flung the kid onto the bed.

He paced across the room with hands on his hips. "You're right! I do know all about it. I know exactly how you feel right now – all warm and fuzzy, right? Like all you wanna do is just curl up and sleep cause the only time you really sleep anymore is after a fix. Otherwise, those creepy-crawly's start jumpin' around in your gut. Yeah, I know all about it!" He pushed his bed in front of the door and began to undress. "Us adults talked it over and we decided to let you go ahead and play your big dance tomorrow night."

"Adults? Like hell," Thomas shouted, still glaring. "I don't give a shit what you think you decided. You can't make me do nothing I don't want to."

"Cut the crap. I heard you make a deal with Curtis. You're

in to him for some money, and he'd be pissed as hell if his star musician didn't show up." He could see Thomas was struggling to concentrate, so Sonny shut off the light and let him sleep.

* * * * * *

The next day was the 4th of July. The town was decked out in full regalia, complete with carnival rides, corn roasts, and band concerts in the park. There was a parade at noon, tractor pulls all afternoon, and of course, the annual street dance at night.

Thomas was allowed to sleep late. Sonny packed the pick-up and went to Dr. Lamp's cabin for a couple of hours. He said he needed to get the place ready, such as hiding the knifes and locking the windows and shutters from the outside. And when Thomas awakened at 3:45 in the afternoon, everyone ignored him, no questions, no hassles. He didn't suspect a thing.

Thomas changed into clean blue jeans and a tie-dyed T-shirt and headed outside. But Sonny appeared on the scene, dressed in nice clothes, and Annie came downstairs in a dress. "We're gonna go listen to ya' play, Thomas," Annie said, smiling. "We can take you into town, okay?"

"Nah, that's all right. Curtis and Kitty will be here soon to pick me up. They got the truck with all the equipment."

Sonny picked up the phone and motioned for Thomas to use it. "Just call 'em and say you'll meet 'em later."

An hour later, Sonny and Annie delivered Thomas to the bandstand, where the members of the band were setting up. Sonny remained very visible, lounging near by. "Hey, what's that all about?" Curtis sneered. "Did you tell him something?"

"No, man, I didn't say anything, honest. He just appointed himself my lord and master. I'm cutting out as soon as this is over." Thomas was getting jumpy and nervous, partly because of the show, but also because he was already starting to get the cravings.

"Hey, kid," Kitty said, smiling, "this is our big night, huh? I've been waiting a long time to show this town what I can do."

"I know, but I'm so nervous. You got anything to take off the edge?"

703

"Sure," Curtis retorted, "Kitty's got some nice stuff."

"Thomas!" Jim cried. "My God, they're watching us like a hawk!"

Thomas nonchalantly took two of the little white pills. "Nah, everything's cool. You worry too much." By the time the music started, he was loose and feeling good.

Sonny, Annie, and the rest of the family sat back to listen. The band performed a wide range of music, trying to keep everyone happy. Gauging by the full dance floor, they were very successful. Annie watched her brother carefully. She could see how totally absorbed he was in what he was doing, with so much emotion flowing through his guitar and his singing.

Right before the first intermission, the rest of the band left the stage except for Thomas who sat on a stool with his guitar. He launched into a rendition of Neil Diamond's "I Am, I Said". He started quietly, with people straining to hear the words, but it gradually gained sound and power until his whole body was moving with the rhythm and mood of the song. The whole audience was swept away by the sheer force of the words. It was a stunning success. Annie wiped away a tear, thinking how sad it was that someone with so much passion had so much difficulty expressing it. The greater tragedy was that their father never recognized it or ever took the time to explore it.

* * * * * *

The dance was over at midnight amid uproarious applause and cheering. Thomas and the others packed up the truck as they slapped each other on the back and congratulated each other on the night's huge success. Thomas was having so much fun, basking in the limelight, that he forgot his plan of slipping away undetected. He had no choice but to go home. He paled when they turned into the lane leading to Dr. Lamp's summer cottage. "Hey!" he cried. "What the hell is going on here?"

"You and me are going to spend a few days here, Thomas." Sonny began to unload the truck just as Thomas leaped out of the cab and ran into the brush. Sonny caught him and brought him back.

"Annie!" Thomas pleaded. "Don't leave me with this lunatic."

"No, you need to get rid of this poison. Sonny knows what to do."

"You think I'm a junkie, but I'm not, I swear."

Annie could barely look at her brother. "Listen to me. I don't understand the reasons why you got mixed up in all this, but I know you're in over your head. Sonny says this is the best way to get over it. And when it's over, we can sit down and talk." She reached over to stroke his wavy hair.

He slapped her hand away. "You're nothing but a traitor, and I hate you."

"Oh, Sonny, he's so scared," she implored in low tones. "Are you sure this is the only way? He's so young and--" But Sonny's face was set and there was no reason to continue. "I hate to think of you doing this alone. Let me stay, please. I could help you."

"This is not something you'd wanna see." He opened the driver's side door and motioned for her to climb in. "Now go!"

"You can't do this," Thomas screamed. "There are laws against this sort of thing. You wanna go back to jail? You will! I'll see to it, I swear!"

Sonny didn't answer, which further infuriated the boy. He screamed every abusive, insulting thing he could think of, but Sonny laid down on the couch, folded his arms across his chest, and waited. When Thomas finally wore out and dozed off, Sonny tied a rope around the kid's ankle and the other end around his own. And then he slept.

When the dawn broke, so did the trouble. Thomas woke with tremendous cravings, begging for a fix. By sundown, he was screaming. The vomiting and the convulsion-like spasms began the next morning. Thomas cried that he wanted to die. Sonny stayed by his side, washing his writhing body and protecting him from himself. As the long hours passed and the extreme exhaustion settled upon him, Sonny began to have a sensation of detachment as though he was hovering above, seeing himself lying there screaming and clawing until each spasm of pain that seized Thomas's body seemed to penetrate his, and he couldn't separate the boy's suffering from his own.

By Monday night, Annie couldn't stand it any longer, and drove to the cottage. It seemed quiet when she arrived. The door was still locked but she had a key. She peered through the darkness and could see at a glance that the place was a mess with an overwhelming stench of vomit and perspiration. Thomas was lying on a bare mattress, nearly naked, and Sonny was sitting nearby on a chair, slumped over with his head resting near Thomas'.

She touched Thomas first, just to make sure he was still alive, and then Sonny. He startled at the slightest movement and bolted upright. "Oh, Annie, it's you," he mumbled. "I guess the worst is over, but I thought we agreed you'd stay away until I called." Annie pulled him onto his feet and helped him over to the other bed. He teetered on the edge of the cot while she helped him peel off his soiled and torn clothes. "It was pretty bad, Annie," he said. "The kid did pretty good, though." She said nothing as she helped him to lay down. "He's pissed as hell at me. He's got a lot of stuff to work out."

"I know," she whispered kissing him on the cheek. You both need to sleep. I'll stay here and keep an eye on him." She moved around the cabin, quietly trying to clean up the worst of the mess. She opened a window to remove the oppressively stagnate air. As she worked, she thought of her parents. Perhaps it wasn't fair to blame their father for his lack of concern and failure to nurture his children because Mother had always attended to the emotional needs of the family. For the first time, she wondered if perhaps they were so dependent on her love that they never learned how to care for each other. Maybe she concentrated so much on fostering individuality in each of her children that they never learned how to appreciate each other's talents.

She checked Thomas and then crawled into bed with Sonny, feeling his slow, rhythmic breathing against her. It occurred to her that this man who had known very little love in his life was teaching them to love unconditionally. It was the ultimate paradox.

CHAPTER 85

The next morning, Annie was the first to awaken. Opening the doors and windows, she stepped out onto the porch and stretched her arms, but sensed she was not alone. Huddled in the corner was Jim Mathers. His father did not spare his face this time. The boy was trembling as Annie helped him onto his feet and took him inside. "Oh, Jimmy, I'm so sorry he did this to you. Here, drink some coffee."

"Is Thomas all right?" he asked, staring at his friend.

"Yes, he's going to be fine. He had a pretty rough time of it, but Sonny says the worst is over. C'mon, now, you lie down here and get some rest." He didn't argue and fell asleep quickly.

About noon, Annie was sitting on the porch swing when she heard some movement inside. Moments later, Sonny came strolling out, buttoning a clean shirt. "So, it wasn't a dream," he smiled. "You did come in last night." He reached for her hand and kissed it as though to say he was glad to see her.

"Did you see Jimmy? I came out here this morning and found him curled up in the corner like a kitten in the rain." She handed Sonny her coffee.

He took a long drink and sat quietly for a few moments. "And you know what? He didn't do nothin'. He wasn't into any of that stuff. Guess he just liked hangin' out with Thomas." He sipped the coffee. "His father was just lookin' for an excuse to beat him." They heard movement coming from inside the cabin. "Let's go check the boys."

They were both awake. Jimmy was sitting on the edge of Thomas's cot, talking, but stopped as soon as Sonny and Annie walked in.

"Mornin', boys," Sonny said. "How's the stomach, Thomas? Ready for some soup?" Thomas scowled at him and turned away without answering. "You gotta eat something," Sonny tried again, touching his shoulder.

"Don't you touch me, you crazy sonofabitch!" Thomas screamed. "After what you did to me? You come walking in here, all cozy with my sister! You can both go straight to hell!"

"Thomas, listen to me," Annie began. "Sonny did this --"

"Piss on your precious Sonny! I begged him—give me something, anything. God! This asshole would have let me die."

Sonny listened to Thomas' tirade, his hands on his hips, obviously trying to control his temper. But then, he crossed the room in two quick steps and flung Thomas onto the floor. "This is all my fault? Oh, yeah, I was the one who stuffed those pills down your throat and held you down while I shot that junk into your veins, right?"

Thomas leaped to his feet. "I didn't say that! Who asked you anyway. Just get the fuck out of my business!"

"I'll tell you why it's my business, you piss ass idiot! You're not just destroying your own life, kid. You're screwing up the whole family, so it will always be my business!. And let me tell you something, this was nothin'. Oh, you puked a little and had some cramps, but this was Sunday school compared to the real thing -- like shootin' up everything and anything until your brain is so fried, your body ain't even your own any more."

"Till one day, you take a long, hard look at yourself and say, this has got to stop. But quitting? Jesus, even the thought of it makes you feel like you got kicked in the nuts, but you figure you got no choice. Either way, you might die. So you shoot up with your last piece of juice, and real quick before ya' lose your nerve, you find some place to lock yourself in like you're a sick animal. You sit and wait – all alone. No baby-sitter to help you in case you choke – nothin'. You puke and shake and bash into the walls until you're covered with your own blood and vomit. You bite down on your own tongue so many times, it's like raw meat. Your fingers are cut and bleeding from trying to dig yourself out. You don't even know how long you were in there. Hours? Days? And when it's over, you don't ever forget! You remember every awful, disgusting minute."

He stopped to compose himself. "The bottom line, kid, is that you have no one to blame except yourself. You needed to stop before you destroy yourself. Now go take a shower and try to eat something." Then he left.

* * * * * *

Thomas and Jim ate their lunch silently. Annie tried to get Jimmy to tell her what had happened between him and his father, but he was not ready to talk about it. The soup didn't settle very well in Thomas's stomach, so he excused himself and went back to bed. Annie was relieved because she had no idea what to say to him anyway.

She went looking for Sonny and found him stretched out in the sun by the river. He heard her coming and held out his hand, inviting her to join him.

They sat quietly for a few minutes, but then Annie asked, "Is that how you did it?"

He sighed deeply. "After I got out of prison and came back here, I knew I had to get off the junk. I figured that was the only way I could do it."

"God, Sonny, you might have died."

"I guess so, but it was worth it. When Danny got into those honey bees, and we went out to burn all that junk, I torched that corn crib and watched it burn. That's when I knew."

"Knew what, Sonny?"

"That I was home."

* * * * * *

Sonny caught some catfish in the river and Annie fried them for supper. Thomas watched the others eat. His stomach was not ready for fried foods. He sat at the table and stared at his plate.

Sonny didn't talk either. He finished eating and pushed away from the table. "You guys help clean up. I'll be back."

Twenty minutes later he stuck his head in the door and said, "I got a fire goin' down by the river. Come on out here." He retrieved a package he had hidden in the brush and placed it on Thomas' lap. "Annie showed this to me when you came back from New York. I think it was your grandfather's," he explained. Thomas unwrapped a wooden guitar, the polished veneer glistening in the firelight. "Everyone thought it was junk, but you

709

know your sister. She never wants to throw anything away.
There's a man in Dubuque who showed me how to re-glue it and
fix the big hole in the back. Old Mr. Schmidt – that's the guy in
town—says it's a beautiful instrument. Your music is the thing
that could help you get through this. You're good, Thomas, but a
nice acoustical guitar is better than screeching thing you usually
play."

Thomas' hands trembled as he took the instrument,
inspected and tuned it. He tried a couple of different melodies,
and then cleared his throat and began singing a new John Denver
song he had heard on the radio.

> *This old guitar gave me my lovely lady*
> *It opened up her eyes and ears to me.*
> *It brought us close together*
> *And I guess it broke her heart.*

They were mesmerized by the rich clarity that resonated in
his voice and the seemingly effortless way that his fingers danced
across the strings of the old guitar. After he finished that song, he
launched into another, playing the folk songs that Annie loved,
like *Where Have All the Flowers Gone* and *Scarborough Fair*.
She and Jim joined in with harmony on the songs they knew.
Sonny sat quietly, occasionally throwing another log on the fire.
Thomas laughed at their feeble attempts to sing. They were
having fun.

Thomas grew tired and stopped singing, strumming the
guitar softly. "It's a really nice instrument. Thank you." No one
said anything so he continued. "At least I know one thing. I can
still play without the junk,"

"Is that what you thought, Thomas?" Annie asked.

"Sure. I think that's why so many entertainers use all the
time. They're afraid to do it alone – without the stuff, I mean.
You drop some pills, get up on stage, you feel so loose and
reckless. If gives you that freedom to create. You think you need
that edge to play."

"But, I've been listening to you play for a long time now,"
Jimmy retorted, "and I'm telling' ya' you were good before. You

don't need that junk."

"It don't matter none anyway, Jim. The band is done. Kitty and Curtis left town after the gig. They'll never come back. Where we gonna get another lead singer like her?"

"I wouldn't be real sure about them leaving," Sonny spoke up for the first time. "Mack spoke to Sheriff Wilkerson. I think Curtis Peet might be cooling his heels in jail by now."

"What about Kitty?" Thomas pressed. "She used, but she never sold it or nothing."

"Yeah, that was pretty clear by the way she was talking. Maybe if she gets away from that jerk, she can get clean herself. She sure can sing!"

"I've never heard her sing sober. I don't know if she can still rock it without the juice."

"Of course, she can." Annie cried. Thomas said nothing, only stared at the fire. "Is that why you started drugs?" she asked, "Because of your music?"

Thomas hesitated before he answered. "I used to sneak some of Pop's booze and smoke some weed, but I never started using the hard stuff until we went back to New York. I really liked the whole lifestyle – nothing but playing, sleeping, and drugs. It was so wild and free, and my music was getting' better and better, and Pop wasn't paying any attention."

"Did you really hate him like you said?" Annie asked.

"Nah, I didn't hate him – I don't hate the kids either. I don't know why I said that shit. I mean, there were times I wished – like, I knew this kid at the Music Institute who was an only child. His mother was a cellist and his father could play every brass instrument there was. Everything revolved around that kid and music. I always thought he had a prefect life."

"You can't pick your family," Annie said.

"That's for sure!" Jim added emphatically.

"I was so angry when Mother died. I blamed Pop for everything," Thomas continued. "I mean, you had to blame someone, didn't you?"

"You know, for the longest time, I felt guilty that I was so angry that she died – mad at her, I mean," Annie said. "Isn't that stupid?"

Thomas stopped playing abruptly and moved away from the fire. "You know what the worst part is? I never talked to him once after I got back. And now he's dead, and I can't take any of it back. I could have said something – anything."

Annie crossed the clearing and sat next to him. "Did you ever stop to think that he should have been the one to approach you? He was an adult – your father, for heaven's sake. But this is a new start for you. Things are going to be different. I want you to get some counseling, Thomas. There are places you can go to with people who can help you understand this stuff. You gotta go back to school to get your diploma. I have plans for you, kid. Hey, if you get rich and famous, you can support us all, right?" She turned her attention to Jim. "What are you going to do? You're not going home, are you?"

"No way, man! That asshole has beat up on me for the last time. I'm worried about my mom, though. He treats her something awful."

"Why doesn't she leave him?" Annie asked. "I mean, why would she stay with him? It doesn't make any sense."

Jim picked up a stick and snapped it in two. "I don't know. I thought I had to stay if she did, but I just can't anymore

"Don't knock yourself up over this, kid," Sonny said. "Believe me, you can't fix it. The best thing you can do is just walk away. We could give you some money to take to your mom. Tell her to get the hell out of there, start over somewhere new."

"But, Jimmy," Annie added, "you're welcome to stay with us as long as you want, if you think you can stand all the noise and confusion and--"

"Annie's cooking," Thomas teased. "Although I must say, she has improved."

They laughed and talked a little longer, but then it was time to go to bed. It had gone well and Annie was very pleased. She actually had hope that her most troubled brother might be on the right path. As Ginny would say, only time would tell.

* * * * * *

The next morning, they were still all asleep when they heard loud yelling and honking outside. It was Penny, slamming up the driveway in her Jeep. "Annie, you gotta get back to the house," she cried as she ran up the porch steps. "That social worker called twice already this morning. She wants to make an appointment. She'll be calling back soon."

"Okay, then," Annie exclaimed, trying not to panic. "I'll go back home with Penny, and you guys clean this place and lock up. Come home as soon as you can, okay?"

"I didn't think that social worker would come this soon, did you?" Thomas said after Annie and Penny left.

"No, me neither." Sonny scowled. "And I thought we'd have more time here at the cottage before you'd have to head back. Do ya' think you're ready?"

"As ready as I'll ever be," Thomas replied gamely. "You should have known, with this family, there's always something going on. C'mon, lets go home. Penny's probably made Annie a nervous wreck by now."

Chapter 86

Annie *was* a nervous wreck. She flew out the door to meet the truck when they drove onto the yard. "Sonny, I talked to her – she wants to come Monday. My God. She asked me if we were married yet and I said just as cool as a cucumber, that our wedding is Saturday. I can't believe I said that!" She was pacing and flaying her arms around as she spoke, her face bright red. "Is that okay?"

Sonny stepped up and caught her mid-swing and gave her a hug. "I guess things really do move fast around here."

"C'mon, you guys," Penny insisted, "we have to plan this wedding and what we're gonna do with this old house and--"

"Hey!" cut in Mack. "This is their wedding and their house. Don't you think you should let them plan it?"

"Well, sure. Of course! But there's a lot to consider here."

"Like what, for instance!"

"Like carpeting! This house has got to have new

carpeting."

"And painting," someone else said. "Most of the rooms have never been touched."

"What about the holes in the plaster? We gotta fix them before we paint."

"And the library. We could really impress that social worker if we could fix the library and unpack all of the books that are still in boxes upstairs."

"See?" Penny said. "There's a lot to consider."

"We're supposed to get all this done and have a wedding, too, by Monday?" Mack asked incredulously. "You're nuts."

"But we have to," Annie cried. "That social worker comes in here and takes one look at this dump and she'll send us all packing'. Anyway, I already called Sears and they're sending out a carpet salesman at 11:00. And after he leaves, we're going into town to get our license and you a suit! Oh, don't look so disgusted. You gotta have one for court anyway."

"Do you really think we can do all that?" Andrew asked, with a look of skepticism.

No one said anything until Annie started thinking out loud. "Simple! We clean and paint stuff on Thursday and Friday and get the wedding planned, which will be small and informal – except the groom will wear a suit. We can get married right here – in the back yard. At sun up – sure, why not. Just like our first Easter in Shanny when they had a wonderful sunrise service. The sunrise was gorgeous, remember? And besides, that's Sonny's favorite part of the day. We'll roll up our sleeves and keep working till it's done. There, that wasn't so bad, was it?"

Everyone sat in stunned silence, until they broke out laughing. She wasn't listening. She squared her shoulders, and picked up her pen and paper. "We just have to be organized. All we need is--"

"Lists!" they all yelled.

* * * * * *

No doubt, the carpet salesman would remember that sales

call for a very long time. When he walked into the house, he was plunged into the middle of a bewildering mix of chaos. There was to be a major shift in bedroom assignments again. Penny suggested that Annie and Sonny take the large master bedroom, but Annie wanted to keep her old room. She didn't want to give up her corner room with her special window. Besides, she said, she wanted to convert the old nursery into an adjacent sitting room like the one her parents had in New York. The nursery for her baby could be in the bedroom across the hall with Joey in the other one. Give Becky the big room, someone suggested. It was big enough for all her enormous piles of dolls and toys. Luke, Thomas, Peter, and Danny could each have a room on the other side. John and Andrew, both of whom were seldom around any more, could have their rooms on the third floor.

After all that was settled, there was the relatively simple task of figuring out color schemes. Mr. Carlson, the hapless carpet salesman, was reduced to following the ladies around with armloads of samples and an order book, which was written and re-written several times before it was finally done. Three hours after he arrived, Annie finally wrote out the check with the contract in hand. Mr. Carlson promised the carpeting would be delivered and laid Saturday.

* * * * * *

Annie changed into a pretty sundress and demanded her fiancé change and shower as well so they could go into town. He would have preferred staying home and getting some work done, but she insisted.

"We can't get the license," Sonny complained. "We need blood tests."

"Not to worry, my dear," she chirped. "Penny has all the paperwork at Doc's office, signed and sealed. We both had our blood drawn a lot recently. We don't have any diseases."

"Okay, then, what about a birth certificate? Remember, I'm sort of a non-person."

"Well, I'm happy to report that even a non-person such as yourself has a paper trail which can be tracked down by a smart lawyer like Mr. Freedman. He got all of that when you were in jail. He'll meet us at the Courthouse." She began checking things off her lists.

They stopped in Shanny to see Father Fritz. Annie didn't think of it until she saw the white, gleaming steeple on the hillside. They knocked at the door of the rectory and were ushered into the pastor's office. Annie, who had many conversations with the sympathetic priest in this room before, was very comfortable and began explaining their plans. Sonny said nothing as he sat ill-at ease, surrounded by the trappings of Catholicism. His apprehension was easily discerned by Father Fritz.

"Mr. Blackstone?" he called for the third time. "You haven't said much. I'm wondering that you think of all this. Annie tells me you're not familiar with the Catholic religion. Would you be willing to take some instruction?"

Sonny shifted in his chair and cleared his throat. "No, sir, I would not. I've only been in church a couple of times before, and that was for funerals. My people don't go to church much, and I don't see any reason to start now."

This time it was Fr. Fritz who moved uncomfortably in his chair. He cleared his throat before he spoke. "Annie, are you aware of his opinion on the subject? Are you sure you should enter into a marriage when your religious ideals are so different? Perhaps you're rushing into this marriage ill-advised--"

"Father, I'm sure you're supposed to ask these questions," Annie interjected quickly. "But to be honest, I don't think God is sitting up there in heaven, saying good little Catholic girls are only supposed to fall in love with good little Catholic boys. That's your rule, not His. Maybe Sonny's religious attitudes don't fit into a nice little package like ours, but he's a good and honest man—more so than a lot of people who show up for Mass every Sunday. We're getting married Saturday at sun up."

"But Ann, you know as well as I do that for a marriage to be recognized by the Church, you have to be married here, in the Sanctuary. I can't marry you outside. You'll need a special dispensation from the Archdiocese. That type of thing takes a lot of paperwork."

"We don't have time for all that. The County social worker is coming next Monday, and we have to be married to get guardianship. You've seen our house, Father. We've got to get in into shape before Monday. If we get married first thing in the morning, we'll have the whole day to work on the house."

"Then get married here, in the church."

"No, we want to get married at home, right when the sun comes up. It'll be so beautiful. You say Mass in the park at Easter. Why can't you do this?"

The kindly priest shook his head. "I can't do that. You know the rules--"

"Father, this is not *my* wedding, it's *our* wedding. It's not just about my beliefs, but Sonny's, too. You've been a wonderful friend to me and my family, and I want you to marry us. But we can get a judge or a justice of the peace if we have to."

Ft. Fritz sat quietly for a few minutes and then said, "Very well, I can see you are very determined. I would be happy to marry you. Just humor me by stopping by and letting me bless the marriage here in the Church. Would you have a problem with that, Mr. Blackstone?"

"No, I guess not," Sonny said. "Whatever it takes to make her happy."

* * * * * *

They drove into Dubuque and met Mr. Freedman at the courthouse. The marriage license was obtained without any difficulty. "You're gonna come to our wedding, aren't you?" Annie asked. "Obviously, there's no time for invitations, but please come."

Next, they stopped at the florists and then to the dry cleaners, where she dropped off her mother's wedding dress. "Now your suit!" she commanded.

"Let's get the rings first."

They decided on plain, gold wedding bands. They told the stunned salesman that there was no need for a diamond since their engagement was less than a week. Finally, it was time to purchase the dreaded suit. They chose a plain black one with a white dress

717

shirt, a silk tie, and new shoes. It was nearly sundown when they started for home.

"Are you hungry?" she asked. "I'm starving! I'm craving a Big Mac." He happily complied and they drove up to the Dubuque Monument to eat their supper. Annie was quiet for several minutes until she asked, "Do you believe in God, Sonny?"

"So all that big talk was just a big smoke screen, huh?" He grinned as her gave her a playful nudge. "What were you trying to do, convince yourself or the priest?"

"No, I meant what I said, but I was bluffing about the Justice of the Peace part. My mom would be disappointed if I wasn't married by a priest. The Church was very important to her. My dad never cared, but her family would have never allowed her to marry him if he hadn't converted."

"Is that what you think I should do? Sounds like a hypocrisy to me. It's fine if Father What's-His-Name marries us. You go off to church any time you want, but not me." He toned it down a little before he continued. "Your dad didn't always go. I bet a hundred times or more, I saw him down in the bottom on Sunday mornings. I'd hear him talkin' to the fields or the river. That was his religion, and mine, too. Now drink this milk. You want our kid to have strong bones, don't ya'?" He watched as she downed a whole cartoon. "We got this wedding pretty well set. So tomorrow I can get some work done, right?"

"Sure, but I was wondering..." She picked up a long blade of grass and twisted it around her finger without looking at him. "How would you feel about writing our own vows? None of that traditional repeat-after-me stuff."

"You mean, you want me to stand up in front of a bunch of people and read a poem?"

"No, of course not – use your own words. This is our wedding, and I want it to be our own way. We'll marry ourselves."

He didn't answer at first. "So that priest would just sorta stands there while we do our own thing? I guess we could try."

* * * * * *

Later that night, Sonny couldn't sleep. Write their own vows? What would he say? He took paper and pen and began working on some ideas.

Across the yard, Annie sat at her desk, too. She smiled when she saw Sonny's light flick on. She had already written her vows and was picking out the readings. She had some very definite ideas of how she wanted the ceremony to proceed. She wrote it all out in detail and planned to drop it off at the rectory in the morning. This was definitely going to be a unique wedding.

The next two days were very hectic. Should they clean the house so it was presentable for their guests, or should they begin demolition? They had to begin somewhere, so they decided to work upstairs and clean the downstairs, which became counter-productive as clean surfaces soon became caked with plaster dust floating down from above.

Friday night came much too quickly. The house was in total disarray, looking worse than when they had started. There was panic showing on everyone's face. They cleaned up what they could, and began setting up for the wedding. At least the gazebo had a new coat of paint. Chairs were assembled on the yard, but it was hoped that whoever came would bring their own lawn chairs. Annie and Penny fussed in the kitchen, making preparations for the wedding breakfast. Since no one was exactly sure who was coming, it was difficult to make plans.

Annie went to her room late that night and even though she was bone tired, she knelt at her bed to pray the Rosary. But then she began to cry. "Oh, Mama," she gasped, "help me do this. There's so much to manage and so much at stake." Wearily, she got into bed. This was the last time she would sleep alone. Sonny would be lying at her side tomorrow night, the night after that, and forever. That word had a finality that was comforting somehow. It was in God's hands now. There was nothing more to do but sleep.

CHAPTER 87

Annie's alarm went off at 5:30. A quick glance out her window told her that Sonny's light was on, too. He'd be choring soon. She showered and did her hair, make-up, and even her nails. She put on her robe and started down the hall, pounding on doors. Penny and Mack arrived with the sleepy-eyed Katie. Annie gave her matron of honor a quick hug. "Are you nervous?" Penny asked. "I think I'm almost as excited as you are. Look, I'm shaking."

One by one the kids passed inspection and allowed downstairs. Lori Bean was managing the kitchen with Ginny's help. Annie could hear Andy and old Jake laughing downstairs, too. But then she glanced out a front window and was horror struck to see several cars arriving. They were parked on both sides of the driveway and down the road.

"My, God!" she cried. "Where are all these people coming from? There's Doc Adams and his wife! Nancy and Brian Garvey. There's Billie, and the Dunlevy's, the Bishops. My God! We don't have enough food! What are we gonna do?"

"Look!" Penny laughed. "Everyone's bringing something. There'll be plenty! See?" It was true. Everyone walking toward the house was carrying baskets and boxes of food, "I think the whole damn town is coming! Look, there's the mayor and his family."

Annie slipped back into her room and put on her dress. She looked in the mirror and felt a shiver. There was strong feeling of her parents' presence with her, and she welcomed it. She remembered the day soon after she learned of her mother's illness when they went together to the attic and Mother took out a box containing her wedding dress. "I kept it for you," she said. "I won't be there to see it, but I know you'll be so beautiful!" They both cried then, and Annie felt a tear trailing down her cheek now, too.

She heard Penny calling to her from the bottom of the stairs where she and Andrew were waiting for her. They gasped as she descended

"Do you think anyone can tell?"

"Tell what?"

"That I'm pregnant?" she retorted, patting her abdomen.

"No, you don't show at all, but everyone will mark their calendars anyway," Penny giggled.

"Is that a recording?" Annie asked. "That sounds like choir music."

"No, look!" Penny said, signaling Annie to peek through the curtain. "It's the ecumenical choir. You know, they sing at Easter services and things." The group of singers was standing near the gazebo. accompanied by Thomas who was playing the small electric organ.

"Where did they come from?" Annie cried. "Did Thomas set this up?"

"I don't know if he did, or if they asked him."

Penny went to the door and gave the sign that they were ready to begin. A hush fell over the yard as Thomas began to play the *Wedding March*. Sonny and Mack took their places on the steps of the gazebo as Penny began down the grassy aisle.

"Come on, gorgeous," Andrew whispered. "Let's do this." Annie took her twin's arm and together they walked out. She was a little unnerved by the large amount of people, so she concentrated only on Sonny's face as she walked toward him.

The groom was clearly overwhelmed by the sight of his bride. They rehearsed that Andrew would escort her to the steps of the gazebo and give her arm to him, but Sonny walked toward them and took her hand to lead her the rest of the way. Together they stepped up onto the top step of the gazebo and stood before the priest. The sun had just appeared above the horizon, as though God was embracing them with streamers of gold and scarlet. It was perfect.

Father Fritz began with a prayer and a blessing, as Annie had scripted. She and Sonny stated their intentions, promising to love, comfort, honor, and keep each other forever. Then Luke and Maggie stepped forward to begin the readings. Annie could feel Ginny's reassuring smile as Luke read the first one:

Two are better than one, because they have good reward for their toil. And if they fall, one will lift up the other; but woe is he who is alone when he falls and has not another to lift him up.

Again, if two lie together, they are warm; but how can one be warm alone? And though a man might prevail against one who is alone, two will withstand him. A threefold cord is not easily broken.

Margaret read the second reading, verses from Corinthians which Annie found circled in her mother's Bible.

Love is patient, love is kind.
It is never jealous, and never pompous.
It is not inflated. It is not rude.
It does not seek its own interests.
It is not quick-tempered.
It does not brood over injury.
It does not rejoice over wrongdoing, but rejoices
*   with the truth*
It bears all things, believes all things, hopes all things,
*   and endures all things.*

\

After the Responsorial was sang beautifully by Thomas and the choir, Fr. Fritz opened his Bible and read the Gospel.

Therefore, I tell you, do not be anxious about your life.
What you shall eat, or about your body and what you shall
*   wear.*
Consider the ravens: they neither reap nor sow,
*   and yet the Lord feeds them...*
Consider the lilies of the field and how they grow,
They neither toil nor spin, and yet, even Solomon in all
*   his glory was never arrayed like one of these.*

The words floated over the soft morning air and mingled

with the songs of the birds and gentle rustling of the wind in the trees. Then Fr. Fritz closed his Bible and said, "Since it's your intention to enter into marriage, then join your right hands and declare your vows before God and His church."

Sonny was trembling slightly as he turned toward her. He took a deep breath and began to whisper his oath. "I wish I could give you the world, but I can't. I wish I could promise you riches and fortune, but I can't. What I give to you is all that I've been, all that I am, and all that I will ever be. And I take unto myself all that you've been, all that you are, and all that you'll ever be. And I swear to you, if you're sick, I will care for you. If you're afraid, I will protect you. If you're cold, I will warm you. I will take care of you for the rest of my life because I love you."

Overwhelmed by the simplicity and beauty of his words, Annie stood stunned for a few moments, unable to speak. But then Fr. Fritz nudged her gently, telling her it was her turn. She said, "Sonny, take my life and make it beautiful. Take my world and make it complete. Take my hand and walk with me through the sunlight and darkness of all the days to come. For I say to you, wherever you go, I will go, and wherever you lodge, I will lodge. Your dreams will be my dreams, and your sadness will be my sadness. Today, as we start our life together, we give so completely of ourselves that our union will be stronger and more steadfast than life itself, and will last longer than forever. Because I, Ann Marie Kathleen Winston, take thee, Sonny Jack Blackstone, to be my lawfully wedded husband, to have and to hold from this day forward. For better, for worse, for richer and for poorer, in sickness and in health, to love and to cherish form this day forth until death do us part, according to God's holy ordinance, and there, too, I give thee my pledge."

Father Fritz took the rings and blessed them. Sonny placed it on her finger and said, "I give you this ring to wear forever."

Annie's pledge was more traditional. She slipped the ring on his finger and said, "In token and pledge of our constant faith and abiding love, with this ring, I thee wed, in the name of the Father, the Son, and the Holy Spirit."

In a beautiful, lyrical confirmation of their pledge and vows of marriage, Thomas began to sing Annie's favorite song from

Westside Story.

Make of our hands, one hand.
Make of our hearts, one heart.
Make of our vows, one last vow.
Only death can part us now.

After the Intentions were read and affirmed by the people assembled there, the prayers offered, the blessings given, Thomas began playing again. Accompanied beautifully by the choir, he sang *Ave Maria,* which is what their mother would have wanted. And then, finally, it was over.

"What God has joined, let no man put asunder! I present Mr. and Mrs. Sonny Jack Blackstone," Fr. Fritz proclaimed. "You may kiss the bride."

A happy sigh fell across the crowd but it grew quickly to a loud cheer as the groom kissed his pretty bride. Everyone clapped and rushed forward to congratulate them. There were not many dry eyes, especially Annie who wept joyously. Even the carpet layers who had arrived during the ceremony, cheered and applauded.

They all hugged and chatted as Lori and the self-appointed committee of church ladies brought out the food. The table was heaped with a fabulous array of meats, fruits, breads and pastries of every description. They mayor made a great show of cases of Champaign unloaded from his car. The bottles were uncorked and paper cups were raised to toast the happy couple.

Sonny was characteristically reserved and said very little. He co-operated with the attention and endured the endless picture taking, but retreated to an unobtrusive corner as soon as possible. He was content to watch her as she moved through the crowd, as gracious to the carpet layers as she was to the mayor.

"Here's to my best friend, Matthew!" Billie called out. "I'm sorry he missed this."

"Here! Here!" everyone said, raising their glasses.

"Oh," Annie gasped. "That reminds me. I want to put flowers on my mother's grave."

"You want to go out there in your dress?"

"We'll have to go the long way, or you could carry me across the barn lot," she giggled.

They made their apologies, explaining they would be back in a few minutes. Soon they were standing on the hilltop cemetery. There was gentle breeze that stirred the layers of the lace and satin of Annie's dress and veil so that she looked like a sweet angel as she knelt to place a bouquet gently by her mother's headstone. "You were right, Mama," she murmured. "It was beautiful." She then turned to place a rose at the grotto for the Blessed Virgin that Luke was building near by. Sonny stood back and watched respectfully as she made the sign of the cross and whispered a quick prayer.

"I wish we could stay here," Sonny sighed. "It's so quiet up here."

"I know, but we can't be rude to our guests. I wonder if these people know we have work to do. What are we going to do if they don't leave?"

When they arrived back at the house, there was no signs of the crowd disbanding. Dismayed and alarmed, the newly weds continued to socialize until finally they had no choice but to announce they were going upstairs to change their clothes. "Maybe people will take the hint," Annie whispered.

As they reached the top of the stairs they became aware that there was giggling from behind the closed doors. They were even more confused when Annie's bedroom was locked. "I didn't even know there was a key," she said incredulously. "If I did, I would have used it long ago."

They tried the door to what used to be the nursery next and were completely caught off guard when they stepped inside and were greeted by a roomful of people shouting "Surprise!"

"Oh, my God!" Annie cried. "Look at this!" The room was completely different. The furniture from her parents' sitting room was nicely arranged with new emerald green drapes on the window. Annie walked from one piece of furniture to the next, lovingly touching everything. The door to their bedroom was open. Annie gasped again. Her own things had been replaced by her parents' bedroom furniture, along with new drapes and accessories.

Obviously Penny was the mastermind behind the project. She was so excited, she could hardly contain herself. "Do you like it?" she exclaimed. "It's less frilly than your old stuff.. I thought--"

"It's terrific," Annie cried. "I love it! But how did --"

"They came up here and started working the moment you went downstairs," Penny exclaimed, pointing to Ginny's cousin, Mildred, and several of her friends. "We were trying to stall you as long as we could." Penny gushed. "This was a big job. Doesn't it look wonderful?"

Annie and Sonny were stunned. It was a magnificent gift, and it was accomplished by virtual strangers. And that was not the last surprise of the day. As they descended down stairs, wearing jeans and T-shirts, they were amazed to see choir robes coming off to reveal bib overalls and work clothes. The ladies in the crowd were tying on aprons and kerchiefs around their hair. People brought step ladders, scrub buckets, and paint brushes from their cars.

"Danny," Mrs. Bishop began. "Why don't you show me which room is yours. Does it need painting? Say, do you like football? I have some very nice curtains with a matching bedspread that's covered with footballs," she chatted as Danny led her upstairs. Others were doing the same thing with the other children. Billie took a crew into the library and started measuring for new shelves. Others began removing the furniture from the dining room and the living room so that painting could begin. There was a committee working on the staircase and setting up ladders with planks to work on the high ceiling and walls in the foyer. Everywhere there was painting and plastering, measuring and cutting. Even the water stained, decrepit bedrooms on the third floor were getting a facelift.

Annie, who pictured herself wall papering all afternoon into the late night hours, was busy answering questions and dispensing coffee and sandwiches all afternoon. Even Sonny was reduced to chief advisor and gofer for materials and supplies. It was the most incredible thing any of them had ever seen. At sundown, people began to trudge home wearily. There were no more holes in the plaster, doors with one hinge, or plywood patches on the stairs. The once shabby, barely habitable old house was now a beautiful home.

Later that night, Penny and Mack sat with Andrew, Annie, and Sonny for a last cup of coffee. They were so amazed at the amount of work that was accomplished, it was difficult to comprehend.

"Doesn't seem like your wedding day, does it?" Penny sighed wearily. "This morning seems like an eternity ago."

"Well, it certainly is a day I'll never forget," Annie smiled. "For a lot of reasons! It was great, wasn't it?"

"Did you see Patricia Dunlevy screaming at her husband for puttin' the wrong finish on those base boards upstairs?" Mack laughed. "Like it really mattered! That wood was bare for 50 years!"

"And did you see Mavis Gherkin having words with Marilyn Kennedy over which curtains to put up in the Becky's room?" Andrew snickered. "These people really came through for us today. It was just unbelievable."

Sonny got up from the table and stood in his usual spot in the back corner. "I sure hope it wasn't for nothin'," he spat.

"What do you mean?" Annie asked.

"None of this is going to matter if that social worker comes in here with her mind made up. How much stuff do you think she can lay her hands on – about me, I mean." His throat seemed tight and his words were forced.

"Sonny," said Mack, "you're setting yourself up for a big guilt trip. I think realistically they'd have reservations about awarding the custody of five children to any young, newly wed couple. We just have to convince them that you can handle it. Look what a great job you did with Thomas--"

"You're never gonna tell anyone about that!" Sonny fired. "There's no official record of his drug use, and it's gonna stay that way."

"Mack's right." Everyone turned to see Thomas standing in the doorway. "I wasn't eavesdropping. I couldn't go to sleep so I came down for something to eat." No one said anything as they watched him go to the refrigerator and pour himself a glass of milk. "The whole damn town knows I was a junkie -- a bona fide, $50 a day, slime ball junkie."

"So, what do you want us to do?" Andrew asked. "Take out a billboard saying Thomas Winston was a druggie, but now he's clean! Telling the social worker about your problem wouldn't help anyone."

"Yes, it would. It would show her what good Sonny and Annie can do for us, better than anyone else. If she asks me, I'm gonna tell her. So will the rest of the kids. How can they make any decisions without asking us first?" Everyone sat startled for a few moments, shocked by his unsolicited testimony. Annie gave him a quick hug. "Thanks for saying those things. It makes us all feel better. By the way, you were great today. You really helped to make our wedding perfect."

"Oh, jeez!" Mack teased. "I'm sure the last thing you want to do is sit around having coffee on your wedding night. Come along, dear, let's go home." He motioned for his wife to follow him out the door. The room cleared quickly.

Annie unplugged the coffee pot and turned off the lights. She put her arms around her husband and whispered, "C'mon, there's nothin' more we can do tonight anyway." She took his hand and led upstairs.

He swept her up into her arms and carried her across the threshold into their room. "What do you mean, there's nothing more we can do tonight." He smiled and laid her on their bed. Slowly, gently, he unbuttoned her blouse. She slipped it off with her bra. Her breasts were larger and firmer since she became pregnant and when he kissed them, it was like an exquisite electric shock shot through her body. But she wanted this night to go slow and last forever, so she pushed him onto his back. It was her turn to do the undressing and caressing. She wanted to touch him and love him like he had never known before.

And later, when she fell exhausted into his arms, she was sure that she finally understood what the words "making love" really meant. No fear, no guilt, no doubts or confusion. She waited for him to say something, wondering what his reaction would be. But she could feel the muscles in his arms and chest beginning to tighten again. "Sonny, what--" she began as he sat up on the side of the bed. The light shone through the window so that for the first time she saw the deep furrows of the scars across his lower back. He turned to say something and saw her staring. He quickly put on his pants and T-shirt and went outside onto the balcony.

She put on her robe and followed him. "Oh, Sonny, I wanted this night to be perfect. I'm sorry if--"

"Sorry for what?" he murmured.

"I'm sorry for expecting we could forget everything else that's going on. Sorry for making you feel uncomfortable by…I just never saw you naked before." He moved away from her. "Please don't pull away from me like this. You said you were giving me everything that you were, what you are, and will be. Remember? Those scars are part of you. Oh, Sonny, how could a father do that to a child?" she cried.

He stood silently for a time, trying to compose himself. "You can't understand how much he hated everything, even me. I thought he cut hate into me, and that I was going to be just like--"

She pressed her fingers to his lips. "No, Sonny, you're nothing like him. Look at this," she whispered as she swept her arm to embrace the wide valley that laid at their feet. "Look at everything you've given me."

"Look at what? I didn't give you anything. I didn't buy it or earn it!"

"That's not true! You gave me a roof that doesn't leak, furnace that heats, and this room with my window. All these mornings when I wake up to beautiful sunrises – you gave them all to me. And now we can share those mornings together! My God, Sonny, don't do this! You're scaring me." She walked back into the house, crying softly.

Her tone of frustration stunned him and jolted him into taking a quick inventory. They weren't talking about if's or maybe's anymore. This is the real thing. This house is where he will live the rest of his life if he can coax it into standing that long. This is his wife, beautiful and pregnant with his child.

He found her sitting by her desk, staring out the window that looked over the yard. He held her and kissed her. "I'm sorry," he said over and over, begging her to stop crying.

"Do you know how many times I came to this window

when I couldn't sleep. I'd look across the yard and I'd wonder about you. I wanted to know what made you tick, why were you so quiet and serious all the time. And later, when my feelings began to change, I longed to be near you and touch you. Oh God, sometimes I wanted you so badly, I ached! And now here you are, in this room, in my bed, and you're still so far away."

"No, I'm not!" he cried. "I'm right here, where I want to be." He lifted her trembling body back into bed. He took off his clothes and stood naked in full view of her for a few moments until he crawled into bed. Taking her into his arms, he said. "If I ever start getting like this again, just remind me what an idiot I am, okay? I just got to get used to being happy, that's all."

"Are you – happy, I mean?" she murmured.

"Yes, I am very happy." To chase the tears away, he made love to her again, giving himself to her completely and unafraid.

CHAPTER 88

Sunday morning saw more activity around the old house, but much less hectic or frantic. After two years of being stacked in the attic and nearly forgotten, boxes and crates from the brownstone were opened. Childhood memories were relived as pictures and remembrances were unpacked. Family portraits and pieces of their parents' art collection were hung throughout the house. The newly refurbished library was stocked with dozens of books, and mother's lovely china and stemware were placed carefully in the buffets. They hung flower baskets in the windows and put a welcome mat at the door. They actually used the word "decorating" as they put finishing touches in every room.

They gathered on the back porch at suppertime to eat grilled hot-dogs and hamburgers because Annie refused to cook anything in her immaculate kitchen. They were tired, but everyone was extremely happy.

"I cannot believe after living here for three years, we actually have a toilet paper dispenser in the bathroom upstairs," Annie said, with mocked disbelief ringing her voice.

"Hey!" John laughed. "What's wrong with that nail Pop

put in there?"

"I'm not real happy that the big whole in the wall in my room is gone," quipped Peter. "Now I got no place to put my stuff."

"And you know what?" Danny jeered. "With all that carpeting, you can sneak up on people better. I tried it before, but the floor always creaked."

"Oh!" smiled Annie, casting a playful glance at her husband. "I'll have to remember that!"

They ate and drank, laughed and planned, until Annie announced it was time for everyone to go to bed. No one mentioned the next day or spoke of their apprehension. But later, as she was walking down the quiet hallway, she heard whispering coming from Peter's bedroom. She was surprised to see Danny had climbed into bed with him, and they were talking in very solemn tones.

"Hey," she called, "I thought you boys were happy to have your own rooms. Should we move you back together?"

"Heck, no!" Peter protested. "He bothers me all the time."

"I do not!"

"Yes, you do!"

"Danny," Annie asked, "do you have something on your mind you want to talk about?"

The boy hesitated for a moment, but then said, "Well, yeah, we were talking about that woman coming tomorrow."

"You don't have to worry about that, Danny," Annie replied.

"Why do you always say that?" Peter retorted. "Every time there's something going on around here, you just say, 'There's nothing to worry about.' We're not babies. We hear stuff. Why don't you just tell us the truth?"

"Yeah, the lady's coming to talk about us, right?" Danny agreed. "So how come no one tells us what's happening?"

Annie was stunned by the forceful resentment in their voices. "But, boys," she began, trying not to sound patronizing, "you are--"

"See! You're doing it again!" Peter muttered. "You said, don't worry and mother died. You said, don't worry, and Luke

731

left and almost died. Then Pop died and Sonny left. Not knowing stuff is worse. You should tell us! At least Ginny tells us the truth. She knows we're not babies! Jake, too."

Annie gathered her thoughts carefully before she spoke. "Boys, listen to me. I'm sorry if you think I don't tell you things. I guess we all thought we were protecting you, but maybe we're making it worse. I promise we'll never do that again, all right? This lady that's coming tomorrow is a social worker. That means she talks to people to find out how they're doing. The judge wants her to decide if this is a good place for you kids to live, and if Sonny and me would make good parents."

"Course, you're good parents!" Danny cried. "How does she know anything anyway. She don't know us!"

"I agree, Danny, but that's the way it is. We have a lawyer, Mr. Freedman, who's going to help us, and we're all going to do our best to convince her that we all belong here together. I have to tell you that Sonny did some bad things before we knew him, and that's all written down on his record. That's why we're a little nervous."

"What if this social worker says no?" Peter asked, his eyes as big as saucers.

"Well, that's the problem. I honestly don't know. I guess Aunt Esther wanted all you kids once before, so they might ask her, or--"

"No way!" Danny scowled. "I ain't gonna live with that damn, dried up old biddy!"

"Daniel!"

"I heard Pop say that once! She's too old. We won't have to go live by her, will we?"

"Danny, I didn't say that. I just said they'll be looking at other possibilities. We just have to hope that everything will be alright. I honestly believe it will." She stood up and tried to smile reassuringly. "I'm going to bed now, okay. I love you." She gave them each a kiss.

But as she stepped out of the room, she stopped outside their door, wondering what they'd say.

"Should we pray?" Danny asked.

"Sure," Peter said, sounding very authoritarian, "but not out loud. Prayin' out loud is for church!"

"I think Mama hears our prayers. Don't you?"

"I suppose."

"Then everything's gotta be all right. She'd fix it, don't you think?"   "Sure, Danny. Now go to sleep."

Annie crept down the hallway, smiling and crying at the same time. She crawled into bed next to her sleeping husband and prayed, too. "Mama," she whispered, "please, please, fix this. Amen."

* * * * * *

The morning dawned and in spite of their brave, confident words, everyone was nervous. There was much debate over what they should wear. Some said dress casual, while others wanted Sunday best. Even Annie lingered at her closet. She finally decided on a nice pant suit rather than a dress. She felt sick, but tried to ignore the waves of nausea. All the beds were made, cereal bowls hidden in the dish washer, and clean towels hung in every bathroom. Sonny and the boys finished the chores early, rushing in to shower and change before the appointed hour. Annie fussed over the little ones, reminding them for the hundredth time to keep quiet when "the nice lady comes to visit," and only speak if spoken to.

Penny and Mack arrived at about 9:00. "Oh, God, I can't believe how nervous I am," Penny exclaimed as she rushed in the back door with the baby. "You must be a wreck!"

"I just wish I knew what to expect from this woman," Annie cried. "She sounded so crisp and efficient on the phone. People like that scare me. Oh, Penny, if our petition gets turned down, Sonny will be devastated."

Mr. Freedman drove on the yard about 9:30. He seemed surprisingly relaxed and casual. He helped himself to coffee and a donut, telling everyone how great the place looked. He teased them about the rather poignant odor of paint in the air, but no one thought it was funny. They had put box fans in every window of the house, but the fumes were still evident.

"That's okay, Annie," he said. "She'll know that you tried

hard to make the house look nice. Where's our star contestant?"

"You mean Sonny?" Annie retorted. "He was the last one into the shower. And do you have to refer to him like that? He's already jittery." "Okay, I'm sorry. I just wanted to remind him again not to loose his cool, no matter what happens. He can't get real defensive about any of her questions. Contrary to my earlier comment, this whole thing is not riding on him exclusively."

"Try telling him that. This just has to go well, it just has to!"

The door bell rang. "My God!" Annie exclaimed. "She's early! Now, I'm really leery of this woman." She steadied herself and opened the door smiling. "Hello, Miss Rausch? Come in, won't you?" She ushered their guest in, stopping to ask Peter to call everyone to the living room.

To her horror, he walked five feet to the bottom of the stairs and screamed at the top of his lungs, "That woman's here! Everybody come down!" Annie said nothing, just kept smiling.

"What a lovely home," Miss Rausch said cordially. "and my goodness, it's so large!"

"We have rather a large family, as you know," Annie replied politely.

Mr. Freedman sauntered in, donut powder in his lapel. Annie introduced them and they shook hands. "Well, Mr. Freeman," Miss Rausch said, looking over the top of her bifocals. "I must say, I am a little surprised to find you here. It is not usually customary or necessary to have an attorney present during these informal fact-finding sessions."

"Well, I have been associated with this family for a while now. I am familiar with the family's finances, among other things. I am handling the disposition of funds and since I assume the financial support of these children is one of your primary concerns, I thought I should be on hand to answer any questions you might have."

"Yes, well, I suppose that's a good idea. But then, we can talk about that later." She readjusted her glasses and opened up the large folder of papers she ha brought with her. "Now, let's meet everyone, shall we?" she said, her lips pressed tightly across her mouth. "Let's see. The youngest of the family is little

Rebecca Elizabeth, correct?" One by one, she went through the list.

"And the oldest of the minor children is Thomas Phillip?" This time she did not smile and stared at him longer than the others. "Hmm," she murmured, writing furiously. There was a collective, non-verbal moan as they realized Thomas's history was well known to their illustrious visitor. "Yes, I was having dinner with my brother and his wife last night, Mr. and Mrs. John Rausch," she said with mocked pleasantries. "He's the principal of the high school, you know. He mentioned to me that you never finished school, Thomas. You've recently returned home? My, my, but, we can discuss that later."

She moved on to the non-minor members of the family. "John Joseph – Oh yes, you will be a sophomore this fall at the University of Iowa under a full football scholarship. An excellent student as well as an outstanding athlete. Isn't that wonderful? You're a good looking fella. I bet you have no shortage of girlfriends, right?" Again she was smiling, but the Winston's were squirming uncomfortably in their seats. Mr. and Mrs. Rausch must have had a lot to say over dinner last night.

"Luke, I see here that you served in Vietnam, incarcerated as a POW camp for nearly two years. Tut, tut, tut," she clicked her teeth, looking at him piteously. "I've read that so many of our boys are having difficulty coping with re-entry into society. How are we doing?"

"My brother is doing just fine," Annie said. "He's working hard here on the farm, and he's building his own cabin nearby. He's getting strong and healthy again. We're so happy to have him home where he belongs."

"Yes, I'm sure that's true," Miss Rausch said without looking up from her writing. "Now, where's Andrew?" She scanned the group until Andrew smiled an acknowledgement. "You graduated from Loras this spring. You have a double major – Pre-seminary and business? My, what an odd combination." She continued without giving Andrew a chance to respond.

"Matthew McAllister Winston, III, and his wife, Penelope Sue. Maiden name, Lamp. Your father is Dr. Dennis Lamp, the orthopedic surgeon, correct? What a wonderful man. He did my mother's hip surgery last year. And you're a nurse? How nice. You work in Dr. Adam's office part time and you do have a two year old daughter, Kathleen. My, but you're a busy little mother."

"And now, Mr. and Mrs. Jack Blackstone – and where is Mr. Blackstone? I don't believe I've met him yet."

"I'm right here, Miss Rausch," Sonny said, walking into the room and looking as though he had been caught playing hooky.

"Yes, well, I've met Mrs. Blackstone. She was here when I arrived." She went back to writing. "I understand that you two have petitioned the court to become legal guardians for the five minor children. Hmmm, we can get to that later. Right now, I'd love to have a tour of this grand old house. I need to become familiar with the sleeping arrangements and so forth."

"Of course, Miss Rausch," Annie said smoothly. "Just follow me. Boys, why don't you take Becky outside and play for awhile, okay?" They clearly wanted to stay, but they took the hint and filed out.

Miss Rausch was impressed with the house. "But, it's a lot to keep up. My goodness, how do you manage all the cleaning and so forth? It must be a burden, especially for someone so young." She said that last word like it was an indictment of wrong doing. Annie began to explain, but again Miss Rausch rushed on without waiting for a reply. "But you do very well. It's a lovely home, much nicer than I expected." Annie wondered what that meant.

They re-joined the others in the living room, and Miss Rausch immediately launched into a more substantive conversation. "Mr. and Mrs. Blackstone, you must realize that this is rather an unusual request, considering your ages and situation. The court may have some reservation granting your petitions. Of course, we realize that these are your brothers and sisters, Mrs. Blackstone, so you would naturally be concerned about their welfare, as are we," she smiled thinly. "But, Mr. Blackstone, how long have you been associated with this family?"

Sonny cleared his throat as though he were having difficulty speaking. "For three years now. I met their father in New York, and since I had some experience in farming, he asked me to come along. I guess you could say I was their hired hand."

"But now he is part owner of this property," Mr. Freedman spoke up for the first time. "One third of the total acreage has been deeded to him. The rest of the acreage belongs to whomever lives in the house. Mack and Penny own 220 acres west of here. Each of the minor children have a substantial trust fund to do with what they wish when they turn 18. The remainder of Mr. Winston's estate is in reserve."

Miss Rausch was writing fast and furiously. "Did Mr. Winston have all of this stipulated in his will? Did he specifically say who he wanted to take over guardianship of his children?"

"No, I'm afraid not. Matthew was only 57 years old. His death was very unexpected and he did not make those kinds of arrangements. His family believes that he would have wanted this family, as well as this farm, to remain intact."

Miss Rausch did not look up from her writing when she asked, "Mr. Blackstone, as a hired hand, did you handle any of the family's money?"

Sonny was obviously unsettled by this line of questioning, but answered evenly. "Yes, my name and signature have been accepted at the bank since Matthew opened that account three years ago. I think the largest check I ever wrote was for $79,000 for a new tractor." They all smiled, thinking he had done well that round.

"But there has been some financial difficulty, hasn't there?" she asked shrewdly as though it was a test or trick question.

Mr. Freedman spoke quickly before anyone else had a chance. "Upon what information are you basing that question? Official documentation or hearsay. Yes, two years ago, Mr. Winston and his family went through a period of readjustment whereas Matthew Winston made the very difficult decision to sever all ties with his company in New York so that this farm became their sole means of income. There were some hard times in the beginning, but now they are on very good, solid ground."

"Yes, well," she persisted, "who will take over that part of the operation now that Mr. Winston is no longer here to make financial decisions."

"We will," Annie replied. "I run the household, and Sonny will be in charge of the farm, like any other couple. Like Sonny said, my father trusted him with all that before."

"But that was before anyone was aware of your past, isn't that true, Mr. Blackstone?" she retorted. "You must have known that part of my job as a court appointed investigator is to check police records."

"Then your records much also show that all charges dismissed because of his exemplary conduct these past three years," countered Mr. Freedman.

"Oh, yes, I read the court records thoroughly. The testimony given in his behalf was very noteworthy. However, this is an entirely different situation. We are talking about the health and welfare of five children. Mr. Blackstone's record has several areas which raise serious questions. For instance, he was mistreated badly as a child--"

"Miss Rausch, surely he cannot be held accountable for the acts of violence which were levied against him twenty years ago!" Mr. Freedman exclaimed, jumping up from his chair as though he cross-examining an unfriendly witness.

"Mr. Freedman, you are aware of the high statistics that show the alarming cycle of abused children that exhibit that same behavior as adults," she refuted sharply, ignoring the shocked gasped that echoed through the room. Only Sonny seemed to be unaffected by her accusations and innuendos.

Just then, they became aware that there was yelling and fighting outside. The back door flung open and Joey came rushing in. He went straight to Sonny. "The boys won't let me play," he wailed. "I wanna play!"

Sonny lifted the boy onto his lap, and said, "Excuse me, I'd better go take care of this."

"Ride me, Sonny! Ride me!" Joey screamed incessantly.

Just as he had done a thousand other times, Sonny swung the little boy onto his shoulders as Joey giggled with delight. Annie stood up and gave them a quick kiss as they were walking out of the room. "You tell those boys to be nice! We'll be having lunch soon, okay?" She smiled bravely for her husband, but as soon as she heard the back door close, she turned to their guest

738

with a less than friendly glare.

"I have never in all my life heard such ridiculous, rude behavior from someone who's supposed to have an understanding of people and their feelings," she fired. Mr. Freedman tried to intercede, but Annie brushed him aside. "If you had read my husband's record thoroughly, then I should think you would be congratulating him, not ridiculing him. Yes, it's true, my father knew nothing about him when he hired him, but his instincts told him that he could trust Sonny, and he did. He trusted him with his money, his family, even with the thing that meant the most to him – this land. Without Sonny, my father would have gone back to New York a failure. And it's absurd to think he would ever hurt anyone." She was trembling and her voice was shaky. She was afraid she was going to begin to cry, so she said, "I don't know why I'm bothering to say any of this because it's obvious that you had your mind made up before you even set foot in this house."

Miss Rausch cleared her throat, and gave Annie a long, hard look before she answered. "I assure you, Mrs. Blackstone, I did not have any pre-conceived idea when I came here. As I told you before, my job is to do a thorough and objective investigation. Obviously there are some legitimate concerns that I cannot ignore. You're newly married – just the day before yesterday, correct? You're both very young. I'm just afraid that so much responsibility would be a tremendous burden to you – and your husband as well, of course." She paused before she continued. "I'm just wondering if some other arrangements shouldn't at least be considered."

"Like what?" Mack exploded, having remained silent longer than anyone expected. "Who else is there? Me and Penny? That wouldn't make any sense. We have our lives set. We're nearby to help, but we can't--"

"Our mother died three and a half years ago," Luke cut in tersely. "Annie has raised these kids ever since. She's the one who takes care of them when they're sick, feeds and clothes them, everything. She loves these kids, and so does Sonny."

"This is what our father would have wanted," John insisted. "He went to court to keep this family together on this farm once before. What more proof do you want?"

"That's right!" chimed in Penny. "Their father may have been the head of this family, but Sonny and Annie are the ones who made it work. Sonny was never just the hired hand. Even Matthew listened to him."

Thomas came forward and gave the others a decisive glare that told them to sit down. "As the oldest of the minor children, I think I should be able to speak," he began. "As you obviously already know, I've had some trouble these past couple of years. I was into drugs pretty heavy. I blamed everyone else for a long time – my dad, my mother's death, leaving New York, all of that. Everyone in this room knew I had a problem, but do you know who finally did something about it? Sonny. He got me off the stuff so that I'm clean now for the first time in months. No one else could have done that – nobody. He'll help me stay clean cause he cares. They both do."

There were a few moments of stunned silence. That was the longest, most passionate speech anyone had ever heard him give. They waited to see how Miss Rausch would respond.

"Let me assure you, young man," she said, still very crisp and unemotional, "I am simply trying to do my job. It is a grave responsibility. What if I were to recommend that these two assume guardianship, and then in a few months or even years from now it turned out to be a mistake. What if they get a divorce, or there are severe financial problems or--"

"Miss Rausch," Mr. Freedman interrupted with obvious controlled anger, "how can you possibly presume to predict that any of those things will happen? What are you, some kind of prophet of doom? That is not your job. As you have said repeatedly, you are doing an impartial investigation, and it should be very obvious that there is only one option here. This family has just suffered the tragic death of their father. They simply want to continue what he started. Giving Annie and Sonny custody is the only logical step."

Miss Rausch said nothing as she began packing up her briefcase so Mr. Freedman continued. "You should tell them what you've decided to recommend – right here, now."

All eyes were focused on the austere Miss Rausch as she snapped her briefcase closed and stood up. "Well," she said, her words agonizingly slow. "I would say, based on everything I've seen and heard here this morning, I will--" She paused and inhaled deeply, "recommend that Judge Henson accept your petitions."

She appeared to want to add something, but Annie never gave her the chance. "Oh, thank you, Miss Rausch. Oh, thank you. We'll be fine, honest. You won't regret this! If you'll excuse me, I think the kids are calling me," she cried merrily, as she was skipping out the door. "Penny, would you see our guest out, please?"

Miss Rausch paused in the foyer, watching out the large bay windows into the backyard as Annie ran across the lawn toward her husband. Both of them picked up a child and embraced joyously. "Yes," Miss Rausch murmured. "I'm sure you'll be just fine."

* * * * * *

Annie had trouble sleeping. Too many thoughts were whirling around in her head. She laid there, watching her husband sleep. He was totally relaxed. It had been a good day. Finally, they could go on with the business of living.

Off in the distance she heard thunder. The wind was picking up a little as the spindly shadows of the swaying branches seemed to be alive as they danced on the bedroom wall. She got out of bed and made her rounds as she had done a hundred other times on such stormy nights. The creaking noises that accompanied her from room to room no longer frightened her. Rather, it assured her that these aging timbers were ready to stand battle against the storm, and all who slept within these walls would be kept safe and warm. She crept back into their bedroom and sat down in her rocking chair. It would be daybreak soon, so she decided to forget trying to sleep.

Now that this whole situation with guardianship was successfully resolved, it was very pleasant to be able to think about the future, something she had not allowed herself to do in a long time. She thought of her brothers and sister, making a mental inventory of their needs and plans.

Becky and the little boys seemed happier and more content than they had in a long time. Danny and Peter were very relieved when told the social worker's recommendation. Annie was reminded again that she had long under-estimated their perceptions of events and, by her failure to discuss things honestly with them, she had caused them undue apprehension. She vowed she would pay more attention to that sort of thing in the future.

She smiled when she thought of Thomas' speech that morning. She wished she had it on tape so when they started having battles she could use it to remind him that he had defended their right to parent him. Sonny had awarded him domain of the shed where his band could practice as much as they wanted. She would like to see him go to college like John, but she doubted he ever would. She wondered if those two will ever become close. Perhaps that was asking too much, although she had noticed them speaking to each other in passing, which was a definite improvement.

She had guarded optimism concerning Luke, too. He was determined to finish the exterior of his cabin this summer, and she was apprehensive about him living there alone now that he was beginning to become more communicative. However, she was sure he was going to have one regular visitor – Margaret. They had become quite close, and she was his confidant and soul mate. Annie hoped for both their sakes that Luke was on the road to recovery.

Annie turned her attention toward her twin. Andrew would be leaving for New York at the end of the week. Aunt Esther must be ecstatic, Annie thought. She remembered her aunt on the witness stand, insisting with so much anguish that at least one of Matthew's sons should assume leadership of the company. Of all her brothers, it never occurred to her that Andrew would be the one who would someday sit at her father's desk. Well, she thought, it was in good hands.

Penny and Mack seemed happier than Annie had ever seen them. Penny had told her a secret a few days ago that she thought she may be pregnant again, something she desperately wanted. Annie smiled, thinking how their children would grow up together on this land.

She rested her hand on the small mound in her tummy. If she sat very quietly, she could feel his little movements. She was positive she was carrying a son, so she always referred to this baby that way. He would be the vessel of so many hopes and dreams to carry forth in his lifetime, dreams that had taken seed long ago.

Sonny began to arouse. He turned toward where she should have been, and not finding her, his eyes shot open.

"I'm right here, Sonny," she called out softly as she climbed into bed.

"Are you all right? It's the middle of the night," he said, still looking alarmed.

"No, it's nearly dawn, and yes, I'm fine. I just couldn't sleep. The rain's almost here. I was just thinking about how frightened I used to be during these storms. Now it's like music."

Sonny smiled as he nestled close to her. "Why couldn't you sleep? You're not worried anymore, are you?"

"About the guardianship? No, thank God, that's all settled. But I was thinking about the kids, and Luke and Andrew, and of course, Thomas."

"Thinking or worrying? It's not good for our kid if you worry all the time."

"I'm not worried, not like before. I just want us all to be happy, especially our baby. It's a him, you know, I'm sure of it."

"Oh, you are, aye?"

"I was thinking how having a child completes the circle. It's like Ginny says, you spend your time on this earth and do the best you can. But even after you're gone, the sun still rises and sets, the river will keep flowing. We just borrow it for a while and then pass it on."

She got up then and went out onto the balcony. He followed her and but his arms around her as they gazed at the valley as they had done so many times before. It was bathed in a fresh, misty blanket of faint pastels even though the rising sun was hidden by a veil of blue-gray clouds. The river, constant and powerful, cut like a blue ribbon across the green floor. There was a dark, contrasting frame of trees and brush along the bluff that was yet untouched by the morning light.

It was all there – the land, the waters and the skies, lying there as they had for millions of years and will be there still, thousands of years from now. But at this moment in time, it belonged to them. And what she saw was mirrored in her husband's face – the hope, the joy, and belief in a new day.

THE END

14634529R00396

Made in the USA
Lexington, KY
12 April 2012